DETECTIVES
and
CRIMINALS

THE MOONSTONE *by Wilkie Collins*

THE AMATEUR CRACKSMAN *by E.W.Hornung*

ROOM 13 *by Edgar Wallace*

CHANCELLOR
PRESS

The Moonstone was first published in Great Britain in 1868
The Amateur Cracksman was first published in Great Britain in 1899
Room 13 was first published in Great Britain in 1923

This collected volume first published in 1993 by Chancellor Press
an imprint of
Reed Consumer Books Limited
Michelin House, 81 Fulham Road, London SW3 6RB
and Auckland, Melbourne, Singapore and Toronto

Design and arrangement copyright © 1993 by
Reed International Books Limited

ISBN 1 85152 298 0

A CIP catalogue record for this book is available at the British Library

Printed in Great Britain by The Bath Press.

CONTENTS

THE MOONSTONE

by Wilkie Collins

AUTHOR'S PREFACES

In some of my former novels, the object proposed has been to trace the influence of circumstances upon character. In the present story I have reversed the process. The attempt made, here, is to trace the influence of character on circumstances. The conduct pursued, under a sudden emergency, by a young girl, supplies the foundation on which I have built this book.

The same object has been kept in view, in the handling of the other characters which appear in these pages. Their course of thought and action under the circumstances which surround them, is shown to be (what it would most probably have been in real life) sometimes right, and sometimes wrong. Right, or wrong, their conduct, in either event, equally directs the course of those portions of the story in which they are concerned.

In the case of the physiological experiment which occupies a prominent place in the closing scenes of *The Moonstone*, the same principle has guided me once more. Having first ascertained, not only from books, but from living authorities as well, what the result of that experiment would really have been, I have declined to avail myself of the novelist's privilege of supposing something which might have happened, and have so shaped the story as to make it grow out of what actually would have happened—which, I beg to inform my readers, is also what actually does happen, in these pages.

With reference to the story of the Diamond, as here set forth, I have to acknowledge that it is founded, in some important particulars, on the stories of two of the royal diamonds of Europe. The magnificent stone which adorns the top of the Russian Imperial Sceptre, was once the eye of an Indian idol. The famous Koh-i-Noor is also supposed to have been one of the sacred gems of India; and, more than this, to have been the subject of a prediction, which prophesied certain misfortune to the persons who should divert it from its ancient uses.

Gloucester Place, Portman Square, *June* 30, 1868.

———

The circumstances under which *The Moonstone* was originally written, have invested the book—in the author's mind—with an interest peculiarly its own.

While this work was still in course of periodical publication in England, and in the United States, and when not more than one third of it was completed, the bitterest affliction of my life and the severest illness from which I have ever suffered, fell on me together. At the time when my mother lay dying in her little cottage in the country, I was struck prostrate, in London; crippled in every limb by the torture of rheumatic gout. Under the weight of this double calamity, I had my duty to the public still to bear in mind. My good readers in England and in America, whom I had never yet disappointed, were expecting their regular weekly instalments of the new story. I held to the story—for my own sake, as well as for theirs. In the intervals of grief, in the occasional remissions of pain, I dictated from my bed that portion of *The Moonstone* which has since proved most successful in amusing the public—the 'Narrative of Miss Clack.' Of the physical sacrifice which the effort cost me I shall say nothing. I only look back now at the blessed relief which my occupation (forced as it was) brought to my mind. The Art which had been always the pride and the pleasure of my life, became now more than ever 'its own exceeding great reward.' I doubt if I should have lived to write another book, if the responsibility of the weekly publication of this story had not forced me to rally my sinking energies of body and mind—to dry my useless tears, and to conquer my merciless pains.

The novel completed, I awaited its reception by the public with an eagerness of anxiety, which I have never felt before or since for the fate of any other writings of mine. If *The Moonstone* had failed, my mortification would have been bitter indeed. As it was, the welcome accorded to the story in England, in America, and on the Continent of Europe was instantly and universally favourable. Never have I had better reason than this work has given me to feel gratefully to novel-readers of all nations. Everywhere my characters made friends, and my story roused interest. Everywhere the public favour looked over my faults—and repaid me a hundred-fold for the hard toil which these pages cost me in the dark time of sickness and grief.

I have only to add that the present edition has had the benefit of my careful revision. All that I can do towards making the book worthy of the readers' continued approval has now been done.

W.C.

May, 1871.

PROLOGUE

THE STORMING OF SERINGAPATAM (1799)

Extracted from a Family Paper

I

I address these lines—written in India—to my relatives in England.

My object is to explain the motive which has induced me to refuse the right hand of friendship to my cousin, John Herncastle. The reserve which I have hitherto maintained in this matter has been misinterpreted by members of my family whose good opinion I cannot consent to forfeit. I request them to suspend their decision until they have read my narrative. And I declare, on my word of honour, that what I am now about to write is, strictly and literally, the truth.

The private difference between my cousin and me took its rise in a great public event in which we were both concerned—the storming of Seringapatam, under General Baird, on the 4 May 1799.

In order that the circumstances may be clearly understood, I must revert for a moment to the period before the assault, and to the stories current in our camp of the treasure in jewels and gold stored up in the Palace of Seringapatam.

II

One of the wildest of these stories related to a Yellow Diamond—a famous gem in the native annals of India.

The earliest known traditions describe the stone as having been set in the forehead of the four-handed Indian god who typifies the Moon. Partly from its peculiar colour, partly from a superstition which represented it as feeling the influence of the deity whom it adorned, and growing and lessening in lustre with the waxing and waning of the moon, it first gained the name by which it continues to be known in India to this day—the name of The Moonstone. A similar superstition was once prevalent, as I have heard, in ancient Greece and Rome; not applying, however (as in India), to a diamond devoted to the service of a god, but to a semi-transparent stone of the inferior order of gems, supposed to be affected by the lunar influences—the moon, in this latter case also, giving the name by which the stone is still known to collectors in our own time.

The adventures of the Yellow Diamond begin with the eleventh century of the Christian era.

At that date, the Mohammedan conqueror, Mahmoud of Ghizni, crossed India; seized on the holy city of Somnauth; and stripped of its treasures the famous temple, which had stood for centuries—the shrine of Hindoo pilgrimage, and the wonder of the eastern world.

Of all the deities worshipped in the temple, the moon-god alone escaped the rapacity of the conquering Mohammedans. Preserved by three Brahmins, the inviolate deity, bearing the Yellow Diamond in its forehead, was removed by night, and was transported to the second of the sacred cities of India—the city of Benares.

Here, in a new shrine—in a hall inlaid with precious stones, under a roof supported by pillars of gold—the moon-god was set up and worshipped. Here, on the night when the shrine was completed, Vishnu the Preserver appeared to the three Brahmins in a dream.

The deity breathed the breath of his divinity on the Diamond in the forehead of the god. And the Brahmins knelt and hid their faces in their robes. The deity commanded that the Moonstone should be watched, from that time forth, by three priests in turn, night and day, to the end of the generations of men. And the Brahmins heard, and bowed before his will. The deity predicted certain disaster to the presumptuous mortal who laid hands on the sacred gem, and to all of his house and name who received it after him. And the Brahmins caused the prophecy to be written over the gates of the shrine in letters of gold.

One age followed another—and still, generation after generation, the successors of the three Brahmins watched their priceless Moonstone, night and day. One age followed another, until the first years of the eighteenth Christian century saw the reign of Aurungzebe, Emperor of the Moguls. At his command, havoc and rapine were let loose once more among the temples of the worship of Brahmah. The shrine of the four-handed god was polluted by the slaughter of sacred animals; the images of the deities were broken in pieces; and the Moonstone was seized by an officer of rank in the army of Aurungzebe.

Powerless to recover their lost treasure by open force, the three guardian priests followed and watched it in disguise. The generations succeeded each other; the warrior who had committed the sacrilege perished miserably; the Moonstone passed (carrying its curse with it) from one lawless Mohammedan hand to another; and still, through all chances and changes, the successors of the three guardian priests kept their watch, waiting the day when the will of Vishnu the Preserver should restore to them their sacred gem. Time rolled on from the first to the last years of the eighteenth Christian century. The Diamond fell into the possession of Tippoo, Sultan of Seringapatam, who caused it to be placed as an ornament in the handle of a dagger, and who commanded it to be kept among the choicest treasures of his armoury. Even then—in the palace of the Sultan himself—the three guardian priests still kept their watch in secret. There were three officers of Tippoo's household, strangers to the rest, who had won their master's confidence by conforming, or appearing to conform, to the Mussulman faith; and to those three men report pointed as the three priests in disguise.

III

So, as told in our camp, ran the fanciful story of the Moonstone. It made no serious impression on any of us except my cousin—whose love of the marvellous induced him to believe it. On the night before the assault on Seringapatam, he was absurdly angry with me, and with others, for treating the whole thing as a fable. A foolish wrangle followed; and Herncastle's unlucky temper got the better of him. He declared, in his boastful way, that we should see the Diamond on his finger, if the English army took Seringapatam. The sally was saluted by a roar of laughter, and there, as we all thought that night, the thing ended.

Let me now take you on to the day of the assault.

My cousin and I were separated at the outset. I never saw him when we forded the river; when we planted the English flag in the first breach; when we crossed the ditch beyond; and, fighting every inch of our way, entered the town. It was only at dusk, when the place was ours, and after General Baird himself had found the dead body of Tippoo under a heap of the slain, that Herncastle and I met.

We were each attached to a party sent out by the General's orders to prevent the plunder and confusion which followed our conquest. The camp-followers committed deplorable excesses; and, worse still, the soldiers found their way, by an unguarded door, into the treasury of the Palace, and loaded themselves with gold and jewels. It was in the court outside the treasury that my cousin and I met, to enforce the laws of discipline on our own soldiers. Herncastle's fiery temper had been, as I could plainly see, exasperated to a kind of frenzy by the terrible slaughter through which we had passed. He was very unfit, in my opinion, to perform the duty that had been entrusted to him.

There was riot and confusion enough in the treasury, but no violence that I saw. The men (if I may use such an expression) disgraced themselves good-humouredly. All sorts of rough jests and catchwords were bandied about among them; and the story of the Diamond turned up again unexpectedly, in the form of a mischievous joke. 'Who's got the Moonstone?' was the rallying cry which perpetually caused the plundering, as soon as it was stopped in one place, to break out in another. While I was still vainly trying to establish order, I heard a frightful yelling on the other side of the court-yard, and at once ran towards the cries, in dread of finding some new outbreak of the pillage in that direction.

I got to an open door, and saw the bodies of two Indians (by their dress, as I guessed, officers of the palace) lying across the entrance, dead.

A cry inside hurried me into a room, which appeared to serve as an armoury. A third Indian, mortally wounded, was sinking at the feet of a man whose back was towards me. The man turned at the instant when I came in, and I saw John Herncastle, with a torch in one hand, and a dagger dripping with blood in the other. A stone, set like a pommel, in the end of the dagger's handle, flashed in the torchlight, as he turned on me, like a gleam of fire. The dying Indian sank to his knees, pointed to the dagger in Herncastle's hand, and said, in his native language:—'The Moonstone will have its vengeance yet on you and yours!' He spoke those words, and fell dead on the floor.

Before I could stir in the matter, the men who had followed me across the courtyard crowded in. My cousin rushed to meet them, like a madman. 'Clear the room!' he shouted to me, 'and set a guard on the door!' The men fell back as he threw himself on them with his torch and his dagger. I put two sentinels of my own company, on whom I could rely, to keep the door. Through the remainder of the night, I saw no more of my cousin.

Early in the morning, the plunder still going on, General Baird announced publicly by beat of drum, that any thief detected in the fact, be he whom he might, should be hung. The provost-marshal was in attendance, to prove that the General was in earnest; and in the throng that followed the proclamation, Herncastle and I met again.

He held out his hand, as usual, and said, 'Good morning.'

I waited before I gave him my hand in return.

'Tell me first,' I said, 'how the Indian in the armoury met his death, and what those last words meant, when he pointed to the dagger in your hand.'

'The Indian met his death, as I suppose, by a mortal wound,' said Herncastle. 'What his last words meant I know no more than you do.'

I looked at him narrowly. His frenzy of the previous day had all calmed down. I determined to give him another chance.

'Is that all you have to tell me?' I asked.

He answered, 'That is all.'

I turned my back on him; and we have not spoken since.

IV

I beg it to be understood that what I write here about my cousin (unless some necessity should arise for making it public) is for the information of the family only. Herncastle has said nothing that can justify me in speaking to our commanding officer. He has been taunted more than once about the Diamond, by those who recollect his angry outbreak before the assault; but, as may easily be imagined, his own remembrance of the circumstances under which I surprised him in the armoury has been enough to keep him silent. It is reported that he means to exchange into another regiment, avowedly for the purpose of separating himself from *me*.

Whether this be true or not, I cannot prevail upon myself to become his accuser—and I think with good reason. If I made the matter public, I have no evidence but moral evidence to bring forward. I have not only no proof that he killed the two men at the door; I cannot even declare that he killed the third man inside—for I cannot say that my own eyes saw the deed committed. It is true that I heard the dying Indian's words; but if those words were pronounced to be the ravings of delirium, how could I contradict the assertion from my own knowledge? Let our relatives, on either side, form their own opinion on what I have written, and decide for themselves whether the aversion I now feel towards this man is well or ill founded.

Although I attach no sort of credit to the fantastic Indian legend of the gem, I must acknowledge, before I conclude, that I am influenced by a certain superstition of my own in this matter. It is my conviction, or my delusion, no matter which, that crime brings ts own fatality with it. I am not only persuaded of Herncastle's guilt; I am even fanciful enough to believe that he will live to regret it, if he keeps the Diamond; and that others will live to regret taking it from him, if he gives the Diamond away.

THE STORY

FIRST PERIOD

THE LOSS OF THE DIAMOND (1848)

The Events related by Gabriel Betteredge, *House-Steward in the service of* Julia, Lady Verinder

CHAPTER 1

In the first part of *Robinson Crusoe*, at page one hundred and twenty-nine, you will find it thus written:

'Now I saw, though too late, the Folly of beginning a Work before we count the Cost, and before we judge rightly of our own Strength to go through with it.'

Only yesterday, I opened my *Robinson Crusoe* at that place. Only this morning (May twenty-first, Eighteen hundred and fifty), came my lady's nephew, Mr Franklin Blake, and held a short conversation with me, as follows:—

'Betteredge,' says Mr Franklin, 'I have been to the lawyer's about some family matters; and, among other things, we have been talking of the loss of the Indian Diamond, in my aunt's house in Yorkshire, two years since. Mr Bruff thinks, as I think, that the whole story ought, in the interests of truth, to be placed on record in writing—and the sooner the better.'

Not perceiving his drift yet, and thinking it always desirable for the sake of peace and quietness to be on the lawyer's side, I said I thought so too. Mr Franklin went on.

'In this matter of the Diamond,' he said, 'the characters of innocent people have suffered under suspicion already—as you know. The memories of innocent people may suffer, hereafter, for want of a record of the facts to which those who come after us can appeal. There can be no doubt that this strange family story of ours ought to be told. And I think, Betteredge, Mr Bruff and I together have hit on the right way of telling it.'

Very satisfactory to both of them, no doubt. But I failed to see what I myself had to do with it, so far.

'We have certain events to relate,' Mr Franklin proceeded; 'and we have certain persons concerned in those events who are capable of relating them. Starting from these plain facts, the idea is that we should all write the story of the Moonstone in turn—as far as our own personal experience extends, and no farther. We must begin by showing how the Diamond first fell into the hands of my uncle Herncastle, when he was serving in

India fifty years since. This prefatory narrative I have already got by me in the form of an old family paper, which relates the necessary particulars on the authority of an eye-witness. The next thing to do is to tell how the Diamond found its way into my aunt's house in Yorkshire, two years ago, and how it came to be lost in little more than twelve hours afterwards. Nobody knows as much as you do, Betteredge, about what went on in the house at that time. So you must take the pen in hand, and start the story.'

In those terms I was informed of what my personal concern was with the matter of the Diamond. If you are curious to know what course I took under the circumstances, I beg to inform you that I did what you would probably have done in my place. I modestly declared myself to be quite unequal to the task imposed upon me—and I privately felt, all the time, that I was quite clever enough to perform it, if I only gave my own abilities a fair chance. Mr Franklin, I imagine, must have seen my private sentiments in my face. He declined to believe in my modesty; and he insisted on giving my abilities a fair chance.

Two hours have passed since Mr Franklin left me. As soon as his back was turned, I went to my writing-desk to start the story. There I have sat helpless (in spite of my abilities) ever since; seeing what Robinson Crusoe saw, as quoted above—namely, the folly of beginning a work before we count the cost, and before we judge rightly of our own strength to go through with it. Please to remember, I opened the book by accident, at that bit, only the day before I rashly undertook the business now in hand; and, allow me to ask—if *that* isn't prophecy, what is?

I am not superstitious; I have read a heap of books in my time; I am a scholar in my own way. Though turned seventy, I possess an active memory, and legs to correspond. You are not to take it, if you please, as the saying of an ignorant man, when I express my opinion that such a book as *Robinson Crusoe* never was written, and never will be written again. I have tried that book for years—generally in combination with a pipe of tobacco—and I have found it my friend in need in all the necessities of this mortal life. When my spirits are bad—*Robinson Crusoe*. When I want advice—*Robinson Crusoe*. In past times, when my wife plagued me; in present times, when I have had a drop too much—*Robinson Crusoe*. I have worn out six stout *Robinson Crusoe*s with hard work in my service. On my lady's last birthday she gave me a seventh. I took a drop too much on the strength of it; and *Robinson Crusoe* put me right again. Price four shillings and sixpence, bound in blue, with a picture into the bargain.

Still, this don't look much like starting the story of the Diamond—does it? I seem to be wandering off in search of Lord knows what, Lord knows where. We will take a new sheet of paper, if you please, and begin over again, with my best respects to you.

CHAPTER 2

I spoke of my lady a line or two back. Now the Diamond could never have been in our house, where it was lost, if it had not been made a present of to my lady's daughter; and my lady's daughter would never have been in existence to have the present, if it had not been for my lady who (with pain and travail) produced her into the world. Consequently, if we begin with my lady, we are pretty sure of beginning far enough back. And that, let me tell you, when you have got such a job as mine in hand, is a real comfort at starting.

If you know anything of the fashionable world, you have heard tell of the three beautiful Miss Herncastles. Miss Adelaide; Miss Caroline; and Miss Julia—this last being the youngest and the best of the three sisters, in my opinion; and I had opportunities of judging, as you shall presently see. I went into the service of the old lord, their father (thank God, we have got nothing to do with *him*, in this business of the Diamond; he had the longest tongue and the shortest temper of any man, high or low, I ever met with)—I say, I went into the service of the old lord, as page-boy in waiting on the three honourable young ladies, at the age of fifteen years. There I lived, till Miss Julia married the late Sir John Verinder. An excellent man, who only wanted somebody to manage him; and, between ourselves, he found somebody to do it; and what is more, he throve on it, and grew fat on it, and lived happy and died easy on it, dating from the day when my lady took him to church to be married, to the day when she relieved him of his last breath, and closed his eyes for ever.

I have omitted to state that I went with the bride to the bride's busband's house and lands down here. 'Sir John,' she says, 'I can't do without Gabriel Betteredge.' 'My lady,' says Sir John, 'I can't do without him, either.' That was his way with her—and that was how I went into his service. It was all one to me where I went, so long as my mistress and I were together.

Seeing that my lady took an interest in the out-of-door work, and the farms, and such like, I took an interest in them too—with all the more reason that I was a small farmer's seventh son myself. My lady got me put under the bailiff, and I did my best, and gave satisfaction, and got promotion accordingly. Some years later, on the Monday as it might be, my lady says, 'Sir John, your bailiff is a stupid old man. Pension him liberally, and let Gabriel Betteredge have his place.' On the Tuesday as it might be, Sir John says, 'My lady, the bailiff is pensioned liberally; and Gabriel Betteredge has got his place.' You hear more than enough of married people living together miserably. Here is an example to the contrary. Let it be a warning to some of you, and an encouragement to others. In the meantime, I will go on with my story.

Well, there I was in clover, you will say. Placed in a position of trust and honour, with a little cottage of my own to live in, with my rounds on the estate to occupy me in the morning, and my accounts in the afternoon, and my pipe and my *Robinson Crusoe* in the evening—what more could I possibly want to make me happy? Remember what Adam wanted when he was alone in the Garden of Eden; and if you don't blame it in Adam, don't blame it in me.

The woman I fixed my eye on, was the woman who kept house for me at my cottage. Her name was Selina Goby. I agree with the late William Cobbett about picking a wife. See that she chews her food well, and sets her foot down firmly on the ground when she walks, and you're all right. Selina Goby was all right in both these respects, which was one reason for marrying her. I had another reason, likewise, entirely of my own discovering. Selina, being a single woman, made me pay so much a week for her board and services. Selina, being my wife, couldn't charge for her board, and would have to give me her services for nothing. That was the point of view I looked at it from. Economy—with a dash of love. I put it to my mistress, as in duty bound, just as I had put it to myself.

'I have been turning Selina Goby over in my mind,' I said, 'and I think, my lady, it will be cheaper to marry her than to keep her.'

My lady burst out laughing, and said she didn't know which to be most shocked at—my language or my principles. Some joke tickled her, I suppose, of the sort that you can't take unless you are a person of quality. Understanding nothing myself but that I was free to put it next to Selina, I went and put it accordingly. And what did Selina say? Lord! how little you must know of women, if you ask that. Of course she said, Yes.

As my time drew nearer, and there got to be talk of my having a new coat for the ceremony, my mind began to misgive me. I have compared notes with other men as to what they felt while they were in my interesting situation; and they have all acknowledged that, about a week before it happened, they privately wished themselves out of it. I went a trifle further than that myself; I actually rose up, as it were, and tried to get out of it. Not for nothing! I was too just a man to expect she would let me off for nothing. Compensation to the woman when the man gets out of it, is one of the laws of England. In obedience to the laws, and after turning it over carefully in my mind, I offered Selina Goby a feather-bed and fifty shillings to be off the bargain. You will hardly believe it, but it is nevertheless true—she was fool enough to refuse.

After that it was all over with me, of course. I got the new coat as cheap as I could, and I went through all the rest of it as cheap as I could. We were not a happy couple, and not a miserable couple. We were six of one and half-a-dozen of the other. How it was I don't understand, but we always seemed to be getting, with the best of motives, in one another's way. When I wanted to go upstairs, there was my wife coming down; or when my wife wanted to go down, there was I coming up. That is married life, according to my experience of it.

After five years of misunderstandings on the stairs, it pleased an all-wise Providence to relieve us of each other by taking my wife. I was left with my little girl Penelope, and with no other child. Shortly afterwards Sir John died, and my lady was left with her little girl, Miss Rachel, and no other child. I have written to very poor purpose of my lady, if you require to be told that my little Penelope was taken care of, under my good mistress's own eye, and was sent to school, and taught, and made a sharp girl, and promoted, when old enough, to be Miss Rachel's own maid.

As for me, I went on with my business as bailiff year after year up to Christmas, 1847, when there came a change in my life. On that day, my lady invited herself to a cup of tea alone with me in my cottage. She remarked that, reckoning from the year when I started as page-boy in the time of the old lord, I had been more than fifty years in her service, and she put into my hands a beautiful waistcoat of wool that she had worked herself, to keep me warm in the bitter winter weather.

I received this magnificent present quite at a loss to find words to thank my mistress with for the honour she had done me. To my great astonishment, it turned out, however, that the waistcoat was not an honour, but a bribe. My lady had discovered that I was getting old before I had discovered it myself, and she had come to my cottage to wheedle me (if I may use such an expression) into giving up my hard out-of-door work as bailiff, and taking my ease for the rest of my days as steward in the house. I made as good a fight of it against the indignity of taking my ease as I could. But my mistress knew the weak side of me; she put it as a favour to herself. The dispute between us ended, after that, in my wiping my eyes, like an old fool, with my new woollen waistcoat, and saying I would think about it.

The perturbation in my mind, in regard to thinking about it, being truly dreadful after my lady had gone away, I applied the remedy which I have never yet found to fail me in cases of doubt and emergency. I smoked a pipe and took a turn at *Robinson Crusoe*. Before I had occupied myself with that extraordinary book five minutes, I came on a comforting bit (page one hundred and fifty-eight), as follows: 'To-day we love, what to-morrow we hate.' I saw my way clear directly. To-day I was all for continuing to be farm-bailiff; to-morrow, on the authority of *Robinson Crusoe*, I should be all the other way. Take myself to-morrow while in to-morrow's humour, and the thing was done. My mind being relieved in this manner, I went to sleep that night in the character of Lady Verinder's farm-bailiff, and I woke up the next morning in the character of Lady Verinder's house-steward. All quite comfortable, and all through *Robinson Crusoe*!

My daughter Penelope has just looked over my shoulder to see what I have done so far. She remarks that it is beautifully written and every word of it true. But she points out one objection. She says what I have done so far isn't in the least what I was wanted to do. I am asked to tell the story of the Diamond, and, instead of that, I have been telling the story of my own self. Curious, and quite beyond me to account for. I wonder whether the gentlemen who make a business and a living out of writing books, ever find their own selves getting in the way of their subjects, like me? If they do, I can feel for them. In the meantime, here is another false start, and more waste of good writing-paper. What's to be done now? Nothing that I know of, except for you to keep your temper, and for me to begin it all over again for the third time.

CHAPTER 3

The question of how I am to start the story properly I have tried to settle in two ways. First, by scratching my head, which led to nothing. Second, by consulting my daughter Penelope, which has resulted in an entirely new idea.

Penelope's notion is that I should set down what happened, regularly day by day, beginning with the day when we got the news that Mr Franklin Blake was expected on a visit to the house. When you come to fix your memory with a date in this way, it is wonderful what your memory will pick up for you upon that compulsion. The only difficulty is to fetch out the dates, in the first place. This Penelope offers to do for me by looking into her own diary, which she was taught to keep when she was at school, and which she has gone on keeping ever since. In answer to an improvement on this notion, devised by myself, namely, that she should tell the story instead of me, out of her own diary, Penelope observes, with a fierce look and a red face, that her journal is for her own private eye, and that no living creature shall ever know what is in it but herself. When I inquire what this means, Penelope says, 'Fiddlesticks!' I say, Sweethearts.

Beginning, then, on Penelope's plan, I beg to mention that I was specially called one Wednesday morning into my lady's own sitting-room, the date being the twenty-fourth of May, Eighteen hundred and forty-eight.

'Gabriel,' says my lady, 'here is news that will surprise you. Franklin Blake has come back from abroad. He has been staying with his father in London, and he is coming to us to-morrow to stop till next month, and keep Rachel's birthday.'

If I had had a hat in my hand, nothing but respect would have prevented me from throwing that hat up to the ceiling. I had not seen Mr Franklin since he was a boy, living along with us in this house. He was, out of all sight (as I remembered him), the nicest boy that ever spun a top or broke a window. Miss Rachel, who was present, and to whom I made that remark, observed, in return, that *she* remembered him as the most atrocious tyrant that ever tortured a doll, and the hardest driver of an exhausted little girl in string harness that England could produce. 'I burn with indignation, and I ache with fatigue,' was the way Miss Rachel summed it up, 'when I think of Franklin Blake.'

Hearing what I now tell you, you will naturally ask how it was that Mr Franklin should have passed all the years, from the time when he was a boy to the time when he was a man, out of his own country. I answer, because his father had the misfortune to be next heir to a Dukedom, and not to be able to prove it.

In two words, this was how the thing happened:

My lady's eldest sister married the celebrated Mr Blake—equally famous for his great riches, and his great suit at law. How many years he went on worrying the tribunals of his country to turn out the Duke in possession, and to put himself in the Duke's place—how many lawyers' purses he filled to bursting, and how many otherwise harmless people he set by the ears together disputing whether he was right or wrong—is more by a great deal than I can reckon up. His wife died, and two of his three children died, before the tribunals could make up their minds to show him the door and take no more of his money. When it was all over, and the Duke in possession was left in possession, Mr Blake discovered that the only way of being even with his country for the manner in which it had treated him, was not to let his country have the honour of educating his son. 'How can I trust my native institutions,' was the form in which he put it, 'after the way in which my native institutions have behaved to *me*?' Add to this, that Mr Blake disliked all boys, his own included, and you will admit that it could only end in one way. Master Franklin was taken from us in England, and was sent to institutions which his father *could* trust, in that superior country, Germany; Mr Blake himself, you will observe, remaining snug in England, to improve his fellow-countrymen in the Parliament House, and to publish a statement on the subject of the Duke in possession, which has remained an unfinished statement from that day to this.

There! thank God, that's told! Neither you nor I need trouble our heads any more about Mr Blake, senior. Leave him to the Dukedom; and let you and I stick to the Diamond.

The Diamond takes us back to Mr Franklin, who was the innocent means of bringing that unlucky jewel into the house.

Our nice boy didn't forget us after he went abroad. He wrote every now and then;

sometimes to my lady, sometimes to Miss Rachel, and sometimes to me. We had had a transaction together, before he left, which consisted in his borrowing of me a ball of string, a four-bladed knife, and seven-and-sixpence in money—the colour of which last I have not seen, and never expect to see again. His letters to me chiefly related to borrowing more. I heard, however, from my lady, how he got on abroad, as he grew in years and stature. After he had learnt what the institutions of Germany could teach him, he gave the French a turn next, and the Italians a turn after that. They made him among them a sort of universal genius, as well as I could understand it. He wrote a little; he painted a little; he sang and played and composed a little—borrowing, as I suspect, in all these cases, just as he had borrowed from me. His mother's fortune (seven hundred a year) fell to him when he came of age, and ran through him, as it might be through a sieve. The more money he had, the more he wanted: there was a hole in Mr Franklin's pocket that nothing would sew up. Wherever he went, the lively, easy way of him made him welcome. He lived here, there, and everywhere; his address (as he used to put it himself) being, 'Post Office, Europe—to be left till called for.' Twice over, he made up his mind to come back to England and see us; and twice over (saving your presence), some unmentionable woman stood in the way and stopped him. His third attempt succeeded, as you know already from what my lady told me. On Thursday the twenty-fifth of May, we were to see for the first time what our nice boy had grown to be as a man. He came of good blood; he had a high courage; and he was five-and-twenty years of age, by our reckoning. Now you know as much of Mr Franklin Blake as I did—before Mr Franklin Blake came down to our house.

The Thursday was as fine a summer's day as ever you saw: and my lady and Miss Rachel (not expecting Mr Franklin till dinner-time) drove out to lunch with some friends in the neighbourhood.

When they were gone, I went and had a look at the bedroom which had been got ready for our guest, and saw that all was straight. Then, being butler in my lady's establishment, as well as steward (at my own particular request, mind, and because it vexed me to see anybody but myself in possession of the key of the late Sir John's cellar)—then, I say, I fetched up some of our famous Latour claret, and set it in the warm summer air to take off the chill before dinner. Concluding to set myself in the warm summer air next—seeing that what is good for old claret is equally good for old age—I took up my beehive chair to go out into the back court, when I was stopped by hearing a sound like the soft beating of a drum, on the terrace in front of my lady's residence.

Going round to the terrace, I found three mahogany-coloured Indians, in white linen frocks and trousers looking up at the house.

The Indians, as I saw on looking closer, had small hand-drums slung in front of them. Behind them stood a little delicate-looking light-haired English boy carrying a bag. I judged the fellows to be strolling conjurors, and the boy with the bag to be carrying the tools of their trade. One of the three, who spoke English, and who exhibited, I must own, the most elegant manners, presently informed me that my judgment was right. He requested permission to show his tricks in the presence of the lady of the house.

Now I am not a sour old man. I am generally all for amusement, and the last person in the world to distrust another person because he happens to be a few shades darker than myself. But the best of us have our weaknesses—and my weakness, when I know a family plate-basket to be out on a pantry table, is to be instantly reminded of that basket by the sight of a strolling stranger whose manners are superior to my own. I accordingly informed the Indian that the lady of the house was out; and I warned him and his party off the premises. He made me a beautiful bow in return; and he and his party went off the premises. On my side, I returned to my beehive chair, and set myself down on the sunny side of the court, and fell (if the truth must be owned), not exactly into a sleep, but into the next best thing to it.

I was roused up by my daughter Penelope running out at me as if the house was on fire. What do you think she wanted? She wanted to have the three Indian jugglers instantly taken up; for this reason, namely, that they knew who was coming from London to visit us, and that they meant some mischief to Mr Franklin Blake.

Mr Franklin's name roused me. I opened my eyes, and made my girl explain herself.

It appeared that Penelope had just come from our lodge, where she had been having a gossip with the lodge-keeper's daughter. The two girls had seen the Indians pass out, after I had warned them off, followed by their little boy. Taking it into their heads that the boy was ill-used by the foreigners—for no reason that I could discover, except that he was pretty and delicate-looking—the two girls had stolen along the inner side of the hedge between us and the road, and had watched the proceedings of the foreigners on the outer side. Those proceedings resulted in the performance of the following extraordinary tricks.

They first looked up the road, and down the road, and made sure that they were alone. Then they all three faced about, and stared hard in the direction of our house. Then they jabbered and disputed in their own language, and looked at each other like men in doubt. Then they all turned to their little English boy, as if they expected *him* to help them. And then the chief Indian, who spoke English, said to the boy, 'Hold out your hand.'

On hearing those dreadful words, my daughter Penelope said she didn't know what prevented her heart from flying straight out of her. I thought privately that it might have been her stays. All I said, however, was, 'You make my flesh creep.' (*Nota bene*: Women like these little compliments.)

Well, when the Indian said, 'Hold out your hand,' the boy shrunk back, and shook his head, and said he didn't like it. The Indian, thereupon, asked him (not at all unkindly), whether he would like to be sent back to London, and left where they had found him, sleeping in an empty basket in a market—a hungry, ragged, and forsaken little boy. This, it seems, ended the difficulty. The little chap unwillingly held out his hand. Upon that, the Indian took a bottle from his bosom, and poured out of it some black stuff, like ink, into the palm of the boy's hand. The Indian—first touching the boy's head, and making signs over it in the air—then said, 'Look.' The boy became quite stiff, and stood like a statue, looking into the ink in the hollow of his hand.

(So far, it seemed to me to be juggling, accompanied by a foolish waste of ink. I was beginning to feel sleepy again, when Penelope's next words stirred me up.)

The Indians looked up the road and down the road once more—and then the chief Indian said these words to the boy: 'See the English gentleman from foreign parts.'

The boy said, 'I see him.'

The Indian said, 'Is it on the road to this house, and on no other, that the English gentleman will travel to-day?'

The boy said, 'It is on the road to this house, and on no other, that the English gentleman will travel to-day.'

The Indian put a second question—after waiting a little first. He said: 'Has the English gentleman got It about him?'

The boy answered—also, after waiting a little first—'Yes.'

The Indian put a third and last question: 'Will the English gentleman come here, as he has promised to come, at the close of day?'

The boy said, 'I can't tell.'

The Indian asked why.

The boy said, 'I am tired. The mist rises in my head, and puzzles me. I can see no more to-day.'

With that, the catechism ended. The chief Indian said something in his own language to the other two, pointing to the boy, and pointing towards the town, in which (as we afterwards discovered) they were lodged. He then, after making more signs on the boy's head, blew on his forehead, and so woke him up with a start. After that, they all went on their way towards the town, and the girls saw them no more.

Most things they say have a moral, if you only look for it. What was the moral of this?

The moral was, as I thought: First, that the chief juggler had heard Mr Franklin's arrival talked of among the servants out-of-doors, and saw his way to making a little money by it. Second, that he and his men and boy (with a view to making the said money) meant to hang about till they saw my lady drive home, and then to come back, and foretell Mr Franklin's arrival by magic. Third, that Penelope had heard them rehearsing their hocus-pocus, like actors rehearsing a play. Fourth, that I should do well to have an eye, that evening, on the plate-basket. Fifth, that Penelope would do well to cool down, and leave me, her father, to doze off again in the sun.

That appeared to me to be the sensible view. If you know anything of the ways of young women, you won't be surprised to hear that Penelope wouldn't take it. The moral of the thing was serious, according to my daughter. She particularly reminded me of the Indian's third question, Has the English gentleman got It about him? 'Oh, father!' says Penelope, clasping her hands, 'don't joke about this! What does "It" mean?'

'We'll ask Mr Franklin, my dear,' I said, 'if you can wait till Mr Franklin comes.' I winked to show I meant that in joke. Penelope took it quite seriously. My girl's earnestness tickled me. 'What on earth should Mr Franklin know about it?' I inquired. 'Ask him,' says Penelope. 'And see whether *he* thinks it a laughing matter, too.' With that parting shot, my daughter left me.

I settled it with myself, when she was gone, that I really would ask Mr Franklin—mainly to set Penelope's mind at rest. What was said between us, when I did ask him, later on that same day, you will find set out fully in its proper place. But as I don't wish to raise your expectations and then disappoint them, I will take leave to warn you here—before we go any further—that you won't find the ghost of a joke in our conversation on the subject of the jugglers. To my great surprise, Mr Franklin, like Penelope, took the thing seriously. How seriously, you will understand, when I tell you that, in his opinion, 'It' meant the Moonstone.

CHAPTER 4

I am truly sorry to detain you over me and my beehive chair. A sleepy old man, in a sunny back yard, is not an interesting object, I am well aware. But things must be put down in their places, as things actually happened—and you must please to jog on a little while longer with me, in expectation of Mr Franklin Blake's arrival later in the day.

Before I had time to doze off again, after my daughter Penelope had left me, I was disturbed by a rattling of plates and dishes in the servants' hall, which meant that dinner was ready. Taking my own meals in my own sitting-room, I had nothing to do with the servants' dinner, except to wish them a good stomach to it all round, previous to composing myself once more in my chair. I was just stretching my legs, when out bounced another woman on me. Not my daughter again; only Nancy, the kitchen-maid, this time. I was straight in her way out; and I observed, as she asked me to let her by, that she had a sulky face—a thing which, as head of the servants, I never allow, on principle, to pass me without inquiry.

'What are you turning your back on your dinner for?' I asked. 'What's wrong now, Nancy?'

Nancy tried to push by, without answering; upon which I rose up, and took her by the ear. She is a nice plump young lass, and it is customary with me to adopt that manner of showing that I personally approve of a girl.

'What's wrong now?' I said once more.

'Rosanna's late again for dinner,' says Nancy. 'And I'm sent to fetch her in. All the hard work falls on my shoulders in this house. Let me alone, Mr Betteredge!'

The person here mentioned as Rosanna was our second housemaid. Having a kind of pity for our second housemaid (why, you shall presently know), and seeing in Nancy's face that she would fetch her fellow-servant in with more hard words than might be needful under the circumstances, it struck me that I had nothing particular to do, and that I might as well fetch Rosanna myself; giving her a hint to be punctual in future, which I knew she would take kindly from *me*.

'Where is Rosanna?' I inquired.

'At the sands, of course!' says Nancy, with a toss of her head. 'She had another of her fainting fits this morning, and she asked to go out and get a breath of fresh air. I have no patience with her!'

'Go back to your dinner, my girl,' I said. 'I have patience with her, and I'll fetch her in.'

Nancy (who has a fine appetite) looked pleased. When she looks pleased, she looks nice. When she looks nice, I chuck her under the chin. It isn't immorality—it's only habit.

Well, I took my stick, and set off for the sands.

No! it won't do to set off yet. I am sorry again to detain you: but you really must hear the story of the sands, and the story of Rosanna—for this reason, that the matter of the Diamond touches them both nearly. How hard I try to get on with my statement without stopping by the way, and how badly I succeed! But, there! —Persons and Things do turn up so vexatiously in this life, and will in a manner insist on being noticed. Let us take it easy, and let us take it short; we shall be in the thick of the mystery soon, I promise you!

Rosanna (to put the Person before the Thing, which is but common politeness) was the only new servant in our house. About four months before the time I am writing of, my lady had been in London, and had gone over a Reformatory, intended to save forlorn women from drifting back into bad ways, after they had got released from prison. The matron, seeing my lady took an interest in the place, pointed out a girl to her, named Rosanna Spearman, and told her a most miserable story, which I haven't the heart to repeat here; for I don't like to be made wretched without any use, and no more do you. The upshot of it was, that Rosanna Spearman had been a thief, and not being of the sort that get up Companies in the City, and rob from thousands, instead of only robbing from one, the law laid hold of her, and the prison and the reformatory followed the lead of the law. The matron's opinion of Rosanna was (in spite of what she had done) that the girl was one in a thousand, and that she only wanted a chance to prove herself worthy of any Christian woman's interest in her. My lady (being a Christian woman, if ever there was one yet) said to the matron, upon that, 'Rosanna Spearman shall have her chance, in my service.' In a week afterwards, Rosanna Spearman entered this establishment as our second housemaid.

Not a soul was told the girl's story, excepting Miss Rachel and me. My lady, doing me the honour to consult me about most things, consulted me about Rosanna. Having fallen a good deal latterly into the late Sir John's way of always agreeing with my lady, I agreed with her heartily about Rosanna Spearman.

A fairer chance no girl could have had than was given to this poor girl of ours. None of the servants could cast her past life in her teeth, for none of the servants knew what it had been. She had her wages and her privileges, like the rest of them; and every now and then a friendly word from my lady, in private, to encourage her. In return, she showed herself, I am bound to say, well worthy of the kind treatment bestowed upon her. Though far from strong, and troubled occasionally with those fainting-fits already mentioned, she went about her work modestly and uncomplainingly, doing it carefully, and doing it well. But, somehow, she failed to make friends among the other women servants, excepting my daughter Penelope, who was always kind to Rosanna, though never intimate with her.

I hardly know what the girl did to offend them. There was certainly no beauty about her to make the others envious; she was the plainest woman in the house, with the additional misfortune of having one shoulder bigger than the other. What the servants chiefly resented, I think, was her silent tongue and her solitary ways. She read or worked in leisure hours when the rest gossiped. And when it came to her turn to go out, nine times out of ten she quietly put on her bonnet, and had her turn by herself. She never quarrelled, she never took offence; she only kept a certain distance, obstinately and civilly, between the rest of them and herself. Add to this that, plain as she was, there was just a dash of something that wasn't like a housemaid, and that *was* like a lady, about her. It might have been in her voice, or it might have been in her face. All I can say is, that the other women pounced on it like lightning the first day she came into the house, and said (which was most unjust) that Rosanna Spearman gave herself airs.

Having now told the story of Rosanna, I have only to notice one of the many queer ways of this strange girl to get on next to the story of the sands.

Our house is high up on the Yorkshire coast, and close by the sea. We have got beautiful walks all round us, in every direction but one. That one I acknowledge to be a horrid walk. It leads, for a quarter of a mile, through a melancholy plantation of firs, and brings you out between low cliffs on the loneliest and ugliest little bay on all our coast.

The sandhills here run down to the sea, and end in two spits of rock jutting out opposite each other, till you lose sight of them in the water. One is called the North Spit, and one the South. Between the two, shifting backwards and forwards at certain seasons of the year, lies the most horrible quicksand on the shores of Yorkshire. At the turn of the tide, something goes on in the unknown deeps below, which sets the whole face of the quicksand shivering and trembling in a manner most remarkable to see, and which has given to it, among the people in our parts, the name of The Shivering Sand. A great bank, half a mile out, nigh the mouth of the bay, breaks the force of the main ocean coming in from the offing. Winter and summer, when the tide flows over the quicksand, the sea seems to leave the waves behind it on the bank, and rolls its waters in smoothly with a heave, and covers the sand in silence. A lonesome and a horrid retreat, I can tell you! No boat ever ventures into this bay. No children from our fishing-village, called Cobb's Hole, ever come here to play. The very birds of the air, as it seems to me, give the Shivering Sand a wide berth. That a young woman, with dozens of nice walks to choose from, and company to go with her, if she only said 'Come!' should prefer this place, and should sit and work or read in it, all alone, when it's her turn out, I grant you, passes belief. It's true, nevertheless, account for it as you may, that this was Rosanna Spearman's favourite walk, except when she went once or twice to Cobb's Hole, to see the only friend she had in our neighbourhood, of whom more anon. It's also true that I was now setting out for this same place, to fetch the girl in to dinner, which brings us round happily to our former point, and starts us fair again on our way to the sands.

I saw no sign of the girl in the plantation. When I got out, through the sandhills, on to the beach, there she was, in her little straw bonnet, and her plain grey cloak that she always wore to hide her deformed shoulder as much as might be—there she was, all alone, looking out on the quicksand and the sea.

She started when I came up with her, and turned her head away from me. Not looking me in the face being another of the proceedings which, as head of the servants, I never allow, on principle, to pass without inquiry—I turned her round my way, and saw that she was crying. My bandanna handkerchief—one of six beauties given to me by me lady—was handy in my pocket. I took it out, and I said to Rosanna, 'Come and sit down, my dear, on the slope of the beach along with me. I'll dry your eyes for you first, and then I'll make so bold as to ask what you have been crying about.'

When you come to my age, you will find sitting down on the slope of a beach a much longer job than you think it now. By the time I was settled, Rosanna had dried her own eyes with a very inferior handkerchief to mine—cheap cambric. She looked very quiet, and very wretched; but she sat down by me like a good girl, when I told her. When you want to comfort a woman by the shortest way, take her on your knee. I thought of this golden rule. But there! Rosanna wasn't Nancy, and that's the truth of it!

'Now, tell me, my dear,' I said, 'what are you crying about?'

'About the years that are gone, Mr Betteredge,' says Rosanna quietly. 'My past life still comes back to me sometimes.'

'Come, come, my girl,' I said, 'your past life is all sponged out. Why can't you forget it?'

She took me by one of the lappets of my coat. I am a slovenly old man, and a good deal of my meat and drink gets splashed about on my clothes. Sometimes one of the women, and sometimes another, cleans me of my grease. The day before, Rosanna had taken out a spot for me on the lappet of my coat, with a new composition, warranted to remove any-thing. The grease was gone, but there was a little dull place left on the nap of the cloth where the grease had been. The girl pointed to that place, and shook her head.

'The stain is taken off,' she said. 'But the place shows, Mr Betteredge—the place shows!'

A remark which takes a man unawares by means of his own coat is not an easy remark to answer. Something in the girl herself, too, made me particularly sorry for her just then. She had nice brown eyes, plain as she was in other ways—and she looked at me with a sort of respect for my bappy old age and my good character, as things for ever out of her own reach, which made my heart heavy for our second housemaid. Not feeling myself able to comfort her, there was only one other thing to do. That thing was—to take her in to dinner.

'Help me up,' I said. 'You're late for dinner, Rosanna—and I have come to fetch you in.'

'You, Mr Betteredge!' says she.

'They told Nancy to fetch you,' I said. 'But I thought you might like your scolding better, my dear, if it came from me.'

Instead of helping me up, the poor thing stole her hand into mine, and gave it a little squeeze. She tried hard to keep from crying again, and succeeded—for which I respected her. 'You're very kind, Mr Betteredge,' she said. 'I don't want any dinner to-day—let me bide a little longer here.'

'What makes you like to be here?' I asked. 'What is it that brings you everlastingly to this miserable place.'

'Something draws me to it,' says the girl, making images with her finger in the sand. 'I try to keep away from it, and I can't. Sometimes,' says she in a low voice, as if she was frightened at her own fancy, 'sometimes, Mr Betteredge, I think that my grave is waiting for me here.'

'There's roast mutton and suet-pudding waiting for you!' says I. 'Go in to dinner directly. This is what comes, Rosanna, of thinking on an empty stomach!' I spoke severely, being naturally indignant (at my time of life) to hear a young woman of five-and-twenty talking about her latter end!

She didn't seem to hear me: she put her hand on my shoulder, and kept me where I was, sitting by her side.

'I think the place has laid a spell on me,' she said. 'I dream of it night after night; I think of it when I sit stitching at my work. You know I am grateful, Mr Betteredge—you know I try to deserve your kindness, and my lady's confidence in me. But I wonder some-times whether the life here is too quiet and too good for such a woman as I am, after all I have gone through, Mr Betteredge —after all I have gone through. It's more lonely to me to be among the other servants, knowing I am not what they are, than it is to be here. My lady doesn't know, the matron at the reformatory doesn't know, what a dreadful reproach honest people are in themselves to a woman like me. Don't scold me, there's a dear good man. I do my work, don't I? Please not to tell my lady I am discontented—I am not. My mind's unquiet, sometimes, that's all.' She snatched her hand off my shoulder, and suddenly pointed down to the quicksand. 'Look!' she said. 'Isn't it wonderful? isn't it terrible? I have seen it dozens of times, and it's always as new to me as if I had never seen it before!'

I looked where she pointed. The tide was on the turn, and the horrid sand began to shiver. The broad brown face of it heaved slowly, and then dimpled and quivered all over. 'Do you know what it looks like to *me*?' says Rosanna, catching me by the shoulder again. 'It looks as if it had hundreds of suffocating people under it—all struggling to get to the surface, and all sinking lower and lower in the dreadful deeps! Throw a stone in, Mr Betteredge! Throw a stone in, and let's see the sand suck it down!'

Here was unwholesome talk! Here was an empty stomach feeding on an unquiet mind! My answer—a pretty sharp one, in the poor girl's own interests, I promise you!—was at my tongue's end, when it was snapped short off on a sudden by a voice among the sand-hills shouting for me by my name. 'Betteredge!' cries the voice, 'where are you?' 'Here!' I shouted out in return, without a notion in my mind of who it was. Rosanna started to her feet, and stood looking towards the voice. I was just thinking of getting on my own legs next, when I was staggered by a sudden change in the girl's face.

Her complexion turned of a beautiful red, which I had never seen in it before; she brightened all over with a kind of speechless and breathless surprise. 'Who is it?' I asked. Rosanna gave me back my own question. 'Oh! who is it?' she said softly, more to herself than to me. I twisted round on the sand, and looked behind me. There, coming out on us from among the hills, was a bright-eyed young gentleman, dressed in a beautiful fawn-coloured suit, with gloves and hat to match, with a rose in his button-hole, and a smile on his face that might have set the Shivering Sand itself smiling at him in return. Before I could get on my legs, he plumped down on the sand by the side of me, put his arm round my neck, foreign fashion, and gave me a hug that fairly squeezed the breath out of my body. 'Dear old Betteredge!' says he. 'I owe you seven-and-sixpence. Now do you know who I am?'

Lord bless us and save us! Here—four good hours before we expected him—was Mr Franklin Blake!

Before I could say a word, I saw Mr Franklin, a little surprised to all appearance, look up from me to Rosanna. Following his lead, I looked at the girl too. She was blushing of a deeper red than ever, seemingly at having caught Mr Franklin's eye; and she turned and left us suddenly, in a confusion quite unaccountable to my mind, without either making her curtsey to the gentleman or saying a word to me. Very unlike her usual self: a civiller and better-behaved servant, in general, you never met with.

'That's an odd girl,' says Mr Franklin. 'I wonder what she sees in me to surprise her?'

'I suppose, sir,' I answered, drolling on our young gentleman's Continental education, 'it's the varnish from foreign parts.'

I set down here Mr Franklin's careless question, and my foolish answer, as a consolation and encouragement to all stupid people—it being, as I have remarked, a great satisfaction to our inferior fellow-creatures to find that their betters are, on occasions, no brighter than they are. Neither Mr Franklin, with his wonderful foreign training, nor I, with my age, experience, and natural mother-wit, had the ghost of an idea of what Rosanna Spearman's unaccountable behaviour really meant. She was out of our thoughts, poor soul, before we had seen the last flutter of her little grey cloak among the sandhills. And what of that? you will ask, naturally enough. Read on, good friend, as patiently as you can, and perhaps you will be as sorry for Rosanna Spearman as I was, when I found out the truth.

CHAPTER 5

The first thing I did, after we were left together alone, was to make a third attempt to get up from my seat on the sand. Mr Franklin stopped me.

'There is one advantage about this horrid place,' he said; 'we have got it all to ourselves. Stay where you are, Betteredge; I have something to say to you.'

While he was speaking, I was looking at him, and trying to see something of the boy I remembered, in the man before me. The man put me out. Look as I might, I could see no more of his boy's rosy cheeks than of his boy's trim little jacket. His complexion had got pale: his face, at the lower part, was covered, to my great surprise and disappointment, with a curly brown beard and mustachios. He had a lively touch-and-go way with him, very pleasant and engaging, I admit; but nothing to compare with his free-and-easy manners of other times. To make matters worse, he had promised to be tall, and had not kept his promise. He was neat, and slim, and well made; but he wasn't by an inch or two up to the middle height. In short, he baffled me altogether. The years that had passed had left nothing of his old self, except the bright, straightforward look in his eyes. There I found our nice boy again, and there I concluded to stop in my investigation.

'Welcome back to the old place, Mr Franklin,' I said. 'All the more welcome, sir, that you have come some hours before we expected you.'

'I have a reason for coming before you expected me,' answered Mr Franklin. 'I suspect, Betteredge, that I have been followed and watched in London, for the last three or four days; and I have travelled by the morning instead of the afternoon train, because I wanted to give a certain dark-looking stranger the slip.'

Those words did more than surprise me. They brought back to my mind, in a flash, the three jugglers, and Penelope's notion that they meant some mischief to Mr Franklin Blake.

'Who's watching you, sir,—and why?' I inquired.

'Tell me about the three Indians you have had at the house to-day,' says Mr Franklin, without noticing my question. 'It's just possible, Betteredge, that my stranger and your three jugglers may turn out to be pieces of the same puzzle.'

'How do you come to know about the jugglers, sir?' I asked, putting one question on the top of another, which was bad manners, I own. But you don't expect much from poor human nature—so don't expect much from me.

'I saw Penelope at the house,' says Mr Franklin; 'and Penelope told me. Your daughter promised to be a pretty girl, Betteredge, and she has kept her promise. Penelope has got a small ear and a small foot. Did the late Mrs Betteredge possess those inestimable advantages?'

'The late Mrs Betteredge possessed a good many defects, sir,' says I. 'One of them (if you will pardon my mentioning it) was never keeping to the matter in hand. She was more like a fly than a woman: she couldn't settle on anything.'

'She would just have suited me,' says Mr Franklin. 'I never settle on anything either. Betteredge, your edge is better than ever. Your daughter said as much, when I asked for particulars about the jugglers.' Father will tell you, sir. He's a wonderful man for his age; and he expresses himself beautifully.' Penelope's own words—blushing divinely. Not even my respect for you prevented me from—never mind; I knew her when she was a child, and she's none the worse for it. Let's be serious. What did the jugglers do?'

I was something dissatisfied with my daughter—not for letting Mr Franklin kiss her; Mr Franklin was welcome to *that*—but for forcing me to tell her foolish story at second hand. However, there was no help for it now but to mention the circumstances. Mr Franklin's merriment all died away as I went on. He sat knitting his eyebrows, and twisting his beard. When I had done, he repeated after me two of the questions which the chief juggler had put to the boy—seemingly for the purpose of fixing them well in his mind.

' "Is it on the road to this house, and on no other, that the English gentleman will travel to-day?" "Has the English gentleman got It about him?" 'I suspect,' says Mr Franklin, pulling a little sealed paper parcel out of his pocket, 'that "It" means *this*. And "this," Betteredge, means my uncle Herncastle's famous Diamond.'

'Good Lord, sir!' I broke out, 'how do you come to be in charge of the wicked Colonel's Diamond?'

'The wicked Colonel's will has left his Diamond as a birthday present to my cousin Rachel,' says Mr Franklin. 'And my father, as the wicked Colonel's executor, has given it in charge to me to bring down here.'

If the sea, then oozing in smoothly over the Shivering Sand, had been changed into dry land before my own eyes, I doubt if I could have been more surprised than I was when Mr Franklin spoke those words.

'The Colonel's Diamond left to Miss Rachel!' says I. 'And your father, sir, the Colonel's executor! Why, I would have laid any bet you like, Mr Franklin, that your father wouldn't have touched the Colonel with a pair of tongs!'

'Strong language, Betteredge! What was there against the Colonel? He belonged to your time, not to mine. Tell me what you know about him, and I'll tell you how my father came to be his executor, and more besides. I have made some discoveries in London about my uncle Herncastle and his Diamond, which have rather an ugly look to my eyes; and I want you to confirm them. You called him the "wicked Colonel" just now. Search your memory, my old friend, and tell me why.'

I saw he was in earnest, and I told him.

Here follows the substance of what I said, written out entirely for your benefit. Pay attention to it, or you will be all abroad, when we get deeper into the story. Clear your mind of the children, or the dinner, or the new bonnet, or what not. Try if you can't forget politics, horses, prices in the City, and grievances at the club. I hope you won't take this freedom on my part amiss; it's only a way I have of appealing to the gentle reader.

Lord! haven't I seen you with the greatest authors in your hands, and don't I know how ready your attention is to wander when it's a book that asks for it, instead of a person?

I spoke, a little way back, of my lady's father, the old lord with the short temper and the long tongue. He had five children in all. Two sons to begin with; then, after a long time, his wife broke out breeding again, and the three young ladies came briskly one after the other, as fast as the nature of things would permit; my mistress, as before mentioned, being the youngest and best of the three. Of the two sons, the eldest, Arthur, inherited the title and estates. The second, the Honourable John, got a fine fortune left him by a relative, and went into the army.

It's an ill bird, they say, that fouls its own nest. I look on the noble family of the Herncastles as being my nest; and I shall take it as a favour if I am not expected to enter into particulars on the subject of the Honourable John. He was, I honestly believe, one of the greatest blackguards that ever lived. I can hardly say more or less for him than that. He went into the army, beginning in the Guards. He had to leave the Guards before he was two-and-twenty—never mind why. They are very strict in the army, and they were too strict for the Honourable John. He went out to India to see whether they were equally strict there, and to try a little active service. In the matter of bravery (to give him his due), he was a mixture of bull-dog and game-cock, with a dash of the savage. He was at the taking of Seringapatam. Soon afterwards he changed into another regiment, and, in course of time, changed again into a third. In the third he got his last step as lieutenant-colonel, and, getting that, got also a sunstroke, and came home to England.

He came back with a character that closed the doors of all his family against him, my lady (then just married) taking the lead, and declaring (with Sir John's approval, of course) that her brother should never enter any house of hers. There was more than one slur on the Colonel that made people shy of him; but the blot of the Diamond is all I need mention here.

It was said he had got possession of his Indian jewel by means which, bold as he was, he didn't dare acknowledge. He never attempted to sell it—not being in need of money, and not (to give him his due again) making money an object. He never gave it away; he never even showed it to any living soul. Some said he was afraid of its getting him into a difficulty with the military authorities; others (very ignorant indeed of the real nature of the man) said he was afraid, if he showed it, of its costing him his life.

There was perhaps a grain of truth mixed up with this last report. It was false to say that he was afraid; but it was a fact that his life had been twice threatened in India; and it was firmly believed that the Moonstone was at the bottom of it. When he came back to England, and found himself avoided by everybody, the Moonstone was thought to be at the bottom of it again. The mystery of the Colonel's life got in the Colonel's way, and outlawed him, as you may say, among his own people. The men wouldn't let him into their clubs; the women—more than one—whom he wanted to marry, refused him; friends and relations got too near-sighted to see him in the street.

Some men in this mess would have tried to set themselves right with the world. But to give in, even when he was wrong, and had all society against him, was not the way of the Honourable John. He had kept the Diamond, in flat defiance of assassination, in India. He kept the Diamond, in flat defiance of public opinion, in England. There you have the portrait of the man before you, as in a picture: a character that braved everything; and a face, handsome as it was, that looked possessed by the devil.

We heard different rumours about him from time to time. Sometimes they said he was given up to smoking opium and collecting old books; sometimes he was reported to be trying strange things in chemistry; sometimes he was seen carousing and amusing himself among the lowest people in the lowest slums of London. Anyhow, a solitary, vicious, underground life was the life the Colonel led. Once, and once only, after his return to England, I myself saw him, face to face.

About two years before the time of which I am now writing, and about a year and a half before the time of his death, the Colonel came unexpectedly to my lady's house in London. It was the night of Miss Rachel's birthday, the twenty-first of June; and there was a party in honour of it, as usual. I received a message from the footman to say that a gentleman wanted to see me. Going up into the hall, there I found the Colonel, wasted, and worn, and old, and shabby, and as wild and as wicked as ever.

'Go up to my sister,' says he; 'and say that I have called to wish my niece many happy returns of the day.'

He had made attempts by letter, more than once already, to be reconciled with my lady, for no other purpose, I am firmly persuaded, than to annoy her. But this was the first time he had actually come to the house. I had it on the tip of my tongue to say that my mistress had a party that night. But the devilish look of him daunted me. I went upstairs with his message, and left him, by his own desire, waiting in the hall. The servants stood staring at him, at a distance, as if he was a walking engine of destruction, loaded with powder and shot, and likely to go off among them at a moment's notice.

My lady had a dash—no more—of the family temper. 'Tell Colonel Herncastle,' she said, when I gave her her brother's message, 'that Miss Verinder is engaged, and that *I* decline to see him.' I tried to plead for a civiller answer than that; knowing the Colonel's constitutional superiority to the restraints which govern gentlemen in general. Quite useless! The family temper flashed out at me directly. 'When I want your advice,' says my lady, 'you know that I always ask for it. I don't ask for it now.' I went down-stairs with the message, of which I took the liberty of presenting a new and amended edition of my own contriving, as follows: 'My lady and Miss Rachel regret that they are engaged, Colonel; and beg to be excused having the honour of seeing you.'

I expected him to break out, even at that polite way of putting it. To my surprise he did nothing of the sort; he alarmed me by taking the thing with an unnatural quiet. His eyes, of a glittering bright grey, just settled on me for a moment; and he laughed, not *out* of himself, like other people, but *into* himself, in a soft, chuckling, horridly mischievous way. 'Thank you, Betteredge,' he said. 'I shall remember my niece's birthday.' With that, he turned on his heel, and walked out of the house.

The next birthday came round, and we heard he was ill in bed. Six months afterwards —that is to say, six months before the time I am now writing of—there came a letter from a highly respectable clergyman to my lady. It communicated two wonderful things in the way of family news. First, that the Colonel had forgiven his sister on his death-bed. Second, that he had forgiven everybody else, and had made a most edifying end. I have myself (in spite of the bishops and the clergy) an unfeigned respect for the Church; but I am firmly persuaded, at the same time, that the devil remained in undisturbed possession of the Honourable John, and that the last abominable act in the life of that abominable man was (saving your presence) to take the clergyman in!

This was the sum-total of what I had to tell Mr Franklin. I remarked that he listened more and more eagerly the longer I went on. Also, that the story of the Colonel being sent away from his sister's door, on the occasion of his niece's birthday, seemed to strike Mr Franklin like a shot that had hit the mark. Though he didn't acknowledge it, I saw that I had made him uneasy, plainly enough, in his face.

'You have said your say, Betteredge,' he remarked. 'It's my turn now. Before, however, I tell you what discoveries I have made in London, and how I came to be mixed up in this matter of the Diamond, I want to know one thing. You look, my old friend, as if you didn't quite understand the object to be answered by this consultation of ours. Do your looks belie you?'

'No, sir,' I said. 'My looks, on this occasion at any rate, tell the truth.'

'In that case,' says Mr Franklin, 'suppose I put you up to my point of view, before we go any further. I see three very serious questions involved in the Colonel's birthday-gift to my cousin Rachel. Follow me carefully, Betteredge; and count me off on your fingers, if it will help you,' says Mr Franklin, with a certain pleasure in showing how clear-headed he could be, which reminded me wonderfully of old times when he was a boy. 'Question the first: Was the Colonel's Diamond the object of a conspiracy in India? Question the second: Has the conspiracy followed the Colonel's Diamond to England? Question the third: Did the Colonel know the conspiracy followed the Diamond; and has he purposely left a legacy of trouble and danger to his sister, through the innocent medium of his sister's child? *That* is what I am driving at, Betteredge. Don't let me frighten you.'

It was all very well to say that, but he *had* frightened me.

If he was right, here was our quiet English house suddenly invaded by a devilish Indian Diamond—bringing after it a conspiracy of living rogues, set loose on us by the vengeance of a dead man. There was our situation, as revealed to me in Mr Franklin's last words! Who ever heard the like of it—in the nineteenth century, mind; in an age of progress, and in a country which rejoices in the blessings of the British constitution? Nobody ever heard the like of it, and, consequently, nobody can be expected to believe it. I shall go on with my story, however, in spite of that.

When you get a sudden alarm, of the sort that I had got now, nine times out of ten the place you feel it in is your stomach. When you feel it in your stomach, your attention wanders, and you begin to fidget. I fidgeted silently in my place on the sand. Mr Franklin noticed me, contending with a perturbed stomach or mind—which you please; they mean the same thing—and, checking himself just as he was starting with his part of the story, said to me sharply, 'What do you want?'

What did I want? I didn't tell *him*; but I'll tell *you*, in confidence. I wanted a whiff of my pipe, and a turn at *Robinson Crusoe*.

CHAPTER 6

Keeping my private sentiments to myself, I respectfully requested Mr Franklin to go on. Mr Franklin replied, 'Don't fidget, Betteredge,' and went on.

Our young gentleman's first words informed me that his discoveries, concerning the wicked Colonel and the Diamond, had begun with a visit which he had paid (before he came to us) to the family lawyer, at Hampstead. A chance word dropped by Mr Franklin, when the two were alone, one day, after dinner, revealed that he had been charged by his father with a birthday present to be taken to Miss Rachel. One thing led to another; and it ended in the lawyer mentioning what the present really was, and how the friendly connection between the late Colonel and Mr Blake, Senior, had taken its rise. The facts here are really so extraordinary, that I doubt if I can trust my own language to do justice to them. I prefer trying to report Mr Franklin's discoveries, as nearly as may be, in Mr Franklin's own words.

'You remember the time, Betteredge,' he said, 'when my father was trying to prove his title to that unlucky Dukedom? Well! that was also the time when my uncle Herncastle returned from India. My father discovered that his brother-in-law was in possession of certain papers which were likely to be of service to him in his lawsuit. He called on the Colonel, on pretence of welcoming him back to England. The Colonel was not to be deluded in that way. 'You want something,' he said, 'or you would never have compromised your reputation by calling on *me*.' My father saw that the one chance for him was to show his hand: he admitted, at once, that he wanted the papers. The Colonel asked for a day to consider his answer. His answer came in the shape of a most extraordinary letter, which my friend the lawyer showed me. The Colonel began by saying that he wanted something of my father, and that he begged to propose an exchange of friendly services between them. The fortune of war (that was the expression he used) had placed him in possession of one of the largest Diamonds in the world; and he had reason to believe that neither he nor his precious jewel was safe in any house, in any quarter of the globe, which they occupied together. Under these alarming circumstances, he had determined to place his Diamond in the keeping of another person. That person was not expected to run any risk. He might deposit the precious stone in any place especially guarded and set apart— like a banker's or jeweller's strong-room—for the safe custody of valuables of high price. His main personal responsibility in the matter was to be of the passive kind. He was to undertake—either by himself, or by a trustworthy representative—to receive at a pre-arranged address, on certain pre-arranged days in every year, a note from the Colonel, simply stating the fact that he was a living man at that date. In the event of the date passing over without the note being received, the Colonel's silence might be taken as a sure token of the Colonel's death by murder. In that case, and in no other, certain sealed instructions relating to the disposal of the Diamond, and deposited with it, were to be opened, and followed implicitly. If my father chose to accept this strange charge, the Colonel's papers were at his disposal in return. That was the letter.'

'What did your father do, sir?' I asked.

'Do?' says Mr Franklin. 'I'll tell you what he did. He brought the invaluable faculty, called common sense, to bear on the Colonel's letter. The whole thing, he declared, was simply absurd. Somewhere in his Indian wanderings, the Colonel had picked up with some wretched crystal which he took for a diamond. As for the danger of his being murdered, and the precautions devised to preserve his life and his piece of crystal, this was the nineteenth century, and any man in his senses had only to apply to the police. The Colonel had been a notorious opium-eater for years past; and, if the only way of getting at the valuable papers he possessed was by accepting a matter of opium as a matter of fact, my father was quite willing to take the ridiculous responsibility imposed on him—all the more readily that it involved no trouble to himself. The Diamond and the sealed instructions went into his banker's strong-room, and the Colonel's letters, periodically reporting him a living man, were received and opened by our family lawyer, Mr Bruff, as my father's representative. No sensible person, in a similar position, could have viewed the matter in any other way. Nothing in this world, Betteredge, is probable unless it appeals to our own trumpery experience; and we only believe in a romance when we see it in a newspaper.'

It was plain to me from this, that Mr Franklin thought his father's notion about the Colonel hasty and wrong.

'What is your own private opinion about the matter, sir?' I asked.

'Let's finish the story of the Colonel first,' says Mr Franklin. 'There is a curious want of system, Betteredge, in the English mind; and your question, my old friend, is an instance of it. When we are not occupied in making machinery, we are (mentally speaking) the most slovenly people in the universe.'

'So much,' I thought to myself, 'for a foreign education! He has learned that way of girding at us in France, I suppose.'

Mr Franklin took up the lost thread, and went on.

'My father,' he said, 'got the papers he wanted, and never saw his brother-in-law again from that time. Year after year, on the prearranged days, the prearranged letter came from the Colonel, and was opened by Mr Bruff. I have seen the letters, in a heap, all of them written in the same brief, business-like form of words: "Sir,—This is to certify that I am still a living man. Let the Diamond be. John Herncastle." That was all he ever wrote, and that came regularly to the day; until some six or eight months since, when the form of the letter varied for the first time. It ran now:—"Sir,—They tell me I am dying. Come to me, and help me to make my Will." Mr Bruff went, and found him, in the little suburban villa, surrounded by its own grounds, in which he had lived alone, ever since he had left India. He had dogs, cats, and birds to keep him company; but no human being near him, except the person who came daily to do the house-work, and the doctor at the bedside. The Will was a very simple matter. The Colonel had dissipated the greater part of his fortune in his chemical investigations. His Will began and ended in three clauses, which he dictated from his bed, in perfect possession of his faculties. The first clause provided for the safe keeping and support of his animals. The second founded a professorship of experimental chemistry at a northern university. The third bequeathed the Moonstone as a birthday present to his niece, on condition that my father would act as executor. My father at first refused to act. On second thoughts, however, he gave way, partly because he was assured that the executorship would involve him in no trouble; partly because Mr Bruff suggested, in Rachel's interest, that the Diamond might be worth something, after all.'

'Did the Colonel give any reason, sir,' I inquired, 'why he left the Diamond to Miss Rachel?'

'He not only gave the reason—he had the reason written in his Will,' said Mr Franklin.

'I have got an extract, which you shall see presently. Don't be slovenly-minded, Betteredge! One thing at a time. You have heard about the Colonel's Will; now you must hear what happened after the Colonel's death. It was formally necessary to have the Diamond valued, before the Will could be proved. All the jewellers consulted, at once confirmed the Colonel's assertion that he possessed one of the largest diamonds in the world. The question of accurately valuing it presented some serious difficulties. Its size made it a phenomenon in the diamond-market; its colour placed it in a category by itself; and, to add to these elements of uncertainty, there was a defect, in the shape of a flaw, in the very heart of the stone. Even with this last serious drawback, however, the lowest of the various estimates given was twenty thousand pounds. Conceive my father's astonishment! He had been within a hair's-breadth of refusing to act as executor, and of allowing this magnificent jewel to be lost to the family. The interest he took in the matter now, induced him to open the sealed instructions which had been deposited with the Diamond. Mr Bruff showed this document to me, with the other papers; and it suggests (to my mind) a clue to the nature of the conspiracy which threatened the Colonel's life.'

'Then you do believe, sir,' I said, 'that there was a conspiracy?'

'Not possessing my father's excellent common sense,' answered Mr Franklin, 'I believe the Colonel's life was threatened, exactly as the Colonel said. The sealed instructions, as I think, explain how it was that he died, after all, quietly in his bed. In the event of his death by violence (that is to say, in the absence of the regular letter from him at the appointed date), my father was then directed to send the Moonstone secretly to Amsterdam. It was to be deposited in that city with a famous diamond-cutter, and it was to be cut up into from four to six separate stones. The stones were then to be sold for what they would fetch, and the proceeds were to be applied to the founding of that professorship of experimental chemistry, which the Colonel has since endowed by his Will. Now, Betteredge, exert those sharp wits of yours, and observe the conclusion to which the Colonel's instructions point!'

I instantly exerted my wits. They were of the slovenly English sort; and they consequently muddled it all, until Mr Franklin took them in hand, and pointed out what they ought to see.

'Remark,' says Mr Franklin, 'that the integrity of the Diamond, as a whole stone, is here artfully made dependent on the preservation from violence of the Colonel's life. He is not satisfied with saying to the enemies he dreads, "Kill me—and you will be no nearer to the Diamond than you are now; it is where you can't get at it—in the guarded strong-room of a bank." He says instead, "Kill me—and the Diamond will be the Diamond no longer; its identity will be destroyed." What does that mean?'

Here I had (as I thought) a flash of the wonderful foreign brightness.

'I know,' I said. 'It means lowering the value of the stone and cheating the rogues in that way!'

'Nothing of the sort,' says Mr Franklin. 'I have inquired about that. The flawed Diamond, cut up, would actually fetch more than the Diamond as it now is; for this plain reason—that from four to six perfect brilliants might be cut from it, which would be, collectively, worth more money than the large—but imperfect—single stone. If robbery for the purpose of gain was at the bottom of the conspiracy, the Colonel's instructions absolutely made the Diamond better worth stealing. More money could have been got for it, and the disposal of it in the diamond-market would have been infinitely easier, if it had passed through the hands of the workmen of Amsterdam.'

'Lord bless us, sir!' I burst out. 'What was the plot, then?'

'A plot organized among the Indians who originally owned the jewel,' says Mr Franklin —'a plot with some old Hindoo superstition at the bottom of it. That is my opinion, confirmed by a family paper which I have about me at this moment.'

I saw, now, why the appearance of the three Indian jugglers at our house had presented itself to Mr Franklin in the light of a circumstance worth noting.

'I don't want to force my opinion on you,' Mr Franklin went on. 'The idea of certain chosen servants of an old Hindoo superstition devoting themselves, through all difficulties and dangers, to watching the opportunity of recovering their sacred gem, appears to *me* to be perfectly consistent with everything that we know of the patience of Oriental races, and the influence of Oriental religions. But then I am an imaginative man; and the butcher, the baker, and the tax-gatherer, are not the only credible realities in existence to *my* mind. Let the guess I have made at the truth in this matter go for what it is worth, and let us get on to the only practical question that concerns us. Does the conspiracy against the Moonstone survive the Colonel's death? And did the Colonel know it, when he left the birthday gift to his niece?'

I began to see my lady and Miss Rachel at the end of it all, now. Not a word he said escaped me.

'I was not very willing, when I discovered the story of the Moonstone,' said Mr Franklin, 'to be the means of bringing it here. But Mr Bruff reminded me that somebody must put my cousin's legacy into my cousin's hands—and that I might as well do it as anybody else. After taking the Diamond out of the bank, I fancied I was followed in the streets by a shabby, dark-complexioned man. I went to my father's house to pick up my luggage, and found a letter there, which unexpectedly detained me in London. I went back to the bank with the Diamond, and thought I saw the shabby man again. Taking the Diamond once more out of the bank this morning, I saw the man for the third time, gave him the slip, and started (before he recovered the trace of me) by the morning instead of the afternoon train. Here I am, with the Diamond safe and sound—and what is the first news that meets me? I find that three strolling Indians have been at the house, and that my arrival from London, and something which I am expected to have about me, are two special objects of investigation to them when they believe themselves to be alone. I don't waste time and words on their pouring the ink into the boy's hand, and telling him to look in it for a man at a distance, and for something in that man's pocket. The thing (which I have often seen done in the East) is "hocus-pocus" in my opinion, as it is in yours. The present question for us to decide is, whether I am wrongly attaching a meaning to a mere accident? or whether we really have evidence of the Indians being on the track of the Moonstone, the moment it is removed from the safe keeping of the bank?'

Neither he nor I seemed to fancy dealing with this part of the inquiry. We looked at each other, and then we looked at the tide, oozing in smoothly, higher and higher, over the Shivering Sand.

'What are you thinking of?' says Mr Franklin, suddenly.

'I was thinking, sir,' I answered, 'that I should like to shy the Diamond into the quicksand, and settle the question in *that* way.'

'If you have got the value of the stone in your pocket,' answered Mr Franklin, 'say so, Betteredge, and in it goes!'

It's curious to note, when your mind's anxious, how very far in the way of relief a very small joke will go. We found a fund of merriment, at the time, in the notion of making away with Miss Rachel's lawful property, and getting Mr Blake, as executor, into dreadful trouble—though where the merriment was, I am quite at a loss to discover now.

Mr Franklin was the first to bring the talk back to the talk's proper purpose. He took an envelope out of his pocket, opened it, and handed to me the paper inside.

'Betteredge,' he said, 'we must face the question of the Colonel's motive in leaving this legacy to his niece, for my aunt's sake. Bear in mind how Lady Verinder treated her brother from the time when he returned to England, to the time when he told you he should remember his niece's birthday. And read that.'

He gave me the extract from the Colonel's Will. I have got it by me while I write these words; and I copy it, as follows, for your benefit:

'Thirdly, and lastly, I give and bequeath to my niece, Rachel Verinder, daughter and only child of my sister, Julia Verinder, widow—if her mother, the said Julia Verinder, shall be living on the said Rachel Verinder's next birthday after my death—the yellow Diamond belonging to me, and known in the East by the name of The Moonstone: subject to this condition, that her mother, the said Julia Verinder, shall be living at the time. And I hereby desire my executor to give my Diamond, either by his own hands or by the hands of some trustworthy representative whom he shall appoint, into the personal possession of my said niece Rachel, on her next birthday after my death, and in the presence, if possible, of my sister, the said Julia Verinder. And I desire that my said sister may be informed, by means of a true copy of this, the third and last clause of my Will, that I give the Diamond to her daughter Rachel, in token of my free forgiveness of the injury which her conduct towards me has been the means of inflicting on my reputation in my lifetime; and especially in proof that I pardon, as becomes a dying man, the insult offered to me as an officer and a gentleman, when her servant, by her orders, closed the door of her house against me, on the occasion of her daughter's birthday.'

More words followed these, providing, if my lady was dead, or if Miss Rachel was dead, at the time of the testator's decease, for the Diamond being sent to Holland, in accordance with the sealed instructions originally deposited with it. The proceeds of the sale were, in that case, to be added to the money already left by the Will for the professorship of chemistry at the university in the north.

I handed the paper back to Mr Franklin, sorely troubled what to say to him. Up to that moment, my own opinion had been (as you know) that the Colonel had died as wickedly as he had lived. I don't say the copy from his Will actually converted me from that opinion: I only say it staggered me.

'Well,' says Mr Franklin, 'now you have read the Colonel's own statement, what do you say? In bringing the Moonstone to my aunt's house, am I serving his vengeance blindfold, or am I vindicating him in the character of a penitent and Christian man?'

'It seems hard to say, sir,' I answered, 'that he died with a horrid revenge in his heart, and a horrid lie on his lips. God alone knows the truth. Don't ask *me*.'

Mr Franklin sat twisting and turning the extract from the Will in his fingers, as if he expected to squeeze the truth out of it in that manner. He altered quite remarkably, at the same time. From being brisk and bright, he now became, most unaccountably, a slow, solemn, and pondering young man.

'This question has two sides,' he said. 'An Objective side, and a Subjective side. Which are we to take?'

He had had a German education as well as a French. One of the two had been in undisturbed possession of him (as I supposed) up to this time. And now (as well as I could make out) the other was taking its place. It is one of my rules in life, never to notice what I don't understand. I steered a middle course between the Objective side and the Subjective side. In plain English I stared hard, and said nothing.

'Let's extract the inner meaning of this,' says Mr Franklin. 'Why did my uncle leave the Diamond to Rachel? Why didn't he leave it to my aunt?'

'That's not beyond guessing, sir, at any rate,' I said. 'Colonel Herncastle knew my lady well enough to know that she would have refused to accept any legacy that came to her from *him*.'

'How did he know that Rachel might not refuse to accept it, too?'

'Is there any young lady in existence, sir, who could resist the temptation of accepting such a birthday present as The Moonstone?'

'That's the Subjective view,' says Mr Franklin. 'It does you great credit, Betteredge, to be able to take the Subjective view. But there's another mystery about the Colonel's legacy which is not accounted for yet. How are we to explain his only giving Rachel her birthday present conditionally on her mother being alive?'

'I don't want to slander a dead man, sir,' I answered. 'But if he *has* purposely left a legacy of trouble and danger to his sister, by the means of her child, it must be a legacy made conditional on his sister's being alive to feel the vexation of it.'

'Oh! That's your interpretation of his motive, is it? The Subjective interpretation again! Have you ever been in Germany, Betteredge?'

'No, sir. What's your interpretation, if you please?'

'I can see,' says Mr Franklin, 'that the Colonel's object may, quite possibly, have been—not to benefit his niece, whom he had never even seen—but to prove to his sister that he had died forgiving her, and to prove it very prettily by means of a present made to her child. There is a totally different explanation from yours, Betteredge, taking its rise in a Subjective-Objective point of view. From all I can see, one interpretation is just as likely to be right as the other.'

Having brought matters to this pleasant and comforting issue, Mr Franklin appeared to think that he had completed all that was required of him. He laid down flat on his back on the sand, and asked what was to be done next.

He had been so clever, and clear-headed (before he began to talk the foreign gibberish), and had so completely taken the lead in the business up to the present time, that I was quite unprepared for such a sudden change as he now exhibited in this helpless leaning upon *me*. It was not till later that I learned—by assistance of Miss Rachel, who was the first to make the discovery—that these puzzling shifts and transformations in Mr Franklin were due to the effect on him of his foreign training. At the age when we are all of us most apt to take our colouring, in the form of a reflection from the colouring of other people, he had been sent abroad, and had been passed on from one nation to another, before there was time for any one colouring more than another to settle itself on him firmly. As a consequence of this, he had come back with so many different sides to his character, all more or less jarring with each other, that he seemed to pass his life in a state of perpetual contradiction with himself. He could be a busy man, and a lazy man; cloudy in the head, and clear in the head; a model of determination, and a spectacle of helplessness, all together. He had his French side, and his German side, and his Italian side—the original English foundation showing through, every now and then, as much as to say, 'Here I am, sorely transmogrified, as you see, but there's something of me left at the bottom of him still.' Miss Rachel used to remark that the Italian side of him was uppermost, on those occasions when he unexpectedly gave in, and asked you in his nice sweet-tempered way to take his own responsibilities on your shoulders. You will do him no injustice, I think, if you conclude that the Italian side of him was uppermost now.

'Isn't it your business, sir,' I asked, 'to know what to do next? Surely it can't be mine?'

Mr Franklin didn't appear to see the force of my question—not being in a position, at the time, to see anything but the sky over his head.

'I don't want to alarm my aunt without reason,' he said. 'And I don't want to leave her without what may be a needful warning. If you were in my place, Betteredge, tell me, in one word, what would you do?'

In one word, I told him: 'Wait.'

'With all my heart,' says Mr Franklin. 'How long?'

I proceeded to explain myself.

'As I understand it, sir,' I said, 'somebody is bound to put this plaguy Diamond into Miss Rachel's hands on her birthday—and you may as well do it as another. Very good. This is the twenty-fifth of May, and the birthday is on the twenty-first of June. We have got close on four weeks before us. Let's wait and see what happens in that time; and let's warn my lady or not, as the circumstances direct us.'

'Perfect, Betteredge, as far as it goes!' says Mr Franklin. 'But, between this and the birthday, what's to be done with the Diamond?'

'What your father did with it, to be sure, sir!' I answered. 'Your father put it in the safe keeping of a bank in London. You put it in the safe keeping of the bank at Frizinghall.' (Frizinghall was our nearest town, and the Bank of England wasn't safer than the bank there.) 'If I were you, sir,' I added, 'I would ride straight away with it to Frizinghall before the ladies come back.'

The prospect of doing something—and, what is more, of doing that something on a horse—brought Mr Franklin up like lightning from the flat of his back. He sprang to his feet, and pulled me up, without ceremony, on to mine. 'Betteredge, you are worth your weight in gold,' he said. 'Come along, and saddle the best horse in the stables directly!'

Here (God bless it!) was the original English foundation of him showing through all the foreign varnish at last! Here was the Master Franklin I remembered, coming out again in the good old way at the prospect of a ride, and reminding me of the good old times! Saddle a horse for him? I would have saddled a dozen horses, if he could only have ridden them all!

We went back to the house in a hurry; we had the fleetest horse in the stables saddled in a hurry; and Mr Franklin rattled off in a hurry, to lodge the cursed Diamond once more in the strong-room of a bank. When I heard the last of his horse's hoofs on the drive, and when I turned about in the yard and found I was alone again, I felt half inclined to ask myself if I hadn't woke up from a dream.

CHAPTER 7

While I was in this bewildered frame of mind, sorely needing a little quiet time by myself to put me right again, my daughter Penelope got in my way (just as her late mother used to get in my way on the stairs), and instantly summoned me to tell her all that had passed at the conference between Mr Franklin and me. Under present circumstances, the one thing to be done was to clap the extinguisher upon Penelope's curiosity on the spot. I accordingly replied that Mr Franklin and I had both talked of foreign politics, till we could talk no longer, and had then mutually fallen asleep in the heat of the sun. Try that sort of answer when your wife or your daughter next worries you with an awkward question at an awkward time, and depend on the natural sweetness of women for kissing and making it up again at the next opportunity.

The afternoon wore on, and my lady and Miss Rachel came back.

Needless to say how astonished they were, when they heard that Mr Franklin Blake had arrived, and had gone off again on horseback. Needless also to say, that *they* asked awkward questions directly, and that the 'foreign politics' and the 'falling asleep in the sun' wouldn't serve a second time over with *them*. Being at the end of my invention, I said Mr Franklin's arrival by the early train was entirely attributable to one of Mr Franklin's freaks. Being asked, upon that, whether his galloping off again on horseback was another of Mr Franklin's freaks, I said, 'Yes, it was'; and slipped out of it—I think very cleverly—in that way.

Having got over my difficulties with the ladies, I found more difficulties waiting for me when I went back to my own room. In came Penelope—with the natural sweetness of women—to kiss and make it up again; and—with the natural curiosity of women—to ask another question. This time she only wanted me to tell her what was the matter with our second housemaid, Rosanna Spearman.

After leaving Mr Franklin and me at the Shivering Sand, Rosanna, it appeared, had returned to the house in a very unaccountable state of mind. She had turned (if Penelope was to be believed) all the colours of the rainbow. She had been merry without reason, and sad without reason. In one breath she asked hundreds of questions about Mr Franklin Blake, and in another breath she had been angry with Penelope for presuming to suppose that a strange gentleman could possess any interest for her. She had been surprised, smiling, and scribbling Mr Franklin's name inside her workbox. She had been surprised again, crying and looking at her deformed shoulder in the glass. Had she and Mr Franklin known anything of each other before to-day? Quite impossible! Had they heard anything of each other? Impossible again! I could speak to Mr Franklin's astonishment as genuine, when he saw how the girl stared at him. Penelope could speak to the girl's inquisitiveness as genuine, when she asked questions about Mr Franklin. The conference between us, conducted in this way, was tiresome enough, until my daughter suddenly ended it by bursting out with what I thought the most monstrous supposition I had ever heard in my life.

'Father!' says Penelope, quite seriously, 'there's only one explanation of it. Rosanna has fallen in love with Mr Franklin Blake at first sight!'

You have heard of beautiful young ladies falling in love at first sight, and have thought it natural enough. But a housemaid out of a reformatory, with a plain face and a deformed shoulder, falling in love, at first sight, with a gentleman who comes on a visit to her mistress's house, match me that, in the way of an absurdity, out of any story-book in Christendom, if you can! I laughed till the tears rolled down my cheeks. Penelope resented my merriment, in rather a strange way. 'I never knew you cruel before, father,' she said, very gently, and went out.

My girl's words fell upon me like a splash of cold water. I was savage with myself, for feeling uneasy in myself the moment she had spoken them—but so it was. We will change the subject, if you please. I am sorry I drifted into writing about it; and not without reason, as you will see when we have gone on together a little longer.

The evening came, and the dressing-bell for dinner rang, before Mr Franklin returned from Frizinghall. I took his hot water up to his room myself, expecting to hear, after this extraordinary delay, that something had happened. To my great disappointment (and no doubt to yours also), nothing had happened. He had not met with the Indians, either going or returning. He had deposited the Moonstone in the bank—describing it merely as a valuable of great price—and he had got the receipt for it safe in his pocket. I went down-stairs, feeling that this was rather a flat ending, after all our excitement about the Diamond earlier in the day.

How the meeting between Mr Franklin and his aunt and cousin went off, is more than I can tell you.

I would have given something to have waited at table that day. But, in my position in the household, waiting at dinner (except on high family festivals) was letting down my dignity in the eyes of the other servants—a thing which my lady considered me quite prone enough to do already, without seeking occasions for it. The news brought to me from the upper regions, that evening, came from Penelope and the footman. Penelope mentioned that she had never known Miss Rachel so particular about the dressing of her hair, and had never seen her look so bright and pretty as she did when she went down to meet Mr Franklin in the drawing-room. The footman's report was, that the preservation of a respectful composure in the presence of his betters, and the waiting on Mr Franklin Blake at dinner, were two of the hardest things to reconcile with each other that had ever tried his training in service. Later in the evening, we heard them singing and playing duets, Mr Franklin piping high, Miss Rachel piping higher, and my lady, on the piano, following them, as it were over hedge and ditch, and seeing them safe through it in a manner most wonderful and pleasant to hear through the open windows, on the terrace at night. Later still, I went to Mr Franklin in the smoking-room, with the soda-water and brandy, and found that Miss Rachel had put the Diamond clean out of his head. 'She's the most charming girl I have seen since I came back to England!' was all I could extract from him, when I endeavoured to lead the conversation to more serious things.

Towards midnight, I went round the house to lock up, accompanied by my second in command (Samuel, the footman), as usual. When all the doors were made fast, except the side door that opened on the terrace, I sent Samuel to bed, and stepped out for a breath of fresh air before I too went to bed in my turn.

The night was still and close, and the moon was at the full in the heavens. It was so silent out of doors, that I heard from time to time, very faint and low, the fall of the sea, as the ground-swell heaved it in on the sandbank near the mouth of our little bay. As the house stood, the terrace side was the dark side; but the broad moonlight showed fair on the gravel walk that ran along the next side to the terrace. Looking this way, after looking up at the sky, I saw the shadow of a person in the moonlight thrown forward from behind the corner of the house.

Being old and sly, I forbore to call out; but being also, unfortunately, old and heavy, my feet betrayed me on the gravel. Before I could steal suddenly round the corner, as I had proposed, I heard lighter feet than mine—and more than one pair of them as I thought—retreating in a hurry. By the time I had got to the corner, the trespassers, who-ever they were, had run into the shrubbery at the off side of the walk, and were hidden from sight among the thick trees and bushes in that part of the grounds. From the shrubbery, they could easily make their way, over our fence, into the road. If I had been forty years younger, I might have had a chance of catching them before they got clear of our premises. As it was, I went back to set a-going a younger pair of legs than mine. With-out disturbing anybody, Samuel and I got a couple of guns, and went all round the house and through the shrubbery. Having made sure that no persons were lurking about any-where in our grounds, we turned back. Passing over the walk where I had seen the shadow, now noticed, for the first time, a little bright object, lying on the clean gravel, under the light of the moon. Picking the object up, I discovered it was a small bottle, containing a thick sweet-smelling liquor, as black as ink.

I said nothing to Samuel. But, remembering what Penelope had told me about the jugglers, and the pouring of the little pool of ink into the palm of the boy's hand, I instantly suspected that I had disturbed the three Indians, lurking about the house, and bent, in their heathenish way, on discovering the whereabouts of the Diamond that night.

CHAPTER 8

Here, for one moment, I find it necessary to call a halt.

On summoning up my own recollections—and on getting Penelope to help me, by consulting her journal—I find that we may pass pretty rapidly over the interval between Mr Franklin Blake's arrival and Miss Rachel's birthday. For the greater part of that time the days passed, and brought nothing with them worth recording. With your good leave, then, and with Penelope's help, I shall notice certain dates only in this place; reserving to myself to tell the story day by day, once more, as soon as we get to the time when the business of the Moonstone became the chief business of everybody in our house.

This said, we may now go on again—beginning, of course, with the bottle of sweet-smelling ink which I found on the gravel walk at night.

On the next morning (the morning of the twenty-sixth) I showed Mr Franklin this article of jugglery, and told him what I have already told you. His opinion was, not only that the Indians had been lurking about after the Diamond, but also that they were actually foolish enough to believe in their own magic—meaning thereby the making of signs on a boy's head, and the pouring of ink into a boy's hand, and then expecting him to see persons and things beyond the reach of human vision. In our country, as well as in the East, Mr Franklin informed me, there are people who practise this curious hocus-pocus (without the ink, however); and who call it by a French name, signifying something like brightness of sight. 'Depend upon it,' says Mr Franklin, 'the Indians took it for granted that we should keep the Diamond here; and they brought their clairvoyant boy to show them the way to it, if they succeeded in getting into the house last night.'

'Do you think they'll try again, sir?' I asked.

'It depends,' says Mr Franklin, 'on what the boy can really do. If he can see the Diamond through the iron-safe of the bank at Frizinghall, we shall be troubled with no more visits from the Indians for the present. If he can't, we shall have another chance of catching them in the shrubbery, before many more nights are over our heads.'

I waited pretty confidently for that latter chance; but, strange to relate, it never came.

Whether the jugglers heard, in the town, of Mr Franklin having been seen at the bank, and drew their conclusions accordingly; or whether the boy really did see the Diamond where the Diamond was now lodged (which I, for one, flatly disbelieve); or whether, after all, it was a mere effect of chance, this at any rate is the plain truth—not the ghost of an Indian came near the house again, through the weeks that passed before Miss Rachel's birthday. The jugglers remained in and about the town plying their trade; and Mr Franklin and I remained waiting to see what might happen, and resolute not to put the rogues on their guard by showing our suspicions of them too soon. With this report of the proceedings on either side, ends all that I have to say about the Indians for the present.

On the twenty-ninth of the month, Miss Rachel and Mr Franklin hit on a new method of working their way together through the time which might otherwise have hung heavy on their hands. There are reasons for taking particular notice here of the occupation that amused them. You will find it has a bearing on something that is still to come.

Gentlefolks in general have a very awkward rock ahead in life—the rock ahead of their own idleness. Their lives being, for the most part, passed in looking about them for something to do, it is curious to see—especially when their tastes are of what is called the intellectual sort—how often they drift blindfold into some nasty pursuit. Nine times out of ten they take to torturing something, or to spoiling something—and they firmly believe they are improving their minds, when the plain truth is, they are only making a mess in the house. I have seen them (ladies, I am sorry to say, as well as gentlemen) go out, day after day, for example, with empty pill-boxes, and catch newts, and beetles, and spiders, and frogs, and come home and stick pins through the miserable wretches, or cut them up, without a pang of remorse, into little pieces. You see my young master, or my young mistress, poring over one of their spiders' insides with a magnifying-glass; or you meet one of their frogs walking down-stairs without his head—and when you wonder what this cruel nastiness means, you are told that it means a taste in my young master or my young mistress for natural history. Sometimes, again, you see them occupied for hours together in spoiling a pretty flower with pointed instruments, out of a stupid curiosity to know what the flower is made of. Is its colour any prettier, or its scent any sweeter, when you *do* know? But there! the poor souls must get through the time, you see—they must get through the time. You dabbled in nasty mud, and made pies, when you were a child; and you dabble in nasty science, and dissect spiders, and spoil flowers, when you grow up. In the one case and in the other, the secret of it is, that you have got nothing to think of in your poor empty head, and nothing to do with your poor idle hands. And so it ends in your spoiling canvas with paints, and making a smell in the house; or in keeping tadpoles in a glass box full of dirty water, and turning everybody's stomach in the house; or in chipping off bits of stone here, there, and everywhere, and dropping grit into all the victuals in the house; or in staining your fingers in the pursuit of photography, and doing justice without mercy on everybody's face in the house. It often falls heavy enough, no doubt, on people who are really obliged to get their living, to be forced to work for the clothes that cover them, the roof that shelters them, and the food that keeps them going. But compare the hardest day's work you ever did with the idleness that splits flowers and pokes its way into spiders' stomachs, and thank your stars that your head has got something it *must* think of, and your hands something that they *must* do.

As for Mr Franklin and Miss Rachel, they tortured nothing, I am glad to say. They simply confined themselves to making a mess; and all they spoilt, to do them justice, was the panelling of a door.

Mr Franklin's universal genius, dabbling in everything, dabbled in what he called 'decorative painting.' He had invented, he informed us, a new mixture to moisten paint with, which he described as a 'vehicle.' What it was made of, I don't know. What it did, I can tell you in two words—it stank. Miss Rachel being wild to try her hand at the new process, Mr Franklin sent to London for the materials; mixed them up, with accompaniment of a smell which made the very dogs sneeze when they came into the room; put an apron and a bib over Miss Rachel's gown, and set her to work decorating her own little sitting-room—called, for want of English to name it in, her 'boudoir.' They began with the inside of the door. Mr Franklin scraped off all the nice varnish with pumice-stone, and made what he described as a surface to work on. Miss Rachel then covered the surface, under his directions and with his help, with patterns and devices—griffins, birds, flowers, cupids, and such like—copied from designs made by a famous Italian painter, whose name escapes me: the one, I mean, who stocked the world with Virgin Maries, and had a sweetheart at the baker's. Viewed as work, this decoration was slow to do, and dirty to deal with. But our young lady and gentleman never seemed to tire of it. When they were not riding, or seeing company, or taking their meals, or piping their songs, there they were with their heads together, as busy as bees, spoiling the door. Who was the poet who said that Satan finds some mischief still for idle hands to do? If he had occupied my place in the family, and had seen Miss Rachel with her brush, and Mr Franklin with his vehicle, he could have written nothing truer of either of them than that.

The next date worthy of notice is Sunday the fourth of June.

On that evening we, in the servants' hall, debated a domestic question for the first time, which, like the decoration of the door, has its bearing on something that is still to come.

Seeing the pleasure which Mr Franklin and Miss Rachel took in each other's society, and noting what a pretty match they were in all personal respects, we naturally speculated on the chance of their putting their heads together with other objects in view besides the ornamenting of a door. Some of us said there would be a wedding in the house before the summer was over. Others (led by me) admitted it was likely enough Miss Rachel might be married; but we doubted (for reasons which will presently appear) whether her bridegroom would be Mr Franklin Blake.

That Mr Franklin was in love, on his side, nobody who saw and heard him could doubt. The difficulty was to fathom Miss Rachel. Let me do myself the honour of making you acquainted with her; after which, I will leave you to fathom her yourself—if you can.

My young lady's eighteenth birthday was the birthday now coming, on the twenty-first of June. If you happen to like dark women (who, I am informed, have gone out of fashion latterly in the gay world), and if you have no particular prejudice in favour of size, I answer for Miss Rachel as one of the prettiest girls your eyes ever looked on. She was small and slim, but all in fine proportion from top to toe. To see her sit down, to see her get up, and specially to see her walk, was enough to satisfy any man in his senses that the graces of her figure (if you will pardon me the expression) were in her flesh and not in her clothes. Her hair was the blackest I ever saw. Her eyes matched her hair. Her nose was not quite large enough, I admit. Her mouth and chin were (to quote Mr Franklin) morsels for the gods; and her complexion (on the same undeniable authority) was as warm as the sun itself, with this great advantage over the sun, that it was always in nice order to look at. Add to the foregoing that she carried her head as upright as a dart, in a dashing, spirited, thoroughbred way—that she had a clear voice, with a ring of the right metal in it, and a smile that began very prettily in her eyes before it got to her lips—and there behold the portrait of her, to the best of my painting, as large as life!

And what about her disposition next? Had this charming creature no faults? She had just as many faults as you have, ma'am—neither more nor less.

To put it seriously, my dear pretty Miss Rachel, possessing a host of graces and attractions, had one defect, which strict impartiality compels me to acknowledge. She was unlike most other girls of her age, in this—that she had ideas of her own, and was stiff-necked enough to set the fashions themselves at defiance, if the fashions didn't suit her views. In trifles, this independence of hers was all well enough; but in matters of importance, it carried her (as my lady thought, and as I thought) too far. She judged for herself, as few women of twice her age judge in general; never asked your advice; never told you beforehand what she was going to do; never came with secrets and confidences to anybody, from her mother downwards. In little things and great, with people she loved, and people she hated (and she did both with equal heartiness), Miss Rachel always went on a way of her own, sufficient for herself in the joys and sorrows of her life. Over and over again I have heard my lady say, 'Rachel's best friend and Rachel's worst enemy are, one and the other—Rachel herself.'

Add one thing more to this, and I have done.

With all her secrecy, and self-will, there was not so much as the shadow of anything false in her. I never remember her breaking her word; I never remember her saying No, and meaning Yes. I can call to mind, in her childhood, more than one occasion when the good little soul took the blame, and suffered the punishment, for some fault committed by a playfellow whom she loved. Nobody ever knew her to confess to it, when the thing was found out, and she was charged with it afterwards. But nobody ever knew her to lie about it, either. She looked you straight in the face, and shook her little saucy head, and said plainly, 'I won't tell you!' Punished again for this, she would own to being sorry for saying 'won't '; but, bread and water notwithstanding, she never told you. Self-willed—devilish self-willed sometimes—I grant; but the finest creature, nevertheless, that ever walked the ways of this lower world. Perhaps you think you see a certain contradiction here? In that case, a word in your ear. Study your wife closely, for the next four-and-twenty hours. If your good lady doesn't exhibit something in the shape of a contradiction in that time, Heaven help you!—you have married a monster.

I have now brought you acquainted with Miss Rachel, which you will find puts us face to face, next, with the question of that young lady's matrimonial views.

On June the twelfth, an invitation from my mistress was sent to a gentleman in London, to come and help to keep Miss Rachel's birthday. This was the fortunate individual on whom I believed her heart to be privately set! Like Mr Franklin, he was a cousin of hers. His name was Mr Godfrey Ablewhite.

My lady's second sister (don't be alarmed; we are not going very deep into family matters this time)—my lady's second sister, I say, had a disappointment in love; and taking a husband afterwards, on the neck or nothing principle, made what they call a misalliance. There was terrible work in the family when the Honourable Caroline insisted on marrying plain Mr Ablewhite, the banker at Frizinghall. He was very rich and very respectable, and he begot a prodigious large family—all in his favour, so far. But he had presumed to raise himself from a low station in the world—and that was against him. However, Time and the progress of modern enlightenment put things right; and the misalliance passed muster very well. We are all getting liberal now; and (provided you can scratch me, if I scratch you) what do I care, in or out of Parliament, whether you are a Dustman or a Duke? That's the modern way of looking at it—and I keep up with the modern way. The Ablewhites lived in a fine house and grounds, a little out of Frizinghall. Very worthy people, and greatly respected in the neighbourhood. We shall not be much troubled with them in these pages—excepting Mr Godfrey, who was Mr Ablewhite's second son, and who must take his proper place here, if you please, for Miss Rachel's sake.

With all his brightness and cleverness and general good qualities, Mr Franklin's chance of topping Mr Godfrey in our young lady's estimation was, in my opinion, a very poor chance indeed.

In the first place, Mr Godfrey was, in point of size, the finest man by far of the two. He stood over six feet high; he had a beautiful red and white colour; a smooth round face, shaved as bare as your hand; and a head of lovely long flaxen hair, falling negligently over the poll of his neck. But why do I try to give you this personal description of him? If you ever subscribed to a Ladies' Charity in London, you know Mr Godfrey Ablewhite as well as I do. He was a barrister by profession; a ladies' man by temperament; and a good Samaritan by choice. Female benevolence and female destitution could do nothing without him. Maternal societies for confining poor women; Magdalen societies for rescuing poor women; strong-minded societies for putting poor women into poor men's places, and leaving the men to shift for themselves;—he was vice-president, manager, referee to them all. Wherever there was a table with a committee of ladies sitting round it in council, there was Mr Godfrey at the bottom of the board, keeping the temper of the

THE MOONSTONE

committee, and leading the dear creatures along the thorny ways of business, hat in hand.
I do suppose this was the most accomplished philanthropist (on a small independence)
that England ever produced. As a speaker at charitable meetings the like of him for
drawing your tears and your money was not easy to find. He was quite a public character.
The last time I was in London, my mistress gave me two treats. She sent me to the theatre
to see a dancing woman who was all the rage; and she sent me to Exeter Hall to hear Mr
Godfrey. The lady did it, with a band of music. The gentleman did it, with a handkerchief and a glass of water. Crowds at the performance with the legs. Ditto at the performance with the tongue. And with all this, the sweetest-tempered person (I allude to Mr
Godfrey)—the simplest and pleasantest and easiest to please—you ever met with. He
loved everybody. And everybody loved *him*. What chance had Mr Franklin—what
chance had anybody of average reputation and capacities—against such a man as this?

On the fourteenth, came Mr Godfrey's answer.

He accepted my mistress's invitation, from the Wednesday of the birthday to the
evening of Friday—when his duties to the Ladies' Charities would oblige him to return to
town. He also enclosed a copy of verses on what he elegantly called his cousin's 'natal
day.' Miss Rachel, I was informed, joined Mr Franklin in making fun of the verses at
dinner; and Penelope, who was all on Mr Franklin's side, asked me, in great triumph,
what I thought of that. 'Miss Rachel has led *you* off on a false scent, my dear,' I replied;
'but my nose is not so easily mystified. Wait till Mr Ablewhite's verses are followed by
Mr Ablewhite himself.'

My daughter replied, that Mr Franklin might strike in, and try his luck, before the verses
were followed by the poet. In favour of this view, I must acknowledge that Mr Franklin
left no chance untried of winning Miss Rachel's good graces.

Though one of the most inveterate smokers I ever met with, he gave up his cigar,
because she said, one day, she hated the stale smell of it in his clothes. He slept so badly,
after this effort of self-denial, for want of the composing effect of the tobacco to which he
was used, and came down morning after morning looking so haggard and worn, that Miss
Rachel herself begged him to take to his cigars again. No! he would take to nothing again
that could cause her a moment's annoyance; he would fight it out resolutely, and get back
his sleep, sooner or later, by main force of patience in waiting for it. Such devotion as this,
you may say (as some of them said downstairs), could never fail of producing the right
effect on Miss Rachel—backed up, too, as it was, by the decorating work every day on the
door. All very well—but she had a photograph of Mr Godfrey in her bedroom; represented speaking at a public meeting, with all his hair blown out by the breath of his own
eloquence, and his eyes, most lovely, charming the money out of your pockets. What do
you say to that? Every morning—as Penelope herself owned to me—there was the man
whom the women couldn't do without, looking on, in effigy, while Miss Rachel was
having her hair combed. He would be looking on, in reality, before long—that was my
opinion of it.

June the sixteenth brought an event which made Mr Franklin's chance look, to my mind,
a worse chance than ever.

A strange gentleman, speaking English with a foreign accent, came that morning to

49

the house, and asked to see Mr Franklin Blake on business. The business could not possibly have been connected with the Diamond, for these two reasons—first, that Mr Franklin told me nothing about it; secondly, that he communicated it (when the gentleman had gone, as I suppose) to my lady. She probably hinted something about it next to her daughter. At any rate, Miss Rachel was reported to have said some severe things to Mr Franklin, at the piano that evening, about the people he had lived among, and the principles he had adopted in foreign parts. The next day, for the first time, nothing was done towards the decoration of the door. I suspect some imprudence of Mr Franklin's on the Continent—with a woman or a debt at the bottom of it—had followed him to England. But that is all guesswork. In this case, not only Mr Franklin, but my lady too, for a wonder, left me in the dark.

On the seventeenth, to all appearance, the cloud passed away again. They returned to their decorating work on the door, and seemed to be as good friends as ever. If Penelope was to be believed, Mr Franklin had seized the opportunity of the reconciliation to make an offer to Miss Rachel, and had neither been accepted nor refused. My girl was sure (from signs and tokens which I need not trouble you with) that her young mistress had fought Mr Franklin off by declining to believe that he was in earnest, and had then secretly regretted treating him in that way afterwards. Though Penelope was admitted to more familiarity with her young mistress than maids generally are—for the two had been almost brought up together as children—still I knew Miss Rachel's reserved character too well to believe that she would show her mind to anybody in this way. What my daughter told me, on the present occasion, was, as I suspected, more what she wished than what she really knew.

On the nineteenth another event happened. We had the doctor in the house professionally. He was summoned to prescribe for a person whom I have had occasion to present to you in these pages—our second housemaid, Rosanna Spearman.

This poor girl—who had puzzled me, as you know already, at the Shivering Sand—puzzled me more than once again, in the interval time of which I am now writing. Penelope's notion that her fellow-servant was in love with Mr Franklin (which my daughter, by my orders, kept strictly secret) seemed to me just as absurd as ever. But I must own that what I myself saw, and what my daughter saw also, of our second housemaid's conduct, began to look mysterious, to say the least of it.

For example, the girl constantly put herself in Mr Franklin's way—very slyly and quietly, but she did it. He took about as much notice of her as he took of the cat: it never seemed to occur to him to waste a look on Rosanna's plain face. The poor thing's appetite, never much, fell away dreadfully; and her eyes in the morning showed plain signs of waking and crying at night. One day Penelope made an awkward discovery, which we hushed up on the spot. She caught Rosanna at Mr Franklin's dressing-table, secretly removing a rose which Miss Rachel had given him to wear in his button-hole, and putting another rose like it, of her own picking, in its place. She was, after that, once or twice impudent to me, when I gave her a well-meant general hint to be careful in her conduct; and, worse still, she was not over-respectful now, on the few occasions when Miss Rachel accidentally spoke to her.

My lady noticed the change, and asked me what I thought about it. I tried to screen the girl by answering that I thought she was out of health; and it ended in the doctor being sent for, as already mentioned, on the nineteenth. He said it was her nerves, and doubted if she was fit for service. My lady offered to remove her for change of air to one of our farms, inland. She begged and prayed, with the tears in her eyes, to be let to stop; and, in an evil hour, I advised my lady to try her for a little longer. As the event proved, and as you will soon see, this was the worst advice I could have given. If I could only have looked a little way into the future, I would have taken Rosanna Spearman out of the house, then and there, with my own hand.

On the twentieth, there came a note from Mr Godfrey. He had arranged to stop at Frizinghall that night, having occasion to consult his father on business. On the afternoon of the next day, he and his two eldest sisters would ride over to us on horseback, in good time before dinner. An elegant little casket in China accompanied the note, presented to Miss Rachel, with her cousin's love and best wishes. Mr Franklin had only given her a plain locket not worth half the money. My daughter Penelope, nevertheless—such is the obstinacy of women—still backed him to win.

Thanks be to Heaven, we have arrived at the eve of the birthday at last! You will own, I think, that I have got you over the ground this time, without much loitering by the way. Cheer up! I'll ease you with another new chapter here—and, what is more, that chapter shall take you straight into the thick of the story.

CHAPTER 9

June twenty-first, the day of the birthday, was cloudy and unsettled at sunrise, but towards noon it cleared up bravely.

We, in the servants' hall, began this happy anniversary, as usual, by offering our little presents to Miss Rachel, with the regular speech delivered annually by me as the chief. I follow the plan adopted by the Queen in opening Parliament—namely, the plan of saying much the same thing regularly every year. Before it is delivered, my speech (like the Queen's) is looked for as eagerly as if nothing of the kind had ever been heard before. When it is delivered, and turns out not to be the novelty anticipated, though they grumble a little, they look forward hopefully to something newer next year. An easy people to govern, in the Parliament and in the Kitchen—that's the moral of it.

After breakfast, Mr Franklin and I had a private conference on the subject of the Moonstone—the time having now come for removing it from the bank at Frizinghall, and placing it in Miss Rachel's own hands.

Whether he had been trying to make love to his cousin again, and had got a rebuff—or whether his broken rest, night after night, was aggravating the queer contradictions and uncertainties in his character—I don't know. But certain it is, that Mr Franklin failed to show himself at his best on the morning of the birthday. He was in twenty different minds about the Diamond in as many minutes. For my part, I stuck fast by the plain facts as we knew them. Nothing had happened to justify us in alarming my lady on the subject of the jewel; and nothing could alter the legal obligation that now lay on Mr Franklin to put it in his cousin's possession. That was my view of the matter; and, twist and turn it as he might, he was forced in the end to make it his view too. We arranged that he was to ride over, after lunch, to Frizinghall, and bring the Diamond back, with Mr Godfrey and the two young ladies, in all probability, to keep him company on the way home again.

This settled, our young gentleman went back to Miss Rachel.

They consumed the whole morning, and part of the afternoon, in the everlasting business of decorating the door, Penelope standing by to mix the colours, as directed; and my lady, as luncheon time drew near, going in and out of the room, with her handkerchief to her nose (for they used a deal of Mr Franklin's vehicle that day), and trying vainly to get the two artists away from their work. It was three o'clock before they took off their aprons, and released Penelope (much the worse for the vehicle), and cleaned themselves of their mess. But they had done what they wanted—they had finished the door on the birthday, and proud enough they were of it. The griffins, cupids, and so on, were, I must own, most beautiful to behold; though so many in number, so entangled in flowers and devices, and so topsy-turvy in their actions and attitudes, that you felt them unpleasantly in your head for hours after you had done with the pleasure of looking at them. If I add that Penelope ended her part of the morning's work by being sick in the back-kitchen, it is in no unfriendly spirit towards the vehicle. No! no! It left off stinking when it dried; and if Art requires these sort of sacrifices—though the girl is my own daughter—I say, let Art have them!

Mr Franklin snatched a morsel from the luncheon-table, and rode off to Frizinghall— to escort his cousins, as he told my lady. To fetch the Moonstone, as was privately known to himself and to me.

This being one of the high festivals on which I took my place at the sideboard, in command of the attendance at table, I had plenty to occupy my mind while Mr Franklin was away. Having seen to the wine, and reviewed my men and women who were to wait at dinner, I retired to collect myself before the company came. A whiff of—you know what, and a turn at a certain book which I have had occasion to mention in these pages, composed me, body and mind. I was aroused from what I am inclined to think must have been, not a nap, but a reverie, by the clatter of horses' hoofs outside; and, going to the door, received a cavalcade comprising Mr Franklin and his three cousins, escorted by one of old Mr Ablewhite's grooms.

Mr Godfrey struck me, strangely enough, as being like Mr Franklin in this respect— that he did not seem to be in his customary spirits. He kindly shook hands with me as usual, and was most politely glad to see his old friend Betteredge wearing so well. But there was a sort of cloud over him, which I couldn't at all account for; and when I asked how he had found his father in health, he answered rather shortly, 'Much as usual.' However, the two Miss Ablewhites were cheerful enough for twenty, which more than restored the balance. They were nearly as big as their brother; spanking, yellow-haired, rosy lasses, overflowing with superabundant flesh and blood; bursting from head to foot with health and spirits. The legs of the poor horses trembled with carrying them; and when they jumped from their saddles (without waiting to be helped), I declare they bounced on the ground as if they were made of india-rubber. Everything the Miss Ablewhites said began with a large O; everything they did was done with a bang; and they giggled and screamed, in season and out of season, on the smallest provocation. Bouncers—that's what I call them.

Under cover of the noise made by the young ladies, I had an opportunity of saying a private word to Mr Franklin in the hall.

'Have you got the Diamond safe, sir?'

He nodded, and tapped the breast-pocket of his coat.

'Have you seen anything of the Indians?'

'Not a glimpse.' With that answer, he asked for my lady, and, hearing she was in the small drawing-room, went there straight. The bell rang, before he had been a minute in the room, and Penelope was sent to tell Miss Rachel that Mr Franklin Blake wanted to speak to her.

Crossing the hall, about half an hour afterwards, I was brought to a sudden standstill by an outbreak of screams from the small drawing-room. I can't say I was at all alarmed; for I recognized in the screams the favourite large O of the Miss Ablewhites. However, I went in (on pretence of asking for instructions about the dinner) to discover whether anything serious had really happened.

There stood Miss Rachel at the table, like a person fascinated, with the Colonel's unlucky Diamond in her hand. There, on either side of her, knelt the two Bouncers, devouring the jewel with their eyes, and screaming with ecstasy every time it flashed on them in a new light. There, at the opposite side of the table, stood Mr Godfrey, clapping his hands like a large child, and singing out softly, 'Exquisite! exquisite!' There sat Mr Franklin, in a chair by the bookcase, tugging at his beard, and looking anxiously towards the window. And there, at the window, stood the object he was contemplating—my lady, having the extract from the Colonel's Will in her hand, and keeping her back turned on the whole of the company.

She faced me, when I asked for my instructions; and I saw the family frown gathering over her eyes, and the family temper twitching at the corners of her mouth.

'Come to my room in half an hour,' she answered. 'I shall have something to say to you then.'

With those words, she went out. It was plain enough that she was posed by the same difficulty which had posed Mr Franklin and me in our conference at the Shivering Sand. Was the legacy of the Moonstone a proof that she had treated her brother with cruel injustice? or was it a proof that he was worse than the worst she had ever thought of him? Serious questions those for my lady to determine, while her daughter, innocent of all knowledge of the Colonel's character, stood there with the Colonel's birthday gift in her hand.

Before I could leave the room, in my turn, Miss Rachel, always considerate to the old servant who had been in the house when she was born, stopped me. 'Look, Gabriel!' she said, and flashed the jewel before my eyes in a ray of sunlight that poured through the window.

Lord bless us! it *was* a Diamond! As large, or nearly, as a plover's egg! The light that streamed from it was like the light of the harvest moon. When you looked down into the stone, you looked into a yellow deep that drew your eyes into it so that they saw nothing else. It seemed unfathomable; this jewel, that you could hold between your finger and thumb, seemed unfathomable as the heavens themselves. We set it in the sun, and then shut the light out of the room, and it shone awfully out of the depths of its own brightness, with a moony gleam, in the dark. No wonder Miss Rachel was fascinated: no wonder her cousins screamed. The Diamond laid such a hold on *me* that I burst out with as large an 'O' as the Bouncers themselves. The only one of us who kept his senses was Mr Godfrey. He put an arm round each of his sisters' waists, and, looking compassionately backwards and forwards between the Diamond and me, said, 'Carbon, Betteredge! mere carbon, my good friend, after all!'

His object, I suppose, was to instruct me. All he did, however, was to remind me of the dinner. I hobbled off to my army of waiters downstairs. As I went out, Mr Godfrey said, 'Dear old Betteredge, I have the truest regard for him!' He was embracing his sisters, and ogling Miss Rachel, while he honoured me with that testimony of affection. Something like a stock of love to draw on *there!* Mr Franklin was a perfect savage by comparison with him.

At the end of half an hour, I presented myself, as directed, in my lady's room.

What passed between my mistress and me, on this occasion, was, in the main, a repetition of what had passed between Mr Franklin and me at the Shivering Sand—with this difference, that I took care to keep my own counsel about the jugglers, seeing that nothing had happened to justify me in alarming my lady on this head. When I received my dismissal, I could see that she took the blackest view possible of the Colonel's motives, and that she was bent on getting the Moonstone out of her daughter's possession at the first opportunity.

On my way back to my own part of the house, I was encountered by Mr Franklin: He wanted to know if I had seen anything of his cousin Rachel. I had seen nothing of her. Could I tell him where his cousin Godfrey was? I didn't know; but I began to suspect that Cousin Godfrey might not be far away from Cousin Rachel. Mr Franklin's suspicions apparently took the same turn. He tugged hard at his beard, and went and shut himself up in the library, with a bang of the door that had a world of meaning in it.

I was interrupted no more in the business of preparing for the birthday dinner till it was time for me to smarten myself up for receiving the company. Just as I had got my white waistcoat on, Penelope presented herself at my toilet, on pretence of brushing what little hair I have got left, and improving the tie of my white cravat. My girl was in high spirits, and I saw she had something to say to me. She gave me a kiss on the top of my bald head, and whispered, 'News for you, father! Miss Rachel has refused him.'

'Who's "*him?*"' I asked.

'The ladies' committee-man, father,' says Penelope. 'A nasty sly fellow! I hate him for trying to supplant Mr Franklin!'

If I had had breath enough, I should certainly have protested against this indecent way of speaking of an eminent philanthropic character. But my daughter happened to be improving the tie of my cravat at that moment, and the whole strength of her feelings found its way into her fingers. I never was more nearly strangled in my life.

'I saw him take her away alone into the rose-garden,' says Penelope. 'And I waited behind the holly to see how they came back. They had gone out arm-in-arm, both laughing. They came back, walking separate, as grave as grave could be, and looking straight away from each other in a manner which there was no mistaking. I never was more delighted, father, in my life! There's one woman in the world who can resist Mr Godfrey Ablewhite, at any rate; and, if I was a lady, I should be another!'

Here I should have protested again. But my daughter had got the hair-brush by this time, and the whole strength of her feelings had passed into *that*. If you are bald, you will understand how she scarified me. If you are not, skip this bit, and thank God you have got something in the way of a defence between your hair-brush and your head.

'Just on the other side of the holly,' Penelope went on, 'Mr Godfrey came to a standstill. "You prefer," says he, "that I should stop here as if nothing had happened?" Miss Rachel turned on him like lightning. "You have accepted my mother's invitation," she said; "and you are here to meet her guests. Unless you wish to make a scandal in the house, you will remain, of course!" She went on a few steps, and then seemed to relent a little. "Let us forget what has passed, Godfrey," she said, "and let us remain cousins still." She gave him her hand. He kissed it, which *I* should have considered taking a liberty, and then she left him. He waited a little by himself, with his head down, and his heel grinding a hole slowly in the gravel walk; you never saw a man look more put out in your life. "Awkward!" he said between his teeth, when he looked up, and went on to the house —"very awkward!" If that was his opinion of himself, he was quite right. Awkward enough, I'm sure. And the end of it is, father, what I told you all along,' cries Penelope, finishing me off with a last scarification, the hottest of all. ' Mr Franklin's the man!'

I got possession of the hair-brush, and opened my lips to administer the reproof which, you will own, my daughter's language and conduct richly deserved.

Before I could say a word, the crash of carriage-wheels outside struck in, and stopped me. The first of the dinner-company had come. Penelope instantly ran off. I put on my coat, and looked in the glass. My head was as red as a lobster; but, in other respects, I was as nicely dressed for the ceremonies of the evening as a man need be. I got into the hall just in time to announce the two first of the guests. You needn't feel particularly interested about them. Only the philanthropist's father and mother—Mr and Mrs Ablewhite.

CHAPTER 10

One on the top of the other, the rest of the company followed the Ablewhites, till we had the whole tale of them complete. Including the family, they were twenty-four in all. It was a noble sight to see, when they were settled in their places round the dinner-table, and the Rector of Frizinghall (with beautiful elocution) rose and said grace.

There is no need to worry you with a list of the guests. You will meet none of them a second time—in my part of the story, at any rate—with the exception of two.

Those two sat on either side of Miss Rachel, who, as queen of the day, was naturally the great attraction of the party. On this occasion, she was more particularly the centre-point towards which everybody's eyes were directed; for (to my lady's secret annoyance) she wore her wonderful birthday present, which eclipsed all the rest—the Moonstone. It was without any setting when it had been placed in her hands; but that universal genius, Mr Franklin, had contrived, with the help of his neat fingers and a little bit of silver wire, to fix it as a brooch in the bosom of her white dress. Everybody wondered at the prodigious size and beauty of the Diamond, as a matter of course. But the only two of the company who said anything out of the common way about it, were those two guests I have mentioned, who sat by Miss Rachel on her right hand and her left.

The guest on her left was Mr Candy, our doctor at Frizinghall.

This was a pleasant, companionable little man, with the drawback, however, I must own, of being too fond, in season and out of season, of his joke, and of his plunging in rather a headlong manner into talk with strangers, without waiting to feel his way first. In society he was constantly making mistakes, and setting people unintentionally by the ears together. In his medical practice he was a more prudent man; picking up his discretion (as his enemies said) by a kind of instinct, and proving to be generally right where more carefully conducted doctors turned out to be wrong. What *he* said about the Diamond to Miss Rachel was said, as usual, by way of a mystification or joke. He gravely entreated her (in the interests of science) to let him take it home and burn it. 'We will first heat it, Miss Rachel,' says the doctor, 'to such and such a degree; then we will expose it to a current of air; and, little by little—puff!—we evaporate the Diamond, and spare you a world of anxiety about the safe keeping of a valuable precious stone!' My lady, listening with rather a careworn expression on her face, seemed to wish that the doctor had been in earnest, and that he could have found Miss Rachel zealous enough in the cause of science to sacrifice her birthday gift.

The other guest, who sat on my young lady's right hand, was an eminent public character—being no other than the celebrated Indian traveller, Mr Murthwaite, who, at risk of his life, had penetrated in disguise where no European had ever set foot before.

This was a long, lean, wiry, brown, silent man. He had a weary look, and a very steady, attentive eye. It was rumoured that he was tired of the humdrum life among the people in our parts, and longing to go back and wander off on the tramp again in the wild places of the East. Except what he said to Miss Rachel about her jewel, I doubt if he spoke six words or drank so much as a single glass of wine, all through the dinner. The Moonstone was the only object that interested him in the smallest degree. The fame of it seemed to have reached him, in some of those perilous Indian places where his wanderings had lain. After looking at it silently for so long a time that Miss Rachel began to get confused, he said to her in his cool immovable way, 'If you ever go to India, Miss Verinder, don't take your uncle's birthday gift with you. A Hindoo diamond is sometimes part of a Hindoo religion. I know a certain city, and a certain temple in that city, where, dressed as you are now, your life would not be worth five minutes' purchase.' Miss Rachel, safe in England, was quite delighted to hear of her danger in India. The Bouncers were more delighted still; they dropped their knives and forks with a crash, and burst out together vehemently, 'O! how interesting!' My lady fidgeted in her chair, and changed the subject.

As the dinner got on, I became aware, little by little, that this festival was not prospering as other like festivals had prospered before it.

Looking back at the birthday now, by the light of what happened afterwards, I am half inclined to think that the cursed Diamond must have cast a blight on the whole company. I plied them well with wine; and being a privileged character, followed the unpopular dishes round the table, and whispered to the company confidentially, 'Please to change your mind and try it; for I know it will do you good.' Nine times out of ten they changed their minds—out of regard for their old original Betteredge, they were pleased to say— but all to no purpose. There were gaps of silence in the talk, as the dinner got on, that made me feel personally uncomfortable. When they did use their tongues again, they used them innocently, in the most unfortunate manner and to the worst possible purpose. Mr Candy, the doctor, for instance, said more unlucky things than I ever knew him to say before. Take one sample of the way in which he went on, and you will understand what I had to put up with at the sideboard, officiating as I was in the character of a man who had the prosperity of the festival at heart.

One of our ladies present at dinner was worthy Mrs Threadgall, widow of the late Professor of that name. Talking of her deceased husband perpetually, this good lady never mentioned to strangers that he *was* deceased. She thought, I suppose, that every able-bodied adult in England ought to know as much as that. In one of the gaps of silence, somebody mentioned the dry and rather nasty subject of human anatomy; whereupon good Mrs Threadgall straightway brought in her late husband as usual, without mentioning that he was dead. Anatomy she described as the Professor's favourite recreation in his leisure hours. As ill-luck would have it, Mr Candy, sitting opposite (who knew nothing of the deceased gentleman), heard her. Being the most polite of men, he seized the opportunity of assisting the Professor's anatomical amusements on the spot.

'They, have got some remarkably fine skeletons lately at the College of Surgeons,' says Mr Candy, across the table, in a loud cheerful voice. 'I strongly recommend the Professor, ma'am, when he next has an hour to spare, to pay them a visit.'

You might have heard a pin fall. The company (out of respect to the Professor's memory) all sat speechless. I was behind Mrs Threadgall at the time, plying her confidentially with a glass of hock. She dropped her head, and said in a very low voice, 'My beloved husband is no more.'

Unlucky Mr Candy, hearing nothing, and miles away from suspecting the truth, went on across the table louder and politer than ever.

'The Professor may not be aware,' says he, 'that the card of a member of the College will admit him, on any day but Sunday, between the hours of ten and four.'

Mrs Threadgall dropped her head right into her tucker, and, in a lower voice still, repeated the solemn words, 'My beloved husband is no more.'

I winked hard at Mr Candy across the table. Miss Rachel touched his arm. My lady looked unutterable things at him. Quite useless! On he went, with a cordiality that there was no stopping anyhow. 'I shall be delighted,' says he, 'to send the Professor my card, if you will oblige me by mentioning his present address.'

'His present address, sir, is *the grave*,' says Mrs Threadgall, suddenly losing her temper, and speaking with an emphasis and fury that made the glasses ring again. 'The Professor has been dead these ten years!'

'Oh, good heavens!' says Mr Candy. Excepting the Bouncers, who burst out laughing, such a blank now fell on the company, that they might all have been going the way of the Professor, and hailing as he did from the direction of the grave.

So much for Mr Candy. The rest of them were nearly as provoking in their different ways as the doctor himself. When they ought to have spoken, they didn't speak; or when they did speak they were perpetually at cross purposes. Mr Godfrey, though so eloquent in public, declined to exert himself in private. Whether he was sulky, or whether he was bashful, after his discomfiture in the rose-garden, I can't say. He kept all his talk for the private ear of the lady (a member of our family) who sat next to him. She was one of his committee-women—a spiritually-minded person, with a fine show of collar-bone and a pretty taste in champagne; liked it dry, you understand, and plenty of it. Being close behind these two at the sideboard, I can testify, from what I heard pass between them, that the company lost a good deal of very improving conversation, which I caught up while drawing the corks, and carving the mutton, and so forth. What they said about their Charities I didn't hear. When I had time to listen to them, they had got a long way beyond their women to be confined, and their women to be rescued, and were disputing on serious subjects. Religion (I understand Mr Godfrey to say, between the corks and the carving) meant love. And love meant religion. And earth was heaven a little the worse for wear. And heaven was earth, done up again to look like new. Earth had some very objectionable people in it; but, to make amends for that, all the women in heaven would be members of a prodigious committee that never quarrelled, with all the men in attendance on them as ministering angels. Beautiful! beautiful! But why the mischief did Mr Godfrey keep it all to his lady and himself?

Mr Franklin again—surely, you will say, Mr Franklin stirred the company up into making a pleasant evening of it?

Nothing of the sort! He had quite recovered himself, and he was in wonderful force and spirits, Penelope having informed him, I suspect, of Mr Godfrey's reception in the rose-garden. But, talk as he might, nine times out of ten he pitched on the wrong subject, or he addressed himself to the wrong person; the end of it being that he offended some, and puzzled all of them. That foreign training of his—those French and German and Italian sides of him, to which I have already alluded—came out, at my lady's hospitable board, in a most bewildering manner.

What do you think, for instance, of his discussing the lengths to which a married woman might let her admiration go for a man who was not her husband, and putting it in his clear-headed witty French way to the maiden aunt of the Vicar of Frizinghall? What do you think, when he shifted to the German side, of his telling the lord of the manor, while that great authority on cattle was quoting his experience in the breeding of bulls, that experience, properly understood, counted for nothing, and that the proper way to breed bulls was to look deep into your own mind, evolve out of it the idea of a perfect bull, and produce him? What do you say, when our county member, growing hot, at cheese and salad time, about the spread of democracy in England, burst out as follows: 'If we once lose our ancient safeguards, Mr Blake, I beg to ask you, what have we got left?'—what do you say to Mr Franklin answering, from the Italian point of view: 'We have got three things left, sir—Love, Music, and Salad'? He not only terrified the company with such outbreaks as these, but, when the English side of him turned up in due course, he lost his foreign smoothness; and, getting on the subject of the medical profession, said such downright things in ridicule of doctors, that he actually put good-humoured little Mr Candy in a rage.

The dispute between them began in Mr Franklin being led—I forget how—to acknowledge that he had latterly slept very badly at night. Mr Candy thereupon told him that his nerves were all out of order, and that he ought to go through a course of medicine immediately. Mr Franklin replied that a course of medicine, and a course of groping in the dark, meant, in his estimation, one and the same thing. Mr Candy, hitting back smartly, said that Mr Franklin himself was, constitutionally speaking, groping in the dark after sleep, and that nothing but medicine could help him to find it. Mr Franklin, keeping the ball up on his side, said he had often heard of the blind leading the blind, and now, for the first time, he knew what it meant. In this way, they kept it going briskly, cut and thrust, till they both of them got hot—Mr Candy, in particular, so completely losing his self-control, in defence of his profession, that my lady was obliged to interfere, and forbid the dispute to go on. This necessary act of authority put the last extinguisher on the spirits of the company. The talk spurted up again here and there, for a minute or two at a time; but there was a miserable lack of life and sparkle in it. The Devil (or the Diamond) possessed that dinner-party; and it was a relief to everybody when my mistress rose, and gave the ladies the signal to leave the gentlemen over their wine.

I had just ranged the decanters in a row before old Mr Ablewhite (who represented the master of the house), when there came a sound from the terrace which startled me out of my company manners on the instant. Mr Franklin and I looked at each other; it was the sound of the Indian drum. As I live by bread, here were the jugglers returning to us with the return of the Moonstone to the house!

As they rounded the corner of the terrace, and came in sight, I hobbled out to warn them off. But, as ill-luck would have it, the two Bouncers were beforehand with me. They whizzed out on to the terrace like a couple of skyrockets, wild to see the Indians exhibit their tricks. The other ladies followed; the gentlemen came out on their side. Before you could say, 'Lord bless us!' the rogues were making their salaams; and the Bouncers were kissing the pretty little boy.

Mr Franklin got on one side of Miss Rachel, and I put myself behind her. If our suspicions were right, there she stood, innocent of all knowledge of the truth, showing the Indians the Diamond in the bosom of her dress!

I can't tell you what tricks they performed, or how they did it. What with the vexation about the dinner, and what with the provocation of the rogues coming back just in the nick of time to see the jewel with their own eyes, I own I lost my head. The first thing that I remember noticing was the sudden appearance on the scene of the Indian traveller, Mr Murthwaite. Skirting the half-circle in which the gentlefolks stood or sat, he came quietly behind the jugglers, and spoke to them on a sudden in the language of their own country.

If he had pricked them with a bayonet, I doubt if the Indians could have started and turned on him with a more tigerish quickness than they did, on hearing the first words that passed his lips. The next moment, they were bowing and salaaming to him in their most polite and snaky way. After a few words in the unknown tongue had passed on either side, Mr Murthwaite withdrew as quietly as he had approached. The chief Indian, who acted as interpreter, thereupon wheeled about again towards the gentlefolks. I noticed that the fellow's coffee-coloured face had turned grey since Mr Murthwaite had spoken to him. He bowed to my lady, and informed her that the exhibition was over. The Bouncers, indescribably disappointed, burst out with a loud 'O!' directed against Mr Murthwaite for stopping the performance. The chief Indian laid his hand humbly on his breast, and said a second time that the juggling was over. The little boy went round with the hat. The ladies withdrew to the drawing-room; and the gentlemen (excepting Mr Franklin and Mr Murthwaite) returned to their wine. I and the footman followed the Indians, and saw them safe off the premises.

Going back by way of the shrubbery, I smelt tobacco, and found Mr Franklin and Mr Murthwaite (the latter smoking a cheroot) walking slowly up and down among the trees. Mr Franklin beckoned to me to join them.

'This,' says Mr Franklin, presenting me to the great traveller, 'is Gabriel Betteredge, the old servant and friend of our family of whom I spoke to you just now. Tell him, if you please, what you have just told me.'

Mr Murthwaite took his cheroot out of his mouth, and leaned, in his weary way, against the trunk of a tree.

'Mr Betteredge,' he began, 'those three Indians are no more jugglers than you and I are.'

Here was a new surprise! I naturally asked the traveller if he had ever met with the Indians before.

'Never,' says Mr Murthwaite; 'but I know what Indian juggling really is. All you have seen to-night is a very bad and clumsy imitation of it. Unless, after long experience, I am utterly mistaken, those men are high-caste Brahmins. I charged them with being disguised, and you saw how it told on them, clever as the Hindoo people are in concealing their feelings. There is a mystery about their conduct that I can't explain. They have doubly sacrificed their caste—first, in crossing the sea; secondly, in disguising themselves as jugglers. In the land they live in, that is a tremendous sacrifice to make. There must be some very serious motive at the bottom of it, and some justification of no ordinary kind to plead for them, in recovery of their caste, when they return to their own country.'

I was struck dumb. Mr Murthwaite went on with his cheroot. Mr Franklin, after what looked to me like a little private veering about between the different sides of his character, broke the silence as follows:

'I feel some hesitation, Mr Murthwaite, in troubling you with family matters, in which you can have no interest and which I am not very willing to speak of out of our own circle. But, after what you have said, I feel bound, in the interests of Lady Verinder and her daughter, to tell you something which may possibly put the clue into your hands. I speak to you in confidence; you will oblige me, I am sure, by not forgetting that?'

With this preface, he told the Indian traveller all that he had told me at the Shivering Sand. Even the immovable Mr Murthwaite was so interested in what he heard, that he let his cheroot go out.

'Now,' says Mr Franklin, when he had done, 'what does your experience say?'

'My experience,' answered the traveller, 'says that you have had more narrow escapes of your life, Mr Franklin Blake, than I have had of mine; and that is saying a great deal.'

'It was Mr Franklin's turn to be astonished now.

'Is it really as serious as that?' he asked.

'In my opinion it is,' answered Mr Murthwaite. 'I can't doubt, after what you have told me, that the restoration of the Moonstone to its place on the forehead of the Indian idol, is the motive and the justification of that sacrifice of caste which I alluded to just now. Those men will wait their opportunity with the patience of cats, and will use it with the ferocity of tigers. How you have escaped them I can't imagine,' says the eminent traveller, lighting his cheroot again, and staring hard at Mr Franklin. 'You have been carrying the Diamond backwards and forwards, here and in London, and you are still a living man! Let us try and account for it. It was daylight, both times, I suppose, when you took the jewel out of the bank in London?'

'Broad daylight,' says Mr Franklin.

'And plenty of people in the streets?'

'Plenty.'

'You settled, of course, to arrive at Lady Verinder's house at a certain time? It's a lonely country between this and the station. Did you keep your appointment?'

'No. I arrived four hours earlier than my appointment.'

'I beg to congratulate you on that proceeding! When did you take the Diamond to the bank at the town here?'

'I took it an hour after I had brought it to this house—and three hours before anybody was prepared for seeing me in these parts.'

'I beg to congratulate you again! Did you bring it back here alone?'

'No. I happened to ride back with my cousins and the groom.'

'I beg to congratulate you for the third time! If you ever feel inclined to travel beyond the civilized limits, Mr Blake, let me know, and I will go with you. You are a lucky man.'

Here I struck in. This sort of thing didn't at all square with my English ideas.

'You don't really mean to say, sir,' I asked, 'that they would have taken Mr Franklin's life, to get their Diamond, if he had given them the chance?'

'Do you smoke, Mr Betteredge?' says the traveller.

'Yes, sir.'

'Do you care much for the ashes left in your pipe, when you empty it?'

'No, sir.'

'In the country those men came from, they care just as much about killing a man, as you care about emptying the ashes out of your pipe. If a thousand lives stood between them and the getting back of their Diamond—and if they thought they could destroy those lives without discovery—they would take them all. The sacrifice of caste is a serious thing in India, if you like. The sacrifice of life is nothing at all.'

I expressed my opinion, upon this, that they were a set of murdering thieves. Mr Murthwaite expressed *his* opinion that they were a wonderful people. Mr Franklin, expressing no opinion at all, brought us back to the matter in hand.

'They have seen the Moonstone on Miss Verinder's dress,' he said. 'What is to be done?'

'What your uncle threatened to do,' answered Mr Murthwaite. 'Colonel Herncastle understood the people he had to deal with. Send the Diamond to-morrow (under guard of more than one man) to be cut up at Amsterdam. Make half a dozen diamonds of it, instead of one. There is an end of its sacred identity as The Moonstone—and there is an end of the conspiracy.'

Mr Franklin turned to me.

'There is no help for it,' he said. 'We must speak to Lady Verinder to-morrow.'

'What about to-night, sir?' I asked. 'Suppose the Indians come back?'

Mr Murthwaite answered me, before Mr Franklin could speak.

'The Indians won't risk coming back to-night,' he said. 'The direct way is hardly ever the way they take to anything—let alone a matter like this, in which the slightest mistake might be fatal to their reaching their end.'

'But suppose the rogues are bolder than you think, sir?' I persisted.

'In that case,' says Mr Murthwaite, 'let the dogs loose. Have you got any big dogs in the yard?'

'Two, sir. A mastiff and a bloodhound.'

'They will do. In the present emergency, Mr Betteredge, the mastiff and the blood-hound have one great merit—they are not likely to be troubled with your scruples about the sanctity of human life.'

The strumming of the piano reached us from the drawing-room, as he fired that shot at me. He threw away his cheroot, and took Mr Franklin's arm, to go back to the ladies. I noticed that the sky was clouding over fast, as I followed them to the house. Mr Murthwaite noticed it too. He looked round at me, in his dry, drolling way, and said:

'The Indians will want their umbrellas, Mr Betteredge, to-night!'

It was all very well for *him* to joke. But I was not an eminent traveller—and my way in this world had not led me into playing ducks and drakes with my own life, among thieves and murderers in the outlandish places of the earth. I went into my own little room, and sat down in my chair in a perspiration, and wondered helplessly what was to be done next. In this anxious frame of mind, other men might have ended by working themselves up into a fever; I ended in a different way. I lit my pipe, and took a turn at *Robinson Crusoe*.

Before I had been at it five minutes, I came to this amazing bit—page one hundred and sixty-one—as follows:

'Fear of Danger is ten thousand times more terrifying than Danger itself, when apparent to the Eyes; and we find the Burthen of Anxiety greater, by much, than the Evil which we are anxious about.'

The man who doesn't believe in *Robinson Crusoe*, after *that*, is a man with a screw loose in his understanding, or a man lost in the mist of his own self-conceit! Argument is thrown away upon him; and pity is better reserved for some person with a livelier faith.

I was far on with my second pipe, and still lost in admiration of that wonderful book, when Penelope (who had been handing round the tea) came in with her report from the drawing-room. She had left the Bouncers singing a duet—words beginning with a large 'O,' and music to correspond. She had observed that my lady made mistakes in her game of whist for the first time in our experience of her. She had seen the great traveller asleep in a corner. She had overheard Mr Franklin sharpening his wits on Mr Godfrey, at the expense of Ladies' Charities in general; and she had noticed that Mr Godfrey hit him back again rather more smartly than became a gentleman of his benevolent character. She had detected Miss Rachel, apparently engaged in appeasing Mrs Threadgall by showing her some photographs, and really occupied in stealing looks at Mr Franklin, which no intel-ligent lady's maid could misinterpret for a single instant. Finally, she had missed Mr Candy, the doctor, who had mysteriously disappeared from the drawing-room, and had then mysteriously returned, and entered into conversation with Mr Godfrey. Upon the whole, things were prospering better than the experience of the dinner gave us any right to expect. If we could only hold on for another hour, old Father Time would bring up their carriages, and relieve us of them altogether.

Everything wears off in this world; and even the comforting effect of *Robinson Crusoe* wore off, after Penelope left me. I got fidgety again, and resolved on making a survey of the grounds before the rain came. Instead of taking the footman, whose nose was human, and therefore useless in any emergency, I took the bloodhound with me. *His* nose for a stranger was to be depended on. We went all round the premises, and out into the road—and returned as wise as we went, having discovered no such thing as a lurking human creature anywhere.

The arrival of the carriages was the signal for the arrival of the rain. It poured as if it meant to pour all night. With the exception of the doctor, whose gig was waiting for him, the rest of the company went home snugly, under cover, in close carriages. I told Mr Candy that I was afraid he would get wet through. He told me, in return, that he wondered I had arrived at my time of life, without knowing that a doctor's skin was waterproof. So he drove away in the rain, laughing over his own little joke; and so we got rid of our dinner company.

The next thing to tell is the story of the night.

CHAPTER 11

When the last of the guests had driven away, I went back into the inner hall, and found Samuel at the side-table, presiding over the brandy and soda-water. My lady and Miss Rachel came out of the drawing-room, followed by the two gentlemen. Mr Godfrey had some brandy and soda-water. Mr Franklin took nothing. He sat down, looking dead tired; the talking on this birthday occasion had, I suppose, been too much for him.

My lady, turning round to wish them good-night, looked hard at the wicked Colonel's legacy shining in her daughter's dress.

'Rachel,' she asked, 'where are you going to put your Diamond to-night?'

Miss Rachel was in high good spirits, just in that humour for talking nonsense, and perversely persisting in it as if it was sense, which you may sometimes have observed in young girls, when they are highly wrought up, at the end of an exciting day. First, she declared she didn't know where to put the Diamond. Then she said, 'On her dressing-table, of course, along with her other things.' Then she remembered that the Diamond might take to shining of itself, with its awful moony light, in the dark—and that would terrify her in the dead of night. Then she bethought herself of an Indian cabinet which stood in her sitting-room; and instantly made up her mind to put the Indian diamond in the Indian cabinet, for the purpose of permitting two beautiful native productions to admire each other. Having let her little flow of nonsense run on as far as that point, her mother interposed and stopped her.

'My dear! your Indian cabinet has no lock to it,' says my lady.

'Good Heavens, mamma!' cried Miss Rachel, 'is this an hotel? Are there thieves in the house?'

Without taking notice of this fantastic way of talking, my lady wished the gentlemen good-night. She next turned to Miss Rachel, and kissed her. 'Why not let *me* keep the Diamond for you to-night?' she asked.

Miss Rachel received that proposal as she might, ten years since, have received a proposal to part her from a new doll. My lady saw there was no reasoning with her that night. 'Come into my room, Rachel, the first thing to-morrow morning,' she said. 'I shall have something to say to you.' With those last words she left us slowly; thinking her own thoughts, and, to all appearance, not best pleased with the way by which they were leading her.

Miss Rachel was the next to say good-night. She shook hands first with Mr Godfrey, who was standing at the other end of the hall, looking at a picture. Then she turned back to Mr Franklin, still sitting weary and silent in a corner.

What words passed between them I can't say. But standing near the old oak frame which holds our large looking-glass, I saw her reflected in it, slyly slipping the locket which Mr Franklin had given to her, out of the bosom of her dress, and showing it to him for a moment, with a smile which certainly meant something out of the common, before she tripped off to bed. This incident staggered me a little in the reliance I had previously felt on my own judgment. I began to think that Penelope might be right about the state of her young lady's affections, after all.

As soon as Miss Rachel left him eyes to see with, Mr Franklin noticed me. His variable humour, shifting about everything, had shifted about the Indians already.

'Betteredge,' he said, 'I'm half inclined to think I took Mr Murthwaite too seriously, when we had that talk in the shrubbery. I wonder whether he has been trying any of his traveller's tales on us? Do you really mean to let the dogs loose?'

'I'll relieve them of their collars, sir,' I answered, 'and leave them free to take a turn in the night, if they smell a reason for it.'

'All right,' says Mr Franklin. 'We'll see what is to be done to-morrow. I am not at all disposed to alarm my aunt, Betteredge, without a very pressing reason for it. Good-night.'

He looked so worn and pale as he nodded to me, and took his candle to go upstairs, that I ventured to advise his having a drop of brandy-and-water, by way of nightcap. Mr Godfrey, walking towards us from the other end of the hall, backed me. He pressed Mr Franklin, in the friendliest manner, to take something, before he went to bed.

I only note these trifling circumstances, because, after all I had seen and heard, that day, it pleased me to observe that our two gentlemen were on just as good terms as ever. Their warfare of words (heard by Penelope in the drawing-room), and their rivalry for the best place in Miss Rachel's good graces, seemed to have set no serious difference between them. But there! they were both good-tempered, and both men of the world. And there is certainly this merit in people of station, that they are not nearly so quarrelsome among each other as people of no station at all.

Mr Franklin declined the brandy-and-water, and went upstairs with Mr Godfrey, their rooms being next door to each other. On the landing, however, either his cousin persuaded him, or he veered about and changed his mind as usual. 'Perhaps I may want it in the night,' he called down to me. 'Send up some brandy-and-water into my room.'

I sent up Samuel with the brandy-and-water; and then went out, and unbuckled the dogs' collars. They both lost their heads with astonishment on being set loose at that time of night, and jumped upon me like a couple of puppies! However, the rain soon cooled them down again: they lapped a drop of water each, and crept back into their kennels. As I went into the house, I noticed signs in the sky which betokened a break in the weather for the better. For the present, it still poured heavily, and the ground was in a perfect sop.

Samuel and I went all over the house, and shut up as usual. I examined everything myself, and trusted nothing to my deputy on this occasion. All was safe and fast, when I rested my old bones in bed, between midnight and one in the morning.

The worries of the day had been a little too much for me, I suppose. At any rate, I had a touch of Mr Franklin's malady that night. It was sunrise, before I fell off at last into a sleep. All the time I lay awake, the house was as quiet as the grave. Not a sound stirred but the splash of the rain, and the sighing of the wind among the trees as a breeze sprang up with the morning.

About half-past seven I woke, and opened my window on a fine sunshiny day. The clock had struck eight, and I was just going out to chain up the dogs again, when I heard a sudden whisking of petticoats on the stairs behind me.

I turned about, and there was Penelope flying down after me like mad. 'Father!' she screamed, 'come upstairs, for God's sake! *The Diamond is gone!*'

'Are you out of your mind?' I asked her.

'Gone!' says Penelope. 'Gone, nobody knows how! Come up and see.'

She dragged me after her into our young lady's sitting-room, which opened into her bedroom. There, on the threshold of her bedroom door, stood Miss Rachel, almost as white in the face as the white dressing-gown that clothed her. There also stood the two doors of the Indian cabinet, wide open. One of the drawers inside was pulled out as far as it would go.

'Look!' says Penelope. 'I myself saw Miss Rachel put the Diamond into that drawer last night.'

I went to the cabinet. The drawer was empty.

'Is this true, miss?' I asked.

With a look that was not like herself, with a voice that was not like her own, Miss Rachel answered, as my daughter had answered: 'The Diamond is gone!'

Having said those words, she withdrew into her bedroom, and shut and locked the door.

Before we knew which way to turn next, my lady came in, hearing my voice in her daughter's sitting-room, and wondering what had happened. The news of the loss of the Diamond seemed to petrify her. She went straight to Miss Rachel's bedroom, and insisted on being admitted. Miss Rachel let her in.

The alarm, running through the house like fire, caught the two gentlemen next.

Mr Godfrey was the first to come out of his room. All he did when he heard what had happened was to hold up his hands in a state of bewilderment, which didn't say much for his natural strength of mind. Mr Franklin, whose clear head I had confidently counted on to advise us, seemed to be as helpless as his cousin when he heard the news in his turn. For a wonder, he had had a good night's rest at last; and the unaccustomed luxury of sleep had, as he said himself, apparently stupefied him. However, when he had swallowed his cup of coffee—which he always took, on the foreign plan, some hours before he ate any breakfast—his brains brightened; the clear-headed side of him turned up, and he took the matter in hand, resolutely and cleverly, much as follows:

He first sent for the servants, and told them to leave all the lower doors and windows (with the exception of the front door, which I had opened) exactly as they had been left when we locked up overnight. He next proposed to his cousin and to me to make quite sure, before we took any further steps, that the Diamond had not accidentally dropped somewhere out of sight—say at the back of the cabinet, or down behind the table on which the cabinet stood. Having searched in both places, and found nothing—having also questioned Penelope, and discovered from her no more than the little she had already told me—Mr Franklin suggested next extending our inquiries to Miss Rachel, and sent Penelope to knock at her bedroom door.

My lady answered the knock, and closed the door behind her. The moment after, we heard it locked inside by Miss Rachel. My mistress came out among us, looking sorely puzzled and distressed. 'The loss of the Diamond seems to have quite overwhelmed Rachel,' she said, in reply to Mr Franklin. 'She shrinks, in the strangest manner, from speaking of it, even to *me*. It is impossible you can see her for the present.'

Having added to our perplexities by this account of Miss Rachel, my lady, after a little effort, recovered her usual composure, and acted with her usual decision.

'I suppose there is no help for it?' she said, quietly. 'I suppose I have no alternative but to send for the police?'

'And the first thing for the police to do,' added Mr Franklin, catching her up, 'is to lay hands on the Indian jugglers who performed here last night'

My lady and Mr Godfrey (not knowing what Mr Franklin and I knew) both started, and both looked surprised.

'I can't stop to explain myself now,' Mr Franklin went on. 'I can only tell you that the Indians have certainly stolen the Diamond. Give me a letter of introduction,' says he, addressing my lady, 'to one of the magistrates at Frizinghall—merely telling him that I represent your interests and wishes, and let me ride off with it instantly. Our chance of catching the thieves may depend on our not wasting one unnecessary minute.' (*Nota bene:* Whether it was the French side or the English, the right side of Mr Franklin seemed to be uppermost now. The only question was, How long would it last?)

He put pen, ink, and paper before his aunt, who (as it appeared to me) wrote the letter he wanted a little unwillingly. If it had been possible to overlook such an event as the loss of a jewel worth twenty thousand pounds, I believe—with my lady's opinion of her late brother, and her distrust of his birthday-gift—it would have been privately a relief to her to let the thieves get off with the Moonstone scot free.

I went out with Mr Franklin to the stables, and took the opportunity of asking him how the Indians (whom I suspected, of course, as shrewdly as he did) could possibly have got into the house.

'One of them might have slipped into the hall, in the confusion, when the dinner company were going away,' says Mr Franklin. 'The fellow may have been under the sofa while my aunt and Rachel were talking about where the Diamond was to be put for the night. He would only have to wait till the house was quiet, and there it would be in the cabinet, to be had for the taking.' With those words, he called to the groom to open the gate, and galloped off.

This seemed certainly to be the only rational explanation. But how had the thief contrived to make his escape from the house? I had found the front door locked and bolted, as I had left it at night, when I went to open it, after getting up. As for the other doors and windows, there they were still, all safe and fast, to speak for themselves. The dogs, too? Suppose the thief had got away by dropping from one of the upper windows, how had he escaped the dogs? Had he come provided for them with drugged meat? As the doubt crossed my mind, the dogs themselves came galloping at me round a corner, rolling each other over on the wet grass, in such lively health and spirits that it was with no small difficulty I brought them to reason, and chained them up again. The more I turned it over in my mind, the less satisfactory Mr Franklin's explanation appeared to be.

We had our breakfasts—whatever happens in a house, robbery or murder, it doesn't matter, you must have your breakfast. When we had done, my lady sent for me; and I found myself compelled to tell her all that I had hitherto concealed, relating to the Indians and their plot. Being a woman of a high courage, she soon got over the first startling effect of what I had to communicate. Her mind seemed to be far more perturbed about her daughter than about the heathen rogues and their conspiracy. 'You know how odd Rachel is, and how differently she behaves sometimes from other girls,' my lady said to me. 'But I have never, in all my experience, seen her so strange and so reserved as she is now. The loss of her jewel seems almost to have turned her brain. Who would have thought that horrible Diamond could have laid such a hold on her in so short a time?'

It was certainly strange. Taking toys and trinkets in general, Miss Rachel was nothing like so mad after them as most young girls. Yet there she was, still locked up inconsolably in her bedroom. It is but fair to add that she was not the only one of us in the house who was thrown out of the regular groove. Mr Godfrey, for instance—though professionally a sort of consoler-general— seemed to be at a loss where to look for his own resources. Having no company to amuse him, and getting no chance of trying what his experience of women in distress could do towards comforting Miss Rachel, he wandered hither and thither about the house and gardens in an aimless uneasy way. He was in two different minds about what it became him to do, after the misfortune that had happened to us. Ought he to relieve the family, in their present situation, of the responsibility of him as a guest, or ought he to stay on the chance that even his humble services might be of some use? He decided ultimately that the last course was perhaps the most customary and considerate course to take, in such a very peculiar case of family distress as this was. Circumstances try the metal a man is really made of. Mr Godfrey, tried by circumstances, showed himself of weaker metal than I had thought him to be. As for the women-servants—excepting Rosanna Spearman, who kept by herself—they took to whispering together in corners, and staring at nothing suspiciously, as is the manner of that weaker half of the human family, when anything extraordinary happens in a house. I myself acknowledge to have been fidgety and ill-tempered. The cursed Moonstone had turned us all upside down.

A little before eleven, Mr Franklin came back. The resolute side of him had, to all appearance, given way, in the interval since his departure, under the stress that had been laid on it. He had left us at a gallop; he came back to us at a walk. When he went away, he was made of iron. When he returned, he was stuffed with cotton, as limp as limp could be.

'Well,' says my lady, 'are the police coming?'

'Yes,' says Mr Franklin; 'they said they would follow me in a fly. Superintendent Seegrave, of your local police force, and two of his men. A mere form! The case is hopeless.'

'What! have the Indians escaped, sir?' I asked.

'The poor ill-used Indians have been most unjustly put in prison,' says Mr Franklin. 'They are as innocent as the babe unborn. My idea that one of them was hidden in the house, has ended, like all the rest of my ideas, in smoke. It's been proved,' says Mr Franklin, dwelling with great relish on his own incapacity, 'to be simply impossible.'

After astonishing us by announcing this totally new turn in the matter of the Moonstone, our young gentleman, at his aunt's request, took a seat, and explained himself.

It appeared that the resolute side of him had held out as far as Frizinghall. He had put the whole case plainly before the magistrate, and the magistrate had at once sent for the police. The first inquiries instituted about the Indians showed that they had not so much as attempted to leave the town. Further questions addressed to the police, proved that all three had been seen returning to Frizinghall with their boy, on the previous night between ten and eleven—which (regard being had to hours and distances) also proved that they had walked straight back, after performing on our terrace. Later still, at midnight, the police, having occasion to search the common lodging-house where they lived, had seen them all three again, and their little boy with them as usual. Soon after midnight I myself had safely shut up the house. Plainer evidence than this, in favour of the Indians, there could not well be. The magistrate said there was not even a case of suspicion against them so far. But, as it was just possible, when the police came to investigate the matter, that discoveries affecting the jugglers might be made, he would contrive, by committing them as rogues and vagabonds, to keep them at our disposal, under lock and key, for a week. They had ignorantly done something (I forget what) in the town, which barely brought them within the operation of the law. Every human institution (Justice included) will stretch a little, if you only pull it the right way. The worthy magistrate was an old friend of my lady's— and the Indians were 'committed' for a week, as soon as the court opened that morning.

Such was Mr Franklin's narrative of events at Frizinghall. The Indian clue to the mystery of the lost jewel was now, to all appearance, a clue that had broken in our hands. If the jugglers were innocent, who, in the name of wonder, had taken the Moonstone out of Miss Rachel's drawer?

Ten minutes later, to our infinite relief, Superintendent Seegrave arrived at the house. He reported passing Mr Franklin on the terrace, sitting in the sun (I suppose with the Italian side of him uppermost); and warning the police, as they went by, that the investigation was hopeless, before the investigation had begun.

For a family in our situation, the Superintendent of the Frizinghall police was the most comforting officer you could wish to see. Mr Seegrave was tall and portly, and military in his manners. He had a fine commanding voice, and a mighty resolute eye, and a grand frock-coat which buttoned beautifully up to his leather stock. 'I'm the man you want!'

was written all over his face; and he ordered his two inferior policemen about with a severity which convinced us all that there was no trifling with *him*.

He began by going round the premises, outside and in; the result of that investigation proving to him that no thieves had broken in upon us from outside, and that the robbery, consequently, must have been committed by some person in the house. I leave you to imagine the state the servants were in when this official announcement first reached their ears. The Superintendent decided to begin by examining the boudoir; and, that done, to examine the servants next. At the same time, he posted one of his men on the staircase which led to the servants' bedrooms, with instructions to let nobody in the house pass him, till further orders.

At this latter proceeding, the weaker half of the human family went distracted on the spot. They bounced out of their corners; whisked upstairs in a body to Miss Rachel's room (Rosanna Spearman being carried away among them this time); burst in on Superintendent Seegrave; and all looking equally guilty, summoned him to say which of them he suspected, at once.

Mr Superintendent proved equal to the occasion—he looked at them with his resolute eye, and he cowed them with his military voice.

'Now, then, you women, go downstairs again, every one of you. I won't have you here. Look!' says Mr Superintendent, suddenly pointing to a little smear of the decorative painting on Miss Rachel's door—at the outer edge, just under the lock. 'Look what mischief the petticoats of some of you have done already. Clear out! clear out!' Rosanna Spearman, who was nearest to him, and nearest to the little smear on the door, set the example of obedience, and slipped off instantly to her work. The rest followed her out. The Superintendent finished his examination of the room; and, making nothing of it, asked me who had first discovered the robbery. My daughter had first discovered it. My daughter was sent for.

Mr Superintendent proved to be a little too sharp with Penelope at starting. 'Now, young woman, attend to me—and mind you speak the truth.' Penelope fired up instantly. 'I've never been taught to tell lies, Mr Policeman!—and if father can stand there and hear me accused of falsehood and thieving, and my own bedroom shut against me, and my character taken away, which is all a poor girl has left, he's not the good father I take him for!' A timely word from me put Justice and Penelope on a pleasanter footing together. The questions and answers went swimmingly; and ended in nothing worth mentioning. My daughter had seen Miss Rachel put the Diamond in the drawer of the cabinet, the last thing at night. She had gone in with Miss Rachel's cup of tea, at eight the next morning, and had found the drawer open and empty. Upon that, she had alarmed the house—and there was an end of Penelope's evidence.

Mr Superintendent next asked to see Miss Rachel herself. Penelope mentioned his request through the door. The answer reached us by the same road—'I have nothing to tell the policeman—I can't see anybody.' Our experienced officer looked equally surprised and offended when he heard that reply. I told him my young lady was ill, and begged him to wait a little and see her later. We thereupon went downstairs again, and were met by Mr Godfrey and Mr Franklin, crossing the hall.

The two gentlemen, being inmates of the house, were summoned to say if they could throw any light on the matter. Neither of them knew anything about it. Had they heard any suspicious noises during the previous night? They had heard nothing but the pattering of the rain. Had I, lying awake longer than either of them, heard nothing either? Nothing! Released from examination, Mr Franklin (still sticking to the helpless view of our difficulty) whispered to me,—'That man will be of no earthly use to us. Superintendent Seegrave is an ass.' Released in his turn, Mr Godfrey whispered to me,— 'Evidently a most competent person. Betteredge, I have the greatest faith in him!' Many men, many opinions, as one of the ancients said, before my time.

Mr Superintendent's next proceeding took him back to the 'boudoir' again, with my daughter and me at his heels. His object was to discover whether any of the furniture had been moved, during the night, out of its customary place—his previous investigation in the room having, apparently, not gone quite far enough to satisfy his mind on this point.

While we were still poking about among the chairs and tables, the door of the bedroom was suddenly opened. After having denied herself to everybody, Miss Rachel, to our astonishment, walked into the midst of us of her own accord. She took up her garden hat from a chair, and then went straight to Penelope with this question:—

'Mr Franklin Blake sent you with a message to me this morning?'

'Yes, miss.'

'He wished to speak to me, didn't he?'

'Yes, miss.'

'Where is he now?'

Hearing voices on the terrace below, I looked out of window, and saw the two gentlemen walking up and down together. Answering for my daughter, I said, 'Mr Franklin is on the terrace, miss.'

Without another word, without heeding Mr Superintendent, who tried to speak to her; pale as death, and wrapped up strangely in her own thoughts, she left the room, and went down to her cousins on the terrace.

It showed a want of due respect, it showed a breach of good manners, on my part; but, for the life of me, I couldn't help looking out of the window when Miss Rachel met the gentlemen outside. She went up to Mr Franklin without appearing to notice Mr Godfrey, who thereupon drew back and left them by themselves. What she said to Mr Franklin appeared to be spoken vehemently. It lasted but for a short time; and (judging by what I saw of his face from the window) seemed to astonish him beyond all power of expression. While they were still together, my lady appeared on the terrace. Miss Rachel saw her—said a few last words to Mr Franklin—and suddenly went back into the house again, before her mother came up with her. My lady, surprised herself, and noticing Mr Franklin's surprise, spoke to him. Mr Godfrey joined them, and spoke also. Mr Franklin walked away a little, between the two, telling them what had happened, I suppose; for they both stopped short, after taking a few steps, like persons struck with amazement. I had just seen as much as this, when the door of the sitting-room was opened violently. Miss Rachel walked swiftly through to her bedroom, wild and angry, with fierce eyes and flaming cheeks. Mr Superintendent once more attempted to question her. She turned round on him at her bedroom door. 'I have not sent for you!' she cried out, vehemently. 'I don't want you. My Diamond is lost. Neither you nor anybody else will ever find it!' With those words she went in, and locked the door in our faces. Penelope, standing nearest to it, heard her burst out crying the moment she was alone again.

In a rage, one moment; in tears, the next! What did it mean?

I told the Superintendent it meant that Miss Rachel's temper was upset by the loss of her jewel. Being anxious for the honour of the family, it distressed me to see my young lady forget herself— even with a police-officer—and I made the best excuse I could, accordingly. In my own private mind, I was more puzzled by Miss Rachel's extraordinary language and conduct than words can tell. Taking what she had said at her bedroom door as a guide to guess by, I could only conclude that she was mortally offended by our sending for the police, and that Mr Franklin's astonishment on the terrace was caused by her having expressed herself to him (as the person chiefly instrumental in fetching the police) to that effect. If this guess was right, why—having lost her Diamond—should she object to the presence in the house of the very people whose business it was to recover it for her? And how, in Heaven's name, could *she* know that the Moonstone would never be found again?

As things stood, at present, no answer to those questions was to be hoped for from anybody in the house. Mr Franklin appeared to think it a point of honour to forbear repeating to a servant—even to so old a servant as I was—what Miss Rachel had said to him on the terrace. Mr Godfrey, who, as a gentleman and a relative, had been probably admitted into Mr Franklin's confidence, respected that confidence as he was bound to do. My lady, who was also in the secret no doubt, and who alone had access to Miss Rachel, owned openly that she could make nothing of her. 'You madden me when you talk of the Diamond!' All her mother's influence failed to extract from her a word more than that.

Here we were, then, at a deadlock about Miss Rachel—and at a deadlock about the Moonstone. In the first case, my lady was powerless to help us. In the second (as you shall presently judge), Mr Seegrave was fast approaching the condition of a superintendent at his wits' end.

Having ferreted about all over the 'boudoir,' without making any discoveries among the furniture, our experienced officer applied to me to know, whether the servants in general were or were not acquainted with the place in which the Diamond had been put for the night.

'I knew where it was put, sir,' I said, 'to begin with. Samuel, the footman, knew also—for he was present in the hall, when they were talking about where the Diamond was to be kept that night. My daughter knew, as she has already told you. She or Samuel may have mentioned the thing to the other servants—or the other servants may have heard the talk for themselves, through the side-door of the hall, which might have been open to the back staircase. For all I can tell, everybody in the house may have known where the jewel was, last night.'

My answer presenting rather a wide field for Mr Superintendent's suspicions to range over, he tried to narrow it by asking about the servants' characters next.

I thought directly of Rosanna Spearman. But it was neither my place nor my wish to direct suspicion against a poor girl, whose honesty had been above all doubt as long as I had known her. The matron at the Reformatory had reported her to my lady as a sincerely penitent and thoroughly trustworthy girl. It was the Superintendent's business to discover reason for suspecting her first—and then, and not till then, it would be my duty to tell him how she came into my lady's service. 'All our people have excellent characters,' I said. 'And all have deserved the trust their mistress has placed in them.' After that, there was but one thing left for Mr Seegrave to do—namely, to set to work, and tackle the servants' characters himself.

One after another, they were examined. One after another, they proved to have nothing to say—and said it (so far as the women were concerned) at great length, and with a very angry sense of the embargo laid on their bedrooms. The rest of them being sent back to their places downstairs, Penelope was then summoned, and examined separately a second time.

My daughter's little outbreak of temper in the 'boudoir,' and her readiness to think herself suspected, appeared to have produced an unfavourable impression on Superintendent Seegrave. It seemed also to dwell a little on his mind, that she had been the last person who saw the Diamond at night. When the second questioning was over, my girl came back to me in a frenzy. There was no doubt of it any longer—the police-officer had almost as good as told her she was the thief! I could scarcely believe him (taking Mr Franklin's view) to be quite such an ass as that. But, though he said nothing, the eye with which he looked at my daughter was not a very pleasant eye to see. I laughed it off with poor Penelope, as something too ridiculous to be treated seriously—which it certainly was. Secretly, I am afraid I was foolish enough to be angry too. It was a little trying—it was, indeed. My girl sat down in a corner, with her apron over her head, quite broken-hearted. Foolish of her, you will say: she might have waited till he openly accused her. Well, being a man of just and equal temper, I admit that. Still Mr Superintendent might have remembered—never mind what he might have remembered. The devil take him!

The next and last step in the investigation brought matters, as they say, to a crisis. The officer had an interview (at which I was present) with my lady. After informing her that the Diamond must have been taken by somebody in the house, he requested permission for himself and his men to search the servants' rooms and boxes on the spot. My good mistress, like the generous high-bred woman she was, refused to let us be treated like thieves. 'I will never consent to make such a return as that,' she said, 'or all I owe to the faithful servants who are employed in my house.'

Mr Superintendent made his bow, with a look in my direction, which said plainly, 'Why employ me, if you are to tie my hands in this way?' As head of the servants, I felt directly that we were bound, in justice to all parties, not to profit by our mistress's generosity. 'We gratefully thank your ladyship,' I said; 'but we ask permission to do what is right in this matter, by giving up our keys. When Gabriel Betteredge sets the example,' says I, stopping Superintendent Seegrave at the door, 'the rest of the servants will follow, I promise you. There are my keys, to begin with!' My lady took me by the hand, and thanked me with the tears in her eyes. Lord! what would I not have given, at that moment, for the privilege of knocking Superintendent Seegrave down!

As I had promised for them, the other servants followed my lead, sorely against the grain, of course, but all taking the view that I took. The women were a sight to see, while the police-officers were rummaging among their things. The cook looked as if she could grill Mr Superintendent alive on a furnace, and the other women looked as if they could eat him when he was done.

The search over, and no Diamond or sign of a Diamond being found, of course, anywhere, Superintendent Seegrave retired to my little room to consider with himself what he was to do next. He and his men had now been hours in the house, and had not advanced us one inch towards a discovery of how the Moonstone had been taken, or of whom we were to suspect as the thief.

While the police-officer was still pondering in solitude, I was sent for to see Mr Franklin in the library. To my unutterable astonishment, just as my hand was on the door, it was suddenly opened from the inside, and out walked Rosanna Spearman!

After the library had been swept and cleaned in the morning, neither first nor second housemaid had any business in that room at any later period of the day. I stopped Rosanna Spearman, and charged her with a breach of domestic discipline on the spot.

'What might you want in the library at this time of day?' I inquired.

'Mr Franklin Blake dropped one of his rings upstairs,' says Rosanna; 'and I have been into the library to give it to him.' The girl's face was all in a flush as she made me that answer; and she walked away with a toss of her head and a look of self-importance which I was quite at a loss to account for. The proceedings in the house had doubtless upset all the women-servants more or less; but none of them had gone clean out of their natural characters, as Rosanna, to all appearance, had now gone out of hers.

I found Mr Franklin writing at the library-table. He asked for a conveyance to the railway station the moment I entered the room. The first sound of his voice informed me that we now had the resolute side of him uppermost once more. The man made of cotton had disappeared; and the man made of iron sat before me again.

'Going to London, sir?' I asked.

'Going to telegraph to London,' says Mr Franklin. 'I have convinced my aunt that we must have a cleverer head than Superintendent Seegrave's to help us; and I have got her permission to despatch a telegram to my father. He knows the Chief Commissioner of Police, and the Commissioner can lay his hand on the right man to solve the mystery of the Diamond. Talking of mysteries, by-the-by,' says Mr Franklin, dropping his voice, 'I have another word to say to you before you go to the stables. Don't breathe a word of it to anybody as yet; but either Rosanna Spearman's head is not quite right, or I am afraid she knows more about the Moonstone than she ought to know.'

I can hardly tell whether I was more startled or distressed at hearing him say that. If I had been younger, I might have confessed as much to Mr Franklin. But when you are old, you acquire one excellent habit. In cases where you don't see your way clearly, you hold your tongue.

'She came in here with a ring I dropped in my bedroom,' Mr Franklin went on. 'When I had thanked her, of course I expected her to go. Instead of that, she stood opposite to me at the table, looking at me in the oddest manner—half frightened, and half familiar—I couldn't make it out. "This is a strange thing about the Diamond, sir," she said, in a curiously sudden, headlong way. I said, "Yes, it was," and wondered what was coming next. Upon my honour, Betteredge, I think she must be wrong in the head! She said, "They will never find the Diamond, sir, will they? No! nor the person who took it—I'll answer for that.' She actually nodded and smiled at me! Before I could ask her what she meant, we heard your step outside. I suppose she was afraid of your catching her here. At any rate, she changed colour, and left the room. What on earth does it mean?'

I could not bring myself to tell him the girl's story, even then. It would have been almost as good as telling him that she was the thief. Besides, even if I had made a clean breast of it, and even supposing she was the thief, the reason why she should let out her secret to Mr Franklin, of all the people in the world, would have been still as far to seek as ever.

'I can't bear the idea of getting the poor girl into a scrape, merely because she has a flighty way with her, and talks very strangely,' Mr Franklin went on. 'And yet if she had said to the Superintendent what she said to me, fool as he is, I'm afraid—' He stopped there, and left the rest unspoken.

'The best way, sir,' I said, 'will be for me to say two words privately to my mistress about it at the first opportunity. My lady has a very friendly interest in Rosanna; and the girl may only have been forward and foolish, after all. When there's a mess of any kind in a house, sir, the women-servants like to look at the gloomy side—it gives the poor wretches a kind of importance in their own eyes. If there's anybody ill, trust the women for prophesying that the person will die. If it's a jewel lost, trust them for prophesying that it will never be found again.'

This view (which, I am bound to say, I thought a probable view myself, on reflection) seemed to relieve Mr Franklin mightily: he folded up his telegram, and dismissed the subject. On my way to the stables, to order the pony-chaise, I looked in at the servants' hall, where they were at dinner. Rosanna Spearman was not among them. On inquiry, I found that she had been suddenly taken ill, and had gone upstairs to her own room to lie down.

'Curious! She looked well enough when I saw her last,' I remarked.

Penelope followed me out. 'Don't talk in that way before the rest of them, father,' she said. 'You only make them harder on Rosanna than ever. The poor thing is breaking her heart about Mr Franklin Blake.'

Here was another view of the girl's conduct. If it was possible for Penelope to be right, the explanation of Rosanna's strange language and behaviour might have been all in this—that she didn't care what she said, so long as she could surprise Mr Franklin into speaking to her. Granting that to be the right reading of the riddle, it accounted, perhaps, for her flighty self-conceited manner when she passed me in the hall. Though he had only said three words, still she had carried her point, and Mr Franklin *had* spoken to her.

I saw the pony harnessed myself. In the infernal network of mysteries and uncertainties that now surrounded us, I declare it was a relief to observe how well the buckles and straps understood each other! When you had seen the pony backed into the shafts of the chaise, you had seen something there was no doubt about. And that, let me tell you, was becoming a treat of the rarest kind in our household.

Going round with the chaise to the front door, I found not only Mr Franklin, but Mr Godfrey and Superintendent Seegrave also waiting for me on the steps.

Mr Superintendent's reflections (after failing to find the Diamond in the servants' rooms or boxes) had led him, it appeared, to an entirely new conclusion. Still sticking to his first text, namely, that somebody in the house had stolen the jewel, our experienced officer was now of opinion that the thief (he was wise enough not to name poor Penelope, whatever he might privately think of her!) had been acting in concert with the Indians; and he accordingly proposed shifting his inquiries to the jugglers in the prison at Frizinghall. Hearing of this new move, Mr Franklin had volunteered to take the Superintendent back to the town, from which he could telegraph to London as easily as from our station. Mr Godfrey, still devoutly believing in Mr Seegrave, and greatly interested in witnessing the examination of the Indians, had begged leave to accompany the officer to Frizinghall. One of the two inferior policemen was to be left at the house, in case anything happened. The other was to go back with the Superintendent to the town. So the four places in the pony-chaise were just filled.

Before he took the reins to drive off, Mr Franklin walked me away a few steps out of hearing of the others.

'I will wait to telegraph to London,' he said, 'till I see what comes of our examination of the Indians. My own conviction is, that this muddle-headed local police-officer is as much in the dark as ever, and is simply trying to gain time. The idea of any of the servants being in league with the Indians is a preposterous absurdity, in my opinion. Keep about the house, Betteredge, till I come back, and try what you can make of Rosanna Spearman. I don't ask you to do anything degrading to your own self-respect, or anything cruel towards the girl. I only ask you to exercise your observation more carefully than usual. We will make as light of it as we can before my aunt—but this is a more important matter than you may suppose.'

'It's a matter of twenty thousand pounds, sir,' I said, thinking of the value of the Diamond.

'It's a matter of quieting Rachel's mind,' answered Mr Franklin gravely. 'I am very uneasy about her.'

He left me suddenly, as if he desired to cut short any further talk between us. I thought I understood why. Further talk might have let me into the secret of what Miss Rachel had said to him on the terrace.

So they drove away to Frizinghall. I was ready enough, in the girl's own interest, to have a little talk with Rosanna in private. But the needful opportunity failed to present itself. She only came downstairs again at tea-time. When she did appear, she was flighty and excited, had what they call an hysterical attack, took a dose of sal-volatile by my lady's order, and was sent back to her bed.

The day wore on to its end drearily and miserably enough, I can tell you. Miss Rachel still kept her room, declaring that she was too ill to come down to dinner that day. My lady was in such low spirits about her daughter, that I could not bring myself to make her additionally anxious, by reporting what Rosanna Spearman had said to Mr Franklin. Penelope persisted in believing that she was to be forthwith tried, sentenced, and transported for theft. The other women took to their Bibles and hymn-books, and looked as sour as verjuice over their reading—a result, which I have observed, in my sphere of life, to follow generally on the performance of acts of piety at unaccustomed periods of the day. As for me, I hadn't even heart enough to open my *Robinson Crusoe*. I went out into the yard, and, being hard up for a little cheerful society, set my chair by the kennels, and talked to the dogs.

Half an hour before dinner-time, the two gentlemen came back from Frizinghall, having arranged with Superintendent Seegrave that he was to return to us the next day. They had called on Mr Murthwaite, the Indian traveller, at his present residence, near the town. At Mr Franklin's request, he had kindly given them the benefit of his knowledge of the language, in dealing with those two, out of the three Indians, who knew nothing of

English. The examination, conducted carefully, and at great length, had ended in nothing; not the shadow of a reason being discovered for suspecting the jugglers of having tampered with any of our servants. On reaching that conclusion, Mr Franklin had sent his telegraphic message to London, and there the matter now rested till to-morrow came.

So much for the history of the day that followed the birthday. Not a glimmer of light had broken in on us, so far. A day or two after, however, the darkness lifted a little. How, and with what result, you shall presently see.

CHAPTER 12

The Thursday night passed, and nothing happened. With the Friday morning came two pieces of news.

Item the first: the baker's man declared he had met Rosanna Spearman, on the previous afternoon, with a thick veil on, walking towards Frizinghall by the footpath way over the moor. It seemed strange that anybody should be mistaken about Rosanna, whose shoulder marked her out pretty plainly, poor thing—but mistaken the man must have been; for Rosanna, as you know, had been all the Thursday afternoon ill upstairs in her room.

Item the second came through the postman. Worthy Mr Candy had said one more of his many unlucky things, when he drove off in the rain on the birthday night, and told me that a doctor's skin was waterproof. In spite of his skin, the wet had got through him. He had caught a chill that night, and was now down with a fever. The last accounts, brought by the postman, represented him to be light-headed—talking nonsense as glibly, poor man, in his delirium as he often talked it in his sober senses. We were all sorry for the little doctor; but Mr Franklin appeared to regret his illness, chiefly on Miss Rachel's account. From what he said to my lady, while I was in the room at breakfast-time, he appeared to think that Miss Rachel—if the suspense about the Moonstone was not soon set at rest—might stand in urgent need of the best medical advice at our disposal.

Breakfast had not been over long, when a telegram from Mr Blake, the elder, arrived, in answer to his son. It informed us that he had laid hands (by help of his friend, the Commissioner) on the right man to help us. The name of him was Sergeant Cuff; and the arrival of him from London might be expected by the morning train.

At reading the name of the new police-officer, Mr Franklin gave a start. It seems that he had heard some curious anecdotes about Sergeant Cuff, from his father's lawyer, during his stay in London. 'I begin to hope we are seeing the end of our anxieties already,' he said. 'If half the stories I have heard are true, when it comes to unravelling a mystery, there isn't the equal in England of Sergeant Cuff!'

We all got excited and impatient as the time drew near for the appearance of this renowned and capable character. Superintendent Seegrave, returning to us at his appointed time, and hearing that the Sergeant was expected, instantly shut himself up in a room, with pen, ink, and paper, to make notes of the Report which would be certainly expected from him. I should have liked to have gone to the station myself, to fetch the Sergeant. But my lady's carriage and horses were not to be thought of, even for the celebrated Cuff; and the pony-chaise was required later for Mr Godfrey. He deeply regretted being obliged to leave his aunt at such an anxious time; and he kindly put off the hour of his departure till as late as the last train, for the purpose of hearing what the clever London police officer thought of the case. But on Friday night he must be in town, having a Ladies' Charity, in difficulties, waiting to consult him on Saturday morning.

When the time came for the Sergeant's arrival, I went down to the gate to look out for him.

A fly from the railway drove up as I reached the lodge; and out got a grizzled, elderly man, so miserably lean that he looked as if he had not got an ounce of flesh on his bones in any part of him. He was dressed all in decent black, with a white cravat round his neck. His face was as sharp as a hatchet, and the skin of it was as yellow and dry and withered as an autumn leaf. His eyes, of a steely light grey, had a very disconcerting trick, when they encountered your eyes, of looking as if they expected something more from you than you were aware of yourself. His walk was soft; his voice was melancholy; his long lanky fingers were hooked like claws. He might have been a parson, or an undertaker—or anything else you like, except what he really was. A more complete opposite to Superintendent Seegrave than Sergeant Cuff, and a less comforting officer to look at, for a family in distress, I defy you to discover, search where you may.

'Is this Lady Verinder's?' he asked.

'Yes, sir.'

'I am Sergeant Cuff.'

'This way, sir, if you please.'

On our road to the house, I mentioned my name and position in the family, to satisfy him that he might speak to me about the business on which my lady was to employ him. Not a word did he say about the business, however, for all that. He admired the grounds, and remarked that he felt the sea air very brisk and refreshing. I privately wondered, on my side, how the celebrated Cuff had got his reputation. We reached the house, in the temper of two strange dogs, coupled up together for the first time in their lives by the same chain.

Asking for my lady, and hearing that she was in one of the conservatories, we went round to the gardens at the back, and sent a servant to seek her. While we were waiting, Sergeant Cuff looked through the evergreen arch on our left, spied out our rosery, and walked straight in, with the first appearance of anything like interest that he had shown yet. To the gardener's astonishment, and to my disgust, this celebrated policeman proved to be quite a mine of learning on the trumpery subject of rose-gardens.

'Ah, you've got the right exposure here to the south and sou'-west,' says the Sergeant, with a wag of his grizzled head, and a streak of pleasure in his melancholy voice. 'This is the shape for a rosery—nothing like a circle set in a square. Yes, yes; with walks between all the beds. But they oughtn't to be gravel walks like these. Grass, Mr Gardener—grass walks between your roses; gravel's too hard for them. That's a sweet pretty bed of white roses and blush roses. They always mix well together, don't they? Here's the white musk rose, Mr Betteredge—our old English rose holding up its head along with the best and the newest of them. Pretty dear!' says the Sergeant, fondling the Musk Rose with his lanky fingers, and speaking to it as if he was speaking to a child.

This was a nice sort of man to recover Miss Rachel's Diamond, and to find out the thief who stole it!

'You seem to be fond of roses, Sergeant?' I remarked.

'I haven't much time to be fond of anything,' says Sergeant Cuff. 'But when I have a moment's fondness to bestow, most times, Mr Betteredge, the roses get it. I began my life among them in my father's nursery garden, and I shall end my life among them, if I can. Yes. One of these days (please God) I shall retire from catching thieves, and try my hand at growing roses. There will be grass walks, Mr Gardener, between my beds,' says the Sergeant, on whose mind the gravel paths of our rosery seemed to dwell unpleasantly.

'It seems an odd taste, sir,' I ventured to say, 'for a man in your line of life.'

'If you will look about you (which most people won't do),' says Sergeant Cuff, 'you will see that the nature of a man's tastes is, most times, as opposite as possible to the nature of a man's business. Show me any two things more opposite one from the other than a rose and a thief; and I'll correct my tastes accordingly—if it is'nt too late at any time of life. You find the damask rose a goodish stock for most of the tender sorts, don't you, Mr Gardener? Ah! I thought so. Here's a lady coming. Is it Lady Verinder?'

He had seen her before either I or the gardener had seen her—though we knew which way to look, and he didn't. I began to think him rather a quicker man than he appeared to be at first sight.

The Sergeant's appearance, or the Sergeant's errand—one or both—seemed to cause my lady some little embarrassment. She was, for the first time in all my experience of her, at a loss what to say at an interview with a stranger. Sergeant Cuff put her at ease directly. He asked if any other person had been employed about the robbery before we sent for him; and hearing that another person had been called in, and was now in the house, begged leave to speak to him before anything else was done.

My lady led the way back. Before he followed her, the Sergeant relieved his mind on the subject of the gravel walks by a parting word to the gardener. 'Get her ladyship to try grass,' he said, with a sour look at the paths. 'No gravel! no gravel!'

Why Superintendent Seegrave should have appeared to be several sizes smaller than life, on being presented to Sergeant Cuff, I can't undertake to explain. I can only state the fact. They retired together; and remained a weary long time shut up from all mortal intrusion. When they came out, Mr Superintendent was excited, and Mr Sergeant was yawning.

'The Sergeant wishes to see Miss Verinder's sitting-room,' says Mr Seegrave, addressing me with great pomp and eagerness. 'The Sergeant may have some questions to ask. Attend the Sergeant, if you please!'

While I was being ordered about in this way, I looked at the great Cuff. The great Cuff, on his side, looked at Superintendent Seegrave in that quietly expecting way which I have already noticed I can't affirm that he was on the watch for his brother-officer's speedy appearance in the character of an Ass—I can only say that I strongly suspected it.

I led the way upstairs. The Sergeant went softly all over the Indian cabinet and all round the 'boudoir'; asking questions (occasionally only of Mr Superintendent, and continually of me), the drift of which I believe to have been equally unintelligible to both of us. In due time, his course brought him to the door, and put him face to face with the decorative painting that you know of. He laid one lean inquiring finger on the small smear, just under the lock, which Superintendent Seegrave had already noticed, when he reproved the women-servants for all crowding together into the room.

'That's a pity,' says Sergeant Cuff. 'How did it happen?'

He put the question to me. I answered that the women-servants had crowded into the room on the previous morning, and that some of their petticoats had done the mischief 'Superintendent Seegrave ordered them out, sir,' I added, 'before they did any more harm.'

'Right!' says Mr Superintendent in his military way. 'I ordered them out. The petticoats did it, Sergeant—the petticoats did it.'

'Did you notice which petticoat did it?' asked Sergeant Cuff, still addressing himself, not to his brother-officer, but to me.

'No, sir.'

He turned to Superintendent Seegrave upon that, and said, 'You noticed, I suppose?'

Mr Superintendent looked a little taken aback; but he made the best of it. 'I can't charge my memory, Sergeant,' he said, 'a mere trifle—a mere trifle.'

Sergeant Cuff looked at Mr Seegrave as he had looked at the gravel walks in the rosery, and gave us, in his melancholy way, the first taste of his quality which we had had yet.

'I made a private inquiry last week, Mr Superintendent,' he said. 'At one end of the inquiry there was a murder, and at the other end there was a spot of ink on a tablecloth that nobody could account for. In all my experience along the dirtiest ways of this dirty little world, I have never met with such a thing as a trifle yet. Before we go a step further in this business we must see the petticoat that made the smear, and we must know for certain when that paint was wet.'

Mr Superintendent—taking his set-down rather sulkily—asked if he should summon the women. Sergeant Cuff, after considering a minute, sighed, and shook his head.

'No,' he said, 'we'll take the matter of the paint first. It's a question of Yes or No with the paint—which is short. It's a question of petticoats with the women—which is long. What o'clock was it when the servants were in this room yesterday morning? Eleven o'clock—eh? Is there anybody in the house who knows whether that paint was wet or dry, at eleven yesterday morning?'

'Her ladyship's nephew, Mr Franklin Blake, knows,' I said.

'Is the gentleman in the house?'

Mr Franklin was as close at hand as could be—waiting for his first chance of being introduced to the great Cuff. In half a minute he was in the room, and was giving his evidence as follows:

'That door, Sergeant,' he said, 'has been painted by Miss Verinder, under my inspection, with my help, and in a vehicle of my own composition. The vehicle dries whatever colours may be used with it, in twelve hours.'

'Do you remember when the smeared bit was done, sir?' asked the Sergeant.

'Perfectly,' answered Mr Franklin. 'That was the last morsel of the door to be finished.

We wanted to get it done, on Wednesday last—and I myself completed it by three in the afternoon, or soon after.'

'To-day is Friday,' said Sergeant Cuff, addressing himself to Superintendent Seegrave. 'Let us reckon back, sir. At three on the Wednesday afternoon, that bit of the painting was completed. The vehicle dried it in twelve hours—that is to say, dried it by three o'clock on Thursday morning. At eleven on Thursday morning you held your inquiry here. Take three from eleven, and eight remains. That paint had been *eight hours dry*, Mr Superintendent, when you supposed that the women-servants' petticoats smeared it.'

First knock down blow for Mr Seegrave! If he had not suspected poor Penelope, I should have pitied him.

Having settled the question of the paint, Sergeant Cuff, from that moment, gave his brother-officer up as a bad job—and addressed himself to Mr Franklin, as the more promising assistant of the two.

'It's quite on the cards, sir,' he said, 'that you have put the clue into our hands.'

As the words passed his lips, the bedroom door opened, and Miss Rachel came out among us suddenly.

She addressed herself to the Sergeant, without appearing to notice (or to heed) that he was a perfect stranger to her.

'Did you say,' she asked, pointing to Mr Franklin, 'that *he* had put the clue into your hands?'

('This is Miss Verinder,' I whispered, behind the Sergeant.)

'That gentleman, miss,' says the Sergeant—with his steely-grey eyes carefully studying my young lady's face—'has possibly put the clue into our hands.'

She turned for one moment, and tried to look at Mr Franklin. I say, tried, for she suddenly looked away again before their eyes met. There seemed to be some strange disturbance in her mind. She coloured up, and then she turned pale again. With the paleness, there came a new look into her face—a look which it startled me to see.

'Having answered your question, miss,' says the Sergeant, 'I beg leave to make an inquiry in my turn. There is a smear on the painting of your door, here. Do you happen to know when it was done? or who did it?'

Instead of making any reply, Miss Rachel went on with her questions, as if he had not spoken, or as if she had not heard him.

'Are you another police-officer?' she asked.

'I am Sergeant Cuff, miss, of the Detective Police.'

'Do you think a young lady's advice worth having?'

'I shall be glad to hear it, miss.'

'Do your duty by yourself—and don't allow Mr Franklin Blake to help you!'

She said those words so spitefully, so savagely, with such an extraordinary outbreak of ill-will towards Mr Franklin, in her voice and in her look, that—though I had known her from a baby, though I loved and honoured her next to my lady herself—I was ashamed of Miss Rachel for the first time in my life.

Sergeant Cuff's immovable eyes never stirred from off her face.

'Thank you, miss,' he said. 'Do you happen to know anything about the smear? Might you have done it by accident yourself?

'I know nothing about the smear.'

With that answer, she turned away, and shut herself up again in her bedroom. This time, I heard her—as Penelope had heard her before—burst out crying as soon as she was alone again.

I couldn't bring myself to look at the Sergeant—I looked at Mr Franklin, who stood nearest to me. He seemed to be even more sorely distressed at what had passed than I was.

'I told you I was uneasy about her,' he said. 'And now you see why.'

'Miss Verinder appears to be a little out of temper about the loss of her Diamond,' remarked the Sergeant. 'It's a valuable jewel. Natural enough! natural enough!'

Here was the excuse that I had made for her (when she forgot herself before Superintendent Seegrave, on the previous day) being made for her over again, by a man who couldn't have had *my* interest in making it—for he was a perfect stranger! A kind of cold shudder ran through me, which I couldn't account for at the time. I know, now, that I must have got my first suspicion, at that moment, of a new light (and a horrid light) having suddenly fallen on the case, in the mind of Sergeant Cuff—purely and entirely in consequence of what he had seen in Miss Rachel, and heard from Miss Rachel, at that first interview between them.

'A young lady's tongue is a privileged member, sir,' says the Sergeant to Mr Franklin. 'Let us forget what has passed, and go straight on with this business. Thanks to you, we know when the paint was dry. The next thing to discover is when the paint was last seen without that smear. *You* have got a head on your shoulders—and you understand what I mean.'

Mr Franklin composed himself, and came back with an effort from Miss Rachel to the matter in hand.

'I think I do understand,' he said. 'The more we narrow the question of time, the more we also narrow the field of inquiry.'

'That's it, sir,' said the Sergeant. 'Did you notice your work here, on the Wednesday afternoon, after you had done it?'

Mr Franklin shook his head, and answered, 'I can't say I did.'

'Did *you?*' inquired Sergeant Cuff, turning to me.

'I can't say I did either, sir.'

'Who was the last person in the room, the last thing on Wednesday night?'

'Miss Rachel, I suppose, sir.'

Mr Franklin struck in there, ' Or possibly your daughter, Betteredge.' He turned to Sergeant Cuff, and explained that my daughter was Miss Verinder's maid.

'Mr Betteredge, ask your daughter to step up. Stop!' says the Sergeant, taking me away to the window, out of earshot. 'Your Superintendent here,' he went on, in a whisper, 'has made a pretty full report to me of the manner in which he has managed this case. Among other things, he has, by his own confession, set the servants' backs up. It's very important to smooth them down again. Tell your daughter, and tell the rest of them, these two things, with my compliments: First, that I have no evidence before me, yet, that the Diamond has been stolen; I only know that the Diamond has been lost. Second, that *my* business here with the servants is simply to ask them to lay their heads together and help me to find it.'

My experience of the women-servants, when Superintendent Seegrave laid his embargo on their rooms, came in handy here.

'May I make so bold, Sergeant, as to tell the women a third thing?' I asked. 'Are they free (with your compliments) to fidget up and downstairs, and whisk in and out of their bedrooms, if the fit takes them?'

'Perfectly free,' says the Sergeant.

'*That* will smooth them down, sir,' I remarked, 'from the cook to the scullion.'

'Go, and do it at once, Mr Betteredge.'

I did it in less than five minutes. There was only one difficulty when I came to the bit about the bedrooms. It took a pretty stiff exertion of my authority, as chief, to prevent the whole of the female household from following me and Penelope upstairs, in the character of volunteer witnesses in a burning fever of anxiety to help Sergeant Cuff.

The Sergeant seemed to approve of Penelope. He became a trifle less dreary; and he looked much as he had looked when he noticed the white musk rose in the flower-garden. Here is my daughter's evidence, as drawn off from her by the Sergeant. She gave it, I think, very prettily—but, there! she is my child all over: nothing of her mother in her; Lord bless you, nothing of her mother in her!

Penelope examined: Took a lively interest in the painting on the door, having helped to mix the colours. Noticed the bit of work under the lock,, because it was the last bit done. Had seen it, some hours afterwards, without a smear. Had left it, as late as twelve at night, without a smear. Had, at that hour, wished her young lady good-night in the bedroom; had heard the clock strike in the 'boudoir'; had her hand at the time on the handle of the painted door; knew the paint was wet (having helped to mix the colours, as aforesaid); took particular pains not to touch it; could swear that she held up the skirts of her dress, and that there was no smear on the paint then; could *not* swear that her dress mightn't have touched it accidentally in going out; remembered the dress she had on, because it was new, a present from Miss Rachel; her father remembered, and could speak to it, too; could, and would, and did fetch it; dress recognized by her father as the dress she wore that night; skirts examined, a long job from the size of them; not the ghost of a paint-stain discovered anywhere. End of Penelope's evidence—and very pretty and convincing, too. Signed, Gabriel Betteredge.

The Sergeant's next proceeding was to question me about any large dogs in the house who might have got into the room, and done the mischief with a whisk of their tails. Hearing that this was impossible, he next sent for a magnifying-glass, and tried how the smear looked, seen that way. No skin-mark (as of a human hand) printed off on the paint. All the signs visible—signs which told that the paint had been smeared by some loose article of somebody's dress touching it in going by. That somebody (putting together Penelope's evidence and Mr Franklin's evidence) must have been in the room, and done the mischief, between midnight and three o'clock on the Thursday morning.

Having brought his investigation to this point, Sergeant Cuff discovered that such a person as Superintendent Seegrave was still left in the room, upon which he summed up the proceedings for his brother-officer's benefit, as follows:

'This trifle of yours, Mr Superintendent,' says the Sergeant, pointing to the place on the door, 'has grown a little in importance since you noticed it last. At the present stage of the inquiry there are, as I take it, three discoveries to make, starting from that smear. Find out (first) whether there is any article of dress in this house with the smear of the paint on it. Find out (second) who that dress belongs to. Find out (third) how the person can account for having been in this room, and smeared the paint, between midnight and three in the morning. If the person can't satisfy you, you haven't far to look for the hand that has got the Diamond. I'll work this by myself, if you please, and detain you no longer from your regular business in the town. You have got one of your men here, I see. Leave him here at my disposal, in case I want him—and allow me to wish you good morning.'

Superintendent Seegrave's respect for the Sergeant was great; but his respect for himself was greater still. Hit hard by the celebrated Cuff, he hit back smartly, to the best of his ability, on leaving the room.

'I have abstained from expressing any opinion, so far,' says Mr Superintendent, with his military voice still in good working order. 'I have now only one remark to offer, on leaving this case in your hands. There is such a thing, Sergeant, as making a mountain out of a molehill. Good morning.'

'There is also such a thing as making nothing out of a molehill, in consequence of your head being too high to see it.' Having returned his brother-officer's compliments in those terms, Sergeant Cuff wheeled about, and walked away to the window by himself.

Mr Franklin and I waited to see what was coming next. The Sergeant stood at the window with his hands in his pockets, looking out, and whistling the tune of 'The Last Rose of Summer' softly to himself. Later in the proceedings, I discovered that he only forgot his manners so far as to whistle, when his mind was hard at work, seeing its way inch by inch to its own private ends, on which occasions 'The Last Rose of Summer' evidently helped and encouraged him. I suppose it fitted in somehow with his character. It reminded him, you see, of his favourite roses, and, as he whistled it, it was the most melancholy tune going.

Turning from the window, after a minute or two, the Sergeant walked into the middle of the room, and stopped there, deep in thought, with his eyes on Miss Rachel's bedroom door. After a little he roused himself, nodded his head, as much as to say, 'That will do!' and, addressing me, asked for ten minutes' conversation with my mistress, at her ladyship's earliest convenience.

Leaving the room with this message, I heard Mr Franklin ask the Sergeant a question, and stopped to hear the answer also at the threshold of the door.

'Can you guess yet,' inquired Mr Franklin, 'who has stolen the Diamond?'

'*Nobody has stolen the Diamond*,' answered Sergeant Cuff.

We both started at that extraordinary view of the case, and both earnestly begged him to tell us what he meant.

'Wait a little,' said the Sergeant. 'The pieces of the puzzle are not all put together yet.'

CHAPTER 13

I found my lady in her own sitting-room. She started and looked annoyed when I mentioned that Sergeant Cuff wished to speak to her.

'*Must* I see him?' she asked. 'Can't you represent me, Gabriel?'

I felt at a loss to understand this, and showed it plainly, I suppose, in my face. My lady was so good as to explain herself.

'I am afraid my nerves are a little shaken,' she said. 'There is something in that police-officer from London which I recoil from—I don't know why. I have a presentiment that he is bringing trouble and misery with him into the house. Very foolish, and very unlike *me*—but so it is.'

I hardly knew what to say to this. The more *I* saw of Sergeant Cuff, the better I liked him. My lady rallied a little after having opened her heart to me—being, naturally, a woman of a high courage, as I have already told you.

'If I must see him, I must,' she said. 'But I can't prevail on myself to see him alone. Bring him in, Gabriel, and stay here as long as he stays.'

This was the first attack of the megrims that I remembered in my mistress since the time when she was a young girl. I went back to the 'boudoir.' Mr Franklin strolled out into the garden, and joined Mr Godfrey, whose time for departure was now drawing near. Sergeant Cuff and I went straight to my mistress's room.

I declare my lady turned a shade paler at the sight of him! She commanded herself, however, in other respects, and asked the Sergeant if he had any objection to my being present. She was so good as to add, that I was her trusted adviser, as well as her old servant, and that in anything which related to the household I was the person whom it might be most profitable to consult. The Sergeant politely answered that he would take my presence as a favour, having something to say about the servants in general, and having found my experience in that quarter already of some use to him. My lady pointed to two chairs, and we set in for our conference immediately.

'I have already formed an opinion on this case,' says Sergeant Cuff, 'which I beg your ladyship's permission to keep to myself for the present. My business now is to mention what I have discovered upstairs in Miss Verinder's sitting-room, and what I have decided (with your ladyship's leave) on doing next.'

He then went into the matter of the smear on the paint, and stated the conclusions he drew from it—just as he had stated them (only with greater respect of language) to Superintendent Seegrave. 'One thing,' he said, in conclusion, 'is certain. The Diamond is missing out of the drawer in the cabinet. Another thing is next to certain. The marks from the smear on the door must be on some article of dress belonging to somebody in this house. We must discover that article of dress before we go a step further.'

'And that discovery,' remarked my mistress, 'implies, I presume, the discovery of the thief?'

'I beg your ladyship's pardon—I don't say the Diamond is stolen. I only say, at present, that the Diamond is missing. The discovery of the stained dress may lead the way to finding it.'

Her ladyship looked at me. 'Do you understand this?' she said.

'Sergeant Cuff understands it, my lady,' I answered.

84

'How do you propose to discover the stained dress?' inquired my mistress, addressing herself once more to the Sergeant. 'My good servants, who have been with me for years, have, I am ashamed to say, had their boxes and rooms searched already by the other officer. I can't and won't permit them to be insulted in that way a second time!'

(There was a mistress to serve! There was a woman in ten thousand, if you like!)

'That is the very point I was about to put to your ladyship,' said the Sergeant. 'The other officer has done a world of harm to this inquiry, by letting the servants see that he suspected them. If I give them cause to think themselves suspected a second time, there's no knowing what obstacles they may not throw in my way—the women especially. At the same time, their boxes *must* be searched again—for this plain reason, that the first investigation only looked for the Diamond, and that the second investigation must look for the stained dress. I quite agree with you, my lady, that the servants' feelings ought to be consulted. But I am equally clear that the servants' wardrobes ought to be searched.'

This looked very like a deadlock. My lady said so, in choicer language than mine.

'I have got a plan to meet the difficulty,' said Sergeant Cuff, 'if your ladyship will consent to it. I propose explaining the case to the servants.'

'The women will think themselves suspected directly,' I said, interrupting him.

'The women won't, Mr Betteredge,' answered the Sergeant, 'if I can tell them I am going to examine the wardrobes of *every*body—from her ladyship downwards—who slept in the house on Wednesday night. It's a mere formality,' he added, with a sidelook at my mistress; 'but the servants will accept it as even dealing between them and their betters; and, instead of hindering the investigation, they will make a point of honour of assisting it.'

I saw the truth of that. My lady, after her first surprise was over, saw the truth of it also.

'You are certain the investigation is necessary?' she said.

'It's the shortest way that I can see, my lady, to the end we have in view.'

My mistress rose to ring the bell for her maid. 'You shall speak to the servants,' she said, 'with the keys of my wardrobe in your hand.'

Sergeant Cuff stopped her by a very unexpected question.

'Hadn't we better make sure first,' he asked, 'that the other ladies and gentlemen in the house will consent, too?'

'The only other lady in the house is Miss Verinder,' answered my mistress, with a look of surprise. 'The only gentlemen are my nephews, Mr Blake and Mr Ablewhite. There is not the least fear of a refusal from any of the three.'

I reminded my lady here that Mr Godfrey was going away. As I said the words, Mr Godfrey himself knocked at the door to say good-bye, and was followed in by Mr Franklin, who was going with him to the station. My lady explained the difficulty. Mr Godfrey settled it directly. He called to Samuel, through the window, to take his portmanteau upstairs again, and he then put the key himself into Sergeant Cuff's hand. 'My luggage can follow me to London,' he said, 'when the inquiry is over.' The Sergeant received the key with a becoming apology. 'I am sorry to put you to any inconvenience, sir, for a mere formality; but the example of their betters will do wonders in reconciling the servants to this inquiry.' Mr Godfrey, after taking leave of my lady, in a most sympathizing manner, left a farewell message for Miss Rachel, the terms of which made it clear to my mind that he had not taken No for an answer, and that he meant to put the marriage question to her once more, at the next opportunity. Mr Franklin, on following his cousin out, informed the Sergeant that all his clothes were open to examination, and that nothing he possessed was kept under lock and key. Sergeant Cuff made his best acknowledgments. His views, you will observe, had been met with the utmost readiness by my lady, by Mr Godfrey, and by Mr Franklin. There was only Miss Rachel now wanting to follow their lead, before we called the servants together, and began the search for the stained dress.

My lady's unaccountable objection to the Sergeant seemed to make our conference more distasteful to her than ever, as soon as we were left alone again. 'If I send you down Miss Verinder's keys,' she said to him, 'I presume I shall have done all you want of me for the present?'

'I beg your ladyship's pardon,' said Sergeant Cuff. 'Before we begin, I should like, if convenient, to have the washing-book. The stained article of dress may be an article of linen. If the search leads to nothing, I want to be able to account next for all the linen in the house, and for all the linen sent to the wash. If there is an article missing, there will be at least a presumption that it has got the paint-stain on it, and that it has been purposely made away with, yesterday or to-day, by the person owning it. Superintendent Seegrave,' added the Sergeant, turning to me, 'pointed the attention of the women-servants to the smear, when they all crowded into the room on Thursday morning. That *may* turn out, Mr Betteredge, to have been one more of Superintendent Seegrave's many mistakes.'

My lady desired me to ring the bell, and order the washing-book. She remained with us until it was produced, in case Sergeant Cuff had any further request to make of her after looking at it.

The washing-book was brought in by Rosanna Spearman. The girl had come down to breakfast that morning miserably pale and haggard, but sufficiently recovered from her illness of the previous day to do her usual work. Sergeant Cuff looked attentively at our second housemaid—at her face, when she came in; at her crooked shoulder, when she went out.

'Have you anything more to say to me?' asked my lady, still as eager as ever to be out of the Sergeant's society.

The great Cuff opened the washing-book, understood it perfectly in half a minute, and shut it up again. 'I venture to trouble your ladyship with one last question,' he said. 'Has the young woman who brought us this book been in your employment as long as the other servants?'

'Why do you ask?' said my lady.

'The last time I saw her,' answered the Sergeant, 'she was in prison for theft.'

After that, there was no help for it, but to tell him the truth. My mistress dwelt strongly on Rosanna's good conduct in her service, and on the high opinion entertained of her by the matron at the reformatory. 'You don't suspect her, I hope?' my lady added, in conclusion, very earnestly.

'I have already told your ladyship that I don't suspect any person in the house of thieving—up to the present time.'

After that answer, my lady rose to go upstairs, and ask for Miss Rachel's keys. The Sergeant was beforehand with me in opening the door for her. He made a very low bow. My lady shuddered as she passed him.

We waited, and waited, and no keys appeared. Sergeant Cuff made no remark to me. He turned his melancholy face to the window; he put his lanky hands into his pockets; and he whistled 'The Last Rose of Summer' softly to himself.

At last, Samuel came in, not with the keys, but with a morsel of paper for me. I got at my spectacles, with some fumbling and difficulty, feeling the Sergeant's dismal eyes fixed on me all the time. There were two or three lines on the paper, written in pencil by my lady. They informed me that Miss Rachel flatly refused to have her wardrobe examined. Asked for her reasons, she had burst out crying. Asked again, she had said: 'I won't, because I won't. I must yield to force if you use it, but I will yield to nothing else.' I understood my lady's disinclination to face Sergeant Cuff with such an answer from her daughter as that. If I had not been too old for the amiable weaknesses of youth, I believe I should have blushed at the notion of facing him myself.

'Any news of Miss Verinder's keys?' asked the Sergeant.

'My young lady refuses to have her wardrobe examined.'

'Ah!' said the Sergeant.

His voice was not quite in such a perfect state of discipline as his face. When he said 'Ah!' he said it in the tone of a man who had heard something which he expected to hear. He half angered and half frightened me—why, I couldn't tell, but he did it.

'Must the search be given up?' I asked.

'Yes,' said the Sergeant, 'the search must be given up, because your young lady refuses to submit to it like the rest. We must examine all the wardrobes in the house or none. Send Mr Ablewhite's portmanteau to London by the next train, and return the washing-book, with my compliments and thanks, to the young woman who brought it in.'

He laid the washing-book on the table, and, taking out his penknife, began to trim his nails.

'You don't seem to be much disappointed,' I said.

'No,' said Sergeant Cuff; 'I am not much disappointed.'

I tried to make him explain himself.

'Why should Miss Rachel put an obstacle in your way?' I inquired. 'Isn't it her interest to help you?'

'Wait a little, Mr Betteredge—wait a little.'

Cleverer heads than mine might have seen his drift. Or a person less fond of Miss Rachel than I was, might have seen his drift. My lady's horror of him might (as I have since thought) have meant that *she* saw his drift (as the scripture says) 'in a glass darkly.' I didn't see it yet—that's all I know.

'What's to be done next?' I asked.

Sergeant Cuff finished the nail on which he was then at work, looked at it for a moment with a melancholy interest, and put up his penknife.

'Come out into the garden,' he said, 'and let's have a look at the roses.'

CHAPTER 14

The nearest way to the garden, on going out of my lady's sitting-room, was by the shrubbery path, which you already know of. For the sake of your better understanding of what is now to come, I may add to this, that the shrubbery path was Mr Franklin's favourite walk. When he was out in the grounds, and when we failed to find him anywhere else, we generally found him here.

I am afraid I must own that I am rather an obstinate old man. The more firmly Sergeant Cuff kept his thoughts shut up from me, the more firmly I persisted in trying to look in at them. As we turned into the shrubbery path, I attempted to circumvent him in another way.

'As things are now,' I said, 'if I was in your place, I should be at my wits' end.'

'If you were in my place,' answered the Sergeant, 'you would have formed an opinion—and, as things are now, any doubt you might previously have felt about your own conclusions, would be completely set at rest. Never mind for the present what those conclusions are, Mr Betteredge. I haven't brought you out here to draw me like a badger; I have brought you out here to ask for some information. You might have given it to me no doubt, in the house, instead of out of it. But doors and listeners have a knack of getting together; and, in my line of life, we cultivate a healthy taste for the open air.'

'Who was to circumvent *this* man? I gave in—and waited as patiently as I could to hear what was coming next.

'We won't enter into your young lady's motives,' the Sergeant went on; 'we will only say it's a pity she declines to assist me, because, by so doing, she makes this investigation more difficult than it might otherwise have been. We must now try to solve the mystery of the smear on the door—which, you may take my word for it, means the mystery of the Diamond also—in some other way. I have decided to see the servants, and to search their thoughts and actions, Mr Betteredge, instead of searching their wardrobes. Before I begin, however, I want to ask you a question or two. You are an observant man—did you notice anything strange in any of the servants (making due allowance, of course, for fright and fluster), after the loss of the Diamond was found out? Any particular quarrel among them? Any one of them not in his or her usual spirits? Unexpectedly out of temper, for instance? or unexpectedly taken ill?'

I had just time to think of Rosanna Spearman's sudden illness at yesterday's dinner— but not time to make any answer—when I saw Sergeant Cuff's eyes suddenly turn aside towards the shrubbery; and I heard him say softly to himself, 'Hullo!'

'What's the matter?' I asked.

'A touch of the rheumatics in my back,' said the Sergeant, in a loud voice, as if he wanted some third person to hear us. 'We shall have a change in the weather before long.'

A few steps further brought us to the corner of the house. Turning off sharp to the right, we entered on the terrace, and went down, by the steps in the middle, into the garden below. Sergeant Cuff stopped there, in the open space, where we could see round us on every side.

'About that young person, Rosanna Spearman?' he said. 'It isn't very likely, with her personal appearance, that she has got a lover. But, for the girl's own sake, I must ask you at once whether *she* has provided herself with a sweetheart, poor wretch, like the rest of them?'

What on earth did he mean, under present circumstances, by putting such a question to me as that? I stared at him, instead of answering him.

'I saw Rosanna Spearman hiding in the shrubbery as we went by,' said the Sergeant.
'When you said "Hullo"?'

'Yes—when I said "Hullo!" If there's a sweetheart in the case, the hiding doesn't much matter. If there isn't—as things are in this house—the hiding is a highly suspicious circumstance, and it will be my painful duty to act on it accordingly.'

What, in God's name, was I to say to him? I knew the shrubbery was Mr Franklin's favourite walk; I knew he would most likely turn that way when he came back from the station; I knew that Penelope had over and over again caught her fellow-servant hanging about there, and had always declared to me that Rosanna's object was to attract Mr Franklin's attention. If my daughter was right, she might well have been lying in wait for Mr Franklin's return when the Sergeant noticed her. I was put between the two difficulties of mentioning Penelope's fanciful notion as if it was mine, or of leaving an unfortunate creature to suffer the consequences, the very serious consequences, of exciting the suspicion of Sergeant Cuff. Out of pure pity for the girl—on my soul and my character, out of pure pity for the girl—I gave the Sergeant the necessary explanations, and told him that Rosanna had been mad enough to set her heart on Mr Franklin Blake.

Sergeant Cuff never laughed. On the few occasions when anything amused him, he curled up a little at the corners of the lips, nothing more. He curled up now.

'Hadn't you better say she's mad enough to be an ugly girl and only a servant?' he asked. 'The falling in love with a gentleman of Mr Franklin Blake's manners and appearance doesn't seem to me to be the maddest part of her conduct by any means. However, I'm glad the thing is cleared up: it relieves one's mind to have things cleared up. Yes, I'll keep it a secret, Mr Betteredge. I like to be tender to human infirmity—though I don't get many chances of exercising that virtue in my line of life. You think Mr Franklin Blake hasn't got a suspicion of the girl's fancy for him? Ah! he would have found it out fast enough if she had been nice-looking. The ugly women have a bad time of it in this world; let's hope it will be made up to them in another. You have got a nice garden here, and a well-kept lawn. See for yourself how much better the flowers look with grass about them instead of gravel. No, thank you. I won't take a rose. It goes to my heart to break them off the stem. Just as it goes to your heart, you know, when there's something wrong in the servants' hall. Did you notice anything you couldn't account for in any of the servants when the loss of the Diamond was first found out?'

I had got on very fairly well with Sergeant Cuff so far. But the slyness with which he slipped in that last question put me on my guard. In plain English, I didn't at all relish the notion of helping his inquiries, when those inquiries took him (in the capacity of snake in the grass) among my fellow-servants.

'I noticed nothing,' I said, 'except that we all lost our heads together, myself included.'

'Oh,' says the Sergeant, 'that's all you have to tell me, is it?'

I answered, with (as I flattered myself) an unmoved countenance, 'That is all.'

Sergeant Cuff's dismal eyes looked me hard in the face.

'Mr Betteredge,' he said, 'have you any objection to oblige me by shaking hands? I have taken an extraordinary liking to you.'

(Why be should have chosen the exact moment when I was deceiving him to give me that proof of his good opinion, is beyond all comprehension! I felt a little proud—I really did feel a little proud of having been one too many at last for the celebrated Cuff!)

We went back to the house; the Sergeant requesting that I would give him a room to himself, and then send in the servants (the indoor servants only), one after another, in the order of their rank, from first to last.

I showed Sergeant Cuff into my own room, and then called the servants together in the hall. Rosanna Spearman appeared among them, much as usual. She was as quick in her way as the Sergeant in his, and I suspect she had heard what he said to me about the servants in general, just before he discovered her. There she was, at any rate, looking as if she had never heard of such a place as the shrubbery in her life.

I sent them in, one by one, as desired. The cook was the first to enter the Court of Justice, otherwise my room. She remained but a short time. Report, on coming out: 'Sergeant Cuff is depressed in his spirits; but Sergeant Cuff is a perfect gentleman.' My lady's own maid followed. Remained much longer. Report, on coming out: 'If Sergeant Cuff doesn't believe a respectable woman, he might keep his opinion to himself, at any rate!' Penelope went next. Remained only a moment or two. Report, on coming out: 'Sergeant Cuff is much to be pitied. He must have been crossed in love, father, when he was a young man.' The first housemaid followed Penelope. Remained, like my lady's maid, a long time. Report, on coming out: 'I didn't enter her ladyship's service, Mr Betteredge, to be doubted to my face by a low police-officer!' Rosanna Spearman went next. Remained longer than any of them. No report on coming out—dead silence, and lips as pale as ashes. Samuel, the footman, followed Rosanna. Remained a minute or two. Report, on coming out: 'Whoever blacks Sergeant Cuff's boots ought to be ashamed of himself.' Nancy, the kitchenmaid, went last. Remained a minute or two. Report, on coming out: 'Sergeant Cuff has a heart; *he* doesn't cut jokes, Mr Betteredge, with a poor hard-working girl.'

Going into the Court of Justice, when it was all over, to hear if there were any further commands for me, I found the Sergeant at his old trick—looking out of window, and whistling 'The Last Rose of Summer' to himself.

'Any discoveries, sir?' I inquired.

'If Rosanna Spearman asks leave to go out,' said the Sergeant, let the poor thing go; but let me know first.'

I might as well have held my tongue about Rosanna and Mr Franklin! It was plain enough; the unfortunate girl had fallen under Sergeant Cuff's suspicions, in spite of all I could do to prevent it.

'I hope you don't think Rosanna is concerned in the loss of the Diamond?' I ventured to say.

The corners of the Sergeant's melancholy mouth curled up, and he looked hard in my face, just as he had looked in the garden.

'I think I had better not tell you, Mr Betteredge,' he said. 'You might lose your head, you know, for the second time.'

I began to doubt whether I had been one too many for the celebrated Cuff after all! It was rather a relief to me that we were interrupted here by a knock at the door, and a message from the cook. Rosanna Spearman *had* asked to go out, for the usual reason, that her head was bad, and she wanted a breath of fresh air. At a sign from the Sergeant, I said, Yes. 'Which is the servants' way out?' he asked, when the messenger had gone. I showed him the servants' way out. 'Lock the door of your room,' says the Sergeant;' and if anybody asks for me, say I'm in there, composing my mind.' He curled up again at the corners of the lips, and disappeared.

Left alone, under those circumstances, a devouring curiosity pushed me on to make some discoveries for myself.

It was plain that Sergeant Cuff's suspicions of Rosanna had been roused by something that he had found out at his examination of the servants in my room. Now, the only two servants (excepting Rosanna herself) who had remained under examination for any length of time, were my lady's own maid and the first housemaid, those two being also the women who had taken the lead in persecuting their unfortunate fellow-servant from the first. Reaching these conclusions, I looked in on them, casually as it might be, in the servants' hall, and, finding tea going forward, instantly invited myself to that meal. (For, *nota bene*, a drop of tea is to a woman's tongue what a drop of oil is to a wasting lamp.)

My reliance on the tea-pot, as an ally, did not go unrewarded. In less than half an hour I knew as much as the Sergeant himself.

My lady's maid and the housemaid had, it appeared, neither of them believed in Rosanna's illness of the previous day. These two devils—I ask your pardon; but how else *can* you describe a couple of spiteful women?—had stolen upstairs, at intervals during the Thursday afternoon; had tried Rosanna's door and found it locked; had knocked, and not been answered; had listened, and not heard a sound inside. When the girl had come down to tea, and had been sent up, still out of sorts, to bed again, the two devils aforesaid had tried her door once more, and found it locked; had looked at the keyhole, and found it stopped up; had seen a light under the door at midnight, and had heard the crackling of a fire (a fire in a servant's bedroom in the month of June!) at four in the morning. All this they had told Sergeant Cuff, who, in return for their anxiety to enlighten him, had eyed them with sour and suspicious looks, and had shown them plainly that he didn't believe either one or the other. Hence, the unfavourable reports of him which these two women had brought out with them from the examination. Hence, also (without reckoning the influence of the tea-pot), their readiness to let their tongues run to any length on the subject of the Sergeant's ungracious behaviour to them.

Having had some experience of the great Cuff's roundabout ways, and having last seen him evidently bent on following Rosanna privately when she went out for her walk, it seemed clear to me that he had thought it unadvisable to let the lady's maid and the housemaid know how materially they had helped him. They were just the sort of women, if he had treated their evidence as trustworthy, to have been puffed up by it, and to have said or done something which would have put Rosanna Spearman on her guard.

I walked out in the fine summer afternoon, very sorry for the poor girl, and very uneasy in my mind at the turn things had taken. Drifting towards the shrubbery, some time later, there I met Mr Franklin. After returning from seeing his cousin off at the station, he had been with my lady, holding a long conversation with her. She had told him of Miss Rachel's unaccountable refusal to let her wardrobe be examined; and had put him in such low spirits about my young lady, that he seemed to shrink from speaking on the subject. The family temper appeared in his face that evening, for the first time in my experience of him.

'Well, Betteredge,' he said, 'how does the atmosphere of mystery and suspicion in which we are all living now, agree with you? Do you remember that morning when I first came here with the Moonstone? I wish to God we had thrown it into the quicksand!'

After breaking out in that way, he abstained from speaking again until he had composed himself. We walked silently, side by side, for a minute or two, and then he asked me what had become of Sergeant Cuff. It was impossible to put Mr Franklin off with the excuse of the Sergeant being in my room, composing his mind. I told him exactly what had happened, mentioning particularly what my lady's maid and the housemaid had said about Rosanna Spearman.

Mr Franklin's clear head saw the turn the Sergeant's suspicions had taken, in the twinkling of an eye.

'Didn't you tell me this morning,' he said, 'that one of the tradespeople declared he had met Rosanna yesterday, on the footway to Frizinghall, when we supposed her to be ill in her room?'

'Yes, sir.'

'If my aunt's maid and the other woman have spoken the truth, you may depend upon it the tradesman *did* meet her. The girl's attack of illness was a blind to deceive us. She had some guilty reason for going to the town secretly. The paint-stained dress is a dress of hers; and the fire heard crackling in her room at four in the morning was a fire lit to destroy it. Rosanna Spearman has stolen the Diamond. I'll go in directly, and tell my aunt the turn things have taken.'

'Not just yet, if you please, sir,' said a melancholy voice behind us.

We both turned about, and found ourselves face to face with Sergeant Cuff.

'Why not just yet?' asked Mr Franklin.

'Because, sir, if you tell her ladyship, her ladyship will tell Miss Verinder.'

Suppose she does. What then?' Mr Franklin said those words with a sudden heat and vehemence, as if the Sergeant had mortally offended him.

'Do you think it's wise, sir,' said Sergeant Cuff, quietly, 'to put such a question as that to me—at such a time as this?'

There was a moment's silence between them: Mr Franklin walked close up to the Sergeant. The two looked each other straight in the face. Mr Franklin spoke first, dropping his voice as suddenly as he had raised it.

'I suppose you know, Mr Cuff,' he said, 'that you are treading on delicate ground?'

'It isn't the first time, by a good many hundreds, that I find myself treading on delicate ground,' answered the other, as immovable as ever.

'I am to understand that you forbid me to tell my aunt what has happened?'

'You are to understand, if you please, sir, that I throw up the case, if you tell Lady Verinder, or tell anybody, what has happened, until I give you leave.'

That settled it. Mr Franklin had no choice but to submit. He turned away in anger—and left us.

I had stood there listening to them, all in a tremble; not knowing whom to suspect, or what to think next. In the midst of my confusion, two things, however, were plain to me. First, that my young lady was, in some unaccountable manner, at the bottom of the sharp speeches that had passed between them. Second, that they thoroughly understood each other, without having previously exchanged a word of explanation on either side.

'Mr Betteredge,' says the Sergeant, 'you have done a very foolish thing in my absence.

You have done a little detective business on your own account. For the future, perhaps you will be so obliging as to do your detective business along with me.'

He took me by the arm, and walked me away with him along the road by which he had come. I dare say I had deserved his reproof—but I was not going to help him to set traps for Rosanna Spearman, for all that. Thief or no thief, legal or not legal, I don't care—I pitied her.

'What do you want of me?' I asked, shaking him off, and stopping short.

'Only a little information about the country round here,' said the Sergeant.

I couldn't well object to improve Sergeant Cuff in his geography.

'Is there any path, in that direction, leading to the sea-beach from this house?' asked the Sergeant. He pointed, as he spoke, to the fir-plantation which led to the Shivering Sand.

'Yes,' I said, 'there is a path.'

'Show it to me.'

Side by side, in the grey of the summer evening, Sergeant Cuff and I set forth for the Shivering Sand.

CHAPTER 15

The Sergeant remained silent, thinking his own thoughts, till we entered the plantation of firs which led to the quicksand. There he roused himself, like a man whose mind was made up, and spoke to me again.

'Mr Betteredge,' he said, 'as you have honoured me by taking an oar in my boat, and as you may, I think, be of some assistance to me before the evening is out, I see no use in our mystifying one another any longer, and I propose to set you an example of plain speaking on my side. You are determined to give me no information to the prejudice of Rosanna Spearman, because she has been a good girl to *you*, and because you pity her heartily. Those humane considerations do you a world of credit, but they happen in this instance to be humane considerations clean thrown away. Rosanna Spearman is not in the slightest danger of getting into trouble—no, not if I fix her with being concerned in the disappearance of the Diamond, on evidence which is as plain as the nose on your face!'

'Do you mean that my lady won't prosecute?' I asked.

'I mean that your lady *can't* prosecute,' said the Sergeant. Rosanna Spearman is simply an instrument in the hands of another person, and Rosanna Spearman will be held harmless for that other person's sake.'

He spoke like a man in earnest—there was no denying that. Still, I felt something stirring uneasily against him in my mind. 'Can't you give that other person a name?' I said.

'Can't *you*, Mr Betteredge?

'No.'

Sergeant Cuff stood stock-still, and surveyed me with a look of melancholy interest.

'It's always a pleasure to me to be tender towards human infirmity,' he said. I feel particularly tender at the present moment, Mr Betteredge, towards you. And you, with the same excellent motive, feel particularly tender towards Rosanna Spearman, don't you? Do you happen to know whether she has had a new outfit of linen lately?

What he meant by slipping in this extraordinary question unawares, I was at a total loss to imagine. Seeing no possible injury to Rosanna if I owned the truth, I answered that the girl had come to us rather sparely provided with linen, and that my lady, in recompense for her good conduct (I laid a stress on her good conduct), had given her a new outfit not a fortnight since.

'This is a miserable world,' says the Sergeant. 'Human life, Mr Betteredge, is a sort of target—misfortune is always firing at it, and always hitting the mark. But for that outfit, we should have discovered a new nightgown or petticoat among Rosanna's things, and have nailed her in that way. You're not at a loss to follow me, are you? You have examined the servants yourself, and you know what discoveries two of them made outside Rosanna's door. Surely you know what the girl was about yesterday, after she was taken ill? You can't guess? Oh dear me, it's as plain as that strip of light there, at the end of the trees. At eleven, on Thursday morning, Superintendent Seegrave (who is a mass of human infirmity) points out to all the women-servants the smear on the door. Rosanna has her own reasons for suspecting her own things; she takes the first opportunity of getting to her room, finds the paint-stain on her nightgown, or petticoat, or what not, shams ill and slips away to the town, gets the materials for making a new petticoat or nightgown, makes it alone in her room on the Thursday night, lights a fire (not to destroy it; two of her fellow-servants are prying outside her door, and she knows better than to make a smell of burning, and to have a lot of tinder to get rid of)—lights a fire, I say, to dry and iron the substitute dress after wringing it out, keeps the stained dress hidden (probably *on* her), and is at this moment occupied in making away with it, in some convenient place, on that lonely bit of beach ahead of us. I have traced her this evening to your fishing village, and to one particular cottage, which we may possibly have to visit, before we go back. She stopped in the cottage for some time, and she came out with (as I believe) something hidden under her cloak. A cloak (on a woman's back) is an emblem of charity—it covers a multitude of sins. I saw her set off northwards along the coast, after leaving the cottage. Is your sea-shore here considered a fine specimen of marine landscape, Mr Betteredge?

I answered, 'Yes,' as shortly as might be.

'Tastes differ,' says Sergeant Cuff. 'Looking at it from my point of view, I never saw a marine landscape that I admired less. If you happen to be following another person along your sea-coast, and if that person happens to look round, there isn't a scrap of cover to hide you anywhere. I had to chose between taking Rosanna in custody on suspicion, or leaving her, for the time being, with her little game in her own hands. For reasons which I won't trouble you with, I decided on making any sacrifice rather than give the alarm as soon as to-night to a certain person who shall be nameless between us. I came back to the house to ask you to take me to the north-end of the beach by another way. Sand—in respect of its printing off people's footsteps—is one of the best detective officers I know. If we don't meet with Rosanna Spearman by coming round on her in this way, the sand may tell us what she has been at, if the light only lasts long enough. Here is the sand. If you will excuse my suggesting it—suppose you hold your tongue, and let me go first?'

If there is such a thing known at the doctor's shop as a *detective-fever*, that disease had now got fast hold of your humble servant. Sergeant Cuff went on between the hillocks of sand, down to the beach. I followed him (with my heart in my mouth); and waited at a little distance for what was to happen next.

As it turned out, I found myself standing nearly in the same place where Rosanna Spearman and I had been talking together when Mr Franklin suddenly appeared before us, on arriving at our house from London. While my eyes were watching the Sergeant, my mind wandered away in spite of me to what had passed, on that former occasion, between Rosanna and me. I declare I almost felt the poor thing slip her hand again into mine, and give it a little grateful squeeze to thank me for speaking kindly to her. I declare I almost heard her voice telling me again that the Shivering Sand seemed to draw her to it against her own will, whenever she went out—almost saw her face brighten again, as it brightened when she first set eyes upon Mr Franklin coming briskly out on us from among the hillocks. My spirits fell lower and lower as I thought of these things—and the view of the lonesome little bay, when I looked about to rouse myself, only served to make me feel more uneasy still.

The last of the evening light was fading away; and over all the desolate place there hung a still and awful calm. The heave of the main ocean on the great sandbank out in the bay, was a heave that made no sound. The inner sea lay lost and dim, without a breath of wind to stir it. Patches of nasty ooze floated, yellow-white, on the dead surface of the water. Scum and slime shone faintly in certain places, where the last of the light still caught them on the two great spits of rock jutting out, north and south, into the sea. It was now the time of the turn of the tide: and even as I stood there waiting, the broad brown face of the quicksand began to dimple and quiver—the only moving thing in all the horrid place.

I saw the Sergeant start as the shiver of the sand caught his eye. After looking at it for a minute or so, he turned and came back to me.

'A treacherous place, Mr Betteredge,' he said; 'and no signs of Rosanna Spearman anywhere on the beach, look where you may.'

He took me down lower on the shore, and I saw for myself that his footsteps and mine were the only footsteps printed off on the sand.

'How does the fishing village bear, standing where we are now?' asked Sergeant Cuff.

'Cobb's Hole,' I answered (that being the name of the place), 'bears as near as may be, due south.'

'I saw the girl this evening, walking northward along the shore, from Cobb's Hole,' said the Sergeant. 'Consequently, she must have been walking towards this place. Is Cobb's Hole on the other side of that point of land there? And can we get to it—now it's low water—by the beach?'

I answered, 'Yes,' to both those questions.

'If you'll excuse my suggesting it, we'll step out briskly,' said the Sergeant. 'I want to find the place where she left the shore, before it gets dark.'

We had walked, I should say, a couple of hundred yards towards Cobb's Hole, when Sergeant Cuff suddenly went down on his knees on the beach, to all appearance seized with a sudden frenzy for saying his prayers.

'There's something to be said for your marine landscape here, after all,' remarked the Sergeant. 'Here are a woman's footsteps, Mr Betteredge! Let us call them Rosanna's footsteps, until we find evidence to the contrary that we can't resist. Very confused footsteps, you will please to observe—purposely confused, I should say. Ah, poor soul, she understands the detective virtues of sand as well as I do! But hasn't she been in rather too great a hurry to tread out the marks thoroughly? I think she has. Here's one footstep going *from* Cobb's Hole; and here is another going back to it. Isn't that the toe of her shoe pointing straight to the water's edge? And don't I see two heel-marks further down the beach, close at the water's edge also? I don't want to hurt your feelings, but I'm afraid Rosanna is sly. It looks as if she had determined to get to that place you and I have just come from, without leaving any marks on the sand to trace her by. Shall we say that she walked through the water from this point till she got to that ledge of rocks behind us, and came back the same way, and then took to the beach again where those two heel-marks are still left. Yes, we'll say that. It seems to fit in with my notion that she had something under her cloak, when she left the cottage. No! not something to destroy—for, in that case, where would have been the need of all these precautions to prevent my tracing the place at which her walk ended? Something to hide is, I think, the better guess of the two. Perhaps, if we go on to the cottage, we may find out what that something is.'

At this proposal, my detective-fever suddenly cooled. 'You don't want me,' I said. 'What good can I do?'

'The longer I know you, Mr Betteredge,' said the Sergeant, 'the more virtues I discover. Modesty—oh dear me, how rare modesty is in this world! and how much of that rarity you possess! If I go alone to the cottage, the people's tongues will be tied at the first question I put to them. If I go with you, I go introduced by a justly respected neighbour, and a flow of conversation is the necessary result. It strikes me in that light; how does it strike you?'

'Not having an answer of the needful smartness as ready as I could have wished, I tried to gain time by asking him what cottage he wanted to go to.

On the Sergeant describing the place, I recognized it as a cottage inhabited by a fisherman named Yolland, with his wife and two grown-up children, a son and a daughter. If you will look back, you will find that, in first presenting Rosanna Spearman to your notice, I have described her as occasionally varying her walk to the Shivering Sand, by a visit to some friends of hers at Cobb's Hole. Those friends were the Yollands—respectable, worthy people, a credit to the neighbourhood. Rosanna's acquaintance with them had begun by means of the daughter, who was afflicted with a misshapen foot, and who was known in our parts by the name of Limping Lucy. The two deformed girls had, I suppose, a kind of fellow-feeling for each other. Any way, the Yollands and Rosanna always appeared to get on together, at the few chances they had of meeting, in a pleasant and friendly manner. The fact of Sergeant Cuff having traced the girl to *their* cottage, set the matter of my helping his inquiries in quite a new light. Rosanna had merely gone where she was in the habit of going; and to show that she had been in company with the fisherman and his family was as good as to prove that she had been innocently occupied, so far, at any rate. It would be doing the girl a service, therefore, instead of an injury, if I allowed myself to be convinced by Sergeant Cuff's logic. I professed myself convinced by it accordingly.

We went on to Cobb's Hole, seeing the footsteps on the sand, as long as the light lasted.

On reaching the cottage, the fisherman and his son proved to be out in the boat; and Limping Lucy, always weak and weary, was resting on her bed upstairs. Good Mrs Yolland received us alone in her kitchen. When she heard that Sergeant Cuff was a celebrated character in London, she clapped a bottle of Dutch gin and a couple of clean pipes on the table, and stared as if she could never see enough of him.

I sat quiet in a corner, waiting to hear how the Sergeant would find his way to the subject of Rosanna Spearman. His usual roundabout manner of going to work proved, on this occasion, to be more roundabout than ever. How he managed it is more than I could tell at the time, and more than I can tell now. But this is certain, he began with the Royal Family, the Primitive Methodists, and the price of fish; and he got from that (in his dismal, underground way) to the loss of the Moonstone, the spitefulness of our first housemaid, and the hard behaviour of the women-servants generally towards Rosanna Spearman. Having reached his subject in this fashion, he described himself as making his inquiries about the lost Diamond, partly with a view to find it, and partly for the purpose of clearing Rosanna from the unjust suspicions of her enemies in the house. In about a quarter of an hour from the time when we entered the kitchen, good Mrs Yolland was persuaded that she was talking to Rosanna's best friend, and was pressing Sergeant Cuff to comfort his stomach and revive his spirits out of the Dutch bottle.

Being firmly persuaded that the Sergeant was wasting his breath to no purpose on Mrs Yolland, I sat enjoying the talk between them, much as I have sat, in my time, enjoying a stage play. The great Cuff showed a wonderful patience; trying his luck drearily this way and that way, and firing shot after shot, as it were, at random, on the chance of hitting the mark. Everything to Rosanna's credit, nothing to Rosanna's prejudice—that was how it ended, try as he might; with Mrs Yolland talking nineteen to the dozen, and placing the most entire confidence in him. His last effort was made, when we had looked at our watches, and had got on our legs previous to taking leave.

'I shall now wish you good-night, ma'am,' says the Sergeant. And I shall only say, at parting, that Rosanna Spearman has a sincere well-wisher in myself, your obedient servant. But, oh dear me! she will never get on in her present place; and my advice to her is—leave it.'

'Bless your heart alive! she is *going* to leave it!' cries Mrs Yolland. (*Nota bene*—I translate Mrs Yolland out of the Yorkshire language into the English language. When I tell you that the all-accomplished Cuff was every now and then puzzled to understand her until I helped him, you will draw your own conclusions as to what *your* state of mind would be if I reported her in her native tongue.)

Rosanna Spearman going to leave us! I pricked up my ears at that. It seemed strange, to say the least of it, that she should have given no warning, in the first place, to my lady or to me. A certain doubt came up in my mind whether Sergeant Cuff's last random shot might not have hit the mark. I began to question whether my share in the proceedings was quite as harmless a one as I had thought it. It might be all in the way of the Sergeant's business to mystify an honest woman by wrapping her round in a network of lies; but it was my duty to have remembered, as a good Protestant, that the father of lies is the Devil—and that mischief and the Devil are never far apart. Beginning to smell mischief in the air, I tried to take Sergeant Cuff out. He sat down again instantly, and asked for a little drop of comfort out of the Dutch bottle. Mr Yolland sat down opposite to him, and gave him his nip. I went on to the door, excessively uncomfortable, and said I thought I must bid them good-night—and yet I didn't go.

'So she means to leave?' says the Sergeant. 'What is she to do when she does leave? Sad, sad! The poor creature has got no friends in the world, except you and me.'

'Ah, but she has though!' says Mrs Yolland. 'She came in here, as I told you, this evening; and, after sitting and talking a little with my girl Lucy and me, she asked to go upstairs by herself, into Lucy's room. It's the only room in our place where there's pen and ink. "I want to write a letter to a friend," she says, "and I can't do it for the prying and peeping of the servants up at the house." Who the letter was written to I can't tell you: it must have been a mortal long one, judging by the time she stopped upstairs over it. I offered her a postage-stamp when she came down. She hadn't got the letter in her hand, and she didn't accept the stamp. A little close, poor soul (as you know), about herself and her doings. But a friend she has got somewhere, I can tell you; and to that friend, you may depend upon it, she will go.'

'Soon?' asked the Sergeant.

'As soon as she can,' says Mrs Yolland.

Here I stepped in again from the door. As chief of my lady's establishment, I couldn't allow this sort of loose talk about a servant of ours going, or not going, to proceed any longer in my presence, without noticing it.

'You must be mistaken about Rosanna Spearman,' I said. 'If she had been going to leave her present situation, she would have mentioned it, in the first place, to *me*.'

'Mistaken?' cries Mrs Yolland. 'Why, only an hour ago she bought some things she wanted for travelling—of my own self, Mr Betteredge, in this very room. And that reminds me,' says the wearisome woman, suddenly beginning to feel in her pocket, 'of something I have got it on my mind to say about Rosanna and her money. Are you either of you likely to see her when you go back to the house?'

'I'll take a message to the poor thing, with the greatest pleasure,' answered Sergeant Cuff, before I could put in a word edgewise.

Mrs Yolland produced out of her pocket, a few shillings and six pences, and counted them out with a most particular and exasperating carefulness in the palm of her hand. She offered the money to the Sergeant, looking mighty loth to part with it all the while.

'Might I ask you to give this back to Rosanna, with my love and respects?' says Mrs Yolland. 'She insisted on paying me for the one or two things she took a fancy to this evening—and money's welcome enough in our house, I don't deny it. Still, I'm not easy in my mind about taking the poor thing's little savings. And to tell you the truth, I don't think my man would like to hear that I had taken Rosanna Spearman's money, when he comes back to-morrow morning from his work. Please say she's heartily welcome to the things she bought of me—as a gift. And don't leave the money on the table,' says Mrs Yolland, putting it down suddenly before the Sergeant, as if it burnt her fingers—'don't, there's a good man! For times are hard, and flesh is weak; and I *might* feel tempted to put it back in my pocket again.'

'Come along!' I said, 'I can't wait any longer: I must go back to the house.'

'I'll follow you directly,' says Sergeant Cuff.

For the second time, I went to the door; and, for the second time, try as I might, I couldn't cross the threshold.

'It's a delicate matter, ma'am,' I heard the Sergeant say, 'giving money back. You charged her cheap for the things, I'm sure?'

'Cheap!' says Mrs Yolland. 'Come and judge for yourself.'

She took up the candle and led the Sergeant to a corner of the kitchen. For the life of me, I couldn't help following them. Shaken down in the corner was a heap of odds and ends (mostly old metal), which the fisherman had picked up at different times from wrecked ships, and which he hadn't found a market for yet, to his own mind. Mrs Yolland dived into this rubbish, and brought up an old japanned tin case, with a cover to it, and a hasp to hang it up by—the sort of thing they use, on board ship, for keeping their maps and charts, and such-like, from the wet.

'There!' says she. 'When Rosanna came in this evening, she bought the fellow to that. ''It will just do,' she says, to put my cuffs and collars in, and keep them from being crumpled in my box.'' One and nine pence, Mr Cuff. As I live by bread, not a halfpenny more!'

'Dirt cheap!' says the Sergeant, with a heavy sigh.

He weighed the case in his hand. I thought I heard a note or two of 'The Last Rose of Summer' as he looked at it. There was no doubt now! He had made another discovery to the prejudice of Rosanna Spearman, in the place of all others where I thought her character was safest, and all through me! I leave you to imagine what I felt, and how sincerely I repented having been the medium of introduction between Mrs Yolland and Sergeant Cuff.

'That will do,' I said. 'We really must go.'

Without paying the least attention to me, Mrs Yolland took another dive into the rubbish, and came up out of it, this time, with a dog-chain.

'Weigh it in your hand, sir,' she said to the Sergeant. 'We had three of these; and Rosanna has taken two of them. ''What can you want, my dear, with a couple of dog-chains?'' says I. ''If I join them together they'll go round my box nicely,'' says she. ''Rope's cheapest,'' says I. ''Chain's surest,'' says she. ''Who ever heard of a box corded with chain!'' says I. ''Oh, Mrs Yolland, don't make objections!'' says she; ''let me have my chains!'' A strange girl, Mr Cuff—good as gold, and kinder than a sister to my Lucy— but always a little strange. There! I humoured her. Three and sixpence. On the word of an honest woman, three and sixpence, Mr Cuff!'

'Each?' says the Sergeant.

'Both together!' says Mrs Yolland. 'Three and sixpence for the two.'

'Given away, ma'am,' says the Sergeant, shaking his head. 'Clean given away!'

'There's the money,' says Mrs Yolland, getting back sideways to the little heap of silver on the table, as if it drew her in spite of herself. 'The tin case and the dog-chains were all she bought, and all she took away. One and ninepence and three and sixpence—total, five and three. With my love and respects—and I can't find it in my conscience to take a poor girl's savings, when she may want them herself.'

'I can't find it in *my* conscience, ma'am, to give the money back,' says Sergeant Cuff. 'You have as good as made her a present of the things—you have indeed.'

'Is that your sincere opinion, sir?' says Mrs Yolland brightening up wonderfully.

'There can't be a doubt about it,' answered the Sergeant. 'Ask Mr Betteredge.'

It was no use asking *me*. All they got out of *me* was, 'Goodnight.'

'Bother the money!' says Mrs Yolland. With those words, she appeared to lose all command over herself; and, making a sudden snatch at the heap of silver, put it back, holus-bolus, in her pocket. 'It upsets one's temper, it does, to see it lying there, and nobody taking it,' cries this unreasonable woman, sitting down with a thump, and looking at Sergeant Cuff, as much as to say, 'It's in my pocket again now—get it out if you can!'

This time, I not only went to the door, but went fairly out on the road back. Explain it how you may, I felt as if one or both of them had mortally offended me. Before I had taken three steps down the village, I heard the Sergeant behind me.

'Thank you for your introduction, Mr Betteredge,' he said. 'I am indebted to the fisherman's wife for an entirely new sensation. Mrs Yolland has puzzled me.'

It was on the tip of my tongue to have given him a sharp answer, for no better reason than this—that I was out of temper with him, because I was out of temper with myself. But when he owned to being puzzled, a comforting doubt crossed my mind whether any great harm had been done after all. I waited in discreet silence to hear more.

'Yes,' says the Sergeant, as if he was actually reading my thoughts in the dark. 'Instead of putting me on the scent, it may console you to know, Mr Betteredge (with your interest in Rosanna), that you have been the means of throwing me off. What the girl has done, to-night, is clear enough, of course. She has joined the two chains, and has fastened them to the hasp in the tin case. She has sunk the case, in the water or in the quicksand. She has made the loose end of the chain fast to some place under the rocks, known only to herself. And she will leave the case secure at its anchorage till the present proceedings have come to an end; after which she can privately pull it up again out of its hiding-place, at her own leisure and convenience. All perfectly plain, so far. But,' says the Sergeant, with the first tone of impatience in his voice that I had heard yet, 'the mystery is—what the devil has she hidden in the tin case? '

I thought to myself, 'The Moonstone!' But I only said to Sergeant Cuff, 'Can't you guess?'

'It's not the Diamond,' says the Sergeant. 'The whole experience of my life is at fault, if Rosanna Spearman has got the Diamond.'

On hearing those words, the infernal detective-fever began, I suppose, to burn in me again. At any rate, I forgot myself in the interest of guessing this new riddle. I said rashly, 'The stained dress!'

Sergeant Cuff stopped short in the dark, and laid his hand on my arm.

'Is anything thrown into that quicksand of yours, ever thrown up on the surface again?' he asked.

'Never,' I answered. 'Light or heavy, whatever goes into the Shivering Sand is sucked down, and seen no more.'

'Does Rosanna Spearman know that?'

'She knows it as well as I do.'

'Then,' Says the Sergeant, 'what on earth has she got to do but to tie up a bit of stone in the stained dress, and throw it into the quicksand? There isn't the shadow of a reason why she should have hidden it—and yet she *must* have hidden it. Query,' says the Sergeant, walking on again, 'is the paint-stained dress a petticoat or a night-gown? or is it some-thing else which there is a reason for preserving at any risk? Mr Betteredge, if nothing occurs to prevent it, I must go to Frizinghall to-morrow, and discover what she bought in the town, when she privately got the materials for making the substitute dress. It's a risk to leave the house, as things are now—but it's a worse risk still to stir another step in this matter in the dark. Excuse my being a little out of temper; I'm degraded in my own estimation—I have let Rosanna Spearman puzzle me.'

When we got back, the servants were at supper. The first person we saw in the outer yard was the policeman whom Superintendent Seegrave had left at the Sergeant's dis-posal. The Sergeant asked if Rosanna Spearman had returned. Yes. When? Nearly an hour since. What had she done? She had gone upstairs to take off her bonnet and cloak—and she was now at supper quietly with the rest.

Without making any remark, Sergeant Cuff walked on, sinking lower and lower in his own estimation, to the back of the house. Missing the entrance in the dark, he went on (in spite of my calling to him) till he was stopped by a wicket-gate which led into the garden. When I joined him to bring him back by the right way, I found that he was looking up attentively at one particular window, on the bedroom floor, at the back of the house.

Looking up, in my turn, I discovered that the object of his contemplation was the window of Miss Rachel's room, and that lights were passing backwards and forwards there as if something unusual was going on.

'Isn't that Miss Verinder's room?' asked Sergeant Cuff.

I replied that it was, and invited him to go in with me to supper. The Sergeant remained in his place, and said something about enjoying the smell of the garden at night. I left him to his enjoyment. Just as I was turning in at the door, I heard 'The Last Rose of Summer' at the wicket-gate. Sergeant Cuff had made another discovery! And my young lady's window was at the bottom of it this time!

The latter reflection took me back again to the Sergeant, with a polite intimation that I could not find it in my heart to leave him by himself. 'Is there anything you don't under-stand up there?' I added, pointing to Miss Rachel's window.

Judging by his voice, Sergeant Cuff had suddenly risen again to the right place in his own estimation. 'You are great people for betting in Yorkshire, are you not?' he asked.

'Well?' I said. 'Suppose we are?'

'If I was a Yorkshireman,' proceeded the Sergeant, taking my arm, 'I would lay you an even sovereign, Mr Betteredge, that your young lady has suddenly resolved to leave the house. If I won on that event, I should offer to lay another sovereign, that the idea has occurred to her within the last hour.'

The first of the Sergeant's guesses startled me. The second mixed itself up somehow in my head with the report we had heard from the policeman, that Rosanna Spearman had returned from the sands within the last hour. The two together had a curious effect on me as we went in to supper. I shook off Sergeant Cuff's arm, and, forgetting my manners, pushed by him through the door to make my own inquiries for myself.

Samuel, the footman, was the first person I met in the passage.

'Her ladyship is waiting to see you and Sergeant Cuff,' he said, before I could put any questions to him.

'How long has she been waiting?' asked the Sergeant's voice behind me.

'For the last hour, sir.'

There it was again! Rosanna had come back; Miss Rachel had taken some resolution out of the common; and my lady had been waiting to see the Sergeant—all within the last hour! It was not pleasant to find these very different persons and things linking themselves together in this way. I went on upstairs, without looking at Sergeant Cuff, or speaking to him. My hand took a sudden fit of trembling as I lifted it to knock at my mistress's door.

'I shouldn't be surprised,' whispered the Sergeant over my shoulder, 'If a scandal was to burst up in the house to-night. Don't be alarmed! I have put the muzzle on worse family difficulties than this, in my time.'

As he said the words, I heard my mistress's voice calling to us to come in.

CHAPTER 16

We found my lady with no light in the room but the reading-lamp. The shade was screwed down so as to overshadow her face. Instead of looking up at us in her usual straightforward way, she sat close at the table, and kept her eyes fixed obstinately on an open book.

'Officer,' she said, 'is it important to the inquiry you are conducting, to know beforehand if any person now in this house wishes to leave it?'

'Most important, my lady.'

'I have to tell you, then, that Miss Verinder proposes going to stay with her aunt, Mrs Ablewhite, of Frizinghall. She has arranged to leave us the first thing to-morrow morning.'

Sergeant Cuff looked at me. I made a step forward to speak to my mistress—and, feeling my heart fail me (if I must own it), took a step back again, and said nothing.

'May I ask your ladyship *when* Miss Verinder informed you that she was going to her aunt's?' inquired the Sergeant.

'About an hour since,' answered my mistress.

Sergeant Cuff looked at me once more. They say old people's hearts are not very easily moved. *My* heart couldn't have thumped much harder than it did now, if I had been five-and-twenty again!

'I have no claim, my lady,' says the Sergeant, 'to control Miss Verinder's actions. All I can ask you to do is to put off her departure, if possible, till later in the day. I must go to Frizinghall myself to-morrow morning—and I shall be back by two o'clock, if not before. If Miss Verinder can be kept here till that time, I should wish to say two words to her—unexpectedly—before she goes.'

My lady directed me to give the coachman her orders, that the carriage was not to come for Miss Rachel until two o'clock. 'Have you more to say?' she asked of the Sergeant, when this had been done.

'Only one thing, your ladyship. If Miss Verinder is surprised at this change in the arrangements, please not to mention Me as being the cause of putting off her journey.'

My mistress lifted her head suddenly from her book as if she was going to say something—checked herself by a great effort—and, looking back again at the open page, dismissed us with a sign of her hand.

'That's a wonderful woman,' said Sergeant Cuff, when we were out in the hall again. 'But for her self-control, the mystery that puzzles you, Mr Betteredge, would have been at an end to-night.'

At those words, the truth rushed at last into my stupid old head. For the moment, I suppose I must have gone clean out of my senses. I seized the Sergeant by the collar of his coat, and pinned him against the wall.

'Damn you!' I cried out, 'there's something wrong about Miss Rachel—and you have been hiding it from me all this time!'

Sergeant Cuff looked up at me—flat against the wall—without stirring a hand, or moving a muscle of his melancholy face.

'Ah,' he said, 'you've guessed it at last.'

My hand dropped from his collar, and my head sunk on my breast. Please to remember, as some excuse for my breaking out as I did, that I had served the family for fifty years. Miss Rachel had climbed upon my knees, and pulled my whiskers, many and many a time when she was a child. Miss Rachel, with all her faults, had been, to my mind, the dearest and prettiest and best young mistress that ever an old servant waited on, and loved. I begged Sergeant Cuff's pardon, but I am afraid I did it with watery eyes, and not in a very becoming way.

'Don't distress yourself, Mr Betteredge,' says the Sergeant, with more kindness than I had any right to expect from him. 'In my line of life, if we were quick at taking offence, we shouldn't be worth salt to our porridge. If it's any comfort to you, collar me again. You don't in the least know how to do it; but I'll overlook your awkwardness in consideration of your feelings.'

He curled up at the corners of his lips, and, in his own dreary way, seemed to think he had delivered himself of a very good joke.

I led him into my own little sitting-room, and closed the door.

'Tell me the truth, Sergeant,' I said. 'What do you suspect? It's no kindness to hide it from me now.'

'I don't suspect,' said Sergeant Cuff. 'I know.'

My unlucky temper began to get the better of me again.

'Do you mean to tell me, in plain English,' I said, 'that Miss Rachel has stolen her own Diamond?'

'Yes,' says the Sergeant; 'that is what I mean to tell you, in so many words. Miss Verinder has been in secret possession of the Moonstone from first to last; and she has taken Rosanna Spearman into her confidence, because she has calculated on our suspecting Rosanna Spearman of the theft. There is the whole case in a nut-shell. Collar me again, Mr Betteredge. If it's any vent to your feelings, collar me again.'

God help me! my feelings were not to be relieved in that way. 'Give me your reasons!' That was all I could say to him.

'You shall hear my reasons to-morrow,' said the Sergeant. 'If Miss Verinder refuses to put off her visit to her aunt (which you will find Miss Verinder will do), I shall be obliged to lay the whole case before your mistress tomorrow. And, as I don't know what may come of it, I shall request you to be present, and to hear what passes on both sides. Let the matter rest for to-night. No, Mr Betteredge, you don't get a word more on the subject of the Moonstone out of me. There is your table spread for supper. That's one of the many human infirmities which I always treat tenderly. If you will ring the bell, I'll say grace. "For what we are going to receive—" '

'I wish you a good appetite to it, Sergeant,' I said. '*My* appetite is gone. I'll wait and see you served, and then I'll ask you to excuse me, if I go away, and try to get the better of this by myself.'

I saw him served with the best of everything—and I shouldn't have been sorry if the best of everything had choked him. The head gardener (Mr Begbie) came in at the same time, with his weekly account. The Sergeant got on the subject of roses and the merits of grass walks and gravel walks immediately. I left the two together, and went out with a heavy heart. This was the first trouble I remember for many a long year which wasn't to be blown off by a whiff of tobacco, and which was even beyond the reach of *Robinson Crusoe*.

Being restless and miserable, and having no particular room to go to, I took a turn on the terrace, and thought it over in peace and quietness by myself. It doesn't much matter what my thoughts were. I felt wretchedly old, and worn out, and unfit for my place—and began to wonder, for the first time in my life, when it would please God to take me. With all this, I held firm, notwithstanding, to my belief in Miss Rachel. If Sergeant Cuff had been Solomon in all his glory, and had told me that my young lady had mixed herself up in a mean and guilty plot, I should have had but one answer for Solomon, wise as he was, 'You don't know her; and I do.'

My meditations were interrupted by Samuel. He brought me a written message from my mistress.

Going into the house to get a light to read it by, Samuel remarked that there seemed a change coming in the weather. My troubled mind had prevented me from noticing it before. But, now my attention was roused, I heard the dogs uneasy, and the wind moaning low. Looking up at the sky, I saw the rack of clouds getting blacker and blacker, and hurrying faster and faster over a watery moon. Wild weather coming—Samuel was right, wild weather coming.

The message from my lady informed me, that the magistrate at Frizinghall had written to remind her about the three Indians. Early in the coming week, the rogues must needs be released, and left free to follow their own devices. If we had any more questions to ask them, there was no time to lose. Having forgotten to mention this, when she had last seen Sergeant Cuff, my mistress now desired me to supply the omission. The Indians had gone clean out of my head (as they have, no doubt, gone clean out of yours). I didn't see much use in stirring that subject again. However, I obeyed my orders on the spot, as a matter of course.

I found Sergeant Cuff and the gardener, with a bottle of Scotch whisky between them, head over ears in an argument on the growing of roses. The Sergeant was so deeply interested that he held up his hand, and signed to me not to interrupt the discussion, when I came in. As far as I could understand it, the question between them was, whether the white moss-rose did, or did not, require to be budded on the dog-rose to make it grow well. Mr Begbie said, Yes; and Sergeant Cuff said, No. They appealed to me, as hotly as a couple of boys. Knowing nothing whatever about the growing of roses, I steered a middle course—just as her Majesty's judges do, when the scales of justice bother them by hanging even to a hair. 'Gentlemen,' I remarked, 'there is much to be said on both sides.' In the temporary lull produced by that impartial sentence, I laid my lady's written message on the table, under the eyes of Sergeant Cuff.

I had got by this time, as nearly as might be, to hate the Sergeant. But truth compels me to acknowledge that, in respect of readiness of mind, he was a wonderful man.

In half a minute after he had read the message, he had looked back into his memory for Superintendent Seegrave's report; had picked out that part of it in which the Indians were concerned; and was ready with his answer. A certain great traveller, who understood the Indians and their language, had figured in Mr Seegrave's report, hadn't he? Very well. Did I know the gentleman's name and address? Very well again. Would I write them on the back of my lady's message? Much obliged to me. Sergeant Cuff would look that gentleman up, when he went to Frizinghall in the morning.

'Do you expect anything to come of it?' I asked. 'Superintendent Seegrave found the Indians as innocent as the babe unborn.'

'Superintendent Seegrave has been proved wrong, up to this time, in all his conclusions,' answered the Sergeant. 'It may be worth while to find out to-morrow whether Superintendent Seegrave was wrong about the Indians as well.' With that he turned to Mr Begbie, and took up the argument again exactly at the place where it had left off. 'This question between us is a question of soils and seasons, and patience and pains, Mr Gardener. Now let me put it to you from another point of view. You take your white moss rose—'

By that time, I had closed the door on them, and was out of hearing of the rest of the dispute.

In the passage, I met Penelope hanging about, and asked what she was waiting for.

She was waiting for her young lady's bell, when her young lady chose to call her back to go on with the packing for the next day's journey. Further inquiry revealed to me, that Miss Rachel had given it as a reason for wanting to go to her aunt at Frizinghall, that the house was unendurable to her, and that she could bear the odious presence of a police-man under the same roof with herself no longer. On being informed, half an hour since, that her departure would be delayed till two in the afternoon, she had flown into a violent passion. My lady, present at the time, had severely rebuked her, and then (having apparently something to say, which was reserved for her daughter's private ear) had sent Penelope out of the room. My girl was in wretchedly low spirits about the changed state of things in the house. 'Nothing goes right, father; nothing is like what it used to be. I feel as if some dreadful misfortune was hanging over us all.'

That was my feeling too. But I put a good face on it, before my daughter. Miss Rachel's bell rang while we were talking. Penelope ran up the back stairs to go on with the packing. I went by the other way to the hall, to see what the glass said about the change in the weather.

Just as I approached the swing-door leading into the hall from the servants' offices, it was violently opened from the other side; and Rosanna Spearman ran by me, with a miserable look of pain in her face, and one of her hands pressed hard over her heart, as if the pang was in that quarter. 'What's the matter, my girl?' I asked, stopping her. 'Are you ill?' 'For God's sake, don't speak to me,' she answered, and twisted herself out of my hands, and ran on towards the servants' staircase. I called to the cook (who was within hearing) to look after the poor girl. Two other persons proved to be within hearing, as well as the cook. Sergeant Cuff darted softly out of my room, and asked what was the matter. I answered 'Nothing.' Mr Franklin, on the other side, pulled open the swing-door, and beckoning me into the hall, inquired if I had seen anything of Rosanna Spearman.

'She has just passed me, sir, with a very disturbed face, and in a very odd manner.'

'I am afraid I am innocently the cause of that disturbance, Betteredge.'

'You, sir!'

'I can't explain it,' says Mr Franklin; 'but, if the girl *is* concerned in the loss of the Diamond, I do really believe she was on the point of confessing everything—to me, of all the people in the world—not two minutes since.'

Looking towards the swing-door, as he said those last words, I fancied I saw it opened a little way from the inner side.

Was there anybody listening? The door fell to, before I could get to it. Looking through, the moment after, I thought I saw the tails of Sergeant Cuff's respectable black coat disappearing round the corner of the passage. He knew, as well as I did, that he could expect no more help from me, now that I had discovered the turn which his investigations were really taking. Under those circumstances, it was quite in his character to help himself, and to do it by the underground way.

Not feeling sure that I had really seen the Sergeant—and not desiring to make needless mischief, where, Heaven knows, there was mischief enough going on already—I told Mr Franklin that I thought one of the dogs had got into the house—and then begged him to describe what had happened between Rosanna and himself.

'Were you passing through the hall, sir?' I asked. 'Did you meet her accidentally, when she spoke to you?'

Mr Franklin pointed to the billiard-table.

'I was knocking the balls about,' he said, 'and trying to get this miserable business of the Diamond out of my mind. I happened to look up—and there stood Rosanna Spearman at the side of me, like a ghost! Her stealing on me in that way was so strange, that I hardly knew what to do at first. Seeing a very anxious expression in her face, I asked her if she wished to speak to me. She answered, "Yes, if I dare." Knowing what suspicion attached to her, I could only put one construction on such language as that. I confess it made me uncomfortable. I had no wish to invite the girl's confidence. At the same time, in the difficulties that now beset us, I could hardly feel justified in refusing to listen to her, if she was really bent on speaking to me. It was an awkward position; and I dare say I got out of it awkwardly enough. I said to her, "I don't quite understand you. Is there anything you want me to do?" Mind, Betteredge, I didn't speak unkindly! The poor girl can't help being ugly—I felt that, at the time. The cue was still in my hand, and I went on knocking the balls about, to take off the awkwardness of the thing. As it turned out, I only made matters worse still. I'm afraid I mortified her without meaning it! She suddenly turned away. "He looks at the billiard balls," I heard her say. "Anything rather than look at *me*!" Before I could stop her, she had left the hall. I am not quite easy about it, Betteredge. Would you mind telling Rosanna that I meant no unkindness? I have been a little hard on her, perhaps, in my own thoughts—I have almost hoped that the loss of the Diamond might be traced to *her*. Not from any ill-will to the poor girl: but—' He stopped there, and going back to the billiard-table, began to knock the balls about once more.

After what had passed between the Sergeant and me, I knew what it was that he had left unspoken as well as he knew it himself.

Nothing but the tracing of the Moonstone to our second housemaid could now raise Miss Rachel above the infamous suspicion that rested on her in the mind of Sergeant Cuff. It was no longer a question of quieting my young lady's nervous excitement; it was a question of proving her innocence. If Rosanna had done nothing to compromise herself, the hope which Mr Franklin confessed to having felt would have been hard enough on her in all conscience. But this was not the case. She had pretended to be ill, and had gone secretly to Frizinghall. She had been up all night, making something or destroying something, in private. And she had been at the Shivering Sand, that evening, under circumstances which were highly suspicious, to say the least of them. For all these reasons (sorry as I was for Rosanna) I could not but think that Mr Franklin's way of looking at the matter was neither unnatural nor unreasonable, in Mr Franklin's position. I said a word to him to that effect.

'Yes, yes!' he said in return. 'But there is just a chance—a very poor one, certainly— that Rosanna's conduct may admit of some explanation which we don't see at present. I hate hurting a woman's feelings, Betteredge! Tell the poor creature what I told you to tell her. And if she wants to speak to me—I don't care whether I get into a scrape or not— send her to me in the library.' With those kind words he laid down the cue and left me.

Inquiry at the servants' offices informed me that Rosanna had retired to her own room. She had declined all offers of assistance with thanks, and had only asked to be left to rest in quiet. Here, therefore, was an end of any confession on her part (supposing she really had a confession to make) for that night. I reported the result to Mr Franklin, who, thereupon, left the library, and went up to bed.

I was putting the lights out, and making the windows fast, when Samuel came in with news of the two guests whom I had left in my room.

The argument about the white moss rose had apparently come to an end at last. The gardener had gone home, and Sergeant Cuff was nowhere to be found in the lower regions of the house.

I looked into my room. Quite true—nothing was to be discovered there but a couple of empty tumblers and a strong smell of hot grog. Had the Sergeant gone of his own accord to the bed-chamber that was prepared for him? I went upstairs to see.

After reaching the second landing, I thought I heard a sound of quiet and regular breathing on my left-hand side. My left-hand side led to the corridor which communicated with Miss Rachel's room. I looked in, and there, coiled up on three chairs placed right across the passage—there, with a red handkerchief tied round his grizzled head, and his respectable black coat rolled up for a pillow, lay and slept Sergeant Cuff!

He woke, instantly and quietly, like a dog, the moment I approached him.

'Good-night, Mr Betteredge,' he said. 'And mind, if you ever take to growing roses, the white moss rose is all the better for *not* being budded on the dog-rose, whatever the gardener may say to the contrary!'

'What are you doing here?' I asked. 'Why are you not in your proper bed?'

'I am not in my proper bed,' answered the Sergeant, 'because I am one of the many people in this miserable world who can't earn their money honestly and easily at the same time. There was a coincidence, this evening, between the period of Rosanna Spearman's return from the Sands and the period when Miss Verinder stated her resolution to leave the house. Whatever Rosanna may have hidden, it's clear to my mind that your young lady couldn't go away until she knew that it *was* hidden. The two must have communicated privately once already to-night. If they try to communicate again, when the house is quiet, I want to be in the way, and stop it. Don't blame me for upsetting your sleeping arrangements, Mr Betteredge—blame the Diamond.'

'I wish to God the Diamond had never found its way into this house!' I broke out.

Sergeant Cuff looked with a rueful face at the three chairs on which he had condemned himself to pass the night.

'So do I,' he said, gravely.

CHAPTER 17

Nothing happened in the night; and (I am happy to add) no attempt at communication between Miss Rachel and Rosanna rewarded the vigilance of Sergeant Cuff.

I had expected the Sergeant to set off for Frizinghall the first thing in the morning. He waited about, however, as if he had something else to do first. I left him to his own devices; and going into the grounds shortly after, met Mr Franklin on his favourite walk by the shrubbery side.

Before we had exchanged two words, the Sergeant unexpectedly joined us. He made up to Mr Franklin, who received him, I must own, haughtily enough. 'Have you anything to say to me?' was all the return he got for politely wishing Mr Franklin good morning.

'I have something to say to you, sir,' answered the Sergeant, 'on the subject of the inquiry I am conducting here. You detected the turn that inquiry was really taking, yesterday. Naturally enough, in your position, you are shocked and distressed. Naturally enough, also, you visit your own angry sense of your own family scandal upon me.'

'What do you want?' Mr Franklin broke in, sharply enough.

'I want to remind you, sir, that I have at any rate, thus far, not been *proved* to be wrong. Bearing that in mind, be pleased to remember, at the same time, that I am an officer of the law acting here under the sanction of the mistress of the house. Under these circumstances, is it, or is it not, your duty as a good citizen, to assist me with any special information which you may happen to possess?'

'I possess no special information,' says Mr Franklin.

Sergeant Cuff put that answer by him, as if no answer had been made.

'You may save my time, sir, from being wasted on an inquiry at a distance,' he went on, 'if you choose to understand me and speak out.'

'I don't understand you,' answered Mr Franklin; 'and I have nothing to say.'

'One of the female servants (I won't mention names) spoke to you privately, sir, last night.'

Once more Mr Franklin cut him short; once more Mr Franklin answered, 'I have nothing to say.'

Standing by in silence, I thought of the movement in the swing-door on the previous evening, and of the coat-tails which I had seen disappearing down the passage. Sergeant Cuff had, no doubt, just heard enough, before I interrupted him, to make him suspect that Rosanna had relieved her mind by confessing something to Mr Franklin Blake.

This notion had barely struck me—when who should appear at the end of the shrubbery walk but Rosanna Spearman in her own proper person! She was followed by Penelope, who was evidently trying to make her retrace her steps to the house. Seeing that Mr Franklin was not alone, Rosanna came to a standstill, evidently in great perplexity what to do next. Penelope waited behind her. Mr Franklin saw the girls as soon as I saw them. The Sergeant, with his devilish cunning, took on not to have noticed them at all. All this happened in an instant. Before either Mr Franklin or I could say a word, Sergeant Cuff struck in smoothly, with an appearance of continuing the previous conversation.

'You needn't be afraid of harming the girl, sir,' he said to Mr Franklin, speaking in a loud voice, so that Rosanna might hear him. 'On the contrary, I recommend you to honour me with your confidence, if you feel any interest in Rosanna Spearman.'

Mr Franklin instantly took on not to have noticed the girls either. He answered, speaking loudly on his side:

'I take no interest whatever in Rosanna Spearman.'

I looked towards the end of the walk. All I saw at the distance was that Rosanna suddenly turned round, the moment Mr Franklin had spoken. Instead of resisting Penelope, as she had done the moment before, she now let my daughter take her by the arm and lead her back to the house.

The breakfast-bell rang as the two girls disappeared—and even Sergeant Cuff was now obliged to give it up as a bad job! He said to me quietly, 'I shall go to Frizinghall, Mr Betteredge; and I shall be back before two.' He went his way without a word more—and for some few hours we were well rid of him.

'You must make it right with Rosanna,' Mr Franklin said to me, when we were alone. 'I seem to be fated to say or do something awkward, before that unlucky girl. You must have seen yourself that Sergeant Cuff laid a trap for both of us. If he could confuse *me*, or irritate *her* into breaking out, either she or I might have said something which would answer his purpose. On the spur of the moment, I saw no better way out of it than the way I took. It stopped the girl from saying anything, and it showed the Sergeant that I saw through him. He was evidently listening, Betteredge, when I was speaking to you last night.'

He had done worse than listen, as I privately thought to myself. He had remembered my telling him that the girl was in love with Mr Franklin; and he had calculated on *that*, when he appealed to Mr Franklin's interest in Rosanna—in Rosanna's hearing.

'As to listening, sir,' I remarked (keeping the other point to myself), 'we shall all be rowing in the same boat, if this sort of thing goes on much longer. Prying, and peeping, and listening are the natural occupations of people situated as we are. In another day or two, Mr Franklin, we shall all be struck dumb together—for this reason, that we shall all be listening to surprise each other's secrets, and all know it. Excuse my breaking out, sir. The horrid mystery hanging over us in this house gets into my head like liquor, and makes me wild. I won't forget what you have told me. I'll take the first opportunity of making it right with Rosanna Spearman.'

'You haven't said anything to her yet about last night, have you?' Mr Franklin asked.

'No, sir.'

'Then say nothing now. I had better not invite the girl's confidence, with the Sergeant on the look-out to surprise us together. My conduct is not very consistent, Betteredge—is it? I see no way out of this business, which isn't dreadful to think of, unless the Diamond is traced to Rosanna. And yet I can't, and won't, help Sergeant Cuff to find the girl out.'

Unreasonable enough, no doubt. But it was my state of mind as well. I thoroughly understood him. If you will, for once in your life, remember that you are mortal, perhaps you will thoroughly understand him too.

The state of things, indoors and out, while Sergeant Cuff was on his way to Frizinghall, was briefly this:

Miss Rachel waited for the time when the carriage was to take her to her aunt's, still obstinately shut up in her own room. My lady and Mr Franklin breakfasted together. After breakfast, Mr Franklin took one of his sudden resolutions, and went out precipitately to quiet his mind by a long walk. I was the only person who saw him go; and he told me he should be back before the Sergeant returned. The change in the weather, foreshadowed overnight, had come. Heavy rain had been followed, soon after dawn, by high wind. It was blowing fresh as the day got on. But though the clouds threatened more than once, the rain still held off. It was not a bad day for a walk, if you were young and strong, and could breast the great gusts of wind which came sweeping in from the sea.

I attended my lady after breakfast, and assisted her in the settlement of our household accounts. She only once alluded to the matter of the Moonstone, and that was in the way of forbidding any present mention of it between us. 'Wait till that man comes back,' she said, meaning the Sergeant. 'We *must* speak of it then: we are not obliged to speak of it now.'

After leaving my mistress, I found Penelope waiting for me in my room.

'I wish, father, you would come and speak to Rosanna,' she said. 'I am very uneasy about her.'

I suspected what was the matter readily enough. But it is a maxim of mine that men (being superior creatures) are bound to improve women—if they can. When a woman wants me to do anything (my daughter, or not, it doesn't matter), I always insist on knowing why. The oftener you make them rummage their own minds for a reason, the more manageable you will find them in all the relations of life. It isn't their fault (poor wretches!) that they act first, and think afterwards; it's the fault of the fools who humour them.

Penelope's reason why, on this occasion, may be given in her own words. 'I am afraid, father,' she said, 'Mr Franklin has hurt Rosanna cruelly, without intending it.'

'What took Rosanna into the shrubbery walk?' I asked.

'Her own madness,' says Penelope; 'I can call it nothing else. She was bent on speaking to

Mr Franklin, this morning, come what might of it. I did my best to stop her; you saw that. If I could only have got her away before she heard those dreadful words—'

'There! there!' I said, 'don't lose your head. I can't call to mind that anything happened to alarm Rosanna.'

'Nothing to alarm her, father. But Mr Franklin said he took no interest whatever in her—and, oh, he said it in such a cruel voice!'

'He said it to stop the Sergeant's mouth,' I answered.

'I told her that,' says Penelope. 'But you see, father (though Mr Franklin isn't to blame), he's been mortifying and disappointing her for weeks and weeks past; and now this comes on the top of it all! She has no right, of course, to expect him to take any interest in her. It's quite monstrous that she should forget herself and her station in that way. But she seems to have lost pride, and proper feeling, and everything. She frightened me, father, when Mr Franklin said those words. They seemed to turn her into stone. A sudden quiet came over her, and she has gone about her work, ever since, like a woman in a dream.'

I began to feel a little uneasy. There was something in the way Penelope put it which silenced my superior sense. I called to mind, now my thoughts were directed that way, what had passed between Mr Franklin and Rosanna overnight. She looked cut to the heart on that occasion; and now, as ill-luck would have it, she had been unavoidably stung again, poor soul, on the tender place. Sad! sad!—all the more sad because the girl had no reason to justify her, and no right to feel it.

I had promised Mr Franklin to speak to Rosanna, and this seemed the fittest time for keeping my word.

We found the girl sweeping the corridor outside the bedrooms, pale and composed, and neat as ever in her modest print dress. I noticed a curious dimness and dullness in her eyes—not as if she had been crying, but as if she had been looking at something too long. Possibly, it was a misty something raised by her own thoughts. There was certainly no object about her to look at which she had not seen already hundreds on hundreds of times.

'Cheer up, Rosanna!' I said. 'You mustn't fret over your own fancies. I have got something to say to you from Mr Franklin.'

I thereupon put the matter in the right view before her, in the friendliest and most comforting words I could find. My principles, in regard to the other sex, are, as you may have noticed, very severe. But somehow or other, when I come face to face with the women, my practice (I own) is not conformable.

'Mr Franklin is very kind and considerate. Please to thank him.' That was all the answer she made me.

My daughter had already noticed that Rosanna went about her work like a woman in a dream. I now added to this observation, that she also listened and spoke like a woman in a dream. I doubted if her mind was in a fit condition to take in what I had said to her.

'Are you quite sure, Rosanna, that you understand me?' I asked.

'Quite sure.'

She echoed me, not like a living woman, but like a creature moved by machinery. She went on sweeping all the time. I took away the broom as gently and as kindly as I could.

'Come, come, my girl!' I said, 'this is not like yourself. You have got something on your mind. I'm your friend—and I'll stand your friend, even if you have done wrong. Make a clean breast of it, Rosanna—make a clean breast of it!'

The time had been, when my speaking to her in that way would have brought the tears into her eyes. I could see no change in them now.

'Yes,' she said, 'I'll make a clean breast of it.'

'To my lady?' I asked.

'No.'

'To Mr Franklin?'

'Yes; to Mr Franklin.'

I hardly knew what to say to that. She was in no condition to understand the caution against speaking to him in private, which Mr Franklin had directed me to give her. Feeling my way, little by little, I only told her Mr Franklin had gone out for a walk.

'It doesn't matter,' she answered. 'I shan't trouble Mr Franklin, to-day.'

'Why not speak to my lady?' I said. 'The way to relieve your mind is to speak to the merciful and Christian mistress who has always been kind to you.'

She looked at me for a moment with a grave and steady attention, as if she was fixing what I said in her mind. Then she took the broom out of my hands; and moved off with it slowly, a little way down the corridor.

'No,' she said, going on with her sweeping, and speaking to herself; 'I know a better way of relieving my mind than that.'

'What is it?'

'Please to let me go on with my work.'

Penelope followed her, and offered to help her.

She answered, 'No. I want to do my work. Thank you, Penelope.' She looked round at me. 'Thank you, Mr Betteredge.'

There was no moving her—there was nothing more to be said. I signed to Penelope to come away with me. We left her, as we had found her, sweeping the corridor, like a woman in a dream.

'This is a matter for the doctor to look into,' I said. 'It's beyond me.'

My daughter reminded me of Mr Candy's illness, owing (as you may remember) to the chill he had caught on the night of the dinner-party. His assistant—a certain Mr Ezra Jennings—was at our disposal, to be sure. But nobody knew much about him in our parts. He had been engaged by Mr Candy, under rather peculiar circumstances; and, right or wrong, we none of us liked him or trusted him. There were other doctors at Frizinghall. But they were strangers to our house; and Penelope doubted, in Rosanna's present state, whether strangers might not do her more harm than good.

I thought of speaking to my lady. But, remembering the heavy weight of anxiety which she already had on her mind, I hesitated to add to all the other vexations this new trouble. Still, there was a necessity for doing something. The girl's state was, to my thinking, downright alarming—and my mistress ought to be informed of it. Unwilling enough, I went to her sitting-room. No one was there. My lady was shut up with Miss Rachel. It was impossible for me to see her till she came out again.

I waited in vain till the clock on the front staircase struck the quarter to two. Five minutes afterwards, I heard my name called, from the drive outside the house. I knew the voice directly. Sergeant Cuff had returned from Frizinghall.

CHAPTER 18

Going down to the front door, I met the Sergeant on the steps.

It went against the grain with me, after what had passed between us, to show him that I felt any sort of interest in his proceedings. In spite of myself, however, I felt an interest that there was no resisting. My sense of dignity sank from under me, and out came the words: 'What news from Frizinghall?'

'I have seen the Indians,' answered Sergeant Cuff. 'And I have found out what Rosanna bought privately in the town, on Thursday last. The Indians will be set free on Wednesday in next week. There isn't a doubt on my mind, and there isn't a doubt on Mr Murthwaite's mind, that they came to this place to steal the Moonstone. Their calculations were all thrown out, of course, by what happened in the house on Wednesday night; and they have no more to do with the actual loss of the jewel than you have. But I can tell you one thing, Mr Betteredge—if *we* don't find the Moonstone, *they* will. You have not heard the last of the three jugglers yet.'

Mr Franklin came back from his walk as the Sergeant said those startling words. Governing his curiosity better than I had governed mine, he passed us without a word, and went on into the house.

As for me, having already dropped my dignity, I determined to have the whole benefit of the sacrifice. 'So much for the Indians,' I said. 'What about Rosanna next?'

Sergeant Cuff shook his head.

'The mystery in that quarter is thicker than ever,' he said. 'I have traced her to a shop at Frizinghall, kept by a linendraper named Maltby. She bought nothing whatever at any of the other drapers' shops, or at any milliners' or tailors' shops; and she bought nothing at Maltby's but a piece of long cloth. She was very particular in choosing a certain quality. As to quantity, she bought enough to make a nightgown.'

'Whose nightgown?' I asked.

'Her own, to be sure. Between twelve and three, on the Thursday morning, she must have slipped down to your young lady's room, to settle the hiding of the Moonstone while all the rest of you were in bed. In going back to her own room, her nightgown must have brushed the wet paint on the door. She couldn't wash out the stain; and she couldn't safely destroy the nightgown without first providing another like it, to make the inventory of her linen complete.'

'What proves that it was Rosanna's nightgown?' I objected.

'The material she bought for making the substitute dress,' answered the Sergeant. 'If it had been Miss Verinder's nightgown, she would have had to buy lace, and frilling, and Lord knows what besides; and she wouldn't have had time to make it in one night. Plain long cloth means a plain servant's nightgown. No, no, Mr Betteredge—all that is clear enough. The pinch of the question is—why, after having provided the substitute dress, does she hide the smeared nightgown, instead of destroying it? If the girl won't speak out, there is only one way of settling the difficulty. The hiding-place at the Shivering Sand must be searched—and the true state of the case will be discovered there.'

'How are you to find the place?' I inquired.

'I am sorry to disappoint you,' said the Sergeant—'but that's a secret which I mean to keep to myself.'

(Not to irritate your curiosity, as he irritated mine, I may here inform you that he had come back from Frizinghall provided with a search-warrant. His experience in such matters told him that Rosanna was in all probability carrying about her a memorandum of the hiding-place, to guide her, in case she returned to it, under changed circumstances and after a lapse of time. Possessed of this memorandum, the Sergeant would be furnished with all that he could desire.)

'Now, Mr Betteredge,' he went on, 'suppose we drop speculation, and get to business. I told Joyce to have an eye on Rosanna. Where is Joyce?'

Joyce was the Frizinghall policeman, who had been left by Superintendent Seegrave at Sergeant Cuff's disposal. The clock struck two, as he put the question; and, punctual to the moment, the carriage came round to take Miss Rachel to her aunt's.

'One thing at a time,' said the Sergeant, stopping me as I was about to send in search of Joyce. 'I must attend to Miss Verinder first.'

As the rain was still threatening, it was the close carriage that had been appointed to take Miss Rachel to Frizinghall. Sergeant Cuff beckoned Samuel to come down to him from the rumble behind.

'You will see a friend of mine waiting among the trees, on this side of the lodge gate,' he said. 'My friend, without stopping the carriage, will get up into the rumble with you. You have nothing to do but to hold your tongue, and shut your eyes. Otherwise, you will get into trouble.'

With that advice, he sent the footman back to his place. What Samuel thought I don't know. It was plain, to my mind, that Miss Rachel was to be privately kept in view from the time when she left our house—if she did leave it. A watch set on my young lady! A spy behind her in the rumble of her mother's carriage! I could have cut my own tongue out for having forgotten myself so far as to speak to Sergeant Cuff.

The first person to come out of the house was my lady. She stood aside, on the top step, posting herself there to see what happened. Not a word did she say, either to the Sergeant or to me. With her lips closed, and her arms folded in the light garden cloak which she had wrapped round her on coming into the air, there she stood, as still as a statue, waiting for her daughter to appear.

In a minute more, Miss Rachel came downstairs—very nicely dressed in some soft yellow stuff, that set off her dark complexion, and clipped her tight (in the form of a jacket) round the waist. She had a smart little straw hat on her head, with a white veil twisted round it. She had primrose-coloured gloves that fitted her hands like a second skin. Her beautiful black hair looked as smooth as satin under her hat. Her little ears were like rosy shells—they had a pearl dangling from each of them. She came swiftly out to us, as straight as a lily on its stem, and as lithe and supple in every movement she made as a young cat. Nothing that I could discover was altered in her pretty face, but her eyes and her lips. Her eyes were brighter and fiercer than I liked to see; and her lips had so completely lost their colour and their smile that I hardly knew them again. She kissed her mother in a hasty and sudden manner on the cheek. She said, 'Try to forgive me, mamma'—and then pulled down her veil over her face so vehemently that she tore it. In another moment she had run down the steps, and had rushed into the carriage as if it was a hiding-place.

Sergeant Cuff was just as quick on his side. He put Samuel back, and stood before Miss

Rachel, with the open carriage-door in his hand, at the instant when she settled herself in her place.

'What do you want?' says Miss Rachel, from behind her veil.

'I want to say one word to you, miss,' answered the Sergeant, 'before you go. I can't presume to stop your paying a visit to your aunt. I can only venture to say that your leaving us, as things are now, puts an obstacle in the way of my recovering your Diamond. Please to understand that; and now decide for yourself whether you go or stay.'

Miss Rachel never even answered him. 'Drive on, James!' she called out to the coachman.

Without another word, the Sergeant shut the carriage-door. Just as he closed it, Mr Franklin came running down the steps. 'Goodbye, Rachel,' he said, holding out his hand.

'Drive on!' cried Miss Rachel, louder than ever, and taking no more notice of Mr Franklin than she had taken of Sergeant Cuff.

Mr Franklin stepped back thunderstruck, as well he might be. The coachman, not knowing what to do, looked towards my lady, still standing immovable on the top step. My lady, with anger and sorrow and shame all struggling together in her face, made him a sign to start the horses, and then turned back hastily into the house. Mr Franklin, recovering the use of his speech, called after her, as the carriage drove off, 'Aunt! you were quite right. Accept my thanks for all your kindness—and let me go.'

My lady turned as though to speak to him. Then, as if distrusting herself, waved her hand kindly. 'Let me see you, before you leave us, Franklin,' she said, in a broken voice—and went on to her own room.

'Do me a last favour, Betteredge,' says Mr Franklin, turning to me, with the tears in his eyes. 'Get me away to the train as soon as you can!'

He too went his way into the house. For the moment, Miss Rachel had completely unmanned him. Judge from that, how fond he must have been of her!

Sergeant Cuff and I were left face to face, at the bottom of the steps. The Sergeant stood with his face set towards a gap in the trees, commanding a view of one of the windings of the drive which led from the house. He had his hands in his pockets, and he was softly whistling 'The Last Rose of Summer' to himself.

'There's a time for everything,' I said, savagely enough. 'This isn't a time for whistling.'

At that moment, the carriage appeared in the distance, through the gap, on its way to the lodge-gate. There was another man, besides Samuel, plainly visible in the rumble behind.

'All right!' said the Sergeant to himself. He turned round to me. 'It's no time for whistling, Mr Betteredge, as you say. It's time to take this business in hand, now, without sparing anybody. We'll begin with Rosanna Spearman. Where is Joyce?'

We both called for Joyce, and received no answer. I sent one of the stable-boys to look for him.

'You heard what I said to Miss Verinder?' remarked the Sergeant, while we were waiting. 'And you saw how she received it? I tell her plainly that her leaving us will be an obstacle in the way of my recovering her Diamond—and she leaves, in the face of that statement! Your young lady has got a travelling companion in her mother's carriage, Mr Betteredge—and the name of it is, the Moonstone.'

I said nothing. I only held on like death to my belief in Miss Rachel.

The stable-boy came back, followed—very unwillingly, as it appeared to me—by Joyce.

'Where is Rosanna Spearman?' asked Sergeant Cuff.

'I can't account for it, sir,' Joyce began; 'and I am very sorry. But somehow or other—'

'Before I went to Frizinghall,' said the Sergeant, cutting him short, 'I told you to keep your eyes on Rosanna Spearman, without allowing her to discover that she was being watched. Do you mean to tell me that you have let her give you the slip?'

'I am afraid, sir,' says Joyce, beginning to tremble, 'that I was perhaps a little *too* careful not to let her discover me. There are such a many passages in the lower parts of this house—'

'How long is it since you missed her?'

'Nigh on an hour since, sir.'

'You can go back to your regular business at Frizinghall,' said the Sergeant, speaking just as composedly as ever, in his usual quiet and dreary way. 'I don't think your talents are at all in our line, Mr Joyce. Your present form of employment is a trifle beyond you. Good morning.'

The man slunk off. I find it very difficult to describe how I was affected by the discovery that Rosanna Spearman was missing. I seemed to be in fifty different minds about it, all at the same time. In that state, I stood staring at Sergeant Cuff—and my powers of language quite failed me.

'No, Mr Betteredge,' said the Sergeant, as if he had discovered the uppermost thought in me, and was picking it out to be answered, before all the rest. 'Your young friend, Rosanna, won't slip through my fingers so easy as you think. As long as I know where Miss Verinder is, I have the means at my disposal of tracing Miss Verinder's accomplice. I prevented them from communicating last night. Very good. They will get together at Frizinghall, instead of getting together here. The present inquiry must be simply shifted (rather sooner than I had anticipated) from this house, to the house at which Miss Verinder is visiting. In the meantime, I'm afraid I must trouble you to call the servants together again.'

I went round with him to the servants' hall. It is very disgraceful, but it is not the less true, that I had another attack of the detective-fever, when he said those last words. I forgot that I hated Sergeant Cuff. I seized him confidentially by the arm. I said, 'For goodness' sake, tell us what you are going to do with the servants now?'

The great Cuff stood stockstill, and addressed himself in a kind of melancholy rapture to the empty air.

'If this man,' said the Sergeant (apparently meaning me), 'only understood the growing of roses, he would be the most completely perfect character on the face of creation!' After that strong expression of feeling, he sighed, and put his arm through mine. 'This is how it stands,' he said, dropping down again to business. 'Rosanna has done one of two things. She has either gone direct to Frizinghall (before I can get there), or she has gone first to visit her hiding-place at the Shivering Sand. The first thing to find out is, which of the servants, saw the last of her before she left the house.'

On instituting this inquiry, it turned out that the last person who had set eyes on Rosanna was Nancy, the kitchenmaid.

Nancy had seen her slip out with a letter in her hand, and stop the butcher's man who had just been delivering some meat at the back door. Nancy had heard her ask the man to post the letter when he got back to Frizinghall. The man had looked at the address, and had said it was a round-about way of delivering a letter, directed to Cobb's Hole, to post it at Frizinghall—and that, moreover, on a Saturday, which would prevent the letter from getting to its destination until Monday morning. Rosanna had answered that the delivery of the letter being delayed till Monday was of no importance. The only thing she wished to be sure of was that the man would do what she told him. The man had promised to do it, and had driven away. Nancy had been called back to her work in the kitchen. And no other person had seen anything afterwards of Rosanna Spearman.

'Well?' I asked, when we were alone again.

'Well,' says the Sergeant. 'I must go to Frizinghall.'

'About the letter, sir?'

'Yes. The memorandum of the hiding-place is in that letter. I must see the address at the post-office. If it is the address I suspect, I shall pay our friend, Mrs Yolland, another visit on Monday next.'

I went with the Sergeant to order the pony-chaise. In the stable-yard we got a new light thrown on the missing girl.

CHAPTER 19

The news of Rosanna's disappearance had, as it appeared, spread among the out-of-door servants. They too had made their inquiries; and they had just laid hands on a quick little imp, nicknamed 'Duffy'—who was occasionally employed in weeding the garden, and who had seen Rosanna Spearman as lately as half an hour since. Duffy was certain that the girl had passed him in the fir-plantation, not walking, but *running*, in the direction of the sea-shore.

'Does this boy know the coast hereabouts?' asked Sergeant Cuff.

'He has been born and bred on the coast,' I answered.

'Duffy!' says the Sergeant, 'do you want to earn a shilling? If you do, come along with me. Keep the pony-chaise ready, Mr Betteredge, till I come back.'

He started for the Shivering Sand, at a rate that my legs (though well enough preserved for my time of life) had no hope of matching. Little Duffy, as the way is with the young savages in our parts when they are in high spirits, gave a howl, and trotted off at the Sergeant's heels.

Here again, I find it impossible to give anything like a clear account of the state of my mind in the interval after Sergeant Cuff had left us. A curious and stupefying restlessness got possession of me. I did a dozen different needless things in and out of the house, not one of which I can now remember. I don't even know how long it was after the Sergeant had gone to the sands, when Duffy came running back with a message for me. Sergeant Cuff had given the boy a leaf torn out of his pocket-book, on which was written in pencil, 'Send me one of Rosanna Spearman's boots, and be quick about it.'

I despatched the first woman-servant I could find to Rosanna's room; and I sent the boy back to say that I myself would follow him with the boot.

This, I am well aware, was not the quickest way to take of obeying the directions which I had received. But I was resolved to see for myself what new mystification was going on, before I trusted Rosanna's boot in the Sergeant's hands. My old notion of screening the girl, if I could, seemed to have come back on me again, at the eleventh hour. This state of feeling (to say nothing of the detective-fever) hurried me off, as soon as I had got the boot, at the nearest approach to a run which a man turned seventy can reasonably hope to make.

As I got near the shore, the clouds gathered black, and the rain came down, drifting in great white sheets of water before the wind. I heard the thunder of the sea on the sand-bank at the mouth of the bay. A little further on, I passed the boy crouching for shelter under the lee of the sand-hills. Then I saw the raging sea, and the rollers tumbling in on the sand-bank, and the driven rain sweeping over the waters like a flying garment; and the yellow wilderness of the beach with one solitary black figure standing on it—the figure of Sergeant Cuff.

He waved his hand towards the north, when he first saw me. 'Keep on that side' he shouted. 'And come on down here to me!'

I went down to him, choking for breath, with my heart leaping as if it was like to leap out of me. I was past speaking. I had a hundred questions to put to him; and not one of them would pass my lips. His face frightened me. I saw a look in his eyes which was a look of horror. He snatched the boot out of my hand, and set it in a footmark on the sand, bearing south from us as we stood, and pointing straight towards the rocky ledge called the South Spit. The mark was not yet blurred out by the rain—and the girl's boot fitted it to a hair.

The Sergeant pointed to the boot in the footmark, without saying a word.

I caught at his arm, and tried to speak to him, and failed as I had failed when I tried before. He went on, following the footsteps down and down to where the rocks and the sand joined. The South Spit was just awash with the flowing tide; the waters heaved over the hidden face of the Shivering Sand. Now this way and now that, with an obstinate patience that was dreadful to see, Sergeant Cuff tried the boot in the footsteps, and always found it pointing the same way—straight *to* the rocks. Hunt as he might, no sign could he find anywhere of the footsteps walking *from* them.

He gave it up at last. Still keeping silence, he looked again at me; and then he looked out at the waters before us, heaving in deeper and deeper over the quicksand. I looked where he looked—and I saw his thought in his face. A dreadful dumb trembling crawled all over me on a sudden. I fell upon my knees on the beach.

'She has been back at the hiding-place,' I heard the Sergeant say to himself. 'Some fatal accident has happened to her on those rocks.'

The girl's altered looks, and words, and actions—the numbed, deadened way in which she listened to me, and spoke to me—when I had found her sweeping the corridor but a few hours since, rose up in my mind, and warned me, even as the Sergeant spoke, that his guess was wide of the dreadful truth. I tried to tell him of the fear that had frozen me up. I tried to say, 'The death she has died, Sergeant, was a death of her own seeking.' No! the words wouldn't come. The dumb trembling held me in its grip. I couldn't feel the driving rain. I couldn't see the rising tide. As in the vision of a dream, the poor lost creature came back before me. I saw her again as I had seen her in the past time—on the morning when I went to fetch her into the house. I heard her again, telling me that the Shivering Sand seemed to draw her to it against her will, and wondering whether her grave was waiting for her *there*. The horror of it struck at me, in some unfathomable way, through my own child. My girl was just her age. My girl, tried as Rosanna was tried, might have lived that miserable life, and died this dreadful death.

The Sergeant kindly lifted me up, and turned me away from the sight of the place where she had perished.

With that relief, I began to fetch my breath again, and to see things about me, as things really were. Looking towards the sand-hills, I saw the men-servants from out-of-doors, and the fisherman, named Yolland, all running down to us together; and all, having taken the alarm, calling out to know if the girl had been found. In the fewest words, the Sergeant showed them the evidence of the footmarks, and told them that a fatal accident must have happened to her. He then picked out the fisherman from the rest, and put a question to him, turning about again towards the sea: 'Tell me,' he said. 'Could a boat have taken her off, in such weather as this, from those rocks where her footmarks stop?'

The fisherman pointed to the rollers tumbling in on the sandbank, and to the great waves leaping up in clouds of foam against the headlands on either side of us.

'No boat that ever was built,' he answered, 'could have got to her through *that*.'

Sergeant Cuff looked for the last time at the footmarks on the sand, which the rain was now fast blurring out.

'There,' he said, 'is the evidence that she can't have left this place by land. And here,' he went on, looking at the fisherman, 'is the evidence that she can't have got away by sea.' He stopped, and considered for a minute. 'She was seen running towards this place, half an hour before I got here from the house,' he said to Yolland. 'Some time has passed since then. Call it, altogether, an hour ago. How high would the water be, at that time, on this side of the rocks?' He pointed to the south side—otherwise, the side which was not filled up by the quicksand.

'As the tide makes to-day,' said the fisherman, 'there wouldn't have been water enough to drown a kitten on that side of the Spit, an hour since.'

Sergeant Cuff turned about northward, towards the quicksand.

'How much on this side?' he asked.

'Less still,' answered Yolland. 'The Shivering Sand would have been just awash, and no more.'

The Sergeant turned to me, and said that the accident must have happened on the side of the quicksand. My tongue was loosened at that. 'No accident!' I told him. 'When she came to this place, she came, weary of her life, to end it here.'

He started back from me. 'How do you know?' he asked. The rest of them crowded round. The Sergeant recovered himself instantly. He put them back from me; he said I was an old man; he said the discovery had shaken me; he said, 'Let him alone a little.' Then he turned to Yolland, and asked, 'Is there any chance of finding her, when the tide ebbs again?' And Yolland answered, 'None. What the Sand gets, the Sand keeps for ever.' Having said that, the fisherman came a step nearer, and addressed himself to me.

'Mr Betteredge,' he said, 'I have a word to say to you about the young woman's death. Four foot out, broadwise, along the side of the Spit, there's a shelf of rock, about half a fathom down under the sand. My question is—why didn't she strike that? If she slipped, by accident, from off the Spit, she fell in where there's foothold at the bottom, at a depth that would barely cover her to the waist. She must have waded out, or jumped out, into the Deeps beyond—or she wouldn't be missing now. No accident, sir! The Deeps of the Quicksand have got her. And they have got her by her own act.'

After that testimony from a man whose knowledge was to be relied on, the Sergeant was silent. The rest of us, like him, held our peace. With one accord, we all turned back up the slope of the beach.

At the sandhillocks we were met by the under-groom, running to us from the house. The lad is a good lad, and has an honest respect for me. He handed me a little note, with a decent sorrow in his face. 'Penelope sent me with this, Mr Betteredge,' he said. 'She found it in Rosanna's room.'

It was her last farewell word to the old man who had done his best—thank God, always done his best—to befriend her.

'You have often forgiven me, Mr Betteredge, in past times. When you next see the Shivering Sand, try to forgive me once more. I have found my grave where my grave was waiting for me. I have lived, and died, sir, grateful for your kindness.'

There was no more than that. Little as it was, I hadn't manhood enough to hold up against it. Your tears come easy, when you're young, and beginning the world. Your tears come easy, when you're old, and leaving it. I burst out crying.

Sergeant Cuff took a step nearer to me—meaning kindly, I don't doubt. I shrank back from him. 'Don't touch me,' I said. 'It's the dread of you, that has driven her to it.'

'You are wrong, Mr Betteredge,' he answered, quietly. 'But there will be time enough to speak of it when we are indoors again.'

I followed the rest of them, with the help of the groom's arm. Through the driving rain we went back—to meet the trouble and the terror that were waiting for us at the house.

CHAPTER 20

Those in front had spread the news before us. We found the servants in a state of panic. As we passed my lady's door, it was thrown open violently from the inner side. My mistress came out among us (with Mr Franklin following, and trying vainly to compose her), quite beside herself with the horror of the thing.

'You are answerable for this!' she cried out, threatening the Sergeant wildly with her hand. 'Gabriel! give that wretch his money—and release me from the sight of him!'

The Sergeant was the only one among us who was fit to cope with her—being the only one among us who was in possession of himself.

'I am no more answerable for this distressing calamity, my lady, than you are,' he said.

'If, in half an hour from this, you still insist on my leaving the house, I will accept your ladyship's dismissal, but not your ladyship's money.'

It was spoken very respectfully, but very firmly at the same time —and it had its effect on my mistress as well as on me. She suffered Mr Franklin to lead her back into the room. As the door closed on the two, the Sergeant, looking about among the women-servants in his observant way, noticed that while all the rest were merely frightened, Penelope was in tears. 'When your father has changed his wet clothes,' he said to her, 'come and speak to us, in your father's room.'

Before the half-hour was out, I had got my dry clothes on, and had lent Sergeant Cuff such change of dress as he required. Penelope came in to us to hear what the Sergeant wanted with her. I don't think I ever felt what a good dutiful daughter I had, so strongly as I felt it at that moment. I took her and sat her on my knee—and I prayed God bless her. She hid her head on my bosom, and put her arms round my neck—and we waited a little while in silence. The poor dead girl must have been at the bottom of it, I think, with my daughter and with me. The Sergeant went to the window, and stood there looking out. I thought it right to thank him for considering us both in this way—and I did.

People in high life have all the luxuries to themselves—among others, the luxury of indulging their feelings. People in low life have no such privilege. Necessity, which spares our betters, has no pity on *us*. We learn to put our feelings back into ourselves, and to jog on with our duties as patiently as may be. I don't complain of this—I only notice it. Penelope and I were ready for the Sergeant, as soon as the Sergeant was ready on his side. Asked if she knew what had led her fellow-servant to destroy herself, my daughter answered (as you will foresee) that it was for love of Mr Franklin Blake. Asked next, if she had mentioned this notion of hers to any other person, Penelope answered, 'I have not mentioned it, for Rosanna's sake.' I felt it necessary to add a word to this. I said, 'And for Mr Franklin's sake, my dear, as well. If Rosanna *has* died for love of him, it is not with his knowledge or by his fault. Let him leave the house to-day, if he does leave it, without the useless pain of knowing the truth.' Sergeant Cuff said, 'Quite right,' and fell silent again; comparing Penelope's notion (as it seemed to me) with some other notion of his own which he kept to himself.

At the end of the half-hour, my mistress's bell rang.

On my way to answer it, I met Mr Franklin coming out of his aunt's sitting-room. He mentioned that her ladyship was ready to see Sergeant Cuff—in my presence as before— and he added that he himself wanted to say two words to the Sergeant first. On our way back to my room, he stopped, and looked at the railway time-table in the hall.

'Are you really going to leave us, sir?' I asked. 'Miss Rachel will surely come right again, if you only give her time?'

'She will come right again,' answered Mr Franklin, 'when she hears that I have gone away, and that she will see me no more.'

I thought he spoke in resentment of my young lady's treatment of him. But it was not so. My mistress had noticed, from the time when the police first came into the house, that the bare mention of him was enough to set Miss Rachel's temper in a flame. He had been too fond of his cousin to like to confess this to himself, until the truth had been forced on him, when she drove off to her aunt's. His eyes once opened in that cruel way which you know of, Mr Franklin had taken his resolution—the one resolution which a man of any spirit *could* take—to leave the house.

What he had to say to the Sergeant was spoken in my presence. He described her lady-ship as willing to acknowledge that she had spoken over-hastily. And he asked if Sergeant Cuff would consent—in that case—to accept his fee, and to leave the matter of the Diamond where the matter stood now. The Sergeant answered, 'No, sir. My fee is paid me for doing my duty. I decline to take it, until my duty is done.'

'I don't understand you,' says Mr Franklin.

'I'll explain myself, sir,' says the Sergeant. 'When I came here, I undertook to throw the necessary light on the matter of the missing Diamond. I am now ready, and waiting, to redeem my pledge. When I have stated the case to Lady Verinder as the case now stands, and when I have told her plainly what course of action to take for the recovery of the Moonstone, the responsibility will be off my shoulders. Let her ladyship decide, after that, whether she does, or does not, allow me to go on. I shall then have done what I undertook to do—and I'll take my fee.'

In those words Sergeant Cuff reminded us that, even in the Detective Police, a man may have a reputation to lose.

The view he took was so plainly the right one, that there was no more to be said. As I rose to conduct him to my lady's room, he asked if Mr Franklin wished to be present. Mr Franklin answered, 'Not unless Lady Verinder desires it.' He added, in a whisper to me, as I was following the Sergeant out, 'I know what that man is going to say about Rachel; and I am too fond of her to hear it, and keep my temper. Leave me by myself.'

I left him, miserable enough, leaning on the sill of my window, with his face hidden in his hands—and Penelope peeping through the door, longing to comfort him. In Mr Franklin's place, I should have called her in. When you are ill-used by one woman, there is great comfort in telling it to another—because, nine times out of ten, the other always takes your side. Per-haps, when my back was turned, he did call her in? In that case, it is only doing my daughter justice to declare that she would stick at nothing, in the way of comforting Mr Franklin Blake.

In the meantime, Sergeant Cuff and I proceeded to my lady's room.

At the last conference we had held with her, we had found her not over willing to lift her eyes from the book which she had on the table. On this occasion there was a change for the better. She met the Sergeant's eye with an eye that was as steady as his own. The family spirit showed itself in every line of her face; and I knew that Sergeant Cuff would meet his match, when a woman like my mistress was strung up to hear the worst he could say to her.

CHAPTER 21

The first words, when we had taken our seats, were spoken by my lady.

'Sergeant Cuff,' she said, 'there was perhaps some excuse for the inconsiderate manner in which I spoke to you half an hour since. I have no wish, however, to claim that excuse. I say, with perfect sincerity, that I regret it, if I wronged you.'

The grace of voice and manner with which she made him that atonement had its due effect on the Sergeant. He requested permission to justify himself—putting his justification as an act of respect to my mistress. It was impossible, he said, that he could be in any way responsible for the calamity which had shocked us all, for this sufficient reason, that his success in bringing his inquiry to its proper end depended on his neither saying nor doing anything that could alarm Rosanna Spearman. He appealed to me to testify whether he had, or had not, carried that object out. I could, and did, bear witness that he had. And there, as I thought, the matter might have been judiciously left to come to an end.

Sergeant Cuff, however, took it a step further, evidently (as you shall now judge) with the purpose of forcing the most painful of all possible explanations to take place between her ladyship and himself.

'I have heard a motive assigned for the young woman's suicide,' said the Sergeant, 'which may possibly be the right one. It is a motive quite unconnected with the case which I am conducting here. I am bound to add, however, that my own opinion points the other way. Some unbearable anxiety in connection with the missing Diamond, has, I believe, driven the poor creature to her own destruction. I don't pretend to know what that unbearable anxiety may have been. But I think (with your ladyship's permission) I can lay my hand on a person who is capable of deciding whether I am right or wrong.'

'Is the person now in the house?' my mistress asked, after waiting a little.

'The person has left the house, my lady.'

That answer pointed as straight to Miss Rachel as straight could be. A silence dropped on us which I thought would never come to an end. Lord! how the wind howled, and how the rain drove at the window, as I sat there waiting for one or other of them to speak again!

'Be so good as to express yourself plainly,' said my lady. 'Do you refer to my daughter?'

'I do,' said Sergeant Cuff, in so many words.

My mistress had her cheque-book on the table when we entered the room—no doubt to pay the Sergeant his fee. She now put it back in the drawer. It went to my heart to see how her poor hand trembled—the hand that had loaded her old servant with benefits; the hand that, I pray God, may take mine, when my time comes, and I leave my place for ever!

'I had hoped,' said my lady, very slowly and quietly, 'to have recompensed your services, and to have parted with you without Miss Verinder's name having been openly mentioned between us as it has been mentioned now. My nephew has probably said something of this, before you came into my room?'

'Mr Blake gave his message, my lady. And I gave Mr Blake a reason—'

'It is needless to tell me your reason. After what you have just said, you know as well as I do that you have gone too far to go back. I owe it to myself, and I owe it to my child, to insist on your remaining here, and to insist on your speaking out.'

The Sergeant looked at his watch.

'If there had been time, my lady,' he answered, 'I should have preferred writing my report, instead of communicating it by word of mouth. But, if this inquiry is to go on, time is of too much importance to be wasted in writing. I am ready to go into the matter at once. It is a very painful matter for me to speak of, and for you to hear—'

There my mistress stopped him once more.

'I may possibly make it less painful to you, and to my good servant and friend here,' she said, 'if I set the example of speaking boldly, on my side. You suspect Miss Verinder of deceiving us all, by secreting the Diamond for some purpose of her own? Is that true?'

'Quite true, my lady.'

'Very well. Now, before you begin, I have to tell you, as Miss Verinder's mother, that she is *absolutely incapable* of doing what you suppose her to have done. Your knowledge of her character dates from a day or two since. My knowledge of her character dates from the beginning of her life. State your suspicion of her as strongly as you please—it is impossible that you can offend me by doing so. I am sure, beforehand, that (with all your experience) the circumstances have fatally misled you in this case. Mind! I am in possession of no private information. I am as absolutely shut out of my daughter's confidence as you are. My one reason for speaking positively, is the reason you have heard already. I know my child.'

She turned to me, and gave me her hand. I kissed it in silence. 'You may go on,' she said, facing the Sergeant again as steadily as ever.

Sergeant Cuff bowed. My mistress had produced but one effect on him. His hatchet-face softened for a moment, as if he was sorry for her. As to shaking him in his own conviction, it was plain to see that she had not moved him by a single inch. He settled himself in his chair; and he began his vile attack on Miss Rachel's character in these words:

'I must ask your ladyship,' he said, 'to look this matter in the face, from my point of view as well as from yours. Will you please to suppose yourself coming down here, in my place, and with my experience? and will you allow me to mention very briefly what that experience has been?'

My mistress signed to him that she would do this. The Sergeant went on:

'For the last twenty years,' he said, 'I have been largely employed in cases of family scandal, acting in the capacity of confidential man. The one result of my domestic practice which has any bearing on the matter now in hand, is a result which I may state in two words. It is well within my experience, that young ladies of rank and position do occasionally have private debts which they dare not acknowledge to their nearest relatives and friends. Sometimes, the milliner and the jeweller are at the bottom of it. Sometimes, the money is wanted for purposes which I don't suspect in this case, and which I won't shock you by mentioning. Bear in mind what I have said, my lady—and now let us see how events in this house have forced me back on my own experience, whether I liked it or not!'

He considered with himself for a moment, and went on—with a horrid clearness that obliged you to understand him; with an abominable justice that favoured nobody.

'My first information relating to the loss of the Moonstone,' said the Sergeant, 'came to me from Superintendent Seegrave. He proved to my complete satisfaction that he was perfectly incapable of managing the case. The one thing he said which struck me as worth listening to, was this—that Miss Verinder had declined to be questioned by him, and had spoken to him with a perfectly incomprehensible rudeness and contempt. I thought this curious—but I attributed it mainly to some clumsiness on the Superintendent's part which might have offended the young lady. After that, I put it by in my mind, and applied myself, single-handed, to the case. It ended, as you are aware, in the discovery of the smear on the door, and in Mr Franklin Blake's evidence satisfying me, that this same smear, and the loss of the Diamond, were pieces of the same puzzle. So far, if I suspected anything, I suspected that the Moonstone had been stolen, and that one of the servants might prove to be the thief. Very good. In this state of things, what happens? Miss Verinder suddenly comes out of her room, and speaks to me. I observe three suspicious appearances in that young lady. She is still violently agitated, though more than four-and-twenty hours have passed since the Diamond was lost. She treats me, as she has already treated Superintendent Seegrave. And she is mortally offended with Mr Franklin Blake. Very good again. Here (I say to myself) is a young lady who has lost a valuable jewel—a young lady, also, as my own eyes and ears inform me, who is of an impetuous temperament. Under these circumstances, and with that character, what does she do? She betrays an incomprehensible resentment against Mr Blake, Mr Superintendent, and myself—otherwise, the very three people who have all, in their different ways, been trying to help her to recover her lost jewel. Having brought my inquiry to that point—*then*, my lady, and not till then, I begin to look back into my own mind for my own experience. My own experience explains Miss Verinder's otherwise incomprehensible conduct. It associates her with those other young ladies that I know of. It tells me she has debts she daren't acknowledge, that must be paid. And it sets me asking myself, whether the loss of the Diamond may not mean—that the Diamond must be secretly pledged to pay them. That is the conclusion which my experience draws from plain facts. What does your ladyship's experience say against it? '

'What I have said already,' answered my mistress. 'The circumstances have misled you.'

I said nothing on my side. *Robinson Crusoe*—God knows how—had got into my muddled old head. If Sergeant Cuff had found himself, at that moment, transported to a desert island, without a man Friday to keep him company, or a ship to take him off—he would have found himself exactly where I wished him to be! (*Nota bene:*—I am an average good Christian, when you don't push my Christianity too far. And all the rest of you—which is a great comfort—are, in this respect, much the same as I am.)

Sergeant Cuff went on:

'Right or wrong, my lady,' he said, 'having drawn my conclusion, the next thing to do was to put it to the test. I suggested to your ladyship the examination of all the wardrobes in the house. It was a means of finding the article of dress which had, in all probability, made the smear; and it was a means of putting my conclusion to the test. How did it turn out? Your ladyship consented; Mr Blake consented; Mr Ablewhite consented. Miss Verinder alone stopped the whole proceeding by refusing point-blank. That result satisfied me that my view was the right one. If your ladyship and Mr Betteredge persist in not agreeing with me, you must be blind to what happened before you this very day. In your hearing, I told the young lady that her leaving the house (as things were then) would put an obstacle in the way of my recovering her jewel. You saw yourselves that she drove off in the face of that statement. You saw yourselves that, so far from forgiving Mr Blake for having done more than all the rest of you to put the clue into my hands, she publicly insulted Mr Blake, on the steps of her mother's house. What do these things mean? If Miss Verinder is not privy to the suppression of the Diamond, what do these things mean?'

This time he looked my way. It was downright frightful to hear him piling up proof after proof against Miss Rachel, and to know, while one was longing to defend her, that there was no disputing the truth of what he said. I am (thank God!) constitutionally superior to reason. This enabled me to hold firm to my lady's view, which was my view also. This roused my spirit, and made me put a bold face on it before Sergeant Cuff. Profit, good friends, I beseech you, by my example. It will save you from many troubles of the vexing sort. Cultivate a superiority to reason, and see how you pare the claws of all the sensible people when they try to scratch you for your own good!

Finding that I made no remark, and that my mistress made no remark, Sergeant Cuff proceeded. Lord! how it did enrage me to notice that he was not in the least put out by our silence!

'There is the case, my lady, as it stands against Miss Verinder alone,' he said. 'The next thing is to put the case as it stands against Miss Verinder and the deceased Rosanna Spearman, taken together. We will go back for a moment, if you please, to your daughter's refusal to let her wardrobe be examined. My mind being made up, after that circumstance, I had two questions to consider next. First, as to the right method of conducting my inquiry. Second, as to whether Miss Verinder had an accomplice among the female servants in the house. After carefully thinking it over, I determined to conduct the inquiry in, what we should call at our office, a highly irregular manner. For this reason: I had a family scandal to deal with, which it was my business to keep within the family limits. The less noise made, and the fewer strangers employed to help me, the better. As to the usual course of taking people in custody on suspicion, going before the magistrate, and all the rest of it—nothing of the sort was to be thought of, when your ladyship's daughter was (as I believed) at the bottom of the whole business. In this case, I felt that a person of Mr Betteredge's character and position in the house—knowing the servants as he did, and having the honour of the family at heart—would be safer to take as an assistant than any other person whom I could lay my hand on. I should have tried Mr Blake as well—but for one obstacle in the way. *He* saw the drift of my proceedings at a very early date; and, with his interest in Miss Verinder, any mutual understanding was impossible between him and me. I trouble your ladyship with these particulars to show you that I have kept the family secret within the family circle. I am the only outsider who knows it—and my professional existence depends on holding my tongue.'

Here I felt that my professional existence depended on not holding *my* tongue. To be held up before my mistress, in my old age, as a sort of deputy-policeman, was, once again, more than my Christianity was strong enough to hear.

'I beg to inform your ladyship,' I said, 'that I never, to my knowledge, helped this abominable detective business, in any way, from first to last; and I summon Sergeant Cuff to contradict me, if he dares!'

Having given vent in those words, I felt greatly relieved. Her ladyship honoured me by a little friendly pat on the shoulder. I looked with righteous indignation at the Sergeant to see what he thought of such a testimony as *that*. The Sergeant looked back like a lamb, and seemed to like me better than ever.

My lady informed him that he might continue his statement. 'I understand,' she said, 'that you have honestly done your best, in what you believe to be my interest. I am ready to hear what you have to say next.'

'What I have to say next,' answered Sergeant Cuff, 'relates to Rosanna Spearman. I recognized the young woman, as your ladyship may remember, when she brought the washing-book into this room. Up to that time I was inclined to doubt whether Miss Verinder had trusted her secret to any one. When I saw Rosanna, I altered my mind. I suspected her at once of being privy to the suppression of the Diamond. The poor creature has met her death by a dreadful end, and I don't want your ladyship to think, now she's gone, that I was unduly hard on her. If this had been a common case of thieving, I should have given Rosanna the benefit of the doubt just as freely as I should have given it to any of the other servants in the house. Our experience of the Reformatory women is, that when tried in service—and when kindly and judiciously treated—they prove themselves in the majority of cases to be honestly penitent, and honestly worthy of the pains taken with them. But this was not a common case of thieving. It was a case —in my mind—of a deeply planned fraud, with the owner of the Diamond at the bottom of it. Holding this view, the first consideration which naturally presented itself to me, in connection with Rosanna, was this. Would Miss Verinder be satisfied (begging your ladyship's pardon) with leading us all to think that the Moonstone was merely lost? Or would she go a step further, and delude us into believing that the Moonstone was stolen? In the latter event there was Rosanna Spearman—with the character of a thief—ready to her hand; the person of all others to lead your ladyship off, and to lead me off, on a false scent.'

Was it possible (I asked myself) that he could put his case against Miss Rachel and Rosanna in a more horrid point of view than this? It *was* possible, as you shall now see.

'I had another reason for suspecting the deceased woman,' he said, 'which appears to me to have been stronger still. Who would be the very person to help Miss Verinder in raising money privately on the Diamond? Rosanna Spearman. No young lady in Miss Verinder's position could manage such a risky matter as that by herself. A go-between she must have, and who so fit, I ask again, as Rosanna Spearman? Your ladyship's deceased housemaid was at the top of her profession when she was a thief. She had relations, to my certain knowledge, with one of the few men in London (in the money-lending line) who would advance a large sum on such a notable jewel as the Moonstone, without asking awkward questions, or insisting on awkward conditions. Bear this in mind, my lady; and now let me show you how my suspicions have been justified by Rosanna's own acts, and by the plain inferences to be drawn from them.'

He thereupon passed the whole of Rosanna's proceedings under review. You are already as well acquainted with those proceedings as I am; and you will understand how unanswerably this part of his report fixed the guilt of being concerned in the disappearance of the Moonstone on the memory of the poor dead girl. Even my mistress was daunted by what he said now. She made him no answer when he had done. It didn't seem to matter to the Sergeant whether he was answered or not. On he went (devil take him!), just as steady as ever.

'Having stated the whole case as I understand it,' he said, 'I have only to tell your ladyship, now, what I propose to do next. I see two ways of bringing this inquiry successfully to an end. One of those ways I look upon as a certainty. The other, I admit, is a bold experiment, and nothing more. Your ladyship shall decide. Shall we take the certainty first?'

My mistress made him a sign to take his own way, and choose for himself.

'Thank you,' said the Sergeant. 'We'll begin with the certainty, as your ladyship is so good as to leave it to me. Whether Miss Verinder remains at Frizinghall, or whether she returns here, I propose, in either case, to keep a careful watch on all her proceedings—on the people she sees, on the rides and walks she may take, and on the letters she may write and receive.'

'What next?' asked my mistress.

'I shall next,' answered the Sergeant, 'request your ladyship's leave to introduce into the house, as a servant in the place of Rosanna Spearman, a woman accustomed to private inquiries of this sort, for whose discretion I can answer.'

'What next?' repeated my mistress.

'Next,' proceeded the Sergeant, 'and last, I propose to send one of my brother-officers to make an arrangement with that money-lender in London, whom I mentioned just now as formerly acquainted with Rosanna Spearman—and whose name and address, your ladyship may rely on it, have been communicated by Rosanna to Miss Verinder. I don't deny that the course of action I am now suggesting will cost money, and consume time. But the result is certain. We run a line round the Moonstone, and we draw that line closer and closer till we find it in Miss Verinder's possession, supposing she decides to keep it. If her debts press, and she decides on sending it away, then we have our man ready, and we meet the Moonstone on its arrival in London.'

To hear her own daughter made the subject of such a proposal as this, stung my mistress into speaking angrily for the first time.

'Consider your proposal declined, in every particular,' she said. 'And go on to your other way of bringing the inquiry to an end.'

'My other way,' said the Sergeant, going on as easy as ever, 'is to try that bold experiment to which I have alluded. I think I have formed a pretty correct estimate of Miss Verinder's temperament. She is quite capable (according to my belief) of committing a daring fraud. But she is too hot and impetuous in temper, and too little accustomed to deceit as a habit, to act the hypocrite in small things, and to restrain herself under all provocations. Her feelings, in this case, have repeatedly got beyond her control, at the very time when it was plainly her interest to conceal them. It is on this peculiarity in her character that I now propose to act. I want to give her a great shock suddenly, under circumstances that will touch her to the quick. In plain English, I want to tell Miss Verinder, without a word of warning, of Rosanna's death—on the chance that her own better feelings will hurry her into making a clean breast of it. Does your ladyship accept *that* alternative?'

My mistress astonished me beyond all power of expression. She answered him on the instant:

'Yes; I do.'

'The pony-chaise is ready,' said the Sergeant. 'I wish your ladyship good morning.'

My lady held up her hand, and stopped him at the door.

'My daughter's better feelings shall be appealed to, as you propose,' she said. 'But I claim the right, as her mother, of putting her to the test myself. You will remain here, if you please; and I will go to Frizinghall.'

For once in his life, the great Cuff stood speechless with amazement, like an ordinary man.

My mistress rang the bell, and ordered her waterproof things. It was still pouring with rain; and the close carriage had gone, as you know, with Miss Rachel to Frizinghall. I tried to dissuade her ladyship from facing the severity of the weather. Quite useless! I asked leave to go with her, and hold the umbrella. She wouldn't hear of it. The pony-chaise came round, with the groom in charge. 'You may rely on two things,' she said to Sergeant Cuff, in the hall. 'I will try the experiment on Miss Verinder as boldly as you could try it yourself. And I will inform you of the result, either personally or by letter, before the last train leaves for London to-night.'

With that, she stepped into the chaise, and, taking the reins herself, drove off to Frizinghall.

CHAPTER 22

My mistress having left us, I had leisure to think of Sergeant Cuff. I found him sitting in a snug corner of the hall, consulting his memorandum book, and curling up viciously at the corners of the lips.

'Making notes of the case?' I asked.

'No,' said the Sergeant. 'Looking to see what my next professional engagement is.'

'Oh!' I said. 'You think it's all over then, here?'

'I think,' answered Sergeant Cuff, 'that Lady Verinder is one of the cleverest women in England. I also think a rose much better worth looking at than a diamond. Where is the gardener, Mr Betteredge?'

There was no getting a word more out of him on the matter of the Moonstone. He had lost all interest in his own inquiry; and he would persist in looking for the gardener. An hour afterwards, I heard them at high words in the conservatory, with the dog-rose once more at the bottom of the dispute.

In the meantime, it was my business to find out whether Mr Franklin persisted in his resolution to leave us by the afternoon train. After having been informed of the conference in my lady's room, and of how it had ended, he immediately decided on waiting to hear the news from Frizinghall. This very natural alteration in his plans—which, with ordinary people, would have led to nothing in particular—proved, in Mr Franklin's case, to have one objectionable result. It left him unsettled, with a legacy of idle time on his hands, and in so doing, it let out all the foreign sides of his character, one on the top of another, like rats out of a bag.

Now as an Italian-Englishman, now as a German-Englishman, and now as a French-Englishman, he drifted in and out of all the sitting-rooms in the house, with nothing to talk of but Miss Rachel's treatment of him; and with nobody to address himself to but me. I found him (for example) in the library, sitting under the map of Modern Italy, and quite unaware of any other method of meeting his troubles, except the method of talking about them. 'I have several worthy aspirations, Betteredge; but what am I to do with them now? I am full of dormant good qualities, if Rachel would only have helped me to bring them out!' He was so eloquent in drawing the picture of his own neglected merits, and so pathetic in lamenting over it when it was done, that I felt quite at my wits' end how to console him, when it suddenly occurred to me that here was a case for the wholesome application of a bit of *Robinson Crusoe*. I hobbled out to my own room, and hobbled back with that immortal book. Nobody in the library! The map of Modern Italy stared at *me*; and *I* stared at the map of Modern Italy.

I tried the drawing-room. There was his handkerchief on the floor, to prove that he had drifted in. And there was the empty room to prove that he had drifted out again.

I tried the dining-room, and discovered Samuel with a biscuit and a glass of sherry, silently investigating the empty air. A minute since, Mr Franklin had rung furiously for a little light refreshment. On its production, in a violent hurry, by Samuel, Mr Franklin had vanished before the bell downstairs had quite done ringing with the pull he had given to it.

I tried the morning-room, and found him at last. There he was at the window, drawing hieroglyphics with his finger in the damp on the glass.

'Your sherry is waiting for you, sir,' I said to him. I might as well have addressed myself to one of the four walls of the room; he was down in the bottomless deep of his own meditations, past all pulling up. 'How do *you* explain Rachel's conduct, Betteredge?' was the only answer I received. Not being ready with the needful reply, I produced *Robinson Crusoe*, in which I am firmly persuaded some explanation might have been found, if we had only searched long enough for it. Mr Franklin shut up *Robinson Crusoe*, and floundered into his German-English gibberish on the spot. 'Why not look into it?' he said, as if I had personally objected to looking into it. 'Why the devil lose your patience, Betteredge, when patience is all that's wanted to arrive at the truth? Don't interrupt me. Rachel's conduct is perfectly intelligible, if you will only do her the common justice to take the Objective view first, and the Subjective view next, and the Objective-Subjective view to wind up with. What do we know? We know that the loss of the Moonstone, on Thursday morning last, threw her into a state of nervous excitement, from which she has not recovered yet. Do you mean to deny the Objective view, so far? Very well, then—don't interrupt me. Now, being in a state of nervous excitement, how are we to expect that she should behave as she might otherwise have behaved to any of the people about her? Arguing in this way, from within-outwards, what do we reach? We reach the Subjective view. I defy you to controvert the Subjective view. Very well then—what follows? Good Heavens! the Objective-Subjective explanation follows, of course! Rachel, properly speaking, is *not* Rachel, but Somebody Else. Do I mind being cruelly treated by Somebody Else? You are unreasonable enough, Betteredge; but you can hardly accuse me of that. Then how does it end? It ends, in spite of your confounded English narrowness and prejudice, in my being perfectly happy and comfortable. Where's the sherry?'

My head was by this time in such a condition, that I was not quite sure whether it was my own head, or Mr Franklin's. In this deplorable state, I contrived to do, what I take to have been, three Objective things. I got Mr Franklin his sherry; I retired to my own room;

and I solaced myself with the most composing pipe of tobacco I ever remember to have smoked in my life.

Don't suppose, however, that I was quit of Mr Franklin on such easy terms as these. Drifting again, out of the morning-room into the hall, he found his way to the offices next, smelt my pipe, and was instantly reminded that he had been simple enough to give up smoking for Miss Rachel's sake. In the twinkling of an eye, he burst in on me with his cigar-case, and came out strong on the one everlasting subject, in his neat, witty, unbelieving, French way. 'Give me a light, Betteredge. Is it conceivable that a man can have smoked as long as I have, without discovering that there is a complete system for the treatment of women at the bottom of his cigar-case? Follow me carefully, and I will prove it in two words. You choose a cigar, you try it, and it disappoints you. What do you do upon that? You throw it away and try another. Now observe the application! You choose a woman, you try her, and she breaks your heart. Fool! take a lesson from your cigar-case. Throw her away, and try another!'

I shook my head at that. Wonderfully clever, I dare say, but my own experience was dead against it. 'In the time of the late Mrs Betteredge,' I said, 'I felt pretty often inclined to try your philosophy, Mr Franklin. But the law insists on your smoking your cigar, sir, when you have once chosen it.' I pointed that observation with a wink. Mr Franklin burst out laughing—and we were as merry as crickets, until the next new side of his character turned up in due course. So things went on with my young master and me; and so, (while the Sergeant and the gardener were wrangling over the roses) we two spent the interval before the news came back from Frizinghall.

The pony-chaise returned a good half-hour before I had ventured to expect it. My lady had decided to remain for the present, at her sister's house. The groom brought two letters from his mistress; one addressed to Mr Franklin, and the other to me.

Mr Franklin's letter I sent to him in the library—into which refuge his driftings had now taken him for the second time. My own letter, I read in my own room. A cheque, which dropped out when I opened it, informed me (before I had mastered the contents) that Sergeant Cuff's dismissal from the inquiry after the Moonstone was now a settled thing.

I sent to the conservatory to say that I wished to speak to the Sergeant directly. He appeared, with his mind full of the gardener and the dog-rose, declaring that the equal of Mr Begbie for obstinacy never had existed yet, and never would exist again. I requested him to dismiss such wretched trifling as this from our conversation, and to give his best attention to a really serious matter. Upon that he exerted himself sufficiently to notice the letter in my hand. 'Ah!' he said in a weary way, 'you have heard from her ladyship. Have I anything to do with it, Mr Betteredge?'

'You shall judge for yourself, Sergeant.' I thereupon read him the letter (with my best emphasis and discretion), in the following words:

'My good Gabriel,—I request that you will inform Sergeant Cuff, that I have performed the promise I made to him; with this result, so far as Rosanna Spearman is concerned. Miss Verinder solemnly declares, that she has never spoken a word in private to Rosanna, since that unhappy woman first entered my house. They never met, even accidentally, on the night when the Diamond was lost; and no communication of any sort whatever took place between them, from the Thursday morning when the alarm was first raised in the house, to this present Saturday afternoon, when Miss Verinder left us. After telling my daughter suddenly, and in so many words, of Rosanna Spearman's suicide—this is what has come of it.'

Having reached that point, I looked up, and asked Sergeant Cuff what he thought of the letter, so far?

'I should only offend you if I expressed *my* opinion,' answered the Sergeant. 'Go on, Mr Betteredge,' he said, with the most exasperating resignation, 'go on.'

When I remembered that this man had had the audacity to complain of our gardener's obstinacy, my tongue itched to 'go on' in other words than my mistress's. This time, however, my Christianity held firm. I proceeded steadily with her ladyship's letter:

'Having appealed to Miss Verinder in the manner which the officer thought most desirable, I spoke to her next in the manner which I myself thought most likely to impress her. On two different occasions, before my daughter left my roof, I privately warned her that she was exposing herself to suspicion of the most unendurable and most degrading kind. I have now told her, in the plainest terms, that my apprehensions have been realized.

'Her answer to this, on her own solemn affirmation, is as plain as words can be. In the first place, she owes no money privately to any living creature. In the second place, the Diamond is not now, and never has been, in her possession, since she put it into her cabinet on Wednesday night.

'The confidence which my daughter has placed in me goes no further than this. She maintains an obstinate silence, when I ask her if she can explain the disappearance of the Diamond. She refuses, with tears, when I appeal to her to speak out for my sake. "The day will come when you will know why I am careless about being suspected, and why I am silent even to *you*. I have done much to make my mother pity me—nothing to make my mother blush for me." Those are my daughter's own words.

'After what has passed between the officer and me, I think—stranger as he is—that he should be made acquainted with what Miss Verinder has said, as well as you. Read my letter to him, and then place in his hands the cheque which I enclose. In resigning all further claim on his services, I have only to say that I am convinced of his honesty and his intelligence; but I am more firmly persuaded than ever, that the circumstances, in this case, have fatally misled him.'

There the letter ended. Before presenting the cheque, I asked Sergeant Cuff if he had any remark to make.

'It's no part of my duty, Mr Betteredge,' he answered, 'to make remarks on a case, when I have done with it.'

I tossed the cheque across the table to him. 'Do you believe in *that* part of her ladyship's letter?' I said, indignantly.

The Sergeant looked at the cheque, and lifted up his dismal eyebrows in acknowledgment of her ladyship's liberality.

'This is such a generous estimate of the value of my time,' he said, 'that I feel bound to make some return for it. I'll bear in mind the amount in this cheque, Mr Betteredge, when the occasion comes round for remembering it.'

'What do you mean?' I asked.

'Her ladyship has smoothed matters over for the present very cleverly,' said the Sergeant. 'But *this* family scandal is of the sort that bursts up again when you least expect it. We shall have more detective-business on our hands, sir, before the Moonstone is many months older.'

If those words meant anything, and if the manner in which he spoke them meant anything—it came to this. My mistress's letter had proved, to his mind, that Miss Rachel was hardened enough to resist the strongest appeal that could be addressed to her, and that she had deceived her own mother (good God, under what circumstances!) by a series of abominable lies. How other people, in my place, might have replied to the Sergeant, I don't know. I answered what he said in these plain terms:

'Sergeant Cuff, I consider your last observation as an insult to my lady and her daughter!'

'Mr Betteredge, consider it as a warning to yourself, and you will be nearer the mark.'

Hot and angry as I was, the infernal confidence with which he gave me that answer closed my lips.

I walked to the window to compose myself. The rain had given over; and, who should I see in the courtyard, but Mr Begbie, the gardener, waiting outside to continue the dog-rose controversy with Sergeant Cuff.

'My compliments to the Sergent,' said Mr Begbie, the moment he set eyes on me. 'If he's minded to walk to the station, I'm agreeable to go with him.'

'What!' cries the Sergeant, behind me, 'are you not convinced yet?'

'The de'il a bit I'm convinced!' answered Mr Begbie.

'Then I'll walk to the station!' says the Sergeant.

'Then I'll meet you at the gate!' says Mr Begbie.

I was angry enough, as you know—but how was any man's anger to hold out against such an interruption as this? Sergeant Cuff noticed the change in me, and encouraged it by a word in season. 'Come! come!' he said, 'why not treat my view of the case as her ladyship treats it? Why not say, the circumstances have fatally misled me?'

To take anything as her ladyship took it, was a privilege worth enjoying—even with the disadvantage of its having been offered to me by Sergeant Cuff. I cooled slowly down to my customary level. I regarded any other opinion of Miss Rachel, than my lady's opinion or mine, with a lofty contempt. The only thing I could *not* do, was to keep off the subject of the Moonstone! My own good sense ought to have warned me, I know, to let the matter rest—but, there! the virtues which distinguish the present generation were not invented in my time. Sergeant Cuff had hit me on the raw, and, though I did look down upon him with contempt, the tender place still tingled for all that. The end of it was that I perversely led him back to the subject of her ladyship's letter. 'I am quite satisfied myself,' I said. 'But never mind that! Go on, as if I was still open to conviction. You think Miss Rachel is not to be believed on her word; and you say we shall hear of the Moonstone again. Back your opinion, Sergeant,' I concluded, in an airy way. 'Back your opinion.'

Instead of taking offence, Sergeant Cuff seized my hand, and shook it till my fingers ached again.

'I declare to heaven,' says this strange officer solemnly, 'I would take to domestic service to-morrow, Mr Betteredge, if I had a chance of being employed along with you! To say you are as transparent as a child, sir, is to pay the children a compliment which nine out of ten of them don't deserve. There! there! we won't begin to dispute again. You shall have it out of me on easier terms than that. I won't say a word more about her ladyship, or about Miss Verinder—I'll only turn prophet, for once in a way, and for your sake. I have warned you already that you haven't done with the Moonstone yet. Very well. Now I'll tell you, at parting, of three things which will happen in the future, and which, I believe, will force themselves on your attention, whether you like it or not.'

'Go on!' I said, quite unabashed, and just as airy as ever.

'First,' said the Sergeant, 'you will hear something from the Yollands—when the postman delivers Rosanna's letter at Cobb's Hole, on Monday next.'

If he had thrown a bucket of cold water over me, I doubt if I could have felt it much more unpleasantly than I felt those words. Miss Rachel's assertion of her innocence had left Rosanna's conduct —the making the new nightgown, the hiding the smeared nightgown, and all the rest of it—entirely without explanation. And this had never occurred to me, till Sergeant Cuff forced it on my mind all in a moment!

'In the second place,' proceeded the Sergeant, 'you will hear of the three Indians again. You will hear of them in the neighbourhood, if Miss Rachel remains in the neighbourhood. You will hear of them in London, if Miss Rachel goes to London.'

Having lost all interest in the three jugglers, and having thoroughly convinced myself of my young lady's innocence, I took this second prophecy easily enough. 'So much for two of the three things that are going to happen,' I said. 'Now for the third!'

'Third, and last,' said Sergeant Cuff, 'you will, sooner or later, hear something of that money-lender in London, whom I have twice taken the liberty of mentioning already. Give me your pocket-book, and I'll make a note for you of his name and address —so that there may be no mistake about it if the thing really happens.'

He wrote accordingly on a blank leaf:—'Mr Septimus Luker, Middlesex Place, Lambeth, London.'

'There,' he said, pointing to the address, 'are the last words, on the subject of the Moonstone, which I shall trouble you with for the present. Time will show whether I am right or wrong. In the meanwhile, sir, I carry away with me a sincere personal liking for you, which I think does honour to both of us. If we don't meet again before my professional retirement takes place, I hope you will come and see me in a little house near London, which I have got my eye on. There will be grass walks, Mr Betteredge, I promise you, in *my* garden. And as for the white moss-rose—'

'The de'il a bit ye'll get the white moss-rose to grow, unless ye bud him on the dogue-rose first,' cried a voice at the window.

We both turned round. There was the everlasting Mr Begbie, too eager for the controversy to wait any longer at the gate. The Sergeant wrung my hand, and darted out into the courtyard, hotter still on his side. 'Ask him about the moss-rose, when he comes back, and see if I have left him a leg to stand on!' cried the Great Cuff, hailing me through the window in his turn. 'Gentlemen, both!' I answered, moderating them again as I had moderated them once already. 'In the matter of the moss-rose there is a great deal to be said on both sides!' I might as well (as the Irish say) have whistled jigs to a milestone.

Away they went together, fighting the battle of the roses without asking or giving quarter on either side. The last I saw of them, Mr Begbie was shaking his obstinate head, and Sergeant Cuff had got him by the arm like a prisoner in charge. Ah, well! well! I own I couldn't help liking the Sergeant—though I hated him all the time.

Explain that state of mind, if you can. You will soon be rid, now, of me and my contradictions. When I have reported Mr Franklin's departure, the history of the Saturday's events will be finished at last. And when I have next described certain strange things that happened in the course of the new week, I shall have done my part of the Story, and shall hand over the pen to the person who is appointed to follow my lead. If you are as tired of reading this narrative as I am of writing it—Lord, how we shall enjoy ourselves on both sides a few pages further on!

CHAPTER 23

I had kept the pony-chaise ready, in case Mr Franklin persisted in leaving us by the train that night. The appearance of the luggage, followed downstairs by Mr Franklin himself, informed me plainly enough that he had held firm to a resolution for once in his life.

'So you have really made up your mind, sir?' I said, as we met in the hall. 'Why not wait a day or two longer, and give Miss Rachel another chance?'

The foreign varnish appeared to have all worn off Mr Franklin, now that the time had come for saying good-bye. Instead of replying to me in words, he put the letter which her ladyship had addressed to him into my hand. The greater part of it said over again what had been said already in the other communication received by me. But there was a bit about Miss Rachel added at the end, which will account for the steadiness of Mr Franklin's determination, if it accounts for nothing else.

'You will wonder, I dare say' (her ladyship wrote), 'at my allowing my own daughter to keep me perfectly in the dark. A Diamond worth twenty thousand pounds has been lost—and I am left to infer that the mystery of its disappearance is no mystery to Rachel, and that some incomprehensible obligation of silence has been laid on her, by some person or persons utterly unknown to me, with some object in view at which I cannot even guess. Is it conceivable that I should allow myself to be trifled with in this way? It is quite conceivable, in Rachel's present state. She is in a condition of nervous agitation pitiable to see. I dare not approach the subject of the Moonstone again until time has done something to quiet her. To help this end, I have not hesitated to dismiss the police-officer. The mystery which baffles us, baffles him too. This is not a matter in which any stranger can help us. He adds to what I have to suffer; and he maddens Rachel if she only hears his name.

'My plans for the future are as well settled as they can be. My present idea is to take

Rachel to London—partly to relieve her mind by a complete change, partly to try what may be done by consulting the best medical advice. Can I ask you to meet us in town? My dear Franklin, you, in your way, must imitate my patience, and wait, as I do, for a fitter time. The valuable assistance which you rendered to the inquiry after the lost jewel is still an unpardoned offence, in the present dreadful state of Rachel's mind. Moving blindfold in this matter, you have added to the burden of anxiety which she has had to bear, by innocently threatening her secret with discovery, through your exertions. It is impossible for me to excuse the perversity that holds you responsible for consequences which neither you nor I could imagine or foresee. She is not to be reasoned with—she can only be pitied. I am grieved to have to say it, but, for the present, you and Rachel are better apart. The only advice I can offer you is, to give her time.'

I handed the letter back, sincerely sorry for Mr Franklin, for I knew how fond he was of my young lady; and I saw that her mother's account of her had cut him to the heart. 'You know the proverb, sir,' was all I said to him. 'When things are at the worst, they're sure to mend. Things can't be much worse, Mr Franklin, than they are now.'

Mr Franklin folded up his aunt's letter, without appearing to be much comforted by the remark which I had ventured on addressing to him.

'When I came here from London with that horrible Diamond,' he said, 'I don't believe there was a happier household in England than this. Look at the household now! Scattered, disunited—the very air of the place poisoned with mystery and suspicion! Do you remember that morning at the Shivering Sand, when we talked about my uncle Herncastle, and his birthday gift? The Moonstone has served the Colonel's vengeance, Betteredge, by means which the Colonel himself never dreamt of!'

With that he shook me by the hand, and went out to the pony-chaise.

I followed him down the steps. It was very miserable to see him leaving the old place, where he had spent the happiest years of his life, in this way. Penelope (sadly upset by all that had happened in the house) came round crying, to bid him good-bye. Mr Franklin kissed her. I waved my hand as much as to say, 'You're heartily welcome, sir.' Some of the other female servants appeared, peeping after him round the corner. He was one of those men whom the women all like. At the last moment, I stopped the pony-chaise, and begged as a favour that he would let us hear from him by letter. He didn't seem to heed what I said—he was looking round from one thing to another, taking a sort of farewell of the old house and grounds. 'Tell us where you are going to, sir!' I said, holding on by the chaise, and trying to get at his future plans in that way. Mr Franklin pulled his hat down suddenly over his eyes. 'Going?' says he, echoing the word after me. 'I am going to the devil!' The pony started at the word, as if he had felt a Christian horror of it. 'God bless you, sir, go where you may!' was all I had time to say, before he was out of sight and hearing. A sweet and pleasant gentleman! With all his faults and follies, a sweet and pleasant gentleman! He left a sad gap behind him, when he left my lady's house.

It was dull and dreary enough, when the long summer evening closed in, on that Saturday night.

I kept my spirits from sinking by sticking fast to my pipe and my *Robinson Crusoe*. The women (excepting Penelope) beguiled the time by talking of Rosanna's suicide. They were all obstinately of opinion that the poor girl had stolen the Moonstone, and that she had destroyed herself in terror of being found out. My daughter, of course, privately held fast to what she had said all along. Her notion of the motive which was really at the bottom of the suicide failed, oddly enough, just where my young lady's assertion of her innocence failed also. It left Rosanna's secret journey to Frizinghall, and Rosanna's proceedings in the matter of the nightgown entirely unaccounted for. There was no use in pointing this out to Penelope; the objection made about as much impression on her as a shower of rain on a waterproof coat. The truth is, my daughter inherits my superiority to reason—and, in respect to that accomplishment, has got a long way ahead of her own father.

On the next day (Sunday), the close carriage, which had been kept at Mr Ablewhite's, came back to us empty. The coachman brought a message for me, and written instructions for my lady's own maid and for Penelope.

The message informed me that my mistress had determined to take Miss Rachel to her house in London, on the Monday. The written instructions informed the two maids of the clothing that was wanted, and directed them to meet their mistresses in town at a given hour. Most of the other servants were to follow. My lady had found Miss Rachel so unwilling to return to the house, after what had happened in it, that she had decided on going to London direct from Frizinghall. I was to remain in the country, until further orders, to look after things indoors and out. The servants left with me were to be put on board wages.

Being reminded, by all this, of what Mr Franklin had said about our being a scattered and disunited household, my mind was led naturally to Mr Franklin himself. The more I thought of him, the more uneasy I felt about his future proceedings. It ended in my writing, by the Sunday's post, to his father's valet, Mr Jeffco (whom I had known in former years) to beg he would let me know what Mr Franklin had settled to do, on arriving in London.

The Sunday evening was, if possible, duller even than the Saturday evening. We ended the day of rest, as hundreds of thousands of people end it regularly, once a week, in these islands—that is to say, we all anticipated bedtime, and fell asleep in our chairs.

How the Monday affected the rest of the household I don't know. The Monday gave *me* a good shake up. The first of Sergeant Cuff's prophecies of what was to happen—namely, that I should hear from the Yollands—came true on that day.

I had seen Penelope and my lady's maid off on the railway with the luggage for London, and was pottering about the grounds, when I heard my name called. Turning round, I found myself face to face with the fisherman's daughter, Limping Lucy. Bating her lame foot and her leanness (this last a horrid drawback to a woman, in my opinion), the girl had some pleasing qualities in the eye of a man. A dark, keen, clever face, and a nice clear voice, and a beautiful brown head of hair counted among her merits. A crutch appeared in the list of her misfortunes. And a temper reckoned high in the sum-total of her defects.

'Well, my dear,' I said, 'what do you want with me?'

'Where's the man you call Franklin Blake?' says the girl, fixing me with a fierce look, as she rested herself on her crutch.

'That's not a respectful way to speak of any gentleman,' I answered. 'If you wish to inquire for my lady's nephew, you will please to mention him as Mr Franklin Blake.'

She limped a step nearer to me, and looked as if she could have eaten me alive. '*Mr* Franklin Blake?' she repeated after me. 'Murderer Franklin Blake would be a fitter name for him.'

My practice with the late Mrs Betteredge came in handy here. Whenever a woman tries to put *you* out of temper, turn the tables, and put *her* out of temper instead. They are generally prepared for every effort you can make in your own defence, but that. One word does it as well as a hundred; and one word did it with Limping Lucy. I looked her pleasantly in the face; and I said—'Pooh!'

The girl's temper flamed out directly. She poised herself on her sound foot, and she took her crutch, and beat it furiously three times on the ground. 'He's a murderer! he's a murderer! he's a murderer! He has been the death of Rosanna Spearman!' She screamed that answer out at the top of her voice. One or two of the people at work in the grounds near us looked up—saw it was Limping Lucy—knew what to expect from that quarter—and looked away again.

'He has been the death of Rosanna Spearman?' I repeated. 'What makes you say that, Lucy?'

'What do you care? What does any man care? Oh! if she had only thought of the men as I think, she might have been living now!'

'She always thought kindly of *me*, poor soul,' I said; 'and, to the best of my ability, I always tried to act kindly by *her*.'

I spoke those words in as comforting a manner as I could. The truth is, I hadn't the heart to irritate the girl by another of my smart replies. I had only noticed her temper at first. I noticed her wretchedness now—and wretchedness is not uncommonly insolent, you will find, in humble life. My answer melted Limping Lucy. She bent her head down, and laid it on the top of her crutch.

'I loved her,' the girl said softly. 'She had lived a miserable life, Mr Betteredge—vile people had ill-treated her and led her wrong—and it hadn't spoiled her sweet temper. She was an angel. She might have been happy with me. I had a plan for our going to London together like sisters, and living by our needles. That man came here, and spoilt it all. He bewitched her. Don't tell me he didn't mean it, and didn't know it. He ought to have known it. He ought to have taken pity on her. "I can't live without him—and, oh, Lucy, he never even looks at me." That's what she said. Cruel, cruel, cruel. I said, "No man is worth fretting for in that way." And she said, "There are men worth dying for, Lucy, and he is one of them." I had saved up a little money. I had settled things with father and mother. I meant to take her away from the mortification she was suffering here. We should have had a little lodging in London, and lived together like sisters. She had a good education, sir, as you know, and she wrote a good hand. She was quick at her needle. I have a good education, and I write a good hand. I am not as quick at my needle as she was—but I could have done. We might have got our living nicely. And, oh! what happens this morning? what happens this morning? Her letter comes and tells me that she has done with the burden of her life. Her letter comes, and bids me good-bye for ever. Where is he?' cries the girl, lifting her head from the crutch, and flaming out again through her tears. 'Where's this gentleman that I mustn't speak of, except with respect?

Ha, Mr Betteredge, the day is not far off when the poor will rise against the rich. I pray Heaven they may begin with *him*. I pray Heaven they may begin with *him*.'

Here was another of your average good Christians, and here was the usual break-down, consequent on that same average Christianity being pushed too far! The parson himself (though I own this is saying a great deal) could hardly have lectured the girl in the state she was in now. All I ventured to do was to keep her to the point—in the hope of something turning up which might be worth hearing.

'What do you want with Mr Franklin Blake?' I asked.

'I want to see him.'

'For anything particular?'

'I have got a letter to give him.'

'From Rosanna Spearman?'

'Yes.'

'Sent to you in your own letter?'

'Yes.'

Was the darkness going to lift? Were all the discoveries that I was dying to make, coming and offering themselves to me of their own accord? I was obliged to wait a moment. Sergeant Cuff had left his infection behind him. Certain signs and tokens, personal to myself, warned me that the detective-fever was beginning to set in again.

'You can't see Mr Franklin,' I said.

'I must, and will, see him.'

'He went to London last night.'

Limping Lucy looked me hard in the face, and saw that I was speaking the truth. Without a word more, she turned about again instantly towards Cobb's Hole.

'Stop!' I said. 'I expect news of Mr Franklin Blake to-morrow. Give me your letter, and I'll send it on to him by the post.'

Limping Lucy steadied herself on her crutch and looked back at me over her shoulder.

'I am to give it from my hands into his hands,' she said. 'And I am to give it to him in no other way.'

'Shall I write, and tell him what you have said?'

'Tell him I hate him. And you will tell him the truth.'

'Yes, yes. But about the letter—?'

'If he wants the letter, he must come back here, and get it from Me.'

With those words she limped off on the way to Cobb's Hole. The detective-fever burnt up all my dignity on the spot. I followed her, and tried to make her talk. All in vain. It was my misfortune to be a man—and Limping Lucy enjoyed disappointing me. Later in the day, I tried my luck with her mother. Good Mrs Yolland could only cry, and recommend a drop of comfort out of the Dutch bottle. I found the fisherman on the beach. He said it was 'a bad job,' and went on mending his net. Neither father nor mother knew more than I knew. The one way left to try was the chance, which might come with the morning, of writing to Mr Franklin Blake.

I leave you to imagine how I watched for the postman on Tuesday morning. He brought me two letters. One, from Penelope (which I had hardly patience enough to read), announced that my lady and Miss Rachel were safely established in London. The other, from Mr Jeffco, informed me that his master's son had left England already.

On reaching the metropolis, Mr Franklin had, it appeared, gone straight to his father's residence. He arrived at an awkward time. Mr Blake, the elder, was up to his eyes in the business of the House of Commons, and was amusing himself at home that night with the favourite parliamentary plaything which they call 'a private bill.' Mr Jeffco himself showed Mr Franklin into his father's study. 'My dear Franklin! why do you surprise me in this way? Anything wrong?' 'Yes; something wrong with Rachel; I am dreadfully distressed about it.' 'Grieved to hear it. But I can't listen to you now.' 'When *can* you listen?' 'My dear boy! I won't deceive you. I can *listen* at the end of the session, not a moment before. Good-night.' 'Thank you, sir. Good-night.'

Such was the conversation, inside the study, as reported to me by Mr Jeffco. The conversation outside the study, was shorter still. 'Jeffco, see what time the tidal train starts to-morrow morning.' 'At six-forty, Mr Franklin.' 'Have me called at five.' 'Going abroad, sir?' 'Going, Jeffco, wherever the railway chooses to take me.' 'Shall I tell your father, sir?' 'Yes; tell him at the end of the session.'

The next morning Mr Franklin had started for foreign parts. To what particular place he was bound, nobody (himself included) could presume to guess. We might hear of him next in Europe, Asia, Africa, or America. The chances were as equally divided as possible, in Mr Jeffco's opinion, among the four quarters of the globe.

This news—by closing up all prospect of my bringing Limping Lucy and Mr Franklin together—at once stopped any further progress of mine on the way to discovery. Penelope's belief that her fellow-servant had destroyed herself through unrequited love for Mr Franklin Blake, was confirmed—and that was all. Whether the letter which Rosanna had left to be given to him after her death did, or did not, contain the confession which Mr Franklin had suspected her of trying to make to him in her life-time, it was impossible to say. It might be only a farewell word, telling nothing but the secret of her unhappy fancy for a person beyond her reach. Or it might own the whole truth about the strange proceedings in which Sergeant Cuff had detected her, from the time when the Moonstone was lost, to the time when she rushed to her own destruction at the Shivering Sand. A sealed letter it had been placed in Limping Lucy's hands, and a sealed letter it remained to me and to every one about the girl, her own parents included. We all suspected her of having been in the dead woman's confidence; we all tried to make her speak; we all failed. Now one, and now another, of the servants—still holding to the belief that Rosanna had stolen the Diamond and had hidden it—peered and poked about the rocks to which she had been traced, and peered and poked in vain. The tide ebbed, and the tide flowed; the summer went on, and the autumn came. And the Quicksand, which hid her body, hid her secret too.

The news of Mr Franklin's departure from England on the Sunday morning, and the news of my lady's arrival in London with Miss Rachel on the Monday afternoon, had reached me, as you are aware, by the Tuesday's post. The Wednesday came, and brought nothing. The Thursday produced a second budget of news from Penelope.

My girl's letter informed me that some great London doctor had been consulted about her young lady, and had earned a guinea by remarking that she had better be amused. Flower-shows, operas, balls—there was a whole round of gaieties in prospect; and Miss Rachel, to her mother's astonishment, eagerly took to it all. Mr Godfrey had called; evidently as sweet as ever on his cousin, in spite of the reception he had met with, when he tried his luck on the occasion of the birthday. To Penelope's great regret, he had been most graciously received, and had added Miss Rachel's name to one of his Ladies' Charities on the spot. My mistress was reported to be out of spirits, and to have held two long interviews with her lawyer. Certain speculations followed, referring to a poor relation of the family—one Miss Clack, whom I have mentioned in my account of the birthday dinner, as sitting next to Mr Godfrey, and having a pretty taste in champagne. Penelope was astonished to find that Miss Clack had not called yet. She would surely not be long before she fastened herself on my lady as usual—and so forth, and so forth, in the way women have of girding at each other, on and off paper. This would not have been worth mentioning, I admit, but for one reason. I hear you are likely to be turned over to Miss Clack, after parting with me. In that case, just do me the favour of not believing a word she says, if she speaks of your humble servant.

On Friday, nothing happened—except that one of the dogs showed signs of a breaking-out behind the ears. I gave him a dose of syrup of buckthorn, and put him on a diet of pot-liquor and vegetables till further orders. Excuse my mentioning this. It has slipped in somehow. Pass it over please. I am fast coming to the end of my offences against your cultivated modern taste. Besides, the dog was a good creature, and deserved a good physicking; he did indeed.

Saturday, the last day of the week, is also the last day in my narrative.

The morning's post brought me a surprise in the shape of a London newspaper. The handwriting on the direction puzzled me. I compared it with the money-lender's name and address as recorded in my pocket-book, and identified it at once as the writing of Sergeant Cuff.

Looking through the paper eagerly enough, after this discovery, I found an ink-mark drawn round one of the police reports. Here it is, at your service. Read it as I read it, and you will set the right value on the Sergeant's polite attention in sending me the news of the day:

'Lambeth—Shortly before the closing of the court, Mr Septimus Luker, the well-known dealer in ancient gems, carvings, intagli, &c., &c., applied to the sitting magistrate for advice. The applicant stated that he had been annoyed, at intervals throughout the day, by the proceedings of some of those strolling Indians who infest the streets. The persons complained of were three in number. After having been sent away by the police, they had returned again and again, and had attempted to enter the house on pretence of asking for charity. Warned off in the front, they had been discovered again at the back of the premises. Besides the annoyance complained of, Mr Luker expressed himself as being under some apprehension that robbery might be contemplated. His collection contained many unique gems, both classical and Oriental, of the highest value. He had only the day before been compelled to dismiss a skilled workman in ivory carving from his employment (a native of India, as we understood), on suspicion of attempted theft; and he felt by no means sure that this man and the street-jugglers of whom he complained, might not be acting in concert. It might be their object to collect a crowd, and create a disturbance in the street, and, in the confusion thus caused, to obtain access to the house.

In reply to the magistrate, Mr Luker admitted that he had no evidence to produce of any attempt at robbery being in contemplation. He could speak positively to the annoyance and interruption caused by the Indians, but not to anything else. The magistrate remarked that, if the annoyance were repeated, the applicant could summon the Indians to that court, where they might easily be dealt with under the Act. As to the valuables in Mr Luker's possession, Mr Luker himself must take the best measures for their safe custody. He would do well perhaps to communicate with the police, and to adopt such additional precautions as their experience might suggest. The applicant thanked his worship, and withdrew.'

One of the wise ancients is reported (I forget on what occasion) as having recommended his fellow-creatures to 'look to the end.' Looking to the end of these pages of mine, and wondering for some days past how I should manage to write it, I find my plain statement of facts coming to a conclusion, most appropriately, of its own self. We have gone on, in this matter of the Moonstone, from one marvel to another; and here we end with the greatest marvel of all—namely, the accomplishment of Sergeant Cuff's three predictions in less than a week from the time when he had made them.

After hearing from the Yollands on the Monday, I had now heard of the Indians, and heard of the money-lender, in the news from London—Miss Rachel herself, remember, being also in London at the time. You see, I put things at their worst, even when they tell dead against my own view. If you desert me, and side with the Sergeant, on the evidence before you—if the only rational explanation you can see is, that Miss Rachel and Mr Luker must have got together, and that the Moonstone must be now in pledge in the money-lender's house—I own I can't blame you for arriving at that conclusion. In the dark, I have brought you thus far. In the dark I am compelled to leave you, with my best respects.

Why compelled? it may be asked. Why not take the persons who have gone along with me, so far, up into those regions of superior enlightenment in which I sit myself?

In answer to this, I can only state that I am acting under orders, and that those orders have been given to me (as I understand) in the interests of truth. I am forbidden to tell more in this narrative than I knew myself at the time. Or, to put it plainer, I am to keep strictly within the limits of my own experience, and am not to inform you of what other persons told me—for the very sufficient reason that you are to have the information from those other persons themselves, at first hand. In this matter of the Moonstone the plan is, not to present reports, but to produce witnesses. I picture to myself a member of the family reading these pages fifty years hence. Lord! what a compliment he will feel it, to be asked to take nothing on hearsay, and to be treated in all respects like a Judge on the bench.

At this place, then, we part—for the present, at least—after long journeying together, with a companionable feeling, I hope, on both sides. The devil's dance of the Indian Diamond has threaded its way to London; and to London you must go after it, leaving me at the country-house. Please to excuse the faults of this composition—my talking so much of myself, and being too familiar, I am afraid, with you. I mean no harm; and I drink most respectfully (having just done dinner) to your health and prosperity, in a tankard of her ladyship's ale. May you find in these leaves of my writing, what Robinson Crusoe found in his experience on the desert island —namely, 'something to comfort your-selves from, and to set in the Description of Good and Evil, on the Credit Side of the Account.'—Farewell.

THE END OF THE FIRST PERIOD

SECOND PERIOD

THE DISCOVERY OF THE TRUTH (1848–1849)

The Events related in several Narratives

FIRST NARRATIVE

Contributed by Miss Clack; *niece of the late* Sir John Verinder

CHAPTER 1

I am indebted to my dear parents (both now in heaven) for having had habits of order and regularity instilled into me at a very early age.

In that happy bygone time, I was taught to keep my hair tidy at all hours of the day and night, and to fold up every article of my clothing carefully, in the same order, on the same chair, in the same place at the foot of the bed, before retiring to rest. An entry of the day's events in my little diary invariably preceded the folding up. The 'Evening Hymn' (repeated in bed) invariably followed the folding up. And the sweet sleep of childhood invariably followed the 'Evening Hymn.'

In later life (alas!) the Hymn has been succeeded by sad and bitter meditations; and the sweet sleep has been but ill exchanged for the broken slumbers which haunt the uneasy pillow of care. On the other hand, I have continued to fold my clothes, and to keep my little diary. The former habit links me to my happy childhood—before papa was ruined. The latter habit—hitherto mainly useful in helping me to discipline the fallen nature which we all inherit from Adam—has unexpectedly proved important to my humble interests in quite another way. It has enabled poor Me to serve the caprice of a wealthy member of the family into which my late uncle married. I am fortunate enough to be useful to Mr Franklin Blake.

I have been cut off from all news of my relatives by marriage for some time past. When we are isolated and poor, we are not infrequently forgotten. I am now living, for economy's sake, in a little town in Brittany, inhabited by a select circle of serious English friends, and possessed of the inestimable advantages of a Protestant clergyman and a cheap market.

In this retirement—a Patmos amid the howling ocean of popery that surrounds us—a letter from England has reached me at last. I find my insignificant existence suddenly remembered by Mr Franklin Blake. My wealthy relative—would that I could add my spiritually-wealthy relative!—writes, without even an attempt at disguising that he wants something of me. The whim has seized him to stir up the deplorable scandal of the Moonstone: and I am to help him by writing the account of what I myself witnessed while visiting at Aunt Verinder's house in London. Pecuniary remuneration is offered to me—with the want of feeling peculiar to the rich. I am to re-open wounds that Time has barely closed; I am to recall the most intensely painful remembrances—and this done, I am to feel myself compensated by a new laceration, in the shape of Mr Blake's cheque. My nature is weak. It cost me a hard struggle, before Christian humility conquered sinful pride, and self-denial accepted the cheque.

Without my diary, I doubt—pray let me express it in the grossest terms!—if I could have honestly earned my money. With my diary, the poor labourer (who forgives Mr Blake for insulting her) is worthy of her hire. Nothing escaped me at the time I was visiting dear Aunt Verinder. Everything was entered (thanks to my early training) day by day as it happened; and everything down to the smallest particular, shall be told here. My sacred regard for truth is (thank God) far above my respect for persons. It will be easy for Mr Blake to suppress what may not prove to be sufficiently flattering in these pages to the person chiefly concerned in them. He has purchased my time; but not even *his* wealth can purchase my conscience too.*

My diary informs me, that I was accidentally passing Aunt Verinder's house in Montagu Square, on Monday, 3 July 1848.

Seeing the shutters opened, and the blinds drawn up, I felt that it would be an act of polite attention to knock, and make inquiries. The person who answered the door, informed me that my aunt and her daughter (I really cannot call her my cousin!) had arrived from the country a week since, and meditated making some stay in London. I sent up a message at once, declining to disturb them, and only begging to know whether I could be of any use.

The person who answered the door, took my message in insolent silence, and left me standing in the hall. She is the daughter of a heathen old man named Betteredge—long, too long, tolerated in my aunt's family. I sat down in the hall to wait for my answer—and, having always a few tracts in my bag, I selected one which proved to be quite providentially applicable to the person who answered the door. The hall was dirty, and the chair was hard; but the blessed consciousness of returning good for evil raised me quite above any trifling considerations of that kind. The tract was one of a series addressed to young women on the sinfulness of dress. In style it was devoutly familiar. Its title was, 'A Word With You On Your Cap-Ribbons.'

'My lady is much obliged, and begs you will come and lunch to-morrow at two.'

I passed over the manner in which she gave her message, and the dreadful boldness of

* Note. *Added by Franklin Blake.*—Miss Clark may make her mind quite easy on this point. Nothing will be added, altered, or removed, in her manuscript, or in any of the other manuscripts which pass through my hands. Whatever opinions any of the writers may express, whatever peculiarities of treatment may mark, and perhaps in a literary sense, disfigure, the narratives which I am now collecting, not a line will be tampered with anywhere, from first to last. As genuine documents they are sent to me—and as genuine documents I shall preserve them; endorsed by the attestations of witnesses who can speak to the facts. It only remains to be added, that 'the person chiefly concerned' in Miss Clack's narrative, is happy enough at the present moment, not only to brave the smartest exercise of Miss Clack's pen, but even to recognize its unquestionable value as an instrument for the exhibition of Miss Clack's character.

her look. I thanked this young castaway; and I said, in a tone of Christian interest, 'Will you favour me by accepting a tract?'

She looked at the title. 'Is it written by a man or a woman, Miss? If it's written by a woman, I had rather not read it on that account. If it's written by a man, I beg to inform him that he knows nothing about it.' She handed me back the tract, and opened the door. We must sow the good seed somehow. I waited till the door was shut on me, and slipped the tract into the letter-box. When I had dropped another tract through the area railings, I felt relieved, in some small degree, of a heavy responsibility towards others.

We had a meeting that evening of the Select Committee of the Mothers'-Small-Clothes-Conversion-Society The object of this excellent Charity is—as all serious people know—to rescue unredeemed fathers' trousers from the pawnbroker, and to prevent their resumption, on the part of the irreclaimable parent, by abridging them immediately to suit the proportions of the innocent son. I was a member, at that time, of the select committee; and I mention the Society here, because my precious and admirable friend, Mr Godfrey Ablewhite, was associated with our work of moral and material usefulness. I had expected to see him in the board-room, on the Monday evening of which I am now writing, and had proposed to tell him, when we met, of dear Aunt Verinder's arrival in London. To my great disappointment he never appeared. On my expressing a feeling of surprise at his absence, my sisters of the Committee all looked up together from their trousers (we had a great pressure of business that night), and asked in amazement, if I had not heard the news. I acknowledged my ignorance, and was then told, for the first time, of an event which forms, so to speak, the starting-point of this narrative. On the previous Friday, two gentlemen—occupying widely-different positions in society—had been the victims of an outrage which had startled all London. One of the gentlemen was Mr Septimus Luker, of Lambeth. The other was Mr Godfrey Ablewhite.

Living in my present isolation, I have no means of introducing the newspaper-account of the outrage into my narrative. I was also deprived, at the time, of the inestimable advantage of hearing the events related by the fervid eloquence of Mr Godfrey Ablewhite. All I can do is to state the facts as they were stated, on that Monday evening, to me; proceeding on the plan which I have been taught from infancy to adopt in folding up my clothes. Everything shall be put neatly, and everything shall be put in its place. These lines are written by a poor weak woman. From a poor weak woman who will be cruel enough to expect more?

The date—thanks to my dear parents, no dictionary that ever was written can be more particular than I am about dates—was Friday, 30 June 1848.

Early on that memorable day, our gifted Mr Godfrey happened to be cashing a cheque at a banking-house in Lombard Street. The name of the firm is accidentally blotted in my diary, and my sacred regard for truth forbids me to hazard a guess in a matter of this kind. Fortunately, the name of the firm doesn't matter. What does matter is a circumstance that occurred when Mr Godfrey had transacted his business. On gaining the door, he encountered a gentleman—a perfect stranger to him—who was accidentally leaving the office exactly at the same time as himself. A momentary contest of politeness ensued between them as to who should be the first to pass through the door of the bank. The stranger insisted on making Mr Godfrey precede him; Mr Godfrey said a few civil words; they bowed, and parted in the street.

Thoughtless and superficial people may say, Here is surely a very trumpery little incident related in an absurdly circumstantial manner. Oh, my young friends and fellow-sinners! beware of presuming to exercise your poor carnal reason. Oh, be morally tidy! Let your faith be as your stockings, and your stockings as your faith. Both ever spotless, and both ready to put on at a moment's notice!

I beg a thousand pardons. I have fallen insensibly into my Sunday-school style. Most inappropriate in such a record as this. Let me try to be worldly—let me say that trifles, in this case as in many others, led to terrible results. Merely promising that the polite stranger was Mr Luker, of Lambeth, we will now follow Mr Godfrey home to his residence at Kilburn.

He found waiting for him, in the hall, a poorly clad but delicate and interesting-looking little boy. The boy handed him a letter, merely mentioning that he had been entrusted with it by an old lady whom he did not know, and who had given him no instructions to wait for an answer. Such incidents as these were not uncommon in Mr Godfrey's large experience as a promoter of public charities. He let the boy go, and opened the letter.

The handwriting was entirely unfamiliar to him. It requested his attendance, within an hour's time, at a house in Northumberland Street, Strand, which he had never had occasion to enter before. The object sought was to obtain from the worthy manager certain details on the subject of the Mothers'-Small-Clothes-Conversion-Society, and the information was wanted by an elderly lady who proposed adding largely to the resources of the charity, if her questions were met by satisfactory replies. She mentioned her name, and she added that the shortness of her stay in London prevented her from giving any longer notice to the eminent philanthropist whom she addressed.

Ordinary people might have hesitated before setting aside their own engagements to suit the convenience of a stranger. The Christian Hero never hesitates where good is to be done. Mr Godfrey instantly turned back, and proceeded to the house in Northumberland Street. A most respectable though somewhat corpulent man answered the door, and, on hearing Mr Godfrey's name, immediately conducted him into an empty apartment at the back, on the drawing-room floor. He noticed two unusual things on entering the room. One of them was a faint odour of musk and camphor. The other was an ancient Oriental manuscript, richly illuminated with Indian figures and devices, that lay open to inspection on a table.

He was looking at the book, the position of which caused him to stand with his back turned towards the closed folding doors communicating with the front room, when, without the slightest previous noise to warn him, he felt himself suddenly seized round the neck from behind. He had just time to notice that the arm round his neck was naked and of a tawny-brown colour, before his eyes were bandaged, his mouth was gagged, and he was thrown helpless on the floor by (as he judged) two men. A third rifled his pockets, and—if, as a lady, I may venture, to use such an expression—searched him, without ceremony, through and through to his skin.

Here I should greatly enjoy saying a few cheering words on the devout confidence which could alone have sustained Mr Godfrey in an emergency so terrible as this. Perhaps, however, the position and appearance of my admirable friend at the culminating period of the outrage (as above described) are hardly within the proper limits of female discussion. Let me pass over the next few moments, and return to Mr Godfrey at the time when the odious search of his person had been completed. The outrage had been perpetrated throughout in dead silence. At the end of it some words were exchanged, among the invisible wretches, in a language which he did not understand, but in tones which were plainly expressive (to his cultivated ear) of disappointment and rage. He was suddenly lifted from the ground, placed in a chair, and bound there hand and foot. The next moment he felt the air flowing in from the open door, listened, and concluded that he was alone again in the room.

An interval elapsed, and he heard a sound below like the rustling sound of a woman's dress. It advanced up the stairs, and stopped. A female scream rent the atmosphere of guilt. A man's voice below exclaimed, 'Hullo!' A man's feet ascended the stairs. Mr Godfrey felt Christian fingers unfastening his bandage, and extracting his gag. He looked in amazement at two respectable strangers, and faintly articulated, 'What does it mean?' The two respectable strangers looked back, and said, 'Exactly the question we were going to ask *you*.'

The inevitable explanation followed. No! Let me be scrupulously particular. Salvolatile and water followed, to compose dear Mr Godfrey's nerves. The explanation came next.

It appeared, from the statement of the landlord and landlady of the house (persons of good repute in the neighbourhood), that their first- and second-floor apartments had been engaged, on the previous day, for a week certain, by a most respectable-looking gentleman—the same who has been already described as answering the door to Mr Godfrey's knock. The gentleman had paid the week's rent and all the week's extras in advance, stating that the apartments were wanted for three Oriental noblemen, friends of his, who were visiting England for the first time. Early on the morning of the outrage, two of the Oriental strangers, accompanied by their respectable English friend, took possession of the apartments. The third was expected to join them shortly; and the luggage (reported as very bulky) was announced to follow when it had passed through the Custom-house, late in the afternoon. Not more than ten minutes previous to Mr Godfrey's visit, the third foreigner had arrived. Nothing out of the common had happened, to the knowledge of the landlord and landlady downstairs, until within the last five minutes—when they had seen the three foreigners, accompanied by their respectable English friend, all leave the house together, walking quietly in the direction of the Strand. Remembering that a visitor had called, and not having seen the visitor also leave the house, the landlady had thought it rather strange that the gentleman should be left by himself upstairs. After a short discussion with her husband, she had considered it advisable to ascertain whether anything was wrong. The result had followed, as I have already attempted to describe it; and there the explanation of the landlord and the landlady came to an end.

An investigation was next made in the room. Dear Mr Godfrey's property was found scattered in all directions. When the articles were collected, however, nothing was missing; his watch, chain, purse, keys, pocket-handkerchief, note-book, and all his loose papers had been closely examined, and had then been left unharmed to be resumed by the owner. In the same way, not the smallest morsel of property belonging to the proprietors of the house had been abstracted. The Oriental noblemen had removed their own illuminated manuscript, and had removed nothing else.

What did it mean? Taking the worldly point of view, it appeared to mean that Mr Godfrey had been the victim of some incomprehensible error, committed by certain unknown men. A dark conspiracy was on foot in the midst of us; and our beloved and innocent friend had been entangled in its meshes. When the Christian hero of a hundred charitable victories plunges into a pitfall that has been dug for him by mistake, oh, what a warning it is to the rest of us to be unceasingly on our guard! How soon may our own evil passions prove to be Oriental noblemen who pounce on us unawares!

I could write pages of affectionate warning on this one theme, but (alas!) I am not permitted to improve—I am condemned to narrate. My wealthy relative's cheque—henceforth, the incubus of my existence—warns me that I have not done with this record of violence yet. We must leave Mr Godfrey to recover in Northumberland Street, and must follow the proceedings of Mr Luker, at a later period of the day.

After leaving the bank, Mr Luker had visited various parts of London on business errands. Returning to his own residence, he found a letter waiting for him, which was described as having been left a short time previously by a boy. In this case, as in Mr Godfrey's case, the handwriting was strange; but the name mentioned was the name of one of Mr Luker's customers. His correspondent announced (writing in the third person—apparently by the hand of a deputy) that he had been unexpectedly summoned to London. He had just established himself in lodgings in Alfred Place, Tottenham Court Road; and he desired to see Mr Luker immediately, on the subject of a purchase which he contemplated making. The gentleman was an enthusiastic collector of oriental antiquities, and had been for many years a liberal patron of the establishment in Lambeth. Oh, when shall we wean ourselves from the worship of Mammon! Mr Luker called a cab, and drove off instantly to his liberal patron.

Exactly what had happened to Mr Godfrey in Northumberland Street now happened to Mr Luker in Alfred Place. Once more the respectable man answered the door, and showed the visitor upstairs into the back drawing-room. There, again, lay the illuminated manuscript on a table. Mr Luker's attention was absorbed, as Mr Godfrey's attention had been absorbed, by this beautiful work of Indian art. He too was aroused from his studies by a tawny naked arm round his throat, by a bandage over his eyes, and by a gag in his mouth. He too was thrown prostrate, and searched to the skin. A longer interval had then elapsed than had passed in the experience of Mr Godfrey; but it had ended as before, in the persons of the house suspecting something wrong, and going upstairs to see what had happened. Precisely the same explanation which the landlord in Northumberland Street had given to Mr Godfrey, the landlord in Alfred Place now gave to Mr Luker. Both had been imposed on in the same way by the plausible address and well-filled purse of the respectable stranger, who introduced himself as acting for his foreign friends. The one point of difference between the two cases occurred when the scattered contents of Mr Luker's pockets were being collected from the floor. His watch and purse were safe, but (less fortunate than Mr Godfrey) one of the loose papers that he carried about him had been taken away. The paper in question acknowledged the receipt of a valuable of great price which Mr Luker had that day left in the care of his bankers. This document would be useless for purposes of fraud, inasmuch as it provided that the valuable should only be given up on the personal application of the owner. As soon as he recovered himself, Mr Luker hurried to the bank, on the chance that the thieves who had robbed him might ignorantly present themselves with the receipt. Nothing had been seen of them when he arrived at the establishment, and nothing was seen of them afterwards. Their respectable English friend had (in the opinion of the bankers) looked the receipt over before they attempted to make use of it, and had given them the necessary warning in good time.

Information of both outrages was communicated to the police, and the needful investigations were pursued, I believe, with great energy. The authorities held that a robbery had been planned, on insufficient information received by the thieves. They had been plainly not sure whether Mr Luker had, or had not, trusted the transmission of his precious gem to another person; and poor polite Mr Godfrey had paid the penalty of having been seen accidentally speaking to him. Add to this, that Mr Godfrey's absence from our Monday evening meeting had been occasioned by a consultation of the authorities, at which he was requested to assist—and all the explanations required being now given, I may proceed with the simpler story of my own little personal experiences in Montagu Square.

I was punctual to the luncheon hour on Tuesday. Reference to my diary shows this to have been a chequered day—much in it to be devoutly regretted, much in it to be devoutly thankful for.

Dear Aunt Verinder received me with her usual grace and kindness. But I noticed, after a little while, that something was wrong. Certain anxious looks escaped my aunt, all of which took the direction of her daughter. I never see Rachel myself without wondering how it can be that so insignificant-looking a person should be the child of such distinguished parents as Sir John and Lady Verinder. On this occasion, however, she not only disappointed—she really shocked me. There was an absence of all lady-like restraint in her language and manner most painful to see. She was possessed by some feverish excitement which made her distressingly loud when she laughed, and sinfully wasteful and capricious in what she ate and drank at lunch. I felt deeply for her poor mother, even before the true state of the case had been confidentially made known to me.

Luncheon over, my aunt said: 'Remember what the doctor told you, Rachel, about quieting yourself with a book after taking your meals.'

'I'll go into the library, mamma,' she answered. 'But if Godfrey calls, mind I am told of it. I am dying for more news of him, after his adventure in Northumberland Street.' She kissed her mother on the forehead, and looked my way. 'Good-bye, Clack,' she said, carelessly. Her insolence roused no angry feeling in me. I only made a private memorandum to pray for her.

When we were left by ourselves, my aunt told me the whole horrible story of the Indian Diamond, which, I am happy to know, it is not necessary to repeat here. She did not conceal from me that she would have preferred keeping silence on the subject. But when her own servants all knew of the loss of the Moonstone, and when some of the circumstances had actually found their way into the newspapers—when strangers were speculating whether there was any connection between what had happened at Lady Verinder's country-house, and what had happened in Northumberland Street and Alfred Place—concealment was not to be thought of; and perfect frankness became a necessity as well as a virtue.

Some persons, hearing what I now heard, would have been probably overwhelmed with astonishment. For my own part, knowing Rachel's spirit to have been essentially unregenerate from her childhood upwards, I was prepared for whatever my aunt could tell me on the subject of her daughter. It might have gone on from bad to worse till it ended in Murder; and I should still have said to myself, The natural result! oh, dear, dear, the natural result! The one thing that *did* shock me was the course my aunt had taken under the circumstances. Here surely was a case for a clergyman, if ever there was one yet! Lady Verinder had thought it a case for a physician. All my poor aunt's early life had been passed in her father's godless household. The natural result again! Oh, dear, dear, the natural result again!

'The doctors recommend plenty of exercise and amusement for Rachel, and strongly urge me to keep her mind as much as possible from dwelling on the past,' said Lady Verinder.

'Oh, what heathen advice!' I thought to myself. 'In this Christian country, what heathen advice!'

My, aunt went on, 'I do my best to carry out my instructions. But this strange adventure of Godfrey's happens at a most unfortunate time. Rachel has been incessantly restless and excited since she first heard of it. She left me no peace till I had written and asked my nephew Ablewhite to come here. She even feels an interest in the other person who was roughly used—Mr Luker, or some such name—though the man is, of course, a total stranger to her.'

'Your knowledge of the world, dear aunt, is superior to mine,' I suggested diffidently. 'But there must be a reason surely for this extraordinary conduct on Rachel's part. She is keeping a sinful secret from you and from everybody. May there not be something in these recent events which threatens her secret with discovery?'

'Discovery?' repeated my aunt. 'What can you possibly mean? Discovery through Mr Luker? Discovery through my nephew?'

As the word passed her lips, a special providence occurred. The servant opened the door, and announced Mr Godfrey Ablewhite.

CHAPTER 2

Mr Godfrey followed the announcement of his name—as Mr Godfrey does everything else—exactly at the right time. He was not so close on the servant's heels as to startle us. He was not so far behind as to cause us the double inconvenience of a pause and an open door. It is in the completeness of his daily life that the true Christian appears. This dear man was very complete.

'Go to Miss Verinder,' said my aunt, addressing the servant, 'and tell her Mr Ablewhite is here.'

We both inquired after his health. We both asked him together whether he felt like himself again, after his terrible adventure of the past week. With perfect tact, he contrived to answer us at the same moment. Lady Verinder had his reply in words. I had his charming smile.

'What,' he cried, with infinite tenderness, 'have I done to deserve all this sympathy? My dear aunt! my dear Miss Clack! I have merely been mistaken for somebody else. I have only been blindfolded; I have only been strangled; I have only been thrown flat on my back, on a very thin carpet, covering a particularly hard floor. Just think how much worse it might have been! I might have been murdered; I might have been robbed. What have I lost? Nothing but Nervous Force—which the law doesn't recognize as property; so that, strictly speaking, I have lost nothing at all. If I could have had my own way, I would have kept my adventure to myself—I shrink from all this fuss and publicity. But Mr Luker made *his* injuries public, and *my* injuries, as the necessary consequence, have been proclaimed in their turn. I have become the property of the newspapers, until the gentle reader gets sick of the subject. I am very sick indeed of it myself. May the gentle reader soon be like me! And how is dear Rachel? Still enjoying the gaieties of London? So glad to hear it! Miss Clack, I need all your indulgence. I am sadly behind-hand with my Committee Work and my dear Ladies. But I really do hope to look in at the Mothers'-Small-Clothes next week. Did you make cheering progress at Monday's Committee? Was the Board hopeful about future prospects? And are we nicely off for Trousers?'

The heavenly gentleness of his smile made his apologies irresistible. The richness of his deep voice added its own indescribable charm to the interesting business question which he had just addressed to me. In truth, we were almost *too* nicely off for Trousers; we were quite overwhelmed by them. I was just about to say so, when the door opened again, and an element of worldly disturbance entered the room, in the person of Miss Verinder.

She approached dear Mr Godfrey at a most unladylike rate of speed, with her hair shockingly untidy, and her face, what *I* should call, unbecomingly flushed.

'I am charmed to see you, Godfrey,' she said, addressing him, I grieve to add, in the off-hand manner of one young man talking to another. 'I wish you had brought Mr Luker with you. You and he (as long as our present excitement lasts) are the two most interesting men in all London. It's morbid to say this; it's unhealthy; it's all that a well-regulated mind like Miss Clack's most instinctively shudders at. Never mind that. Tell me the whole of the Northumberland Street story directly. I know the newspapers have left some of it out.'

Even dear Mr Godfrey partakes of the fallen nature which we all inherit from Adam—it is a very small share of our human legacy, but, alas! he has it. I confess it grieved me to see him take Rachel's hand in both of his own hands, and lay it softly on the left side of his waistcoat. It was a direct encouragement to her reckless way of talking, and her insolent reference to me.

'Dearest Rachel,' he said, in the same voice which had thrilled me when he spoke of our prospects and our trousers, 'the newspapers have told you everything—and they have told it much better than I can.'

'Godfrey thinks we all make too much of the matter,' my aunt remarked. 'He has just been saying that he doesn't care to speak of it.'

'Why?'

She put the question with a sudden flash in her eyes, and a sudden look up into Mr Godfrey's face. On his side, he looked down at her with an indulgence so injudicious and so ill-deserved, that I really felt called on to interfere.

'Rachel, darling!' I remonstrated, gently, 'true greatness and true courage are ever modest.'

'You are a very good fellow in your way, Godfrey,' she said—not taking the smallest notice, observe, of me, and still speaking to her cousin as if she was one young man addressing another. 'But I am quite sure you are not great; I don't believe you possess any extraordinary courage; and I am firmly persuaded—if you ever had any modesty—that your lady-worshippers relieved you of that virtue a good many years since. You have some private reason for not talking of your adventure in Northumberland Street; and I mean to know it.'

'My reason is the simplest imaginable, and the most easily acknowledged,' he answered, still bearing with her. 'I am tired of the subject.'

'You are tired of the subject? My dear Godfrey, I am going to make a remark.'

'What is it?'

'You live a great deal too much in the society of women. And you have contracted two very bad habits in consequence. You have learnt to talk nonsense seriously, and you have got into a way of telling fibs for the pleasure of telling them. You can't go straight with your lady-worshippers. I mean to make you go straight with *me*. Come, and sit down. I am brimful of downright questions; and I expect you to be brimful of downright answers.'

She actually dragged him across the room to a chair by the window, where the light would fall on his face. I deeply feel being obliged to report such language, and to describe such conduct. But, hemmed in as I am, between Mr Franklin Blake's cheque on one side and my own sacred regard for truth on the other, what am I to do? I looked at my aunt. She sat unmoved; apparently in no way disposed to interfere. I had never noticed this kind of torpor in her before. It was, perhaps, the reaction after the trying time she had had in the country. Not a pleasant symptom to remark, be it what it might, at dear Lady Verinder's age, and with dear Lady Verinder's autumnal exuberance of figure.

In the meantime, Rachel had settled herself at the window with our amiable and forbearing—our too forbearing—Mr Godfrey. She began the string of questions with which she had threatened him, taking no more notice of her mother, or of myself, than if we had not been in the room.

'Have the police done anything, Godfrey?'

'Nothing whatever.'

'It is certain, I suppose, that the three men who laid the trap for you were the same three men who afterwards laid the trap for Mr Luker?'

'Humanly speaking, my dear Rachel, there can be no doubt of it.'

'And not a trace of them has been discovered?'

'Not a trace.'

'It is thought—is it not?—that these three men are the three Indians who came to our house in the country.'

'Some people think so.'

'Do you think so?'

'My dear Rachel, they blindfolded me before I could see their faces. I know nothing whatever of the matter. How can I offer an opinion on it?'

Even the angelic gentleness of Mr Godfrey was, you see, beginning to give way at last under the persecution inflicted on him. Whether unbridled curiosity, or ungovernable dread, dictated Miss Verinder's questions I do not presume to inquire. I only report that, on Mr Godfrey's attempting to rise, after giving her the answer just described, she actually took him by the two shoulders, and pushed him back into his chair—Oh, don't say this was immodest! don't even hint that the recklessness of guilty terror could alone account for such conduct as I have described! We must not judge others. My Christian friends, indeed, indeed, indeed, we must not judge others!

She went on with her questions, unabashed. Earnest Biblical students will perhaps be reminded—as I was reminded—of the blinded children of the devil, who went on with their orgies, unabashed, in the time before the Flood.

'I want to know something about Mr Luker, Godfrey.'

'I am again unfortunate, Rachel. No man knows less of Mr Luker than I do.'

'You never saw him before you and he met accidentally at the bank?'

'Never.'

'You have seen him since?'

'Yes. We have been examined together, as well as separately, to assist the police.'

'Mr Luker was robbed of a receipt which he had got from his banker's—was he not? What was the receipt for?'

'For a valuable gem which he had placed in the safe keeping of the bank.'

'That's what the newspapers say. It may be enough for the general reader; but it is not enough for me. The banker's receipt must have mentioned what the gem was?'

'The banker's receipt, Rachel—as I have heard it described—mentioned nothing of the kind. A valuable gem, belonging to Mr Luker; deposited by Mr Luker; sealed with Mr Luker's seal; and only to be given up on Mr Luker's personal application. That was the form, and that is all I know about it.'

She waited a moment, after he had said that. She looked at her mother, and sighed. She looked back again at Mr Godfrey, and went on.

'Some of our private affairs, at home,' she said, 'seem to have got into the newspapers?'

'I grieve to say, it is so.'

'And some idle people, perfect strangers to us, are trying to trace a connection between what happened at our house in Yorkshire and what has happened since, here in London?'

'The public curiosity, in certain quarters, is, I fear, taking that turn.'

'The people who say that the three unknown men who ill-used you and Mr Luker are the three Indians, also say that the valuable gem—'

There she stopped. She had become gradually, within the last few moments, whiter and whiter in the face. The extraordinary blackness of her hair made this paleness, by contrast, so ghastly to look at, that we all thought she would faint, at the moment when she checked herself in the middle of her question. Dear Mr Godfrey made a second attempt to leave his chair. My aunt entreated her to say no more. I followed my aunt with a modest medicinal peace-offering, in the shape of a bottle of salts. We none of us produced the slightest effect on her. 'Godfrey, stay where you are. Mamma, there is not the least reason to be alarmed about me. Clack, you're dying to hear the end of it—I won't faint, expressly to oblige *you*.'

Those were the exact words she used—taken down in my diary the moment I got home. But, oh, don't let us judge! My Christian friends, don't let us judge!

She turned once more to Mr Godfrey. With an obstinacy dreadful to see, she went back again to the place where she had checked herself, and completed her question in these words:

'I spoke to you, a minute since, about what people were saying in certain quarters. Tell me plainly, Godfrey, do they any of them say that Mr Luker's valuable gem is—the Moonstone?'

As the name of the Indian Diamond passed her lips, I saw a change come over my admirable friend. His complexion deepened. He lost the genial suavity of manner which is one of his greatest charms. A noble indignation inspired his reply.

'They *do* say it,' he answered. 'There are people who don't hesitate to accuse Mr Luker of telling a falsehood to serve some private interests of his own. He has over and over again solemnly declared that, until this scandal assailed him, he had never even heard of the Moonstone. And these vile people reply, without a shadow of proof to justify them, He has his reasons for concealment; we decline to believe him on his oath. Shameful! shameful!'

Rachel looked at him very strangely—I can't well describe how —while he was speaking. When he had done, she said,

'Considering that Mr Luker is only a chance acquaintance of yours, you take up his cause, Godfrey, rather warmly.'

My gifted friend made her one of the most truly evangelical answers I ever heard in my life.

'I hope, Rachel, I take up the cause of all oppressed people rather warmly,' he said.

The tone in which those words were spoken might have melted a stone. But, oh dear, what is the hardness of stone? Nothing, compared to the hardness of the unregenerate human heart! She sneered. I blush to record it—she sneered at him to his face.

'Keep your noble sentiments for your Ladies' Committees, Godfrey. I am certain that the scandal which has assailed Mr Luker, has not spared You.'

Even my aunt's torpor was roused by those words.

'My dear Rachel,' she remonstrated, 'you have really no right to say that!'

'I mean no harm, mamma—I mean good. Have a moment's patience with me, and you will see.'

She looked back at Mr Godfrey, with what appeared to be a sudden pity for him. She went the length—the very unladylike length—of taking him by the hand.

'I am certain,' she said, 'that I have found out the true reason of your unwillingness to speak of this matter before my mother and before me. An unlucky accident has associated you in people's minds with Mr Luker. You have told me what scandal says of *him*. What does scandal say of *you*?'

Even at the eleventh hour, dear Mr Godfrey—always ready to return good for evil—tried to spare her.

'Don't ask me!' he said. 'It's better forgotten, Rachel—it is, indeed.'

'I *will* hear it!' she cried out, fiercely, at the top of her voice.

'Tell her, Godfrey!' entreated my aunt. 'Nothing can do her such harm as your silence is doing now!'

Mr Godfrey's fine eyes filled with tears. He cast one last appealing look at her—and then he spoke the fatal words:

'If you will have it, Rachel—scandal says that the Moonstone is in pledge to Mr Luker, and that I am the man who has pawned it.'

She started to her feet with a scream. She looked backwards and forwards from Mr Godfrey to my aunt, and from my aunt to Mr Godfrey, in such a frantic manner that I really thought she had gone mad.

'Don't speak to me! Don't touch me!' she exclaimed, shrinking back from all of us (I declare like some hunted animal!) into a corner of the room. 'This is my fault! I must set it right. I have sacrificed myself—I had a right to do that, if I liked. But to let an innocent man be ruined; to keep a secret which destroys his character for life—Oh, good God, it's too horrible! I can't bear it!'

My aunt half rose from her chair, then suddenly sat down again. She called to me faintly, and pointed to a little phial in her work-box.

'Quick!' she whispered. 'Six drops, in water. Don't let Rachel see.'

Under other circumstances, I should have thought this strange. There was no time now to think—there was only time to give the medicine. Dear Mr Godfrey unconsciously assisted me in concealing what I was about from Rachel, by speaking composing words to her at the other end of the room.

'Indeed, indeed, you exaggerate,' I heard him say. 'My reputation stands too high to be destroyed by a miserable passing scandal like this. It will be all forgotten in another week. Let us never speak of it again.' She was perfectly inaccessible, even to such generosity as this. She went on from bad to worse.

'I must, and will, stop it,' she said. 'Mamma! hear what I say, Miss Clack! hear what I say. I know the hand that took the Moonstone. I know—' she laid a strong emphasis on the words; she stamped her foot in the rage that possessed her—'*I know that Godfrey Ablewhite is innocent*. Take me to the magistrate, Godfrey! Take me to the magistrate, and I will swear it!'

My aunt caught me by the hand, and whispered, 'Stand between us for a minute or two. Don't let Rachel see me.' I noticed a bluish tinge in her face which alarmed me. She saw I was startled. 'The drops will put me right in a minute or two,' she said, and so closed her eyes, and waited a little.

While this was going on, I heard dear Mr Godfrey still gently remonstrating.

'You must not appear publicly in such a thing as this,' he said. '*Your* reputation, dearest Rachel, is something too pure and too sacred to be trifled with.'

'*My* reputation!' She burst out laughing. 'Why, I am accused, Godfrey, as well as you. The best detective-officer in England declares that I have stolen my own Diamond. Ask him what he thinks—and he will tell you that I have pledged the Moonstone to pay my private debts!' She stopped, ran across the room—and fell on her knees at her mother's feet. 'Oh, mamma! mamma! mamma! I must be mad—mustn't I?—not to own the truth *now*?' She was too vehement to notice her mother's condition—she was on her feet again, and back with Mr Godfrey, in an instant. 'I won't let you—I won't let any innocent Man—be accused and disgraced through my fault. If you won't take me before the magistrate, draw out a declaration of your innocence on paper, and I will sign it. Do as I tell you, Godfrey, or I'll write it to the newspapers—I'll go out, and cry it in the streets!'

We will not say this was the language of remorse—we will say it was the language of hysterics. Indulgent Mr Godfrey pacified her by taking a sheet of paper, and drawing out the declaration. She signed it in a feverish hurry. 'Show it everywhere—don't think of *me*,' she said, as she gave it to him. 'I am afraid, Godfrey, I have not done you justice, hitherto, in my thoughts. You are more unselfish—you are a better man than I believed you to be. Come here when you can, and I will try and repair the wrong I have done you.'

She gave him her hand. Alas, for our fallen nature! Alas, for Mr Godfrey! He not only forgot himself so far as to kiss her hand—he adopted a gentleness of tone in answering her which, in such a case, was little better than a compromise with sin. 'I will come, dearest,' he said, 'on condition that we don't speak of this hateful subject again.' Never had I seen and heard our Christian Hero to less advantage than on this occasion.

Before another word could be said by anybody, a thundering knock at the street door startled us all. I looked through the window, and saw the World, the Flesh, and the Devil waiting before the house—as typified in a carriage and horses, a powdered footman, and three of the most audaciously dressed women I ever beheld in my life.

Rachel started, and composed herself. She crossed the room to her mother.

'They have come to take me to the flower-show,' she said. One word, mamma, before I go. I have not distressed you, have I?'

(Is the bluntness of moral feeling which could ask such a question as that, after what had just happened, to be pitied or condemned? I like to lean towards mercy. Let us pity it.)

The drops had produced their effect. My poor aunt's complexion was like itself again. 'No, no, my dear,' she said. 'Go with our friends, and enjoy yourself.'

Her daughter stooped, and kissed her. I had left the window, and was near the door, when Rachel approached it to go out. Another change had come over her—she was in tears. I looked with interest at the momentary softening of that obdurate heart. I felt inclined to say a few earnest words. Alas! my well-meant sympathy only gave offence. 'What do you mean by pitying me?' she asked, in a bitter whisper, as she passed to the door. 'Don't you see how happy I am? I'm going to the flower-show, Clack; and I've got the prettiest bonnet in London.' She completed the hollow mockery of that address by blowing me a kiss—and so left the room.

I wish I could describe in words the compassion that I felt for this miserable and mis-guided girl. But I am almost as poorly provided with words as with money. Permit me to say—my heart bled for her.

Returning to my aunt's chair, I observed dear Mr Godfrey searching for something softly, here and there, in different parts of the room. Before I could offer to assist him, he had found what he wanted. He came back to my aunt and me, with his declaration of innocence in one hand, and with a box of matches in the other.

'Dear aunt, a little conspiracy!' he said, 'Dear Miss Clack, a pious fraud which even your high moral 'rectitude will excuse! Will you leave Rachel to suppose that I accept the generous self-sacrifice which has signed this paper? And will you kindly bear witness that I

157

destroy it in your presence, before I leave the house?' He kindled a match, and, lighting the paper, laid it to burn in a plate on the table. 'Any trifling inconvenience that I may suffer is as nothing,' he remarked, 'compared with the importance of preserving that pure name from the contaminating contact of the world. There! We have reduced it to a little harmless heap of ashes; and our dear impulsive Rachel will never know what we have done! How do you feel? My precious friends, how do you feel? For my poor part, I am as light-hearted as a boy!'

He beamed on us with his beautiful smile; he held out a hand to my aunt, and a hand to me. I was too deeply affected by his noble conduct to speak. I closed my eyes; I put his hand, in a kind of spiritual self-forgetfulness, to my lips. He murmured a soft remonstrance. Oh, the ecstasy, the pure, unearthly ecstasy of that moment! I sat—I hardly know on what—quite lost in my own exalted feelings. When I opened my eyes again, it was like descending from heaven to earth. There was nobody but my aunt in the room. He had gone.

I should like to stop here—I should like to close my narrative with the record of Mr Godfrey's noble conduct. Unhappily, there is more, much more, which the unrelenting pecuniary pressure of Mr Blake's cheque obliges me to tell. The painful disclosures which were to reveal themselves in my presence, during that Tuesday's visit to Montagu Square, were not at an end yet.

Finding myself alone with Lady Verinder, I turned naturally to the subject of her health; touching delicately on the strange anxiety which she had shown to conceal her indisposition, and the remedy applied to it, from the observation of her daughter.

My aunt's reply greatly surprised me.

'Drusilla,' she said (if I have not already mentioned that my christian name is Drusilla, permit me to mention it now), 'you are touching—quite innocently, I know—on a very distressing subject.'

I rose immediately. Delicacy left me but one alternative—the alternative, after first making my apologies, of taking my leave. Lady Verinder stopped me, and insisted on my sitting down again.

'You have surprised a secret,' she said, 'which I had confided to my sister Mrs Ablewhite, and to my lawyer Mr Bruff, and to no one else. I can trust in their discretion; and I am sure, when I tell you the circumstances, I can trust in yours. Have you any pressing engagement, Drusilla? or is your time your own this afternoon?'

It is needless to say that my time was entirely at my aunt's disposal.

'Keep me company then,' she said, 'for another hour. I have something to tell you which I believe you will be sorry to hear. And I shall have a service to ask of you afterwards, if you don't object to assist me.'

It is again needless to say that, so far from objecting, I was all eagerness to assist her.

'You can wait here,' she went on, 'till Mr Bruff comes at five. And you can be one of the witnesses, Drusilla, when I sign my Will.'

Her Will! I thought of the drops which I had seen in her work-box. I thought of the bluish tinge which I had noticed in her complexion. A light which was not of this world—a light shining prophetically from an unmade grave—dawned on my mind. My aunt's secret was a secret no longer.

CHAPTER 3

Consideration for poor Lady Verinder forbade me even to hint that I had guessed the melancholy truth, before she opened her lips. I waited her pleasure in silence; and, having privately arranged to say a few sustaining words at the first convenient opportunity, felt prepared for any duty that could claim me, no matter how painful it might be.

'I have been seriously ill, Drusilla, for some time past,' my aunt began. 'And, strange to say, without knowing it myself.'

I thought of the thousands and thousands of perishing human creatures who were all at that moment spiritually ill, without knowing it themselves. And I greatly feared that my poor aunt might be one of the number. 'Yes, dear,' I said, sadly. 'Yes.'

'I brought Rachel to London, as you know, for medical advice,' she went on. 'I thought it right to consult two doctors.'

Two doctors! And, oh me (in Rachel's state), not one clergyman! 'Yes, dear?' I said once more. 'Yes?'

'One of the two medical men,' proceeded my aunt, 'was a stranger to me. The other had been an old friend of my husband's, and had always felt a sincere interest in me for my husband's sake. After prescribing for Rachel, he said he wished to speak to me privately in another room. I expected, of course, to receive some special directions for the management of my daughter's health. To my surprise, he took me gravely by the hand, and said, 'I have been looking at you, Lady Verinder, with a professional as well as a personal interest. You are, I am afraid, far more urgently in need of medical advice than your daughter.' He put some questions to me, which I was at first inclined to treat lightly enough, until I observed that my answers distressed him. It ended in his making an appointment to come and see me, accompanied by a medical friend, on the next day, at an hour when Rachel would not be at home. The result of that visit—most kindly and gently conveyed to me—satisfied both the physicians that there had been precious time lost, which could never be regained, and that my case had now passed beyond the reach of their art. For more than two years I have been suffering under an insidious form of heart disease, which, without any symptoms to alarm me, has, by little and little, fatally broken me down. I may live for some months, or I may die before another day has passed over my head—the doctors cannot, and dare not, speak more positively than this. It would be vain to say, my dear, that I have not had some miserable moments since my real situation has been made known to me. But I am more resigned than I was, and I am doing my best to set my worldly affairs in order. My one great anxiety is that Rachel should be kept in ignorance of the truth. If she knew it, she would at once attribute my broken health to anxiety about the Diamond, and would reproach herself bitterly, poor child, for what is in no sense her fault. Both the doctors agree that the mischief began two, if not three years since. I am sure you will keep my secret, Drusilla—for I am sure I see sincere sorrow and sympathy for me in your face.'

Sorrow and sympathy! Oh, what Pagan emotions to expect from a Christian English-woman anchored firmly on her faith!

Little did my poor aunt imagine what a gush of devout thankfulness thrilled through me as she approached the close of her melancholy story. Here was a career of usefulness opened before me! Here was a beloved relative and perishing fellow-creature, on the eve of the great change, utterly unprepared; and led, providentially led, to reveal her situation to Me! How can I describe the joy with which I now remembered that the precious clerical friends on whom I could rely, were to be counted, not by ones or twos, but by tens and twenties! I took my aunt in my arms—my overflowing tenderness was not to be satisfied, *now*, with anything less than an embrace. 'Oh!' I said to her, fervently, 'the indescribable interest with which you inspire me! Oh! the good I mean to do you, dear, before we part!' After another word or two of earnest prefatory warning, I gave her her choice of three precious friends, all plying the work of mercy from morning to night in her own neighbourhood; all equally inexhaustible in exhortation; all affectionately ready to exercise their gifts at a word from *me*. Alas! the result was far from encouraging. Poor Lady Verinder looked puzzled and frightened, and met everything I could say to her with the purely worldly objection that she was not strong enough to face strangers. I yielded—for the moment only, of course. My large experience (as Reader and Visitor, under not less, first and last, than fourteen beloved clerical friends) informed me that this was another case for preparation by books. I possessed a little library of works, all suitable to the present emergency, all calculated to arouse, convince, prepare, enlighten, and fortify my aunt. 'You will read, dear, won't you?' I said, in my most winning way. 'You will read, if I bring you my own precious books? Turned down at all the right places, aunt. And marked in pencil where you are to stop and ask yourself, "Does this apply to me?" ' Even that simple appeal—so absolutely heathenizing is the influence of the world—appeared to startle my aunt. She said, 'I will do what I can, Drusilla, to please you,' with a look of surprise, which was at once instructive and terrible to see. Not a moment was to be lost. The clock on the mantelpiece informed me that I had just time to hurry home; to provide myself with a first series of selected readings (say a dozen only); and to return in time to meet the lawyer, and witness Lady Verinder's Will. Promising faithfully to be back by five o'clock, I left the house on my errand of mercy.

When no interests but my own are involved, I am humbly content to get from place to place by the omnibus. Permit me to give an idea of my devotion to my aunt's interests by recording that, on this occasion, I committed the prodigality of taking a cab.

I drove home, selected and marked my first series of readings, and drove back to Montagu Square, with a dozen works in a carpet-bag, the like of which, I firmly believe, are not to be found in the literature of any other country in Europe. I paid the cabman exactly his fare. He received it with an oath; upon which I instantly gave him a tract. If I had presented a pistol at his head, this abandoned wretch could hardly have exhibited greater consternation. He jumped up on his box, and, with profane exclamations dismay, drove off furiously. Quite useless, I am happy to say! I sowed the good seed, in spite of him, by throwing a second tract in at the window of the cab.

The servant who answered the door—not the person with the cap-ribbons, to my great relief, but the footman—informed me that the doctor had called, and was still shut up with Lady Verinder. Mr Bruff, the lawyer, had arrived a minute since and was waiting in the library. I was shown into the library to wait too.

Mr Bruff looked surprised to see me. He is the family solicitor, and we had met more than once, on previous occasions, under Lady Verinder's roof. A man, I grieve to say, grown old and grizzled in the service of the world. A man who, in his hours of business, was the chosen prophet of Law and Mammon; and who, in his hours of leisure, was equally capable of reading a novel and of tearing up a tract.

'Have you come to stay here, Miss Clack?' he asked, with a look at my carpet-bag.

To reveal the contents of my precious bag to such a person as this would have been simply to invite an outburst of profanity. I lowered myself to his own level, and mentioned my business in the house.

'My aunt has informed me that she is about to sign her Will,' I answered. 'She has been so good as to ask me to be one of the witnesses.'

'Aye? aye? Well, Miss Clack, you will do. You are over twenty-one, and you have not the slightest pecuniary interest in Lady Verinder's Will.'

Not the slightest pecuniary interest in Lady Verinder's Will. Oh, how thankful I felt when I heard that! If my aunt, possessed of thousands, had remembered poor Me, to whom five pounds is an object—if my name had appeared in the Will, with a little comforting legacy attached to it—my enemies might have doubted the motive which had loaded me with the choicest treasures of my library, and had drawn upon my failing resources for the prodigal expenses of a cab. Not the cruellest scoffer of them all could doubt now. Much better as it was! Oh, surely, surely, much better as it was!

I was aroused from these consoling reflections by the voice of Mr Bruff. My meditative silence appeared to weigh upon the spirits of this worldling, and to force him, as it were, into talking to me against his own will.

'Well, Miss Clack, what's the last news in the charitable circles? How is your friend Mr Godfrey Ablewhite, after the, mauling he got from the rogues in Northumberland Street? Egad! they're telling a pretty story about that charitable gentleman at my club!'

I had passed over the manner in which this person had remarked that I was more than twenty-one, and that I had no pecuniary interest in my aunt's Will. But the tone in which he alluded to dear Mr Godfrey was too much for my forbearance. Feeling bound, after what had passed in my presence that afternoon, to assert the innocence of my admirable friend, whenever I found it called in question—I own to having also felt bound to include in the accomplishment of this righteous purpose, a stinging castigation in the case of Mr Bruff.

'I live very much out of the world,' I said; 'and I don't possess the advantage, sir, of belonging to a club. But I happen to know the story to which you allude; and I also know that a viler falsehood than that story never was told.'

'Yes, yes, Miss Clack—you believe in your friend. Natural enough. Mr Godfrey Ablewhite won't find the world in general quite so easy to convince as a committee of charitable ladies. Appearances are dead against him. He was in the house when the Diamond was lost. And he was the first person in the house to go to London afterwards. Those are ugly circumstances, ma'am, viewed by the light of later events.'

I ought, I know, to have set him right before he went any farther. I ought to have told him that he was speaking in ignorance of a testimony to Mr Godfrey's innocence, offered by the only person who was undeniably competent to speak from a positive knowledge of the subject. Alas! the temptation to lead the lawyer artfully on to his own discomfiture was too much for me. I asked what he meant by 'later events'—with an appearance of the utmost innocence.

'By later events, Miss Clack, I mean events in which the Indians are concerned,' proceeded Mr Bruff, getting more and more superior to poor Me, the longer he went on. 'What do the Indians do, the moment they are let out of the prison at Frizinghall? They go straight to London, and fix on Mr Luker. What follows? Mr Luker feels alarmed for the safety of "a valuable of great price," which he has got in the house. He lodges it privately (under a general description) in his bankers' strong-room. Wonderfully clever of him: but the Indians are just as clever on their side. They have their suspicions that the "valuable of great price" is being shifted from one place to another; and they hit on a singularly bold and complete way of clearing those suspicions up. Whom do they seize and search? Not Mr Luker only—which would be intelligible enough—but Mr Godfrey Ablewhite as well. Why? Mr Ablewhite's explanation is, that they acted on blind suspicion, after seeing him accidentally speaking to Mr Luker. Absurd! Half a dozen other people spoke to Mr Luker that morning. Why were they not followed home too, and decoyed into the trap? No! no! The plain inference is, that Mr Ablewhite had his private interest in the "valuable" as well as Mr Luker, and that the Indians were so uncertain as to which of the two had the disposal of it, that there was no alternative but to search them both. Public opinion says that, Miss Clack. And public opinion, on this occasion, is not easily refuted.'

He said those last words, looking so wonderfully wise in his own worldly conceit, that I really (to my shame be it spoken) could not resist leading him a little farther still, before I overwhelmed him with the truth.

'I don't presume to argue with a clever lawyer like you,' I said. 'But is it quite fair, sir, to Mr Ablewhite to pass over the opinion of the famous London police-officer who investigated this case? Not the shadow of a suspicion rested upon anybody but Miss Verinder, in the mind of Sergeant Cuff.'

'Do you mean to tell me, Miss Clack, that you agree with the Sergeant?

'I judge nobody, sir, and I offer no opinion.'

'And I commit both those enormities, ma'am. I judge the Sergeant to have been utterly wrong; and I offer the opinion that, if he had known Rachel's character as I know it, he would have suspected everybody in the house but *her*. I admit that she has her faults—she is secret, and self-willed; odd and wild, and unlike other girls of her age. But true as steel, and high-minded and generous to a fault. If the plainest evidence in the world pointed one way, and if nothing but Rachel's word of honour pointed the other, I would take her word before the evidence, lawyer as I am! Strong language, Miss Clack; but I mean it.'

'Would you object to illustrate your meaning, Mr Bruff, so that I may be sure I understand it? Suppose you found Miss Verinder quite unaccountably interested in what has happened to Mr Ablewhite and Mr Luker? Suppose she asked the strangest questions about this dreadful scandal, and displayed the most ungovernable agitation when she found out the turn it was taking?'

'Suppose anything you please, Miss Clack, it wouldn't shake my belief in Rachel Verinder by a hair's-breadth.'

'She is so absolutely to be relied on as that?'

'So absolutely to be relied on as that.'

'Then permit me to inform you, Mr Bruff, that Mr Godfrey Ablewhite was in this house not two hours since, and that his entire innocence of all concern in the disappearance of the Moonstone was proclaimed by Miss Verinder herself, in the strongest language I ever heard used by a young lady in my life.'

I enjoyed the triumph—the unholy triumph, I fear, I must admit— of seeing Mr Bruff utterly confounded and overthrown by a few plain words from Me. He started to his feet, and stared at me in silence. I kept my seat, undisturbed, and related the whole scene as it had occurred. 'And what do you say about Mr Ablewhite *now*?' I asked, with the utmost possible gentleness, as soon as I had done.

'If Rachel has testified to his innocence, Miss Clack, I don't scruple to say that I believe in his innocence as firmly as you do. I have been misled by appearances, like the rest of the world; and I will make the best atonement I can, by publicly contradicting the scandal which has assailed your friend wherever I meet with it. In the meantime, allow me to congratulate you on the masterly manner in which You have opened the full fire of your batteries on me at the moment when I least expected it. You would have done great things in my profession, ma'am, if you had happened to be a man.'

With those words he turned away from me, and began walking irritably up and down the room.

I could see plainly that the new light I had thrown on the subject had greatly surprised and disturbed him. Certain expressions dropped from his lips, as he became more and more absorbed in his own thoughts, which suggested to my mind the abominable view that he had hitherto taken of the mystery of the lost Moonstone. He had not scrupled to suspect dear Mr Godfrey of the infamy of stealing the Diamond, and to attribute Rachel's conduct to a generous resolution to conceal the crime. On Miss Verinder's own authority—a perfectly unassailable authority, as you are aware, in the estimation of Mr Bruff—that explanation of the circumstances was now shown to be utterly wrong. The perplexity into which I had plunged this high legal authority was so overwhelming that he was quite unable to conceal it from notice. 'What a case!' I heard him say to himself, stopping at the window in his walk, and drumming on the glass with his fingers. 'It not only defies explanation, it's even beyond conjecture.'

There was nothing in these words which made any reply at all needful, on my part—and yet, I answered them! It seems hardly credible that I should not have been able to let Mr Bruff alone, even now. It seems almost beyond mere mortal perversity that I should have discovered, in what he had just said, a new opportunity of making myself personally disagreeable to him. But—ah, my friends! nothing is beyond mortal perversity; and anything is credible when our fallen natures get the better of us!

'Pardon me for intruding on your reflections,' I said to the unsuspecting Mr Bruff. 'But surely there is a conjecture to make which has not occurred to us yet.'

'Maybe, Miss Clack. I own I don't know what it is.'

'Before I was so fortunate, sir, as to convince you of Mr Ablewhite's innocence, you mentioned it as one of the reasons for suspecting him, that he was in the house at the time when the Diamond was lost. Permit me to remind you that Mr Franklin Blake was also in the house at the time when the Diamond was lost.'

The old worldling left the window, took a chair exactly opposite to mine, and looked at me steadily, with a hard and vicious smile.

'You are not so good a lawyer, Miss Clack,' he remarked in a meditative manner, 'as I supposed. You don't know how to let well alone.'

'I am afraid I fail to follow you, Mr Bruff,' I said, modestly.

'It won't do, Miss Clack—it really won't do a second time. Franklin Blake is a prime favourite of mine, as you are well aware. But that doesn't matter. I'll adopt your view, on this occasion, before you have time to turn round on me. You're quite right, ma'am. I have suspected Mr Ablewhite, on grounds which abstractedly justify suspecting Mr Blake too. Very good—let's suspect them together. It's quite in his character, we will say, to be capable of stealing the Moonstone. The only question is, whether it was his interest to do so.'

'Mr Franklin Blake's debts,' I remarked, 'are matters of family notoriety.'

'And Mr Godfrey Ablewhite's debts have not arrived at that stage of development yet. Quite true. But there happen to be two difficulties in the way of your theory, Miss Clack. I manage Franklin Blake's affairs, and I beg to inform you that the vast majority of his creditors (knowing his father to be a rich man) are quite content to charge interest on their debts, and to wait for their money. There is the first difficulty—which is tough enough. You will find the second tougher still. I have it on the authority of Lady Verinder herself, that her daughter was ready to marry Franklin Blake, before that infernal Indian Diamond disappeared from the house. She had drawn him on and put him off again, with the coquetry of a young girl. But she had confessed to her mother that she loved cousin Franklin, and her mother had trusted cousin Franklin with the secret. So there he was, Miss Clack, with his creditors content to wait, and with the certain prospect before him of marrying an heiress. By all means consider him a scoundrel; but tell me, if you please, why he should steal the Moonstone?'

'The human heart is unsearchable,' I said gently. 'Who is to fathom it?'

'In other words, ma'am—though he hadn't the shadow of a reason for taking the Diamond—he might have taken it, nevertheless, through natural depravity. Very well. Say he did. Why the devil—'

'I beg your pardon, Mr Bruff. If I hear the devil referred to in that manner, I must leave the room.'

'I beg *your* pardon, Miss Clack—I'll be more careful in my choice of language for the future. All I meant to ask was this. Why—even supposing he did take the Diamond—should Franklin Blake make himself the most prominent person in the house, in trying to recover it? You may tell me he cunningly did that to divert suspicion from himself. I answer that he had no need to divert suspicion—because nobody suspected him. He first steals the Moonstone (without the slightest reason) through natural depravity; and he then acts a part, in relation to the loss of the jewel, which there is not the slightest necessity to act, and which leads to his mortally offending the young lady who would otherwise have married him. That is the monstrous proposition which you are driven to assert, if you attempt to associate the disappearance of the Moonstone with Franklin Blake. No, no, Miss Clack! After what has passed here to-day, between us two, the dead-lock, in this case, is complete. Rachel's own innocence is (as her mother knows, and as I know) beyond a doubt. Mr Ablewhite's innocence is equally certain—or Rachel would never have testified to it. And Franklin Blake's innocence, as you have just seen, unanswerably asserts itself. On the one hand, we are morally certain of all these things.

And, on the other hand, we are equally sure that somebody has brought the Moonstone to London, and that Mr Luker, or his banker, is in private possession of it at this moment. What is the use of my experience, what is the use of any person's experience, in such a case as that? It baffles me; it baffles you; it baffles everybody.'

No—not everybody. It had not baffled Sergeant Cuff. I was about to mention this, with all possible mildness, and with every necessary protest against being supposed to cast a slur upon Rachel —when the servant came in to say that the doctor had gone, and that my aunt was waiting to receive us.

This stopped the discussion. Mr Bruff collected his papers, looking a little exhausted by the demands which our conversation had made on him. I took up my bag-full of precious publications, feeling as if I could have gone on talking for hours. We proceeded in silence to Lady Verinder's room.

Permit me to add here, before my narrative advances to other events, that I have not described what passed between the lawyer and me, without having a definite object in view. I am ordered to include in my contribution to the shocking story of the Moonstone a plain disclosure, not only of the turn which suspicion took, but even of the names of the persons on whom suspicion rested, at the time when the Indian Diamond was believed to be in London. A report of my conversation in the library with Mr Bruff appeared to me to be exactly what was wanted to answer this purpose—while, at the same time, it possessed the great moral advantage of rendering a sacrifice of sinful self-esteem essentially necessary on my part. I have been obliged to acknowledge that my fallen nature got the better of me. In making that humiliating confession, *I* get the better of my fallen nature. The moral balance is restored; the spiritual atmosphere feels clear once more. Dear friends, we may go on again.

CHAPTER 4

The signing of the Will was a much shorter matter than I had anticipated. It was hurried over, to my thinking, in indecent haste. Samuel, the footman, was sent for to act as second witness—and the pen was put at once into my aunt's hand. I felt strongly urged to say a few appropriate words on this solemn occasion. But Mr Bruff's manner convinced me that it was wisest to check the impulse while he was in the room. In less than two minutes it was all over—and Samuel (unbenefited by what I might have said) had gone downstairs again.

Mr Bruff folded up the Will, and then looked my way; apparently wondering whether I did or did not mean to leave him alone with my aunt. I had my mission of mercy to fulfil, and my bag of precious publications ready on my lap. He might as well have expected to move St Paul's Cathedral by looking at it, as to move Me. There was one merit about him (due no doubt to his worldly training) which I have no wish to deny. He was quick at seeing things. I appeared to produce almost the same impression on him which I had produced on the cabman. *He* too uttered a profane expression, and withdrew in a violent hurry, and left me mistress of the field.

As soon as we were alone, my aunt reclined on the sofa, and then alluded, with some appearance of confusion, to the subject of her Will.

'I hope you won't think yourself neglected, Drusilla,' she said. 'I mean to *give* you your little legacy, my dear, with my own hand.'

Here was a golden opportunity! I seized it on the spot. In other words, I instantly opened my bag, and took out the top publication. It proved to be an early edition—only the twenty-fifth—of the famous anonymous work (believed to be by precious Miss Bellows), entitled *The Serpent at Home*. The design of the book—with which the worldly reader may not be acquainted—is to show how the Evil One lies in wait for us in all the most apparently innocent actions of our daily lives. The chapters best adapted to female perusal are 'Satan in the Hair Brush;' 'Satan behind the Looking Glass;' 'Satan under the Tea Table;' 'Satan out of the Window'—and many others.

'Give your attention, dear aunt, to this precious book—and you will give me all I ask.' With those words, I handed it to her open, at a marked passage—one continuous burst of burning eloquence! Subject: Satan among the Sofa Cushions.

Poor Lady Verinder (reclining thoughtlessly on her own sofa cushions) glanced at the book, and handed it back to me looking more confused than ever.

'I'm afraid, Drusilla,' she said, 'I must wait till I am a little better, before I can read that. The doctor—'

The moment she mentioned the doctor's name, I knew what was coming. Over and over again in my past experience among my perishing fellow-creatures, the members of the notoriously infidel profession of Medicine had stepped between me and my mission of mercy—on the miserable pretence that the patient wanted quiet, and that the disturbing influence of all others which they most dreaded, was the influence of Miss Clack and her Books. Precisely the same blinded materialism (working treacherously behind my back) now sought to rob me of the only right of property that my property could claim—my right of spiritual property in my perishing aunt.

'The doctor tells me,' my poor misguided relative went on, 'that I am not so well to-day. He forbids me to see any strangers; and he orders me, if I read at all, only to read the lightest and the most amusing books. "Do nothing, Lady Verinder, to wear your head, or to quicken your pulse"—those were his last words, Drusilla, when he left me to-day.'

There was no help for it but to yield again—for the moment only, as before. Any open assertion of the infinitely superior importance of such a ministry as mine, compared with the ministry of the medical man, would only have provoked the doctor to practise on the human weakness of his patient, and to threaten to throw up the case. Happily, there are more ways than one of sowing the good seed, and few persons are better versed in those ways than myself.

'You might feel stronger, dear, in an hour or two,' I said. 'Or you might wake, to-morrow morning, with a sense of something wanting, and even this unpretending volume might be able to supply it. You will let me leave the book, aunt? The doctor can hardly object to that!'

I slipped it under the sofa cushions, half in, and half out, close by her handkerchief, and her smelling-bottle. Every time her hand searched for either of these, it would touch the book; and, sooner or later (who knows?) the book might touch *her*. After making this arrangement, I thought it wise to withdraw. 'Let me leave you to repose, dear aunt; I will call again to-morrow.' I looked accidentally towards the window as I said that. It was full of flowers, in boxes and pots. Lady Verinder was extravagantly fond of these perishable treasures, and had a habit of rising every now and then, and going to look at them and smell them. A new idea flashed across my mind. 'Oh! may I take a flower?' I said—and got to the window unsuspected, in that way. Instead of taking away a flower, I added one, in the shape of another book from my bag, which I left, to surprise my aunt, among the geraniums and roses. The happy thought followed, 'Why not do the same for her, poor dear, in every other room that she enters?' I immediately said good-bye; and, crossing the hall, slipped into the library. Samuel, coming up to let me out, and supposing I had gone, went downstairs again. On the library table I noticed two of the 'amusing books' which the infidel doctor had recommended. I instantly covered them from sight with two of my own precious publications. In the breakfast-room I found my aunt's favourite canary singing in his cage. She was always in the habit of feeding the bird herself. Some groundsel was strewed on a table which stood immediately under the cage. I put a book among the groundsel. In the drawing-room I found more cheering opportunities of emptying my bag. My aunt's favourite musical pieces were on the piano. I slipped in two more books among the music. I disposed of another in the back drawing-room, under some unfinished embroidery, which I knew to be of Lady Verinder's working. A third little room opened out of the back drawing-room, from which it was shut off by curtains instead of a door. My aunt's plain old-fashioned fan was on the chimney-piece. I opened my ninth book at a very special passage, and put the fan in as a marker, to keep the place. The question then came, whether I should go higher still, and try the bedroom floor—at the risk, undoubtedly, of being insulted, if the person with the cap-ribbons happened to be in the upper regions of the house, and to find me out. But oh, what of that? It is a poor Christian that is afraid of being insulted. I went upstairs, prepared to bear anything. All was silent and solitary—it was the servants' tea-time, I suppose. My aunt's room was in front. The miniature of my late dear uncle, Sir John, hung on the wall opposite the bed. It seemed to smile at me; it seemed to say, 'Drusilla! deposit a book.' There were tables on either side of my aunt's bed. She was a bad sleeper, and wanted, or thought she wanted, many things at night. I put a book near the matches on one side, and a book under the box of chocolate drops on the other. Whether she wanted a light, or whether she wanted a drop, there was a precious publication to meet her eye, or to meet her hand, and to say with silent eloquence, in either case, 'Come, try me! try me!' But one book was now left at the bottom of my bag, and but one apartment was still unexplored—the bathroom, which opened out of the bedroom. I peeped in; and the holy inner voice that never deceives, whispered to me, 'You have met her, Drusilla, everywhere else; meet her at the bath, and the work is done.' I observed a dressing-gown thrown across a chair. It had a pocket in it, and in that pocket I put my last book. Can words express my exquisite sense of duty done, when I had slipped out of the house, unsuspected by any of them, and when I found myself in the street with my empty bag under my arm? Oh, my worldly friends, pursuing the phantom, Pleasure, through the guilty mazes of Dissipation, how easy it is to be happy, if you will only be good!

When I folded up my things that night—when I reflected on the *true* riches which I had scattered with such a lavish hand, from top to bottom of the house of my wealthy aunt—I declare I felt as free from all anxiety as if I had been a child again. I was so light-hearted that I sang a verse of the Evening Hymn. I was so light-hearted that I fell asleep before I could sing another. Quite like a child again! quite like a child again!

So I passed that blissful night. On rising the next morning, how young I felt! I might add, how young I looked, if I were capable of dwelling on the concerns of my own perishable body. But I am not capable—and I add nothing.

Towards luncheon time—not for the sake of the creature-comforts, but for the certainty of finding dear aunt—I put on my bonnet to go to Montagu Square. Just as I was ready, the maid at the lodgings in which I then lived looked in at the door, and said, 'Lady Verinder's servant, to see Miss Clack.'

I occupied the parlour-floor, at that period of my residence in London. The front parlour was my sitting-room. Very small, very low in the ceiling, very poorly furnished—but, oh, so neat! I looked into the passage to see which of Lady Verinder's servants had asked for me. It was the young footman, Samuel—a civil fresh-coloured person, with a teachable look and a very obliging manner. I had always felt a spiritual interest in Samuel, and a wish to try him with a few serious words. On this occasion, I invited him into my sitting-room.

He came in, with a large parcel under his arm. When he put the parcel down, it appeared to frighten him. 'My lady's love, Miss; and I was to say that you would find a letter inside.' Having given that message, the fresh-coloured young footman surprised me by looking as if he would have liked to run away.

I detained him to make a few kind inquiries. Could I see my aunt, if I called in Montagu Square? No; she had gone out for a drive. Miss Rachel had gone with her, and Mr Ablewhite had taken a seat in the carriage, too. Knowing how sadly dear Mr Godfrey's charitable work was in arrear, I thought it odd that he should be going out driving, like an idle man. I stopped Samuel at the door, and made a few more kind inquiries. Miss Rachel was going to a ball that night, and Mr Ablewhite had arranged to come to coffee, and go with her. There was a morning concert advertised for to-morrow, and Samuel was ordered to take places for a large party, including a place for Mr Ablewhite. 'All the tickets may be gone, Miss,' said this innocent youth, 'if I don't run and get them at once!' He ran as he said the words—and I found myself alone again, with some anxious thoughts to occupy me.

We had a special meeting of the Mothers' Small-Clothes-Conversion Society, that night, summoned expressly with a view to obtaining Mr Godfrey's advice and assistance. Instead of sustaining our sisterhood, under an overwhelming flow of Trousers which quite prostrated our little community, he had arranged to take coffee in Montagu Square, and to go to a ball afterwards! The afternoon of the next day had been selected for the Festival of the British-Ladies'-Servants'-Sunday-Sweetheart-Supervision Society. Instead of being present, the life and soul of that struggling Institution, he had engaged to make one of a party of worldlings at a morning concert! I asked myself what did it mean? Alas! it meant that our Christian Hero was to reveal himself to me in a new character, and to become associated in my mind with one of the most awful back-slidings of modern times.

To return, however, to the history of the passing day. On finding myself alone in my room, I naturally turned my attention to the parcel which appeared to have so strangely intimidated the fresh-coloured young footman. Had my aunt sent me my promised legacy? and had it taken the form of cast-off clothes, or worn-out silver spoons, or unfashionable jewellery, or anything of that sort? Prepared to accept all, and to resent nothing, I opened the parcel—and what met my view? The twelve precious publications which I had scattered through the house, on the previous day; all returned to me by the doctor's orders! Well might the youthful Samuel shrink when he brought his parcel into my room! Well might he run when he had performed his miserable errand! As to my aunt's letter, it simply amounted, poor soul, to this—that she dare not disobey her medical man.

What was to be done now? With my training and my principles, I never had a moment's doubt.

Once self-supported by conscience, once embarked on a career of manifest usefulness, the true Christian never yields. Neither public nor private influences produce the slightest effect on us, when we have once got our mission. Taxation may be the consequence of a mission; riots may be the consequence of a mission; wars may be the consequence of a mission: we go on with our work, irrespective of every human consideration which moves the world outside us. We are above reason; we are beyond ridicule; we see with nobody's eyes, we hear with nobody's ears, we feel with nobody's hearts, but our own. Glorious, glorious privilege! And how is it earned? Ah, my friends, you may spare yourselves the useless inquiry! We are the only people who can earn it—for we are the only people who are always right.

In the case of my misguided aunt, the form which pious perseverance was next to take revealed itself to me plainly enough.

Preparation by clerical friends had failed, owing to Lady Verinder's own reluctance. Preparation by books had failed, owing to the doctor's infidel obstinacy. So be it! What was the next thing to try? The next thing to try was—Preparation by Little Notes. In other words, the books themselves having been sent back, select extracts from the books, copied by different hands, and all addressed as letters to my aunt, were, some to be sent by post, and some to be distributed about the house on the plan I had adopted on the previous day. As letters they would excite no suspicion; as letters they would be opened—and, once opened, might be read. Some of them I wrote myself. 'Dear aunt, may I ask your attention to a few lines?' &c. 'Dear aunt, I was reading last night, and I chanced on the following passage,' &c. Other letters were written for me by my valued fellow-workers, the sisterhood at the Mothers' Small-Clothes. 'Dear madam, pardon the interest taken in you by a true, though humble, friend.' 'Dear madam, may a serious person surprise you by saying a few cheering words?' Using these and other similar forms of courteous appeal, we reintroduced all my precious passages under a form which not even the doctor's watchful materialism could suspect. Before the shades of evening had closed around us, I had a dozen awakening letters for my aunt, instead of a dozen awakening books. Six I made immediate arrangements for sending through the post, and six I kept in my pocket for personal distribution in the house the next day.

Soon after two o'clock I was again on the field of pious conflict, addressing more kind inquiries to Samuel at Lady Verinder's door.

My aunt had had a bad night. She was again in the room in which I had witnessed her Will, resting on the sofa, and trying to get a little sleep.

I said I would wait in the library, on the chance of seeing her. In the fervour of my zeal to distribute the letters, it never occurred to me to inquire about Rachel. The house was quiet, and it was past the hour at which the musical performance began. I took it for granted that she and her party of pleasure-seekers (Mr Godfrey, alas! included) were all at the concert, and eagerly devoted myself to my good work, while time and opportunity were still at my own disposal.

My aunt's correspondence of the morning—including the six awakening letters which I had posted overnight—was lying unopened on the library table. She had evidently not felt herself equal to dealing with a large mass of letters—and she might be daunted by the number of them, if she entered the library later in the day. I put one of my second set of six letters on the chimney-piece by itself; leaving it to attract her curiosity, by means of its solitary position, apart from the rest. A second letter I put purposely on the floor in the breakfast-room. The first servant who went in after me would conclude that my aunt had dropped it, and would be specially careful to restore it to her. The field thus sown on the basement story, I ran lightly upstairs to scatter my mercies next over the drawing-room floor.

Just as I entered the front room, I heard a double-knock at the street-door—a soft, fluttering, considerate little knock. Before I could think of slipping back to the library (in which I was supposed to be waiting), the active young footman was in the hall, answering the door. It mattered little, as I thought. In my aunt's state of health, visitors in general were not admitted. To my horror and amazement, the performer of the soft little knock proved to be an exception to general rules. Samuel's voice below me (after apparently answering some questions which I did not hear) said, unmistakably, 'Upstairs, if you please, sir.' The next moment I heard footsteps—a man's footsteps—approaching the drawing-room floor. Who could this favoured male, visitor possibly be? Almost as soon as I asked myself the question, the answer occurred to me. Who *could* it be but the doctor?

In the case of any other visitor, I should have allowed myself to be discovered in the drawing-room. There would have been nothing out of the common in my having got tired of the library, and having gone upstairs for a change. But my own self-respect stood in the way of my meeting the person who had insulted me by sending me back my books. I slipped into the little third room, which I have mentioned as communicating with the back drawing-room, and dropped the curtains which closed the open doorway. If I only waited there for a minute or two, the usual result in such cases would take place. That is to say, the doctor would be conducted to his patient's room.

I waited a minute or two, and more than a minute or two. I heard the visitor walking restlessly backwards and forwards. I also heard him talking to himself. I even thought I recognized the voice. Had I made a mistake? Was it not the doctor, but somebody else? Mr Bruff, for instance? No! an unerring instinct told me it was not Mr Bruff. Whoever he was, he was still talking to himself. I parted the heavy curtains the least little morsel in the world, and listened.

The words I heard were, 'I'll do it to-day!' And the voice that spoke them was Mr Godfrey Ablewhite's.

CHAPTER 5

My hand dropped from the curtain. But don't suppose—oh, don't suppose—that the dreadful embarrassment of my situation was the uppermost idea in my mind! So fervent still was the sisterly interest I felt in Mr Godfrey, that I never stopped to ask myself why he was not at the concert. No! I thought only of the words—the startling words—which had just fallen from his lips. He would do it to-day. He had said, in a tone of terrible resolution, he would do it to-day. What, oh what, would he do! Something even more deplorably unworthy of him than what he had done already? Would he apostatize from the faith? Would he abandon us at the Mothers' Small-Clothes? Had we seen the last of his angelic smile in the committee-room? Had we heard the last of his unrivalled eloquence at Exeter Hall? I was so wrought up by the bare idea of such awful eventualities as these in connection with such a man, that I believe I should have rushed from my place of concealment, and implored him in the name of all the Ladies' Committees in London to explain himself—when I suddenly heard another voice in the room. It penetrated through the curtains; it was loud, it was bold, it was wanting in every female charm. The voice of Rachel Verinder!

'Why have you come up here, Godfrey?' she asked. 'Why didn't you go into the library?'

He laughed softly, and answered, 'Miss Clack is in the library.'

'Clack in the library!' She instantly seated herself on the ottoman in the back drawing-room. 'You are quite right, Godfrey. We had much better stop here.'

I had been in a burning fever, a moment since, and in some doubt what to do next. I became extremely cold now, and felt no doubt whatever. To show myself, after what I had heard, was impossible. To retreat—except into the fireplace—was equally out of the question. A martyrdom was before me. In justice to myself, I noiselessly arranged the curtains so that I could both see and hear. And then I met my martyrdom, with the spirit of a primitive Christian.

'Don't sit on the ottoman,' the young lady proceeded. 'Bring a chair, Godfrey. I like people to be opposite to me when I talk to them.'

He took the nearest seat. It was a low chair. He was very tall, and many sizes too large for it. I never saw his legs to such disadvantage before.

'Well?' she went on. 'What did you say to them?'

'Just what you said, dear Rachel, to me.'

'That mamma was not at all well to-day? And that I didn't quite like leaving her to go to the concert?'

'Those were the words. They were grieved to lose you at the concert, but they quite understood. All sent their love; and all expressed a cheering belief that Lady Verinder's indisposition would soon pass away.'

'*You* don't think it's serious, do you, Godfrey?'

'Far from it! In a few days, I feel quite sure, all will be well again.'

'I think so, too. I was a little frightened at first, but I think so too. It was very kind to go and make my excuses for me to people who are almost strangers to you. But why not have gone with them to the concert? It seems very hard that you should miss the music too.'

'Don't say that, Rachel! If you only knew how much happier I am—here, with you!'

He clasped his hands, and looked at her. In the position which he occupied, when he did that, he turned my way. Can words describe how I sickened when I noticed exactly the same pathetic expression on his face, which had charmed me when he was pleading for destitute millions of his fellow-creatures on the platform at Exeter Hall!

'It's hard to get over one's bad habits, Godfrey. But do try to get over the habit of paying compliments—do, to please me.'

'I never paid *you* a compliment, Rachel, in my life. Successful love may sometimes use the language of flattery, I admit. But hopeless love, dearest, always speaks the truth.'

He drew his chair close, and took her hand, when he said 'hopeless love.' There was a momentary silence. He, who thrilled everybody, had doubtless thrilled *her*. I thought I now understood the words which had dropped from him when he was alone in the drawing-room, 'I'll do it to-day.' Alas! the most rigid propriety could hardly have failed to discover that he was doing it now.

'Have you forgotten what we agreed on, Godfrey, when you spoke to me in the country? We agreed that we were to be cousins, and nothing more.'

'I break the agreement, Rachel, every time I see you.'

'Then don't see me.'

'Quite useless! I break the agreement every time I think of you. Oh, Rachel! how kindly you told me, only the other day, that my place in your estimation was a higher place than it had ever been yet! Am I mad to build the hopes I do on those dear words? Am I mad to dream of some future day when your heart may soften to me? Don't tell me so, if I am! Leave me my delusion, dearest! I must have *that* to cherish, and to comfort me, if I have nothing else!'

His voice trembled, and he put his white handkerchief to his eyes. Exeter Hall again! Nothing wanting to complete the parallel but the audience, the cheers, and the glass of water.

Even *her* obdurate nature was touched. I saw her lean a little nearer to him. I heard a new tone of interest in her next words.

'Are you really sure, Godfrey, that you are so fond of me as that?'

'Sure! You know what I was, Rachel. Let me tell you what I am. I have lost every interest in life, but my interest in you. A transformation has come over me which I can't account for, myself. Would you believe it? My charitable business is an unendurable nuisance to me; and when I see a Ladies' Committee now, I wish myself at the uttermost ends of the earth!'

If the annals of apostasy offer anything comparable to such a declaration as that, I can only say that the case in point is not producible from the stores of *my* reading. I thought of the Mothers' Small-Clothes. I thought of the Sunday-Sweetheart-Supervision. I thought of the other Societies, too numerous to mention, all built up on this man as on a tower of strength. I thought of the struggling Female Boards, who, so to speak, drew the breath of their business-life through the nostrils of Mr Godfrey—of that same Mr Godfrey who had just reviled our good work as a 'nuisance'— and just declared that he wished he was at the uttermost ends of the earth when he found himself in our company! My young female friends will feel encouraged to persevere, when I mention that it tried even My discipline before I could devour my own righteous indignation in silence. At the same time, it is only justice to myself to add, that I didn't lose a syllable of the conversation. Rachel was the next to speak.

'You have made your confession,' she said. 'I wonder whether it would cure you of your unhappy attachment to me, if I made mine?'

He started. I confess I started too. He thought, and I thought, that she was about to divulge the mystery of the Moonstone.

'Would you think, to look at me,' she went on, 'that I am the wretchedest girl living? It's true, Godfrey. What greater wretchedness can there be than to live degraded in your own estimation? That is my life now.'

'My dear Rachel! it's impossible you can have any reason to speak of yourself in that way!'

'How do you know I have no reason?'

'Can you ask me the question! I know it, because I know *you*. Your silence, dearest, has never lowered you in the estimation of your true friends. The disappearance of your precious birthday gift may seem strange; your unexplained connection with that event may seem stranger still—'

'Are you speaking of the Moonstone, Godfrey?'

'I certainly thought that you referred—'

'I referred to nothing of the sort. I can hear of the loss of the Moonstone, let who will speak of it, without feeling degraded in my own estimation. If the story of the Diamond ever comes to light, it will be known that I accepted a dreadful responsibility; it will be known that I involved myself in the keeping of a miserable secret— but it will be as clear as the sun at noonday that I did nothing mean! You have misunderstood me, Godfrey. It's my fault for not speaking more plainly. Cost me what it may, I will be plainer now. Suppose you were not in love with me? Suppose you were in love with some other woman?'

'Yes?'

'Suppose you discovered that woman to be utterly unworthy of you? Suppose you were quite convinced that it was a disgrace to you to waste another thought on her? Suppose the bare idea of ever marrying such a person made your face burn, only with thinking of it?'

'Yes?'

'And, suppose, in spite of all that—you couldn't tear her from your heart? Suppose the feeling she had roused in you (in the time when you believed in her) was not a feeling to be hidden? Suppose the love this wretch had inspired in you—? Oh, how can I find words to say it in! How can I make a *man* understand that a feeling which horrifies me at myself, can be a feeling that fascinates me at the same time? It's the breath of my life, Godfrey, and it's the poison that kills me—both in one! Go away! I must be out of my mind to talk as I am talking now. No! you mustn't leave me—you mustn't carry away a wrong impression. I must say, what is to be said in my own defence. Mind this! *He* doesn't know—he never will know, what I have told *you*. I will never see him—I don't care what happens—I will never, never, never see him again! Don't ask me his name! Don't ask me any more! Let's change the subject. Are you doctor enough, Godfrey, to tell me why I feel as if I was stifling for want of breath? Is there a form of hysterics that bursts into words instead of tears? I dare say! What does it matter? You will get over any trouble I have caused you,

173

easily enough now. I have dropped to my right place in your estimation, haven't I? Don't notice me! Don't pity me! For God's sake, go away!'

She turned round on a sudden, and beat her hands wildly on the back of the ottoman. Her head dropped on the cushions; and she burst out crying. Before I had time to feel shocked at this, I was horror-struck by an entirely unexpected proceeding on the part of Mr Godfrey. Will it be credited that he fell on his knees at her feet?—on *both* knees, I solemnly declare! May modesty mention that he put his arms round her next? And may reluctant admiration acknowledge that he electrified her with two words?

'Noble creature!'

No more than that! But he did it with one of the bursts which have made his fame as a public speaker. She sat, either quite thunderstruck, or quite fascinated—I don't know which—without even making an effort to put his arms back where his arms ought to have been. As for me, my sense of propriety was completely bewildered. I was so painfully uncertain whether it was my first duty to close my eyes, or to stop my ears, that I did neither. I attribute my being still able to hold the curtain in the right position for looking and listening, entirely to suppressed hysterics. In suppressed hysterics, it is admitted, even by the doctors, that one must hold something.

'Yes,' he said, with all the fascination of his evangelical voice and manner, 'you are a noble creature! A woman who can speak the truth, for the truth's own sake—a woman who will sacrifice her pride, rather than sacrifice an honest man who loves her—is the most priceless of all treasures. When such a woman marries, if her husband only wins her esteem and regard, he wins enough to ennoble his whole life. You have spoken, dearest, of your place in my estimation. Judge what that place is—when I implore you on my knees, to let the cure of your poor wounded heart be my care. Rachel! will you honour me, will you bless me, by being my wife?'

By this time I should certainly have decided on stopping my ears, if Rachel had not encouraged me to keep them open, by answering him in the first sensible words I had ever heard fall from her lips.

'Godfrey!' she said, 'you must be mad!'

'I never spoke more reasonably, dearest—in your interests, as well as in mine. Look for a moment to the future. Is your happiness to be sacrificed to a man who has never known how you feel towards him, and whom you are resolved never to see again? Is it not your duty to yourself to forget this ill-fated attachment? and is forgetfulness to be found in the life you are leading now? You have tried that life, and you are wearying of it already. Surround yourself with nobler interests than the wretched interests of the world. A heart that loves and honours you; a home whose peaceful claims and happy duties win gently on you day by day—try the consolation, Rachel, which is to be found *there*! I don't ask for your love—I will be content with your affection and regard. Let the rest be left, confidently left, to your husband's devotion, and to Time that heals even wounds as deep as yours.'

She began to yield already. Oh, what a bringing-up she must have had! Oh, how differently I should have acted in her place!

'Don't tempt me, Godfrey,' she said; 'I am wretched enough and reckless enough as it is. Don't tempt me to be more wretched and more reckless still!'

'One question, Rachel. Have you any personal objection to me?'

'I! I always liked you. After what you have just said to me, I should be insensible indeed if I didn't respect and admire you as well.'

'Do you know many wives, my dear Rachel, who respect and admire their husbands? And yet they and their husbands get on very well. How many brides go to the altar with hearts that would bear inspection by the men who take them there? And yet it doesn't end unhappily—somehow or other the nuptial establishment jogs on. The truth is, that women try marriage as a Refuge, far more numerously than they are willing to admit; and, what is more, they find that marriage has justified their confidence in it. Look at your own case once again. At your age, and with your attractions, is it possible for you to sentence yourself to a single life? Trust my knowledge of the world—nothing is less possible. It is merely a question of time. You may marry some other man, some years hence. Or you may marry the man, dearest, who is now at your feet, and who prizes your respect and admiration above the love of any other woman on the face of the earth.'

'Gently, Godfrey! you are putting something into my head which I never thought of before. You are tempting me with a new prospect, when all my other prospects are closed before me. I tell you again, I am miserable enough and desperate enough, if you say another word, to marry you on your own terms. Take the warning, and go!'

'I won't even rise from my knees, till you have said yes!'

'If I say yes you will repent, and I shall repent, when it is too late!'

'We shall both bless the day, darling, when I pressed, and when you yielded.'

'Do you feel as confidently as you speak?'

'You shall judge for yourself. I speak from what I have seen in my own family. Tell me what you think of our household at Frizinghall. Do my father and mother live unhappily together?'

'Far from it—so far as I can see.'

'When my mother was a girl, Rachel (it is no secret in the family), she had loved as you love—she had given her heart to a man who was unworthy of her. She married my father, respecting him, admiring him, but nothing more. Your own eyes have seen the result. Is there no encouragement in it for you and for me?'*

'You won't hurry me, Godfrey?'

'My time shall be yours.'

'You won't ask me for more than I can give?'

'My angel! I only ask you to give me yourself.'

'Take me!'

In those two words she accepted him!

He had another burst—a burst of unholy rapture this time. He drew her nearer and nearer to him till her face touched his; and then—No! I really cannot prevail upon myself to carry this shocking disclosure any farther. Let me only say, that I tried to close my eyes before it happened, and that I was just one moment too late. I had calculated, you see, on her resisting. She submitted. To every right-feeling person of my own sex, volumes could say no more.

Even my innocence in such matters began to see its way to the end of the interview now. They understood each other so thoroughly by this time, that I fully expected to see them walk

---

* See Betteredge's Narrative, chapter viii.

off together, arm in arm, to be married. There appeared, however, judging by Mr Godfrey's next words, to be one more trifling formality which it was necessary to observe. He seated himself—unforbidden this time— on the ottoman by her side. 'Shall I speak to your dear mother?'

She asked. 'Or will you?'

She declined both alternatives.

'Let my mother hear nothing from either of us, until she is better. I wish it to be kept a secret for the present, Godfrey. Go now, and come back this evening. We have been here alone together quite long enough.'

She rose, and, in rising, looked for the first time towards the little room in which my martyrdom was going on.

'Who has drawn those curtains?' she exclaimed. 'The room is close enough, as it is, without keeping the air out of it in that way.'

She advanced to the curtains. At the moment when she laid her hand on them—at the moment when the discovery of me appeared to be quite inevitable—the voice of the fresh-coloured young footman, on the stairs, suddenly suspended any further proceedings on her side or on mine. It was unmistakably the voice of a man in great alarm.

'Miss Rachel!' he called out, 'where are you, Miss Rachel?'

She sprang back from the curtains, and ran to the door.

The footman came just inside the room. His ruddy colour was all gone. He said, 'Please to come downstairs, Miss! My lady has fainted, and we can't bring her to again.'

In a moment more I was alone, and free to go downstairs in my turn, quite unobserved.

Mr Godfrey passed me in the hall, hurrying out, to fetch the doctor. 'Go in, and help them!' he said, pointing to the room. I found Rachel on her knees by the sofa, with her mother's head on her bosom. One look at my aunt's face (knowing what I knew) was enough to warn me of the dreadful truth. I kept my thoughts to myself till the doctor came in. It was not long before he arrived. He began by sending Rachel out of the room— and then he told the rest of us that Lady Verinder was no more. Serious persons, in search of proofs of hardened scepticism, may be interested in hearing that he showed no signs of remorse when he looked at Me.

At a later hour I peeped into the breakfast-room, and the library. My aunt had died without opening one of the letters which I had addressed to her. I was so shocked at this, that it never occurred to me, until some days afterwards, that she had also died without giving me my little legacy.

CHAPTER 6

(1) 'Miss Clack presents her compliments to Mr Franklin Blake; and, in sending him the fifth chapter of her humble narrative, begs to say that she feels quite unequal to enlarge as she could wish on an event so awful, under the circumstances, as Lady Verinder's death. She has, therefore, attached to her own manuscript, copious Extracts from precious publications in her possession, all bearing on this terrible subject. And may those Extracts (Miss Clack fervently hopes) sound as the blast of a trumpet in the ears of her respected kinsman, Mr Franklin Blake.'

(2) 'Mr Franklin Blake presents his compliments to Miss Clack, and begs to thank her for the fifth chapter of her narrative. In returning the extracts sent with it, he will refrain from mentioning any personal objection which he may entertain to this species of literature, and will merely say that the proposed additions to the manuscript are not necessary to the fulfilment of the purpose that he has in view.'

(3) 'Miss Clack begs to acknowledge the return of her Extracts. She affectionately reminds Mr Franklin Blake that she is a Christian, and that it is, therefore, quite impossible for him to offend her. Miss C. persists in feeling the deepest interest in Mr Blake, and pledges herself, on the first occasion when sickness may lay him low, to offer him the use of her Extracts for the second time. In the meanwhile she would be glad to know, before beginning the final chapters of her narrative, whether she may be permitted to make her humble contribution complete, by availing herself of the light which later discoveries have thrown on the mystery of the Moonstone.'

(4) 'Mr Franklin Blake is sorry to disappoint Miss Clack. He can only repeat the instructions which he had the honour of giving her when she began her narrative. She is requested to limit herself to her own individual experience of persons and events, as recorded in her diary. Later discoveries she will be good enough to leave to the pens of those persons who can write in the capacity of actual witnesses.'

(5) 'Miss Clack is extremely sorry to trouble Mr Franklin Blake with another letter. Her Extracts have been returned, and the expression of her matured views on the subject of the Moonstone has been forbidden. Miss Clack is painfully conscious that she ought (in the worldly phrase) to feel herself put down. But, no—Miss C. has learnt Perseverance in the School of Adversity. Her object in writing is to know whether Mr Blake (who prohibits everything else) prohibits the appearance of the present correspondence in Miss Clack's narrative? Some explanation of the position in which Mr Blake's interference has placed her as an authoress, seems due on the ground of common justice. And Miss Clack, on her side, is most anxious that her letters should be produced to speak for themselves.'

(6) 'Mr Franklin Blake agrees to Miss Clack's proposal, on the understanding that she will kindly consider this intimation of his consent as closing the correspondence between them.'

(7) 'Miss Clack feels it an act of Christian duty (before the correspondence closes) to inform Mr Franklin Blake that his last letter—evidently intended to offend her—has not succeeded in accomplishing the object of the writer. She affectionately requests Mr Blake to retire to the privacy of his own room, and to consider with himself whether the training which can thus elevate a poor weak woman above the reach of insult, be not worthy of

greater admiration than he is now disposed to feel for it. On being favoured with an intimation to that effect, Miss C. solemnly pledges herself to send back the complete series of her Extracts to Mr Franklin Blake.'

[To this letter no answer was received. Comment is needless.

(Signed)　　Drusilla Clack.]

CHAPTER 7

The foregoing correspondence will sufficiently explain why no choice is left to me but to pass over Lady Verinder's death with the simple announcement of the fact which ends my fifth chapter.

Keeping myself for the future strictly within the limits of my own personal experience, I have next to relate that a month elapsed from the time of my aunt's decease before Rachel Verinder and I met again. That meeting was the occasion of my spending a few days under the same roof with her. In the course of my visit, something happened, relating to her marriage-engagement with Mr Godfrey Ablewhite, which is important enough to require special notice in these pages. When this last of many painful family circumstances has been disclosed, my task will be completed; for I shall then have told all that I know, as an actual (and most unwilling) witness of events.

My aunt's remains were removed from London, and were buried in the little cemetery attached to the church in her own park. I was invited to the funeral with the rest of the family. But it was impossible (with my religious views) to rouse myself in a few days only from the shock which this death had caused me. I was informed, moreover, that the rector of Frizinghall was to read the service. Having myself in past times seen this clerical castaway making one of the players at Lady Verinder's whist-table, I doubt, even if I had been fit to travel, whether I should have felt justified in attending the ceremony.

Lady Verinder's death left her daughter under the care of her brother-in-law, Mr Ablewhite the elder. He was appointed guardian by the will, until his niece married, or came of age. Under these circumstances, Mr Godfrey informed his father, I suppose, of the new relation in which he stood towards Rachel. At any rate, in ten days from my aunt's death, the secret of the marriage engagement was no secret at all within the circle of the family, and the grand question for Mr Ablewhite senior—another confirmed castaway!— was how to make himself and his authority most agreeable to the wealthy young lady who was going to marry his son.

Rachel gave him some trouble at the outset, about the choice of a place in which she could be prevailed upon to reside. The house in Montagu Square was associated with the calamity of her mother's death. The house in Yorkshire was associated with the scandalous affair of the lost Moonstone. Her guardian's own residence at Frizinghall was open to neither of these objections. But Rachel's presence in it, after her recent bereavement, operated as a check on the gaieties of her cousins, the Miss Ablewhites—and she herself requested that her visit might be deferred to a more favourable opportunity. It ended in a proposal, emanating from old Mr Ablewhite, to try a furnished house at Brighton. His wife, an invalid daughter, and Rachel were to inhabit it together, and were to expect him to join them later in the season. They would see no society but a few old friends, and they would have his son Godfrey, travelling backwards and forwards by the London train, always at their disposal.

I describe this aimless flitting about from one place of residence to another—this insatiate restlessness of body and appalling stagnation of soul—merely with the view to arriving at results. The event which (under Providence) proved to be the means of bringing Rachel Verinder and myself together again, was no other than the hiring of the house at Brighton.

My Aunt Ablewhite is a large, silent, fair-complexioned woman, with one noteworthy point in her character. From the hour of her birth she has never been known to do anything for herself. She has gone through life, accepting everybody's help, and adopt-ing everybody's opinions. A more hopeless person, in a spiritual point of view, I have never met with—there is absolutely, in this perplexing case, no obstructive material to work upon. Aunt Ablewhite would listen to the Grand Lama of Thibet exactly as she listens to Me, and would reflect his views quite as readily as she reflects mine. She found the furnished house at Brighton by stopping at an hotel in London, composing herself on a sofa, and sending for her son. She discovered the necessary servants by breakfasting in bed one morning (still at the hotel), and giving her maid a holiday on condition that the girl 'would begin enjoying herself by fetching Miss Clack.' I found her placidly fanning herself in her dressing-gown at eleven o'clock. 'Drusilla, dear, I want some servants. You are so clever—please get them for me.' I looked round the untidy room. The church-bells were going for a week-day service; they suggested a word of affectionate remonstrance on my part. 'Oh, aunt!' I said sadly. 'Is *this* worthy of a Christian Englishwoman? Is the passage from time to eternity to be made in *this* manner?' My aunt answered, 'I'll put on my gown, Drusilla, if you will be kind enough to help me.' What was to be said after that? I have done wonders with murderesses—I have never advanced an inch with Aunt Ablewhite. 'Where is the list,' I asked, 'of the servants whom you require?' My aunt shook her head; she hadn't even energy enough to keep the list. 'Rachel has got it, dear,' she said, 'in the next room.' I went into the next room, and so saw Rachel again, for the first time since we had parted in Montagu Square.

She looked pitiably small and thin in her deep mourning. If I attached any serious importance to such a perishable trifle as personal appearance, I might be inclined to add that hers was one of those unfortunate complexions which always suffers when not relieved by a border of white next the skin. But what are our complexions and our looks? Hindrances and pitfalls, dear girls, which beset us on our way to higher things! Greatly to my surprise, Rachel rose when I entered the room, and came forward to meet me with outstretched hand.

'I am glad to see you,' she said. 'Drusilla, I have been in the habit of speaking very foolishly and very rudely to you, on former occasions. I beg your pardon. I hope you will forgive me.'

My face, I suppose, betrayed the astonishment I felt at this. She coloured up for a moment, and then proceeded to explain herself.

'In my poor mother's lifetime,' she went on, 'her friends were not always my friends, too. Now I have lost her, my heart turns for comfort to the people she liked. She liked you. Try to be friends with me, Drusilla, if you can.'

To any rightly-constituted mind, the motive thus acknowledged was simply shocking. Here in Christian England was a young woman in a state of bereavement, with so little idea of where to look for true comfort, that she actually expected to find it among her mother's friends! Here was a relative of mine, awakened to a sense of her shortcomings towards others, under the influence, not of conviction and duty, but of sentiment and impulse! Most deplorable to think of—but, still, suggestive of something hopeful, to a person of my experience in plying the good work. There could be no harm, I thought, in ascertaining the extent of the change which the loss of her mother had wrought in Rachel's character. I decided, as a useful test, to probe her on the subject of her marriage engagement to Mr Godfrey Ablewhite.

Having first met her advances with all possible cordiality, I sat by her on the sofa, at her own request. We discussed family affairs and future plans—always excepting that one future plan which was to end in her marriage. Try as I might to turn the conversation that way, she resolutely declined to take the hint. Any open reference to the question, on my part, would have been premature at this early stage of our reconciliation. Besides, I had discovered all I wanted to know. She was no longer the reckless, defiant creature whom I had heard and seen, on the occasion of my martyrdom in Montagu Square. This was, of itself, enough to encourage me to take her future conversion in hand—beginning with a few words of earnest warning directed against the hasty formation of the marriage tie, and so getting on to higher things. Looking at her, now, with this new interest—and calling to mind the headlong suddenness with which she had met Mr Godfrey's matrimonial views—I felt the solemn duty of interfering, with a fervour which assured me that I should achieve no common results. Rapidity of proceeding was, as I believed, of importance in this case. I went back at once to the question of the servants wanted for the furnished house.

'Where is the list, dear?'

Rachel produced it.

'Cook, kitchen-maid, housemaid, and footman,' I read. 'My dear Rachel, these servants are only wanted for a term—the term during which your guardian has taken the house. We shall have great difficulty in finding persons of character and capacity to accept a temporary engagement of that sort, if we try in London. Has the house in Brighton been found yet?'

'Yes. Godfrey has taken it; and persons in the house wanted him to hire them as servants. He thought they would hardly do for us, and came back having settled nothing.'

'And you have no experience yourself in these matters, Rachel?'

'None whatever.'

'And Aunt Ablewhite won't exert herself?'

No, poor dear. Don't blame her, Drusilla. I think she is the only really happy woman I have ever met with.'

'There are degrees in happiness, darling. We must have a little talk, some day, on that subject. In the meantime I will undertake to meet the difficulty about the servants. Your aunt will write a letter to the people of the house—'

'She will sign a letter, if I write it for her, which comes to the same thing.'

'Quite the same thing. I shall get the letter, and I will go to Brighton to-morrow.'

How extremely kind of you! We will join you as soon as you are ready for us. And you will stay, I hope, as *my* guest. Brighton is so lively; you are sure to enjoy it.'

In those words the invitation was given, and the glorious prospect of interference was opened before me.

It was then the middle of the week. By Saturday afternoon the house was ready for them. In that short interval I had sifted, not the characters only, but the religious views as well, of all the disengaged servants who applied to me, and had succeeded in making a selection which my conscience approved. I also discovered, and called on, two serious friends of mine, residents in the town, to whom I knew I could confide the pious object which had brought me to Brighton. One of them—a clerical friend—kindly helped me to take sittings for our little party in the church in which he himself ministered. The other—a single lady, like myself—placed the resources of her library (composed throughout of precious publications) entirely at my disposal. I borrowed half a dozen works, all carefully chosen with a view to Rachel. When these had been judiciously distributed in the various rooms she would be likely to occupy, I considered that my preparations were complete. Sound doctrine in the servants who waited on her; sound doctrine in the minister who preached to her; sound doctrine in the books that lay on her table—such was the treble welcome which my zeal had prepared for the motherless girl! A heavenly composure filled my mind, on that Saturday afternoon, as I sat at the window waiting the arrival of my relatives. The giddy throng passed and repassed before my eyes. Alas! how many of them felt my exquisite sense of duty done? An awful question. Let us not pursue it.

Between six and seven the travellers arrived. To my indescribable surprise, they were escorted, not by Mr Godfrey (as I had anticipated) but by the lawyer, Mr Bruff.

'How do you do, Miss Clack?' he said. 'I mean to stay this time.'

That reference to the occasion on which I had obliged him to postpone his business to mine, when we were both visiting in Montagu Square, satisfied me that the old worldling had come to Brighton with some object of his own in view. I had prepared quite a little Paradise for my beloved Rachel—and here was the Serpent already!

'Godfrey was very much vexed, Drusilla, not to be able to come with us,' said my Aunt Ablewhite. 'There was something in the way which kept him in town. Mr Bruff volunteered to take his place, and make a holiday of it till Monday morning. By-the-by, Mr Bruff, I'm ordered to take exercise, and I don't like it. That,' added Aunt Ablewhite, pointing out of window to an invalid going by in a chair on wheels, drawn by a man, 'is my idea of exercise. If it's air you want, you get it in your chair. And if it's fatigue you want, I am sure it's fatiguing enough to look at the man.'

Rachel stood silent, at a window by herself, with her eyes fixed on the sea.

'Tired, love?' I inquired.

'No. Only a little out of spirits,' she answered. 'I have often seen the sea, on our Yorkshire coast, with that light on it. And I was thinking, Drusilla, of the days that can never come again.'

Mr Bruff remained to dinner, and stayed through the evening. The more I saw of him, the more certain I felt that he had some private end to serve in coming to Brighton. I watched him carefully. He maintained the same appearance of ease, and talked the same godless gossip, hour after hour, until it was time to take leave. As he shook hands with Rachel, I caught his hard and cunning eye resting on her for a moment with a peculiar interest and attention. She was plainly concerned in the object that he had in view. He said nothing out of the common to her or to any one on leaving. He invited himself to luncheon the next day, and then he went away to his hotel.

It was impossible the next morning to get my Aunt Ablewhite out of her dressing-gown in time for church. Her invalid daughter (suffering from nothing, in my opinion, but incurable laziness, inherited from her mother) announced that she meant to remain in bed for the day. Rachel and I went alone together to church. A magnificent sermon was preached by my gifted friend on the heathen indifference of the world to the sinfulness of little sins. For more than an hour his eloquence (assisted by his glorious voice) thundered through the sacred edifice. I said to Rachel, when we came out, 'Has it found its way to your heart, dear?' And she answered, 'No; it has only made my head ache.' This might have been discouraging to some people; but, once embarked on a career of manifest usefulness, nothing discourages Me.

We found Aunt Ablewhite and Mr Bruff at luncheon. When Rachel declined eating anything, and gave as a reason for it that she was suffering from a headache, the lawyer's cunning instantly saw, and seized, the chance that she had given him.

'There is only one remedy for a headache,' said this horrible old man. 'A walk, Miss Rachel, is the thing to cure you. I am entirely at your service, if you will honour me by accepting my arm.'

'With the greatest pleasure. A walk is the very thing I was longing for.'

'It's past two,' I gently suggested. 'And the afternoon service, Rachel, begins at three.'

'How can you expect me to go to church again,' she asked, petulantly, 'with such a headache as mine?'

Mr Bruff officiously opened the door for her. In another minute more they were both out of the house. I don't know when I have felt the solemn duty of interfering so strongly as I felt it at that moment. But what was to be done? Nothing was to be done but to interfere at the first opportunity, later in the day.

On my return from the afternoon service I found that they had just got back. One look at them told me that the lawyer had said what he wanted to say. I had never before seen Rachel so silent and so thoughtful. I had never before seen Mr Bruff pay her such devoted attention, and look at her with such marked respect. He had (or pretended that he had) an engagement to dinner that day—and he took an early leave of us all; intending to go back to London by the first train the next morning.

'Are you sure of your own resolution?' he said to Rachel at the door.

'Quite sure,' she answered—and so they parted.

The moment his back was turned, Rachel withdrew to her own room. She never appeared at dinner. Her maid (the person with the cap-ribbons) was sent downstairs to announce that her headache had returned. I ran up to her and made all sorts of sisterly offers through the door. It was locked, and she kept it locked. Plenty of obstructive material to work on here! I felt greatly cheered and stimulated by her locking the door.

When her cup of tea went up to her the next morning, I followed it in. I sat by her bedside and said a few earnest words. She listened with languid civility. I noticed my serious friend's precious publications huddled together on a table in a corner. Had she chanced to look into them?—I asked. Yes—and they had not interested her. Would she allow me to read a few passages of the deepest interest, which had probably escaped her eye? No, not now —she had other things to think of. She gave these answers, with her attention apparently absorbed in folding and refolding the frilling of her night-gown. It was plainly necessary to rouse her by some reference to those worldly interests which she still had at heart.

'Do you know, love,' I said, 'I had an odd fancy, yesterday, about Mr Bruff? I thought, when I saw you after your walk with him, that he had been telling you some bad news.'

Her fingers dropped from the frilling of her night-gown, and her fierce black eyes flashed at me.

'Quite the contrary!' she said. 'It was news I was interested in hearing—and I am deeply indebted to Mr Bruff for telling me of it.'

'Yes?' I said, in a tone of gentle interest.

Her fingers went back to the frilling, and she turned her head sullenly away from me. I had been met in this manner, in the course of plying the good work, hundreds of times. She merely stimulated me to try again. In my dauntless zeal for her welfare, I ran the great risk, and openly alluded to her marriage engagement.

'News you were interested in hearing?' I repeated. 'I suppose, my dear Rachel, that must be news of Mr Godfrey Ablewhite?'

She started up in the bed, and turned deadly pale. It was evidently on the tip of her tongue to retort on me with the unbridled insolence of former times. She checked herself—laid her head back on the pillow—considered a minute—and then answered in these remarkable words:

'*I shall never marry Mr Godfrey Ablewhite.*'

It was my turn to start at that.

'What can you possibly mean?' I exclaimed. 'The marriage is considered by the whole family as a settled thing!'

'Mr Godfrey Ablewhite is expected here to-day,' she said, doggedly. 'Wait till he comes—and you will see.'

'But my dear Rachel—'

She rang the bell at the head of her bed. The person with the cap-ribbons appeared.

'Penelope! my bath.'

Let me give her her due. In the state of my feelings at that moment, I do sincerely believe that she had hit on the only possible way of forcing me to leave the room.

By the mere worldly mind my position towards Rachel might have been viewed as presenting difficulties of no ordinary kind. I had reckoned on leading her to higher things by means of a little earnest exhortation on the subject of her marriage. And now, if she was to be believed, no such event as her marriage was to take place at all. But ah, my friends! a working Christian of my experience (with an evangelizing prospect before her) takes broader views than these. Supposing Rachel really broke off the marriage, on which the Ablewhites, father and son, counted as a settled thing, what would be the result? It could only end, if she held firm, in an exchanging of hard words and bitter accusations on both sides. And what would be the effect on Rachel when the stormy interview was over? A salutary moral depression would be the effect. Her pride would be exhausted, her stubbornness would be exhausted, by the resolute resistance which it was in her character to make under the circumstances. She would turn for sympathy to the nearest person who had sympathy to offer. And I was that nearest person— brimful of comfort, charged to overflowing with seasonable and reviving words. Never had the evangelizing prospect looked brighter, to *my* eyes, than it looked now.

She came down to breakfast, but she ate nothing, and hardly uttered a word.

After breakfast she wandered listlessly from room to room—then suddenly roused herself, and opened the piano. The music she selected to play was of the most scandalously profane sort, associated with performances on the stage which it curdles one's blood to think of. It would have been premature to interfere with her at such a time as this. I privately ascertained the hour at which Mr Godfrey Ablewhite was expected, and then I escaped the music by leaving the house.

Being out alone, I took the opportunity of calling upon my two resident friends. It was an indescribable luxury to find myself indulging in earnest conversation with serious persons. Infinitely encouraged and refreshed, I turned my steps back again to the house, in excellent time to await the arrival of our expected visitor. I entered the dining-room, always empty at that hour of the day, and found myself face to face with Mr Godfrey Ablewhite!

He made no attempt to fly the place. Quite the contrary. He advanced to meet me with the utmost eagerness.

'Dear Miss Clack, I have been only waiting to see *you*! Chance set me free of my London engagements to-day sooner than I had expected, and I have got here, in consequence, earlier than my appointed time.'

Not the slightest embarrassment encumbered his explanation, though this was his first meeting with me after the scene in Montagu Square. He was not aware, it is true, of my having been a witness of that scene. But he knew, on the other hand, that my attendances at the Mothers' Small-Clothes, and my relations with friends attached to other charities, must have informed me of his shameless neglect of his Ladies and of his Poor. And yet there he was before me, in full possession of his charming voice and his irresistible smile!

'Have you seen Rachel yet?' I asked.

He sighed gently, and took me by the hand. I should certainly have snatched my hand away, if the manner in which he gave his answer had not paralysed me with astonishment.

'I have seen Rachel,' he said with perfect tranquillity. 'You are aware, dear friend, that she was engaged to me? Well, she has taken a sudden resolution to break the engagement. Reflection has convinced her that she will best consult her welfare and mine by retracting a rash promise, and leaving me free to make some happier choice elsewhere. That is the only reason she will give, and the only answer she will make to every question that I can ask of her.'

'What have you done on your side?' I inquired. 'Have you submitted?'

'Yes,' he said with the most unruffled composure, 'I have submitted.'

His conduct, under the circumstances, was so utterly inconceivable, that I stood bewildered with my hand in his. It is a piece of rudeness to stare at anybody, and it is an act of indelicacy to stare at a gentleman. I committed both those improprieties. And I said, as if in a dream, 'What does it mean?'

'Permit me to tell you,' he replied. 'And suppose we sit down?'

He led me to a chair. I have an indistinct remembrance that he was very affectionate. I don't think he put his arm round my waist to support me—but I am not sure. I was quite helpless, and his ways with ladies were very endearing. At any rate, we sat down. I can answer for that, if I can answer for nothing more.

CHAPTER 8

'I have lost a beautiful girl, an excellent social position, and a handsome income,' Mr Godfrey began; 'and I have submitted to it without a struggle. What can be the motive for such extraordinary conduct as that? My precious friend, there is no motive.'

'No motive?' I repeated.

'Let me appeal, my dear Miss Clack, to your experience of children,' he went on. 'A child pursues a certain course of conduct. You are greatly struck by it, and you attempt to get at the motive. The dear little thing is incapable of telling you its motive. You might as well ask the grass why it grows, or the birds why they sing. Well! in this matter, I am like the dear little thing—like the grass—like the birds. I don't know why I made a proposal of marriage to Miss Verinder. I don't know why I have shamefully neglected my dear Ladies. I don't know why I have apostatized from the Mothers'-Small-Clothes. You say to the child, Why have you been naughty? And the little angel puts its finger into its mouth, and doesn't know. My case exactly, Miss Clack! I couldn't confess it to anybody else. I feel impelled to confess it to *you!*'

I began to recover myself. A mental problem was involved here. I am deeply interested in mental problems—and I am not, it is thought, without some skill in solving them.

'Best of friends, exert your intellect, and help me,' he proceeded. 'Tell me—why does a time come when these matrimonial proceedings of mine begin to look like something done in a dream? Why does it suddenly occur to me that my true happiness is in helping my dear Ladies, in going my modest round of useful work, in saying my few earnest words when called on by my Chairman? What do I want with a position? I have got a position. What do I want with an income? I can pay for my bread and cheese, and my nice little lodging, and my two coats a year. What do I want with Miss Verinder? She has told me with her own lips (this, dear lady, is between ourselves) that she loves another man, and that her only idea in marrying me is to try and put that other man out of her head. What a horrid union is this! Oh, dear me, what a horrid union is this! Such are my reflections, Miss Clack, on my way to Brighton. I approach Rachel with the feeling of a criminal who is going to receive his sentence. When I find that she has changed her mind too—when I hear her propose to break the engagement—I experience (there is no sort of doubt about it) a most overpowering sense of relief. A month ago I was pressing her rapturously to my bosom. An hour ago, the happiness of knowing that I shall never press her again, intoxicates me like strong liquor. The thing seems impossible —the thing can't be. And yet there are the facts, as I had the honour of stating them when we first sat down together in these two chairs. I have lost a beautiful girl, an excellent social position, and a handsome income; and I have submitted to it without a struggle. Can *you* account for it, dear friend? It's quite beyond *me*.'

His magnificent head sank on his breast, and he gave up his own mental problem in despair.

I was deeply touched. The case (if I may speak as a spiritual physician) was now quite plain to me. It is no uncommon event, in the experience of us all, to see the possessors of exalted ability occasionally humbled to the level of the most poorly-gifted people about them. The object, no doubt, in the wise economy of Providence, is to remind greatness that it is mortal, and that the power which has conferred, it can also take it away. It was now—to my mind—easy to discern one of these salutary humiliations in the deplorable proceedings on dear Mr Godfrey's part, of which I had been the unseen witness. And it was equally easy to recognize the welcome reappearance of his own finer nature in the horror with which he recoiled from the idea of a marriage with Rachel, and in the charming eagerness which he showed to return to his Ladies and his Poor.

I put this view before him in a few simple and sisterly words. His joy was beautiful to see. He compared himself, as I went on, to a lost man emerging from the darkness into the light. When I answered for a loving reception of him at the Mothers' Small-Clothes, the grateful heart of our Christian Hero overflowed. He pressed my hands alternately to his lips. Overwhelmed by the exquisite triumph of having got him back among us, I let him do what he liked with my hands. I closed my eyes. I felt my head, in an ecstasy of spiritual self-forgetfulness, sinking on his shoulder. In a moment more I should certainly have swooned away in his arms, but for an interruption from the outer world, which brought me to myself again. A horrid rattling of knives and forks sounded outside the door, and the footman came in to lay the table for luncheon.

Mr Godfrey started up, and looked at the clock on the mantelpiece.

'How time flies with *you!*' he exclaimed. 'I shall barely catch the train.'

I ventured on asking why he was in such a hurry to get back to town. His answer reminded me of family difficulties that were still to be reconciled, and of family disagreements that were yet to come.

'I have heard from my father,' he said. 'Business obliges him to leave Frizinghall for London to-day, and he proposes coming on here, either this evening or to-morrow. I must tell him what has happened between Rachel and me. His heart is set on our marriage—there will be great difficulty, I fear, in reconciling him to the breaking-off of the engagement. I must stop him, for all our sakes, from coming here till he is reconciled. Best and dearest of friends, we shall meet again!'

With those words he hurried out. In equal haste on my side, I ran upstairs to compose myself in my own room before meeting Aunt Ablewhite and Rachel at the luncheon-table.

I am well aware—to dwell for a moment yet on the subject of Mr Godfrey—that the all-profaning opinion of the world has charged him with having his own private reasons for releasing Rachel from her engagement, at the first opportunity she gave him. It has also reached my ears, that his anxiety to recover his place in my estimation has been attributed, in certain quarters, to a mercenary eagerness to make his peace (through me) with a venerable committee-woman at the Mothers' Small-Clothes, abundantly blessed with the goods of this world, and a beloved and intimate friend of my own. I only notice these odious slanders for the sake of declaring that they never had a moment's influence on my mind. In obedience to my instructions, I have exhibited the fluctuations in my opinion of our Christian Hero, exactly as I find them recorded in my diary. In justice to myself, let me here add that, once reinstated in his place in my estimation, my gifted friend never lost that place again. I write with the tears in my eyes, burning to say more. But no—I am cruelly limited to my actual experience of persons and things. In less than a month from the time of which I am now writing, events in the money-market (which diminished even *my* miserable little income) forced me into foreign exile, and left me with nothing but a loving remembrance of Mr Godfrey which the slander of the world has assailed, and assailed in vain.

Let me dry my eyes, and return to my narrative.

I went downstairs to luncheon, naturally anxious to see how Rachel was affected by her release from her marriage engagement.

It appeared to me—but I own I am a poor authority in such matters—that the recovery of her freedom had set her thinking again of that other man whom she loved, and that she was furious with herself for not being able to control a revulsion of feeling of which she was secretly ashamed. Who was the man? I had my suspicions—but it was needless to waste time in idle speculation. When I had converted her, she would, as a matter of course, have no concealments from Me. I should hear all about the man; I should hear all about the Moonstone. If I had had no higher object in stirring her up to a sense of spiritual things, the motive of relieving her mind of its guilty secrets would have been enough of itself to encourage me to go on.

Aunt Ablewhite took her exercise in the afternoon in an invalid chair. Rachel accompanied her. 'I wish I could drag the chair,' she broke out, recklessly. 'I wish I could fatigue myself till I was ready to drop.'

She was in the same humour in the evening. I discovered in one of my friend's precious publications—the Life, Letters, and Labours of Miss Jane Ann Stamper, forty-fourth edition—passages which bore with a marvellous appropriateness on Rachel's present position. Upon my proposing to read them, she went to the piano. Conceive how little she must have known of serious people, if she supposed that my patience was to be exhausted in that way! I kept Miss Jane Ann Stamper by me, and waited for events with the most unfaltering trust in the future.

Old Mr Ablewhite never made his appearance that night. But I knew the importance which his worldly greed attached to his son's marriage with Miss Verinder—and I felt a positive conviction (do what Mr Godfrey might to prevent it) that we should see him the next day. With his interference in the matter, the storm on which I had counted would certainly come, and the salutary exhaustion of Rachel's resisting powers would as certainly follow. I am not ignorant that old Mr Ablewhite has the reputation generally (especially among his inferiors) of being a remarkably good-natured man. According to my observation of him, he deserves his reputation as long as he has his own way, and not a moment longer.

The next day, exactly as I had foreseen, Aunt Ablewhite was as near to being astonished as her nature would permit, by the sudden appearance of her husband. He had barely been a minute in the house, before he was followed, to *my* astonishment this time, by an unexpected complication, in the shape of Mr Bruff.

I never remember feeling the presence of the lawyer to be more unwelcome than I felt it at that moment. He looked ready for anything in the way of an obstructive proceeding—capable even of keeping the peace, with Rachel for one of the combatants!

'This is a pleasant surprise, sir,' said Mr Ablewhite, addressing himself with his deceptive cordiality to Mr Bruff. 'When I left your office yesterday, I didn't expect to have the honour of seeing you at Brighton to-day.'

'I turned over our conversation in my mind, after you had gone,' replied Mr Bruff. 'And it occurred to me that I might perhaps be of some use on this occasion. I was just in time to catch the train, and I had no opportunity of discovering the carriage in which you were travelling.'

Having given that explanation, he seated himself by Rachel. I retired modestly to a corner—with Miss Jane Ann Stamper on my lap, in case of emergency. My aunt sat at the window; placidly fanning herself as usual. Mr Ablewhite stood up in the middle of the room, with his bald head much pinker than I had ever seen it yet, and addressed himself in the most affectionate manner to his niece.

'Rachel, my dear,' he said, 'I have heard some very extraordinary news from Godfrey. And I am here to inquire about it. You have a sitting-room of your own in this house. Will you honour me by showing me the way to it?'

Rachel never moved. Whether she was determined to bring matters to a crisis, or whether she was prompted by some private sign from Mr Bruff, is more than I can tell. She declined doing old Mr Ablewhite the honour of conducting him into her sitting-room.

'Whatever you wish to say to me,' she answered, 'can be said here—in the presence of my relatives, and in the presence' (she looked at Mr Bruff) 'of my mother's trusted old friend.'

'Just as you please, my dear,' said the amiable Mr Ablewhite. He took a chair. The rest of them looked at his face—as if they expected it, after seventy years of worldly training, to speak the truth. *I* looked at the top of his bald head; having noticed on other occasions that the temper which was really in him had a habit of registering itself *there*.

'Some weeks ago,' pursued the old gentleman, 'my son informed me that Miss Verinder had done him the honour to engage herself to marry him. Is it possible, Rachel, that he can have misinterpreted—or presumed upon—what you really said to him?'

'Certainly not,' she replied. 'I did engage myself to marry him.'

'Very frankly answered!' said Mr Ablewhite. 'And most satisfactory, my dear, so far. In respect to what happened some weeks since, Godfrey has made no mistake. The error is evidently in what he told me yesterday. I begin to see it now. You and he have had a lovers' quarrel—and my foolish son has interpreted it seriously. Ah! I should have known better than that at his age.'

The fallen nature in Rachel—the mother Eve, so to speak—began to chafe at this.

'Pray let us understand each other, Mr Ablewhite,' she said. 'Nothing in the least like a quarrel took place yesterday between your son and me. If he told you that I proposed breaking off our marriage engagement, and that he agreed on his side—he told you the truth.'

The self-registering thermometer at the top of Mr Ablewhite's bald head, began to indicate a rise of temper. His face was more amiable than ever—but *there* was the pink at the top of his face, a shade deeper already!

'Come, come, my dear!' he said, in his most soothing manner, 'now don't be angry, and don't be hard on poor Godfrey! He has evidently said some unfortunate thing. He was always clumsy from a child—but he means well, Rachel, he means well!'

'Mr Ablewhite, I have either expressed myself very badly, or you are purposely mistaking me. Once for all, it is a settled thing between your son and myself that we remain, for the rest of our lives, cousins and nothing more. Is that plain enough?'

The tone in which she said those words made it impossible, even for old Mr Ablewhite, to mistake her any longer. His thermometer went up another degree, and his voice when he next spoke, ceased to be the voice which is appropriate to a notoriously good-natured man.

'I am to understand, then,' he said, 'that your marriage engagement is broken off?'

'You are to understand that, Mr Ablewhite, if you please.'

'I am also to take it as a matter of fact that the proposal to withdraw from the engagement came, in the first instance, from *you?*'

'It came, in the first instance, from me. And it met, as I have told you, with your son's consent and approval.'

The thermometer went up to the top of the register. I mean, the pink changed suddenly to scarlet.

'My son is a mean-sprited hound!' cried this furious old worldling. 'In justice to myself as his father—not in justice to *him*—beg to ask you, Miss Verinder, what complaint you have to make of Mr Godfrey Ablewhite?

Here Mr Bruff interfered for the first time.

'You are not bound to answer that question,' he said to Rachel.

Old Mr Ablewhite fastened on him instantly.

Don't forget, sir,' he said, 'that you are a self-invited guest here. Your interference would have come with a better grace if you had waited until it was asked for.'

Mr Bruff took no notice. The smooth varnish on *his* wicked old face never cracked. Rachel thanked him for the advice he had given to her, and then turned to old Mr Ablewhite— preserving her composure in a manner which (having regard to her age and her sex) was simply awful to see.

'Your son put the same question to me which you have just asked,' she said. 'I had only one answer for him, and I have only one answer for you. I proposed that we should release each other, because reflection had convinced me that I should best consult his welfare and mine by retracting a rash promise, and leaving him free to make his choice elsewhere.'

'What has my son done?' persisted Mr Ablewhite. 'I have a right to know that. What has my son done?'

She persisted just as obstinately on her side.

'You have had the only explanation which I think it necessary to give to you, or to him,' she answered.

'In plain English, it's your sovereign will and pleasure, Miss Verinder, to jilt my son?'

Rachel was silent for a moment. Sitting close behind her, I heard her sigh. Mr Bruff took her hand, and gave it a little squeeze. She recovered herself, and answered Mr Ablewhite as boldly as ever.

'I have exposed myself to worse misconstruction than that,' she said. 'And I have borne it patiently. The time has gone by, when you could mortify me by calling me a jilt.'

She spoke with a bitterness of tone which satisfied me that the scandal of the Moonstone had been in some way recalled to her mind. 'I have no more to say,' she added, wearily, not addressing the words to any one in particular, and looking away from us all, out of the window that was nearest to her.

Mr Ablewhite got upon his feet, and pushed away his chair so violently that it toppled over and fell on the floor.

'I have something more to say on my side,' he announced, bringing down the flat of his hand on the table with a bang. 'I have to say that if my son doesn't feel this insult, I do!'

Rachel started, and looked at him in sudden surprise.

'Insult?' she repeated. 'What do you mean?'

'Insult!' reiterated Mr Ablewhite. 'I know your motive, Miss Verinder, for breaking your promise to my son! I know it as certainly as if you had confessed it in so many words. Your cursed family pride is insulting Godfrey, as it insulted *me* when I married your aunt. Her family—her beggarly family—turned their backs on her for marrying an honest man, who had made his own place and won his own fortune. I had no ancestors. I wasn't descended from a set of cut-throat scoundrels who lived by robbery and murder. I couldn't point to the time when the Ablewhites hadn't a shirt to their backs, and couldn't sign their own names. Ha! ha! I wasn't good enough for the Herncastles, when *I* married. And, now it comes to the pinch, my son isn't good enough for *you*. I suspected it, all along. You have got the Herncastle blood in you, my young lady! I suspected it all along.'

'A very unworthy suspicion,' remarked Mr Bruff. 'I am astonished that you have the courage to acknowledge it.'

Before Mr Ablewhite could find words to answer in, Rachel spoke in a tone of the most exasperating contempt.

'Surely,' she said to the lawyer, 'this is beneath notice. If he can think in *that* way, let us leave him to think as he pleases.'

From scarlet, Mr Ablewhite was now becoming purple. He gasped for breath; he looked backwards and forwards from Rachel to Mr Bruff in such a frenzy of rage with both of them that he didn't know which to attack first. His wife, who had sat impenetrably fanning herself up to this time, began to be alarmed, and attempted, quite uselessly, to quiet him. I had, throughout this distressing interview, felt more than one inward call to interfere with a few earnest words, and had controlled myself under a dread of the possible results, very unworthy of a Christian Englishwoman who looks, not to what is meanly prudent, but to what is morally right. At the point at which matters had now arrived, I rose superior to all considerations of mere expediency. If I had contemplated interposing any remonstrance of my own humble devising, I might possibly have still hesitated. But the distressing domestic emergency which now confronted me, was most marvellously and beautifully provided for in the Correspondence of Miss Jane Ann Stamper—Letter one thousand and one, on 'Peace in Families.' I rose in my modest corner, and I opened my precious book.

'Dear Mr Ablewhite,' I said, 'one word!'

When I first attracted the attention of the company by rising, I could see that he was on the point of saying something rude to me. My sisterly form of address checked him. He stared at me in heathen astonishment.

'As an affectionate well-wisher and friend,' I proceeded, 'and as one long accustomed to arouse, convince, prepare, enlighten, and fortify others, permit me to take the most pardonable of all liberties—the liberty of composing your mind.'

He began to recover himself; he was on the point of breaking out—he *would* have broken out, with anybody else. But my voice (habitually gentle) possesses a high note or so, in emergencies. In this emergency, I felt imperatively called upon to have the highest voice of the two.

I held up my precious book before him; I rapped the open page impressively with my forefinger. 'Not my words!' I exclaimed, in a burst of fervent interruption. 'Oh, don't suppose that I claim attention for My humble words! Manna in the wilderness, Mr Ablewhite! Dew on the parched earth! Words of comfort, words of wisdom, words of love—the blessed, blessed, blessed words of Miss Jane Ann Stamper!'

I was stopped there by a momentary impediment of the breath. Before I could recover myself, this monster in human form shouted out furiously,—

'Miss Jane Ann Stamper be—!'

It is impossible for me to write the awful word, which is here represented by a blank. I shrieked as it passed his lips; I flew to my little bag on the side-table; I shook out all my tracts; I seized the one particular tract on profane swearing, entitled, 'Hush, for Heaven's Sake!'; I handed it to him with an expression of agonized entreaty. He tore it in two, and threw it back at me across the table. The rest of them rose in alarm, not knowing what might happen next. I instantly sat down again in my corner. There had once been an occasion, under somewhat similar circumstances, when Miss Jane Ann Stamper had been taken by the two shoulders and turned out of a room. I waited, inspired by *her* spirit, for a repetition of *her* martyrdom.

But no—it was not to be. His wife was the next person whom he addressed. 'Who—who—who,' he said, stammering with rage, 'asked this impudent fanatic into the house? Did you?'

Before Aunt Ablewhite could say a word, Rachel answered for her.

'Miss Clack is here,' she said, 'as my guest.'

Those words had a singular effect on Mr Ablewhite. They suddenly changed him from a man in a state of red-hot anger to a man in a state of icy-cold contempt. It was plain to everybody that Rachel had said something—short and plain as her answer had been—which gave him the upper hand of her at last.

'Oh?' he said. 'Miss Clack is here as *your* guest—in *my* house?'

It was Rachel's turn to lose her temper at that. Her colour rose, and her eyes brightened fiercely. She turned to the lawyer, and, pointing to Mr Ablewhite, asked haughtily, 'What does he mean?'

Mr Bruff interfered for the third time.

'You appear to forget,' he said, addressing Mr Ablewhite, 'that you took this house as Miss Verinder's guardian, for Miss Verinder's use.'

'Not quite so fast,' interposed Mr Ablewhite. 'I have a last word to say, which I should have said some time since, if this—' he looked my way, pondering what abominable name he should call me—'if this Rampant Spinster had not interrupted us. I beg to inform you, sir, that, if my son is not good enough to be Miss Verinder's husband, I cannot presume to consider his father good enough to be Miss Verinder's guardian. Understand, if you please, that I refuse to accept the position which is offered to me by Lady Verinder's will. In your legal phrase, I decline to act. This house has necessarily been hired in my name. I take the entire responsibility of it on my shoulders. It is my house. I can keep it, or let it, just as I please. I have no wish to hurry Miss Verinder. On the contrary, I beg her to remove her guest and her luggage, at her own entire convenience.' He made a low bow, and walked out of the room.

That was Mr Ablewhite's revenge on Rachel, for refusing to marry his son!

The instant the door closed, Aunt Ablewhite exhibited a phenomenon which silenced us all. She became endowed with energy enough to cross the room!

'My dear,' she said, taking Rachel by the hand, 'I should be ashamed of my husband, if I didn't know that it is his temper which I has spoken to you, and not himself. You,' continued Aunt Ablewhite, turning on me in my corner with another endownment of energy, in her looks this time instead of her limbs—'you are the mischievous person who irritated him. I hope I shall never see you or your tracts again.' She went back to Rachel and kissed her. I beg your pardon, my dear,' she said, 'in my husband's name. What can I do for you?'

Consistently perverse in everything—capricious and unreasonable in all the actions of her life—Rachel melted into tears at those commonplace words, and returned her aunt's kiss in silence.

'If I may be permitted to answer for Miss Verinder,' said Mr Bruff, 'might I ask you, Mrs Ablewhite, to send Penelope down with her mistress's bonnet and shawl. Leave us ten minutes together,' he added, in a lower tone, 'and you may rely on my setting matters right, to your satisfaction as well as to Rachel's.'

The trust of the family in this man was something wonderful to see. Without a word more, on her side, Aunt Ablewhite left the room.

'Ah!' said Mr Bruff, looking after her. 'The Herncastle blood has its drawbacks, I admit. But there *is* something in good breeding after all!'

Having made that purely worldly remark, he looked hard at my corner, as if he expected me to go. My interest in Rachel—an infinitely higher interest than his—riveted me to my chair.

Mr Bruff gave it up, exactly as he had given it up at Aunt Verinder's, in Montagu Square. He led Rachel to a chair by the window, and spoke to her there.

'My dear young lady,' he said, 'Mr Ablewhite's conduct has naturally shocked you, and taken you by surprise. If it was worth while to contest the question with such a man, we might soon show him that he is not to have things all his own way. But it isn't worth while. You were quite right in what you said just now; he is beneath our notice.'

He stopped, and looked round at my corner. I sat there quite immovable, with my tracts at my elbow, and with Miss Jane Ann Stamper on my lap.

'You know,' he resumed, turning back again to Rachel, 'that it was part of your poor mother's fine nature always to see the best of the people about her, and never the worst. She named her brother-in-law your guardian because she believed in him, and because she thought it would please her sister. I had never liked Mr Ablewhite myself, and I induced your mother to let me insert a clause in the will, empowering her executors, in certain events, to consult with me about the appointment of a new guardian. One of those events has happened to-day; and I find myself in a position to end all these dry business details, I hope agreeably, with a message from my wife. Will you honour Mrs Bruff by becoming her guest? And will you remain under my roof, and be one of my family, until we wise people have laid our heads together, and have settled what is to be done next?'

At those words, I rose to interfere. Mr Bruff had done exactly what I had dreaded he would do, when he asked Mrs Ablewhite for Rachel's bonnet and shawl.

Before I could interpose a word, Rachel had accepted his invitation in the warmest terms. If I suffered the arrangement thus made between them to be carried out—if she once passed the threshold of Mr Bruff's door—farewell to the fondest hope of my life, the hope of bringing my lost sheep back to the fold! The bare idea of such a calamity as this quite overwhelmed me. I cast the miserable trammels of worldly discretion to the winds, and spoke with the fervour that filled me, in the words that came first.

'Stop!' I said—'Stop! I must be heard. Mr Bruff! you are not related to her, and I am. *I* invite her—I summon the executors to appoint *me* guardian. Rachel, dearest Rachel, I offer you my modest home; come to London by the next train, love, and share it with me!'

Mr Bruff said nothing. Rachel looked at me with a cruel astonishment which she made no effort to conceal.

'You are very kind, Drusilla,' she said. 'I shall hope to visit you whenever I happen to be in London. But I have accepted Mr Bruff's invitation, and I think it will be best, for the present, if I remain under Mr Bruff's care.'

'Oh, don't say so!' I pleaded. 'I can't part with you, Rachel,—I can't part with you!'

I tried to fold her in my arms. But she drew back. My fervour did not communicate itself; it only alarmed her.

'Surely,' she said, 'this is a very unnecessary display of agitation? I don't understand it.'

'No more do I,' said Mr Bruff.

Their hardness—their hideous, worldly hardness—revolted me.

'Oh, Rachel! Rachel!' I burst out. 'Haven't you seen *yet*, that my heart yearns to make a Christian of you? Has no inner voice told you that I am trying to do for *you*, what I was trying to do for your dear mother when death snatched her out of my hands?'

Rachel advanced a step nearer, and looked at me very strangely.

'I don't understand your reference to my mother,' she said. 'Miss Clack, will you have the goodness to explain yourself?'

Before I could answer, Mr Bruff came forward, and offering his arm to Rachel, tried to lead her out of the room.

'You had better not pursue the subject, my dear,' he said. 'And Miss Clack had better not explain herself.'

If I had been a stock or a stone, such an interference as this must have roused me into testifying to the truth. I put Mr Bruff aside indignantly with my own hand, and, in solemn and suitable language, I stated the view with which sound doctrine does not scruple to regard the awful calamity of dying unprepared.

Rachel started back from me—I blush to write it—with a scream of horror.

'Come away!' she said to Mr Bruff. 'Come away, for God's sake, before that woman can say any more! Oh, think of my poor mother's harmless, useful, beautiful life! You were at the funeral, Mr Bruff; you saw how everybody loved her; you saw the poor helpless people crying at her grave over the loss of their best friend. And that wretch stands there, and tries to make me doubt that my mother, who was an angel on earth, is an angel in heaven now! Don't stop to talk about it! Come away! It stifles me to breathe the same air with her! It frightens me to feel that we are in the same room together!'

Deaf to all remonstrance, she ran to the door.

At the same moment, her maid entered with her bonnet and shawl. She huddled them on anyhow. 'Pack my things,' she said, 'and bring them to Mr Bruff's.' I attempted to approach her—I was shocked and grieved, but, it is needless to say, not offended. I only wished to say to her, 'May your hard heart be softened! I freely forgive you!' She pulled down her veil, and tore her shawl away from my hand, and, hurrying out, shut the door in my face. I bore the insult with my customary fortitude. I remember it now with my customary superiority to all feeling of offence.

Mr Bruff had his parting word of mockery for me, before he too hurried out, in his turn.

'You had better not have explained yourself, Miss Clack,' he said, and bowed, and left the room.

The person with the cap-ribbons followed.

'It's easy to see who has set them all by the ears together,' she said. 'I'm only a poor servant—but I declare I'm ashamed of you!' She too went out, and banged the door after her.

I was left alone in the room. Reviled by them all, deserted by them all, I was left alone in the room.

Is there more to be added to this plain statement of facts—to this touching picture of a Christian persecuted by the world? No! my diary reminds me that one more of the many chequered chapters in my life, ends here. From that day forth, I never saw Rachel Verinder again. She had my forgiveness at the time when she insulted me. She has had my prayerful good wishes ever since. And when I die—to complete the return on my part of good for evil—she will have the *Life, Letters, and Labours of Miss Jane Ann Stamper* left her as a legacy by my will.

SECOND NARRATIVE

Contributed by Mathew Bruff, *Solicitor, of Gray's Inn Square.*

CHAPTER 1

My fair friend, Miss Clack, having laid down the pen, there are two reasons for my taking it up next, in my turn.

In the first place, I am in a position to throw the necessary light on certain points of interest which have thus far been left in the dark. Miss Verinder had her own private reason for breaking her marriage engagement—and I was at the bottom of it. Mr Godfrey Ablewhite had his own private reason for withdrawing all claim to the hand of his charming cousin—and I discovered what it was.

In the second place, it was my good or ill fortune, I hardly know which, to find myself personally involved—at the period of which I am now writing—in the mystery of the Indian Diamond. I had the honour of an interview, at my own office, with an Oriental stranger of distinguished manners, who was no other, unquestionably, than the chief of the three Indians. Add to this, that I met with the celebrated traveller, Mr Murthwaite, the day afterwards, and that I held a conversation with him on the subject of the Moonstone, which has a very important bearing on later events. And there you have the statement of my claims to fill the position which I occupy in these pages.

The true story of the broken marriage engagement comes first in point of time, and must therefore take the first place in the present narrative. Tracing my way back along the chain of events, from one end to the other, I find it necessary to open the scene, oddly enough as you will think, at the bedside of my excellent client and friend, the late Sir John Verinder.

Sir John had his share—perhaps rather a large share—of the more harmless and amiable of the weaknesses incidental to humanity. Among these, I may mention as applicable to the matter in hand, an invincible reluctance—so long as he enjoyed his usual good health—to face the responsibility of making his will. Lady Verinder exerted her influence to rouse him to a sense of duty in this matter; and I exerted my influence. He admitted the justice of our views—but he went no further than that, until he found himself afflicted with the illness which ultimately brought him to his grave. Then, I was sent for at last, to take my client's instructions on the subject of his will. They proved to be the simplest instructions I had ever received in the whole of my professional career.

Sir John was dozing, when I entered the room. He roused himself at the sight of me.

'How do you do, Mr Bruff?' he said. 'I shan't be very long about this. And then I'll go to sleep again.' He looked on with great interest while, I collected pens, ink, and paper. 'Are you ready?' he asked. I bowed, and took a dip of ink, and waited for my instructions.

'I leave everything to my wife,' said Sir John. 'That's all.' He turned round on his pillow, and composed himself to sleep again.

I was obliged to disturb him.

'Am I to understand,' I asked, 'that you leave the whole of the property, of every sort and description, of which you die possessed, absolutely to Lady Verinder?'

'Yes,' said Sir John. 'Only, *I* put it shorter. Why can't *you* put it shorter, and let me go to sleep again? Everything to my wife. That's my Will.'

His property was entirely at his own disposal, and was of two kinds. Property in land (I purposely abstain from using technical language), and property in money. In the majority of cases, I am afraid I should have felt it my duty to my client to ask him to reconsider his Will. In the case of Sir John, I knew Lady Verinder to be, not only worthy of the unreserved trust which her husband had placed in her (all good wives are worthy of that)—but to be also capable of properly administering a trust (which, in my experience of the fair sex, not one in a thousand of them is competent to do). In ten minutes, Sir John's Will was drawn, and executed, and Sir John himself, good man, was finishing his interrupted nap.

Lady Verinder amply justified the confidence which her husband had placed in her. In the first days of her widowhood, she sent for me, and made her Will. The view she took of her position was so thoroughly sound and sensible, that I was relieved of all necessity for advising her. My responsibility began and ended with shaping her instructions into the proper legal form. Before Sir John had been a fortnight in his grave, the future of his daughter had been most wisely and most affectionately provided for.

The Will remained in its fireproof box at my office, through more years than I like to reckon up. It was not till the summer of eighteen hundred and forty-eight that I found occasion to look at it again under very melancholy circumstances.

At the date I have mentioned, the doctors pronounced the sentence on poor Lady Verinder, which was literally a sentence of death. I was the first person whom she informed of her situation; and I found her anxious to go over her Will again with me.

It was impossible to improve the provisions relating to her daughter. But, in the lapse of time, her wishes in regard to certain minor legacies, left to different relatives, had undergone some modification; and it became necessary to add three or four Codicils to the original document. Having done this at once, for fear of accidents, I obtained her ladyship's permission to embody her recent instructions in a second Will. My object was to avoid certain inevitable confusions and repetitions which now disfigured the original document, and which, to own the truth, grated sadly on my professional sense of the fitness of things.

The execution of this second Will has been described by Miss Clack, who was so obliging as to witness it. So far as regarded Rachel Verinder's pecuniary interests, it was, word for word, the exact counterpart of the first Will. The only changes introduced related to the appointment of a guardian, and to certain provisions concerning that appointment, which were made under my advice. On Lady Verinder's death, the Will was placed in the hands of my proctor to be 'proved' (as the phrase is) in the usual way.

In about three weeks from that time—as well as I can remember—the first warning reached me of something unusual going on under the surface. I happened to be looking in at my friend the proctor's office, and I observed that he received me with an appearance of greater interest than usual.

'I have some news for you,' he said. 'What do you think I heard at Doctors' Commons this morning? Lady Verinder's Will has been asked for, and examined, already!'

This was news indeed! There was absolutely nothing which could be contested in the Will; and there was nobody I could think of who had the slightest interest in examining it. (I shall perhaps do well if I explain in this place, for the benefit of the few people who don't know it already, that the law allows all Wills to be examined at Doctors' Commons by anybody who applies, on the payment of a shilling fee.)

'Did you hear who asked for the Will?' I asked.

'Yes; the clerk had no hesitation in telling *me*. Mr Smalley, of the firm of Skipp and Smalley, asked for it. The Will has not been copied yet into the great Folio Registers. So there was no alternative but to depart from the usual course, and to let him see the original document. He looked it over carefully, and made a note in his pocket-book. Have you any idea of what he wanted with it?'

I shook my head. 'I shall find out,' I answered, 'before I am a day older.' With that I went back at once to my own office.

If any other firm of solicitors had been concerned in this unaccountable examination of my deceased client's Will, I might have found some difficulty in making the necessary discovery. But I had a hold over Skipp and Smalley which made my course in this matter a comparatively easy one. My common-law clerk (a most competent and excellent man) was a brother of Mr Smalley's; and, owing to this sort of indirect connection with me, Skipp and Smalley had, for some years past, picked up the crumbs that fell from my table, in the shape of cases brought to my office, which, for various reasons, I did not think it worth while to undertake. My professional patronage was, in this way, of some importance to the firm. I intended, if necessary, to remind them of that patronage, on the present occasion.

The moment I got back I spoke to my clerk; and, after telling him what had happened, I sent him to his brother's office, 'with Mr Bruff's compliments, and he would be glad to know why Messrs Skipp and Smalley had found it necessary to examine Lady Verinder's Will.'

This message brought Mr Smalley back to my office, in company with his brother. He acknowledged that he had acted under instructions received from a client. And then he put it to me, whether it would not be a breach of professional confidence on his part to say more.

We had a smart discussion upon that. He was right, no doubt; and I was wrong. The truth is, I was angry and suspicious—and I insisted on knowing more. Worse still, I declined to consider any additional information offered me, as a secret placed in my keeping: I claimed perfect freedom to use my own discretion. Worse even than that, I took an unwarrantable advantage of my position. 'Choose, sir,' I said to Mr Smalley, 'between the risk of losing your client's business and the risk of losing Mine.' Quite indefensible, I admit—an act of tyranny, and nothing less. Like other tyrants, I carried my point. Mr Smalley chose his alternative, without a moment's hesitation. He smiled resignedly, and gave up the name of his client:

Mr Godfrey Ablewhite.

That was enough for me—I wanted to know no more.

Having reached this point in my narrative, it now becomes necessary to place the reader of these lines—so far as Lady Verinder's Will is concerned—on a footing of perfect equality, in respect of information, with myself.

Let me state, then, in the fewest possible words, that Rachel Verinder had nothing but a life-interest in the property. Her mother's excellent sense, and my long experience, had combined to relieve her of all responsibility, and to guard her from all danger of becoming the victim in the future of some needy and unscrupulous man. Neither she, nor her husband (if she married), could raise sixpence, either on the property in land, or on the property in money. They would have the houses in London and in Yorkshire to live in, and they would have the handsome income—and that was all.

When I came to think over what I had discovered, I was sorely perplexed what to do next.

Hardly a week had passed since I had heard (to my surprise and distress) of Miss Verinder's proposed marriage. I had the sincerest admiration and affection for her; and I had been inexpressibly grieved when I heard that she was about to throw herself away on Mr Godfrey Ablewhite. And now, here was the man—whom I had always believed to be a smooth-tongued impostor—justifying the very worst that I had thought of him, and plainly revealing the mercenary object of the marriage, on his side! And what of that?— you may reply—the thing is done every day. Granted, my dear sir. But would you think of it quite as lightly as you do, if the thing was done (let us say) with your own sister?

The first consideration which now naturally occurred to me was this. Would Mr Godfrey Ablewhite hold to his engagement, after what his lawyer had discovered for him?

It depended entirely on his pecuniary position, of which I knew nothing. If that position was not a desperate one, it would be well worth his while to marry Miss Verinder for her income alone. If, on the other hand, he stood in urgent need of realizing a large sum by a given time, then Lady Verinder's Will would exactly meet the case, and would preserve her daughter from falling into a scoundrel's hands.

In the latter event, there would be no need for me to distress Miss Rachel, in the first days of her mourning for her mother, by an immediate revelation of the truth. In the former event, if I remained silent, I should be conniving at a marriage which would make her miserable for life.

My doubts ended in my calling at the hotel in London, at which I knew Mrs Ablewhite and Miss Verinder to be staying. They informed me that they were going to Brighton the next day, and that an unexpected obstacle prevented Mr Godfrey Ablewhite from accompanying them. I at once proposed to take his place. While I was only thinking of Rachel Verinder, it was possible to hesitate. When I actually saw her, my mind was made up directly, come what might of it, to tell her the truth.

I found my opportunity, when I was out walking with her, on the day after my arrival.

'May I speak to you,' I asked, 'about your marriage engagement?'

'Yes,' she said, indifferently, 'if you have nothing more interesting to talk about.'

'Will you forgive an old friend and servant of your family, Miss Rachel, if I venture on asking whether your heart is set on this marriage?'

'I am marrying in despair, Mr Bruff—on the chance of dropping into some sort of stagnant happiness which may reconcile me to my life.'

Strong language! and suggestive of something below the surface, in the shape of a romance. But I had my own object in view, and I declined (as we lawyers say) to pursue the question into its side-issues.

'Mr Godfrey Ablewhite can hardly be of your way of thinking,' I said. '*His* heart must be set on the marriage at any rate?'

'He says so, and I suppose I ought to believe him. He would hardly marry me, after what I have owned to him, unless he was fond of me.'

Poor thing! the bare idea of a man marrying her for his own selfish and mercenary ends had never entered her head. The task I had set myself began to look like a harder task than I had bargained for.

'It sounds strangely,' I went on, 'in my old-fashioned ears—'

'What sounds strangely?' she asked.

'To hear you speak of your future husband as if you were not quite sure of the sincerity of his attachment. Are you conscious of any reason in your own mind for doubting him?'

Her astonishing quickness of perception, detected a change in my voice, or my manner, when I put that question, which warned her that I had been speaking all along with some ulterior object in view. She stopped, and taking her arm out of mine, looked me searchingly in the face.

'Mr Bruff,' she said, 'you have something to tell me about Godfrey Ablewhite. Tell it.'

I knew her well enough to take her at her word. I told it.

She put her arm again into mine, and walked on with me slowly. I felt her hand tightening its grasp mechanically on my arm, and I saw her getting paler and paler as I went on—but, not a word passed her lips while I was speaking. When I had done, she still kept silence. Her head drooped a little, and she walked by my side, unconscious of my presence, unconscious of everything about her; lost—buried, I might almost say—in her own thoughts.

I made no attempt to disturb her. My experience of her disposition warned me, on this, as on former occasions, to give her time.

The first instinct of girls in general, on being told of anything which interests them, is to ask a multitude of questions, and then to run off, and talk it all over with some favourite friend. Rachel Verinder's first instinct, under similar circumstances, was to shut herself up in her own mind, and to think it over by herself. This absolute self-dependence is a great virtue in a man. In a woman it has the serious drawback of morally separating her from the mass of her sex, and so exposing her to misconstruction by the general opinion. I strongly suspect myself of thinking as the rest of the world think in this matter—except in the case of Rachel Verinder. The self-dependence in *her* character, was one of its virtues in my estimation; partly, no doubt, because I sincerely admired and liked her; partly, because the view I took of her connection with the loss of the Moonstone was based on my own special knowledge of her disposition. Badly as appearances might look, in the matter of the Diamond—shocking as it undoubtedly was to know that she was associated in any way with the mystery of an undiscovered theft—I was satisfied nevertheless that she had done nothing unworthy of her, because I was also satisfied that she had not stirred a step in the business, without shutting herself up in her own mind, and thinking it over first.

We had walked on, for nearly a mile I should say, before Rachel roused herself. She suddenly looked up at me with a faint reflection of her smile of happier times—the most irresistible smile I have ever seen on a woman's face.

'I owe much already to your kindness,' she said. 'And I feel more deeply indebted to it now than ever. If you hear any rumours of my marriage when you get back to London, contradict them at once, on my authority.'

Have you resolved to break your engagement?' I asked.

'Can you doubt it?' she returned proudly, 'after what you have told me!'

'My dear Miss Rachel, you are very young—and you may find more difficulty in withdrawing from your present position than you anticipate. Have you no one—I mean a lady, of course—whom you could consult?'

'No one,' she answered.

It distressed me, it did indeed distress me, to hear her say that. She was so young and so lonely—and she bore it so well! The impulse to help her got the better of any sense of my own unfitness which I might have felt under the circumstances; and I stated such ideas on the subject as occurred to me on the spur of the moment, to the best of my ability. I have advised a prodigious number of clients, and have dealt with some exceedingly awkward difficulties, in my time. But this was the first occasion on which I had ever found myself advising a young lady how to obtain her release from a marriage engagement. The suggestion I offered amounted briefly to this. I recommended her to tell Mr Godfrey Ablewhite at a private interview, of course—that he had, to her certain knowledge, betrayed the mercenary nature of the motive on his side. She was then to add that their marriage, after what she had discovered, was a simple impossibility—and she was to put it to him, whether he thought it wisest to secure her silence by falling in with her views, or to force her, by opposing them, to make the motive under which she was acting generally known. If he attempted to defend himself, or to deny the facts, she was, in that event, to refer him to *me*.

Miss Verinder listened attentively till I had done. She then thanked me very prettily for my advice, but informed me at the same time that it was impossible for her to follow it.

'May I ask,' I said, 'what objection you see to following it?'

She hesitated—and then met me with a question on her side.

'Suppose you were asked to express your opinion of Mr Godfrey Ablewhite's conduct?' she began.

'Yes?'

'What would you call it?'

'I should call it the conduct of a meanly deceitful man.'

'Mr Bruff! I have believed in that man. I have promised to marry that man. How can I tell him he is mean, how can I tell him he has deceived me, how can I disgrace him in the eyes of the world after that? I have degraded myself by ever thinking of him as my husband. If I say what you tell me to say to him—I am owning that I have degraded myself to his face. I can't do that. After what has passed between us, I can't do that! The shame of it would be nothing to *him*. But the shame of it would be unendurable to *me*.'

Here was another of the marked peculiarities in her character disclosing itself to me without reserve. Here was her sensitive horror of the bare contact with anything mean, blinding her to every consideration of what she owed to herself, hurrying her into a false position which might compromise her in the estimation of all her friends! Up to this time, I had been a little diffident about the propriety of the advice I had given to her. But, after what she had just said, I had no sort of doubt that it was the best advice that could have been offered; and I felt no sort of hesitation in pressing it on her again.

She only shook her head, and repeated her objection in other words.

'He has been intimate enough with me to ask me to be his wife. He has stood high enough in my estimation to obtain my consent. I can't tell him to his face that he is the most contemptible of living creatures, after that!'

'But, my dear Miss Rachel,' I remonstrated, 'it's equally impossible for you to tell him that you withdraw from your engagement without giving some reason for it.'

'I shall say that I have thought it over, and that I am satisfied it will be best for both of us if we part.'

'No more than that?'

'No more.'

'Have you thought of what he may say, on his side?'

'He may say what he pleases.'

It was impossible not to admire her delicacy and her resolution, and it was equally impossible not to feel that she was putting herself in the wrong. I entreated her to consider her own position. I reminded her that she would be exposing herself to the most odious misconstruction of her motives. 'You can't brave public opinion,' I said, 'at the command of private feeling.'

'I can,' she answered. 'I have done it already.'

'What do you mean?'

'You have forgotten the Moonstone, Mr Bruff. Have I not braved public opinion, *there*, with my own private reasons for it?'

Her answer silenced me for the moment. It set me trying to trace the explanation of her conduct, at the time of the loss of the Moonstone, out of the strange avowal which had just escaped her. I might perhaps have done it when I was younger. I certainly couldn't do it now.

I tried a last remonstrance before we returned to the house. She was just as immovable as ever. My mind was in a strange conflict of feelings about her when I left her that day. She was obstinate; she was wrong. She was interesting; she was admirable; she was deeply to be pitied. I made her promise to write to me the moment she had any news to send. And I went back to my business in London, with a mind exceedingly ill at ease.

On the evening of my return, before it was possible for me to receive my promised letter, I was surprised by a visit from Mr Ablewhite the elder, and was informed that Mr Godfrey had got his dismissal—*and had accepted it*—that very day.

With the view I already took of the case, the bare fact stated in the words that I have underlined, revealed Mr Godfrey Ablewhite's motive for submission as plainly as if he had acknowledged it himself. He needed a large sum of money; and he needed it by a given time. Rachel's income, which would have helped him to anything else, would not help him here; and Rachel had accordingly released herself, without encountering a moment's serious opposition on his part. If I am told that this is a mere speculation, I ask, in my turn, What other theory will account for his giving up a marriage which would have maintained him in splendour for the rest of his life?

Any exultation I might otherwise have felt at the lucky turn which things had now taken, was effectually checked by what passed at my interview with old Mr Ablewhite.

He came, of course, to know whether I could give him any explanation of Miss

Verinder's extraordinary conduct. It is needless to say that I was quite unable to afford him the information he wanted. The annoyance which I thus inflicted, following on the irritation produced by a recent interview with his son, threw Mr Ablewhite off his guard. Both his looks and his language convinced me that Miss Verinder would find him a merciless man to deal with, when he joined the ladies at Brighton the next day.

I had a restless night, considering what I ought to do next. How my reflections ended, and how thoroughly well founded my distrust of Mr Ablewhite proved to be, are items of information which (as I am told) have already been put tidily in their proper places, by that exemplary person, Miss Clack. I have only to add—in completion of her narrative—that Miss Verinder found the quiet and repose which she sadly needed, poor thing, in my house at Hampstead. She honoured us by making a long stay. My wife and daughters were charmed with her; and, when the executors decided on the appointment of a new guardian, I feel sincere pride and pleasure in recording that my guest and my family parted like old friends, on either side.

CHAPTER 2

The next thing I have to do, is to present such additional information as I possess on the subject of the Moonstone, or, to speak more correctly, on the subject of the Indian plot to steal the Diamond. The little that I have to tell is (as I think I have already said) of some importance, nevertheless, in respect of its bearing very remarkably on events which are still to come.

About a week or ten days after Miss Verinder had left us, one of my clerks entered the private room at my office, with a card in his hand, and informed me that a gentleman was below, who wanted to speak to me.

I looked at the card. There was a foreign name written on it, which has escaped my memory. it was followed by a line written in English at the bottom of the card, which I remember perfectly well:

'Recommended by Mr Septimus Luker.'

The audacity of a person in Mr Luker's position presuming to recommend anybody to *me*, took me so completely by surprise, that I sat silent for the moment, wondering whether my own eyes had not deceived me. The clerk, observing my bewilderment, favoured me with the result of his own observation of the stranger who was waiting downstairs.

'He is rather a remarkable-looking man, sir. So dark in the complexion that we all set him down in the office for an Indian, or something of that sort.'

Associating the clerk's idea with the line inscribed on the card in my hand, I thought it possible that the Moonstone might be at the bottom of Mr Luker's recommendation, and of the stranger's visit at my office. To the astonishment of my clerk, I at once decided on granting an interview to the gentleman below.

In justification of the highly unprofessional sacrifice to mere curiosity which I thus made, permit me to remind anybody who may read these lines, that no living person (in England, at any rate) can claim to have had such an intimate connection with the romance of the Indian Diamond as mine has been. I was trusted with the secret of Colonel Herncastle's plan for escaping assassination. I received the Colonel's letters, periodically reporting himself a living man. I drew his Will, leaving the Moonstone to Miss Verinder. I persuaded his executor to act, on the chance that the jewel might prove to be a valuable acquisition to the fanlily. And, lastly, I combated Mr Franklin Blake's scruples, and induced him to be the means of transporting the Diamond to Lady Verinder's house. If any one can claim a prescriptive right of interest in the Moonstone, and in everything connected with it, I think it is hardly to be denied that I am the man.

The moment my mysterious client was shown in, I felt an inner conviction that I was in the presence of one of the three Indians—probably of the chief. He was carefully dressed in European costume. But his swarthy complexion, his long lithe figure, and his grave and graceful politeness of manner were enough to betray his Oriental origin to any intelligent eyes that looked at him.

I pointed to a chair, and begged to be informed of the nature of his business with me.

After first apologizing—in an excellent selection of English words—for the liberty which he had taken in disturbing me, the Indian produced a small parcel the outer covering of which was of cloth of gold. Removing this and a second wrapping of some silken fabric, he placed a little box, or casket, on my table, most beautifully and richly inlaid in jewels, on an ebony ground.

'I have come, sir,' he said, 'to ask you to lend me some money. And I leave this as an assurance to you that my debt will be paid back.'

I pointed to his card. 'And you apply to me,' I rejoined, 'at Mr Luker's recommendation?'

The Indian bowed.

'May I ask how it is that Mr Luker himself did not advance the money that you require?'

'Mr Luker informed me, sir, that he had no money to lend.'

'And so he recommended you to come to me?'

The Indian, in his turn, pointed to the card. 'It is written there,' he said.

Briefly answered, and thoroughly to the purpose! If the Moonstone had been in my possession, this Oriental gentleman would have murdered me, I am well aware, without a moment's hesitation. At the same time, and barring that slight drawback, I am bound to testify that he was the perfect model of a client. He might not have respected my life. But he did what none of my own countrymen had ever done, in all my experience of them— he respected my time.

'I am sorry,' I said, 'that you should have had the trouble of coming to me. Mr Luker is quite mistaken in sending you here. I am trusted, like other men in my profession, with money to lend. But I never lend it to strangers, and I never lend it on such a security as you have produced.'

Far from attempting, as other people would have done, to induce me to relax my own rules, the Indian only made me another bow, and wrapped up his box in its two coverings without a word of protest. He rose—this admirable assassin rose to go, the moment I had answered him!

'Will your condescension towards a stranger, excuse my asking one question,' he said, 'before I take my leave?'

I bowed on my side. Only one question at parting! The average in my experience was fifty.

'Supposing, sir, it had been possible (and customary) for *you* to lend me the money,' he said, 'in what space of time would it have been possible (and customary) for *me* to pay it back?'

'According to the usual course pursued in this country,' I answered, 'you would have been entitled to pay the money back (if you liked) in one year's time from the date at which it was first advanced to you.'

The Indian made me a last bow, the lowest of all—and suddenly and softly walked out of the room.

It was done in a moment, in a noiseless, supple, cat-like way, which a little startled me, I own. As soon as I was composed enough to think, I arrived at one distinct conclusion in reference to the othewise incomprehensible visitor who had favoured me with a call.

His face, voice, and manner—while I was in his company—were under such perfect control that they set all scrutiny at defiance. But he had given me one chance of looking under the smooth outer surface of him, for all that. He had not shown the slightest sign of attempting to fix anything that I had said to him in his mind, until I mentioned the time at which it was customary to permit the earliest repayment, on the part of a debtor, of money that had been advanced as a loan. When I gave him that piece of information, he looked me straight in the face, while I was speaking, for the first time. The inference I drew from this was—that he had a special purpose in asking me his last question, and a special interest in hearing my answer to it. The more carefully I reflected on what had passed between us, the more shrewdly I suspected the production of the casket, and the application for the loan, of having been mere formalities, designed to pave the way for the parting inquiry addressed to me.

I had satisfied myself of the correctness of this conclusion—and was trying to get on a step further, and penetrate the Indian's motives next—when a letter was brought to me, which proved to be from no less a person than Mr Septimus Luker himself. He asked my pardon in terms of sickening servility, and assured me that he could explain matters to my satisfaction, if I would honour him by consenting to a personal interview.

I made another unprofessional sacrifice to mere curiosity. I honoured him by making an appointment at my office, for the next day.

Mr Luker was, in every respect, such an inferior creature to the Indian—he was so vulgar, so ugly, so cringing, and so prosy—that he is quite unworthy of being reported, at any length, in these pages. The substance of what he had to tell me may be fairly stated as follows:

The day before I had received the visit of the Indian, Mr Luker had been favoured with a call from that accomplished gentleman. In spite of his European disguise, Mr Luker had instantly identified his visitor with the chief of the three Indians, who had formerly annoyed him by loitering about his house, and who had left him no alternative but to consult a magistrate. From this startling discovery he had rushed to the conclusion (naturally enough I own) that he must certainly be in the company of one of the three men who had blindfolded him, gagged him, and robbed him of his banker's receipt. The result was that he became quite paralysed with terror, and that he firmly believed his last hour had come.

On his side, the Indian preserved the character of a perfect stranger. He produced the little casket, and made exactly the same application which he had afterwards made to me. As the speediest way of getting rid of him, Mr Luker had at once declared that he had no money. The Indian had thereupon asked to be informed of the best and safest person to apply to for the loan he wanted. Mr Luker had answered that the best and safest person, in such cases, was usually a respectable solicitor. Asked to name some individual of that character and profession, Mr Luker had mentioned me—for the one simple reason that, in the extremity of his terror, mine was the first name which occurred to him. 'The perspiration was pouring off me like rain, sir,' the wretched creature concluded. 'I didn't know what I was talking about. And I hope you'll look over it, Mr Bruff, sir, in consideration of my having been really and truly frightened out of my wits.'

I excused the fellow graciously enough. It was the readiest way of releasing myself from the sight of him. Before he left me, I detained him to make one inquiry. Had the Indian said anything noticeable, at the moment of quitting Mr Luker's house?

Yes! The Indian had put precisely the same question to Mr Luker, at parting, which he had put to me; receiving, of course, the same answer as the answer which I had given him.

What did it mean? Mr Luker's explanation gave me no assistance towards solving the problem. My own unaided ingenuity, consulted next, proved quite unequal to grapple with the difficulty. I had a dinner engagement that evening; and I went upstairs, in no very genial frame of mind, little suspecting that the way to my dressing-room and the way to discovery, meant, on this particular occasion, one and the same thing.

CHAPTER 3

The prominent personage among the guests at the dinner-party I found to be Mr Murthwaite.

On his appearance in England, after his wanderings, society had been greatly interested in the traveller, as a man who had passed through many dangerous adventures, and who had escaped to tell the tale. He had now announced his intention of returning to the scene of his exploits, and of penetrating into regions left still unexplored. This magnificent indifference to placing his safety in peril for the second time, revived the flagging interest of the worshippers in the hero. The law of chances was clearly against his escaping on this occasion. It is not every day that we can meet an eminent person at dinner, and feel that there is a reasonable prospect of the news of his murder being the news that we hear of him next.

When the gentlemen were left by themselves in the dining-room, I found myself sitting next to Mr Murthwaite. The guests present being all English, it is needless to say that, as soon as the wholesome check exercised by the presence of the ladies was removed, the conversation turned on politics as a necessary result.

In respect to this all-absorbing national topic, I happen to be one of the most un-English Englishmen living. As a general rule, political talk appears to me to be of all talk the most dreary and the most profitless. Glancing at Mr Murthwaite, when the bottles had made their first round of the table, I found that he was apparently of my way of thinking. He was doing it very dexterously—with all possible consideration for the feelings of his host—but it is not the less certain that he was composing himself for a nap. It struck me as an experiment worth attempting, to try whether a judicious allusion to the subject of the Moonstone would keep him awake, and, if it did, to see what *he* thought of the last new complication in the Indian conspiracy, as revealed in the prosaic precincts of my office.

'If I am not mistaken, Mr Murthwaite,' I began, 'you were acquainted with the late Lady Verinder, and you took some interest in the strange succession of events which ended in the loss of the Moonstone?'

The eminent traveller did me the honour of waking up in an instant, and asking me who I was.

I informed him of my professional connection with the Herncastle family, not forgetting the curious position which I had occupied towards the Colonel and his Diamond in the bygone time.

Mr Murthwaite shifted round in his chair, so as to put the rest of the company behind him (Conservatives and Liberals alike), and concentrated his whole attention on plain Mr Bruff, of Gray's Inn Square.

'Have you heard anything, lately, of the Indians?' he asked.

'I have every reason to believe,' I answered, 'that one of them had an interview with me, in my office, yesterday.'

Mr Murthwaite was not an easy man to astonish; but that last answer of mine completely staggered him. I described what had happened to Mr Luker, and what had happened to myself, exactly as I have described it here. 'It is clear that the Indian's parting inquiry had an object,' I added. 'Why should he be so anxious to know the time at which a borrower of money is usually privileged to pay the money back?'

'Is it possible that you don't see his motive, Mr Bruff?'

'I am ashamed of my stupidity, Mr Murthwaite—but I certainly don't see it.'

The great traveller became quite interested in sounding the immense vacuity of my dullness to its lowest depths.

'Let me ask you one question,' he said. 'In what position does the conspiracy to seize the Moonstone now stand?'

'I can't say,' I answered. 'The Indian plot is a mystery to me.'

'The Indian plot, Mr Bruff, can only be a mystery to you, because you have never seriously examined it. Shall we run it over together, from the time when you drew Colonel Herncastle's Will, to the time when the Indian called at your office? In your position, it may be of very serious importance to the interests of Miss Verinder, that you should be able to take a clear view of this matter in case of need. Tell me, bearing that in mind, whether you will penetrate the Indian's motive for yourself? or whether you wish me to save you the trouble of making any inquiry into it?'

It is needless to say that I thoroughly appreciated the practical purpose which I now saw that he had in view, and that the first of the two alternatives was the alternative I chose.

'Very good,' said Mr Murthwaite. 'We will take the question of the ages of the three Indians first. I can testify that they all look much about the same age—and you can decide for yourself, whether the man whom you saw was, or was not, in the prime of life. Not forty, you think? My idea too. We will say not forty. Now look back to the time when Colonel Herncastle came to England, and when you were concerned in the plan he adopted to preserve his life. I don't want you to count the years. I will only say, it is clear that these present Indians, at their age, must be the successors of three other Indians (high caste Brahmins all of them, Mr Bruff, when they left their native country!) who followed the Colonel to these shores. Very well. These present men of ours have succeeded to the men who were here before them. If they had only done that, the matter would not have been worth inquiring into. But they have done more. They have succeeded to the organization which their predecessors established in this country. Don't start! The organization is a very trumpery affair, according to our ideas, I have no doubt. I should reckon it up as including the command of money; the services, when needed, of that shady sort of Englishman, who lives in the byways of foreign life in London; and, lastly, the secret sympathy of such few men of their own country, and (formerly, at least) of their own religion, as happen to be employed in ministering to some of the multitudinous wants of this great city. Nothing very formidable, as you see! But worth notice at starting, because we *may* find occasion to refer to this modest little Indian organization as we go on. Having now cleared the ground, I am going to ask you a question; and I expect your experience to answer it. What was the event which gave the Indians their first chance of seizing the Diamond?'

I understood the allusion to my experience.

'The first chance they got,' I replied, 'was clearly offered to them by Colonel Herncastle's death. They would be aware of his death, I suppose, as a matter of course?'

'As a matter of course. And his death, as you say, gave them their first chance. Up to that time the Moonstone was safe in the strong-room of the bank. You drew the Colonel's Will leaving his jewel to his niece; and the Will was proved in the usual way. As a lawyer, you can be at no loss to know what course the Indians would take (under English advice) after *that*.'

'They would provide themselves with a copy of the Will from Doctors' Commons,' I said.

'Exactly. One or other of those shady Englishmen to whom I have alluded, would get them the copy you have described. That copy would inform them that the Moonstone was bequeathed to the daughter of Lady Verinder, and that Mr Blake the elder, or some person appointed by him, was to place it in her hands. You will agree with me that the necessary information about persons in the position of Lady Verinder and Mr Blake, would be perfectly easy information to obtain. The one difficulty for the Indians would be to decide, whether they should make their attempt on the Diamond when it was in course of removal from the keeping of the bank, or whether they should wait until it was taken down to Yorkshire to Lady Verinder's house. The second way would be manifestly the safest way—and there you have the explanation of the appearance of the Indians at

Frizinghall, disguised as jugglers, and waiting their time. In London, it is needless to say, they had their organization at their disposal to keep them informed of events. Two men would do it. One to follow anybody who went from Mr Blake's house to the bank. And one to treat the lower men servants with beer, and to hear the news of the house. These commonplace precautions would readily inform them that Mr Franklin Blake had been to the bank, and that Mr Franklin Blake was the only person in the house who was going to visit Lady Verinder. What actually followed upon that discovery, you remember, no doubt, quite as correctly as I do.'

I remembered that Franklin Blake had detected one of the spies, in the street—that he had, in consequence, advanced the time of his arrival in Yorkshire by some hours—and that (thanks to old Betteredge's excellent advice) he had lodged the Diamond in the bank at Frizinghall, before the Indians were so much as prepared to see him in the neighbourhood. All perfectly clear so far. But, the Indians being ignorant of the precaution thus taken, how was it that they had made no attempt on Lady Verinder's house (in which they must have supposed the Diamond to be) through the whole of the interval that elapsed before Rachel's birthday?

In putting this difficulty to Mr Murthwaite, I thought it right to add that I had heard of the little boy, and the drop of ink, and the rest of it, and that any explanation based on the theory of clairvoyance was an explanation which would carry no conviction whatever with it, to *my* mind.

'Nor to mine either,' said Mr Murthwaite. 'The clairvoyance in this case is simply a development of the romantic side of the Indian character. It would be a refreshment and an encouragement to those men—quite inconceivable, I grant you, to the English mind—to surround their wearisome and perilous errand in this country with a certain halo of the marvellous and the supernatural. Their boy is unquestionably a sensitive subject to the mesmeric influence—and, under that influence, he has no doubt reflected what was already in the mind of the person mesmerizing him. I have tested the theory of clairvoyance—and I have never found the manifestations get beyond that point. The Indians don't investigate the matter in this way; the Indians look upon their boy as a Seer of things invisible to their eyes—and, I repeat, in that marvel they find the source of a new interest in the purpose that unites them. I only notice this as offering a curious view of human character, which must be quite new to you. We have nothing whatever to do with clairvoyance, or with mesmerism, or with anything else that is hard of belief to a practical man, in the inquiry that we are now pursuing. My object in following the Indian plot, step by step, is to trace results back, by rational means, to natural causes. Have I succeeded to your satisfaction so far?'

'Not a doubt—of it, Mr Murthwaite! I am waiting, however, with some anxiety, to hear the rational explanation of the difficulty which I have just bad the honour of submitting to you.'

Mr Murthwaite smiled. 'It's the easiest difficulty to deal with of all,' he said. 'Permit me to begin by admitting your statement of the case as a perfectly correct one. The Indians were undoubtedly not aware of what Mr Franklin Blake had done with the Diamond—for we find them making their first mistake, on the first night of Mr Blake's arrival at his aunt's house.'

'Their first mistake ?' I repeated.

'Certainly! The mistake of allowing themselves to be surprised, lurking about the terrace at night, by Gabriel Betteredge. However, they had the merit of seeing for themselves that they had taken a false step—for, as you say, again, with plenty of time at their disposal, they never came near the house for weeks afterwards.'

'Why, Mr Murthwaite? That's what I want to know! Why?'

'Because no Indian, Mr Bruff, ever runs an unnecessary risk. The clause you drew in Colonel Herncastle's Will, informed them (didn't it?) that the Moonstone was to pass absolutely into Miss Verinder's possession on her birthday. Very well. Tell me which was the safest course for men in their position? To make their attempt on the Diamond while it was under the control of Mr Franklin Blake, who had shown already that he could suspect and outwit them? Or to wait till the Diamond was at the disposal of a young girl, who would innocently delight in wearing the magnificent jewel at every possible opportunity? Perhaps you want a proof that my theory is correct? Take the conduct of the Indians themselves as the proof. They appeared at the house, after waiting all those weeks, on Miss Verinder's birthday; and they were rewarded for the patient accuracy of their calculations by seeing the Moonstone in the bosom of her dress! When I heard the story of the Colonel and the Diamond, later in the evening, I felt so sure about the risk Mr Franklin Blake had run (they would have certainly attacked him, if he had not happened to ride back to Lady Verinder's in the company of other people); and I was so strongly convinced of the worse risks still, in store for Miss Verinder, that I recommended following the Colonel's plan, and destroying the identity of the gem by having it cut into separate stones. How its extraordinary disappearance, that night, made my advice useless, and utterly defeated the Hindoo plot—and how all further action on the part of the Indians was paralyzed the next day by their confinement in prison as rogues and vagabonds—you know as well as I do. The first act in the conspiracy closes there. Before we go on to the second, may I ask whether I have met your difficulty, with an explanation which is satisfactory to the mind of a practical man?'

It was impossible to deny that he had met my difficulty fairly; thanks to his superior knowledge of the Indian character—and thanks to his not having had hundreds of other Wills to think of since Colonel Herncastle's time!

'So far, so good,' resumed Mr Murthwaite. 'The first chance the Indians had of seizing the Diamond was a chance lost, on the day when they were committed to the prison at Frizinghall. When did the second chance offer itself? The second chance offered itself—as I am in a condition to prove—while they were still in confinement.'

He took out his pocket-book, and opened it at a particular leaf, before he went on.

I was staying,' he resumed, 'with some friends at Frizinghall, at the time. A day or two before the Indians were set free (on a Monday, I think), the governor of the prison came to me with a letter. It had been left for the Indians by one Mrs Macann, of whom they had hired the lodging in which they lived; and it had been delivered at Mrs Macann's door, in ordinary course of post, on the previous morning. The prison authorities had noticed that the post-mark was 'Lambeth,' and that the address on the outside, though expressed in correct English, was, in form, oddly at variance with the customary method of directing a letter. On opening it, they had found the contents to be written in a foreign language, which they rightly guessed at as Hindustani. Their object in coming to me was, of course, to have the letter translated to them. I took a copy in my pocket-book of the original, and of my translation—and there they are at your service.'

He handed me the open pocket-book. The address on the letter was the first thing copied. It was all written in one paragraph, without any attempt at punctuation, thus: 'To the three Indian men living with the lady called Macann at Frizinghall in Yorkshire.' The Hindoo characters followed; and the English translation appeared at the end, expressed in these mysterious words:

'In the name of the Regent of the Night, whose seat is on the Antelope, whose arms embrace the four corners of the earth.

'Brothers, turn your faces to the south, and come to me in the street of many noises, which leads down to the muddy river.

'The reason is this.

'My own eyes have seen it.'

There the letter ended, without either date or signature. I handed it back to Mr Murthwaite, and owned that this curious specimen of Hindoo correspondence rather puzzled me.

'I can explain the first sentence to you,' he said; 'and the conduct of the Indians themselves will explain the rest. The god of the moon is represented, in the Hindoo mythology, as a four-armed deity, seated on an antelope; and one of his titles is the regent of the night. Here, then, to begin with, is something which looks suspiciously like an indirect reference to the Moonstone. Now, let us see what the Indians did, after the prison authorities had allowed them to receive their letter. On the very day when they were set free they went at once to the railway station, and took their places in the first train that started for London. We all thought it a pity at Frizinghall that their proceedings were not privately watched. But, after Lady Verinder had dismissed the police officer, and had stopped all further inquiry into the loss of the Diamond, no one else could presume to stir in the matter. The Indians were free to go to London, and to London they went. What was the next news we heard of them, Mr Bruff?'

'They were annoying Mr Luker,' I answered, 'by loitering about the house at Lambeth.'

'Did you read the report of Mr Luker's application to the magistrate?'

'Yes.'

'In the course of his statement he referred, if you remember, to a foreign workman in his employment, whom he had just dismissed on suspicion of attempted theft, and whom he also distrusted as possibly acting in collusion with the Indians who had annoyed him. The inference is pretty plain, Mr Bruff, as to who wrote that letter which puzzled you just now, and as to which of Mr Luker's Oriental treasures the workman had attempted to steal.'

The inference (as I hastened to acknowledge) was too plain to need being pointed out. I had never doubted that the Moonstone had found its way into Mr Luker's hands, at the time Mr Murthwaite alluded to. My only question had been, How had the Indians discovered the circumstance? This question (the most difficult to deal with of all, as I had thought) had now received its answer, like the rest. Lawyer as I was, I began to feel that I might trust Mr Murthwaite to lead me blindfold through the last windings of the labyrinth, along which he had guided me thus far. I paid him the compliment of telling him this, and found my little concession very graciously received.

'You shall give me a piece of information in your turn before we go on,' he said. 'Somebody must have taken the Moonstone from Yorkshire to London. And somebody

must have raised money on it, or it would never have been in Mr Luker's possession. Has there been any discovery made of who that person was?'

'None that I know of.'

'There was a story (was there not?) about Mr Godfrey Ablewhite. I am told he is an eminent philanthropist—which is decidedly against him, to begin with.'

I heartily agreed in this with Mr Murthwaite. At the same time, I felt bound to inform him (without, it is needless to say, mentioning Miss Verinder's name) that Mr Godfrey Ablewhite had been cleared of all suspicion, on evidence which I could answer for as entirely beyond dispute.

'Very well,' said Mr Murthwaite, quietly, 'let us leave it to time to clear the matter up. In the meanwhile, Mr Bruff, we must get back again to the Indians, on your account. Their journey to London simply ended in their becoming the victims of another defeat. The loss of their second chance of seizing the Diamond is mainly attributable, as I think, to the cunning and foresight of Mr Luker—who doesn't stand at the top of the prosperous and ancient profession of usury for nothing! By the prompt dismissal of the man in his employment, he deprived the Indians of the assistance which their confederate would have rendered them in getting into the house. By the prompt transport of the Moonstone to his banker's, he took the conspirators by surprise before they were prepared with a new plan for robbing him. How the Indians, in this latter case, suspected what he had done, and how they contrived to possess themselves of his banker's receipt, are events too recent to need dwelling on. Let it be enough to say that they know the Moonstone to be once more out of their reach; deposited (under the general description of 'a valuable of great price') in a banker's strong-room. Now, Mr Bruff, what is their third chance of seizing the Diamond? and when will it come?'

As the question passed his lips, I penetrated the motive of the Indian's visit to my office at last!

'I see it!' I exclaimed. 'The Indians take it for granted, as we do, that the Moonstone has been pledged; and they want to be certainly informed of the earliest period at which the pledge can be redeemed—because that will be the earliest period at which the Diamond can be removed from the safe keeping of the bank!'

'I told you you would find it out for yourself, Mr Bruff, if I only gave you a fair chance. In a year from the time when the Moonstone was pledged, the Indians will be on the watch for their third chance. Mr Luker's own lips have told them how long they will have to wait, and your respectable authority has satisfied them that Mr Luker has spoken the truth. When do we suppose, at a rough guess, that the Diamond found its way into the money-lender's hands?'

'Towards the end of last June,' I answered, 'as well as I can reckon it.'

'And we are now in the year 'forty-eight. Very good. If the unknown person who has pledged the Moonstone can redeem it in a year, the jewel will be in that person's possession again at the end of June, 'forty-nine. I shall be thousands of miles away from England and English news at that date. But it may be worth your while to take a note of it, and to arrange to be in London at the time.'

'You think something serious will happen?' I said.

'I think I shall be safer,' he answered, 'among the fiercest fanatics of Central Asia than I should be if I crossed the door of the bank with the Moonstone in my pocket. The

Indians have been defeated twice running, Mr Bruff. It's my firm belief that they won't be defeated a third time.'

Those were the last words he said on the subject. The coffee came in; the guests rose, and dispersed themselves about the room; and we joined the ladies of the dinner-party upstairs.

I made a note of the date, and it may not be amiss if I close my narrative by repeating that note here

June, 'forty-nine. Expect news of the Indians, towards the end of the month.

And that done, I hand the pen, which I have now no further claim to use, to the writer who follows me next.

THIRD NARRATIVE

Contributed by Franklin Blake

CHAPTER 1

In the spring of the year eighteen hundred and forty-nine I was wandering in the East, and had then recently altered the travelling plans which I had laid out some months before, and which I had communicated to my lawyer and my banker in London.

This change made it necessary for me to send one of my servants to obtain my letters and remittances from the English consul in a certain city, which was no longer included as one of my resting-places in my new travelling scheme. The man was to join me again at an appointed place and time. An accident, for which he was not responsible, delayed him on his errand. For a week I and my people waited, encamped on the borders of a desert. At the end of that time the missing man made his appearance, with the money and the letters, at the entrance of my tent.

'I am afraid I bring you bad news, sir,' he said, and pointed to one of the letters, which had a mourning border round it, and the address on which was in the handwriting of Mr Bruff.

I know nothing, in a case of this kind, so unendurable as suspense. The letter with the mourning border was the letter that I opened first.

It informed me that my father was dead, and that I was heir to his great fortune. The wealth which had thus fallen into my hands brought its responsibilities with it; and Mr Bruff entreated me to lose no time in returning to England.

By daybreak the next morning I was on my way back to my own country.

The picture presented of me, by my old friend Betteredge, at the time of my departure from England, is (as I think) a little overdrawn. He has, in his own quaint way, interpreted seriously one of his young mistress's many satirical references to my foreign education; and has persuaded himself that he actually saw those French, German, and Italian sides to my character, which my lively cousin only professed to discover in jest, and which never had any real existence, except in our good Betteredge's own brain. But, barring this drawback, I am bound to own that he has stated no more than the truth in representing me as wounded to the heart by Rachel's treatment, and as leaving England in the first keenness of suffering caused by the bitterest disappointment of my life.

I went abroad, resolved—if change and absence could help me—to forget her. It is, I am persuaded, no true view of human nature which denies that change and absence *do* help a man under these circumstances: they force his attention away from the exclusive contemplation of his own sorrow. I never forgot her; but the pang of remembrance lost its worst bitterness, little by little, as time, distance, and novelty interposed themselves more and more effectually between Rachel and me.

On the other hand, it is no less certain that, with the act of turning homeward, the remedy which had gained its ground so steadily, began now, just as steadily, to drop back. The nearer I drew to the country which she inhabited, and to the prospect of seeing her again, the more irresistibly her influence began to recover its hold on me. On leaving England, she was the last person in the world, whose name I would have suffered to pass my lips. On returning to England, she was the first person I inquired after, when Mr Bruff and I met again.

I was informed, of course, of all that had happened in my absence: in other words of all that has been related here in continuation of Betteredge's narrative—one circumstance only being excepted. Mr Bruff did not, at that time, feel himself at liberty to inform me of the motives which had privately influenced Rachel and Godfrey Ablewhite in recalling the marriage promise, on either side. I troubled him with no embarrassing questions on this delicate subject. It was relief enough to me, after the jealous disappointment caused by hearing that she had ever contemplated being Godfrey's wife, to know that reflection had convinced her of acting rashly, and that she had effected her own release from her marriage engagement.

Having heard the story of the past, my next inquiries (still inquiries after Rachel!) advanced naturally to the present time. Under whose care had she been placed after leaving Mr Bruff's house? and where was she living now?

She was living under the care of a widowed sister of the late Sir John Verinder—one Mrs Merridew—whom her mother's executors had requested to act as guardian, and who had accepted the proposal. They were reported to me, as getting on together admirably well, and as being now established, for the season, in Mrs Merridew's house in Portland Place.

Half an hour after receiving this information, I was on my way to Portland Place—without having had the courage to own it to Mr Bruff!

The man who answered the door was not sure whether Miss Verinder was at home or not. I sent him upstairs with my card, as the speediest way of setting the question at rest. The man came down again with an impenetrable face, and informed me that Miss Verinder was out.

I might have suspected other people of purposely denying themselves to me. But it was impossible to suspect Rachel. I left word that I would call again at six o'clock that evening.

At six o'clock I was informed for the second time that Miss Verinder was not at home. Had any message been left for me? No message had been left for me. Had Miss Verinder not received My card? The servant begged my pardon—Miss Verinder *had* received it.

The inference was too plain to be resisted. Rachel declined to see me.

On my side, I declined to be treated in this way, without making an attempt, at least, to discover a reason for it. I sent up my name to Mrs Merridew, and requested her to favour me with a personal interview at any hour which it might be most convenient to her to name.

Mrs Merridew made no difficulty about receiving me at once. I was shown into a comfortable little sitting-room, and found myself in the presence of a comfortable little elderly lady. She was so good as to feel great regret and much surprise, entirely on my account. She was at the same time, however, not in a position to offer me any explanation, or to press Rachel on a matter which appeared to relate to a question of private feeling alone. This was said over and over again, with a polite patience that nothing could tire; and this was all I gained by applying to Mrs Merridew.

My last chance was to write to Rachel. My servant took a letter to her the next day, with strict instructions to wait for an answer.

The answer came back, literally in one sentence.

'Miss Verinder begs to decline entering into any correspondence with Mr Franklin Blake.'

Fond as I was of her, I felt indignantly the insult offered to me in that reply. Mr Bruff came in to speak to me on business, before I had recovered possession of myself. I dismissed the business on the spot, and laid the whole case before him. He proved to be as incapable of enlightening me as Mrs Merridew herself. I asked him if any slander had been spoken of me in Rachel's hearing. Mr Bruff was not aware of any slander of which I was the object. Had she referred to me in any way, while she was staying under Mr Bruff's roof? Never. Had she not so much as asked, during all my long absence, whether I was living or dead? No such question had ever passed her lips. I took out of my pocket-book the letter which poor Lady Verinder had written to me from Frizinghall, on the day when I left her house in Yorkshire. And I pointed Mr Bruff's attention to these two sentences in it:

'The valuable assistance which you rendered to the inquiry after the lost jewel is still an unpardoned offence, in the present dreadful state of Rachel's mind. Moving blindfold in this matter, you have added to the burden of anxiety which she has had to bear, by innocently threatening her secret with discovery through your exertions.'

'Is it possible,' I asked, 'that the feeling towards me which is there described, is as bitter as ever against me now?'

Mr Bruff looked unaffectedly distressed.

'If you insist on an answer,' he said, 'I own I can place no other interpretation on her conduct than that.'

I rang the bell, and directed my servant to pack my portmanteau, and to send out for a railway guide. Mr Bruff asked, in astonishment, what I was going to do.

'I am going to Yorkshire,' I answered, 'by the next train.'

'May I ask for what purpose?'

'Mr Bruff, the assistance I innocently rendered to the inquiry after the Diamond was an unpardoned offence, in Rachel's mind, nearly a year since; and it remains an unpardoned offence still. I won't accept that position! I am determined to find out the secret of her silence towards her mother, and her enmity towards *me*. If time, pains, and money can do it, I will lay my hand on the thief who took the Moonstone!'

The worthy old gentleman attempted to remonstrate—to induce me to listen to reason —to do his duty towards me, in short. I was deaf to everything that he could urge. No earthly consideration would, at that moment, have shaken the resolution that was in me.

'I shall take up the inquiry again,' I went on, 'at the point where I dropped it; and I shall follow it onwards, step by step, till I come to the present time. There are missing links in the evidence, as *I* left it, which Gabriel Betteredge can supply, and to Gabriel Betteredge I go!'

Towards sunset, that evening, I stood again on the well-remembered terrace, and looked once more at the peaceful old country house. The gardener was the first person whom I saw in the deserted grounds. He had left Betteredge, an hour since, sunning himself in the customary corner of the back yard. I knew it well; and I said I would go and seek him myself.

I walked round by the familiar paths and passages, and looked in at the open gate of the yard.

There he was—the dear old friend of the happy days that were never to come again— there he was in the old corner, on the old beehive chair, with his pipe in his mouth, and his *Robinson Crusoe* on his lap, and his two friends, the dogs, dozing on either side of him! In the position in which I stood, my shadow was projected in front of me by the last slanting rays of the sun. Either the dogs saw it, or their keen scent informed them of my approach: they started up with a growl. Starting in his turn, the old man quieted them by a word, and then shaded his failing eyes with his hand, and looked inquiringly at the figure at the gate.

My own eyes were full of tears. I was obliged to wait for a moment before I could trust myself to speak to him.

CHAPTER 2

'Betteredge!' I said, pointing to the well-remembered book on his knee, 'has *Robinson Crusoe* informed you, this evening, that you might expect to see Franklin Blake?'

By the lord Harry, Mr Franklin!' cried the old man, 'that's exactly what *Robinson Crusoe* has done!'

He struggled to his feet with my assistance, and stood for a moment, looking backwards and forwards between *Robinson Crusoe* and me, apparently at a loss to discover which of us had surprised him most. The verdict ended in favour of the book. Holding it open before him in both hands, he surveyed the wonderful volume with a stare of unutterable anticipation—as if he expected to see Robinson Crusoe himself walk out of the pages, and favour us with a personal interview.

'Here's the bit, Mr Franklin!' he said, as soon as he had recovered the use of his speech. 'As I live by bread, sir, here's the bit I was reading, the moment before you came in! Page one hundred and fifty-six as follows—"I stood like one Thunderstruck, or as if I had seen an Apparition." If that isn't as much as to say: "Expect the sudden appearance of Mr Franklin Blake"—there's no meaning in the English language!' said Betteredge, closing the book with a bang, and getting one of his hands free at last to take the hand which I offered him.

I had expected him, naturally enough under the circumstances, to overwhelm me with questions. But no—the hospitable impulse was the uppermost impulse in the old servant's mind, when a member of the family appeared (no matter how!) as a visitor at the house.

'Walk in, Mr Franklin,' he said, opening the door behind him, with his quaint old-fashioned bow. 'I'll ask what brings you here afterwards—I must make you comfortable first. There have been sad changes, since you went away. The house is shut up, and the servants are gone. Never mind that! I'll cook your dinner; and the gardener's wife will make your bed—and if there's a bottle of our famous Latour claret left in the cellar, down your throat, Mr Franklin, that bottle shall go. I bid you welcome, sir! I bid you heartily welcome!' said the poor old fellow, fighting manfully against the gloom of the deserted house, and receiving me with the sociable and courteous attention of the bygone time.

It vexed me to disappoint him. But the house was Rachel's house, now. Could I eat in it, or sleep in it, after what had happened in London? The commonest sense of self-respect forbade me—properly forbade me—to cross the threshold.

I took Betteredge by the arm, and led him out into the garden. There was no help for it. I was obliged to tell him the truth. Between his attachment to Rachel, and his attachment to me, he was sorely puzzled and distressed at the turn things had taken. His opinion, when he expressed it, was given in his usual downright manner, and was agreeably redolent of the most positive philosophy I know—the philosophy of the Betteredge school.

'Miss Rachel has her faults—I've never denied it,' he began. 'And riding the high horse, now and then, is one of them. She has been trying to ride over *you*—and you have put up with it. Lord, Mr Franklin, don't you know women by this time better than that? You have heard me talk of the late Mrs Betteredge?'

I had heard him talk of the late Mrs Betteredge pretty often—invariably producing her as his one undeniable example of the inbred frailty and perversity of the other sex. In that capacity he exhibited her now.

'Very well, Mr Franklin. Now listen to me. Different women have different ways of riding the high horse. The late Mrs Betteredge took her exercise on that favourite female animal whenever I happened to deny her anything that she had set her heart on. So sure as I came home from my work on these occasions, so sure was my wife to call to me up the kitchen stairs, and to say that, after my brutal treatment of her, she hadn't the heart to cook me my dinner. I put up with it for some time—just as you are putting up with it now from Miss Rachel. At last my patience wore out. I went downstairs, and I took Mrs Betteredge—affectionately, you understand—up in my arms, and carried her, holus-bolus, into the best parlour, where she received her company. I said, 'That's the right place for you, my dear,' and so went back to the kitchen. I locked myself in, and took off my coat, and turned up my shirt-sleeves, and cooked my own dinner. When it was done, I served it up in my best manner, and enjoyed it most heartily. I had my pipe and my drop of grog afterwards; and then I cleared the table, and washed the crockery, and cleaned the knives and forks, and put the things away, and swept up the hearth. When things were as bright and clean again, as bright and clean could be, I opened the door, and let Mrs Betteredge in. 'I've had my dinner, my dear,' I said; 'and I hope you will find that I have left the kitchen all that your fondest wishes can desire.' For the rest of that woman's life, Mr Franklin, I never had to cook my dinner again! Moral: You have put up with Miss Rachel in London; don't put up with her in Yorkshire. Come back to the house.'

Quite unanswerable! I could only assure my good friend that even *his* powers of persuasion were, in this case, thrown away on me.

'It's a lovely evening,' I said. 'I shall walk to Frizinghall, and stay at the hotel, and you must come to-morrow morning and breakfast with me. I have something to say to you.'

Betteredge shook his head gravely.

'I'm heartily sorry for this,' he said. 'I had hoped, Mr Franklin, to hear that things were all smooth and pleasant again between you and Miss Rachel. If you must have your own way, sir,' he continued, after a moment's reflection, 'there is no need to go to Frizinghall to-night for a bed. It's to be had nearer than that. There's Hotherstone's Farm, barely two miles from here. You can hardly object to *that* on Miss Rachel's account,' the old man added slily. 'Hotherstone lives, Mr Franklin, on his own freehold.'

I remembered the place the moment Betteredge mentioned it. The farm-house stood in a sheltered inland valley, on the banks of the prettiest stream in that part of Yorkshire: and the farmer had a spare bedroom and parlour, which he was accustomed to let to artists, anglers, and tourists in general. A more agreeable place of abode, during my stay in the neighbourhood, I could not have wished to find.

'Are the rooms to let?' I inquired.

'Mrs Hotherstone herself, sir, asked for my good word to recommend the rooms, yesterday.'

'I'll take them, Betteredge, with the greatest pleasure.'

We went back to the yard, in which I had left my travelling-bag. After putting a stick through the handle, and swinging the bag over his shoulder, Betteredge appeared to relapse into the bewilderment which my sudden appearance had caused, when I surprised him in the beehive chair. He looked incredulously at the house, and then he wheeled about, and looked more incredulously still at me.

'I've lived a goodish long time in the world,' said this best and dearest of all old servants—'but the like of this, I never did expect to see. There stands the house, and here stands Mr Franklin Blake—and, Damme, if one of them isn't turning his back on the other, and going to sleep in a lodging!'

He led the way out, wagging his head and growling ominously. 'There's only one more miracle that *can* happen,' he said to me, over his shoulder. 'The next thing you'll do,

Mr Franklin, will be to pay me back that seven-and-sixpence you borrowed of me when you were a boy.'

This stroke of sarcasm put him in a better humour with himself and with me. We left the house, and passed through the lodge gates. Once clear of the grounds, the duties of hospitality (in Betteredge's code of morals) ceased, and the privileges of curiosity began.

He dropped back, so as to let me get on a level with him. 'Fine evening for a walk, Mr Franklin,' he said, as if we had just accidentally encountered each other at that moment. 'Supposing you had gone to the hotel at Frizinghall, sir?'

'Yes?'

'I should have had the honour of breakfasting with you, to-morrow morning.'

'Come and breakfast with me at Hotherstone's Farm, instead.'

'Much obliged to you for your kindness, Mr Franklin. But it wasn't exactly breakfast that I was driving at. I think you mentioned that you had something to say to me? If it's no secret, sir,' said Betteredge, suddenly abandoning the crooked way, and taking the straight one, 'I'm burning to know what's brought you down here, if you please, in this sudden way.'

'What brought me here before? 'I asked.

'The Moonstone, Mr Franklin. But what brings you now, sir?'

'The Moonstone again, Betteredge.'

The old man suddenly stood still, and looked at me in the grey twilight as if he suspected his own ears of deceiving him.

'If that's a joke, sir,' he said, 'I'm afraid I'm getting a little dull in my old age. I don't take it.'

'It's no joke,' I answered. 'I have come here to take up the inquiry which was dropped when I left England. I have come here to do what nobody has done yet—to find out who took the Diamond.'

'Let the Diamond be, Mr Franklin! Take my advice, and let the Diamond be! That cursed Indian jewel has misguided everybody who has come near it. Don't waste your money and your temper—in the fine springtime of your life, sir—by meddling with the Moonstone. How can *you* hope to succeed (saving your presence), when Sergeant Cuff himself made a mess of it? Sergeant Cuff!' repeated Betteredge, shaking his forefinger at me sternly. 'The greatest policeman in England!'

'My mind is made up, my old friend. Even Sergeant Cuff doesn't daunt me.—By-the-by, I may want to speak to him, sooner or later. Have you heard anything of him lately?'

'The Sergeant won't help you,' Mr Franklin.

'Why not?'

'There has been an event, sir, in the police-circles, since you went away. The great Cuff has retired from business. He has got a little cottage at Dorking; and he's up to his eyes in the growing of roses. I have it in his own handwriting, Mr Franklin. He has grown the white moss-rose, without budding it on the dog-rose first. And Mr Begbie the gardener is to go to Dorking, and own that the Sergeant has beaten him at last.'

'It doesn't much matter,' I said. 'I must do without Sergeant Cuff's help. And I must trust to you, at starting.'

It is likely enough that I spoke rather carelessly. At any rate, Betteredge seemed to be piqued by something in the reply which I had just made to him. 'You might trust to worse than me, Mr Franklin—I can tell you that,' he said a little sharply.

The tone in which he retorted, and a certain disturbance, after he had spoken, which I detected in his manner, suggested to me that he was possessed of some information which he hesitated to communicate.

'I expect you to help me,' I said, 'in picking up the fragments of evidence which Sergeant Cuff has left behind him. I know you can do that. Can you do no more?'

'What more can you expect from me, sir? 'asked Betteredge, with an appearance of the utmost humility.

'I expect more—from what you said just now.'

'Mere boasting, Mr Franklin,' returned the old man obstinately. 'Some people are born boasters, and they never get over it to their dying day. I'm one of them.'

There was only one way to take with him. I appealed to his interest in Rachel, and his interest in me.

'Betteredge, would you be glad to hear that Rachel and I were good friends again?'

'I have served your family, sir, to mighty little purpose, if you doubt it!'

'Do you remember how Rachel treated me, before I left England?'

'As well as if it was yesterday! My lady herself wrote you a letter about it; and you were so good as to show the letter to me. It said that Miss Rachel was mortally offended with you, for the part you had taken in trying to recover her jewel. And neither my lady, nor you, nor anybody else could guess why.'

'Quite true, Betteredge! And I come back from my travels, and find her mortally offended with me still. I knew that the Diamond was at the bottom of it, last year, and I know that the Diamond is at the bottom of it now. I have tried to speak to her, and she won't see me. I have tried to write to her, and she won't answer me. How, in Heaven's name, am I to clear the matter up? The chance of searching into the loss of the Moonstone, is the one chance of inquiry that Rachel herself has left me!'

Those words evidently put the case before him, as he had not seen it yet. He asked a question which satisfied me that I had shaken him.

'There is no ill-feeling in this, Mr Franklin, on your side—is there?'

'There was some anger,' I answered, 'when I left London. But that is all worn out now. I want to make Rachel come to an understanding with me—and I want nothing more.'

'You don't feel any fear, sir—supposing you make any discoveries—in regard to what you may find out about Miss Rachel?'

I understood the jealous belief in his young mistress which prompted those words.

'I am as certain of her as you are,' I answered. 'The fullest disclosure of her secret will reveal nothing that can alter her place in your estimation, or in mine.'

Betteredge's last-left scruples vanished at that.

'If I am doing wrong to help you, Mr Franklin,' he exclaimed, 'all I can say is—I am as innocent of seeing it as the babe unborn! I can put you on the road to discovery, if you can only go on by yourself. You remember that poor girl of ours—Rosanna Spearman?'

'Of course!'

'You always thought she had some sort of confession, in regard to this matter of the Moonstone, which she wanted to make to you?'

'I certainly couldn't account for her strange conduct in any other way.'

'You may set that doubt at rest, Mr Franklin, whenever you please.'

It was my turn to come to a standstill now. I tried vainly, in the gathering darkness, to see his face. In the surprise of the moment, I asked a little impatiently what he meant.

'Steady, sir!' proceeded Betteredge. 'I mean what I say. Rosanna Spearman left a sealed letter behind her—a letter addressed to *you*.'

'Where is it?'

'In the possession of a friend of hers, at Cobb's Hole. You must have heard tell, when you were here last, sir, of Limping Lucy—a lame girl with a crutch.'

'The fisherman's daughter?'

'The same, Mr Franklin.'

'Why wasn't the letter forwarded to me?'

'Limping Lucy has a will of her own, sir. She wouldn't give it into any hands but yours. And you had left England before I could write to you.'

'Let's go back, Betteredge, and get it at once!'

'Too late, sir, to-night. They're great savers of candles along our coast; and they go to bed early at Cobb's Hole.'

'Nonsense! We might get there in half an hour.'

'*You* might, sir. And when you did get there, you would find the door locked.' He pointed to a light, glimmering below us; and, at the same moment, I heard through the stillness of the evening the bubbling of a stream. 'There's the Farm, Mr Franklin! Make yourself comfortable for to-night, and come to me to-morrow morning—if you'll be so kind?'

'You will go with me to the fisherman's cottage?'

'Yes, sir.'

'Early?'

'As early, Mr Franklin, as you like.'

We descended the path that led to the Farm.

CHAPTER 3

I have only the most indistinct recollection of what happened at Hotherstone's Farm.

I remember a hearty welcome; a prodigious supper, which would have fed a whole village in the East; a delightfully clean bedroom, with nothing in it to regret but that detestable product of the folly of our forefathers—a feather-bed; a restless night, with much kindling of matches, and many lightings of one little candle; and an immense sensation of relief when the sun rose, and there was a prospect of getting up.

It had been arranged over-night with Betteredge, that I was to call for him, on our way to Cobb's Hole, as early as I liked—which, interpreted by my impatience to get possession of the letter, meant as early as I could. Without waiting for breakfast at the Farm, I took a crust of bread in my hand, and set forth, in some doubt whether I should not surprise the excellent Betteredge in his bed. To my great relief he proved to be quite as excited about the coming event as I was. I found him ready, and waiting for me, with his stick in his hand.

'How are you this morning, Betteredge?'

'Very poorly, sir.'

'Sorry to hear it. What do you complain of?'

'I complain of a new disease, Mr Franklin, of my own inventing. I don't want to alarm you, but you're certain to catch it before the morning is out.'

'The devil I am!'

'Do you feel an uncomfortable heat at the pit of your stomach, sir? and a nasty thumping at the top of your head? Ah! not yet? It will lay hold of you at Cobb's Hole, Mr Franklin. I call it the detective-fever; and I first caught it in the company of Sergeant Cuff.'

'Aye! aye! and the cure in this instance is to open Rosanna Spearman's letter, I suppose? Come along, and let's get it.'

Early as it was, we found the fisherman's wife astir in her kitchen. On my presentation by Betteredge, good Mrs Yolland performed a social ceremony, strictly reserved (as I afterwards learnt) for strangers of distinction. She put a bottle of Dutch gin and a couple of clean pipes on the table, and opened the conversation by saying, 'What news from London, sir?'

Before I could find an answer to this immensely comprehensive question, an apparition advanced towards me, out of a dark corner of the kitchen. A wan, wild, haggard girl, with remarkably beautiful hair, and with a fierce keenness in her eyes, came limping up on a crutch to the table at which I was sitting, and looked at me as if I was an object of mingled interest and horror, which it quite fascinated her to see.

'Mr Betteredge,' she said, without taking her eyes off me, 'mention his name again, if you please.'

'This gentleman's name,' answered Betteredge (with a strong emphasis on *gentleman*), 'is Mr Franklin Blake.'

The girl turned her back on me, and suddenly left the room. Good Mrs Yolland—as I believe—made some apologies for her daughter's odd behaviour, and Betteredge (probably) translated them into polite English. I speak of this in complete uncertainty. My attention was absorbed in following the sound of the girl's crutch. Thump-thump, up the wooden stairs; thump-thump across the room above our heads; thump-thump down the stairs again—and there stood the apparition at the open door, with a letter in its hand, beckoning me out!

I left more apologies in course of delivery behind me, and followed this strange creature—limping on before me, faster and faster—down the slope of the beach. She led me behind some boats, out of sight and hearing of the few people in the fishing-village, and then stopped, and faced me for the first time.

'Stand there,' she said, 'I want to look at you.'

There was no mistaking the expression on her face. I inspired her with the strongest emotions of abhorrence and disgust. Let me not be vain enough to say that no woman had ever looked at me in this manner before. I will only venture on the more modest assertion that no woman had ever let me perceive it yet. There is a limit to the length of the inspection which a man can endure, under certain circumstances. I attempted to direct Limping Lucy's attention to some less revolting object than my face.

'I think you have got a letter to give me,' I began. 'Is it the letter there, in your hand?'

221

'Say that again,' was the only answer I received.

I repeated the words, like a good child learning its lesson.

'No,' said the girl, speaking to herself, but keeping her eyes still mercilessly fixed on me. 'I can't find out what she saw in his face. I can't guess what she heard in his voice.' She suddenly looked away from me, and rested her head wearily on the top of her crutch. 'Oh, my poor dear! 'she said, in the first soft tones which had fallen from her, in my hearing. 'Oh, my lost darling! what could you see in this man?' She lifted her head again fiercely, and looked at me once more. 'Can you eat and drink?' she asked.

I did my best to preserve my gravity, and answered, 'Yes.'

'Can you sleep?'

'Yes.'

'When you see a poor girl in service, do you feel no remorse?'

'Certainly not. Why should I?'

She abruptly thrust the letter (as the phrase is) into my face.

'Take it!' she exclaimed furiously. 'I never set eyes on you before. God Almighty forbid I should ever set eyes on you again.'

With those parting words she limped away from me at the top of her speed. The one interpretation that I could put on her conduct has, no doubt, been anticipated by everybody. I could only suppose that she was mad.

Having reached that inevitable conclusion, I turned to the more interesting object of investigation which was presented to me by Rosanna Spearman's letter. The address was written as follows:—'For Franklin Blake, Esq. To be given into his own hands (and not to be trusted to any one else), by Lucy Yolland.'

I broke the seal. The envelope contained a letter: and this, in its turn, contained a slip of paper. I read the letter first:—

'Sir—If you are curious to know the meaning of my behaviour to you, whilst you were staying in the house of my mistress, Lady Verinder, do what you are told to do in the memorandum enclosed with this—and do it without any person being present to overlook you. Your humble servant,

'Rosanna Spearman.'

I turned to the slip of paper next. Here is the literal copy of it, word for word:

'Memorandum:—To go to the Shivering Sand at the turn of the tide. To walk out on the South Spit, until I get the South Spit Beacon, and the flagstaff at the Coast-guard station above Cobb's Hole in a line together. To lay down on the rocks, a stick, or any straight thing to guide my hand, exactly in the line of the beacon and the flagstaff. To take care, in doing this, that one end of the stick shall be at the edge of the rocks, on the side of them which overlooks the quicksand. To feel along the stick, among the seaweed (beginning from the end of the stick which points towards the beacon), for the Chain. To run my hand along the Chain, when found, until I come to the part of it which stretches over the edge of the rocks, down into the quicksand. *And then, to pull the chain.*'

Just as I had read the last words—underlined in the original—I heard the voice of Betteredge behind me. The inventor of the detective-fever had completely succumbed to that irresistible malady. 'I can't stand it any longer, Mr Franklin. What does her letter say? For mercy's sake, sir, tell us, what does her letter say?'

I handed him the letter, and the memorandum. He read the first without appearing to be much interested in it. But the second—the memorandum—produced a strong impression on him.

'The Sergeant said it!' cried Betteredge. 'From first to last, sir, the Sergeant said she had got a memorandum of the hiding-place. And here it is! Lord save us, Mr Franklin, here is the secret that puzzled everybody, from the great Cuff downwards, ready and waiting, as one may say, to show itself to *you*! It's the ebb now, sir, as anybody may see for themselves. How long will it be till the turn of the tide?' He looked up, and observed a lad at work, at some little distance from us, mending a net. 'Tammie Bright!' he shouted, at the top of his voice.

'I hear you!' Tammie shouted back.

'When's the, turn of the tide?'

'In an hour's time.'

We both looked at our watches.

'We can go round by the coast, Mr Franklin,' said Betteredge; 'and get to the quick-sand in that way, with plenty of time to spare. What do you say, sir?'

'Come along?'

On our way to the Shivering Sand, I applied to Betteredge to revive my memory of events (as affecting Rosanna Spearman) at the period of Sergeant Cuff's inquiry. With my old friend's help, I soon had the succession of circumstances clearly registered in my mind. Rosanna's journey to Frizinghall, when the whole household believed her to be ill in her own room—Rosanna's mysterious employment of the night-time, with her door locked, and her candle burning till the morning—Rosanna's suspicious purchase of the japanned tin case, and the two dog-chains from Mrs Yolland—the Sergeant's positive conviction that Rosanna had hidden something at the Shivering Sand, and the Sergeant's absolute ignorance as to what that something might be—all these strange results of the abortive inquiry into the loss of the Moonstone, were clearly present to me again, when we reached the quicksand, and walked out together on the low ledge of rocks called the South Spit.

With Betteredge's help, I soon stood in the right position to see the Beacon and the Coast-guard flagstaff in a line together. Following the memorandum as our guide, we next laid my stick in the necessary direction, as neatly as we could, on the uneven surface of the rocks. And then we looked at our watches once more.

It wanted nearly twenty minutes yet of the turn of the tide. I suggested waiting through this interval on the beach, instead of on the wet and slippery surface of the rocks. Having reached the dry sand, I prepared to sit down; and, greatly to my surprise, Betteredge prepared to leave me.

'What are you going away for?' I asked.

'Look at the letter again, sir, and you will see.'

A glance at the letter reminded me that I was charged, when I made my discovery, to make it alone.

'It's hard enough for me to leave you, at such a time as this,' said Betteredge. 'But she died a dreadful death, poor soul—and I feel a kind of call on me, Mr Franklin, to humour that fancy of hers. Besides,' he added, confidentially, 'there's nothing in the letter against your letting out the secret afterwards. I'll hang about in the fir plantation, and wait till you pick me up. Don't be longer than you can help, sir. The detective-fever isn't an easy disease to deal with, under *these* circumstances.'

With that parting caution, he left me.

The interval of expectation, short as it was when reckoned by the measure of time, assumed formidable proportions when reckoned by the measure of suspense. This was one of the occasions on which the invaluable habit of smoking becomes especially precious and consolatory. I lit a cigar, and sat down on the slope of the beach.

The sunlight poured its unclouded beauty on every object that I could see. The exquisite freshness of the air made the mere act of living and breathing a luxury. Even the lonely little bay welcomed the morning with a show of cheerfulness; and the bared wet surface of the quicksand itself, glittering with a golden brightness, hid the horror of its false brown face under a passing smile. It was the finest day I had seen since my return to England.

The turn of the tide came, before my cigar was finished. I saw the preliminary heaving of the Sand, and then the awful shiver that crept over its surface—as if some spirit of terror lived and moved and shuddered in the fathomless deeps beneath. I threw away my cigar, and went back again to the rocks.

My directions in the memorandum instructed me to feel along the line traced by the stick, beginning with the end which was nearest to the beacon.

I advanced, in this manner, more than half-way along the stick, without encountering anything but the edges of the rocks. An inch or two further on, however, my patience was rewarded. In a narrow little fissure, just within reach of my forefinger, I felt the chain. Attempting, next, to follow it, by touch, in the direction of the quicksand, I found my progress stopped by a thick growth of seaweed—which had fastened itself into the fissure, no doubt, in the time that had elapsed since Rosanna Spearman had chosen her hiding-place.

It was equally impossible to pull up the seaweed, or to force my hand through it. After marking the spot indicated by the end of the stick which was placed nearest to the quicksand, I determined to pursue the search for the chain on a plan of my own. My idea was to 'sound' immediately under the rocks, on the chance of recovering the lost trace of the chain at the point at which it entered the sand. I took up the stick, and knelt down on the brink of the South Spit.

In this position, my face was within a few feet of the surface of the quicksand. The sight of it so near me, still disturbed at intervals by its hideous shivering fit, shook my nerves for the moment. A horrible fancy that the dead woman might appear on the scene of her suicide, to assist my search—an unutterable dread of seeing her rise through the heaving surface of the sand, and point to the place—forced itself into my mind, and turned me cold in the warm sunlight. I own I closed my eyes at the moment when the point of the stick first entered the quicksand.

The instant afterwards, before the stick could have been submerged more than a few inches, I was free from the hold of my own superstitious terror, and was throbbing with excitement, from head to foot. Sounding blindfold, at my first attempt—at that first attempt I had sounded right! The stick struck the chain.

Taking a firm hold of the roots of the seaweed with my left hand, I laid myself down over the brink, and felt with my right hand under the overhanging edges of the rock. My right hand found the chain.

I drew it up without the slightest difficulty. And there was the japanned tin case fastened to the end of it.

The action of the water had so rusted the chain, that it was impossible for me to unfasten it from the hasp which attached it to the case. Putting the case between my knees, and exerting my utmost strength, I contrived to draw off the cover. Some white substance filled the whole interior when I looked in. I put in my hand, and found it to be linen.

In drawing out the linen, I also drew out a letter crumpled up with it. After looking at the direction, and discovering that it bore my name, I put the letter in my pocket, and, completely removed the linen. It came out in a thick roll, moulded, of course, to the shape of the case in which it had been so long confined, and perfectly preserved from any injury by the sea.

I carried the linen to the dry sand of the beach, and there unrolled and smoothed it out. There was no mistaking it as an article of dress. It was a nightgown.

The uppermost side, when I spread it out, presented to view innumerable folds and creases, and nothing more. I tried the undermost side, next—and instantly discovered the smear of the paint from the door of Rachel's boudoir!

My eyes remained riveted on the stain, and my mind took me back at a leap from present to past. The very words of Sergeant Cuff recurred to me, as if the man himself was at my side again, pointing to the unanswerable inference which he drew from the smear on the door.

'Find out whether there is any article of dress in this house with the stain of paint on it. Find out who that dress belongs to. Find out how the person can account for having been in the room, and smeared the paint, between midnight and three in the morning. If the person can't satisfy you, you haven't far to look for the hand that took the Diamond.'

One after another those words travelled over my memory, repeating themselves again and again with a wearisome, mechanical reiteration. I was roused from what felt like a trance of many hours—from what was really, no doubt, the pause of a few moments only—by a voice calling to me. I looked up, and saw that Betteredge's patience had failed him at last. He was just visible between the sand hills, returning to the beach.

The old man's appearance recalled me, the moment I perceived it, to my—sense of present things, and reminded me that the inquiry which I had pursued thus far, still remained incomplete. I had discovered the smear on the nightgown. To whom did the nightgown belong?

My first impulse was to consult the letter in my pocket—the letter which I had found in the case.

As I raised my hand to take it out, I remembered that there was a shorter way to discovery than this. The nightgown itself would reveal the truth; for, in all probability, the nightgown was marked with its owner's name.

I took it up from the sand, and looked for the mark.

I found the mark, and read—

MY OWN NAME.

There were the familiar letters which told me that the nightgown was mine. I looked up from them. There was the sun; there were the glittering waters of the bay; there was old Betteredge, advancing nearer and nearer to me. I looked back again at the letters. My own name. Plainly confronting me—my own name.

'If time, pains, and money can do it, I will lay my hand on the thief who took the Moonstone.'—I had left London, with those words on my lips. I had penetrated the secret which the quicksand had kept from every other living creature. And, on the unanswerable evidence of the paint-stain, I had discovered Myself as the Thief.

CHAPTER 4

I have not a word to say about my own sensations.

My impression is, that the shock inflicted on me completely suspended my thinking and feeling power. I certainly could not have known what I was about, when Betteredge joined me—for I have it on his authority that I laughed, when he asked what was the matter, and, putting the nightgown into his hands, told him to read the riddle for himself.

Of what was said between us on the beach, I have not the faintest recollection. The first place in which I can now see myself again plainly is the plantation of firs. Betteredge and I are walking back together to the house; and Betteredge is telling me that I shall be able to face it, and he will be able to face it, when we have had a glass of grog.

The scene shifts from the plantation, to Betteredge's little sitting-room. My resolution not to enter Rachel's house is forgotten. I feel gratefully the coolness and shadiness and quiet of the room. I drink the grog (a perfectly new luxury to me, at that time of day), which my good old friend mixes with icy-cold water from the well. Under any other circumstances, the drink would simply stupify me. As things are, it strings up my nerves. I begin to 'face it,' as Betteredge has predicted. And Betteredge, on his side, begins to face it,' too.

The picture which I am now presenting of myself, will, I suspect, be thought a very strange one, to say the least of it. Placed in a situation which may, I think, be described as entirely without parallel, what is the first proceeding to which I resort? Do I seclude myself from all human society? Do I set my mind to analyse the abominable impossibility which, nevertheless, confronts me as an undeniable fact? Do I hurry back to London by the first train to consult the highest authorities, and to set a searching inquiry on foot immediately? No. I accept the shelter of a house which I had resolved never to degrade myself by entering again; and I sit, tippling spirits and water in the company of an old servant, at ten o'clock in the morning. Is this the conduct that might have been expected from a man placed in my horrible position? I can only answer that the sight of old Betteredge's familiar face was an inexpressible comfort to me, and that the drinking of old Betteredge's grog helped me, as I believe nothing else would have helped me, in the state of complete bodily and mental prostration into which I had fallen. I can only offer this excuse for myself; and I can only admire that invariable preservation of dignity, and that strictly logical consistency of conduct which distinguish every man and woman who may read these lines, in every emergency of their lives from the cradle to the grave.

'Now, Mr Franklin, there's one thing certain, at any rate,' said Betteredge, throwing the nightgown down on the table between us, and pointing to it as if it was a living creature that could hear him. '*He's* a liar, to begin with.'

This comforting view of the matter was not the view that presented itself to my mind.

'I am as innocent of all knowledge of having taken the Diamond as you are,' I said. 'But there is the witness against me! The paint on the nightgown, and the name on the nightgown are facts.'

Betteredge lifted my glass, and put it persuasively into my hand.

'Facts?' he repeated. 'Take a drop more grog, Mr Franklin, and you'll get over the weakness of believing in facts! Foul play, sir!' he continued, dropping his voice confidentially. 'That is how I read the riddle. Foul play somewhere—and you and I must find it out. Was there nothing else in the tin case, when you put your hand into it?'

The question instantly reminded me of the letter in my pocket. I took it out, and opened it. It was a letter of many pages, closely written. I looked impatiently for the signature at the end. 'Rosanna Spearman.'

As I read the name, a sudden remembrance illuminated my mind, and a sudden suspicion rose out of the new light.

'Stop!' I exclaimed. 'Rosanna Spearman came to my aunt out of a Reformatory? Rosanna Spearman had once been a thief?'

'There's no denying that, Mr Franklin. What of it now, if you please?'

'What of it now? How do we know she may not have stolen the Diamond after all? How do we know she may not have smeared my nightgown purposely with the paint—?'

Betteredge laid his hand on my arm, and stopped me before I could say any more.

'You will be cleared of this, Mr Franklin, beyond all doubt. But I hope you won't be cleared in *that* way. See what the letter says, sir. In justice to the girl's memory, see what it says.'

I felt the earnestness with which he spoke—felt it as a friendly rebuke to me. 'You shall form your own judgment on her letter,' I said, 'I will read it out.'

I began—and read these lines:

'Sir—I have something to own to you. A confession which means much misery, may sometimes be made in very few words. This confession can be made in three words. I love you.'

The letter dropped from my hand. I looked at Betteredge. 'In the name of Heaven,' I said, 'what does it mean?'

He seemed to shrink from answering the question.

'You and Limping Lucy were alone together this morning, sir,' he said. 'Did she say nothing about Rosanna Spearman?'

'She never even mentioned Rosanna Spearman's name.'

'Please to go back to the letter, Mr Franklin. I tell you plainly, I can't find it in my heart to distress you, after what you have had to bear already. Let her speak for herself, sir. And get on with your grog. For your own sake, get on with your grog.'

I resumed the reading of the letter.

'It would be very disgraceful to me to tell you this, if I was a living woman when you read it. I shall be dead and gone, sir, when you find my letter. It is that which makes me bold. Not even my grave will be left to tell of me. I may own the truth—with the quicksand waiting to hide me when the words are written.

'Besides, you will find your nightgown in my hiding-place, with the smear of the paint on it; and you will want to know how it came to be hidden by me? and why I said nothing to you about it in my life-time? I have only one reason to give. I did these strange things, because I loved you.

'I won't trouble you with much about myself, or my life, before you came to my lady's house. Lady Verinder took me out of a reformatory. I had gone to the reformatory from the prison. I was put in the prison, because I was a thief. I was a thief, because my mother went on the streets when I was quite a little girl. My mother went on the streets, because the gentleman who was my father deserted her. There is no need to tell such a common story as this, at any length. It is told quite often enough in the newspapers.

'Lady Verinder was very kind to me, and Mr Betteredge was very kind to me. Those two, and the matron at the reformatory are the only good people I have ever met with in all my life. I might have got on in my place—not happily—but I might have got on, if you had not come visiting. I don't blame *you*, sir. It's my fault—all my fault.

'Do you remember when you came out on us from among the sand hills, that morning, looking for Mr Betteredge? You were like a prince in a fairy-story. You were like a lover in a dream. You were the most adorable human creature I had ever seen. Something that felt like the happy life I had never led yet, leapt up in me at the instant I set eyes on you. Don't laugh at this if you can help it. Oh, if I could only make you feel how serious it is to *me!*

'I went back to the house, and wrote your name and mine in my work-box, and drew a true lovers' knot under them. Then, some devil—no, I ought to say some good angel— whispered to me, "Go and look in the glass." The glass told me—never mind what. I was too foolish to take the warning. I went on getting fonder and fonder of you, just as if I was a lady in your own rank of life, and the most beautiful creature your eyes ever rested on. I tried—oh, dear, how I tried—to get you to look at me. If you had known how I used to cry at night with the misery and the mortification of your never taking any notice of me, you would have pitied me perhaps, and have given me a look now and then to live on.

'It would have been no very kind look, perhaps, if you had known how I hated Miss Rachel. I believe I found out you were in love with her, before you knew it yourself. She used to give you roses to wear in your button-hole. Ah, Mr Franklin, you wore *my* roses oftener than either you or she thought! The only comfort I had at that time, was putting my rose secretly in your glass of water, in place of hers—and then throwing her rose away.

'If she had been really as pretty as you thought her, I might have borne it better. No; I believe I should have been more spiteful against her still. Suppose you put Miss Rachel into a servant's dress, and took her ornaments off? I don't know what is the use of my writing in this way. It can't be denied that she had a bad figure; she was too thin. But who can tell what the men like? And young ladies may behave in a manner which would cost a servant her place. It's no business of mine. I can't expect you to read my letter, if I write it in this way. But it does stir one up to hear Miss Rachel called pretty, when one knows all the time that it's her dress does it, and her confidence in herself.

'Try not to lose patience with me, sir. I will get on as fast as I can to the time which is sure to interest you—the time when the Diamond was lost.

'But there is one thing which I have got it on my mind to tell you first.

'My life was not a very hard life to bear, while I was a thief. It was only when they had taught me at the reformatory to feel my own degradation, and to try for better things, that the days grew long and weary. Thoughts of the future forced themselves on me now. I felt the dreadful reproach that honest people—even the kindest of honest people—were to me in themselves. A heart-breaking sensation of loneliness kept with me, go where I might, and do what I might, and see what persons I might. It was my duty, I know, to try and get on with my fellow-servants in my new place. Somehow, I couldn't make friends with them. They looked (or I thought they looked) as if they suspected what I had been. I don't regret, far from it, having been roused to make the effort to be a reformed woman—but, indeed, indeed it was a weary life. You had come across it like a beam of sunshine at first—and then you too failed me. I was mad enough to love you; and I couldn't even attract your notice. There was great misery—there really was great misery in that.

'Now I am coming to what I wanted to tell you. In those days of bitterness, I went two or three times, when it was my turn to go out, to my favourite place—the beach above the Shivering Sand. And I said to myself, "I think it will end here. When I can bear it no longer, I think it will end here." You will understand, sir, that the place had laid a kind of spell on me before you came. I had always had a notion that something would happen to me at the quicksand. But I had never looked at it, with the thought of its being the means of my making away with myself, till the time came of which I am now writing. Then I did think that here was a place which would end all my troubles for me in a moment or two—and hide me for ever afterwards.

'This is all I have to say about myself, reckoning from the morning when I first saw you, to the morning when the alarm was raised in the house that the Diamond was lost.

'I was so aggravated by the foolish talk among the women servants, all wondering who was to be suspected first; and I was so angry with you (knowing no better at that time) for the pains you took in hunting for the jewel, and sending for the police, that I kept as much as possible away by myself, until later in the day, when the officer from Frizinghall came to the house.

'Mr Seegrave began, as you may remember, by setting a guard on the women's bed-rooms; and the women all followed him upstairs in a rage, to know what he meant by the insult he had put on them. I went with the rest, because if I had done anything different from the rest, Mr Seegrave was the sort of man who would have suspected me directly. We found him in Miss Rachel's room. He told us he wouldn't have a lot of women there; and he pointed to the smear on the painted door, and said some of our petticoats had done the mischief, and sent us all downstairs again.

'After leaving Miss Rachel's room, I stopped a moment on one of the landings, by myself, to see if I had got the paint-stain by any chance on *my* gown. Penelope Betteredge (the only one of the women with whom I was on friendly terms) passed, and noticed what I was about.

' "You needn't trouble yourself, Rosanna,' she said. "The paint on Miss Rachel's door has been dry for hours. If Mr Seegrave hadn't set a watch on our bedrooms, I might have told him as much. I don't know what *you* think—*I* was never so insulted before in my life!"

'Penelope was a hot-tempered girl. I quieted her, and brought her back to what she had said about the paint on the door having been dry for hours.

' "How do you know that?" I asked.

' "I was with Miss Rachel, and Mr Franklin, all yesterday morning," Penelope said, "mixing the colours, while they finished the door. I heard Miss Rachel ask whether the door would be dry that evening, in time for the birthday company to see it. And Mr Franklin shook his head, and said it wouldn't be dry in less than twelve hours. It was long past luncheon-time—it was three o'clock before they had done. What does your arithmetic say, Rosanna? Mine says the door was dry by three this morning."

' "Did some of the ladies go upstairs yesterday evening to see it?" I asked. "I thought I heard Miss Rachel warning them to keep clear of the door."

' "None of the ladies made the smear," Penelope answered. "I left Miss Rachel in bed at twelve last night. And I noticed the door, and there was nothing wrong with it then."

' "Oughtn't you to mention this to Mr Seegrave, Penelope?"

' "I wouldn't say a word to help Mr Seegrave for anything that could be offered to me!"

'She went to her work, and I went to mine.

'My work, sir, was to make your bed, and to put your room tidy. It was the happiest hour I had in the whole day. I used to kiss the pillow on which your head had rested all night. No matter who has done it since, you have never had your clothes folded as nicely as I folded them for you. Of all the little knick-knacks in your dressing-case, there wasn't one that had so much as a speck on it. You never noticed it, any more than you noticed me. I beg your pardon; I am forgetting myself. I will make haste, and go on again.

'Well, I went in that morning to do my work in your room. There was your nightgown tossed across the bed, just as you had thrown it off. I took it up to fold it—and I saw the stain of the paint from Miss Rachel's door!

'I was so startled by the discovery that I ran out, with the nightgown in my hand, and made for the back stairs, and locked myself into my own room, to look at it in a place where nobody could intrude and interrupt me.

'As soon as I got my breath again, I called to mind my talk with Penelope, and I said to myself, "Here's the proof that he was in Miss Rachel's sitting-room between twelve last night, and three this morning!"

'I shall not tell you in plain words what was the first suspicion that crossed my mind, when I had made that discovery. You would only be angry—and, if you were angry, you might tear my letter up and read no more of it.

'Let it be enough, if you please, to say only this. After thinking it over to the best of my ability, I made it out that the thing wasn't likely, for a reason that I will tell you. If you had been in Miss Rachel's sitting-room, at that time of night, with Miss Rachel's knowledge (and if you had been foolish enough to forget to take care of the wet door) *she* would have reminded you—*she* would never have let you carry away such a witness against her, as the witness I was looking at now! At the same time, I own I was not completely certain in my own mind that I had proved my own suspicion to be wrong. You will not have forgotten that I have owned to hating Miss Rachel. Try to think, if you can, that there was a little of that hatred in all this. It ended in my determining to keep the nightgown, and to wait, and watch, and see what use I might make of it. At that time, please to remember, not the ghost of an idea entered my head that *you* had stolen the Diamond.'

There, I broke off in the reading of the letter for the second time.

I had read those portions of the miserable woman's confession which related to myself, with unaffected surprise, and, I can honestly add, with sincere distress. I had regretted, truly regretted, the aspersion which I had thoughtlessly cast on her memory, before I had seen a line of her letter. But when I had advanced as far as the passage which is quoted above, I own I felt my mind growing bitterer and bitterer against Rosanna Spearman as I went on. 'Read the rest for yourself,' I said, handing the letter to Betteredge across the table. 'If there is anything in it that I *must* look at, you can tell me as you go on.'

'I understand you, Mr Franklin,' he answered. 'It's natural, sir, in *you*. And, God help us all!' he added, in a lower tone, 'it's no less natural in *her*.'

I proceed to copy the continuation of the letter from the original, in my own possession:—

'Having determined to keep the nightgown, and to see what use my love, or my revenge (I hardly know which) could turn it to in the future, the next thing to discover was how to keep it without the risk of being found out.

'There was only one way—to make another nightgown exactly like it, before Saturday came, and brought the laundry-woman and her inventory to the house.

'I was afraid to put it off till next day (the Friday); being in doubt lest some accident might happen in the interval. I determined to make the new nightgown on that same day (the Thursday), while I could count, if I played my cards properly, on having my time to myself. The first thing to do (after locking up your nightgown in my drawer) was to go back to your bedroom—not so much to put it to rights (Penelope would have done that for me, if I had asked her) as to find out whether you had smeared off any of the paint-stain from your nightgown, on the bed, or on any piece of furniture in the room.

'I examined everything narrowly, and at last, I found a few faint streaks of the paint on the inside of your dressing-gown—not the linen dressing-gown you usually wore in that summer season, but a flannel dressing-gown which you had with you also. I suppose you felt chilly after walking to and fro in nothing but your night-dress, and put on the warmest thing you could find. At any rate, there were the stains, just visible, on the inside of the dressing-gown. I easily got rid of these by scraping away the stuff of the flannel. This done, the only proof left against you was the proof locked up in my drawer.

'I had just finished your room when I was sent for to be questioned by Mr Seegrave, along with the rest of the servants. Next came the examination of all our boxes. And then followed the most extraordinary event of the day—to *me*—since I had found the paint on your nightgown. This event came out of the second questioning of Penelope Betteredge by Superintendent Seegrave.

'Penelope returned to us quite beside herself with rage at the manner in which Mr Seegrave had treated her. He had hinted, beyond the possibility of mistaking him, that he suspected her of being the thief. We were all equally astonished at hearing this, and we all asked, Why?

' "Because the Diamond was in Miss Rachel's sitting-room," Penelope answered. "And because I was the last person in the sitting-room at night!"

'Almost before the words had left her lips, I remembered that another person had been in the sitting-room later than Penelope. That person was yourself. My head whirled round, and my thoughts were in dreadful confusion. In the midst of it all, something in my mind whispered to me that the smear on your nightgown might have a meaning entirely different to the meaning which I had given to it up to that time. "If the last person who was in the room is the person to be suspected," I thought to myself, "the thief is not Penelope, but Mr Franklin Blake!"

'In the case of any other gentleman, I believe I should have been ashamed of suspecting him of theft, almost as soon as the suspicion had passed through my mind.

'But the bare thought that you had let yourself down to my level, and that I, in possessing myself of your nightgown, had also possessed myself of the means of shielding you from being discovered, and disgraced for life—I say, sir, the bare thought of this seemed to open such a chance before me of winning your good will, that I passed blind-fold, as one may say, from suspecting to believing. I made up my mind, on the spot, that you had shown yourself the busiest of anybody in fetching the police, as a blind to deceive us all; and that the hand which had taken Miss Rachel's jewel could by no possibility be any other hand than yours.

'The excitement of this new discovery of mine must I think, have turned my head for awhile. I felt such a devouring eagerness to see you—to try you with a word or two about the Diamond and to *make* you look at me, and speak to me, in that way—that I put my hair tidy, and made myself as nice as I could, and went to you boldly in the library where I knew you were writing.

'You had left one of your rings upstairs, which made as good an excuse for my intrusion as I could have desired. But, oh, sir! if you have ever loved, you will understand how it was that all my courage cooled, when I walked into the room, and found myself in your presence. And then, you looked up at me so coldly, and you thanked me for finding your ring in such an indifferent manner, that my knees trembled under me, and I felt as if I should drop on the floor at your feet. When you had thanked me, you looked back, if you remember, at your writing. I was so mortified at being treated in this way, that I plucked up spirit enough to speak. I said, "This is a strange thing about the Diamond, sir." And you looked up again, and said, "Yes, it is!" You spoke civilly (I can't deny that); but still you kept a distance—a cruel distance between us. Believing, as I did, that you had got the lost Diamond hidden about you, while you were speaking, your coolness so provoked me that I got bold enough, in the heat of the moment, to give you a hint. I said, "They will never find the Diamond, sir, will they? No! nor the person who took it—I'll answer for that." I nodded, and smiled at you, as much as to say, "I know!" *This* time, you looked up at me with something like interest in your eyes; and I felt that a few more words on your side and mine might bring out the truth. Just at that moment, Mr Betteredge spoilt it all by coming to the door. I knew his footstep, and I also knew that it was against his rules for me to be in the library at that time of day—let alone being there along with you. I had only just time to get out of my own accord, before he could come in and tell me to go. I was angry and disappointed; but I was not entirely without hope for all that. The ice, you see, was broken between us—and I thought I would take care, on the next occasion, that Mr Betteredge was out of the way.

'When I got back to the servants' hall, the bell was going for our dinner. Afternoon already! and the materials for making the new nightgown were still to be got! There was but one chance of getting them. I shammed ill at dinner; and so secured the whole of the interval from then till tea-time to my own use.

'What I was about, while the household believed me to be lying down in my own room; and how I spent the night, after shamming ill again at tea-time, and having been sent up to bed, there is no need to tell you. Sergeant Cuff discovered that much, if he discovered nothing more. And I can guess how. I was detected (though I kept my veil down) in the draper's shop at Frizinghall. There was a glass in front of me, at the counter where I was buying the longcloth; and—in that glass—I saw one of the shopmen point to my shoulder and whisper to another. At night again, when I was secretly at work, locked into my room, I heard the breathing of the women servants who suspected me, outside my door.

'It didn't matter then; it doesn't matter now. On the Friday morning, hours before Sergeant Cuff entered the house, there was the new nightgown—to make up your number in place of the nightgown that I had got—made, wrung out, dried, ironed, marked, and folded as the laundry woman folded all the others, safe in your drawer. There was no fear (if the linen in the house was examined) of the newness of the nightgown betraying me. All your underclothing had been renewed, when you came to our house—I suppose on your return home from foreign parts.

'The next thing was the arrival of Sergeant Cuff; and the next great surprise was the announcement of what he thought about the smear on the door.

'I had believed you to be guilty (as I have owned) more because I wanted you to be guilty than for any other reason. And now, the Sergeant had come round by a totally different way to the same conclusion (respecting the nightgown) as mine! And I had got the dress that was the only proof against you! And not a living creature knew it—yourself included! I am afraid to tell you how I felt when I called these things to mind—you would hate my memory for ever afterwards.'

At that place, Betteredge looked up from the letter.

'Not a glimmer of light so far, Mr Franklin,' said the old man, taking off his heavy tortoiseshell spectacles, and pushing Rosanna Spearman's confession a little away from him. 'Have you come to any conclusion, sir, in your own mind, while I have been reading?'

'Finish the letter first, Betteredge; there may be something to lighten us at the end of it. I shall have a word or two to say to you after that.'

'Very good, sir. I'll just rest my eyes, and then I'll go on again. In the meantime, Mr Franklin—I don't want to hurry you—but would you mind telling me, in one word, whether you see your way out of this dreadful mess yet?'

'I see my way back to London,' I said, 'to consult Mr Bruff. If he can't help me—'

'Yes, sir?'

'And if the Sergeant won't leave his retirement at Dorking—'

'He won't, Mr Franklin!'

'Then, Betteredge—as far as I can see now—I am at the end of my resources. After Mr Bruff and the Sergeant, I don't know of a living creature who can be of the slightest use to me.'

As the words passed my lips, some person outside knocked at the door of the room.

Betteredge looked surprised as well as annoyed by the interruption.

'Come in,' he called out, irritably, 'whoever you are!'

The door opened, and there entered to us, quietly, the most remarkable-looking man that I had ever seen. Judging him by his figure and his movements, he was still young. Judging him by his face, and comparing him with Betteredge, he looked the elder of the two. His complexion was of a gipsy darkness; his fleshless cheeks had fallen into deep hollows, over which the bone projected like a pent-house. His nose presented the fine shape and modelling so often found among the ancient people of the East, so seldom visible among the newer races of the West. His forehead rose high and straight from the brow. His marks and wrinkles were innumerable. From this strange face, eyes, stranger still, of the softest brown—eyes dreamy and mournful, and deeply sunk in their orbits—looked out at you, and (in my case, at least) took your attention captive at their will. Add to this a quantity of thick closely-curling hair, which, by some freak of Nature, had lost its colour in the most startlingly partial and capricious manner. Over the top of his head it was still of the deep black which was its natural colour. Round the sides of his head—without the slightest gradation of grey to break the force of the extraordinary contrast—it had turned completely white. The line between the two colours preserved no sort of regularity. At one place, the white hair ran up into the black; at another, the black hair ran down into the white. I looked at the man with a curiosity which, I am ashamed to say, I found it quite impossible to control. His soft brown eyes looked back at me gently; and he met my involuntary rudeness in staring at him, with an apology which I was conscious that I had not deserved.

'I beg your pardon,' he said. 'I had no idea that Mr Betteredge was engaged.' He took a slip of paper from his pocket, and handed it to Betteredge. 'The list for next week,' he said. His eyes just rested on me again—and he left the room as quietly as he had entered it.

'Who is that?' I asked.

'Mr Candy's assistant,' said Betteredge. 'By-the-by, Mr Franklin, you will be sorry to hear that the little doctor has never recovered from that illness he caught, going home from the birthday dinner. He's pretty well in health; but he lost his memory in the fever, and he has never recovered more than the wreck of it since. The work all falls on his assistant. Not much of it now, except among the poor. *They* can't help themselves, you know. *They* must put up with the man with the piebald hair, and the gipsy complexion—or they would get no doctoring at all.'

'You don't seem to like him, Betteredge?'

'Nobody likes him, sir.'

'Why is he so unpopular?'

'Well, Mr Franklin, his appearance is against him, to begin with. And then there's a story that Mr Candy took him with a very doubtful character. Nobody knows who he is— and he hasn't a friend in the place. How can you expect one to like him, after that?'

'Quite impossible, of course! May I ask what he wanted with you, when he gave you that bit of paper?'

'Only to bring me the weekly list of the sick people about here, sir, who stand in need of a little wine. My lady always had a regular distribution of good sound port and sherry among the infirm poor; and Miss Rachel wishes the custom to be kept up. Times have changed! times have changed! I remember when Mr Candy himself brought the list to my mistress. Now it's Mr Candy's assistant who brings the list to me. I'll go on with the letter, if you will allow me, sir,' said Betteredge, drawing Rosanna Spearman's confession back to him. 'It isn't lively reading, I grant you. But, there! it keeps me from getting sour with thinking of the past.' He put on his spectacles, and wagged his head gloomily. 'There's a bottom of good sense, Mr Franklin, in our conduct to our mothers, when they first start us on the journey of life. We are all of us more or less unwilling to be brought into the world. And we are all of us right.'

Mr Candy's assistant had produced too strong an impression on me to be immediately dismissed from my thoughts. I passed over the last unanswerable utterance of the Betteredge philosophy; and returned to the subject of the man with the piebald hair.

'What is his name?' I asked.

'As ugly a name as need be,' Betteredge answered, gruffly. 'Ezra Jennings.'

CHAPTER 5

Having told me the name of Mr Candy's assistant, Betteredge appeared to think that we had wasted enough of our time on an insignificant subject. He resumed the perusal of Rosanna Spearman's letter.

On my side, I sat at the window, waiting until he had done. Little by little, the impression produced on me by Ezra Jennings—it seemed perfectly unaccountable, in such a situation as mine, that any human being should have produced an impression on me at all!—faded from my mind. My thoughts flowed back into their former channel. Once more, I forced myself to look my own incredible position resolutely in the face. Once more, I reviewed in my own mind the course which I had at last summoned composure enough to plan out for the future.

To go back to London that day; to put the whole case before Mr Bruff; and, last and most important, to obtain (no matter by what means or at what sacrifice) a personal interview with Rachel—this was my plan of action, so far as I was capable of forming it at the time. There was more than an hour still to spare before the train started. And there was the bare chance that Betteredge might discover something in the unread portion of Rosanna Spearman's letter, which it might be useful for me to know before I left the house in which the Diamond had been lost. For that chance I was now waiting.

The letter ended in these terms:

'You have no need to be angry, Mr Franklin, even if I did feel some little triumph at knowing that I held all your prospects in life in my own hands. Anxieties and fears soon came back to me. With the view Sergeant Cuff took of the loss of the Diamond, he would be sure to end in examining our linen and our dresses. There was no place in my room—there was no place in the house—which I could feel satisfied would be safe from him. How to hide the nightgown so that not even the Sergeant could find it? and how to do that without losing one moment of precious time?—these were not easy questions to answer. My uncertainties ended in my taking a way that may make you laugh. I undressed, and put the nightgown on me. You had worn it—and I had another little moment of pleasure in wearing it after you.

'The next news that reached us in the servants' hall showed that I had not made sure of the nightgown a moment too soon. Sergeant Cuff wanted to see the washing-book.

'I found it, and took it to him in my lady's sitting-room. The Sergeant and I had come across each other more than once in former days. I was certain he would know me again—and I was *not* certain of what he might do when he found me employed as servant in a house in which a valuable jewel had been lost. In this suspense, I felt it would be a relief to me to get the meeting between us over, and to know the worst of it at once.

'He looked at me as if I was a stranger, when I handed him the washing-book; and he was very specially polite in thanking me for bringing it. I thought those were both bad signs. There was no knowing what he might say of me behind my back; there was no knowing how soon I might not find myself taken in custody on suspicion, and searched. It was then time for your return from seeing Mr Godfrey Ablewhite off by the railway; and I went to your favourite walk in the shrubbery, to try for another chance of speaking to you—the last chance, for all I knew to the contrary, that I might have.

'You never appeared; and, what was worse still, Mr Betteredge and Sergeant Cuff passed by the place where I was hiding—and the Sergeant saw me.

'I had no choice, after that, but to return to my proper place and my proper work, before more disasters happened to me. Just as I was going to step across the path, you came back from the railway. You were making straight for the shrubbery, when you saw me—I am certain, sir, you saw me—and you turned away as if I had got the plague, and went into the house.*

'I made the best of my way indoors again, returning by the servants' entrance. There was nobody in the laundry-room at that time; and I sat down there alone. I have told you already of the thoughts which the Shivering Sand put into my head. Those thoughts came back to me now. I wondered in myself which it would be hardest to do, if things went on in this manner—to bear Mr Franklin Blake's indifference to me, or to jump into the quicksand and end it for ever in that way?

'It's useless to ask me to account for my own conduct, at this time. I try—and I can't understand it myself.

'Why didn't I stop you, when you avoided me in that cruel manner? Why didn't I call out, "Mr Franklin, I have got something to say to you; it concerns yourself, and you must,

* Note. by Franklin Blake.—The writer is entirely mistaken, poor creature. I never noticed her. My intention was certainly to have taken a turn in the shrubbery. But, remembering at the same moment that my aunt might wish to see me, after my return from the railway, I altered my mind, and went into the house.

and shall, hear it?'' You were at my mercy—I had got the whip-hand of you, as they say. And better than that, I had the means (if I could only make you trust me) of being useful to you in the future. Of course, I never supposed that you—a gentleman—had stolen the Diamond for the mere pleasure of stealing it. No. Penelope had heard Miss Rachel, and I had heard Mr Betteredge, talk about your extravagance and your debts. It was plain enough to me that you had taken the Diamond to sell it, or pledge it, and so to get the money of which you stood in need. Well! I could have told you of a man in London who would have advanced a good large sum on the jewel, and who would have asked no awkward questions about it either.

'Why didn't I speak to you! why didn't I speak to you!

'I wonder whether the risks and difficulties of keeping the nightgown were as much as I could manage, without having other risks and difficulties added to them? This might have been the case with some women—but how could it be the case with me? In the days when I was a thief, I had run fifty times greater risks, and found my way out of difficulties to which *this* difficulty was mere child's play. I had been apprenticed, as you may say, to frauds and deceptions—some of them on such a grand scale, and managed so cleverly, that they became famous, and appeared in the newspapers. Was such a little thing as the keeping of the nightgown likely to weigh on my spirits, and to set my heart sinking within me, at the time when I ought to have spoken to you? What nonsense to ask the question! The thing couldn't be.

'Where is the use of my dwelling in this way on my own folly? The plain truth is plain enough, surely? Behind your back, I loved you with all my heart and soul. Before your face—there's no denying it—I was frightened of you; frightened of making you angry with me; frightened of what you might say to me (though you *had* taken the Diamond) if I presumed to tell you that I had found it out. I had gone as near to it as I dared when I spoke to you in the library. You had not turned your back on me then. You had not started away from me as if I had got the plague. I tried to provoke myself into feeling angry with you, and to rouse up my courage in that way. No! I couldn't feel anything but the misery and the mortification of it. ''You're a plain girl; you have got a crooked shoulder; you're only a housemaid—what do you mean by attempting to speak to Me?'' You never uttered a word of that, Mr Franklin; but you said it all to me, nevertheless! Is such madness as this to be accounted for? No. There is nothing to be done but to confess it, and let it be.

'I ask your pardon, once more, for this wandering of my pen. There is no fear of its happening again. I am close at the end now.

'The first person who disturbed me by coming into the empty room was Penelope. She had found out my secret long since, and she had done her best to bring me to my senses—and done it kindly too.

' ''Ah!'' she said, ''I know why you're sitting here, and fretting, all by yourself. The best thing that can happen for your advantage, Rosanna, will be for Mr Franklin's visit here to come to an end. It's my belief that he won't be long now before he leaves the house.''

'In all my thoughts of you I had never thought of your going away. I couldn't speak to Penelope. I could only look at her.

' ''I've just left Miss Rachel,'' Penelope went on. ''And a hard matter I have had of it to put up with her temper. She says the house is unbearable to her with the police in it;

and she's determined to speak to my lady this evening, and to go to her Aunt Ablewhite to-morrow. If she does that, Mr Franklin will be the next to find a reason for going away, you may depend on it!''

'I recovered the use of my tongue at that. ''Do you mean to say Mr Franklin will go with her?'' I asked.

' ''Only too gladly, if she would let him; but she won't. *He* has been made to feel her temper; *he* is in her black books too— and that after having done all he can to help her, poor fellow! No! no! If they don't make it up before to-morrow, you will see Miss Rachel go one way, and Mr Franklin another. Where he may betake himself to I can't say. But he will never stay here, Rosanna, after Miss Rachel has left us.''

'I managed to master the despair I felt at the prospect of your going away. To own the truth, I saw a little glimpse of hope for myself if there was really a serious disagreement between Miss Racbel and you. ''Do you know,'' I asked, ''what the quarrel is between them?''

' ''It is all on Miss Rachel's side,'' Penelope said. ''And, for anything I know to the contrary, it's all Miss Rachel's temper, and nothing else. I am loth to distress you, Rosanna; but don't run away with the notion that Mr Franklin is ever likely to quarrel with *her*. He's a great deal too fond of her for that!''

'She had only just spoken those cruel words when there came a call to us from Mr Betteredge. All the indoor servants were to assemble in the hall. And then we were to go in, one by one, and be questioned in Mr Betteredge's room by Sergeant Cuff.

'It came to my turn to go in, after her ladyship's maid and the upper housemaid had been questioned first. Sergeant Cuff's inquiries—though he wrapped them up very cunningly—soon showed me that those two women (the bitterest enemies I had in the house) had made their discoveries outside my door, on the Tuesday afternoon, and again on the Thursday night. They had told the Sergeant enough to open his eyes to some part of the truth. He rightly believed me to have made a new nightgown secretly, but he wrongly believed the paint-stained nightgown to be mine. I felt satisfied of another thing, from what he said, which it puzzled me to understand. He suspected me, of course, of being concerned in the disappearance of the Diamond. But, at the same time, he let me see—purposely, as I thought—that he did not consider me as the person chiefly answerable for the loss of the jewel. He appeared to think that I had been acting under the direction of somebody else. Who that person might be, I couldn't guess then, and can't guess now.

'In this uncertainty, one thing was plain—that Sergeant Cuff was miles away from knowing the whole truth. You were safe as long as the nightgown was safe—and not a moment longer.

'I quite despair of making you understand the distress and terror which pressed upon me now. It was impossible for me to risk wearing your nightgown any longer. I might find myself taken off, at a moment's notice, to the police court at Frizinghall, to be charged on suspicion, and searched accordingly. While Sergeant Cuff still left me free, I had to choose—and at once—between destroying the nightgown, or hiding it in some safe place, at some safe distance from the house.

'If I had only been a little less fond of you, I think I should have destroyed it. But oh! how could I destroy the only thing I had which proved that I had saved you from discovery? If we did come to an explanation together, and if you suspected me of having some bad motive, and denied it all, how could I win upon you to trust me, unless I had the nightgown to produce? Was it wronging you to believe, as I did, and do still, that you might hesitate to let a poor girl like me be the sharer of your secret, and your accomplice in the theft which your money-troubles had tempted you to commit? Think of your cold behaviour to me, sir, and you will hardly wonder at my unwillingness to destroy the only claim on your confidence and your gratitude which it was my fortune to possess.

'I determined to hide it; and the place I fixed on was the place I knew best—the Shivering Sand.

'As soon as the questioning was over, I made the first excuse that came into my head, and got leave to go out for a breath of fresh air. I went straight to Cobb's Hole, to Mr Yolland's cottage. His wife and daughter were the best friends I had. Don't suppose I trusted them with your secret—I have trusted nobody. All I wanted was to write this letter to you, and to have a safe opportunity of taking the nightgown off me. Suspected as I was, I could do neither of those things, with any sort of security, up at the house.

'And now I have nearly got through my long letter, writing it alone in Lucy Yolland's bedroom. When it is done, I shall go downstairs with the nightgown rolled up, and hidden under my cloak. I shall find the means I want for keeping it safe and dry in its hiding-place, among the litter of old things in Mrs Yolland's kitchen. And then I shall go to the Shivering Sand—don't be afraid of my letting my footmarks betray me!—and hide the nightgown down in the sand, where no living creature can find it without being first let into the secret by myself.

'And, when that's done, what then?

'Then, Mr Franklin, I shall have two reasons for making another attempt to say the words to you which I have not said yet. If you leave the house, as Penelope believes you will leave it, and if I haven't spoken to you before that, I shall lose my opportunity forever. That is one reason. Then, again, there is the comforting knowledge—if my speaking does make you angry—that I have got the nightgown ready to plead my cause for me as nothing else can. That is my other reason. If these two together don't harden my heart against the coldness which has hitherto frozen it up (I mean the coldness of your treatment of me), there will be the end of my efforts—and the end of my life.

'Yes. If I miss my next opportunity—if you are as cruel as ever, and if I feel it again as I have felt it already—goodbye to the world which has grudged me the happiness that it gives to others. Goodbye to life, which nothing but a little kindness from *you* can ever make pleasurable to me again. Don't blame yourself, sir, if it ends in this way. But try— do try—to feel some forgiving sorrow for me! I shall take care that you find out what I have done for you, when I am past telling you of it myself. Will you say something kind of me then—in the same gentle way that you have when you speak to Miss Rachel? If you do that, and if there are such things as ghosts, I believe my ghost will hear it, and tremble with the pleasure of it.

'It's time I left off. I am making myself cry. How am I to see my way to the hiding-place if I let these useless tears come and blind me?

'Besides, why should I look at the gloomy side? Why not believe, while I can, that it will end well after all? I may find you in a good humour to-night—or, if not, I may succeed better to-morrow morning. I shan't improve my plain face by fretting—shall I?

Who knows but I may have filled all these weary long pages of paper for nothing? They will go, for safety's sake (never mind now for what other reason) into the hiding-place along with the nightgown. It has been hard, hard work writing my letter. Oh! if we only end in understanding each other, how I shall enjoy tearing it up!

'I beg to remain, sir, your true lover and humble servant,

'Rosanna Spearman.'

The reading of the letter was completed by Betteredge in silence. After carefully putting it back in the envelope, he sat thinking, with his head bowed down, and his eyes on the ground.

'Betteredge,' I said, 'is there any hint to guide me at the end of the letter?'

He looked up slowly, with a heavy sigh.

'There is nothing to guide you, Mr Franklin,' he answered. 'If you take my advice you will keep the letter in the cover till these present anxieties of yours have come to an end. It will sorely distress you, whenever you read it. Don't read it now.'

I put the letter away in my pocket-book.

A glance back at the sixteenth and seventeenth chapters of Betteredge's Narrative will show that there really was a reason for my thus sparing myself, at a time when my fortitude had been already cruelly tried. Twice over, the unhappy woman had made her last attempt to speak to me. And twice over, it had been my misfortune (God knows how innocently!) to repel the advances she had made to me. On the Friday night, as Betteredge truly describes it, she had found me alone at the billiard-table. Her manner and language suggested to me—and would have suggested to any man, under the circumstances—that she was about to confess a guilty knowledge of the disappearance of the Diamond. For her own sake, I had purposely shown no special interest in what was coming; for her own sake, I had purposely looked at the billiard balls, instead of looking at *her*—and what had been the result? I had sent her away from me, wounded to the heart! On the Saturday again— on the day when she must have foreseen, after what Penelope had told her, that my departure was close at hand—the same fatality still pursued us. She had once more attempted to meet me in the shrubbery walk, and she had found me there in company with Betteredge and Sergeant Cuff. In her hearing, the Sergeant, with his own under- hand object in view, had appealed to my interest in Rosanna Spearman. Again for the poor creature's own sake, I had met the police-officer with a flat denial, and had declared—loudly declared, so that she might hear me too—that I felt 'no interest what- ever in Rosanna Spearman.' At those words, solely designed to warn her against attempt- ing to gain my private ear, she had turned away and left the place: cautioned of her danger, as I then believed; self-doomed to destruction, as I know now. From that point, I have already traced the succession of events which led me to the astounding discovery at the quicksand. The retrospect is now complete. I may leave the miserable story of Rosanna Spearman—to which, even at this distance of time, I cannot revert without a pang of distress—to suggest for itself all that is here purposely left unsaid. I may pass from the suicide at the Shivering Sand, with its strange and terrible influence on my present posi- tion and future prospects, to interests which concern the living people of this narrative, and to events which were already paving my way for the slow and toilsome journey from the darkness to the light.

CHAPTER 6

I walked to the railway station accompanied, it is needless to say, by Gabriel Betteredge. I had the letter in my pocket, and the nightgown safely packed in a little bag—both to be submitted, before I slept that night, to the investigation of Mr Bruff.

We left the house in silence. For the first time in my experience of him, I found old Betteredge in my company without a word to say to me. Having something to say on my side, I opened the conversation as soon as we were clear of the lodge gates.

'Before I go to London,' I began, 'I have two questions to ask you. They relate to myself, and I believe they will rather surprise you.'

'If they will put that poor creature's letter out of my head, Mr Franklin, they may do anything else they like with me. Please to begin surprising me, sir, as soon as you can.'

'My first question, Betteredge, is this. Was I drunk on the night of Rachel's Birthday?'

'*You* drunk!' exclaimed the old man. 'Why it's the great defect of your character, Mr Franklin, that you only drink with your dinner, and never touch a drop of liquor afterwards!'

'But the birthday was a special occasion. I might have abandoned my regular habits, on that night of all others.'

Betteredge considered for a moment.

'You did go out of your habits, sir,' he said. 'And I'll tell you how. You looked wretchedly ill—and we persuaded you to have a drop of brandy and water to cheer you up a little.'

'I am not used to brandy and water. It is quite possible——'

'Wait a bit, Mr Franklin. I knew you were not used, too. I poured you out half a wineglass-full of our fifty-year-old Cognac; and (more shame for me!) I drowned that noble liquor in nigh on a tumbler-full of cold water. A child couldn't have got drunk on it—let alone a grown man!'

I knew I could depend on his memory, in a matter of this kind. It was plainly impossible that I could have been intoxicated. I passed on to the second question.

'Before I was sent abroad, Betteredge, you saw a great deal of me when I was a boy? Now tell me plainly, do you remember anything strange of me, after I had gone to bed at night? Did you ever discover me walking in my sleep?'

Betteredge stopped, looked at me for a moment, nodded his head, and walked on again.

'I see your drift now, Mr Franklin!' he said. 'You're trying to account for how you got the paint on your nightgown, without knowing it yourself. It won't do, sir. You're miles away still from getting at the truth. Walk in your sleep? You never did such a thing in your life!'

Here again, I felt that Betteredge must be right. Neither at home nor abroad had my life ever been of the solitary sort. If I had been a sleep-walker, there were hundreds on hundreds of people who must have discovered me, and who, in the interest of my own safety, would have warned me of the habit, and have taken precautions to restrain it.

Still, admitting all this, I clung—with an obstinacy which was surely natural and excusable, under the circumstances—to one or other of the only two explanations that I could see which accounted for the unendurable position in which I then stood. Observing that I was not yet satisfied, Betteredge shrewdly adverted to certain later events in the history of the Moonstone; and scattered both my theories to the wind at once and for ever.

'Let's try it another way, sir,' he said. 'Keep your own opinion, and see how far it will take you towards finding out the truth. If we are to believe the nightgown—which I don't for one—you not only smeared off the paint from the door, without knowing it, but you also took the Diamond without knowing it. Is that right, so far?'

'Quite right. Go on.'

'Very good, sir. We'll say you were drunk, or walking in your sleep, when you took the jewel. That accounts for the night and morning, after the birthday. But how does it account for what has happened since that time? The Diamond has been taken to London, since that time. The Diamond has been pledged to Mr Luker, since that time. Did you do those two things, without knowing it, too? Were you drunk when I saw you off in the pony-chaise on that Saturday evening? And did you walk in your sleep to Mr Luker's, when the train had brought you to your journey's end? Excuse me for saying it, Mr Franklin, but this business has so upset you, that you're not fit yet to judge for yourself. The sooner you lay your head alongside of Mr Bruff's head, the sooner you will see your way out of the deadlock that has got you now.'

We reached the station, with only a minute or two to spare.

I hurriedly gave Betteredge my address in London, so that he might write to me, if necessary; promising, on my side, to inform him of any news which I might have to communicate. This done, and just as I was bidding him farewell, I happened to glance towards the book-and-newspaper stall. There was Mr Candy's remarkable-looking assistant again, speaking to the keeper of the stall! Our eyes met at the same moment. Ezra Jennings took off his hat to me. I returned the salute, and got into a carriage just as the train started. It was a relief to my mind, I suppose, to dwell on any subject which appeared to be, personally, of no sort of importance to me. At all events, I began the momentous journey back which was to take me to Mr Bruff, wondering—absurdly enough, I admit—that I should have seen the man with the piebald hair twice in one day!

The hour at which I arrived in London precluded all hope of my finding Mr Bruff at his place of business. I drove from the railway to his private residence at Hampstead, and disturbed the old lawyer dozing alone in his dining-room, with his favourite pug-dog on his lap, and his bottle of wine at his elbow.

I shall best describe the effect which my story produced on the mind of Mr Bruff by relating his proceedings when he had heard it to the end. He ordered lights, and strong tea, to be taken into his study; and he sent a message to the ladies of his family, forbidding them to disturb us on any pretence whatever. These preliminaries disposed of, he first examined the nightgown, and then devoted himself to the reading of Rosanna Spearman's letter.

The reading completed, Mr Bruff addressed me for the first time since we had been shut up together in the seclusion of his own room.

'Franklin Blake,' said the old gentleman, 'this is a very serious matter, in more respects than one. In my opinion, it concerns Rachel quite as nearly as it concerns you. Her extraordinary conduct is no mystery *now*. She believes you have stolen the Diamond.'

I had shrunk from reasoning my own way fairly to that revolting conclusion. But it had forced itself on me, nevertheless. My resolution to obtain a personal interview with

Rachel, rested really and truly on the ground just stated by Mr Bruff.

'The first step to take in this investigation,' the lawyer proceeded, 'is to appeal to Rachel. She has been silent all this time, from motives which I (who know her character) can readily understand. It is impossible, after what has happened, to submit to that silence any longer. She must be persuaded to tell us, or she must be forced to tell us, on what grounds she bases her belief that you took the Moonstone. The chances are, that the whole of this case, serious as it seems now, will tumble to pieces, if we can only break through Rachel's inveterate reserve, and prevail upon her to speak out.'

'That is a very comforting opinion for *me*,' I said. 'I own I should like to know—'

'You would like to know how I can justify it,' interposed Mr Bruff. 'I can tell you in two minutes. Understand, in the first place, that I look at this matter from a lawyer's point of view. It's a question of evidence, with me. Very well. The evidence breaks down, at the outset, on one important point.'

'On what point?'

'You shall hear. I admit that the mark of the name proves the nightgown to be yours. I admit that the mark of the paint proves the nightgown to have made the smear on Rachel's door. But what evidence is there to prove that you are the person who wore it, on the night when the Diamond was lost?'

The objection struck me, all the more forcibly that it reflected an objection which I had felt myself.

'As to this,' pursued the lawyer, taking up Rosanna Spearman's confession, 'I can understand that the letter is a distressing one to *you*. I can understand that you may hesitate to analyse it from a purely impartial point of view. But *I* am not in your position. I can bring my professional experience to bear on this document, just as I should bring it to bear on any other. Without alluding to the woman's career as a thief, I will merely remark that her letter proves her to have been an adept at deception, on her own showing; and I argue from that, that I am justified in suspecting her of not having told the whole truth. I won't start any theory, at present, as to what she may or may not have done. I will only say that, if Rachel has suspected you *on the evidence of the nightgown only*, the chances are ninety-nine to a hundred that Rosanna Spearman was the person who showed it to her. In that case, there is the woman's letter, confessing that she was jealous of Rachel, confessing that she changed the roses, confessing that she saw a glimpse of hope for herself, in the prospect of a quarrel between Rachel and you. I don't stop to ask who took the Moonstone (as a means to her end, Rosanna Spearman would have taken fifty Moonstones)—I only say that the disappearance of the jewel gave this reclaimed thief who was in love with you, an opportunity of setting you and Rachel at variance for the rest of your lives. She had not decided on destroying herself, *then*, remember; and, having the opportunity, I distinctly assert that it was in her character, and in her position at the time, to take it. What do you say to that?'

'Some such suspicion,' I answered, 'crossed my own mind, as soon as I opened the letter.'

'Exactly! And when you had read the letter, you pitied the poor creature, and couldn't find it in your heart to suspect her. Does you credit, my dear sir—does you credit!'

'But suppose it turns out that I did wear the nightgown? What then?'

'I don't see how that fact is to be proved,' said Mr Bruff. 'But assuming the proof to be possible, the vindication of your innocence would be no easy matter. We won't go into that, now. Let us wait and see whether Rachel hasn't suspected you on the evidence of the nightgown only.'

'Good God, how coolly. you talk of Rachel suspecting me!' I broke out. 'What right has she to suspect Me, on any evidence, of being a thief?'

'A very sensible question, my dear sir. Rather hotly put—but well worth considering for all that. What puzzles you, puzzles me too. Search your memory, and tell me this. Did anything happen while you were staying at the house—not, of course, to shake Rachel's belief in your honour—but, let us say, to shake her belief (no matter with how little reason) in your principles generally?'

I started, in ungovernable agitation, to my feet. The lawyer's question reminded me, for the first time since I had left England, that something *had* happened.

In the eighth chapter of Betteredge's Narrative, an allusion will be found to the arrival of a foreigner and a stranger at my aunt's house, who came to see me on business. The nature of his business was this.

I had been foolish enough (being, as usual, straitened for money at the time) to accept a loan from the keeper of a small restaurant in Paris, to whom I was well known as a customer. A time was settled between us for paying the money back; and when the time came, I found it (as thousands of other honest men have found it) impossible to keep my engagement. I sent the man a bill. My name was unfortunately too well known on such documents: he failed to negotiate it. His affairs had fallen into disorder, in the interval since I had borrowed of him; bankruptcy stared him in the face; and a relative of his, a French lawyer, came to England to find me, and to insist upon the payment of my debt. He was a man of violent temper; and he took the wrong way with me. High words passed on both sides; and my aunt and Rachel were unfortunately in the next room, and heard us. Lady Verinder came in, and insisted on knowing what was the matter. The Frenchman produced his credentials, and declared me to be responsible for the ruin of a poor man, who had trusted in my honour. My aunt instantly paid him the money, and sent him off. She knew me better of course than to take the Frenchman's view of the transaction. But she was shocked at my carelessness, and justly angry with me for placing myself in a position, which, but for her interference, might have become a very disgraceful one. Either her mother told her, or Rachel heard what passed—I can't say which. She took her own romantic, high-flown view of the matter. I was 'heartless'; I was 'dishonourable'; I had 'no principle'; there was 'no knowing what I might do next'—in short, she said some of the severest things to me which I had ever heard from a young lady's lips. The breach between us lasted for the whole of the next day. The day after, I succeeded in making my peace, and thought no more of it. Had Rachel reverted to this unlucky accident, at the critical moment when my place in her estimation was again, and far more seriously, assailed? Mr Bruff, when I had mentioned the circumstances to him, answered the question at once in the affirmative.

'It would have its effect on her mind,' he said gravely. 'And I wish, for your sake, the thing had not happened. However, we have discovered that there *was* a predisposing influence against you—and there is one uncertainty cleared out of our way, at any rate. I see nothing more that we can do now. Our next step in this inquiry must be the step that takes us to Rachel.'

He rose, and began walking thoughtfully up and down the room. Twice, I was on the point of telling him that I had determined on seeing Rachel personally; and twice, having regard to his age and his character, I hesitated to take him by surprise at an unfavourable moment.

'The grand difficulty is,' he resumed, 'how to make her show her whole mind in this matter, without reserve. Have you any suggestions to offer?'

'I have made up my mind, Mr Bruff, to speak to Rachel myself.'

'You!' He suddenly stopped in his walk, and looked at me as if he thought I had taken leave of my senses. 'You, of all the people in the world!' He abruptly checked himself, and took another turn in the room. 'Wait a little,' he said. 'In cases of this extraordinary kind, the rash way is sometimes the best way.' He considered the question for a moment or two, under that new light, and ended boldly by a decision in my favour. 'Nothing venture, nothing have,' the old gentleman resumed. 'You have a chance in your favour which I don't possess—and you shall be the first to try the experiment.'

'A chance in my favour?' I repeated, in the greatest surprise.

Mr Bruff's face softened, for the first time, into a smile.

'This is how it stands,' he said. 'I tell you fairly, I don't trust your discretion, and I don't trust your temper. But I do trust in Rachel's still preserving, in some remote little corner of her heart, a certain perverse weakness for *you*. Touch that—and trust to the consequences for the fullest disclosures that can flow from a woman's lips! The question is—how are you to see her?'

'She has been a guest of yours at this house,' I answered.

'May I venture to suggest—if nothing was said about me beforehand—that I might see her here?'

'Cool!' said Mr Bruff. With that one word of comment on the reply that I had made to him, he took another turn up and down the room.

'In plain English,' he said, 'my house is to be turned into a trap to catch Rachel; with a bait to tempt her, in the shape of an invitation from my wife and daughters. If you were anybody else but Franklin Blake, and if this matter was one atom less serious than it really is, I should refuse point-blank. As things are, I firmly believe Rachel will live to thank me for turning traitor to her in my old age. Consider me your accomplice. Rachel shall be asked to spend the day here; and you shall receive due notice of it.'

'When? To-morrow?'

'To-morrow won't give us time enough to get her answer. Say the day after.'

'How shall I hear from you?'

'Stay at home all the morning and expect me to call on you.'

I thanked him for the inestimable assistance which he was rendering to me, with the gratitude that I really felt; and, declining a hospitable invitation to sleep that night at Hampstead, returned to my lodgings in London.

Of the day that followed, I have only to say that it was the longest day of my life. Innocent as I knew myself to be, certain as I was that the abominable imputation which rested on me must sooner or later be cleared off, there was nevertheless a sense of self-abasement in my mind which instinctively disinclined me to see any of my friends. We often hear (almost invariably, however, from superficial observers) that guilt can look like innocence. I believe it to be infinitely the truer axiom of the two that innocence can look like guilt. I caused myself to be denied all day, to every visitor who called; and I only ventured out under cover of the night.

The next morning, Mr Bruff surprised me at the breakfast-table. He handed me a large key, and announced that he felt ashamed of himself for the first time in his life.

'Is she coming?'

'She is coming to-day, to lunch and spend the afternoon with my wife and my girls.'

'Are Mrs Bruff, and your daughters, in the secret?'

'Inevitably. But women, as you may have observed, have no principles. My family don't feel my pangs of conscience. The end being to bring you and Rachel together again, my wife and daughters pass over the means employed to gain it, as composedly as if they were Jesuits.'

'I am infinitely obliged to them. What is this key?'

'The key of the gate in my back-garden wall. Be there at three this afternoon. Let yourself into the garden, and make your way in by the conservatory door. Cross the small drawing-room, and open the door in front of you which leads into the music-room. There, you will find Rachel—and find her, alone.'

'How can I thank you!'

'I will tell you how. Don't blame *me* for what happens afterwards.'

With those words, he went out.

I had many weary hours still to wait through. To while away the time, I looked at my letters. Among them was a letter from Betteredge.

I opened it eagerly. To my surprise and disappointment, it began with an apology warning me to expect no news of any importance. In the next sentence the everlasting Ezra Jennings appeared again! He had stopped Betteredge on the way out of the station, and had asked who I was. Informed on this point, he had mentioned having seen me to his master, Mr Candy. Mr Candy hearing of this, had himself driven over to Betteredge, to express his regret at our having missed each other. He had a reason for wishing particularly to speak to me; and when I was next in the neighbourhood of Frizinghall, he begged I would let him know. Apart from a few characteristic utterances of the Betteredge philosophy, this was the sum and substance of my correspondent's letter. The warmhearted, faithful old man acknowledged that he had written 'mainly for the pleasure of writing to me.'

I crumpled up the letter in my pocket, and forgot it the moment after, in the all-absorbing interest of my coming interview with Rachel.

As the clock of Hampstead church struck three, I put Mr Bruff's key into the lock of the door in the wall. When I first stepped into the garden, and while I was securing the door again on the inner side, I own to having felt a certain guilty doubtfulness about what might happen next. I looked furtively on either side of me, suspicious of the presence of some unexpected witness in some unknown corner of the garden. Nothing appeared, to justify my apprehensions. The walks were, one and all, solitudes; and the birds and the bees were the only witnesses.

I passed through the garden; entered the conservatory; and crossed the small drawing-room. As I laid my hand on the door opposite, I heard a few plaintive chords struck on the piano in the room within. She had often idled over the instrument in this way, when I was staying at her mother's house. I was obliged to wait a little, to steady myself. The past and present rose side by side, at that supreme moment—and the contrast shook me.

After the lapse of a minute, I roused my manhood, and opened the door.

CHAPTER 7

At the moment when I showed myself in the doorway, Rachel rose from the piano.

I closed the door behind me. We confronted each other in silence, with the full length of the room between us. The movement she had made in rising appeared to be the one exertion of which she was capable. All use of every other faculty, bodily or mental, seemed to be merged in the mere act of looking at me.

A fear crossed my mind that I had shown myself too suddenly. I advanced a few steps towards her. I said gently, 'Rachel!'

The sound of my voice brought the life back to her limbs, and the colour to her face. She advanced, on her side, still without speaking. Slowly, as if acting under some influence independent of her own will, she came nearer and nearer to me; the warm dusky colour flushing her cheeks, the light of reviving intelligence brightening every instant in her eyes. I forgot the object that had brought me into her presence; I forgot the vile suspicion that rested on my good name; I forgot every consideration, past, present, and future, which I was bound to remember. I saw nothing but the woman I loved coming nearer and nearer to me. She trembled; she stood irresolute. I could resist it no longer—I caught her in my arms, and covered her face with kisses.

There was a moment when I thought the kisses were returned; a moment when it seemed as if she, too, might have forgotten. Almost before the idea could shape itself in my mind, her first voluntary action made me feel that she remembered. With a cry which was like a cry of horror—with a strength which I doubt if I could have resisted if I had tried—she thrust me back from her. I saw merciless anger in her eyes; I saw merciless contempt on her lips. She looked me over, from head to foot, as she might have looked at a stranger who had insulted her.

'You coward!' she said. 'You mean, miserable, heartless coward!'

Those were her first words! The most unendurable reproach that a woman can address to a man, was the reproach that she picked out to address to Me.

'I remember the time, Rachel,' I said, 'when you could have told me that I had offended you, in a worthier way than that. I beg your pardon.'

Something of the bitterness that I felt may have communicated itself to my voice. At the first words of my reply, her eyes, which had been turned away the moment before, looked back at me unwillingly. She answered in a low tone, with a sullen submission of manner which was quite new in my experience of her.

'Perhaps there is some excuse for me,' she said. 'After what you have done, is it a manly action, on your part, to find your way to me as you have found it to-day? It seems a cowardly experiment, to try an experiment on my weakness for you. It seems a cowardly surprise, to surprise me into letting you kiss me. But that is only a woman's view. I ought to have known it couldn't be your view. I should have done better if I had controlled myself, and said nothing.'

The apology was more unendurable than the insult. The most degraded man living would have felt humiliated by it.

'If my honour was not in your hands,' I said, 'I would leave you this instant, and never see you again. You have spoken of what I have done. What have I done?'

'What have you done! *You* ask that question of *me*?'

'I ask it.'

'I have kept your infamy a secret,' she answered. 'And I have suffered the conse-quences of concealing it. Have I no claim to be spared the insult of your asking me what you have done? Is *all* sense of gratitude dead in you? You were once a gentleman. You were once dear to my mother, and dearer still to me—'

Her voice failed her. She dropped into a chair, and turned her back on me, and covered her face with her hands.

I waited a little before I trusted myself to say any more. In that moment of silence, I hardly know which I felt most keenly—the sting which her contempt had planted in me, or the proud resolution which shut me out from all community with her distress.

'If you will not speak first,' I said, 'I must. I have come here with something serious to say to you. Will you do me the common justice of listening while I say it?'

'She neither moved, nor answered. I made no second appeal to her; I never advanced an inch nearer to her chair. With a pride which was as obstinate as her pride, I told her of my discovery at the Shivering Sand, and of all that had led to it. The narrative, of necessity, occupied some little time. From beginning to end, she never looked round at me, and she never uttered a word.

I kept my temper. My whole future depended, in all probability, on my not losing possession of myself at that moment. The time had come to put Mr Bruff's theory to the test. In the breathless interest of trying that experiment, I moved round so as to place myself in front of her.

'I have a question to ask you,' I said. 'It obliges me to refer again to a painful subject. Did Rosanna Spearman show you the nightgown? Yes, or No?'

She started to her feet; and walked close up to me of her own accord. Her eyes looked me searchingly in the face, as if to read something there which they had never read yet.

'Are you mad?' she asked.

I still restrained myself. I said quietly, 'Rachel, will you answer my question?'

She went on, without heeding me.

'Have you some object to gain which I don't understand? Some mean fear about the future, in which I am concerned? They say your father's death has made you a rich man. Have you come here to compensate me for the loss of my Diamond? And have you heart enough left to feel ashamed of your errand? Is *that* the secret of your pretence of innocence, and your story about Rosanna Spearman? Is there a motive of shame at the bottom of all the falsehood, this time?'

I stopped her there. I could control myself no longer.

'You have done me an infamous wrong!' I broke out hotly. 'You suspect me of stealing your Diamond. I have a right to know, and I *will* know, the reason why!'

'Suspect you!' she exclaimed, her anger rising with mine. '*You villain, I saw you take the Diamond with my own eyes!*'

The revelation which burst upon me in those words, the overthrow which they instantly accomplished of the whole view of the case on which Mr Bruff had relied, struck me helpless. Innocent as I was, I stood before her in silence. To her eyes, to any eyes, I must have looked like a man overwhelmed by the discovery of his own guilt.

She drew back from the spectacle of my humiliation, and of her triumph. The sudden silence that had fallen upon me seemed to frighten her. 'I spared you, at the time,' she said. 'I would have spared you now, if you had not forced me to speak.' She moved away as if to leave the room—and hesitated before she got to the door. 'Why did you come here to humiliate yourself?' she asked. 'Why did you come here to humiliate me?' She went on a few steps, and paused once more. 'For God's sake, say something!' she exclaimed, passionately. 'If you have any mercy left, don't let me degrade myself in this way! Say something—and drive me out of the room!'

I advanced towards her, hardly conscious of what I was doing. I had possibly some confused idea of detaining her until she had told me more. From the moment when I knew that the evidence on which I stood condemned in Rachel's mind, was the evidence of her own eyes, nothing—not even my conviction of my own innocence—was clear to my mind. I took her by the hand; I tried to speak firmly and to the purpose. All I could say was, 'Rachel, you once loved me.'

She shuddered, and looked away from me. Her hand lay powerless and trembling in mine. 'Let go of it,' she said faintly.

My touch seemed to have the same effect on her which the sound of my voice had produced when I first entered the room. After she had said the word which called me a coward, after she had made the avowal which branded me as a thief—while her hand lay in mine I was her master still!

I drew her gently back into the middle of the room. I seated her by the side of me. 'Rachel,' I said, 'I can't explain the contradiction in what I am going to tell you. I can only speak the truth as you have spoken it. You saw me—with your own eyes, you saw me take the Diamond. Before God who hears us, I declare that I now know I took it for the first time! Do you doubt me still?'

She had neither heeded nor heard me. 'Let go of my hand,' she repeated faintly. That was her only answer. Her head sank on my shoulder; and her hand unconsciously closed on mine, at the moment when she asked me to release it.

I refrained from pressing the question. But there my forbearance stopped. My chance of ever holding up my head again among honest men depended on my chance of inducing her to make her disclosure complete. The one hope left for me was the hope that she might have overlooked something in the chain of evidence—some mere trifle, perhaps, which might nevertheless, under careful investigation, be made the means of vindicating my innocence in the end. I own I kept possession of her hand. I own I spoke to her with all that I could summon back of the sympathy and confidence of the bygone time.

'I want to ask you something,' I said. 'I want you to tell me everything that happened, from the time when we wished each other good night, to the time when you saw me take the Diamond.'

She lifted her head from my shoulder, and made an effort to release her hand. 'Oh, why go back to it!' she said. 'Why go back to it!'

'I will tell you why, Rachel. You are the victim, and I am the victim, of some monstrous delusion which has worn the mask of truth. If we look at what happened on the night of your birthday, together, we may end in understanding each other yet.'

Her head dropped back on my shoulder. The tears gathered in her eyes, and fell slowly over her cheeks. 'Oh!' she said, 'have I never had that hope? Have I not tried to see it, as you are trying now?'

'You have tried by yourself,' I answered. 'You have not tried with me to help you.'

Those words seemed to awaken in her something of the hope which I felt myself when I uttered them. She replied to my questions with more than docility—she exerted her intelligence; she willingly opened her whole mind to me.

'Let us begin,' I said, 'with what happened after we had wished each other good night. Did you go to bed? or did you sit up?'

'I went to bed.'

'Did you notice the time? Was it late?'

'Not very. About twelve o'clock, I think.'

'Did you fall asleep?'

'No. I couldn't sleep that night.'

'You were restless?'

'I was thinking of you.'

The answer almost unmanned me. Something in the tone, even more than in the words, went straight to my heart. It was only after pausing a little first that I was able to go on.

'Had you any light in your room?' I asked.

'None—until I got up again, and lit my candle.'

'How long was that, after you had gone to bed?'

'About an hour after, I think. About one o'clock.'

'Did you leave your bedroom?'

'I was going to leave it. I had put on my dressing-gown; and I was going into my sitting-room to get a book—'

'Had you opened your bedroom door?'

'I had just opened it.'

'But you had not gone into the sitting-room?'

'No—I was stopped from going into it.'

'What stopped you?'

'I saw a light, under the door; and I heard footsteps approaching it.'

'Were you frightened?'

'Not then. I knew my poor mother was a bad sleeper; and I remembered that she had tried hard, that evening, to persuade me to let her take charge of my Diamond. She was unreasonably anxious about it, as I thought; and I fancied she was coming to me to see if I was in bed, and to speak to me about the Diamond again, if she found that I was up.'

'What did you do?'

'I blew out my candle, so that she might think I was in bed. I was unreasonable, on my side—I was determined to keep my Diamond in the place of my own choosing.'

'After blowing the candle out, did you go back to bed?'

'I had no time to go back. At the moment when I blew the candle out, the sitting-room door opened, and I saw—'

'You saw?'

'You.'

'Dressed as usual?'

'No.'

'In my nightgown?'

'In your nightgown—with your bedroom candle in your hand.'

'Alone?'

'Alone.'

'Could you see my face?'

'Yes.'

'Plainly?'

'Quite plainly. The candle in your hand showed it to me.'

'Were my eyes open?'

'Yes.'

'Did you notice anything strange in them? Anything like a fixed, vacant expression?'

'Nothing of the sort. Your eyes were bright—brighter than usual. You looked about in the room, as if you knew you were where you ought not to be, and as if you were afraid of being found out.'

'Did you observe one thing when I came into the room—did you observe how I walked?'

'You walked as you always do. You came in as far as the middle of the room—and then you stopped and looked about you.'

'What did you do, on first seeing me?'

'I could do nothing. I was petrified. I couldn't speak, I couldn't call out, I couldn't even move to shut my door.'

'Could I see you, where you stood?'

'You might certainly have seen me. But you never looked towards me. It's useless to ask the question. I am sure you never saw me.'

'How are you sure?'

'Would you have taken the Diamond? would you have acted as you did afterwards? would you be here now—if you had seen that I was awake and looking at you? Don't make me talk of that part of it! I want to answer you quietly. Help me to keep as calm as I can. Go on to something else.'

She was right—in every way, right. I went on to other things.

'What did I do, after I had got to the middle of the room, and had stopped there?'

'You turned away, and went straight to the corner near the window—where my Indian cabinet stands.'

'When I was at the cabinet, my back must have been turned towards you. How did you see what I was doing?'

'When you moved, I moved.'

'So as to see what I was about with my hands?'

'There are three glasses in my sitting-room. As you stood there, I saw all that you did, reflected in one of them.'

'What did you see?'

'You put your candle on the top of the cabinet. You opened, and shut, one drawer after another, until you came to the drawer in which I had put my Diamond. You looked at the open drawer for a moment. And then you put your hand in, and took the Diamond out.'

'How do you know I took the Diamond out?'

'I saw your hand go into the drawer. And I saw the gleam of the stone between your finger and thumb, when you took your hand out.'

'Did my hand approach the drawer again—to close it, for instance?'

'No. You had the Diamond in your right hand; and you took the candle from the top of the cabinet with your left hand.'

'Did I look about me again, after that?'

'No.'

'Did I leave the room immediately?'

'No. You stood quite still, for what seemed a long time. I saw your face sideways in the glass. You looked like a man thinking, and dissatisfied with his own thoughts.'

'What happened next?'

'You roused yourself on a sudden, and you went straight out of the room.'

'Did I close the door after me?'

'No. You passed out quickly into the passage, and left the door open.'

'And then?'

'Then, your light disappeared, and the sound of your steps died away, and I was left alone in the dark.'

'Did nothing happen—from that time, to the time when the whole house knew that the Diamond was lost?'

'Nothing.'

'Are you sure of that? Might you not have been asleep a part of the time?'

'I never slept. I never went back to my bed. Nothing happened until Penelope came in, at the usual time in the morning.'

I dropped her hand, and rose, and took a turn in the room. Every question that I could put had been answered. Every detail that I could desire to know had been placed before me. I had even reverted to the idea of sleep-walking, and the idea of intoxication; and, again, the worthlessness of the one theory and the other had been proved—on the authority, this time, of the witness who had seen me. What was to be said next? what was to be done next? There rose the horrible fact of the Theft—the one visible, tangible object that confronted me, in the midst of the impenetrable darkness which enveloped all besides! Not a glimpse of light to guide me, when I had possessed myself of Rosanna Spearman's secret at the Shivering Sand. And not a glimpse of light now, when I had appealed to Rachel herself, and had heard the hateful story of the night from her own lips.

She was the first, this time, to break the silence.

'Well?' she said, 'you have asked, and I have answered. You have made me hope something from all this, because *you* hoped something from it. What have you to say now?'

The tone in which she spoke warned me that my influence over her was a lost influence once more.

'We were to look at what happened on my birthday night, together,' she went on; 'and we were then to understand each other. Have we done that?'

She waited pitilessly for my reply. In answering her I committed a fatal error—I let the exasperating helplessness of my situation get the better of my self-control. Rashly and uselessly, I reproached her for the silence which had kept me until that moment in ignorance of the truth.

'If you had spoken when you ought to have spoken,' I began: 'if you had done me the common justice to explain yourself—'

She broke in on me with a cry of fury. The few words I had said seemed to have lashed her on the instant into a frenzy of rage.

'Explain myself!' she repeated. 'Oh! is there another man like this in the world? I spare him, when my heart is breaking; I screen him when my own character is at stake; and *he*—of all human beings, *he*—turns on me now, and tells me that I ought to have explained myself! After believing in him as I did, after loving him as I did, after thinking of him by day, and dreaming of him by night—he wonders I didn't charge him with his disgrace the first time we met: 'My heart's darling, you are a Thief! My hero whom I love and honour, you have crept into my room under cover of the night, and stolen my Diamond!' That is what I ought to have said. You villain, you mean, mean, mean villain, I would have lost fifty Diamonds, rather than see your face lying to me, as I see it lying now!'

I took up my hat. In mercy to *her*—yes! I can honestly say it—in mercy to *her*, I turned away without a word, and opened the door by which I had entered the room.

She followed, and snatched the door out of my hand; she closed it, and pointed back to the place that I had left.

'No!' she said. 'Not yet! It seems that *I* owe a justification of my conduct to *you*. You shall stay and hear it. Or you shall stoop to the lowest infamy of all, and force your way out.'

It wrung my heart to see her; it wrung my heart to hear her. I answered by a sign—it was all I could do—that I submitted myself to her will.

The crimson flush of anger began to fade out of her face, as I went back, and took my chair in silence. She waited a little, and steadied herself. When she went on, but one sign of feeling was discernible in her. She spoke without looking at me. Her hands were fast clasped in her lap, and her eyes were fixed on the ground.

'I ought to have done you the common justice to explain myself,' she said, repeating my own words. 'You shall see whether I did try to do you justice, or not. I told you just now that I never slept, and never returned to my bed, after you had left my sitting-room. It's useless to trouble you by dwelling on what I thought—you would not understand my thoughts—I will only tell you what I did, when time enough had passed to help me to recover myself. I refrained from alarming the house, and telling everybody what had happened—as I ought to have done. In spite of what I had seen, I was fond enough of you to believe—no matter what!—any impossibility, rather than admit it to my own mind that you were deliberately a thief. I thought and thought—and I ended in writing to you.'

'I never received the letter.'

'I know you never received it. Wait a little, and you shall hear why. My letter would have told you nothing openly. It would not have ruined you for life, if it had fallen into some other person's hands. It would only have said—in a manner which you yourself could not possibly have mistaken—that I had reason to know you were in debt, and that it was in my experience and in my mother's experience of you, that you were not very discreet, or very scrupulous about how you got money when you wanted it. You would have remembered the visit of the French lawyer, and you would have known what I referred to. If you had read on with some interest after that, you would have come to an offer I had to make to you—the offer, privately (not a word, mind, to be said openly about it between us!), of the loan of as large a sum of money as I could get.—And I would have got it!' she exclaimed, her colour beginning to rise again, and her eyes looking up at me once more. 'I would have pledged the Diamond myself, if I could have got the money in no other way! In those words I wrote to you. Wait! I did more than that. I arranged with Penelope to give you the letter when nobody was near. I planned to shut myself into my bedroom, and to have the sitting-room left open and empty all the morning. And I hoped—with all my heart and soul I hoped!—that you would take the opportunity, and put the Diamond back secretly in the drawer.'

I attempted to speak. She lifted her hand impatiently, and stopped me. In the rapid alternations of her temper, her anger was beginning to rise again. She got up from her chair, and approached me.

'I know what you are going to say,' she went on. 'You are going to remind me again that you never received my letter. I can tell you why. I tore it up.'

'For what reason?' I asked.

'For the best of reasons. I preferred tearing it up to throwing it away upon such a man as you! What was the first news that reached me in the morning? Just as my little plan was complete, what did I hear? I heard that you—you!!!—were the foremost person in the house in fetching the police. You were the active man; you were the leader; you were working harder than any of them to recover the jewel! You even carried your audacity far enough to ask to speak to *me* about the loss of the Diamond—the Diamond which you yourself had stolen; the Diamond which was all the time in your own hands! After that proof of your horrible falseness and cunning, I tore up my letter. But even then—even when I was maddened by the searching and questioning of the policeman, whom *you* had sent in—even then, there was some infatuation in my mind which wouldn't let me give you up. I said to myself, "He has played his vile farce before everybody else in the house. Let me try if he can play it before me." Somebody told me you were on the terrace. I went down to the terrace. I forced myself to look at you; I forced myself to speak to you. Have you forgotten what I said?'

I might have answered that I remembered every word of it. But what purpose, at that moment, would the answer have served?

How could I tell her that what she had said had astonished me, had distressed me, had suggested to me that she was in a state of dangerous nervous excitement, had even roused a moment's doubt in my mind whether the loss of the jewel was as much a mystery to her as to the rest of us—but had never once given so much as a glimpse at the truth? Without the shadow of a proof to produce in vindication of my innocence, how could I persuade her that I knew no more than the veriest stranger could have known of what was really in her thoughts when she spoke to me on the terrace?

'It may suit your convenience to forget; it suits my convenience to remember,' she went on. 'I know what I said—for I considered it with myself, before I said it. I gave you one opportunity after another of owning the truth. I left nothing unsaid that I *could* say— short of actually telling you that I knew you had committed the theft. And all the return you made, was to look at me with your vile pretence of astonishment, and your false face of innocence—just as you have looked at me to-day; just as you are looking at me now! I left you, that morning, knowing you at last for what you were—for what you are—as base a wretch as ever walked the earth!'

'If you had spoken out at the time, you might have left me, Rachel, knowing that you had cruelly wronged an innocent man.'

'If I had spoken out before other people,' she retorted, with another burst of indignation, 'you would have been disgraced for life! If I had spoken out to no ears but yours, you would have denied it, as you are denying it now! Do you think I should have believed you? Would a man hesitate at a lie, who had done what I saw *you* do—who had behaved about it afterwards, as I saw *you* behave? I tell you again, I shrank from the horror of hearing you lie, after the horror of seeing you thieve. You talk as if this was a misunderstanding which a few words might have set right! Well! the misunderstanding is at an end. Is the thing set right? No! the thing is just where it was. I don't believe you *now*! I don't believe you found the nightgown, I don't believe in Rosanna Spearman's letter, I don't believe a word you have said. You stole it—I saw you! You affected to help the police—I saw you! You pledged the Diamond to the money-lender in London —I am sure of it! You cast the suspicion of your disgrace (thanks to my base silence!) on an innocent man! You fled to the Continent with your plunder the next morning! After all that vileness, there was but one thing more you *could* do. You could come here with a last falsehood on your lips—you could come here, and tell me that I have wronged you!'

If I had stayed a moment more, I know not what words might have escaped me which I should have remembered with vain repentance and regret. I passed by her, and opened the door for the second time. For the second time—with the frantic perversity of a roused woman—she caught me by the arm, and barred my way out.

'Let me go, Rachel,' I said. 'It will be better for both of us. Let me go.'

The hysterical passion swelled in her bosom—her quickened convulsive breathing almost beat on my face, as she held me back at the door.

'Why did you come here?' she persisted, desperately. 'I ask you again—why did you come here? Are you afraid I shall expose you? Now you are a rich man, now you have got a place in the world, now you may marry the best lady in the land—are you afraid I shall say the words which I have never said yet to anybody but you? I can't say the words! I can't expose you! I am worse, if worse can be, than you are yourself.' Sobs and tears burst from her. She struggled with them fiercely; she held me more and more firmly. 'I can't tear you out of my heart,' she said, 'even now! You may trust in the shameful, shameful weakness which can only struggle against you in this way!' She suddenly let go of me—she threw up her hands, and wrung them frantically in the air. 'Any other woman living would shrink from the disgrace of touching him!' she exclaimed. 'Oh, God! I despise myself even more heartily than I despise *him*!'

The tears were forcing their way into my eyes in spite of me—the horror of it was to be endured no longer.

'You shall know that you have wronged me, yet,' I said. 'Or you shall never see me again!'

With those words, I left her. She started up from the chair on which she had dropped the moment before: she started up—the noble creature!—and followed me across the outer room, with a last merciful word at parting.

'Franklin!' she said, 'I forgive you! Oh, Franklin, Franklin! we shall never meet again. Say you forgive *me*!'

I turned, so as to let my face show her that I was past speaking—I turned, and waved my hand, and saw her dimly, as in a vision, through the tears that had conquered me at last.

The next moment, the worst bitterness of it was over. I was out in the garden again. I saw her, and heard her, no more.

CHAPTER 8

Late that evening, I was surprised at my lodgings by a visit from Mr Bruff.

There was a noticeable change in the lawyer's manner. It had lost its usual confidence and spirit. He shook hands with me, for the first time in his life, in silence.

'Are you going back to Hempstead?' I asked, by way of saying something.

'I have just left Hampstead,' he answered. 'I know, Mr Franklin, that you have got at the truth at last. But, I tell you plainly, if I could have foreseen the price that was to be paid for it, I should have preferred leaving you in the dark.'

'You have seen Rachel?'

'I have come here after taking her back to Portland Place; it was impossible to let her return in the carriage by herself. I can hardly hold you responsible—considering that you saw her in my house and by my permission—for the shock that this unlucky interview has inflicted on her. All I can do is to provide against a repetition of the mischief. She is young— she has a resolute spirit—she will get over this, with time and rest to help her. I want to be assured that you will do nothing to hinder her recovery. May I depend on your making no second attempt to see her—except with my sanction and approval?'

'After what she has suffered, and after what I have suffered,' I said, 'you may rely on me.'

'I have your promise?'

'You have my promise.'

Mr Bruff looked relieved. He put down his hat, and drew his chair nearer to mine.

'That's settled!' he said. 'Now, about the future—*your* future, I mean. To my mind, the result of the extraordinary turn which the matter has now taken is briefly this. In the first place, we are sure that Rachel has told you the whole truth, as plainly as words can tell it. In the second place—though we know that there must be some dreadful mistake somewhere—we can hardly blame her for believing you to be guilty, on the evidence of her own senses; backed, as that evidence has been, by circumstances which appear, on the face of them, to tell dead against you.'

There I interposed. 'I don't blame Rachel,' I said. 'I only regret that she could not prevail on herself to speak more plainly to me at the time.'

'You might as well regret that Rachel is not somebody else,' rejoined Mr Bruff. 'And even then, I doubt if a girl of any delicacy, whose heart had been set on marrying you, could have brought herself to charge you to your face with being a thief. Anyhow, it was not in

THE MOONSTONE

Rachel's nature to do it. In a very different matter to this matter of yours—which placed her, however, in a position not altogether unlike her position towards you—I happen to know that she was influenced by a similar motive to the motive which actuated her conduct in your case. Besides, as she told me herself, on our way to town this evening, if she *had* spoken plainly, she would no more have believed your denial then than she believes it now. What answer can you make to that? There is no answer to be made to it. Come, come, Mr Franklin! my view of the case has been proved to be all wrong, I admit—but, as things are now, my advice may be worth having for all that. I tell you plainly, we shall be wasting our time, and cudgelling our brains to no purpose, if we attempt to try back, and unravel this frightful complication from the beginning. Let us close our minds resolutely to all that happened last year at Lady Verinder's country house; and let us look to what we *can* discover in the future, instead of to what we can *not* discover in the past.'

'Surely you forget,' I said, 'that the whole thing is essentially a matter of the past—so far as I am concerned?'

'Answer me this,' retorted Mr Bruff. 'Is the Moonstone at the bottom of all the mischief—or is it not?'

'It is—of course.'

'Very good. What do we believe was done with the Moonstone, when it was taken to London?'

'It was pledged to Mr Luker.'

'We know that you are not the person who pledged it. Do we know who did?'

'No.'

'Where do we believe the Moonstone to be now?'

'Deposited in the keeping of Mr Luker's bankers.'

'Exactly. Now observe. We are already in the month of June. Towards the end of the month (I can't be particular to a day) a year will have elapsed from the time when we believe the jewel to have been pledged. There is a chance—to say the least—that the year's time has expired. If he redeems it, Mr Luker must himself—according to the terms of his own arrangement—take the Diamond out of his bankers' hands. Under these circumstances, I propose setting a watch at the bank, as the present month draws to an end, and discovering who the person is to whom Mr Luker restores the Moonstone. Do you see it now?'

I admitted (a little unwillingly) that the idea was a new one, at any rate.

'It's Mr Murthwaite's idea quite as much as mine,' said Mr Bruff. 'It might have never entered my head, but for a conversation we had together some time since. If Mr Murthwaite is right, the Indians are likely to be on the look-out at the bank, towards the end of the month too—and something serious may come of it. What comes of it doesn't matter to you and me—except as it may help us to lay our hands on the mysterious Somebody who pawned the Diamond. That person, you may rely on it, is responsible (I don't pretend to know how) for the position in which you stand at this moment; and that person alone can set you right in Rachel's estimation.'

'I can't deny,' I said, 'that the plan you propose meets the difficulty in a way that is very daring, and very ingenious, and very new. But—'

'But you have an objection to make?'

'Yes. My objection is, that your proposal obliges us to wait.'

'Granted. As I reckon the time, it requires you to wait about a fortnight—more or less. Is that so very long?'

'It's a lifetime, Mr Bruff, in such a situation as mine. My existence will be simply unendurable to me, unless I do something towards clearing my character at once.'

'Well, well, I understand that. Have you thought yet of what you can do?'

'I have thought of consulting Sergeant Cuff.'

'He has retired from the police. It's useless to expect the Sergeant to help you.'

'I know where to find him; and I can but try.'

'Try,' said Mr Bruff, after a moment's consideration. 'The case has assumed such an extraordinary aspect since Sergeant Cuff's time, that you *may* revive his interest in the inquiry. Try, and let me hear the result. In the meanwhile,' he continued, rising, 'if you make no discoveries between this, and the end of the month, am I free to try, on my side, what can be done by keeping a look-out at the bank?'

'Certainly,' I answered—'unless I relieve you of an necessity for trying the experiment in the interval.'

'Mr Bruff smiled, and took up his hat.

'Tell Sergeant Cuff,' he rejoined, 'that *I* say the discovery of the truth depends on the discovery of the person who pawned the Diamond. And let me hear what the Sergeant's experience says to that.'

So we parted.

Early the next morning, I set forth for the little town of Dorking—the place of Sergeant Cuff's retirement, as indicated to me by Betteredge.

Inquiring at the hotel, I received the necessary directions for finding the Sergeant's cottage. It was approached by a quiet by-road, a little way out of the town, and it stood snugly in the middle of its own plot of garden ground, protected by a good brick wall at the back and the sides, and by a high quickset hedge in front. The gate, ornamented at the upper part by smartly-painted trellis-work, was locked. After ringing at the bell, I peered through the trellis-work, and saw the great Cuff's favourite flower everywhere; blooming in his garden, clustering over his door, looking in at his windows. Far from the crimes and the mysteries of the great city, the illustrious thief-taker was placidly living out the last Sybarite years of his life, smothered in roses!

A decent elderly woman opened the gate to me, and at once annihilated all the hopes I had built on securing the assistance of Sergeant Cuff. He had started, only the day before, on a journey to Ireland.

'Has he gone there on business?' I asked.

The woman smiled. 'He has only one business now, sir,' she said; 'and that's roses. Some great man's gardener in Ireland has found out something new in the growing of roses—and Mr Cuff's away to inquire into it.'

'Do you know when he will be back?'

'It's quite uncertain, sir. Mr Cuff said he should come back directly, or be away some time, just according as he found the new discovery worth nothing, or worth looking into. If you have any message to leave for him, I'll take care, sir, that he gets it.'

'I gave her my card, having first written on it in pencil: 'I have something to say about the Moonstone. Let me hear from you as soon as you get back.' That done, there was nothing left but to submit to circumstances, and return to London.

In the irritable condition of my mind, at the time of which I am now writing, the abortive result of my journey to the Sergeant's cottage simply aggravated the restless impulse in me to be doing something. On the day of my return from Dorking, I determined that the next morning should find me bent on a new effort at forcing my way, through all obstacles, from the darkness to the light.

What form was my next experiment to take?

If the excellent Betteredge had been present while I was considering that question, and if he had been let into the secret of my thoughts, he would, no doubt, have declared that the German side of me was, on this occasion, my uppermost side. To speak seriously, it is perhaps possible that my German training was in some degree responsible for the labyrinth of useless speculations in which I now involved myself. For the greater part of the night, I sat smoking, and building up theories, one more profoundly improbable than another. When I did get to sleep, my waking fancies pursued me in dreams. I rose the next morning, with Objective-Subjective and Subjective-Objective inextricably entangled together in my mind; and I began the day which was to witness my next effort at practical action of some kind, by doubting whether I had any sort of right (on purely philosophical grounds) to consider any sort of thing (the Diamond included) as existing at all.

How long I might have remained lost in the mist of my own metaphysics, if I had been left to extricate myself, it is impossible for me to say. As the event proved, accident came to my rescue, and happily delivered me. I happened to wear, that morning, the same coat which I had worn on the day of my interview with Rachel. Searching for something else in one of the pockets, I came upon a crumpled piece of paper, and, taking it out, found Betteredge's forgotten letter in my hand.

It seemed hard on my good old friend to leave him without a reply. I went to my writing-table, and read his letter again.

A letter which has nothing of the slightest importance in it, is not always an easy letter to answer. Betteredge's present effort at corresponding with me came within this category. Mr Candy's assistant, otherwise Ezra Jennings, had told his master that he had seen me; and Mr Candy, in his turn, wanted to see me and say something to me, when I was next in the neighbourhood of Frizinghall. What was to be said in answer to that, which would be worth the paper it was written on? I sat idly drawing likenesses from memory of Mr Candy's remarkable-looking assistant, on the sheet of paper which I had vowed to dedicate to Betteredge—until it suddenly occurred to me that here was the irrepressible Ezra Jennings getting in my way again! I threw a dozen portraits, at least, of the man with the piebald hair (the hair in every case, remarkably like), into the waste-paper basket—and then and there, wrote my answer to Betteredge. It was a perfectly commonplace letter—but it had one excellent effect on me. The effort of writing a few sentences, in plain English, completely cleared my mind of the cloudy nonsense which had filled it since the previous day.

Devoting myself once more to the elucidation of the impenetrable puzzle which my own position presented to me, I now tried to meet the difficulty by investigating it from a plainly practical point of view. The events of the memorable night being still unintelligible to me, I looked a little farther back, and searched my memory of the earlier hours of the birthday for any incident which might prove of some assistance to me in finding the clue.

Had anything happened while Rachel and I were finishing the painted door? or, later, when I rode over to Frizinghall? or afterwards, when I went back with Godfrey Ablewhite and his sisters? or, later again, when I put the Moonstone into Rachel's hands? or, later still, when the company came, and we all assembled round the dinner-table? My memory disposed of that string of questions readily enough, until I came to the last. Looking back at the social events of the birthday dinner, I found myself brought to a standstill at the outset of the inquiry. I was not even capable of accurately remembering the number of the guests who had sat at the same table with me.

To feel myself completely at fault here, and to conclude, thereupon, that the incidents of the dinner might especially repay the trouble of investigating them, formed parts of the same mental process, in my case. I believe other people, in a similar situation, would have reasoned as I did. When the pursuit of our own interests causes us to become objects of inquiry to ourselves, we are naturally suspicious of what we don't know. Once in possession of the names of the persons who had been present at the dinner, I resolved—as a means of enriching the deficient resources of my own memory—to appeal to the memory of the rest of the guests; to write down all that they could recollect of the social events of the birthday; and to test the result, thus obtained, by the light of what had happened afterwards, when the company had left the house.

This last and newest of my many contemplated experiments in the art of inquiry— which Betteredge would probably have attributed to the clear-headed, or French, side of me being uppermost for the moment—may fairly claim record here, on its own merits. Unlikely as it may seem, I had now actually groped my way to the root of the matter at last. All I wanted was a hint to guide me in the right direction at starting. Before another day had passed over my head, that hint was given me by one of the company who had been present at the birthday feast!

With the plan of proceeding which I now had in view, it was first necessary to possess the complete list of the guests. This I could easily obtain from Gabriel Betteredge. I determined to go back to Yorkshire on that day, and to begin my contemplated investigation the next morning.

It was just too late to start by the train which left London before noon. There was no alternative but to wait, nearly three hours, for the departure of the next train. Was there anything I could do in London, which might usefully occupy this interval of time?

My thoughts went back again obstinately to the birthday dinner.

Though I had forgotten the numbers, and, in many cases, the names of the guests, I remembered readily enough that by far the larger proportion of them came from Frizinghall, or from its neighbourhood. But the larger proportion was not all. Some few of us were not regular residents in the county. I myself was one of the few. Mr Murthwaite was another. Godfrey Ablewhite was a third. Mr Bruff—no: I called to mind that business had prevented Mr Bruff from making one of the party. Had any ladies been present, whose usual residence was in London? I could only remember Miss Clack as coming within this latter category. However, here were three of the guests, at any rate, whom it was clearly advisable for me to see before I left town. I drove off at once to Mr Bruff's office; not knowing the addresses of the persons of whom I was in search, and thinking it probable that he might put me in the way of finding them.

Mr Bruff proved to be too busy to give me more than a minute of his valuable time. In that minute, however, he contrived to dispose—in the most discouraging manner—of all the questions I had to put to him.

In the first place, he considered my newly-discovered method of finding a clue to the mystery as something too purely fanciful to be seriously discussed. In the second, third, and fourth places, Mr Murthwaite was now on his way back to the scene of his past adventures; Miss Clack had suffered losses, and had settled, from motives of economy, in France; Mr Godfrey Ablewhite might, or might not, be discoverable somewhere in London. Suppose I inquired at his club? And suppose I excused Mr Bruff, if he went back to his business and wished me good morning?

The field of inquiry in London, being now so narrowed as only to include the one necessity of discovering Godfrey's address, I took the lawyer's hint, and drove to his club.

In the hall, I met with one of the members, who was an old friend of my cousin's, and who was also an acquaintance of my own. This gentleman, after enlightening me on the subject of Godfrey's address, told me of two recent events in his life, which were of some importance in themselves, and which had not previously reached my ears.

It appeared that Godfrey, far from being discouraged by Rachel's withdrawal from her engagement to him, had made matrimonial advances soon afterwards to another young lady, reputed to be a great heiress. His suit had prospered, and his marriage had been considered as a settled and certain thing. But, here again, the engagement had been suddenly and unexpectedly broken off—owing, it was said, on this occasion, to a serious difference of opinion between the bridegroom and the lady's father, on the question of settlements.

As some compensation for this second matrimonial disaster, Godfrey had soon afterwards found himself the object of fond pecuniary remembrance, on the part of one of his many admirers. A rich old lady—highly respected at the Mothers' Small-Clothes-Conversion-Society, and a great friend of Miss Clack's (to whom she had left nothing but a mourning ring)—had bequeathed to the admirable and meritorious Godfrey a legacy of five thousand pounds. After receiving this handsome addition to his own modest pecuniary resources, he had been heard to say that he felt the necessity of getting a little respite from his charitable labours, and that his doctor prescribed 'a run on the Continent, as likely to be productive of much future benefit to his health.' If I wanted to see him, it would be advisable to lose no time in paying my contemplated visit.

I went, then and there, to pay my visit.

The same fatality which had made me just one day too late in calling on Sergeant Cuff, made me again one day too late in calling on Godfrey. He had left London, on the previous morning, by the tidal train, for Dover. He was to cross to Ostend; and his servant believed he was going on to Brussels. The time of his return was rather uncertain; but I might be sure he would be away at least three months.

I went back to my lodgings a little depressed in spirits. Three of the guests at the birthday dinner—and those three all exceptionally intelligent people—were out of my reach, at the very time when it was most important to be able to communicate with them. My last hopes now rested on Betteredge, and on the friends of the late Lady Verinder whom I might still find living in the neighbourhood of Rachel's country house.

* * * * *

On this occasion, I travelled straight to Frizinghall—the town being now the central point in my field of inquiry. I arrived too late in the evening to be able to communicate with Betteredge. The next morning, I sent a messenger with a letter, requesting him to join me at the hotel, at his earliest convenience.

Having taken the precaution—partly to save time, partly to accommodate Betteredge —of sending my messenger in a fly, I had a reasonable prospect, if no delays occurred, of seeing the old man within less than two hours from the time when I had sent for him. During this interval, I arranged to employ myself in opening my contemplated inquiry, among the guests present at the birthday dinner who were personally known to me, and who were easily within my reach. These were my relatives, the Ablewhites, and Mr Candy. The doctor had expressed a special wish to see me, and the doctor lived in the next street. So to Mr Candy I went first.

After what Betteredge had told me, I naturally anticipated finding traces in the doctor's face of the severe illness from which he had suffered. But I was utterly unprepared for such a change as I saw in him when he entered the room and shook hands with me. His eyes were dim; his hair had turned completely grey; his face was wizen; his figure had shrunk. I looked at the once lively, rattlepated, humorous little doctor—associated in my remembrance with the perpetration of incorrigible social indiscretions and innumerable boyish jokes—and I saw nothing left of his former self, but the old tendency to vulgar smartness in his dress. The man was a wreck; but his clothes and his jewellery—in cruel mockery of the change in him—were as gay and as gaudy as ever.

'I have often thought of you, Mr Blake,' he said; 'and I am heartily glad to see you again at last. If there is anything I can do for you, pray command my services, sir—pray command my services!'

He said those few commonplace words with needless hurry and eagerness, and with a curiosity to know what had brought me to Yorkshire, which he was perfectly—I might say childishly— incapable of concealing from notice.

With the object that I had in view, I had of course foreseen the necessity of entering into some sort of personal explanation, before I could hope to interest people, mostly strangers to me, in doing their best to assist my inquiry. On the journey to Frizinghall I had arranged what my explanation was to be—and I seized the opportunity now offered to me of trying the effect of it on Mr Candy.

'I was in Yorkshire, the other day, and I am in Yorkshire again now, on rather a romantic errand,' I said. 'It is a matter, Mr Candy, in which the late Lady Verinder's friends all took some interest. You remember the mysterious loss of the Indian Diamond, now nearly a year since? Circumstances have lately happened which lead to the hope that it may yet be found—and I am interesting myself, as one of the family, in recovering it. Among the obstacles in my way, there is the necessity of collecting again all the evidence which was discovered at the time, and more if possible. There are peculiarities in this case which make it desirable to revive my recollection of everything that happened in the house, on the evening of Miss Verinder's birthday. And I venture to appeal to her late mother's friends who were present on that occasion, to lend me the assistance of their memories—'

I had got as far as that in rehearsing my explanatory phrases, when I was suddenly checked by seeing plainly in Mr Candy's face that my experiment on him was a total failure.

The little doctor sat restlessly picking at the points of his fingers all the time I was speaking. His dim watery eyes were fixed on my face with an expression of vacant and wistful inquiry very painful to see. What he was thinking of, it was impossible to divine. The one thing clearly visible was that I had failed, after the first two or three words, in fixing his attention. The only chance of recalling him to himself appeared to lie in changing the subject. I tried a new topic immediately.

'So much,' I said, gaily, 'for what brings me to Frizinghall! Now, Mr Candy, it's your turn. You sent me a message by Gabriel Betteredge—'

He left off picking at his fingers, and suddenly brightened up.

'Yes! yes! yes!' he exclaimed eagerly. 'That's it! I sent you a message!'

'And Betteredge duly communicated it by letter,' I went on. 'You had something to say to me, the next time I was in your neighbourhood. Well, Mr Candy, here I am!'

'Here you are!' echoed the doctor. 'And Betteredge was quite right. I had something to say to you. That was my message. Betteredge is a wonderful man. What a memory! At his age, what a memory!'

He dropped back into silence, and began picking at his fingers again. Recollecting what I had heard from Betteredge about the effect of the fever on his memory, I went on with the conversation, in the hope that I might help him at starting.

'It's a long time since we met,' I said. 'We last saw each other at the last birthday dinner my poor aunt was ever to give.'

'That's it!' cried Mr Candy. 'The birthday dinner!' He started impulsively to his feet, and looked at me. A deep flush suddenly overspread his faded face, and he abruptly sat down again, as if conscious of having betrayed a weakness which he would fain have concealed. It was plain, pitiably plain, that he was aware of his own defect of memory, and that he was bent on hiding it from the observation of his friends.

Thus far, he had appealed to my compassion only. But the words he had just said—few as they were—roused my curiosity instantly to the highest pitch. The birthday dinner had already become the one event in the past, at which I looked back with strangely mixed feelings of hope and distrust. And here was the birthday dinner unmistakably proclaiming itself as the subject on which Mr Candy had something important to say to me!

I attempted to help him out once more. But, this time, my own interests were at the bottom of my compassionate motive, and they hurried me on a little too abruptly to the end I had in view.

'It's nearly a year now,' I said, 'since we sat at that pleasant table. Have you made any memorandum—in your diary, or otherwise—of what you wanted to say to me?'

Mr Candy understood the suggestion, and showed me that he understood it, as an insult.

'I require no memorandums, Mr Blake,' he said, stiffly enough. 'I am not such a very old man, yet—and my memory (thank God) is to be thoroughly depended on!'

It is needless to say that I declined to understand that he was offended with me.

'I wish I could say the same of *my* memory,' I answered. When *I* try to think of matters that are a year old, I seldom find my remembrance as vivid as I could wish it to be. Take the dinner at Lady Verinder's, for instance—'

Mr Candy brightened up again, the moment the allusion passed my lips.

'Ah! the dinner, the dinner at Lady Verinder's!' he exclaimed, more eagerly than ever. 'I have got something to say to you about that.'

His eyes looked at me again with the painful expression of inquiry, so wistful, so vacant, so miserably helpless to see. He was evidently trying hard, and trying in vain, to recover the lost recollection. 'It was a very pleasant dinner,' he burst out suddenly, with an air of saying exactly what he wanted to say. 'A very pleasant dinner, Mr Blake, wasn't it?' He nodded and smiled, and appeared to think, poor fellow, that he had succeeded in concealing the total failure of his memory, by a well-timed exertion of his own presence of mind.

It was so distressing that I at once shifted the talk—deeply as I was interested in his recovering the lost remembrance—to topics of local interest.

Here, he got on glibly enough. Trumpery little scandals and quarrels in the town, some of them as much as a month old, appeared to recur to his memory readily. He chattered on, with something of the smooth gossiping fluency of former times. But there were moments, even in the full flow of his talkativeness, when he suddenly hesitated—looked at me for a moment with the vacant inquiry once more in his eyes—controlled himself—and went on again. I submitted patiently to my martyrdom (it is surely nothing less than martyrdom to a man of cosmopolitan sympathies, to absorb in silent resignation the news of a country town?) until the clock on the chimney-piece told me that my visit had been prolonged beyond half an hour. Having now some right to consider the sacrifice as complete, I rose to take leave. As we shook hands, Mr Candy reverted to the birthday festival of his own accord.

'I am so glad we have met again,' he said. 'I had it on my mind—I really had it on my mind, Mr Blake, to speak to you. About the dinner at Lady Verinder's, you know! A pleasant dinner—really a pleasant dinner now, wasn't it?'

On repeating the phrase, he seemed to feel hardly as certain of having prevented me from suspecting his lapse of memory, as he had felt on the first occasion. The wistful look clouded his face again; and, after apparently designing to accompany me to the street door, he suddenly changed his mind, rang the bell for the servant, and remained in the drawing-room.

I went slowly down the doctor's stairs, feeling the disheartening conviction that he really had something to say which it was vitally important to me to hear, and that he was morally incapable of saying it. The effort of remembering that he wanted to speak to me was, but too evidently, the only effort that his enfeebled memory was now able to achieve.

Just as I had reached the bottom of the stairs, and had turned a corner on my way to the outer hall, a door opened softly somewhere on the ground floor of the house, and a gentle voice said behind me:

'I am afraid, sir, you find Mr Candy sadly changed?'

I turned round, and found myself face to face with Ezra Jennings.

The doctor's pretty housemaid stood waiting for me, with the street-door open in her hand. Pouring brightly into the hall, the morning light fell full on the face of Mr Candy's assistant when I turned, and looked at him.

It was impossible to dispute Betteredge's assertion that the appearance of Ezra Jennings, speaking from the popular point of view, was against him. His gipsy-complexion, his fleshless cheeks, his gaunt facial bones, his dreamy eyes, his extraordinary parti-coloured hair, the puzzling contradiction between his face and figure which made him look old and young both together—were all more or less calculated to produce an unfavourable impression of him on a stranger's mind. And yet—feeling this as I certainly did—it is not to be denied that Ezra Jennings made some inscrutable appeal to my sympathies, which I found it impossible to resist. While my knowledge of the world warned me to answer the question which he had put, acknowledging that I did indeed find Mr Candy sadly changed, and then to proceed on my way out of the house—my interest in Ezra Jennings held me rooted to the place, and gave him the opportunity of speaking to me in private about his employer, for which he had been evidently on the watch.

'Are you walking my way, Mr Jennings?' I said, observing that he held his hat in his hand. 'I am going to call on my aunt, Mrs Ablewhite.'

Ezra Jennings replied that he had a patient to see, and that he was walking my way.

We left the house together. I observed that the pretty servant girl—who was all smiles and amiability, when I wished her good morning on my way out—received a modest little message from Ezra Jennings, relating to the time at which he might be expected to return, with pursed-up lips, and with eyes which ostentatiously looked anywhere rather than look in his face. The poor wretch was evidently no favourite in the house. Out of the house, I had Betteredge's word for it that he was unpopular everywhere. 'What a life!' I thought to myself, as we descended the doctor's doorsteps.

Having already referred to Mr Candy's illness on his side, Ezra Jennings now appeared determined to leave it to me to resume the subject. His silence said significantly, 'It's your turn now.' I, too, had my reasons for referring to the doctor's illness; and I readily accepted the responsibility of speaking first.

'Judging by the change I see in him,' I began, 'Mr Candy's illness must have been far more serious than I had supposed.'

'It is almost a miracle,' said Ezra Jennings, 'that he lived through it.'

'Is his memory never any better than I have found it to-day? He has been trying to speak to me—'

'Of something which happened before he was taken ill?' asked the assistant, observing that I hesitated.

'Yes.'

'His memory of events, at that past time, is hopelessly enfeebled,' said Ezra Jennings. 'It is almost to be deplored, poor fellow, that even the wreck of it remains. While he remembers dimly plans that he formed—things, here and there, that he had to say or do, before his illness—he is perfectly incapable of recalling what the plans were, or what the thing was that he had to say or do. He is painfully conscious of his own deficiency, and painfully anxious, as you must have seen, to hide it from observation. If he could only have recovered in a complete state of oblivion as to the past, he would have been a happier man. Perhaps we should all be happier,' he added, with a sad smile, 'if we could but completely forget!'

'There are some events surely in all men's lives,' I replied, 'the memory of which they would be unwilling entirely to lose?'

'That is, I hope, to be said of most men, Mr Blake. I am afraid it cannot truly be said of *all*. Have you any reason to suppose that the lost remembrance which Mr Candy tried to recover—while you were speaking to him just now—was a remembrance which it was important to *you* that he should recall?'

In saying those words, he had touched, of his own accord, on the very point upon which I was anxious to consult him. The interest I felt in this strange man had impelled me, in the first instance, to give him the opportunity of speaking to me; reserving what I might have to say, on my side, in relation to his employer, until I was first satisfied that he was a person in whose delicacy and discretion I could trust. The little that he had said, thus far, had been sufficient to convince me that I was speaking to a gentleman. He had what I may venture to describe as the *unsought self-possession*, which is a sure sign of good breeding, not in England only, but everywhere else in the civilized world. Whatever the object which he had in view, in putting the question that he had just addressed to me, I felt no doubt that I was justified—so far—in answering him without reserve.

'I believe, I have a strong interest,' I said, 'in tracing the lost remembrance which Mr Candy was unable to recall. May I ask whether you can suggest to me any method by which I might assist his memory?'

Ezra Jennings looked at me, with a sudden flash of interest in his dreamy brown eyes.

'Mr Candy's memory is beyond the reach of assistance,' he said. 'I have tried to help it often enough, since his recovery, to be able to speak positively on that point.'

This disappointed me; and I owned it.

'I confess you led me to hope for a less discouraging answer than that,' I said.

Ezra Jennings smiled. 'It may not, perhaps, be a final answer, Mr Blake. It may be possible to trace Mr Candy's lost recollection, without the necessity of appealing to Mr Candy himself.'

'Indeed? Is it an indiscretion, on my part, to ask: how?'

'By no means. My only difficulty in answering your question, is the difficulty of explaining myself. May I trust to your patience, if I refer once more to Mr Candy's illness: and if I speak of it this time, without sparing you certain professional details?'

'Pray go on! You have interested me already in hearing the details.'

My eagerness seemed to amuse—perhaps, I might rather say, to please him. He smiled again. We had by this time left the last houses in the town behind us. Ezra Jennings stopped for a moment, and picked some wild flowers from the hedge by the roadside. 'How beautiful they are!' he said, simply, showing his little nose-gay to me. 'And how few people in England seem to admire them as they deserve!'

'You have not always been in England?' I said.

'No. I was born, and partly brought up, in one of our colonies. My father was an Englishman; but my mother—We are straying away from our subject, Mr Blake; and it is my fault. The truth is, I have associations vath these modest little hedgeside flowers— It doesn't matter; we were speaking of Mr Candy. To Mr Candy let us return.'

Connecting the few words about himself which thus reluctantly escaped him, with the melancholy view of life which led him to place the conditions of human happiness in complete oblivion of the past, I felt satisfied that the story which I had read in his face was, in two particulars at least, the story that it really told. He had suffered as few men suffer; and there was the mixture of some foreign race in his English blood.

'You have heard, I dare say, of the original cause of Mr Candy's illness?' be resumed. 'The night of Lady Verinder's dinner-party was a night of heavy rain. My employer drove home through it in his gig, and reached the house, wetted to the skin. He found an urgent message from a patient, waiting for him; and he most unfortunately went at once to visit the sick person, without stopping to change his clothes. I was myself professionally detained, that night, by a case at some distance from Frizinghall. When I got back the next morning, I found Mr Candy's groom waiting in great alarm to take me to his master's room. By that time the mischief was done; the illness had set in.'

'The illness has only been described to me, in general terms, as a fever,' I said.

'I can add nothing which will make the description more accurate,' answered Ezra Jennings. 'From first to last the fever assumed no specific form. I sent at once to two of Mr Candy's medical friends in the town, both physicians, to come and give me their opinion of the case. They agreed with me that it looked serious; but they both strongly dissented from the view I took of the treatment. We differed entirely in the conclusions which we drew from the patient's pulse. The two doctors, arguing from the rapidity of the beat, declared that a lowering treatment was the only treatment to be adopted. On my side, I admitted the rapidity of the pulse, but I also pointed to its alarming feebleness as indicating an exhausted condition of the system, and as showing a plain necessity for the administration of stimulants. The two doctors were for keeping him on gruel, lemonade, barley-water, and so on. I was for giving him champagne, or brandy, ammonia, and quinine. A serious difference of opinion, as you see!—a difference between two physicians of established local repute, and a stranger who was only an assistant in the house. For the first few days, I had no choice but to give way to my elders and betters; the patient steadily sinking all the time. I made a second attempt to appeal to the plain, undeniably plain, evidence of the pulse. Its rapidity was unchecked, and its feebleness had increased. The two doctors took offence at my obstinacy. They said, "Mr Jennings, either we manage this case, or you manage it. Which is it to be?" I said, "Gentlemen, give me five minutes to consider, and that plain question shall have a plain reply." When the time expired, I was ready with my answer. I said, "You positively refuse to try the stimulant treatment?" They refused in so many words. "I mean to try it at once, gentlemen."— "Try it, Mr Jennings; and we withdraw from the case." I sent down to the cellar for a bottle of champagne; and I administered half a tumbler-full of it to the patient with my own hand. The two physicians took up their hats in silence, and left the house.'

'You had assumed a serious responsibility,' I said. 'In your place, I am afraid I should have shrunk from it.'

'In my place, Mr Blake, you would have remembered that Mr Candy had taken you into his employment, under circumstances which made you his debtor for life. In my place, you would have seen him sinking, hour by hour; and you would have risked anything, rather than let the one man on earth who had befriended you, die before your eyes. Don't suppose that I had no sense of the terrible position in which I had placed myself! There were moments when I felt all the misery of my friendlessness, all the peril of my dreadful responsibility. If I had been a happy man, if I had led a prosperous life, I believe I should have sunk under the task I had imposed on myself. But I had no happy time to look back at, no past peace of mind to force itself into contrast with my present anxiety and suspense—and I held firm to my resolution through it all. I took an interval in the middle of the day, when my patient's condition was at its best, for the repose I needed. For the rest of the four-and-twenty hours, as long as his life was in danger, I never left his bedside. Towards sunset, as usual in such cases, the delirium incidental to the fever came on. It lasted more or less through the night; and then intermitted, at that terrible time in the early morning—from two o'clock to five—when the vital energies even of the healthiest of us are at their lowest. It is then that Death gathers in his human harvest most abundantly. It was then that Death and I fought our fight over the bed, which should have the man who lay on it. I never hesitated in pursuing the treatment on which I had staked everything. When wine failed, I tried brandy. When the other stimulants lost their influence, I doubled the dose. After an interval of suspense—the like of which I hope to God I shall never feel again—there came a day when the rapidity of the pulse slightly, but appreciably, diminished; and, better still, there came also a change in the beat—an unmistakable change to steadiness and strength. *Then*, I knew that I had saved him; and then I own I broke down. I laid the poor fellow's wasted hand back on the bed, and burst out crying. An hysterical relief, Mr Blake—nothing more! Physiology says, and says truly, that some men are born with female constitutions—and I am one of them!'

He made that bitterly professional apology for his tears, speaking quietly and unaffectedly, as he had spoken throughout. His tone and manner, from beginning to end, showed him to be especially, almost morbidly, anxious not to set himself up as an object of interest to me.

'You may well ask why I have wearied you with all these details,' he went on. 'It is the only way I can see, Mr Blake, of properly introducing to you what I have to say next. Now you know exactly what my position was, at the time of Mr Candy's illness, you will the more readily understand the sore need I had of lightening the burden on my mind by giving it, at intervals, some sort of relief. I have had the presumption to occupy my leisure, for some years past, in writing a book, addressed to the members of my profession—a book on the intricate and delicate subject of the brain and the nervous system. My work will probably never be finished; and it will certainly never be published. It has none the less been the friend of many lonely hours; and it helped me to while away the anxious time—the time of waiting, and nothing else—at Mr Candy's bedside. I told you he was delirious, I think? And I mentioned the time at which his delirium came on?'

'Yes.'

'Well, I had reached a section of my book, at that time, which touched on this same question of delirium. I won't trouble you at any length with my theory on the subject—I will confine myself to telling you only what it is your present interest to know. It has often occurred to me in the course of my medical practice, to doubt whether we can justifiably infer—in cases of delirium—that the loss of the faculty of speaking connectedly, implies of necessity the loss of the faculty of thinking connectedly as well. Poor Mr Candy's illness gave me an opportunity of putting this doubt to the test. I understand the art of writing in shorthand; and I was able to take down the patient's "wanderings," exactly as they fell from his lips.—Do you see, Mr Blake, what I am coming to at last?'

I saw it clearly, and waited with breathless interest to hear more.

'At odds and ends of time,' Ezra Jennings went on, 'I reproduced my shorthand notes, in the ordinary form of writing—leaving large spaces between the broken phrases, and even the single words, as they had fallen disconnectedly from Mr Candy's lips. I then treated the result thus obtained, on something like the principle which one adopts in putting together a child's "puzzle." It is all confusion to begin with; but it may be all brought into order and shape, if you can only find the right way. Acting on this plan, I filled in each blank space on the paper, with what the words or phrases on either side of it suggested to me as the speaker's meaning; altering over and over again, until my additions followed naturally on the spoken words which came before them, and fitted naturally into the spoken words which came after them. The result was, that I not only occupied in this way many vacant and anxious hours, but that I arrived at something which was (as it seemed to me) a confirmation of the theory that I held. In plainer words, after putting the broken sentences together I found the superior faculty of thinking going on, more or less connectedly, in my patient's mind, while the inferior faculty of expression was in a state of almost complete incapacity and confusion.'

'One word!' I interposed, eagerly. 'Did my name occur in any of his wanderings?'

'You shall hear, Mr Blake. Among my written proofs of the assertion which I have just advanced—or, I ought to say, among the written experiments, tending to put my assertion to the proof—there *is* one, in which your name occurs. For nearly the whole of one night, Mr Candy's mind was occupied with *something* between himself and you. I have got the broken words, as they dropped from his lips, on one sheet of paper. And I have got the links of my own discovering which connect those words together, on another sheet of paper. The product (as the arithmeticians would say) is an intelligible statement—first, of something actually done in the past; secondly, of something which Mr Candy contemplated doing in the future, if his illness had not got in the way, and stopped him. The question is whether this does, or does not, represent the lost recollection which he vainly attempted to find when you called on him this morning?'

'Not a doubt of it!' I answered. 'Let us go back directly, and look at the papers!'

'Quite impossible, Mr Blake.'

'Why?'

'Put yourself in my position for a moment,' said Ezra Jennings. 'Would *you* disclose to another person what had dropped unconsciously from the lips of your suffering patient and your helpless friend, without first knowing that there was a necessity to justify you in opening your lips?

I felt that he was unanswerable, here; but I tried to argue the question, nevertheless.

'My conduct in such a delicate matter as you describe,' I replied, 'would depend greatly on whether the disclosure was of a nature to compromise my friend, or not.'

'I have disposed of all necessity for considering that side of the question, long since,' said Ezra Jennings. 'Wherever my notes included anything which Mr Candy might have wished to keep secret, those notes have been destroyed. My manuscript-experiments at my friend's bedside, include nothing, now, which he would have hesitated to communicate to others, if he had recovered the use of his memory. In your case, I have every reason to suppose that my notes contain something which he actually wished to say to you—'

'And yet, you hesitate?'

'And yet, I hesitate. Remember the circumstances, under which I obtained the information which I possess! Harmless as it is, I cannot prevail upon myself to give it up to you, unless you first satisfy me that there is a reason for doing so. He was so miserably ill, Mr Blake! and he was so helplessly dependent upon Me! Is it too much to ask, if I request you only to hint to me what your interest is in the lost recollection—or what you believe that lost recollection to be?'

To have answered him with the frankness which his language and his manner both claimed from me, would have been to commit myself to openly acknowledging that I was suspected of the theft of the Diamond. Strongly as Ezra Jennings had intensified the first impulsive interest which I had felt in him, he had not overcome my unconquerable reluctance to disclose the degrading position in which I stood. I took refuge once more in the explanatory phrases with which I had prepared myself to meet the curiosity of strangers.

This time, I had no reason to complain of a want of attention on the part of the person to whom I addressed myself. Ezra Jennings listened patiently, even anxiously, until I had done.

'I am sorry to have raised your expectations, Mr Blake, only to disappoint them,' he said. 'Throughout the whole period of Mr Candy's illness, from first to last, not one word about the Diamond escaped his lips. The matter with which I heard him connect your name has, I can assure you, no discoverable relation whatever with the loss or the recovery of Miss Verinder's jewel.'

We arrived, as he said those words, at a place where the highway along which we had been walling, branched off into two roads. One led to Mr Ablewhite's house; and the other to a moorland village some two or three miles off. Ezra Jennings stopped at the road which led to the village.

'My way lies in this direction,' he said. 'I am really and truly sorry, Mr Blake, that I can be of no use to you.'

His voice told me that he spoke sincerely. His soft brown eyes rested on me for a moment with a look of melancholy interest. He bowed, and went, without another word, on his way to the village.

For a minute or more, I stood and watched him, walking farther and farther away from me; carrying farther and farther away with him what I now firmly believed to be the clue of which I was in search. He turned, after walking on a little way, and looked back. Seeing me still standing at the place where we had parted, he stopped, as if doubting whether I might not wish to speak to him again. There was no time for me to reason out my own situation—to remind myself that I was losing my opportunity, at what might be the turning-point of my life, and all to flatter nothing more important than my own self-esteem! There was only time to call him back first, and to think afterwards. I suspect I am one of the rashest of existing men. I called him back—and then I said to myself, 'Now there is no help for it. I must tell him the truth!'

He retraced his steps directly. I advanced along the road to meet him.

'Mr Jennings,' I said, 'I have not treated you quite fairly. My interest in tracing Mr Candy's lost recollection, is not the interest of recovering the Moonstone. A serious personal matter is at the bottom of my visit to Yorkshire. I have but one excuse for not having dealt frankly with you in this matter. It is more painful to me than I can say, to mention to anybody what my position really is.'

Ezra Jennings looked at me with the first appearance of embarrassment which I had seen in him yet.

'I have no right, Mr Blake, and no wish,' he said, 'to intrude myself into your private affairs. Allow me to ask your pardon, on my side, for having (most innocently) put you to a painful test.'

'You have a perfect right,' I rejoined, 'to fix the terms on which you feel justified in revealing what you heard at Mr Candy's bedside. I understand, and respect, the delicacy which influences you in this matter. How can I expect to be taken into your confidence, if I decline to admit you into mine? You ought to know, and you shall know, why I am interested in discovering what Mr Candy wanted to say to me. If I turn out to be mistaken in my anticipations, and if you prove unable to help me when you are really aware of what I want, I shall trust to your honour to keep my secret—and something tells me that I shall not trust in vain.'

'Stop, Mr Blake. I have a word to say, which must be said before you go any farther.' I looked at him in astonishment. The grip of some terrible emotion seemed to have seized him, and shaken him to the soul. His gipsy complexion had altered to a livid greyish paleness; his eyes had suddenly become wild and glittering; his voice had dropped to a tone—low, stern, and resolute—which I now heard for the first time. The latent resources in the man, for good or for evil—it was hard, at that moment, to say which—leapt up in him and showed themselves to me, with the suddenness of a flash of light.

'Before you place any confidence in me,' he went on, 'you ought to know, and you *must* know, under what circumstances I have been received into Mr Candy's house. It won't take long. I don't profess, sir, to tell my story (as the phrase is) to any man. My story will die with me. All I ask, is to be permitted to tell you, what I have told Mr Candy. If you are still in the mind, when you have heard that, to say what you have proposed to say, you will command my attention, and command my services. Shall we walk on?'

The suppressed misery in his face, silenced me. I answered his question by a sign. We walked on.

After advancing a few hundred yards, Ezra Jennings stopped at a gap in the rough stone wall which shut off the moor from the road, at this part of it.

'Do you mind resting a little, Mr Blake?' he asked. 'I am not what I was—and some things shake me.'

I agreed of course. He led the way through the gap to a patch of turf on the heathy ground, screened by bushes and dwarf trees on the side nearest to the road, and commanding in the opposite direction a grandly desolate view over the broad brown wilderness of the moor. The clouds had gathered, within the last half-hour. The light was dull; the distance was dim. The lovely face of Nature met us, soft and still and colourless—met us without a smile.

We sat down in silence. Ezra Jennings laid aside his hat, and passed his hand wearily over his forehead, wearily through his startling white and black hair. He tossed his little nosegay of wild flowers away from him, as if the remembrances which it recalled were remembrances which hurt him now.

'Mr Blake!' he said, suddenly. 'You are in bad company. The cloud of a horrible accusation has rested on me for years. I tell you the worst at once. I am a man whose life is a wreck, and whose character is gone.'

I attempted to speak. He stopped me.

'No,' he said. 'Pardon me; not yet. Don't commit yourself to expressions of sympathy which you may afterwards wish to recall. I have mentioned an accusation which has rested on me for years. There are circumstances in connexion with it that tell against me. I cannot bring myself to acknowledge what the accusation is. And I am incapable, perfectly incapable, of proving my innocence. I can only assert my innocence. I assert it, sir, on my oath, as a Christian. It is useless to appeal to my honour as a man.'

He paused again. I looked round at him. He never looked at me in return. His whole being seemed to be absorbed in the agony of recollecting, and in the effort to speak.

'There is much that I might say,' he went on, 'about the merciless treatment of me by my own family, and the merciless enmity to which I have fallen a victim. But the harm is done; the wrong is beyond all remedy. I decline to weary or distress you, sir, if I can help it. At the outset of my career in this country, the vile slander to which I have referred struck me down at once and for ever. I resigned my aspirations in my profession—obscurity was the only hope left for me. I parted with the woman I loved— how could I condemn her to share my disgrace? A medical assistant's place offered itself, in a remote corner of England. I got the place. It promised me peace; it promised me obscurity, as I thought. I was wrong. Evil report, with time and chance to help it, travels patiently, and travels far. The accusation from which I had fled, followed me. I got warning of its approach. I was able to leave my situation voluntarily, with the testimonials that I had earned. They got me another situation in another remote district. Time passed again; and again the slander that was death to my character found me out. On this occasion I had no warning. My employer said, "Mr Jennings, I have no complaint to make against you; but you must set yourself right, or leave me." I had but one choice— I left him. It's useless to dwell on what I suffered after that. I am only forty years old now. Look at my face, and let it tell for me the story of some miserable years. It ended in my drifting to this place, and meeting with Mr Candy. He wanted an assistant. I referred him, on the question of capacity, to my last employer. The question of character remained. I told him what I have told you—and more. I warned him that there were difficulties in the way, even if he believed me. "Here, as elsewhere," I said, "I scorn the guilty evasion of living under an assumed name: I am no safer at Frizinghall than at other places from the cloud that follows me, go where I may." He answered, "I don't do things by halves—I believe you, and I pity you. If *you* will risk what may happen, *I* will risk it too." God Almighty bless him! He has given me shelter, he has given me employment, he has given me rest of mind—and I have the certain conviction (I have had it for some months past) that nothing will happen now to make him regret it.'

'The slander has died out?' I said.

'The slander is as active as ever. But when it follows me here, it will come too late.'

'You will have left the place?'

'No, Mr Blake—I shall be dead. For ten years past, I have suffered from an incurable internal complaint. I don't disguise from you that I should have let the agony of it kill me long since but for one last interest in life, which makes my existence of some importance to me still. I want to provide for a person—very dear to me—whom I shall never see again. My own little patrimony is hardly sufficient to make her independent of the world. The hope, if I could only live long enough, of increasing it to a certain sum, has impelled me to resist the disease by such palliative means as I could devise. The one effectual palliative in my case, is—opium. To that all-potent and all-merciful drug, I am indebted for a respite of many years from my sentence of death. But even the virtues of opium have their limit. The progress of the disease has gradually forced me from the use of opium, to the abuse of it. I am feeling the penalty at last. My nervous system is shattered; my nights are nights of horror. The end is not far off now. Let it come—I have not lived and worked in vain. The little sum is nearly made up; and I have the means of completing it, if my last reserves of life fail me sooner than I expect. I hardly know how I have wandered into telling you this. I don't think I am mean enough to appeal to your pity. Perhaps, I fancy you may be all the readier to believe me, if you know that what I have said to you, I have said with the certain knowledge in me that I am a dying man. There is no disguising, Mr Blake, that you interest me. I have attempted to make my poor friend's loss of memory the means of bettering my acquaintance with you. I have speculated on the chance of your feeling a passing curiosity about what he wanted to say, and of my being able to satisfy it. Is there no excuse for my intruding myself on you? Perhaps there is some excuse. A man who has lived as I have lived has his bitter moments when he ponders over human destiny. You have youth, health, riches, a place in the world, a prospect before you. You, and such as you, show me the sunny side of human life, and reconcile me with the world that I am leaving, before I go. However this talk between us may end, I shall not forget that you have done me a kindness in doing that. It rests with you, sir, to say what you proposed saying, or to wish me good morning.'

I had but one answer to make to that appeal. Without a moment's hesitation, I told him the truth, as unreservedly as I have told it in these pages.

He started to his feet, and looked at me with breathless eagerness as I approached the leading incident of my story.

'It is certain that I went into the room,' I said; 'it is certain that I took the Diamond. I can only meet those two plain facts by declaring that, do what I might, I did it without my own knowledge—'

Ezra Jennings caught me excitedly by the arm.

'Stop!' he said. 'You have suggested more to me than you suppose. Have *you* ever been accustomed to the use of opium?'

'I never tasted it in my life.'

'Were your nerves out of order, at this time last year? Were you unusually restless and irritable?'

'Yes.'

'Did you sleep badly?'

'Wretchedly. Many nights I never slept at all.'

'Was the birthday night an exception? Try, and remember. Did you sleep well on that one occasion?'

'I do remember! I slept soundly.'

He dropped my arm as suddenly as he had taken it—and looked at me with the air of a man whose mind was relieved of the last doubt that rested on it.

'This is a marked day in your life, and in mine,' he said, gravely. 'I am absolutely certain, Mr Blake, of one thing—I have got what Mr Candy wanted to say to you this morning, in the notes that I took at my patient's bedside. Wait! that is not all. I am firmly persuaded that I can prove you to have been unconscious of what you were about, when you entered the room and took the Diamond. Give me time to think, and time to question you. I believe the vindication of your innocence is in my hands!'

'Explain yourself, for God' sake! What do you mean?'

In the excitement of our colloquy, we had walked on a few steps, beyond the clump of dwarf trees which had hitherto screened us from view. Before Ezra Jennings could answer me, he was hailed from the high-road by a man, in great agitation, who had been evidently on the look-out for him.

'I am coming,' he called back; 'I am coming as fast as I can!' He turned to me. 'There is an urgent case waiting for me at the village yonder; I ought to have been there half an hour since—I must attend to it at once. Give me two hours from this time, and call at Mr Candy's again—and I will engage to be ready for you.'

'How am I to wait!' I exclaimed, impatiently. 'Can't you quiet my mind by a word of explanation before we part?'

'This is far too serious a matter to be explained in a hurry, Mr Blake. I am not wilfully trying your patience—I should only be adding to your suspense, if I attempted to relieve it as things are now. At Frizinghall, sir, in two hours' time!'

The man on the high-road hailed him again. He hurried away, and left me.

CHAPTER 10

How the interval of suspense to which I was now condemned might have affected other men in my position, I cannot pretend to say. The influence of the two hours' probation upon *my* temperament, was simply this. I felt physically incapable of remaining still in any one place, and morally incapable of speaking to any one human being, until I had first heard all that Ezra Jennings had to say to me.

In this frame of mind, I not only abandoned my contemplated visit to Mrs Ablewhite—I even shrank from encountering Gabriel Betteredge himself.

Returning to Frizinghall, I left a note for Betteredge, telling him that I had been unexpectedly called away, for a few hours, but that he might certainly expect me to return towards 15.00 in the afternoon. I requested him, in the interval, to order his dinner at the usual hour, and to amuse himself as he pleased. He had, as I well knew, hosts of friends in Frizinghall; and he would be at no loss how to fill up his time until I returned to the hotel.

This done, I made the best of my way out of the town again, and roamed the lonely moorland country which surrounds Frizinghall, until my watch told me that it was time, at last, to return to Mr Candy's house.

I found Ezra Jennings, ready and waiting for me.

He was sitting alone in a bare little room, which communicated by a glazed door with a surgery. Hideous coloured diagrams of the ravages of hideous diseases, decorated the barren buff-coloured walls. A bookcase filled with dingy medical works, and ornamented at the top with a skull, in place of the customary bust; a large deal table copiously splashed with ink; wooden chairs of the sort that are seen in kitchens and cottages; a threadbare drugget in the middle of the floor; a sink of water, with a basin and waste-pipe roughly let into the wall, horribly suggestive of its connection with surgical operations—comprised the entire furniture of the room. The bees were humming among a few flowers placed in pots outside the window; the birds were singing in the garden, and the faint intermittent jingle of a tuneless piano in some neighbouring house, forced itself now and again, on the ear. In any other place, these everyday sounds might have spoken pleasantly of the everyday world outside. Here, they came in as intruders on a silence which nothing but human suffering had the privilege to disturb. I looked at the mahogany instrument case, and at the huge roll of lint, occupying places of their own on the bookshelves, and shuddered inwardly as I thought of the sounds, familiar and appropriate to the everyday use of Ezra Jennings' room.

'I make no apology, Mr Blake, for the place in which I am receiving you,' he said. 'It is the only room in the house, at this hour of the day, in which we can feel quite sure of being left undisturbed. Here are my papers ready for you; and here are two books to which we may have occasion to refer, before we have done. Bring your chair to the table, and we shall be able to consult them together.'

I drew up to the table; and Ezra Jennings handed me his manuscript notes. They consisted of two large folio leaves of paper. One leaf contained writing which only covered the surface at intervals. The other presented writing, in red and black ink, which completely filled the page from top to bottom. In the irritated state of my curiosity, at that moment, I laid aside the second sheet of paper in despair.

'Have some mercy on me!' I said. 'Tell me what I am to expect, before I attempt to read this.'

'Willingly, Mr Blake! Do you mind my asking you one or two more questions?'

'Ask me anything you like!'

'He looked at me with the sad smile on his lips, and the kindly interest in his soft brown eyes.

'You have already told me,' he said, 'that you have never—to your knowledge—tasted opium in your life.'

'To my knowledge,' I repeated.

'You will understand directly, why I speak with that reservation. Let us go on. You are not aware of ever having taken opium. At this time, last year, you were suffering from nervous irritation, and you slept wretchedly at night. On the night of the birthday, however, there was an exception to the rule—you slept soundly. Am I right, so far?'

'Quite right.'

'Can you assign any cause for the nervous suffering, and your want of sleep?'

'I can assign no cause. Old Betteredge made a guess at the cause, I remember. But that is hardly worth mentioning.'

'Pardon me. Anything is worth mentioning in such a case as this. Betteredge attributed your sleeplessness to something. To what?'

'To my leaving off smoking.'

'Had you been an habitual smoker?'

'Yes.'

'Did you leave off the habit suddenly?'

'Yes.'

'Betteredge was perfectly right, Mr Blake. When smoking is a habit, a man must have no common constitution who can leave it off suddenly without some temporary damage to his nervous system. Your sleepless nights are accounted for, to my mind. My next question refers to Mr Candy. Do you remember having entered into anything like a dispute with him—at the birthday dinner, or afterwards—on the subject of his profession?'

The question instantly awakened one of my dormant remembrances, in connection with the birthday festival. The foolish wrangle which took place, on that occasion, between Mr Candy and myself, will be found, described at much greater length than it deserves, in the tenth chapter of Betteredge's Narrative. The details there presented of the dispute—so little had I thought of it afterwards—entirely failed to recur to my memory. All that I could now recall, and all that I could tell Ezra Jennings was, that I had attacked the art of medicine at the dinner-table, with sufficient rashness and sufficient pertinacity to put even Mr Candy out of temper for the moment. I also remembered that Lady Verinder had interfered to stop the dispute, and that the little doctor and I had 'made it up again,' as the children say, and had become as good friends as ever, before we shook hands that night.

'There is one thing more,' said Ezra Jennings, 'which it is very important I should know. Had you any reason for feeling any special anxiety about the Diamond, at this time last year?'

'I had the strongest reasons for feeling anxiety about the Diamond. I knew it to be the object of a conspiracy; and I was warned to take measures for Miss Verinder's protection, as the possessor of the stone.'

'Was the safety of the Diamond the subject of conversation between you and any other person, immediately before you retired to rest on the birthday night?'

'It was the subject of a conversation, between Lady Verinder and her daughter—'

'Which took place in your hearing?'

'Yes.'

Ezra Jennings took up his notes from the table, and placed them in my hands.

'Mr Blake,' he said, 'if you read those notes now, by the light which my questions and your answers have thrown on them, you will make two astounding discoveries, concerning yourself. You will find:—First, that you entered Miss Verinder's sitting-room and took the Diamond, in a state of trance, produced by opium. Secondly, that the opium was given to you by Mr Candy—without your own knowledge—as a practical refutation of the opinions which you had expressed to him at the birthday dinner.'

I sat, with the papers in my hand, completely stupefied.

'Try, and forgive poor Mr Candy,' said the assistant gently. 'He has done dreadful mischief, I own; but he has done it innocently. If you will look at the notes, you will see that—but for his illness—he would have returned to Lady Verinder's the morning after the party, and would have acknowledged the trick that he had played you. Miss Verinder would have heard of it, and Miss Verinder would have questioned him—and the truth which has laid hidden for a year, would have been discovered in a day.'

I began to regain my self-possession. 'Mr Candy is beyond the reach of my resentment,' I said angrily. 'But the trick that he played me is not the less an act of treachery, for all that. I may forgive, but I shall not forget it.'

'Every medical man commits that act of treachery, Mr Blake, in the course of his practice. The ignorant distrust of opium (in England) is by no means confined to the lower and less cultivated classes. Every doctor in large practice finds himself, every now and then, obliged to deceive his patients, as Mr Candy deceived you. I don't defend the folly of playing you a trick under the circumstances. I only plead with you for a more accurate and more merciful construction of motives.'

'How was it done?' I asked. 'Who gave me the laudanum, without my knowing it myself?'

'I am not able to tell you. Nothing relating to that part of the matter dropped from Mr Candy's lips, all through his illness. Perhaps, your own memory may point to the person to be suspected?'

'No.'

'It is useless, in that case, to pursue the inquiry. The laudanum was secretly given to you in some way. Let us leave it there, and go on to matters of more immediate importance. Read my notes, if you can. Familiarize your mind with what has happened in the past. I have something very bold and very startling to propose to you, which relates to the future.'

Those last words roused me.

I looked at the papers, in the order in which Ezra Jennings had placed them in my hands. The paper which contained the smaller quantity of writing was the uppermost of the two. On this, the disconnected words, and fragments of sentences, which had dropped from Mr Candy in his delirium, appeared as follows:

'. . . Mr Franklin Blake . . . and agreeable. . . . down a peg. . . . medicine. . . . confesses . . . sleep at night . . . tell him . . . out of order . . . medicine . . . he tells me . . . and groping in the dark mean one and the same thing . . . all the company at the dinner-table . . . I say . . . groping after sleep . . . nothing but medicine . . . he says . . . leading the blind . . . know what it means . . . witty . . . a night's rest in spite of his teeth . . . wants sleep . . . Lady Verinder's medicine chest . . . five-and-twenty minims . . . without his knowing it . . . to-morrow morning . . . Well, Mr Blake . . . medicine to-day . . . never . . . without it . . . out, Mr Candy . . . excellent . . . without it . . . down on him truth . . . something besides . . . excellent . . . dose of laudanum, sir . . . bed . . . what . . . medicine now.'

There, the first of the two sheets of paper came to an end. I handed it back to Ezra Jennings.

'That is what you heard at his bedside?' I said.

'Literally and exactly what I heard,' he answered—'except that the repetitions are not transferred here from my short-hand notes. He reiterated certain words and phrases a dozen times over, fifty times over, just as he attached more or less importance to the idea which they represented. The repetitions, in this sense, were of some assistance to me in putting together those fragments. Don't suppose,' he added, pointing to the second sheet of paper, 'that I claim to have reproduced the expressions which Mr Candy himself would have used if he had been capable of speaking connectedly. I only say that I have penetrated through the obstacle of the disconnected expression, to the thought which was underlying it connectedly all the time. Judge for yourself.'

I turned to the second sheet of paper, which I now knew to be the key to the first.

Once more, Mr Candy's wanderings appeared, copied in black ink; the intervals between the phrases being filled up by Ezra Jennings in red ink. I reproduce the result here, in one plain form; the original language and the interpretation of it coming close enough together in these pages to be easily compared and verified.

'. . . Mr Franklin Blake is clever and agreeable, but he wants taking down a peg when he talks of medicine. He confesses that he has been suffering from want of sleep at night. I tell him that his nerves are out of order, and that he ought to take medicine. He tells me that taking medicine and groping in the dark mean one and the same thing. This before all the company at the dinner-table. I say to him, you are groping after sleep, and nothing but medicine can help you to find it. He says to me, I have heard of the blind leading the blind, and now I know what it means. Witty—but I can give him a night's rest in spite of his teeth. He really wants sleep; and Lady Verinder's medicine chest is at my disposal. Give him five-and-twenty minims of laudanum to-night, without his knowing it; and then call to-morrow morning. "Well, Mr Blake, will you try a little medicine to-day? You will never sleep without it."—"There you are out, Mr Candy: I have had an excellent night's rest without it." Then, come down on him with the truth! "You have had something besides an excellent night's rest; you had a dose of laudanum, sir, before you went to bed. What do you say to the art of medicine, now?" '

Admiration of the ingenuity which had woven this smooth and finished texture out of the ravelled skein, was naturally the first impression that I felt, on handing the manuscript back to Ezra Jennings. He modestly interrupted the first few words in which my sense of surprise expressed itself, by asking me if the conclusion which he had drawn from his notes was also the conclusion at which my own mind had arrived.

'Do you believe as I believe,' he said, 'that you were acting under the influence of the laudanum in doing all that you did, on the night of Miss Verinder's birthday, in Lady Verinder's house?'

'I am too ignorant of the influence of laudanum to have an opinion of my own,' I answered. 'I can only follow your opinion, and feel convinced that you are right.'

'Very well. The next question is this. You are convinced; and I am convinced—how are we to carry our conviction to the minds of other people?'

I pointed to the two manuscripts, lying on the table between us. Ezra Jennings shook his head.

'Useless, Mr Blake! Quite useless, as they stand now, for three unanswerable reasons. In the first place, those notes have been taken, under circumstances entirely out of the experience of the mass of mankind. Against them, to begin with! In the second place, those notes represent a medical and metaphysical theory. Against them, once more! In the third place, those notes are of *my* making; there is nothing but *my* assertion to the contrary, to guarantee that they are not fabrications. Remember what I told you on the moor—and ask yourself what my assertion is worth. No! my notes have but one value, looking to the verdict of the world outside. Your innocence is to be vindicated; and they show how it can be done. We must put our conviction to the proof—and You are the man to prove it?'

'How?' I asked.

He leaned eagerly nearer to me across the table that divided us. 'Are you willing to try a bold experiment?'

'I will do anything to clear myself of the suspicion that on me now.'

'Will you submit to some personal inconvenience for a time?'

'To any inconvenience, no matter what it may be.'

'Will you be guided implicitly by my advice? It may expose you to the ridicule of fools; it may subject you to the remonstrances of friends whose opinions you are bound to respect—'

'Tell me what to do!' I broke out impatiently. 'And, come what may, I'll do it.'

'You shall do this, Mr Blake,' he answered. 'You shall steal the Diamond, unconsciously, for the second time, in the presence of witnesses whose testimony is beyond dispute!'

I started to my feet. I tried to speak. I could only look at him. 'I believe it *can* be done,' he went on. 'And it *shall* be done—if you will only help me. Try to compose yourself—sit down, and hear what I have to say to you. You have resumed the habit of smoking; I have seen that for myself. How long have you resumed it?'

'For nearly a year.'

'Do you smoke more, or less, than you did?'

'More.'

'Will you give up the habit again? Suddenly, mind!—as you gave it up before.'

I began dimly to see his drift. 'I will give it up, from this moment,' I answered.

'If the same consequences follow, which followed last June,' said Ezra Jennings—'if you suffer once more as you suffered then, from sleepless nights, we shall have gained our first step. We shall have put you back again into something assimilating to your nervous condition on the birthday night. If we can next revive, or nearly revive, the domestic circumstances which surrounded you; and if we can occupy your mind again with the various questions concerning the Diamond which formerly agitated it, we shall have replaced you, as, nearly as possible, in the same position, physically and morally, in which the opium found you last year. In that case we may fairly hope that a repetition of the dose will lead, in a greater or lesser degree, to a repetition of the result. There is my proposal, expressed in a few hasty words. You shall now see what reasons I have to justify me in making it.'

He turned to one of the books at his side, and opened it at a place marked by a small slip of paper.

'Don't suppose that I am going to weary you with a lecture on physiology,' he said. 'I think myself bound to prove, in justice to both of us, that I am not asking you to try this experiment in deference to any theory of my own devising. Admitted principles, and recognized authorities, justify me in the view that I take. Give me five minutes of your attention; and I will undertake to show you that Science sanctions my proposal, fanciful as it may seem. Here, in the first place, is the physiological principle on which I am acting, stated by no less a person than Dr Carpenter. Read it for yourself.'

He handed me the slip of paper which had marked the place in the book. It contained a few lines of writing, as follows:—

'There seems much ground for the belief, that *every* sensory impression which has once been recognized by the perceptive consciousness, is registered (so to speak) in the brain, and may be reproduced at some subsequent time, although there may be no consciousness of its existence in the mind during the whole intermediate period.' 'Is that plain, so far?' asked Ezra Jennings.

'Perfectly plain.'

'He pushed the open book across the table to me, and pointed to a passage, marked by pencil lines.

'Now,' he said, 'read that account of a case, which has—as I believe—a direct bearing on your own position, and on the experiment which I am tempting you to try. Observe, Mr Blake, before you begin, that I am now referring you to one of the greatest of English physiologists. The book in your hand is Doctor Elliotson's *Human Physiology*; and the case which the doctor cites, rests on the well-known authority of Mr Combe.'

The passage pointed out to me, was expressed in these terms:—

'Dr Abel informed me,' says Mr Combe, 'of an Irish porter to a warehouse, who forgot, when sober, what he had done when drunk; but, being drunk, again recollected the transactions of his former state of intoxication. On one occasion, being drunk, he had lost a parcel of some value, and in his sober moments could give no account of it. Next time he was intoxicated, he recollected that he had left the parcel at a certain house, and there being no address on it, it had remained there safely, and was got on his calling for it.'

'Plain again?' asked Ezra Jennings.

'As plain as need be.'

He put back the slip of paper in its place, and closed the book.

'Are you satisfied that I have not spoken without good authority to support me?' he asked. 'If not, I have only to go to those bookshelves, and you have only to read the passages which I can point out to you.'

'I am quite satisfied,' I said, 'without reading a word more.'

'In that case, we may return to your own personal interest in this matter. I am bound to tell you that there is something to be said against the experiment as well as for it. If we could, this year, exactly reproduce, in your case, the conditions as they existed last year, it is physiologically certain that we should arrive at exactly the same result. But this—there is no denying it—is simply impossible. We can only hope to approximate to the conditions; and if we don't succeed in getting you nearly enough back to what you were, this venture of ours will fail. If we do succeed—and I am myself hopeful of success—you may at least so far repeat your proceedings on the birthday night, as to satisfy any reasonable person that you are guiltless, morally speaking, of the theft of the Diamond. I believe, Mr Blake, I have now stated the question, on both sides of it, as fairly as I can, within the limits that I have imposed on myself. If there is anything that I have not made clear to you, tell me what it is—and if I can enlighten you, I will.'

'All that you have explained to me,' I said, 'I understand perfectly. But I own I am puzzled on one point, which you have not made clear to me yet.'

'What is the point?'

'I don't understand the effect of the laudanum on me. I don't understand my walking downstairs, and along corridors, and my opening and shutting the drawers of a cabinet, and my going back again to my own room. All these are active proceedings. I thought the influence of opium was first to stupefy you, and then to send you to sleep.'

'The common error about opium, Mr Blake! I am, at this moment, exerting my intelligence (such as it is) in your service, under the influence of a dose of laudanum, some ten times larger than the dose Mr Candy administered to you. But don't trust to my authority—even on a question which comes within my own personal experience. I anticipated the objection you have just made: and I have again provided myself with independent testimony, which will carry its due weight with it in your own mind, and in the minds of your friends.'

He handed me the second of the two books which he had by him on the table.

'There,' he said, 'are the far-famed *Confessions of an English Opium Eater*! Take the book away with you, and read it. At the passage which I have marked, you will find that when De Quincey had committed what he calls "a debauch of opium," he either went to the gallery at the Opera to enjoy the music, or he wandered about the London markets on Saturday night, and interested himself in observing all the little shifts and bargainings of the poor in providing their Sunday's dinner. So much for the capacity of a man to occupy himself actively, and to move about from place to place under the influence of opium.'

'I am answered so far,' I said; 'but I am not answered yet as to the effect produced by the opium on myself.'

'I will try to answer you in a few words,' said Ezra Jennings. 'The action of opium is comprised, in the majority of cases, in two influences—a stimulating influence first, and a sedative influence afterwards. Under the stimulating influence, the latest and most vivid impressions left on your mind—namely, the impressions relating to the Diamond—would be likely, in your morbidly sensitive nervous condition, to become intensified in your brain, and would subordinate to themselves your judgment and your will—exactly as an ordinary dream subordinates to itself your judgment and your will. Little by little, under this action, any apprehensions about the safety of the Diamond which you might have felt during the day, would be liable to develop themselves from the state of doubt to the state of certainty—would impel you into practical action to preserve the jewel—would direct your steps, with that motive in view, into the room which you entered—and would guide your hand to the drawers of the cabinet, until you had found the drawer which held the stone. In the spiritualized intoxication of opium, you would do all that. Later, as the sedative action began to gain on the stimulant action, you would slowly become inert and stupefied. Later still you would fall into a deep sleep. When the morning came, and the effect of the opium had been all slept off, you would wake as absolutely ignorant of what you had done in the night as if you had been living at the Antipodes.—Have I made it tolerably clear to you, so far?'

'You have made it so clear,' I said, 'that I want you to go farther. You have shown me how I entered the room, and how I came to take the Diamond. But Miss Verinder saw me leave the room again, with the jewel in my hand. Can you trace my proceedings from that moment? Can you guess what I did next?'

'That is the very point I was coming to,' he rejoined. 'It is a question with me whether the experiment which I propose as a means of vindicating your innocence, may not also be made a means of recovering the lost Diamond as well. When you left Miss Verinder's sitting-room, with the jewel in your hand, you went back in all probability to your own room—'

'Yes!—and what then?'

'It is possible, Mr Blake—I dare not say more—that your idea of preserving the Diamond led, by a natural sequence, to the idea of hiding the Diamond, and that the place in which you hid it was somewhere in your bedroom. In that event, the case of the Irish porter may be your case. You may remember, under the influence of the second dose of opium, the place in which you hid the Diamond under the influence of the first.'

It was my turn, now, to enlighten Ezra Jennings. I stopped him, before he could say any more.

'You are speculating,' I said, 'on a result which cannot possibly take place. The Diamond is, at this moment, in London.'

He started, and looked at me in great surprise.

'In London?' he repeated. 'How did it get to London from Lady Verinder's house?'

'Nobody knows.'

'You removed it with your own hand from Miss Verinder's room. How was it taken out of your keeping?'

'I have no idea how it was taken out of my keeping.'

'Did you see it, when you woke in the morning?'

'No.'

'Has Miss Verinder recovered possession of it?'

'No.'

'Mr Blake! there seems to be something here which wants clearing up. May I ask how you know that the Diamond is, at this moment, in London?'

I had put precisely the same question to Mr Bruff, when I made my first inquiries about the Moonstone, on my return to England. In answering Ezra Jennings, I accordingly repeated what I had myself heard from the lawyer's own lips—and what is already familiar to the readers of these pages.

He showed plainly that he was not satisfied with my reply.

'With all deference to you,' he said, 'and with all deference to your legal adviser, I maintain the opinion which I expressed just now. It rests, I am well aware, on a mere assumption. Pardon me for reminding you, that your opinion also rests on a mere assumption as well.'

The view he took of the matter was entirely new to me. I waited anxiously to hear how he would defend it.

'*I* assume,' pursued Ezra Jennings, 'that the influence of the opium—after impelling you to possess yourself of the Diamond, with the purpose of securing its safety—might also impel you, acting under the same influence and the same motive, to hide it somewhere in your own room. *You* assume that the Hindoo conspirators could by no possibility commit a mistake. The Indians went to Mr Luker's house after the Diamond—and, therefore, in Mr Luker's possession the Diamond must be! Have you any evidence to prove that the Moonstone was taken to London at all? You can't even guess how, or by whom, it was removed from Lady Verinder's house! Have you any evidence that the jewel was pledged to Mr Luker? He declares that he never heard of the Moonstone; and his bankers' receipt acknowledges nothing but the deposit of a valuable of great price. The Indians assume that Mr Luker is lying—and you assume again that the Indians are right. All I say, in differing with you, is—that my view is possible. What more, Mr Blake, either logically or legally, can be said for yours?'

It was put strongly; but there was no denying that it was put truly as well.

'I confess you stagger me,' I replied. 'Do you object to my writing to Mr Bruff, and telling him what you have said?'

'On the contrary, I shall be glad if you will write to Mr Bruff. If we consult his experience, we may see the matter under a new light. For the present, let us return to our experiment with the opium. We have decided that you leave off the habit of smoking, from this moment?'

'From this moment.'

'That is the first step. The next step is to reproduce, as nearly as we can, the domestic circumstances which surrounded you last year.'

How was this to be done? Lady Verinder was dead. Rachel and I, so long as the suspicion of theft rested on me, were parted irrevocably. Godfrey Ablewhite was away, travelling on the Continent. It was simply impossible to reassemble the people who had inhabited the house, when I had slept in it last. The statement of this objection did not appear to embarrass Ezra Jennings. He attached very little importance he said to reassembling the same people—seeing that it would be vain to expect them to reassume the various positions which they had occupied towards me in the past times. On the other hand, he considered it essential to the success of the experiment, that I should see the same objects about me which had surrounded me when I was last in the house.

'Above all things,' he said, 'you must sleep in the room which you slept in, on the birthday night, and it must be furnished in the same way. The stairs, the corridors, and Miss Verinder's sitting-room, must also be restored to what they were when you saw them last. It is absolutely necessary, Mr Blake, to replace every article of furniture in that part of the house which may now be put away. The sacrifice of your cigars will be useless, unless we can get Miss Verinder's permission to do that.'

'Who is to apply to her for permission?' I asked.

'Is it not possible for *you* to apply?'

'Quite out of the question. After what has passed between us, on the subject of the lost Diamond, I can neither see her, nor write to her, as things are now.'

Ezra Jennings paused, and considered for a moment.

'May I ask you a delicate question?' he said.

I signed to him to go on.

'Am I right, Mr Blake, in fancying (from one or two things which have dropped from you) that you felt no common interest in Miss Verinder, in former times?'

'Quite right.'

'Was the feeling returned?'

'It was.'

'Do you think Miss Verinder would be likely to feel a strong interest in the attempt to prove your innocence?'

'I am certain of it.'

'In that case, *I* will write to Miss Verinder—if you will give me leave.'

'Telling her of the proposal that you have made to me?'

'Telling her of everything that has passed between us to-day.'

It is needless to say that I eagerly accepted the service which he had offered to me.

'I shall have time to write by to-day's post,' he said, looking at his watch. 'Don't forget to lock up your cigars, when you get back to the hotel! I will call to-morrow morning and hear how you have passed the night.'

I rose to take leave of him; and attempted to express the grateful sense of his kindness which I really felt.

He pressed my hand gently. 'Remember what I told you on the moor,' he answered. 'If I can do you this little service, Mr Blake, I shall feel it like a last gleam of sunshine, falling on the evening of a long and clouded day.'

We parted. It was then the fifteenth of June. The events of the next ten days—every one of them more or less directly connected with the experiment of which I was the passive object—are all placed on record, exactly as they happened, in the Journal habitually kept by Mr Candy's assistant. In the pages of Ezra Jennings, nothing is concealed, and nothing is forgotten. Let Ezra Jennings tell how the venture with the opium was tried, and how it ended.

FOURTH NARRATIVE

Extracted from the Journal of Ezra Jennings

1849.—15 June. . . . With some interruption from patients, and some interruption from pain, I finished my letter to Miss Verinder in time for to-day's post. I failed to make it as short a letter as I could have wished. But I think I have made it plain. It leaves her entirely mistress of her own decision. If she consents to assist the experiment, she consents of her own free will, and not as a favour to Mr Franklin Blake or to me.

16 June.—Rose late, after a dreadful night; the vengeance of yesterday's opium, pursuing me through a series of frightful dreams. At one time, I was whirling through empty space with the phantoms of the dead, friends and enemies together. At another, the one beloved face which I shall never see again, rose at my bedside, hideously phosphorescent in the black darkness, and glared and grinned at me. A slight return of the old pain, at the usual time in the early morning, was welcome as a change. It dispelled the visions—and it was bearable because it did that.

My bad night made it late in the morning, before I could get to Mr Franklin Blake. I found him stretched on the sofa, breakfasting on brandy and soda-water, and a dry biscuit.

'I am beginning, as well as you could possibly wish,' he said. 'A miserable, restless night; and a total failure of appetite this morning. Exactly what happened last year, when I gave up my cigars. The sooner I am ready for my second dose of laudanum, the better I shall be pleased.'

'You shall have it on the earliest possible day,' I answered. 'In the meantime, we must be as careful of your health as we can. If we allow you to become exhausted, we shall fail in that way. You must get an appetite for your dinner. In other words, you must get a ride or a walk this morning, in the fresh air.'

'I will ride, if they can find me a horse here. By-the-by, I wrote to Mr Bruff, yesterday. Have you written to Miss Verinder?

'Yes—by last night's post.'

'Very good. We shall have some news worth hearing, to tell each other to-morrow. Don't go yet! I have a word to say to you. You appeared to think, yesterday, that our experiment with the opium was not likely to be viewed very favourably by some of my friends. You were quite right. I call old Gabriel Betteredge one of my friends; and you will be amused to hear that he protested strongly when I saw him yesterday. "You have done a wonderful number of foolish things in the course of your life, Mr Franklin; but this tops them all!" There is Betteredge's opinion! You will make allowance for his prejudices, I am sure, if you and he happen to meet?'

I left Mr Blake, to go my rounds among my patients; feeling the better and the happier even for the short interview that I had had with him.

What is the secret of the attraction that there is for me in this man? Does it only mean that I feel the contrast between the frankly kind manner in which he has allowed me to become acquainted with him, and the merciless dislike and distrust with which I am met by other people? Or is there really something in him which answers to the yearning that I have for a little human sympathy—the yearning, which has survived the solitude and persecution of many years; which seems to grow keener and keener, as the time comes nearer and nearer when I shall endure and feel no more? How useless to ask these questions! Mr Blake has given me a new interest in life. Let that be enough, without seeking to know what the new interest is.

17 June.—Before breakfast, this morning, Mr Candy informed me that he was going away for a fortnight, on a visit to a friend in the south of England. He gave me as many special directions, poor fellow, about the patients, as if he still had the large practice which he possessed before he was taken ill. The practice is worth little enough now! Other doctors have superseded *him*; and nobody who can help it will employ *me*.

It is perhaps fortunate that he is to be away just at this time. He would have been mortified if I had not informed him of the experiment which I am going to try with Mr Blake. And I hardly know what undesirable results might not have happened, if I had taken him into my confidence. Better as it is. Unquestionably, better as it is.

The post brought me Miss Verinder's answer, after Mr Candy had left the house.

A charming letter! It gives me the highest opinion of her. There is no attempt to conceal the interest that she feels in our proceedings. She tells me, in the prettiest manner, that my letter has satisfied her of Mr Blake's innocence, without the slightest need (so far as she is concerned) of putting my assertion to the proof. She even upbraids herself—most undeservedly, poor thing!—for not having divined at the time what the true solution of the mystery might really be. The motive underlying all this, proceeds evidently from something more than a generous eagerness to make atonement for a wrong which she has innocently inflicted on another person. It is plain that she has loved him, throughout the estrangement between them. In more than one place the rapture of discovering that he has deserved to be loved, breaks its way innocently through the stoutest formalities of pen and ink, and even defies the stronger restraint still of writing to a stranger. Is it possible (I ask myself, in reading this delightful letter) that I, of all men in the world, am chosen to be the means of bringing these two young people together again? My own happiness has been trampled under foot; my own love has been torn from me. Shall I live to see a happiness of others, which is of my making—a love renewed, which is of my bringing back? O merciful Death! let me see it before your arms enfold me, before your voice whispers to me, 'Rest at last!'

There are two requests contained in the letter. One of them prevents me from showing it to Mr Franklin Blake. I am authorized to tell him that Miss Verinder willingly consents to place her house at our disposal; and, that said, I am desired to add no more.

So far, it is easy to comply with her wishes. But the second request embarrasses me seriously.

Not content with having written to Mr Betteredge, instructing him to carry out whatever directions I may have to give, Miss Verinder asks leave to assist me, by personally superintending the restoration of her own sitting-room. She only waits a word of reply from me, to make the journey to Yorkshire, and to be present as one of the witnesses on the night when the opium is tried for the second time.

Here, again, there is a motive under the surface; and, here again, I fancy that I can find it out.

What she has forbidden me to tell Mr Franklin Blake, she is (as I interpret it) eager to tell him with her own lips, *before* he is put to the test which is to vindicate his character in the eyes of other people. I understand and admire this generous anxiety to acquit him, without waiting until his innocence may, or may not, be proved. It is the atonement that she is longing to make, poor girl, after having innocently and inevitably wronged him. But the thing cannot be done. I have no sort of doubt that the agitation which a meeting between them would produce on both sides—reviving dormant feelings, appealing to old memories, awakening new hopes—would, in their effect on the mind of Mr Blake, be almost certainly fatal to the success of our experiment. It is hard enough, as things are, to reproduce in him the conditions as they existed, or nearly as they existed, last year. With new interests and new emotions to agitate him, the attempt would be simply useless.

And yet, knowing this, I cannot find it in my heart to disappoint her. I must try if I can discover some new arrangement, before post-time, which will allow me to say Yes to Miss Verinder, without damage to the service which I have bound myself to tender to Mr Franklin Blake.

Two o'clock.—I have just returned from my round of medical visits; having begun, of course, by calling at the hotel.

Mr Blake's report of the night is the same as before. He has had some intervals of broken sleep, and no more. But he feels it less to-day, having slept after yesterday's dinner. This after-dinner sleep is the result, no doubt, of the ride which I advised him to take. I fear I shall have to curtail his restorative exercise in the fresh air. He must not be too well; he must not be too ill. It is a case (as a sailor would say) of very fine steering.

He has not heard yet from Mr Bruff. I found him eager to know if I had received any answer from Miss Verinder.

I told him exactly what I was permitted to tell, and no more. It was quite needless to invent excuses for not showing him the letter. He told me bitterly enough, poor fellow, that he understood the delicacy which disinclined me to produce it. 'She consents, of course, as a matter of common courtesy and common justice,' he said. 'But she keeps her own opinion of me, and waits to see the result.' I was sorely tempted to hint that he was now wronging her as she had wronged him. On reflection, I shrank from forestalling her in the double luxury of surprising and forgiving him.

My visit was a very short one. After the experience of the other night, I have been compelled once more to give up my dose of opium. As a necessary result, the agony of the disease that is in me has got the upper hand again. I felt the attack coming on, and left abruptly, so as not to alarm or distress him. It only lasted a quarter of an hour this time, and it left me strength enough to go on with my work.

Five o'clock —I have written my reply to Miss Verinder.

The arrangement I have proposed reconciles the interests on both sides, if she will only consent to it. After first stating the objections that there are to a meeting between Mr Blake and herself, before the experiment is tried, I have suggested that she should so time her journey as to arrive at the house privately, on the evening when we make the attempt. Travelling by the afternoon train from London, she would delay her arrival until nine o'clock. At that hour, I have undertaken to see Mr Blake safely into his bedchamber; and so to leave Miss Verinder free to occupy her own rooms until the time comes for administering the laudanum. When that has been done, there can be no objection to her watching the result, with the rest of us. On the next morning, she shall show Mr Blake (if she likes) her correspondence with me, and shall satisfy him in that way that he was acquitted in her estimation, before the question of his innocence was put to the proof.

In that sense, I have written to her. This is all that I can do to-day. To-morrow I must see Mr Betteredge, and give the necessary directions for re-opening the house.

18 June.—Late again, in calling on Mr Franklin Blake. More of that horrible pain in the early morning; followed, this time, by complete prostration, for some hours. I foresee, in spite of the penalties which it exacts from me, that I shall have to return to the opium for the hundredth time. If I had only myself to think of, I should prefer the sharp pains to the frightful dreams. But the physical suffering exhausts me. If I let myself sink, it may end in my becoming useless to Mr Blake at the time when he wants me most.

It was nearly one o'clock before I could get to the hotel to-day. The visit, even in my shattered condition, proved to be a most amusing one—thanks entirely to the presence on the scene of Gabriel Betteredge.

I found him in the room, when I went in. He withdrew to the window and looked out, while I put my first customary question to my patient. Mr Blake had slept badly again, and he felt the loss of rest this morning more than he had felt it yet.

I asked next if he had heard from Mr Bruff.

A letter had reached him that morning. Mr Bruff expressed the strongest disapproval of the course which his friend and client was taking under my advice. It was mischievous—for it excited hopes that might never be realized. It was quite unintelligible to *his* mind, except that it looked like a piece of trickery, akin to the trickery of mesmerism, clairvoyance, and the like. It unsettled Miss Verinder's house, and it would end in unsettling Miss Verinder herself. He had put the case (without mentioning names) to an eminent physician; and the eminent physician had smiled, had shaken his head, and had said—nothing. On these grounds, Mr Bruff entered his protest, and left it there.

My next inquiry related to the subject of the Diamond. Had the lawyer produced any evidence to prove that the jewel was in London?

No, the lawyer had simply declined to discuss the question. He was himself satisfied that the Moonstone had been pledged to Mr Luker. His eminent absent friend, Mr Murthwaite (whose consummate knowledge of the Indian character no one could deny), was satisfied also. Under these circumstances, and with the many demands already made on him, he must decline entering into any disputes on the subject of evidence. Time would show; and Mr Bruff was willing to wait for time.

It was quite plain—even if Mr Blake had not made it plainer still by reporting the substance of the letter, instead of reading what was actually written—that distrust of *me* was at the bottom of all this. Having myself foreseen that result, I was neither mortified nor surprised. I asked Mr Blake if his friend's protest had shaken him. He answered emphatically, that it had not produced the slightest effect on his mind. I was free after that to dismiss Mr Bruff from consideration—and I did dismiss him accordingly.

A pause in the talk between us, followed—and Gabriel Betteredge came out from his retirement at the window.

'Can you favour me with your attention, sir?' he inquired, addressing himself to me.

'I am quite at your service,' I answered.

Betteredge took a chair and seated himself at the table. He produced a huge old-fashioned leather pocket-book, with a pencil of dimensions to match. Having put on his spectacles, he opened the pocket-book, at a blank page, and addressed himself to me once more.

'I have lived,' said Betteredge, looking at me sternly, 'nigh on fifty years in the service of my late lady. I was page-boy before that, in the service of the old lord, her father. I am now somewhere between seventy and eighty years of age—never mind exactly where! I am reckoned to have got as pretty a knowledge and experience of the world as most men. And what does it all end in? It ends, Mr Ezra Jennings, in a conjuring trick being performed on Mr Franklin Blake, by a doctor's assistant with a bottle of laudanum—and by the living jingo, I'm appointed, in my old age, to be conjuror's boy!'

Mr Blake burst out laughing. I attempted to speak. Betteredge held up his hand, in token that he had not done yet.

'Not a word, Mr Jennings!' he said. 'It don't want a word, sir, from you. I have got my principles, thank God. If an order comes to me, which is own brother to an order come from Bedlam, it don't matter. So long as I get it from my master or mistress, as the case may be, I obey it. I may have my own opinion, which is also, you will please to remember, the opinion of Mr Bruff—the Great Mr Bruff!' said Betteredge, raising his voice, and shaking his head at me solemnly. 'It don't matter; I withdraw my opinion, for all that. My young lady says, "Do it." And I say, "Miss, it shall be done." Here I am, with my book and my pencil—the latter not pointed so well as I could wish, but when Christians take leave of their senses, who is to expect that pencils will keep their points? Give me your orders, Mr Jennings. I'll have them in writing, sir. I'm determined not to be behind 'em, or before 'em, by so much as a hair's-breadth. I'm a blind agent—that's what I am. A blind agent!' repeated Betteredge, with infinite relish of his own description of himself.

'I am very sorry,' I began, 'that you and I don't agree—'

'Don't bring *me*, into it!' interposed Betteredge. 'This is not a matter of agreement, it's a matter of obedience. Issue your directions, sir—issue your directions!'

Mr Blake made me a sign to take him at his word. I 'issued my directions' as plainly and as gravely as I could.

'I wish certain parts of the house to be re-opened,' I said, 'and to be furnished, exactly as they were furnished at this time last year.'

Betteredge gave his imperfectly-pointed pencil a preliminary lick with his tongue. 'Name the parts, Mr Jennings!' he said loftily.

First, the inner hall, leading to the chief staircase.'

' "First, the inner hall," ' Betteredge wrote. 'Impossible to furnish that, sir, as it was furnished last year—to begin with.'

'Why?'

'Because there was a stuffed buzzard, Mr Jennings, in the hall last year. When the family left, the buzzard was put away with the other things. When the buzzard was put away—he burst.'

'We will except the buzzard then.'

Betteredge took a note of the exception. ' "The inner hall to be furnished again, as furnished last year. A burst buzzard alone excepted." Please to go on, Mr Jennings.'

'The carpet to be laid down on the stairs, as before.'

' "The carpet to be laid down on the stairs, as before." Sorry to disappoint you, sir. But that can't be done either.'

'Why not?'

'Because the man who laid that carpet down, is dead, Mr Jennings—and the like of him for reconciling together a carpet and a corner, is not to be found in all England, look where you may.'

'Very well. We must try the next best man in England.'

Betteredge took another note; and I went on issuing my directions.

'Miss Verinder's sitting-room to be restored exactly to what it was last year. Also, the corridor leading from the sitting-room to the first landing. Also, the second corridor, leading from the second landing to the best bedrooms. Also, the bedroom occupied last June by Mr Franklin Blake.'

Betteredge's blunt pencil followed me conscientiously, word by word. 'Go on, sir,' he said, with sardonic gravity. 'There's a deal of writing left in the point of this pencil yet.'

I told him that I had no more directions to give. 'Sir,' said Betteredge, 'in that case, I have a point or two to put on my own behalf.' He opened the pocket-book at a new page, and gave the inexhaustible pencil another preliminary lick.

'I wish to know,' he began, 'whether I may, or may not, wash my hands—'

'You may decidedly,' said Mr Blake. 'I'll ring for the waiter.'

'—of certain responsibilities,' pursued Betteredge, impenetrably declining to see anybody in the room but himself and me.

'As to Miss Verinder's sitting-room, to begin with. When we took up the carpet last year, Mr Jennings, we found a surprising quantity of pins. Am I responsible for putting back the pins?

'Certainly not.'

Betteredge made a note of that concession, on the spot.

'As to the first corridor next,' he resumed. 'When we moved the ornaments in that part, we moved a statue of a fat naked child—profanely described in the catalogue of the house as "Cupid, god of Love." He had two wings last year, in the fleshy part of his shoulders. My eye being off him, for the moment, he lost one of them. Am I responsible for Cupid's wing?'

I made another concession, and Betteredge made another note.

'As to the second corridor,' he went on. 'There having been nothing in it, last year, but the doors of the rooms (to every one of which I can swear, if necessary), my mind is easy, I admit, respecting that part of the house only. But, as to Mr Franklin's bedroom (if *that* is to be put back to what it was before), I want to know who is responsible for keeping it in a perpetual state of litter, no matter how often it may be set right—his trousers here, his towels there, and his French novels everywhere. I say, who is responsible for untidying the tidiness of Mr Franklin's room, him or me?'

Mr Blake declared that he would assume the whole responsibility with the greatest pleasure. Betteredge obstinately declined to listen to any solution of the difficulty, without first referring it to my sanction and approval. I accepted Mr Blake's proposal; and Betteredge made a last entry in the pocket-book to that effect.

'Look in when you like, Mr Jennings, beginning from to-morrow,' he said, getting on his legs. 'You will find me at work, with the necessary persons to assist me. I respectfully beg to thank you, sir, for overlooking the case of the stuffed buzzard, and the other case of the Cupid's wing—as also for permitting me to wash my hands of all responsibility in respect of the pins on the carpet, and the litter in Mr Franklin's room. Speaking as a servant, I am deeply indebted to you. Speaking as a man, I consider you to be a person whose head is full of maggots, and I take up my testimony against your experiment as a delusion and a snare. Don't be afraid, on that account, of my feelings as a man getting in the way of my duty as a servant! You shall be obeyed. The maggots notwithstanding, sir, you shall be obeyed. If it ends in your setting the house on fire, Damme if I send for the engines, unless you ring the bell and order them first!'

With that farewell assurance, he made me a bow, and walked out of the room.

'Do you think we can depend on him?' I asked.

'Implicitly,' answered Mr Blake. 'When we go to the house, we shall find nothing neglected, and nothing forgotten.'

19 June.—Another protest against our contemplated proceedings! From a lady this time.

The morning's post brought me two letters. One, from Miss Verinder, consenting, in the kindest manner, to the arrangement that I have proposed. The other from the lady under whose care she is living—one Mrs Merridew.

Mrs Merridew presents her compliments, and does not pretend to understand the subject on which I have been corresponding with Miss Verinder, in its scientific bearings. Viewed in its social bearings, however, she feels free to pronounce an opinion. I am probably, Mrs Merridew thinks, not aware that Miss Verinder is barely nineteen years of age. To allow a young lady, at her time of life, to be present (without a 'chaperone') in a house full of men among whom a medical experiment is being carried on, is an outrage on propriety which Mrs Merridew cannot possibly permit. If the matter is allowed to proceed, she will feel it to be her duty—at a serious sacrifice of her own personal convenience—to accompany Miss Verinder to Yorkshire. Under these circumstances, she ventures to request that I will kindly reconsider the subject; seeing that Miss Verinder declines to be guided by any opinion but mine. Her presence cannot possibly be necessary; and a word from me, to that effect, would relieve both Mrs Merridew and myself of a very unpleasant responsibility.

Translated from polite commonplace, into plain English, the meaning of this is, as I take it, that Mrs Merridew stands in mortal fear of the opinion of the world. She has unfortunately appealed to the very last man in existence who has any reason to regard that opinion with respect. I won't disappoint Miss Verinder; and I won't delay a reconciliation between two young people who love each other, and who have been parted too long already. Translated from plain English into polite commonplace, this means that Mr Jennings presents his compliments to Mrs Merridew, and regrets that he cannot feel justified in interfering any farther in the matter.

Mr Blake's report of himself, this morning, was the same as before. We determined not to disturb Betteredge by overlooking him at the house to-day. To-morrow will be time enough for our first visit of inspection.

20 June.—Mr Blake is beginning to feel his continued restlessness at night. The sooner the rooms are refurnished, now, the better.

On our way to the house, this morning, he consulted me, with some nervous impatience and irresolution, about a letter (forwarded to him from London) which he had received from Sergeant Cuff.

The Sergeant writes from Ireland. He acknowledges the receipt (through his house-keeper) of a card and message which Mr Blake left at his residence near Dorking, and announces his return to England as likely to take place in a week or less. In the meantime, he requests to be favoured with Mr Blake's reasons for wishing to speak to him (as stated in the message) on the subject of the Moonstone. If Mr Blake can convict him of having made any serious mistake, in the course of his last year's inquiry concerning the Diamond, he will consider it a duty (after the liberal manner in which he was treated by the late Lady Verinder) to place himself at that gentleman's disposal. If not, he begs permission to remain in his retirement, surrounded by the peaceful floricultural attractions of a country life.

After reading the letter, I had no hesitation in advising Mr Blake to inform Sergeant Cuff, in reply, of all that had happened since the inquiry was suspended last year, and to leave him to draw his own conclusions from the plain facts.

On second thoughts, I also suggested inviting the Sergeant to be present at the experiment, in the event of his returning to England in time to join us. He would be a valuable witness to have, in any case; and, if I proved to be wrong in believing the Diamond to be hidden in Mr Blake's room, his advice might be of great importance, at a future stage of the proceedings over which I could exercise no control. This last consideration appeared to decide Mr Blake. He promised to follow my advice.

The sound of the hammer informed us that the work of refurnishing was in full progress, as we entered the drive that led to the house.

Betteredge, attired for the occasion in a fisherman's red cap, and an apron of green baize, met us in the outer hall. The moment he saw me, he pulled out the pocket-book and pencil, and obstinately insisted on taking notes of everything that I said to him. Look where we might, we found, as Mr Blake had foretold, that the work was advancing as rapidly and as intelligently as it was possible to desire. But there was still much to be done in the inner hall, and in Miss Verinder's room. It seemed doubtful whether the house would be ready for us before the end of the week.

Having congratulated Betteredge on the progress that he had made (he persisted in taking notes every time I opened my lips; declining, at the same time, to pay the slightest attention to anything said by Mr Blake); and having promised to return for a second visit of inspection in a day or two, we prepared to leave the house, going out by the back way. Before we were clear of the passages downstairs, I was stopped by Betteredge, just as I was passing the door which led into his own room.

'Could I say two words to you in private?' he asked, in a mysterious whisper.

I consented of course. Mr Blake walked on to wait for me in the garden, while I accompanied Betteredge into his room. I fully anticipated a demand for certain new concessions, following the precedent already established in the cases of the stuffed buzzard, and the Cupid's wing. To my great surprise, Betteredge laid his hand confidentially on my arm, and put this extraordinary question to me:

'Mr Jennings, do you happen to be acquainted with *Robinson Crusoe?*'

I answered that I had read *Robinson Crusoe* when I was a child.

'Not since then?' inquired Betteredge.

'Not since then.'

He fell back a few steps, and looked at me with an expression of compassionate curiosity, tempered by superstitious awe.

'He has not read *Robinson Crusoe* since he was a child,' said Betteredge, speaking to himself—not to me. 'Let's try how *Robinson Crusoe* strikes him now!'

He unlocked a cupboard in a corner, and produced a dirty and dog's-eared book, which exhaled a strong odour of stale tobacco as he turned over the leaves. Having found a passage of which he was apparently in search, he requested me to join him in the corner; still mysteriously confidential, and still speaking under his breath.

'In respect to this hocus-pocus of yours, sir, with the laudanum and Mr Franklin Blake,' he began. 'While the workpeople are in the house, my duty as a servant gets the better of my feelings as a man. When the workpeople are gone, my feelings as a man get the better of my duty as a servant. Very good. Last night, Mr Jennings, it was borne in powerfully on my mind that this new medical enterprise of yours would end badly. If I had yielded to that secret Dictate, I should have put all the furniture away again with my own hand, and have warned the workmen off the premises when they came the next morning.'

'I am glad to find, from what I have seen upstairs,' I said, 'that you resisted the secret Dictate.'

'Resisted isn't the word,' answered Betteredge. 'Wrostled is the word. I wrostled, sir, between the silent orders in my bosom pulling me one way, and the written orders in my pocket-book pushing me the other, until (saving your presence) I was in a cold sweat. In that dreadful perturbation of mind and laxity of body, to what remedy did I apply? To the remedy, sir, which has never failed me yet for the last thirty years and more—to This Book!'

He hit the book a sounding blow with his open hand, and struck out of it a stronger smell of stale tobacco than ever.

'What did I find here,' pursued Betteredge, 'at the first page I opened? This awful bit, sir, page one hundred and seventy-eight, as follows:—'Upon these, and many like Reflections, I afterwards made it a certain rule with me, That whenever I found those secret Hints or Pressings of my Mind, to doing, or not doing any Thing that presented; or to going this Way, or that Way, I never failed to obey the secret Dictate.'—As I live by bread, Mr Jennings, those were the first words that met my eye, exactly at the time when I myself was setting the secret Dictate at defiance! You don't see anything at all out of the common in that, do you, sir?'

'I see a coincidence—nothing more.'

'You don't feel at all shaken, Mr Jennings, in respect to this medical enterprise of yours?'

'Not the least in the world.'

Betteredge stared hard at me, in dead silence. He closed the book with great deliberation; he locked it up again in the cupboard with extraordinary care; he wheeled round, and stared hard at me once more. Then he spoke.

'Sir,' he said gravely, 'there are great allowances to be made for a man who has not read *Robinson Crusoe*, since he was a child. I wish you good morning.'

He opened his door with a low bow, and left me at liberty to find my own way into the garden. I met Mr Blake returning to the house.

'You needn't tell me what has happened,' he said. 'Betteredge has played his last card: he has made another prophetic discovery in *Robinson Crusoe*. Have you humoured his favourite delusion? No? You have let him see that you don't believe in *Robinson Crusoe*? Mr Jennings! you have fallen to the lowest possible place in Betteredge's estimation. Say what you like, and do what you like, for the future. You will find that he won't waste another word on you now.'

21 June.—A short entry must suffice in my journal to-day.

Mr Blake has had the worst night that he has passed yet. I have been obliged, greatly against my will, to prescribe for him. Men of his sensitive organization are fortunately quick in feeling the effect of remedial measures. Otherwise, I should be inclined to fear that he will be totally unfit for the experiment when the time comes to try it.

As for myself, after some little remission of my pains for the last two days, I had an attack this morning, of which I shall say nothing but that it has decided me to return to the opium. I shall close this book, and take my full dose—five hundred drops.

22 June.—Our prospects look better to-day. Mr Blake's nervous suffering is greatly allayed. He slept a little last night. *My* night, thanks to the opium, was the night of a man who is stunned. I can't say that I woke this morning; the fitter expression would be, that I recovered my senses.

We drove to the house to see if the refurnishing was done. It will be completed to-morrow—Saturday. As Mr Blake foretold, Betteredge raised no further obstacles. From first to last, he was ominously polite, and ominously silent.

My medical enterprise (as Betteredge calls it) must now, inevitably, be delayed until Monday next. To-morrow evening, the workmen will be late in the house. On the next day, the established Sunday tyranny which is one of the institutions of this free country, so times the trains as to make it impossible to ask anybody to travel to us from London. Until Monday comes, there is nothing to be done but to watch Mr Blake carefully, and to keep him, if possible, in the same state in which I find him to-day.

In the meanwhile, I have prevailed on him to write to Mr Bruff, making a point of it that he shall be present as one of the witnesses. I especially choose the lawyer, because he is strongly prejudiced against us. If we convince *him*, we place our victory beyond the possibility of dispute.

Mr Blake has also written to Sergeant Cuff; and I have sent a line to Miss Verinder. With these, and with old Betteredge (who is really a person of importance in the family) we shall have witnesses enough for the purpose—without including Mrs Merridew, if Mrs Merridew persists in sacrificing herself to the opinion of the world.

23 June.—The vengeance of the opium overtook me again last night. No matter; I must go on with it now till Monday is past and gone.

Mr Blake is not so well again to-day. At two this morning, he confesses that he opened the drawer in which his cigars are put away. He only succeeded in locking it up again by a violent effort. His next proceeding, in case of temptation, was to throw the key out of window. The waiter brought it in this morning, discovered at the bottom of an empty cistern—such is Fate! I have taken possession of the key, until Tuesday next.

24 June.—Mr Blake and I took a long drive in an open carriage. We both felt beneficially the blessed influence of the soft summer air. I dined with him at the hotel. To my great relief—for I found him in an over-wrought, over-excited state, this morning—he had two hours' sound sleep on the sofa after dinner. If he has another bad night, now—I am not afraid of the consequences.

25 June, Monday.—The day of the experiment! It is five o'clock in the afternoon. We have just arrived at the house.

The first and foremost question, is the question of Mr Blake's health.

So far as it is possible for me to judge, he promises (physically speaking) to be quite as susceptible to the action of the opium to-night, as he was at this time last year. He is, this afternoon, in a state of nervous sensitiveness which just stops short of nervous irritation. He changes colour readily; his hand is not quite steady; and he starts at chance noises, and at unexpected appearances of persons and things.

These results have all been produced by deprivation of sleep, which is in its turn the nervous consequence of a sudden cessation in the habit of smoking, after that habit has been carried to an extreme. Here are the same causes at work again, which operated last year; and here are, apparently, the same effects. Will the parallel still hold good, when the final test has been tried? The events of the night must decide.

While I write these lines, Mr Blake is amusing himself at the billiard table in the inner hall, practising different strokes in the game, as he was accustomed to practise them when he was a guest in this house in June last. I have brought my journal here, partly with a view to occupying the idle hours which I am sure to have on my hands between this and to-morrow morning; partly in the hope that something may happen which it may be worth my while to place on record at the time.

Have I omitted anything, thus far? A glance at yesterday's entry shows me that I have forgotten to note the arrival of the morning's post. Let me set this right, before I close these leaves for the present, and join Mr Blake.

I received a few lines then, yesterday, from Miss Verinder. She has arranged to travel by the afternoon train, as I recommended. Mrs Merridew has insisted on accompanying her. The note hints that the old lady's generally excellent temper is a little ruffled, and requests all due indulgence for her, in consideration of her age and her habits. I will endeavour, in my relations with Mrs Merridew, to emulate the moderation which Betteredge displays in his relations with me. He received us to-day, portentously arrayed in his best black suit, and his stiffest white cravat. Whenever he looks my way, he remembers that I have not read *Robinson Crusoe* since I was a child, and he respectfully pities me.

Yesterday, also, Mr Blake had the lawyer's answer. Mr Bruff accepts the invitation— under protest. It is, he thinks, clearly necessary that a gentleman possessed of the average allowance of common sense, should accompany Miss Verinder to the scene of, what he will venture to call, the proposed exhibition. For want of a better escort, Mr Bruff himself will be that gentleman.—So here is poor Miss Verinder provided with two 'chaperons.' It is a relief to think that the opinion of the world must surely be satisfied with this!

Nothing has been heard of Sergeant Cuff. He is no doubt still in Ireland. We must not expect to see him to-night.

Betteredge has just come in, to say that Mr Blake has asked for me. I must lay down my pen for the present.

*   *   *   *   *

Seven o'clock.—We have been all over the refurnished rooms and staircases again; and we have had a pleasant stroll in the shrubbery which was Mr Blake's favourite walk when he was here last. In this way, I hope to revive the old impressions of places and things as vividly as possible in his mind.

We are now going to dine, exactly at the hour at which the birthday dinner was given last year. My object, of course, is a purely medical one in this case. The laudanum must find the process of digestion, as nearly as may be, where the laudanum found it last year.

At a reasonable time after dinner, I propose to lead the conversation back again—as inartificially as I can—to the subject of the Diamond, and of the Indian conspiracy to steal it. When I have filled his mind with these topics, I shall have done all that it is in my power to do, before the time comes for giving him the second dose.

* * * * *

Half-past eight.—I have only this moment found an opportunity of attending to the most important duty of all; the duty of looking in the family medicine chest, for the laudanum which Mr Candy used last year.

Ten minutes since, I caught Betteredge at an unoccupied moment, and told him what I wanted. Without a word of objection, without so much as an attempt to produce his pocket-book, he led the way (making allowances for me at every step) to the store-room in which the medicine chest is kept.

I discovered the bottle, carefully guarded by a glass stopper tied over with leather. The preparation which it contained was, as I had anticipated, the common Tincture of Opium. Finding the bottle still well filled, I have resolved to use it, in preference to employing either of the two preparations with which I had taken care to provide myself, in case of emergency.

The question of the quantity which I am to administer, presents certain difficulties. I have thought it over, and have decided on increasing the dose.

My notes inform me that Mr Candy only administered twenty-five minims. This is a small dose to have produced the results which followed—even in the case of a person so sensitive as Mr Blake. I think it highly probable that Mr Candy gave more than he supposed himself to have given—knowing, as I do, that he has a keen relish of the pleasures of the table, and that he measured out the laudanum on the birthday, after dinner. In any case, I shall run the risk of enlarging the dose to forty minims. On this occasion, Mr Blake knows beforehand that he is going to take the laudanum—which is equivalent, physiologically speaking, to his having (unconsciously to himself) a certain capacity in him to resist the effects. If my view is right, a larger quantity is therefore imperatively required, this time, to repeat the results which the smaller quantity produced, last year.

* * * * *

Ten o'clock.—The witnesses, or the company (which shall I call them?) reached the house an hour since.

A little before nine o'clock, I prevailed on Mr Blake to accompany me to his bedroom; stating, as a reason, that I wished him to look round it, for the last time, in order to make quite sure that nothing had been forgotten in the refurnishing of the room. I had previously arranged with Betteredge, that the bedchamber prepared for Mr Bruff should be the next room to Mr Blake's, and that I should be informed of the lawyer's arrival by a knock at the door. Five minutes after the clock in the hall had struck nine, I heard the knock; and, going out immediately, met Mr Bruff in the corridor.

My personal appearance (as usual) told against me. Mr Bruff's distrust looked at me plainly enough out of Mr Bruff's eyes. Being well used to producing this effect on strangers, I did not hesitate a moment in saying what I wanted to say, before the lawyer found his way into Mr Blake's room.

'You have travelled here, I believe, in company with Mrs Merridew and Miss Verinder?' I said.

'Yes,' answered Mr Bruff, as drily as might be.

'Miss Verinder has probably told you, that I wish her presence in the house (and Mrs Merridew's presence of course), to be kept a secret from Mr Blake, until my experiment on him has been tried first?'

'I know that I am to hold my tongue, sir!' said Mr Bruff, impatiently. 'Being habitually silent on the subject of human folly, I am all the readier to keep my lips closed on this occasion. Does that satisfy you?'

I bowed, and left Betteredge to show him to his room. Betteredge gave me one look at parting, which said, as if in so many words, 'You have caught a Tartar, Mr Jennings—and the name of him is Bruff.'

It was next necessary to get the meeting over with the two ladies. I descended the stairs—a little nervously, I confess—on my way to Miss Verinder's sitting-room.

The gardener's wife (charged with looking after the accommodation of the ladies) met me in the first-floor corridor. This excellent woman treats me with an excessive civility which is plainly the offspring of downright terror. She stares, trembles, and curtseys, whenever I speak to her. On my asking for Miss Verinder, she stared, trembled, and would no doubt have curtseyed next, if Miss Verinder herself had not cut that ceremony short, by suddenly opening her sitting-room door.

'Is that Mr Jennings?' she asked.

Before I could answer, she came out eagerly to speak to me in the corridor. We met under the light of a lamp on a bracket. At the first sight of me, Miss Verinder stopped, and hesitated. She recovered herself instantly, coloured for a moment—and then, with a charming frankness, offered me her hand.

'I can't treat you like a stranger, Mr Jennings,' she said. 'Oh, if you only knew how happy your letters have made me!'

She looked at my ugly wrinkled face, with a bright gratitude so new to me in *my* experience of my fellow-creatures, that I was at a loss how to answer her. Nothing had prepared me for her kindness and her beauty. The misery of many years has not hardened my heart, thank God. I was as awkward and as shy with her, as if I had been a lad in my teens.

'Where is he now?' she asked, giving free expression to her one dominant interest—the interest in Mr Blake. 'What is he doing? Has he spoken of me? Is he in good spirits? How does he bear the sight of the house, after what happened in it last year? When are you going to give him the laudanum? May I see you pour it out? I am so interested; I am so excited—I have ten thousand things to say to you, and they all crowd together so that I don't know what to say first. Do you wonder at the interest I take in this?'

'No,' I said. 'Venture to think that I thoroughly understand it.'

She was far above the paltry affectation of being confused. She answered me as she might have answered a brother or a father.

'You have relieved me of indescribable wretchedness; you have given me a new life. How can I be ungrateful enough to have any concealments from *you*? I love him,' she said simply, 'I have loved him from first to last—even when I was wronging him in my own thoughts; even when I was saying the hardest and the cruellest words to him. Is there any excuse for me, in that? I hope there is—I am afraid it is the only excuse I have. When to-morrow comes, and he knows that I am in the house, do you think—?'

She stopped again, and looked at me very earnestly.

'When to-morrow comes,' I said, 'I think you have only to tell him what you have just told me.'

Her face brightened; she came a step nearer to me. Her fingers trifled nervously with a flower which I had picked in the garden, and which I had put into the button-hole of my coat.

'You have seen a great deal of him lately,' she said. 'Have you, really and truly, seen *that?*'

'Really and truly,' I answered. 'I am quite certain of what will happen to-morrow. I wish I could feel as certain of what will happen to-night.'

At that point in the conversation, we were interrupted by the appearance of Betteredge, with the tea-tray. He gave me another significant look as he passed on into the sitting-room. 'Aye! aye! make your hay while the sun shines. The Tartar's upstairs, Mr Jennings—the Tartar's upstairs!'

We followed him into the room. A little old lady, in a corner, very nicely dressed, and very deeply absorbed over a smart piece of embroidery, dropped her work in her lap, and uttered a faint little scream at the first sight of my gipsy complexion and my piebald hair.

'Mrs Merridew,' said Miss Verinder, 'this is Mr Jennings.'

'I beg Mr Jennings' pardon,' said the old lady, looking at Miss Verinder, and speaking at *me*. 'Railway travelling always makes me nervous. I am endeavouring to quiet my mind by occupying myself as usual. I don't know whether my embroidery is out of place, on this extraordinary occasion. If it interferes with Mr Jennings' medical views, I shall be happy to put it away of course.'

I hastened to sanction the presence of the embroidery, exactly as I had sanctioned the absence of the burst buzzard and the Cupid's wing. Mrs Merridew made an effort—a grateful effort—to look at my hair. No! it was not to be done. Mrs Merridew looked back again at Miss Verinder.

'If Mr Jennings will permit me,' pursued the old lady, 'I should like to ask a favour. Mr Jennings is about to try a scientific experiment to-night. I used to attend scientific experiments when I was a girl at school. They invariably ended in an explosion. If Mr Jennings will be so very kind, I should like to be warned of the explosion this time. With a view to getting it over, if possible, before I go to bed.'

I attempted to assure Mrs Merridew that an explosion was not included in the programme on this occasion.

'No,' said the old lady. 'I am much obliged to Mr Jennings—I am aware that he is only deceiving me for my own good. I prefer plain dealing. I am quite resigned to the explosion—but I *do* want to get it over, if possible, before I go to bed.'

Here the door opened, and Mrs Merridew uttered another little scream. The advent of the explosion? No: only the advent of Betteredge.

'I beg your pardon, Mr Jennings,' said Betteredge, in his most elaborately confidential manner. 'Mr Franklin wishes to know where you are. Being under your orders to deceive him, in respect to the presence of my young lady in the house, I have said I don't know. That, you will please to observe, was a lie. Having one foot already in the grave, sir, the fewer lies you expect me to tell, the more I shall be indebted to you, when my conscience pricks me and my time comes.'

There was not a moment to be wasted on the purely speculative question of Betteredge's conscience. Mr Blake might make his appearance in search of me, unless I went to him at once in his own room. Miss Verinder followed me out into the corridor.

'They seem to be in a conspiracy to persecute you,' she said. 'What does it mean?'

'Only the protest of the world, Miss Verinder—on a very small scale—against anything that is new.'

'What are we to do with Mrs Merridew?'

'Tell her the explosion will take place at nine to-morrow morning.'

'So as to send her to bed?'

'Yes—so as to send her to bed.'

Miss Verinder went back to the sitting-room, and I went upstairs to Mr Blake.

To my surprise, I found him alone; restlessly pacing his room, and a little irritated at being left by himself.

'Where is Mr Bruff?' I asked.

He pointed to the closed door of communication between the two rooms. Mr Bruff had looked in on him, for a moment; had attempted to renew his protest against our proceedings; and had once more failed to produce the smallest impression on Mr Blake. Upon this, the lawyer had taken refuge in a black leather bag, filled to bursting with professional papers. 'The serious business of life,' he admitted, 'was sadly out of place on such an occasion as the present. But the serious business of life must be carried on, for all that. Mr Blake would perhaps kindly make allowance for the old-fashioned habits of a practical man. Time was money—and, as for Mr Jennings, he might depend on it that Mr Bruff would be forthcoming when called upon.' With that apology, the lawyer had gone back to his own room, and had immersed himself obstinately in his black bag.

I thought of Mrs Merridew and her embroidery, and of Betteredge and his conscience. There is a wonderful sameness in the solid side of the English character—just as there is a wonderful sameness in the solid expression of the English face.

'When are you going to give me the laudanum?' asked Mr Blake impatiently.

'You must wait a little longer,' I said. 'I will stay and keep you company till the time comes.'

It was then not ten o'clock. Inquiries which I had made, at various times, of Betteredge and Mr Blake, had led me to the conclusion that the dose of laudanum given by Mr Candy could not possibly have been administered before eleven. I had accordingly determined not to try the second dose until that time.

We talked a little; but both our minds were preoccupied by the coming ordeal. The conversation soon flagged—then dropped altogether. Mr Blake idly turned over the books on his bedroom table. I had taken the precaution of looking at them, when we first entered the room. *The Guardian; The Tatler*; Richardson's *Pamela*; Mackenzie's *Man of Feeling*; Roscoe's *Lorenzo de' Medici*; and Robertson's *Charles the Fifth*—all classical works; all (of course) immeasurably superior to anything produced in later times; and all (from my present point of view) possessing the one great merit of enchaining nobody's interest, and exciting nobody's brain. I left Mr Blake to the composing influence of Standard Literature, and occupied myself in making this entry in my journal.

My watch informs me that it is close on eleven o'clock. I must shut up these leaves once more.

*   *   *   *   *

Two o'clock—The experiment has been tried. With what result, I am now to describe.

At eleven o'clock, I rang the bell for Betteredge, and told Mr Blake that he might at last prepare himself for bed.

I looked out of window at the night. It was mild and rainy resembling, in this respect, the night of the birthday—the twenty-first of June, last year. Without professing to believe in omens, it was at least encouraging to find no direct nervous influences—no stormy or electric perturbations—in the atmosphere. Betteredge joined me at the window, and mysteriously put a little slip of paper into my hand. It contained these lines:

'Mrs Merridew has gone to bed, on the distinct understanding that the explosion is to take place at nine to-morrow morning, and that I am not to stir out of this part of the house until she comes and sets me free. She has no idea that the chief scene of the experiment is my sitting-room—or she would have remained in it for the whole night! I am alone, and very anxious. Pray let me see you measure out the laudanum; I want to have something to do with it, even in the unimportant character of a mere looker-on.—R. V.'

I followed Betteredge out of the room, and told him to remove the medicine-chest into Miss Verinder's sitting-room.

The order appeared to take him completely by surprise. He looked as if he suspected me of some occult medical design on Miss Verinder! 'Might I presume to ask,' he said, 'what my young lady and the medicine-chest have got to do with each other?'

'Stay in the sitting-room, and you will see.'

Betteredge appeared to doubt his own unaided capacity to superintend me effectually, on an occasion when a medicine-chest was included in the proceedings.

'Is there any objection, sir,' he asked, 'to taking Mr Bruff into this part of the business?'

'Quite the contrary! I am now going to ask Mr Bruff to accompany me downstairs.'

Betteredge withdrew to fetch the medicine-chest, without another word. I went back into Mr Blake's room, and knocked at the door of communication. Mr Bruff opened it, with his papers in his hand—immersed in Law; impenetrable to Medicine.

'I am sorry to disturb you,' I said. 'But I am going to prepare the laudanum for Mr Blake; and I must request you to be present, and to see what I do.'

'Yes?' said Mr Bruff, with nine-tenths of his attention riveted on his papers, and with one-tenth unwillingly accorded to me. 'Anything else?'

'I must trouble you to return here with me, and to see me administer the dose.'

'Anything else?'

'One thing more. I must put you to the inconvenience of remaining in Mr Blake's room, and of waiting to see what happens.'

'Oh, very good!' said Mr Bruff. 'My room, or Mr Blake's room—it doesn't matter which; I can go on with my papers anywhere. Unless you object, Mr Jennings, to my importing *that* amount of common sense into the proceedings?'

Before I could answer, Mr Blake addressed himself to the lawyer, speaking from his bed.

'Do you really mean to say that you don't feel any interest in what we are going to do?' he asked. 'Mr Bruff, you have no more imagination than a cow!'

'A cow is a very useful animal, Mr Blake,' said the lawyer. With that reply, he followed me out of the room, still keeping his papers in his hand.

We found Miss Verinder, pale and agitated, restlessly pacing her sitting-room from end to end. At a table in a corner, stood Betteredge, on guard over the medicine-chest. Mr Bruff sat down on the first chair that he could find, and (emulating the usefulness of the cow) plunged back again into his papers on the spot.

Miss Verinder drew me aside, and reverted instantly to her one all-absorbing interest—her interest in Mr Blake.

'How is he now?' she asked. 'Is he nervous? Is he out of temper? Do you think it will succeed? Are you sure it will do no harm?'

'Quite sure. Come, and see me measure it out.'

'One moment! It is past eleven now. How long will it be before anything happens?'

'It is not easy to say. An hour perhaps.'

'I suppose the room must be dark, as it was last year?'

'Certainly.'

'I shall wait in my bedroom—just as I did before. I shall keep the door a little way open. It was a little way open last year. I will watch the sitting-room door; and the moment it moves, I will blow out my light. It all happened in that way, on my birthday night. And it must all happen again in the same way, mustn't it?'

'Are you sure you can control yourself, Miss Verinder?'

'In *his* interests, I can do anything!' she answered fervently.

One look at her face told me that I could trust her. I addressed myself again to Mr Bruff. 'I must trouble you to put your papers aside for a moment,' I said.

'Oh, certainly!' He got up with a start—as if I had disturbed him at a particularly interesting place—and followed me to the medicine-chest. There, deprived of the breathless excitement incidental to the practice of his profession, he looked at Betteredge—and yawned wearily.

Miss Verinder joined me with a glass jug of cold water, which she had taken from a side-table. 'Let me pour out the water,' she whispered. 'I *must* have a hand in it!'

I measured out the forty minims from the bottle, and poured the laudanum into a medicine glass. 'Fill it till it is three parts full,' I said, and handed the glass to Miss Verinder. I then directed Betteredge to lock up the medicine-chest; informing him that I had done with it now. A look of unutterable relief overspread the old servant's countenance. He had evidently suspected me of a medical design on his young lady!

After adding the water as I had directed, Miss Verinder seized a moment—while Betteredge was locking the chest, and while Mr Bruff was looking back at his papers—and slyly kissed the rim of the medicine glass. 'When you give it to him,' said the charming girl, 'give it to him on that side!'

I took the piece of crystal which was to represent the Diamond from my pocket, and gave it to her.

'You must have a hand in this, too,' I said. 'You must put it where you put the Moonstone last year.'

She led the way to the Indian cabinet, and put the mock Diamond into the drawer which the real Diamond had occupied on the birthday night. Mr Bruff witnessed this proceeding, under protest, as he had witnessed everything else. But the strong dramatic interest which the experiment was now assuming, proved (to my great amusement) to be too much for Betteredge's capacity of self-restraint. His hand trembled as he held the candle, and he whispered anxiously, 'Are you sure, miss, it's the right drawer?'

I led the way out again, with the laudanum and water in my hand. At the door, I stopped to address a last word to Miss Verinder.

'Don't be long in putting out the lights,' I said.

'I will put them out at once,' she answered. 'And I will wait in my bedroom, with only one candle alight.'

She closed the sitting-room door behind us. Followed by Mr Bruff and Betteredge, I went back to Mr Blake's room.

We found him moving restlessly from side to side of the bed, and wondering irritably whether he was to have the laudanum that night. In the presence of the two witnesses, I gave him the dose, and shook up his pillows, and told him to lie down again quietly and wait.

His bed, provided with light chintz curtains, was placed, with the head against the wall of the room, so as to leave a good open space on either side of it. On one side, I drew the curtains completely—and in the part of the room thus screened from his view, I placed Mr Bruff and Betteredge, to wait for the result. At the bottom of the bed, I half drew the curtains—and placed my own chair at a little distance, so that I might let him see me or not see me, speak to me or not speak to me, just as the circumstances might direct. Having already been informed that he always slept with a light in the room, I placed one of the two lighted candles on a little table at the head of the bed, where the glare of the light would not strike on his eyes. The other candle I gave to Mr Bruff; the light, in this instance, being subdued by the screen of the chintz curtains. The window was open at the top, so as to ventilate the room. The rain fell softly, the house was quiet. It was twenty minutes past eleven, by my watch, when the preparations were completed, and I took my place on the chair set apart at the bottom of the bed.

Mr Bruff resumed his papers, with every appearance of being as deeply interested in them as ever. But looking towards him now, I saw certain signs and tokens which told me that the Law was beginning to lose its hold on him at last. The suspended interest of the situation in which we were now placed, was slowly asserting its influence even on *his* unimaginative mind. As for Betteredge, consistency of principle and dignity of conduct had become, in his case, mere empty words. He forgot that I was performing a conjuring trick on Mr Franklin Blake; he forgot that I had upset the house from top to bottom; he forgot that I had not read *Robinson Crusoe* since I was a child. 'For the Lord's sake, sir,' he whispered to me, 'tell us when it will begin to work.'

'Not before midnight,' I whispered back. 'Say nothing, and sit still.'

Betteredge dropped to the lowest depth of familiarity with me, without a struggle to save himself. He answered by a wink!

Looking next towards Mr Blake, I found him as restless as ever in his bed; fretfully wondering why the influence of the laudanum had not begun to assert itself yet. To tell him, in his present humour, that the more he fidgeted and wondered, the longer he would delay the result for which we were now waiting, would have been simply useless. The wiser course to take was to dismiss the idea of the opium from his mind, by leading him insensibly to think of something else.

With this view, I encouraged him to talk to me; contriving so to direct the

THE MOONSTONE

conversation, on my side, as to lead it back again to the subject which had engaged us earlier in the evening—the subject of the Diamond. I took care to revert to those portions of the story of the Moonstone, which related to the transport of it from London to Yorkshire; to the risk which Mr Blake had run in removing it from the bank at Frizinghall: and to the unexpected appearance of the Indians at the house, on the evening of the birthday. And I purposely assumed, in referring to these events, to have misunderstood much of what Mr Blake himself had told me a few hours since. In this way, I set him talking on the subject with which it was now vitally important to fill his mind—without allowing him to suspect that I was making him talk for a purpose. Little by little, he became so interested in putting me right that he forgot to fidget in the bed. His mind was far away from the question of the opium, at the all-important time when his eyes first told me that the opium was beginning to lay its hold on his brain.

I looked at my watch. It wanted five minutes to twelve, when the premonitory symptoms of the working of the laudanum first showed themselves to me.

At this time, no unpractised eyes would have detected any change in him. But, as the minutes of the new morning wore away, the swiftly-subtle progress of the influence began to show itself more plainly. The sublime intoxication of opium gleamed in his eyes; the dew of a stealthy perspiration began to glisten on his face. In five minutes more, the talk which he still kept up with me, failed in coherence. He held steadily to the subject of the Diamond; but he ceased to complete his sentences. A little later, the sentences dropped to single words. Then, there was an interval of silence. Then, he sat up in bed. Then, still busy with the subject of the Diamond, he began to talk again—not to me, but to himself. That change told me that the first stage in the experiment was reached. The stimulant influence of the opium had got him.

The time, now, was twenty-three minutes past twelve. The next half-hour, at most, would decide the question of whether he would, or would not, get up from his bed, and leave the room.

In the breathless interest of watching him—in the unutterable triumph of seeing the first result of the experiment declare itself in the manner, and nearly at the time, which I had anticipated—I had utterly forgotten the two companions of my night vigil. Looking towards them now, I saw the Law (as represented by Mr Bruff's papers) lying unheeded on the floor. Mr Bruff himself was looking eagerly through a crevice left in the imperfectly-drawn curtains of the bed. And Betteredge, oblivious of all respect for social distinctions, was peeping over Mr Bruff's shoulder.

They both started back, on finding that I was looking at them, like two boys caught out by their schoolmaster in a fault. I signed to them to take off their boots quietly, as I was taking off mine. If Mr Blake gave us the chance of following him, it was vitally necessary to follow him without noise.

Ten minutes passed—and nothing happened. Then, he suddenly threw the bed-clothes off him. He put one leg out of bed. He waited.

'I wish I had never taken it out of the bank,' he said to himself. 'It was safe in the bank.'

My heart throbbed fast; the pulses at my temples beat furiously. The doubt about the safety of the Diamond was, once more, the dominant impression in his brain! On that one pivot, the whole success of the experiment turned. The prospect thus suddenly

303

opened before me, was too much for my shattered nerves. I was obliged to look away from him—or I should have lost my self-control.

There was another interval of silence.

When I could trust myself to look back at him, he was out of his bed, standing erect at the side of it. The pupils of his eyes were now contracted; his eyeballs gleamed in the light of the candle as he moved his head slowly to and fro. He was thinking; he was doubting—he spoke again.

'How do I know?' he said. 'The Indians may be hidden in the house?'

He stopped, and walked slowly to the other end of the room. He turned—waited—came back to the bed.

'It's not even locked up,' he went on. 'It's in the drawer of her cabinet. And the drawer doesn't lock.'

He sat down on the side of the bed. 'Anybody might take it,' he said.

He rose again restlessly, and reiterated his first words.

'How do I know? The Indians may be hidden in the house.'

He waited again. I drew back behind the half-curtain of the bed. He looked about the room, with a vacant glitter in his eyes. It was a breathless moment. There was a pause of some sort. A pause in the action of the opium? A pause in the action of the brain? Who could tell? Everything depended, now, on what he did next.

He laid himself down again on the bed!

A horrible doubt crossed my mind. Was it possible that the sedative action of the opium was making itself felt already? It was not in my experience that it should do this. But what is experience, where opium is concerned? There are probably no two men in existence on whom the drug acts in exactly the same manner. Was some constitutional peculiarity in him, feeling the influence in some new way? Were we to fail, on the very brink of success?

No! He got up again abruptly. 'How the devil am I to sleep,' he said, 'with *this* on my mind?'

He looked at the light, burning on the table at the head of his bed. After a moment, he took the candle in his hand.

I blew out the second candle, burning behind the closed curtains. I drew back, with Mr Bruff and Betteredge, into the farthest corner by the bed. I signed to them to be silent, as if their lives had depended on it.

We waited—seeing and hearing nothing. We waited, hidden from him by the curtains.

The light which he was holding on the other side of us, moved suddenly. The next moment, he passed us, swift and noiseless, with the candle in his hand.

He opened the bedroom door, and went out.

We followed him along the corridor. We followed him down the stairs. We followed him along the second corridor. He never looked back; he never hesitated.

He opened the sitting-room door, and went in, leaving it open behind him.

The door was hung (like all the other doors in the house) on large old-fashioned hinges. When it was opened, a crevice was opened between the door and the post. I signed to my two companions to look through this, so as to keep them from showing themselves. I placed myself—outside the door also—on the opposite side. A recess in the wall was at my left hand, in which I could instantly hide myself, if he showed any signs of looking back into the corridor.

He advanced to the middle of the room, with the candle still in his hand: he looked about him—but he never looked back.

I saw the door of Miss Verinder's bedroom, standing ajar. She had put out her light. She controlled herself nobly. The dim white outline of her summer dress was all that I could see. Nobody who had not known it beforehand, would have suspected that there was a living creature in the room. She kept back, in the dark: not a word, not a movement escaped her.

It was now ten minutes past one. I heard, through the dead silence, the soft drip of the rain and the tremulous passage of the night air through the trees.

After waiting irresolute, for a minute or more, in the middle of the room, he moved to the corner near the window, where the Indian cabinet stood.

He put his candle on the top of the cabinet. He opened, and shut, one drawer after another, until he came to the drawer in which the mock Diamond was put. He looked into the drawer for a moment. Then, he took the mock Diamond out with his right hand. With the other hand, he took the candle from the top of the cabinet.

He walked back a few steps towards the middle of the room, and stood still again.

Thus far, he had exactly repeated what he had done on the birthday night. Would his next proceeding be the same as the proceeding of last year? Would he leave the room? Would he go back now, as I believed he had gone back then, to his bedchamber? Would he show us what he had done with the Diamond, when he had returned to his own room?

His first action, when he moved once more, proved to be an action which he had *not* performed, when he was under the influence of the opium for the first time. He put the candle down on a table, and wandered on a little towards the farther end of the room. There was a sofa here. He leaned heavily on the back of it, with his left hand—then roused himself, and returned to the middle of the room. I could now see his eyes. They were getting dull and heavy; the glitter in them was fast dying out.

The suspense of the moment proved too much for Miss Verinder's self-control. She advanced a few steps—then stopped again. Mr Bruff and Betteredge looked across the open doorway at me for the first time. The prevision of a coming disappointment was impressing itself on their minds as well as on mine.

Still, so long as he stood where he was, there was hope. We waited, in unutterable expectation, to see what would happen next.

The next event was decisive. He let the mock Diamond drop out of his hand.

It fell on the floor, before the doorway—plainly visible to him, and to every one. He made no effort to pick it up: he looked down at it vacantly, and, as he looked, his head sank on his breast. He staggered—roused himself for an instant—walked back unsteadily to the sofa—and sat down on it. He made a last effort; he tried to rise, and sank back. His head fell on the sofa cushions. It was then twenty-five minutes past one o'clock. Before I had put my watch back in my pocket, he was asleep.

It was all over now. The sedative influence had got him; the experiment was at an end.

I entered the room, telling Mr Bruff and Betteredge that they might follow me. There was no fear of disturbing him. We were free to move and speak.

'The first thing to settle,' I said, 'is the question of what we are to do with him. He will probably sleep for the next six or seven hours, at least. It is some distance to carry him back to his own room. When I was younger, I could have done it alone. But my health and strength are not what they were—I am afraid I must ask you to help me.'

Before they could answer, Miss Verinder called to me softly. She met me at the door of her room, with a light shawl, and with the counterpane from her own bed.

'Do you mean to watch him, while he sleeps?' she asked.

'Yes. I am not sure enough of the action of the opium, in his case, to be willing to leave him alone.'

She handed me the shawl and the counterpane.

'Why should you disturb him?' she whispered. 'Make his bed on the sofa. I can shut my door, and keep in my room.'

It was infinitely the simplest and the safest way of disposing of him for the night. I mentioned the suggestion to Mr Bruff and Betteredge—who both approved of my adopting it. In five minutes, I had laid him comfortably on the sofa, and had covered him lightly with the counterpane and the shawl. Miss Verinder wished us good night, and closed the door. At my request, we three then drew round the table in the middle of the room, on which the candle was still burning, and on which writing materials were placed.

'Before we separate,' I began, 'I have a word to say about the experiment which has been tried to-night. Two distinct objects were to be gained by it. The first of these objects was to prove, that Mr Blake entered this room, and took the Diamond, last year, acting unconsciously and irresponsibly, under the influence of opium. After what you have both seen, are you both satisfied, so far?'

They answered me in the affirmative, without a moment's hesitation.

'The second object,' I went on, 'was to discover what he did with the Diamond, after he was seen by Miss Verinder to leave her sitting-room with the jewel in his hand, on the birthday night. The gaining of this object depended, of course, on his still continuing exactly to repeat his proceedings of last year. He has failed to do that; and the purpose of the experiment is defeated accordingly. I can't assert that I am not disappointed at the result—but I can honestly say that I am not surprised by it. I told Mr Blake from the first, that our complete success in this matter, depended on our completely reproducing in him the physical and moral conditions of last year—and I warned him that this was the next thing to a downright impossibility. We have only partially reproduced the conditions, and the experiment has been only partially successful in consequence. It is also possible that I may have administered too large a dose of laudanum. But I myself look upon the first reason that I have given, as the true reason why we have to lament a failure, as well as to rejoice over a success.'

After saying those words, I put the writing materials before Mr Bruff, and asked him if he had any objection—before we separated for the night—to draw out, and sign, a plain statement of what he had seen. He at once took the pen, and produced the statement with the fluent readiness of a practised hand.

'I owe you this,' he said, signing the paper, 'as some atonement for what passed between us earlier in the evening. I beg your pardon, Mr Jennings, for having doubted you. You have done Franklin Blake an inestimable service. In our legal phrase, you have proved your case.'

Betteredge's apology was characteristic of the man.

'Mr Jennings,' he said, 'when you read *Robinson Crusoe* again (which I strongly recommend you to do), you will find that he never scruples to acknowledge it, when he turns out to have been in the wrong. Please to consider me, sir, as doing what Robinson Crusoe did, on the present occasion.' With those words he signed the paper in his turn.

Mr Bruff took me aside, as we rose from the table.

'One word about the Diamond,' he said. 'Your theory is that Franklin Blake hid the Moonstone in his room. My theory is, that the Moonstone is in the possession of Mr Luker's bankers in London. We won't dispute which of us is right. We will only ask, which of us is in a position to put his theory to the test?'

'The test, in my case,' I answered, 'has been tried to-night, and has failed.'

'The test, in my case,' rejoined Mr Bruff, 'is still in process of trial. For the last two days, I have had a watch set for Mr Luker at the bank; and I shall cause that watch to be continued until the last day of the month. I know that he must take the Diamond himself out of his bankers' hands—and I am acting on the chance that the person who has pledged the Diamond may force him to do this, by redeeming the pledge. In that case, I may be able to lay my hand on the person. If I succeed, I clear up the mystery, exactly at the point where the mystery baffles us now! Do you admit that, so far?'

I admitted it readily.

'I am going back to town by the morning train,' pursued the lawyer. 'I may hear, when I return, that a discovery has been made—and it may be of the greatest importance that I should have Franklin Blake at hand to appeal to, if necessary. I intend to tell him, as soon as he wakes, that he must return with me to London. After all that has happened, may I trust to your influence to back me?'

'Certainly!' I said.

Mr Bruff shook hands with me, and left the room. Betteredge followed him out.

I went to the sofa to look at Mr Blake. He had not moved since I had laid him down and made his bed—he lay locked in a deep and quiet sleep.

While I was still looking at him, I heard the bedroom door softly opened. Once more, Miss Verinder appeared on the threshold, in her pretty summer dress.

'Do me a last favour,' she whispered. 'Let me watch him with you.'

I hesitated—not in the interests of propriety; only in the interest of her night's rest. She came close to me, and took my hand.

'I can't sleep; I can't even sit still, in my own room,' she said. 'Oh, Mr Jennings, if you were me, only think how you would long to sit and look at him. Say, yes! Do!'

Is it necessary to mention that I gave way? Surely not!

She drew a chair to the foot of the sofa. She looked at him, in a silent ecstasy of happiness, till the tears rose in her eyes. She dried her eyes, and said she would fetch her work. She fetched her work, and never did a single stitch of it. It lay in her lap—she was not even able to look away from him long enough to thread her needle. I thought of my own youth; I thought of the gentle eyes which had once looked love at *me*. In the heaviness of my heart, I turned to my journal for relief, and wrote in it what is written here.

So we kept our watch together in silence. One of us absorbed in his writing; the other absorbed in her love.

Hour after hour, he lay in his deep sleep. The light of the new day grew and grew in the room, and still he never moved.

Towards six o'clock, I felt the warning which told me that my pains were coming back. I was obliged to leave her alone with him for a little while. I said I would go upstairs, and fetch another pillow for him out of his room. It was not a long attack, this time. In a little while, I was able to venture back, and let her see me again.

I found her at the head of the sofa, when I returned. She was just touching his forehead with her lips. I shook my head as soberly as I could, and pointed to her chair. She looked back at me with a bright smile, and a charming colour in her face. 'You would have done it,' she whispered, 'in my place!'

*   *   *   *   *

It is just eight o'clock. He is beginning to move for the first time.

Miss Verinder is kneeling by the side of the sofa. She has so placed herself that when his eyes first open, they must open on her face.

Shall I leave them together?

Yes!

*   *   *   *   *

Eleven o'clock.—The house is empty again. They have arranged it among themselves; they have all gone to London by the ten o'clock train. My brief dream of happiness is over. I have awakened again to the realities of my friendless and lonely life.

I dare not trust myself to write down the kind words that have been said to me—especially by Miss Verinder and Mr Blake. Besides, it is needless. Those words will come back to me in my solitary hours, and will help me through what is left of the end of my life. Mr Blake is to write, and tell me what happens in London. Miss Verinder is to return to Yorkshire in the autumn (for her marriage, no doubt); and I am to take a holiday, and be a guest in the house. Oh me, how I felt it, as the grateful happiness looked at me out of her eyes, and the warm pressure of her hand said, 'This is your doing!'

My poor patients are waiting for me. Back again, this morning, to the old routine! Back again, to-night, to the dreadful alternative between the opium and the pain!

God be praised for his mercy! I have seen a little sunshine—I have had a happy time.

FIFTH NARRATIVE

The Story resumed by Franklin Blake

CHAPTER 1

But few words are needed, on my part, to complete the narrative that has been presented in the Journal of Ezra Jennings.

Of myself, I have only to say that I awoke on the morning of the twenty-sixth, perfectly ignorant of all that I had said and done under the influence of the opium—from the time when the drug first laid its hold on me, to the time when I opened my eyes, in Rachel's sitting-room.

Of what happened after my waking, I do not feel called upon to render an account in detail. Confining myself merely to results, I have to report that Rachel and I thoroughly understood each other, before a single word of explanation had passed on either side. I decline to account, and Rachel declines to account, for the extraordinary rapidity of our reconciliation. Sir and Madam, look back at the time when you were passionately attached to each other—and you will know what happened, after Ezra Jennings had shut the door of the sitting-room, as well as I know it myself.

I have, however, no objection to add, that we should have been certainly discovered by Mrs Merridew, but for Rachel's presence of mind. She heard the sound of the old lady's dress in the corridor; and instantly ran out to meet her. I heard Mrs Merridew say, 'What is the matter?' and I heard Rachel answer, 'The explosion!' Mrs Merridew instantly permitted herself to be taken by the arm, and led into the garden, out of the way of the impending shock. On her return to the house, she met me in the hall, and expressed herself as greatly struck by the vast improvement in Science, since the time when she was a girl at school. 'Explosions, Mr Blake, are infinitely milder than they were. I assure you, I barely heard Mr Jennings's explosion from the garden. And no smell afterwards, that I can detect, now we have come back to the house! I must really apologize to your medical friend. It is only due to him to say, that he has managed it beautifully!'

So, after vanquishing Betteredge and Mr Bruff, Ezra Jennings vanquished Mrs Merridew herself. There is a great deal of undeveloped liberal feeling in the world, after all!

At breakfast, Mr Bruff made no secret of his reasons for wishing that I should accompany him to London by the morning train. The watch kept at the bank, and the result which might yet come of it, appealed so irresistibly to Rachel's curiosity, that she at once decided (if Mrs Merridew had no objection) on accompanying us back to town—so as to be within reach of the earliest news of our proceedings.

Mrs Merridew proved to be all pliability and indulgence, after the truly considerate manner in which the explosion had conducted itself; and Betteredge was accordingly informed that we were all four to travel back together by the morning train. I fully expected that he would have asked leave to accompany us. But Rachel had wisely provided her faithful old servant with an occupation that interested him. He was charged with completing the refurnishing of the house, and was too full of his domestic responsibilities to feel the 'detective-fever' as he might have felt it under other circumstances.

Our one subject of regret, in going to London, was the necessity of parting, more abruptly than we could have wished, with Ezra Jennings. It was impossible to persuade him to accompany us. I could only promise to write to him—and Rachel could only insist on his coming to see her when she returned to Yorkshire. There was every prospect of our meeting again in a few months—and yet there was something very sad in seeing our best and dearest friend left standing alone on the platform, as the train moved out of the station.

On our arrival in London, Mr Bruff was accosted at the terminus by a small boy, dressed in a jacket and trousers of threadbare black cloth, and personally remarkable in virtue of the extraordinary prominence of his eyes. They projected so far, and they rolled about so loosely, that you wondered uneasily why they remained in their sockets. After listening to the boy, Mr Bruff asked the ladies whether they would excuse our accompanying them back to Portland Place. I had barely time to promise Rachel that I would return, and tell her everything that had happened, before Mr Bruff seized me by the arm, and hurried me into a cab. The boy with the ill-secured eyes, took his place on the box by the driver, and the driver was directed to go to Lombard Street.

'News from the bank?' I asked, as we started.

'News of Mr Luker,' said Mr Bruff. 'An hour ago, he was seen to leave his house at Lambeth, in a cab, accompanied by two men, who were recognized by *my* men as police officers in plain clothes. If Mr Luker's dread of the Indians is at the bottom of this precaution, the inference is plain enough. He is going to take the Diamond out of the bank.'

'And we are going to the bank to see what comes of it?'

'Yes—or to hear what has come of it, if it is all over by this time. Did you notice my boy—on the box, there?'

'I noticed his eyes.'

Mr Bruff laughed. 'They call the poor little wretch "Gooseberry," at the office,' he said. 'I employ him to go on errands—and I only wish my clerks who have nicknamed him, were as thoroughly to be depended on as he is. Gooseberry is one of the sharpest boys in London, Mr Blake, in spite of his eyes.'

It was twenty minutes to five, when we drew up before the bank in Lombard Street. Gooseberry looked longingly at his master as he opened the cab door.

'Do you want to come in too?' asked Mr Bruff kindly.

'Come in then, and keep at my heels till further orders. He's as quick as lightning,' pursued Mr Bruff, addressing me in a whisper.

'Two words will do with Gooseberry, where twenty would be wanted with another boy.'

We entered the bank. The outer office—with the long counter, behind which the cashiers sat—was crowded with people; all waiting their turn to take money out, or to pay money in, before the bank closed at five o'clock.

Two men among the crowd approached Mr Bruff, as soon as he showed himself.

'Well?' asked the lawyer. 'Have you seen him?'

'He passed us here half an hour since, sir, and went on into the inner office.'

'Has he not come out again yet?'

'No, sir.'

Mr Bruff turned to me. 'Let us wait,' he said.

I looked round among the people about me for the three Indians. Not a sign of them was to be seen anywhere. The only person present with a noticeably dark complexion was a tall man in a pilot coat, and a round hat, who looked like a sailor. Could this be one of them in disguise? Impossible! The man was taller than any of the Indians; and his face, where it was not hidden by a bushy black beard, was at least twice the breadth of any of their faces.

'They must have their spy somewhere,' said Mr Bruff, looking at the dark sailor in his turn. 'And he may be the man.'

Before he could say more, his coat-tail was respectfully pulled by his attendant sprite with the gooseberry eyes. Mr Bruff looked where the boy was looking. 'Hush!' he said. 'Here is Mr Luker!'

The money-lender came out from the inner regions of the bank, followed by his two guardian policemen in plain clothes.

'Keep your eye on him,' whispered Mr Bruff. 'If he passes the Diamond to anybody, he will pass it here.'

Without noticing either of us, Mr Luker slowly made his way to the door—now in the thickest, now in the thinnest part of the crowd. I distinctly saw his hand move, as he passed a short, stout man, respectably dressed in a suit of sober grey. The man started a little, and looked after him. Mr Luker moved on slowly through the crowd. At the door, his guard placed themselves on either side of him. They were all three followed by one of Mr Bruff's men—and I saw them no more.

I looked round at the lawyer, and then looked significantly towards the man in the suit of sober grey. 'Yes!' whispered Mr Bruff, 'I saw it too!' He turned about, in search of his second man. The second man was nowhere to be seen. He looked behind him for his attendant sprite. Gooseberry had disappeared.

'What the devil does it mean?' said Mr Bruff angrily. 'They have both left us at the very time when we want them most.'

It came to the turn of the man in the grey suit to transact his business at the counter. He paid in a cheque—received a receipt for it—and turned to go out.

'What is to be done?' asked Mr Bruff. '*We* can't degrade ourselves by following him.'

'*I* can!' I said. 'I wouldn't lose sight of that man for ten thousand pounds!'

'In that case,' rejoined Mr Bruff, 'I wouldn't lose sight of *you*, for twice the money. A nice occupation for a man in my position,' he muttered to himself, as we followed the stranger out of the bank. 'For Heaven's sake don't mention it. I should be ruined if it was known.'

The man in the grey suit got into an omnibus, going westward. We got in after him. There were latent reserves of youth still left in Mr Bruff. I assert it positively—when he took his seat in the omnibus, he blushed!

The man with the grey suit stopped the omnibus, and got out in Oxford Street. We followed him again. He went into a chemist's shop.

Mr Bruff started. 'My chemist!' he exclaimed. 'I am afraid we have made a mistake.'

We entered the shop. Mr Bruff and the proprietor exchanged a few words in private. The lawyer joined me again, with a very crestfallen face.

'It's greatly to our credit,' he said, as he took my arm, and led me out—' that's one comfort!'

'What is to our credit?' I asked.

'Mr Blake! you and I are the two worst amateur detectives that ever tried their hands at the trade. The man in the grey suit has been thirty years in the chemist's service. He was sent to the bank to pay money to his master's account—and he knows no more of the Moonstone than the babe unborn.'

I asked what was to be done next.

'Come back to my office,' said Mr Bruff. 'Gooseberry, and my second man, have evidently followed somebody else. Let us hope that *they* had their eyes about them at any rate!'

When we reached Gray's Inn Square, the second man had arrived there before us. He had been waiting for more than a quarter of an hour.

'Well?' asked Mr Bruff. 'What's your news?'

'I am sorry to say, sir,' replied the man, 'that I have made a mistake. I could have taken my oath that I saw Mr Luker pass something to an elderly gentleman, in a light-coloured paletot. The elderly gentleman turns out, sir, to be a most respectable master ironmonger in Eastcheap.'

'Where is Gooseberry?' asked Mr Bruff resignedly.

The man stared. 'I don't know, sir. I have seen nothing of him since I left the bank.'

Mr Bruff dismissed the man. 'One of two things,' he said to me. 'Either Gooseberry has run away, or he is hunting on his own account. What do you say to dining here, on the chance that the boy may come back in an hour or two? I have got some good wine in the cellar, and we can get a chop from the coffee-house.'

We dined at Mr Bruff's chambers. Before the cloth was removed, 'a person' was announced as wanting to speak to the lawyer. Was the person, Gooseberry? No: only the man who had been employed to follow Mr Luker when he left the bank.

The report, in this case, presented no feature of the slightest interest. Mr Luker had gone back to his own house, and had there dismissed his guard. He had not gone out again afterwards. Towards dusk, the shutters had been put up, and the doors had been bolted. The street before the house, and the alley behind the house, had been carefully watched. No signs of the Indians had been visible. No person whatever had been seen loitering about the premises. Having stated these facts, the man waited to know whether there were any further orders. Mr Bruff dismissed him for the night.

'Do you think Mr Luker has taken the Moonstone home with him?' I asked.

'Not he,' said Mr Bruff. 'He would never have dismissed his two policemen, if he had run the risk of keeping the Diamond in his own house again.'

We waited another half-hour for the boy, and waited in vain. It was then time for Mr Bruff to go to Hampstead, and for me to return to Rachel in Portland Place. I left my card, in charge of the porter at the chambers, with a line written on it to say that I should be at my lodgings at half-past ten, that night. The card was to be given to the boy, if the boy came back.

Some men have a knack of keeping appointments; and other men have a knack of missing them. I am one of the other men. Add to this, that I passed the evening at Portland Place, on the same seat with Rachel, in a room forty feet long, with Mrs Merridew at the further end of it. Does anybody wonder that I got home at half-past twelve instead of half-past ten? How thoroughly heartless that person must be! And how earnestly I hope I may never make that person's acquaintance!

My servant handed me a morsel of paper when he let me in.

I read, in a neat legal handwriting, these words:—'If you please, sir, I am getting sleepy. I will come back to-morrow morning, between nine and ten.' Inquiry proved that a boy, with very extraordinary-looking eyes, had called, had presented my card and message, had waited an hour, had done nothing but fall asleep and wake up again, had written a line for me, and had gone home—after gravely informing the servant that 'he was fit for nothing unless he got his night's rest.'

At nine, the next morning, I was ready for my visitor. At half-past nine, I heard steps outside my door. 'Come in, Gooseberry!' I called out. 'Thank you, sir,' answered a grave and melancholy voice. The door opened. I started to my feet, and confronted—Sergeant Cuff!

'I thought I would look in here, Mr Blake, on the chance of your being in town, before I wrote to Yorkshire,' said the Sergeant.

He was as dreary and as lean as ever. His eyes had not lost their old trick (so subtly noticed in Betteredge's Narrative) of 'looking as if they expected something more from you than you were aware of yourself.' But, so far as dress can alter a man, the great Cuff was changed beyond all recognition. He wore a broad-brimmed white hat, a light shooting jacket, white trousers, and drab gaiters. He carried a stout oak stick. His whole aim and object seemed to be, to look as if he had lived in the country all his life. When I complimented him on his Metamorphosis, he declined to take it as a joke. He complained, quite gravely, of the noises and the smells of London. I declare I am far from sure that he did not speak with a slightly rustic accent! I offered him breakfast. The innocent countryman was quite shocked. *His* breakfast hour was half-past six—and *he* went to bed with the cocks and hens!

'I only got back from Ireland last night,' said the Sergeant, coming round to the practical object of his visit, in his own impenetrable manner. 'Before I went to bed, I read your letter, telling me what has happened since my inquiry after the Diamond was suspended last year. There's only one thing to be said about the matter, on my side. I completely mistook my case. How any man living was to have seen things in their true light, in such a situation as mine was at the time, I don't profess to know. But that doesn't alter the facts as they stand. I own that I made a mess of it. Not the first mess, Mr Blake, which has distinguished my professional career! It's only in books that the officers of the detective force are superior to the weakness of making a mistake.'

'You have come in the nick of time to recover your reputation,' I said.

'I beg your pardon, Mr Blake,' rejoined the Sergeant. 'Now I have retired from business, I don't care a straw about my reputation. I have done with my reputation, thank God! I am here, sir, in grateful remembrance of the late Lady Verinder's liberality to me. I will go back to my old work—if you want me, and if you will trust me—on that consideration, and on no other. Not a farthing of money is to pass, if you please, from you to me. This is on honour. Now tell me, Mr Blake, how the case stands since you wrote to me last.'

I told him of the experiment with the opium, and of what had occurred afterwards at the bank in Lombard Street. He was greatly struck by the experiment—it was something entirely new in his experience. And he was particularly interested in the theory of Ezra Jennings, relating to what I had done with the Diamond, after I had left Rachel's sitting-room, on the birthday night.

'I don't hold with Mr Jennings that you hid the Moonstone,' said Sergeant Cuff. 'But I agree with him, that you must certainly have taken it back to your own room.'

'Well?' I asked. 'And what happened then?'

'Have you no suspicion yourself of what happened, sir?'

'None whatever.'

'Has Mr Bruff no suspicion?'

'No more than I have.'

Sergeant Cuff rose, and went to my writing-table. He came back with a sealed envelope. It was marked 'Private'; it was addressed to me; and it had the Sergeant's signature in the corner.

'I suspected the wrong person, last year,' he said: 'and I may be suspecting the wrong person now. Wait to open the envelope, Mr Blake, till you have got at the truth. And then compare the name of the guilty person, with the name that I have written in that sealed letter.'

I put the letter into my pocket—and then asked for the Sergeant's opinion of the measures which we had taken at the bank.

'Very well intended, sir,' he answered, 'and quite the right thing to do. But there was another person who ought to have been looked after besides Mr Luker.'

'The person named in the letter you have just given to me?'

'Yes, Mr Blake, the person named in the letter. It can't be helped now. I shall have something to propose to you and Mr Bruff, sir, when the time comes. Let's wait, first, and see if the boy has anything to tell us that is worth hearing.'

It was close on ten o'clock, and the boy had not made his appearance. Sergeant Cuff talked of other matters. He asked after his old friend Betteredge, and his old enemy the gardener. In a minute more, he would no doubt have got from this, to the subject of his favourite roses, if my servant had not interrupted us by announcing that the boy was below.

On being brought into the room, Gooseberry stopped at the threshold of the door, and looked distrustfully at the stranger who was in my company. I told the boy to come to me.

'You may speak before this gentleman,' I said. 'He is here to assist me; and he knows all that has happened. Sergeant Cuff,' I added, 'this is the boy from Mr Bruff's office.'

In our modern system of civilization, celebrity (no matter of what kind) is the lever that will move anything. The fame of the great Cuff had even reached the ears of the small Gooseberry. The boy's ill-fixed eyes rolled, when I mentioned the illustrious name, till I thought they really must have dropped on the carpet.

'Come here, my lad,' said the Sergeant, 'and let's hear what you have got to tell us.'

The notice of the great man—the hero of many a famous story in every lawyer's office in London—appeared to fascinate the boy. He placed himself in front of Sergeant Cuff, and put his hands behind him, after the approved fashion of a neophyte who is examined in his catechism.

'What is your name?' said the Sergeant, beginning with the first question in the catechism.

'Octavius Guy,' answered the boy. 'They call me Gooseberry at the office because of my eyes.'

'Octavius Guy, otherwise Gooseberry,' pursued the Sergeant, with the utmost gravity, 'you were missed at the bank yesterday. What were you about?'

'If you please, sir, I was following a man.'

'Who was he?'

'A tall man, sir, with a big black beard, dressed like a sailor.'

'I remember the man!' I broke in. 'Mr Bruff and I thought he was a spy, employed by the Indians.'

Sergeant Cuff did not appear to be much impressed by what Mr Bruff and I had thought. He went on catechizing Gooseberry.

'Well?' he said—'and why did you follow the sailor?'

'If you please, sir, Mr Bruff wanted to know whether Mr Luker passed anything to anybody on his way out of the bank. I saw Mr Luker pass something to the sailor with the black beard.'

'Why didn't you tell Mr Bruff what you saw?'

'I hadn't time to tell anybody, sir, the sailor went out in such a hurry.'

'And you ran out after him—eh?'

'Yes, sir.'

'Gooseberry,' said the Sergeant, patting his head, 'you have got something in that small skull of yours—and it isn't cotton-wool. I am greatly pleased with you, so far.'

The boy blushed with pleasure. Sergeant Cuff went on:

'Well? and what did the sailor do, when he got into the street?'

'He called a cab, sir.'

'And what did you do?'

'Held on behind, and run after it.'

Before the Sergeant could put his next question, another visitor was announced—the head clerk from Mr Bruff's office.

Feeling the importance of not interrupting Sergeant Cuff's examination of the boy, I received the clerk in another room. He came with bad news of his employer. The agitation and excitement of the last two days had proved too much for Mr Bruff. He had awoke that morning with an attack of gout; he was confined to his room at Hampstead; and, in the present critical condition of our affairs, he was very uneasy at being compelled to leave me without the advice and assistance of an experienced person. The chief clerk had received orders to hold himself at my disposal, and was willing to do his best to replace Mr Bruff.

I wrote at once to quiet the old gentleman's mind, by telling him of Sergeant Cuff's visit: adding that Gooseberry was at that moment under examination; and promising to inform Mr Bruff, either personally or by letter, of whatever might occur later in the day. Having despatched the clerk to Hampstead with my note, I returned to the room which I had left, and found Sergeant Cuff at the fireplace, in the act of ringing the bell.

'I beg your pardon, Mr Blake,' said the Sergeant. 'I was just going to send word by your servant that I wanted to speak to you. There isn't a doubt on my mind that this boy—this most meritorious boy,' added the Sergeant, patting Gooseberry on the head, 'has followed the right man. Precious time has been lost, sir, through your unfortunately not

315

being at home at half-past ten last night. The only thing to do, now, is to send for a cab immediately.'

In five minutes more, Sergeant Cuff and I (with Gooseberry on the box to guide the driver) were on our way eastward, towards the City.

'One of these days,' said the Sergeant, pointing through the front window of the cab, 'that boy will do great things in my late profession. He is the brightest and cleverest little chap I have met with, for many a long year past. You shall hear the substance, Mr Blake, of what he told me while you were out of the room. You were present, I think, when he mentioned that he held on behind the cab, and ran after it?'

'Yes.'

'Well, sir, the cab went from Lombard Street to the Tower Wharf. The sailor with the black beard got out, and spoke to the steward of the Rotterdam steamboat, which was to start next morning. He asked if he could be allowed to go on board at once, and sleep in his berth over-night. The steward said, No. The cabins, and berths, and bedding were all to have a thorough cleaning that evening, and no passenger could be allowed to come on board, before the morning. The sailor turned round, and left the wharf. When he got into the street again, the boy noticed for the first time, a man dressed like a respectable mechanic, walking on the opposite side of the road, and apparently keeping the sailor in view. The sailor stopped at an eating-house in the neighbourhood, and went in. The boy—not being able to make up his mind, at the moment—hung about among some other boys, staring at the good things in the eating-house window. He noticed the mechanic waiting, as he himself was waiting—but still on the opposite side of the street. After a minute, a cab came by slowly, and stopped where the mechanic was standing. The boy could only see plainly one person in the cab, who leaned forward at the window to speak to the mechanic. He described that person, Mr Blake, without any prompting from me, as having a dark face, like the face of an Indian.'

It was plain, by this time, that Mr Bruff and I had made another mistake. The sailor with the black beard was clearly not a spy in the service of the Indian conspiracy. Was he, by any possibility, the man who had got the Diamond?

'After a little,' pursued the Sergeant, 'the cab moved on slowly down the street. The mechanic crossed the road, and went into the eating-house. The boy waited outside till he was hungry and tired—and then went into the eating-house, in his turn. He had a shilling in his pocket; and he dined sumptuously, he tells me, on a black-pudding, an eel-pie, and a bottle of ginger-beer. What can a boy *not* digest? The substance in question has never been found yet.'

'What did he see in the eating-house?' I asked.

'Well, Mr Blake, he saw the sailor reading the newspaper at one table, and the mechanic reading the newspaper at another. It was dusk before the sailor got up, and left the place. He looked about him suspiciously when he got out into the street. The boy—*being* a boy—passed unnoticed. The mechanic had not come out yet. The sailor walked on, looking about him, and apparently not very certain of where he was going next. The mechanic appeared once more, on the opposite side of the road. The sailor went on, till he got to Shore Lane, leading into Lower Thames Street. There he stopped before a public-house, under the sign of "The Wheel of Fortune," and, after examining the place outside, went in. Gooseberry went in too. There were a great many people, mostly of the decent sort, at the bar. "The Wheel of Fortune" is a very respectable house, Mr Blake; famous for its porter and pork-pies.'

The Sergeant's digressions irritated me. He saw it; and confined himself more strictly to Gooseberry's evidence when he went on.

'The sailor,' he resumed, 'asked if he could have a bed. The landlord said "No; they were full." The barmaid corrected him, and said "Number Ten was empty." A waiter was sent for to show the sailor to Number Ten. Just before that, Gooseberry had noticed the mechanic among the people at the bar. Before the waiter had answered the call, the mechanic had vanished. The sailor was taken off to his room. Not knowing what to do next, Gooseberry had the wisdom to wait and see if anything happened. Something did happen. The landlord was called for. Angry voices were heard upstairs. The mechanic suddenly made his appearance again, collared by the landlord, and exhibiting, to Gooseberry's great surprise, all the signs and tokens of being drunk. The landlord thrust him out at the door, and threatened him with the police if he came back. From the altercation between them, while this was going on, it appeared that the man had been discovered in Number Ten, and had declared with drunken obstinacy, that he had taken the room. Gooseberry was so struck by this sudden intoxication of a previously sober person, that he couldn't resist running out after the mechanic into the street. As long as he was in sight of the public-house, the man reeled about in the most disgraceful manner. The moment he turned the corner of the street, he recovered his balance instantly, and became as sober a member of society as you could wish to see. Gooseberry went back to "The Wheel of Fortune," in a very bewildered state of mind. He waited about again, on the chance of something happening. Nothing happened; and nothing more was to be heard, or seen, of the sailor. Gooseberry decided on going back to the office. Just as he came to this conclusion, who should appear, on the opposite side of the street as usual, but the mechanic again! He looked up at one particular window at the top of the public-house, which was the only one that had a light in it. The light seemed to relieve his mind. He left the place directly. The boy made his way back to Gray's Inn—got your card and message—called—and failed to find you. There you have the state of the case, Mr Blake, as it stands at the present time.'

'What is your own opinion of the case, Sergeant?'

'I think it's serious, sir. Judging by what the boy saw, the Indians are in it, to begin with.'

'Yes. And the sailor is evidently the person to whom Mr Luker passed the Diamond. It seems odd that Mr Bruff, and I, and the man in Mr Bruff's employment, should all have been mistaken about who the person was.'

'Not at all, Mr Blake. Considering the risk that person ran, it's likely enough that Mr Luker purposely misled you, by previous arrangement between them.'

'Do you understand the proceedings at the public-house?' I asked. 'The man dressed like a mechanic, was acting of course in the employment of the Indians. But I am as much puzzled to account for his sudden assumption of drunkenness as Gooseberry himself.'

'I think I can give a guess at what it means, sir,' said the Sergeant.

'If you will reflect, you will see that the man must have had some pretty strict instructions from the Indians. They were far too noticeable themselves to risk being seen at the bank, or in the public-house—they were obliged to trust everything to their

317

deputy. Very good. Their deputy hears a certain number named, in the public-house, as the number of the room which the sailor is to have for the night—that being also the room (unless our notion is all wrong) which the Diamond is to have for the night, too. Under those circumstances, the Indians, you may rely on it, would insist on having a description of the room—of its position in the house, of its capability of being approached from the outside, and so on. What was the man to do, with such orders as these? Just what he did! He ran upstairs to get a look at the room, before the sailor was taken into it. He was found there, making his observations—and he shammed drunk, as the easiest way of getting out of the difficulty. That's how I read the riddle. After he was turned out of the public-house, he probably went with his report to the place where his employers were waiting for him. And his employers, no doubt, sent him back to make sure that the sailor was really settled at the public-house till the next morning. As for what happened at "The Wheel of Fortune," after the boy left—we ought to have discovered that last night. It's eleven in the morning, now. We must hope for the best, and find out what we can.'

In a quarter of an hour more, the cab stopped in Shore Lane, and Gooseberry opened the door for us to get out.

'All right?' asked the Sergeant.

'All right,' answered the boy.

The moment we entered 'The Wheel of Fortune,' it was plain even to my inexperienced eyes that there was something wrong in the house.

The only person behind the counter at which the liquors were served, was a bewildered servant girl, perfectly ignorant of the business. One or two customers, waiting for their morning drink, were tapping impatiently on the counter with their money. The barmaid appeared from the inner regions of the parlour, excited and preoccupied. She answered Sergeant Cuff's inquiry for the landlord, by telling him sharply that her master was upstairs, and was not to be bothered by anybody.

'Come along with me, sir,' said Sergeant Cuff, coolly leading the way upstairs, and beckoning to the boy to follow him.

The barmaid called to her master, and warned him that strangers were intruding themselves into the house. On the first floor we were encountered by the landlord, hurrying down, in a highly irritated state, to see what was the matter.

'Who the devil are you? and what do you want here?' he asked.

'Keep your temper,' said the Sergeant, quietly. 'I'll tell you who I am to begin with. I am Sergeant Cuff.'

The illustrious name instantly produced its effect. The angry landlord threw open the door of a sitting-room, and asked the Sergeant's pardon.

'I am annoyed and out of sorts, sir—that's the truth,' he said. 'Something unpleasant has happened in the house this morning. A man in my way of business has a deal to upset his temper, Sergeant Cuff.'

'Not a doubt of it,' said the Sergeant. 'I'll come at once, if you will allow me, to what brings us here. This gentleman and I want to trouble you with a few inquiries, on a matter of some interest to both of us.'

'Relating to what, sir?' asked the landlord.

'Relating to a dark man, dressed like a sailor, who slept here last night.'

'Good God! that's the man who is upsetting the whole house at this moment!' exclaimed the landlord. 'Do you, or does this gentleman know anything about him?'

'We can't be certain till we see him,' answered the Sergeant.

'See him?' echoed the landlord. 'That's the one thing that nobody has been able to do since seven o'clock this morning. That was the time when he left word, last night, that he was to be called. He *was* called—and there was no getting an answer from him, and no opening his door to see what was the matter. They tried again at eight, and they tried again at nine. No use! There was the door still locked—and not a sound to be heard in the room! I have been out this morning—and I only got back a quarter of an hour ago. I have hammered at the door myself—and all to no purpose. The potboy has gone to fetch a carpenter. If you can wait a few minutes, gentlemen, we will have the door opened, and see what it means.'

'Was the man drunk last night?' asked Sergeant Cuff.

'Perfectly sober, sir—or I would never have let him sleep in my house.'

'Did he pay for his bed beforehand?'

'No.'

'Could he leave the room in any way, without going out by the door?'

'The room is a garret,' said the landlord. 'But there's a trap-door in the ceiling, leading out on to the roof—and a little lower down the street, there's an empty house under repair. Do you think, Sergeant, the blackguard has got off in that way, without paying?'

'A sailor,' said Sergeant Cuff, 'might have done it—early in the morning, before the street was astir. He would be used to climbing, and his head wouldn't fail him on the roofs of the houses.'

As he spoke, the arrival of the carpenter was announced. We all went upstairs, at once, to the top story. I noticed that the Sergeant was unusually grave, even for *him*. It also struck me as odd that he told the boy (after having previously encouraged him to follow us), to wait in the room below till we came down again.

The carpenter's hammer and chisel disposed of the resistance of the door in a few minutes. But some article of furniture had been placed against it inside, as a barricade. By pushing at the door, we thrust this obstacle aside, and so got admission to the room. The landlord entered first; the Sergeant second; and I third. The other persons present followed us.

We all looked towards the bed, and all started.

The man had not left the room. He lay, dressed, on the bed—with a white pillow over his face, which completely hid it from view.

'What does that mean?' said the landlord pointing to the pillow.

Sergeant Cuff led the way to the bed, without answering, and removed the pillow.

The man's swarthy face was placid and still; his black hair and beard were slightly, very slightly, discomposed. His eyes stared wide-open, glassy and vacant, at the ceiling. The filmy look and the fixed expression of them horrified me. I turned away, and went to the open window. The rest of them remained, where Sergeant Cuff remained, at the bed.

'He's in a fit!' I heard the landlord say.

'He's dead,' the Sergeant answered. 'Send for the nearest doctor, and send for the police.'

The waiter was despatched on both errands. Some strange fascination seemed to hold

Sergeant Cuff to the bed. Some strange curiosity seemed to keep the rest of them waiting, to see what the Sergeant would do next.

I turned again to the window. The moment afterwards, I felt a soft pull at my coat-tails, and a small voice whispered, 'Look here, sir!'

Gooseberry had followed us into the room. His loose eyes rolled frightfully—not in terror, but in exultation. He had made a detective-discovery on his own account. 'Look here, sir,' he repeated—and led me to a table in the corner of the room.

On the table stood a little wooden box, open, and empty. On one side of the box lay some jewellers' cotton. On the other side, was a torn sheet of white paper, with a seal on it, partly destroyed, and with an inscription in writing, which was still perfectly legible. The inscription was in these words:

'Deposited with Messrs. Bushe, Lysaught, and Bushe, by Mr Septimus Luker, of Middlesex Place, Lambeth, a small wooden box, sealed up in this envelope, and containing a valuable of great price. The box, when claimed, to be only given up by Messrs Bushe and Co. on the personal application of Mr Luker.'

Those lines removed all further doubt, on one point at least. The sailor had been in possession of the Moonstone, when he had left the bank on the previous day.

I felt another pull at my coat-tails. Gooseberry had not done with me yet.

'Robbery!' whispered the boy, pointing, in high delight, to the empty box.

'You were told to wait downstairs,' I said. 'Go away!'

'And Murder!' added Gooseberry, pointing, with a keener relish still, to the man on the bed.

There was something so hideous in the boy's enjoyment of the horror of the scene, that I took him by the two shoulders and put him out of the room.

At the moment when I crossed the threshold of the door, I heard Sergeant Cuff's voice, asking where I was. He met me, as I returned into the room, and forced me to go back with him to the bedside.

'Mr Blake!' he said. 'Look at the man's face. It is a face disguised—and here's a proof of it!'

He traced with his finger a thin line of livid white, running backward from the dead man's forehead, between the swarthy complexion, and the slightly-disturbed black hair. 'Let's see what is under this,' said the Sergeant, suddenly seizing the black hair, with a firm grip of his hand.

My nerves were not strong enough to bear it. I turned away again from the bed.

The first sight that met my eyes, at the other end of the room, was the irrepressible Gooseberry, perched on a chair, and looking with breathless interest, over the heads of his elders, at the Sergeant's proceedings.

'He's pulling off his wig!' whispered Gooseberry, compassionating my position, as the only person in the room who could see nothing.

There was a pause—and then a cry of astonishment among the people round the bed.

'He's pulled off his beard!' cried Gooseberry.

There was another pause—Sergeant Cuff asked for something. The landlord went to the washhand-stand, and returned to the bed with a basin of water and a towel.

Gooseberry danced with excitement on the chair. 'Come up here, along with me, sir! He's washing off his complexion now!'

The Sergeant suddenly burst his way through the people about him, and came, with horror in his face, straight to the place where I was standing.

'Come back to the bed, sir!' he began. He looked at me closer, and checked himself, 'No!' he resumed. 'Open the sealed letter first—the letter I gave you this morning.'

I opened the letter.

'Read the name, Mr Blake, that I have written inside.'

I read the name that he had written. It was—*Godfrey Ablewhite*.

'Now,' said the Sergeant, 'come with me, and look at the man on the bed.'

I went with him, and looked at the man on the bed.

Godfrey Ablewhite!

SIXTH NARRATIVE

Contributed by Sergeant Cuff

I

Dorking, Surrey, 30 July 1849. To Franklin Blake, Esq. Sir,—I beg to apologize for the delay that has occurred in the production of the Report, with which I engaged to furnish you. I have waited to make it a complete Report; and I have been met, here and there, by obstacles which it was only possible to remove by some little expenditure of patience and time.

The object which I proposed to myself has now, I hope, been attained. You will find, in these pages, answers to the greater part—if not all—of the questions, concerning the late Mr Godfrey Ablewhite, which occurred to your mind when I last had the honour of seeing you.

I propose to tell you—in the first place—what is known of the manner in which your cousin met his death; appending to the statement such inferences and conclusions as we are justified (according to my opinion) in drawing from the facts.

I shall then endeavour—in the second place—to put you in possession of such discoveries as I have made, respecting the proceedings of Mr Godfrey Ablewhite, before, during, and after the time, when you and he met as guests at the late Lady Verinder's country-house.

II

As to your cousin's death, then, first.

It appears to me to be established, beyond any reasonable doubt, that he was killed (while he was asleep, or immediately on his waking) by being smothered with a pillow from his bed—that the persons guilty of murdering him are the three Indians—and that the object contemplated (and achieved) by the crime, was to obtain possession of the diamond, called the Moonstone.

The facts from which this conclusion is drawn, are derived partly from an examination of the room at the tavern; and partly from the evidence obtained at the Coroner's Inquest.

On forcing the door of the room, the deceased gentleman was discovered, dead, with the pillow of the bed over his face. The medical man who examined him, being informed of this circumstance, considered the post-mortem appearances as being perfectly compatible with murder by smothering—that is to say, with murder committed by some person, or persons, pressing the pillow over the nose and mouth of the deceased, until death resulted from congestion of the lungs.

Next, as to the motive for the crime.

A small box, with a sealed paper torn off from it (the paper containing an inscription) was found open, and empty, on a table in the room. Mr Luker has himself personally identified the box, the seal, and the inscription. He has declared that the box did actually contain the diamond, called the Moonstone; and he has admitted having given the box (thus sealed up) to Mr Godfrey Ablewhite (then concealed under a disguise), on the afternoon of the twenty-sixth of June last. The fair inference from all this is, that the stealing of the Moonstone was the motive of the crime.

Next, as to the manner in which the crime was committed.

On examination of the room (which is only seven feet high), a trap-door in the ceiling, leading out on to the roof of the house, was discovered open. The short ladder, used for obtaining access to the trap-door (and kept under the bed), was found placed at the opening, so as to enable any person or persons, in the room, to leave it again easily. In the trap-door itself was found a square aperture cut in the wood, apparently with some exceedingly sharp instrument, just behind the bolt which fastened the door on the inner side. In this way, any person from the outside could have drawn back the bolt, and opened the door, and have dropped (or have been noiselessly lowered by an accomplice) into the room—its height, as already observed, being only seven feet. That some person, or persons, must have got admission in this way, appears evident from the fact of the aperture being there. As to the manner in which he (or they) obtained access to the roof of the tavern, it is to be remarked that the third house, lower down in the street, was empty, and under repair—that a long ladder was left by the workmen, leading from the pavement to the top of the house—and that, on returning to their work, on the morning of the 27th, the men found the plank which they had tied to the ladder, to prevent any one from using it in their absence, removed, and lying on the ground. As to the possibility of ascending by this ladder, passing over the roofs of the houses, passing back, and descending again, unobserved—it is discovered, on the evidence of the night policeman, that he only passes through Shore Lane twice in an hour, when out on his beat. The testimony of the inhabitants also declares, that Shore Lane, after midnight, is one of the quietest and loneliest streets in London. Here again, therefore, it seems fair to infer that—with ordinary caution, and presence of mind—any man, or men, might have ascended by the ladder, and might have descended again, unobserved. Once on the roof of the tavern, it has been proved, by experiment, that a man might cut through the trap-door, while lying down on it, and that in such a position, the parapet in front of the house would conceal him from the view of any one passing in the street.

Lastly, as to the person, or persons, by whom the crime was committed.

It is known (1) that the Indians had an interest in possessing themselves of the Diamond. (2) It is at least probable that the man looking like an Indian, whom Octavius Guy saw at the window of the cab, speaking to the man dressed like a mechanic, was one of the three Hindoo conspirators. (3) It is certain that this same man dressed like a mechanic, was seen keeping Mr Godfrey Ablewhite in view, all through the evening of the 26th, and was found in the bedroom (before Mr Ablewhite was shown into it) under circumstances which lead to the suspicion that he was examining the room. (4) A morsel of torn gold thread was picked up in the bedroom, which persons expert in such matters, declare to be of Indian manufacture, and to be a species of gold thread not known in England. (5) On the morning of the 27th, three men, answering to the description of the three Indians, were observed in Lower Thames Street, were traced to the Tower Wharf, and were seen to leave London by the steamer bound for Rotterdam.

There is here, moral, if not legal, evidence, that the murder was committed by the Indians.

Whether the man personating a mechanic was, or was not, an accomplice in the crime, it is impossible to say. That he could have committed the murder alone, seems beyond the limits of probability. Acting by himself, he could hardly have smothered Mr Ablewhite—who was the taller and stronger man of the two—without a struggle taking place, or a cry being heard. A servant girl, sleeping in the next room, heard nothing. The landlord, sleeping in the room below, heard nothing. The whole evidence points to the inference that more than one man was concerned in this crime—and the circumstances, I repeat, morally justify the conclusion that the Indians committed it.

I have only to add, that the verdict at the Coroner's Inquest was Wilful Murder against some person, or persons, unknown. Mr Ablewhite's family have offered a reward, and no effort has been left untried to discover the guilty persons. The man dressed like a mechanic has eluded all inquiries. The Indians have been traced. As to the prospect of ultimately capturing these last, I shall have a word to say to you on that head, when I reach the end of the present Report.

In the meanwhile, having now written all that is needful on the subject of Mr Godfrey Ablewhite's death, I may pass next to the narrative of his proceedings before, during, and after the time, when you and he met at the late Lady Verinder's house.

III

With regard to the subject now in hand, I may state, at the outset, that Mr Godfrey Ablewhite's life had two sides to it.

The side turned up to the public view, presented the spectacle of a gentleman, possessed of considerable reputation as a speaker at charitable meetings, and endowed with administrative abilities, which he placed at the disposal of various Benevolent Societies, mostly of the female sort. The side kept hidden from the general notice, exhibited this same gentleman in the totally different character of a man of pleasure, with a villa in the suburbs which was not taken in his own name, and with a lady in the villa, who was not taken in his own name, either.

My investigations in the villa have shown me several fine pictures and statues; furniture tastefully selected, and admirably made; and a conservatory of the rarest flowers, the match of which it would not be easy to find in all London. My investigation of the lady has resulted in the discovery of jewels which are worthy to take rank with the flowers, and of carriages and horses which have (deservedly) produced a sensation in the Park, among persons well qualified to judge of the build of the one, and the breed of the others.

All this is, so far, common enough. The villa and the lady are such familiar objects in London life, that I ought to apologize for introducing them to notice. But what is not common and not familiar (in my experience), is that all these fine things were not only ordered, but paid for. The pictures, the statues, the flowers, the jewels, the carriages and the horses—inquiry proved, to my indescribable astonishment, that not a sixpence of debt was owing on any of them. As to the villa, it had been bought, out and out, and settled on the lady.

I might have tried to find the right reading of this riddle, and tried in vain—but for Mr Godfrey Ablewhite's death, which caused an inquiry to be made into the state of his affairs.

The inquiry elicited these facts:—

That Mr Godfrey Ablewhite was entrusted with the care of a sum of twenty thousand pounds—as one of two Trustees for a young gentleman, who was still a minor in the year eighteen hundred and forty-eight. That the Trust was to lapse, and that the young gentleman was to receive the twenty thousand pounds on the day when he came of age, in the month of February, eighteen hundred and fifty. That, pending the arrival of this period, an income of six hundred pounds was to be paid to him by his two Trustees, half-yearly—at Christmas and Midsummer Day. That this income was regularly paid by the active Trustee, Mr Godfrey Ablewhite. That the twenty thousand pounds (from which the income was supposed to be derived) had, every farthing of it, been sold out of the Funds, at different periods, ending with the end of the year eighteen hundred and forty-seven. That the power of attorney, authorizing the bankers to sell out the stock, and the various written orders telling them what amounts to sell out, were formally signed by both the Trustees. That the signature of the second Trustee (a retired army officer, living in the country) was a signature forged, in every case, by the active Trustee—otherwise Mr Godfrey Ablewhite.

In these facts, lies the explanation of Mr Godfrey's honourable conduct, in paying the debts incurred for the lady and the villa—and (as you will presently see) of more besides.

We may now advance to the date of Miss Verinder's birthday (in the year eighteen hundred and forty-eight)—the twenty-first of June.

On the day before, Mr Godfrey Ablewhite arrived at his father's house, and asked (as I know from Mr Ablewhite, senior, himself) for a loan of three hundred pounds. Mark the sum; and remember at the same time, that the half-yearly payment to the young gentleman was due on the twenty-fourth of the month. Also, that the whole of the young gentleman's fortune had been spent by his Trustee, by the end of the year 'forty-seven.

Mr Ablewhite, senior, refused to lend his son farthing.

The next day Mr Godfrey Ablewhite rode over, with you, to Lady Verinder's house. A few hours afterwards, Mr Godfrey (as you yourself have told me) made a proposal of marriage to Miss Verinder. Here, he saw his way no doubt—if accepted—to the end of all his money anxieties, present and future. But, as events actually turned out, what happened? Miss Verinder refused him.

On the night of the birthday, therefore, Mr Godfrey Ablewhite's pecuniary position was this. He had three hundred pounds to find on the twenty-fourth of the month, and twenty thousand pounds to find in February eighteen hundred and fifty. Failing to raise these sums, at these times, he was a ruined man.

Under those circumstances, what takes place next?

You exasperate Mr Candy, the doctor, on the sore subject of his profession; and he plays you a practical joke, in return, with a dose of laudanum. He trusts the administration of the dose, prepared in a little phial, to Mr Godfrey Ablewhite—who has himself confessed the share he had in the matter, under circumstances which shall presently be related to you. Mr Godfrey is all the readier to enter into the conspiracy, having himself suffered from your sharp tongue in the course of the evening. He joins Betteredge in persuading you to drink a little brandy and water before you go to bed. He privately drops the dose of laudanum into your cold grog. And you drink the mixture.

Let us now shift the scene, if you please, to Mr Luker's house at Lambeth. And allow me to remark, by way of preface, that Mr Bruff and I, together, have found a means of forcing the money-lender to make a clean breast of it. We have carefully sifted the statement he has addressed to us; and here it is at your service.

IV

Late on the evening of Friday, the twenty-third of June ('forty-eight), Mr Luker was surprised by a visit from Mr Godfrey Ablewhite. He was more than surprised, when Mr Godfrey produced the Moonstone. No such Diamond (according to Mr Luker's experience) was in the possession of any private person in Europe.

Mr Godfrey Ablewhite had two modest proposals to make, in relation to this magnificent gem. First, would Mr Luker be so good as to buy it? Secondly, would Mr Luker (in default of seeing his way to the purchase) undertake to sell it on commission, and to pay a sum down, on the anticipated result?

Mr Luker tested the Diamond, weighed the Diamond, and estimated the value of the Diamond, before he answered a word. *His* estimate (allowing for the flaw in the stone) was thirty thousand pounds.

Having reached that result, Mr Luker opened his lips, and put a question: 'How did you come by this?' Only six words! But what volumes of meaning in them!

Mr Godfrey Ablewhite began a story. Mr Luker opened his lips again, and only said three words, this time. 'That won't do!'

Mr Godfrey Ablewhite began another story. Mr Luker wasted no more words on him. He got up, and rang the bell for the servant, to show the gentleman out.

Upon this compulsion, Mr Godfrey made an effort, and came out with a new and amended version of the affair, to the following effect.

After privately slipping the laudanum into your brandy and water, he wished you good-night, and went into his own room. It was the next room to yours; and the two had a door of communication between them. On entering his own room Mr Godfrey (as he supposed) closed this door. His money-troubles kept him awake. He sat, in his dressing-gown and slippers, for nearly an hour, thinking over his position. Just as he was preparing to get into bed, he heard you, talking to yourself, in your own room, and going to the door of communication, found that he had not shut it as he supposed.

He looked into your room to see what was the matter. He discovered you with the candle in your hand, just leaving your bedchamber. He heard you say to yourself, in a voice quite unlike your own voice, 'How do I know? The Indians may be hidden in the house.'

Up to that time, he had simply supposed himself (in giving you the laudanum) to be helping to make you the victim of a harmless practical joke. It now occurred to him, that the laudanum had taken some effect on you, which had not been foreseen by the doctor, any more than by himself. In the fear of an accident happening, he followed you softly to see what you would do.

He followed you to Miss Verinder's sitting-room, and saw you go in. You left the door open. He looked through the crevice thus produced, between the door and the post, before he ventured into the room himself.

In that position, he not only detected you in taking the Diamond out of the drawer—he also detected Miss Verinder, silently watching you from her bedroom, through her open door. His own eyes satisfied him that *she* saw you take the Diamond, too.

Before you left the sitting-room again, you hesitated a little. Mr Godfrey took advantage of this hesitation to get back again to his bedroom before you come out, and discovered him. He had barely got back, before you got back too. You saw him (as he supposes) just as he was passing through the door of communication. At any rate, you called to him in a strange, drowsy voice.

He came back to you. You looked at him in a dull sleepy way. You put the Diamond into his hand. You said to him, 'Take it back, Godfrey, to your father's bank. It's safe there—it's not safe here.' You turned away unsteadily, and put on your dressing-gown. You sat down in the large arm-chair in your room. You said, '*I* can't take it back to the bank. My head's like lead—and I can't feel my feet under me.' Your head sank on the back of the chair—you heaved a heavy sigh—and you fell asleep.

Mr Godfrey Ablewhite went back, with the Diamond, into his own room. His statement is, that he came to no conclusion, at that time—except that he would wait, and see what happened in the morning.

When the morning came, your language and conduct showed that you were absolutely ignorant of what you had said and done overnight. At the same time, Miss Verinder's language and conduct showed that she was resolved to say nothing (in mercy to you) on her side. If Mr Godfrey Ablewhite chose to keep the Diamond, he might do so with perfect impunity. The Moonstone stood between him and ruin. He put the Moonstone into his pocket.

V

This was the story told by your cousin (under pressure of necessity) to Mr Luker.

Mr Luker believed the story to be, as to all main essentials, true—on this ground, that Mr Godfrey Ablewhite was too great a fool to have invented it. Mr Bruff and I agree with Mr Luker, in considering this test of the truth of the story to be a perfectly reliable one.

The next question, was the question of what Mr Luker would do in the matter of the Moonstone. He proposed the following terms, as the only terms on which he would consent to mix himself up with what was (even in *his* line of business) a doubtful and dangerous transaction.

Mr Luker would consent to lend Mr Godfrey Ablewhite the sum of two thousand pounds, on condition that the Moonstone was to be deposited with him as a pledge. If, at the expiration of one year from that date, Mr Godfrey Ablewhite paid three thousand pounds to Mr Luker, he was to receive back the Diamond, as a pledge redeemed. If he failed to produce the money at the expiration of the year, the pledge (otherwise the Moonstone) was to be considered as forfeited to Mr Luker—who would, in this latter case, generously make Mr Godfrey a present of certain promissory notes of his (relating to former dealings) which were then in the money-lender's possession.

It is needless to say, that Mr Godfrey indignantly refused to listen to these monstrous terms. Mr Luker thereupon, handed him back the Diamond, and wished him good night.

Your cousin went to the door, and came back again. How was he to be sure that the conversation of that evening, would be kept strictly secret between his friend and himself?

Mr Luker didn't profess to know how. If Mr Godfrey had accepted his terms, Mr Godfrey would have made him an accomplice, and might have counted on his silence as on a certainty. As things were, Mr Luker must be guided by his own interests. If awkward inquiries were made, how could he be expected to compromise himself, for the sake of a man who had declined to deal with him?

Receiving this reply, Mr Godfrey Ablewhite did, what all animals (human and otherwise) do, when they find themselves caught in a trap. He looked about him in a state of helpless despair. The day of the month, recorded on a neat little card in a box on the money-lender's chimney-piece, happened to attract his eye. It was the twenty-third of June. On the twenty-fourth, he had three hundred pounds to pay to the young gentleman for whom he was trustee, and no chance of raising the money, except the chance that Mr Luker had offered to him. But for this miserable obstacle, he might have taken the Diamond to Amsterdam, and have made a marketable commodity of it, by having it cut up into separate stones. As matters stood, he had no choice but to accept Mr Luker's terms. After all, he had a year at his disposal, in which to raise the three thousand pounds—and a year is a long time.

Mr Luker drew out the necessary documents on the spot. When they were signed, he gave Mr Godfrey Ablewhite two cheques. One, dated 23 June, for three hundred pounds. Another, dated a week on, for the remaining balance—seventeen hundred pounds.

How the Moonstone was trusted to the keeping of Mr Luker's bankers, and how the Indians treated Mr Luker and Mr Godfrey (after that had been done) you know already.

The next event in your cousin's life, refers again to Miss Verinder. He proposed marriage to her for the second time—and (after having been accepted) he consented, at her request, to consider the marriage as broken off. One of his reasons for making this concession has been penetrated by Mr Bruff. Miss Verinder had only a life interest in her mother's property—and there was no raising the twenty thousand pounds on *that*.

But you will say, he might have saved the three thousand pounds, to redeem the pledged Diamond, if he had married. He might have done so certainly—supposing neither his wife, nor her guardians and trustees, objected to his anticipating more than half of the income at his disposal, for some unknown purpose, in the first year of his marriage. But even if he got over this obstacle, there was another waiting for him in the background. The lady at the Villa, had heard of his contemplated marriage. A superb woman, Mr Blake, of the sort that are not to be trifled with—the sort with the light complexion and the Roman nose. She felt the utmost contempt for Mr Godfrey Ablewhite. It would be silent contempt, if he made a handsome provision for her. Otherwise, it would be contempt with a tongue to it. Miss Verinder's life interest allowed him no more hope of raising the 'provision' than of raising the twenty thousand pounds. He couldn't marry—he really couldn't marry, under all the circumstances.

How he tried his luck again with another lady, and how *that* marriage also broke down on the question of money, you know already. You also know of the legacy of five thousand pounds, left to him shortly afterwards, by one of those many admirers among the soft sex whose good graces this fascinating man had contrived to win. That legacy (as the event has proved) led him to his death.

I have ascertained that when he went abroad, on getting his five thousand pounds, he went to Amsterdam. There, he made all the necessary arrangements for having the Diamond cut into separate stones. He came back (in disguise), and redeemed the Moonstone, on the appointed day. A few days were allowed to elapse (as a precaution agreed to by both parties) before the jewel was actually taken out of the bank. If he had got safe with it to Amsterdam, there would have been just time between July 'forty-nine and February 'fifty (when the young gentleman came of age) to cut the Diamond, and to make a marketable commodity (polished or unpolished) of the separate stones. Judge from this, what motives he had to run the risk which he actually ran. It was 'neck or nothing' with him—if ever it was 'neck or nothing' with a man yet.

I have only to remind you, before closing this Report, that there is a chance of laying hands on the Indians, and of recovering the Moonstone yet. They are now (there is every reason to believe) on their passage to Bombay, in an East Indiaman. The ship (barring accidents) will touch at no other port on her way out; and the authorities at Bombay (already communicated with by letter, overland) will be prepared to board the vessel, the moment she enters the harbour.

I have the honour to remain, dear sir, your obedient servant, Richard Cuff (late sergeant in the Detective Force, Scotland Yard, London).*

SEVENTH NARRATIVE

In a letter from Mr Candy

Frizinghall, Wednesday, 26 September 1849.—Dear Mr Franklin Blake, you will anticipate the sad news I have to tell you, on finding your letter to Ezra Jennings returned to you, unopened, in this enclosure. He died in my arms, at sunrise, on Wednesday last.

I am not to blame for having failed to warn you that his end was at hand. He expressly forbade me to write to you. 'I am indebted to Mr Franklin Blake,' he said, 'for having seen some happy days. Don't distress him, Mr Candy—don't distress him.'

His sufferings, up to the last six hours of his life, were terrible to see. In the intervals of remission, when his mind was clear, I entreated him to tell me of any relatives of his to whom I might write. He asked to be forgiven for refusing anything to *me*. And then he said—not bitterly—that he would die as he had lived, forgotten and unknown. He maintained that resolution to the last. There is no hope now of making any discoveries concerning him. His story is a blank.

The day before he died, he told me where to find all his papers. I brought them to him on his bed. There was a little bundle of old letters which he put aside. There was his unfinished book. There was his Diary—in many locked volumes. He opened the volume for this year, and tore out, one by one, the pages relating to the time when you and he were together. 'Give those,' he said, 'to Mr Franklin Blake. In years to come, he may feel an interest in looking back at what is written there.' Then he clasped his hands, and prayed God fervently to bless you, and those dear to you. He said he should like to see you again. But the next moment, he altered his mind. 'No,' he answered, when I offered to write. 'I won't distress him! I won't distress him!'

At his request, I next collected the other papers—that is to say, the bundle of letters, the unfinished book, and the volumes of the Diary—and enclosed them all in one wrapper, sealed with my own seal. 'Promise,' he said, 'that you will put this into my coffin with your own hand; and that you will see that no other hand touches it afterwards.'

I gave him my promise. And the promise has been performed.

* Note.—Wherever the Report touches on the events of the birthday, or of the three days that followed it, compare with Betteredge's Narrative, chapters viii to xiii.

He asked me to do one other thing for him—which it cost me a hard struggle to comply with. He said, 'Let my grave be forgotten. Give me your word of honour that you will allow no monument of any sort—not even the commonest tombstone—to mark the place of my burial. Let me sleep, nameless. Let me rest, unknown.' When I tried to plead with him to alter his resolution, he became for the first, and only time, violently agitated. I could not bear to see it; and I gave way. Nothing but a little grass mound, marks the place of his rest. In time, the tombstones will rise round it. And the people who come after us will look, and wonder, at the nameless grave.

As I have told you, for six hours before his death his sufferings ceased. He dozed a little. I think he dreamed. Once or twice, he smiled. A woman's name, as I suppose—the name of 'Ella'—was often on his lips at this time. A few minutes before the end came, he asked me to lift him on his pillow, to see the sun rise through the window. He was very weak. His head fell on my shoulder. He whispered, 'It's coming!' Then he said, 'Kiss me!' I kissed his forehead. On a sudden, he lifted his head. The sunlight touched his face. A beautiful expression, an angelic expression, came over it. He cried out three times, 'Peace! peace! peace!' His head sank back again on my shoulder, and the long trouble of his life was at an end.

So he has gone from us. This was, as I think, a great man—though the world never knew him. He bore a hard life bravely. He had the sweetest temper I have ever met with. The loss of him makes me feel very lonely. Perhaps I have never been quite myself again since my illness. Sometimes, I think of giving up my practice, and going away, and trying what some of the foreign baths and waters will do for me.

It is reported here, that you and Miss Verinder are to be married next month. Please to accept my best congratulations.

The pages of my poor friend's Journal are waiting for you at my house—sealed up, with your name on the wrapper. I was afraid to trust them to the post.

My best respects and good wishes attend Miss Verinder. I remain, dear Mr Franklin Blake, truly yours, Thomas Candy.

EIGHTH NARRATIVE

Contributed by Gabriel Betteredge

I am the person (as you remember, no doubt) who led the way in these pages, and opened the story. I am also the person who is left behind, as it were, to close the story up.

Let nobody suppose that I have any last words to say here, concerning the Indian Diamond. I hold that unlucky jewel in abhorrence—and I refer you to other authority than mine, for such news of the Moonstone as you may, at the present time, be expected to receive. My purpose, in this place, is to state a fact in the history of the family, which has been passed over by everybody, and which I won't allow to be disrespectfully smothered up in that way. The fact to which I allude is—the marriage of Miss Rachel and Mr Franklin Blake. This interesting event took place at our house in Yorkshire, on Tuesday, October ninth, eighteen hundred and forty-nine. I had a new suit of clothes on the occasion. And the married couple went to spend the honeymoon in Scotland.

Family festivals having been rare enough at our house, since my poor mistress's death, I own—on this occasion of the wedding—to having (towards the latter part of the day) taken a drop too much on the strength of it.

If you have ever done the same sort of thing yourself, you will understand and feel for me. If you have not, you will very likely say, 'Disgusting old man! why does he tell us this?' The reason why is now to come.

Having, then, taken my drop (bless you! you have got your favourite vice, too; only your vice isn't mine, and mine isn't yours), I next applied the one infallible remedy—that remedy being, as you know, *Robinson Crusoe*. Where I opened that unrivalled book, I can't say. Where the lines of print at last left off running into each other, I know, however, perfectly well. It was at page three hundred and eighteen—a domestic bit concerning Robinson Crusoe's marriage, as follows:

'With those Thoughts, I considered my new Engagement, that I had a Wife'—(Observe! so had Mr Franklin!)—'one Child bore'—(Observe again! that might yet be Mr Franklin's case, too!)—'and my Wife then'—What Robinson Crusoe's wife did, or did not do, 'then,' I felt no desire to discover. I scored the bit about the Child with my pencil, and put a morsel of paper for a mark to keep the place: 'Lie you there,' I said, 'till the marriage of Mr Franklin and Miss Rachel is some months older—and then we'll see!'

The months passed (more than I had bargained for), and no occasion presented itself for disturbing that mark in the book. It was not till this present month of November, eighteen hundred and fifty, that Mr Franklin came into my room, in high good spirits, and said, 'Betteredge! I have got some news for you! Something is going to happen in the house, before we are many months older.'

'Does it concern the, family, sir?' I asked.

'It decidedly concerns the family,' says Mr Franklin.

'Has your good lady anything to do with it, if you please, sir?'

'She has a great deal to do with it,' says Mr Franklin, beginning to look a little surprised.

'You needn't say a word more, sir,' I answered. 'God bless you both! I'm heartily glad to hear it.'

Mr Franklin stared like a person thunderstruck. 'May I venture to inquire where you got your information?' he asked.

'I only got mine (imparted in the strictest secrecy) five minutes since.'

Here was an opportunity of producing *Robinson Crusoe*! Here was a chance of reading that domestic bit about the child which I had marked on the day of Mr Franklin's marriage! I read those miraculous words with an emphasis which did them justice, and then I looked him severely in the face. '*Now*, sir, do you believe in *Robinson Crusoe*?' I asked, with a solemnity suitable to the occasion.

'Betteredge!' says Mr Franklin, with equal solemnity, 'I'm convinced at last.' He shook hands with me—and I felt that I had converted him.

With the relation of this extraordinary circumstance, my reappearance in these pages comes to an end. Let nobody laugh at the unique anecdote here related. You are welcome to be as merry as you please over everything else I have written. But when I write of *Robinson Crusoe*, by the Lord it's serious—and I request you to take it accordingly!

When this is said, all is said. Ladies and gentlemen, I make my bow, and shut up the story.

EPILOGUE

THE FINDING OF THE DIAMOND

I

THE STATEMENT OF SERGEANT CUFF'S MAN (1849)

On the twenty-seventh of June last, I received instructions from Sergeant Cuff to follow three men; suspected of murder, and described as Indians. They had been seen on the Tower Wharf that morning, embarking on board the steamer bound for Rotterdam.

I left London by a steamer belonging to another company, which sailed on the morning of Thursday the twenty-eighth. Arriving at Rotterdam, I succeeded in finding the commander of the Wednesday's steamer. He informed me that the Indians had certainly been passengers on board his vessel—but as far as Gravesend only. Off that place, one of the three had inquired at what time they would reach Calais. On being informed that the steamer was bound to Rotterdam, the spokesman of the party expressed the greatest surprise and distress at the mistake which he and his two friends had made. They were all willing (he said) to sacrifice their passage money, if the commander of the steamer would only put them ashore. Commiserating their position, as foreigners in a strange land, and knowing no reason for detaining them, the commander signalled for a shore boat, and the three men left the vessel.

This proceeding of the Indians having been plainly resolved on beforehand, as a means of preventing their being traced, I lost no time in returning to England. I left the steamer at Gravesend, and discovered that the Indians had gone from that place to London. Thence, I again traced them as having left for Plymouth. Inquiries made at Plymouth, proved that they had sailed, forty-eight hours previously, in the *Bewley Castle*, East Indiaman, bound direct to Bombay.

On receiving this intelligence, Sergeant Cuff caused the authorities at Bombay to be communicated with, overland—so that the vessel might be boarded by the police immediately on her entering the port. This step having been taken, my connection with the matter came to an end. I have heard nothing more of it since that time.

II

THE STATEMENT OF THE CAPTAIN (1849)

I am requested by Sergeant Cuff to set in writing certain facts, concerning three men (believed to be Hindoos) who were passengers, last summer, in the ship *Bewley Castle*, bound for Bombay direct, under my command.

The Hindoos joined us at Plymouth. On the passage out, I heard no complaint of their conduct, They were berthed in the forward part of the vessel. I had but few occasions myself of personally noticing them.

In the latter part of the voyage, we had the misfortune to be becalmed for three days and nights, off the coast of India. I have not got the ship's journal to refer to, and I cannot now call to mind the latitude and longitude. As to our position, therefore, I am only able to state generally that the currents drifted us in towards the land, and that when the wind found us again, we reached our port in twenty-four hours afterwards.

The discipline of a ship (as all seafaring persons know) becomes relaxed in a long calm. The discipline of my ship became relaxed. Certain gentlemen among the passengers got some of the smaller boats lowered, and amused themselves by rowing about, and swimming, when the sun at evening time was cool enough to let them divert themselves in that way. The boats when done with, ought to have been slung up again in their places. Instead of this they were left moored to the ship's side. What with the heat, and what with the vexation of the weather, neither officers nor men seemed to be in heart for their duty while the calm lasted.

On the third night, nothing unusual was heard or seen by the watch on deck. When the morning came, the smallest of the boats was missing—and the three Hindoos were next reported to be missing too.

If these men had stolen the boat shortly after dark (which I have no doubt they did), we were near enough to the land to make it vain to send in pursuit of them, when the discovery was made in the morning. I have no doubt they got ashore, in that calm weather (making all due allowance for fatigue and clumsy rowing), before day-break.

On reaching our port, I there learnt, for the first time, the reason these passengers had for seizing their opportunity of escaping from the ship. I could only make the same statement to the authorities which I have made here. They considered me to blame for allowing the discipline of the vessel to be relaxed. I have expressed my regret on this score to them, and to my owners. Since that time, nothing has been heard to my knowledge of the three Hindoos. I have no more to add to what is here written.

III

THE STATEMENT OF MR MURTHWAITE (1850)

(*In a letter to* Mr Bruff)

Have any recollection, my dear sir, of a semi-savage person whom you met out at dinner, in London, in the autumn of 'forty-eight? Permit me to remind you that the person's name was Murthwaite, and that you and he had a long conversation together after dinner. The talk related to an Indian Diamond, called the Moonstone, and to a conspiracy then in existence to get possession of the gem.

Since that time, I have been wandering in Central Asia. Thence I have drifted back to the scene of some of my past adventures in the north and north-west of India. About a fortnight since, I found myself in a certain district or province (but little known to Europeans) called Kattiawar.

Here an adventure befell me, in which (incredible as it may appear) you are personally interested.

In the wild regions of Kattiawar (and how wild they are, you will understand, when I tell you that even the husbandmen plough the land, armed to the teeth), the population is fanatically devoted to the old Hindoo religion—to the ancient worship of Bramah and Vishnu. The few Mahometan families, thinly scattered about the villages in the interior, are afraid to taste meat of any kind. A Mahometan even suspected of killing that sacred animal, the cow, is, as a matter of course, put to death without mercy in these parts by the pious Hindoo neighbours who surround him. To strengthen the religious enthusiasm of the people, two of the most famous shrines of Hindoo pilgrimage are contained within the boundaries of Kattiawar. One of them is Dwarka, the birthplace of the god Krishna. The other is the sacred city of Somnauth—sacked, and destroyed, as long since as the eleventh century, by the Mahometan conqueror, Mahmoud of Ghizni.

Finding myself, for the second time, in these romantic regions, I resolved not to leave Kattiawar, without looking once more on the magnificent desolation of Somnauth. At the place where I planned to do this, I was (as nearly as I could calculate it) some three days distant, journeying on foot, from the sacred city.

I had not been long on the road, before I noticed that other people—by twos and threes—appeared to be travelling in the same direction as myself.

To such of these as spoke to me, I gave myself out as a Hindoo-Boodhist, from a distant province, bound on a pilgrimage. It is needless to say that my dress was of the sort to carry out this description. Add, that I know the language as well as I know my own, and that I am lean enough and brown enough to make it no easy matter to detect my European origin—and you will understand that I passed muster with the people readily: not as one of themselves, but as a stranger from a distant part of their own country.

On the second day, the number of Hindoos travelling in my direction, had increased to fifties and hundreds. On the third day, the throng had swollen to thousands; all slowly converging to one point—the city of Somnauth.

A trifling service which I was able to render to one of my fellow-pilgrims, during the third day's journey, proved the means of introducing me to certain Hindoos of the higher caste. From these men I learnt that the multitude was on its way to a great religious ceremony, which was to take place on a hill at a little distance from Somnauth. The ceremony was in honour of the god of the Moon; and it was to be held at night.

The crowd detained us as we drew near to the place of celebration. By the time we reached the hill, the moon was high in the heaven. My Hindoo friends possessed some special privileges which enabled them to gain access to the shrine. They kindly allowed me to accompany them. When we arrived at the place, we found the shrine hidden from our view by a curtain hung between two magnificent trees. Beneath the trees, a flat projection of rock jutted out, and formed a species of natural platform. Below this, I stood, in company with my Hindoo friends.

Looking back down the hill, the view presented the grandest spectacle of Nature and Man, in combination, that I have ever seen. The lower slopes of the eminence melted imperceptibly into a grassy plain, the place of the meeting of three rivers. On one side, the graceful winding of the waters stretched away, now visible, now hidden by trees, as far as the eye could see. On the other, the waveless ocean slept in the calm of the night. People this lovely scene with tens of thousands of human creatures, all dressed in white, stretching down the sides of the hill, overflowing into the plain, and fringing the nearer banks of the winding rivers. Light this halt of the pilgrims by the wild red flames of cressets and torches, streaming up at intervals from every part of the innumerable throng. Imagine the moonlight of the East, pouring in unclouded glory over all—and you will form some idea of the view that met me when I looked forth from the summit of the hill.

A strain of plaintive music, played on stringed instruments and flutes, recalled my attention to the hidden shrine.

I turned, and saw on the rocky platform, the figures of three men. In the central figure of the three I recognized the man to whom I had spoken in England, when the Indians appeared on the terrace at Lady Verinder's house. The other two who had been his companions on that occasion, were no doubt his companions also on this.

One of the spectators, near whom I was standing, saw me start. In a whisper, he explained to me the apparition of the three figures on the platform of rock.

They were Brahmins (he said) who had forfeited their caste, in the service of the god. The god had commanded that their purification should be the purification by pilgrimage. On that night, the three men were to part. In three separate directions, they were to set forth as pilgrims to the shrines of India. Never more were they to look on each other's faces. Never more were they to rest on their wanderings, from the day which witnessed their separation, to the day which witnessed their death.

As those words were whispered to me, the plaintive music ceased. The three men prostrated themselves on the rock, before the curtain which hid the shrine. They rose—they looked on one another—they embraced. Then they descended separately among the people. The people made way for them in dead silence. In three different directions, I saw the crowd part, at one and the same moment. Slowly the grand white mass of the people closed together again. The track of the doomed men through the ranks of their fellow mortals was obliterated. We saw them no more.

A new strain of music, loud and jubilant, rose from the hidden shrine. The crowd around me shuddered, and pressed together.

The curtain between the trees was drawn aside, and the shrine was disclosed to view.

There, raised high on a throne—seated on his typical antelope, with his four arms stretching towards the four corners of the earth—there, soared above us, dark and awful in the mystic light of heaven, the god of the Moon. And there, in the forehead of the deity, gleamed the yellow Diamond, whose splendour had last shone on me in England, from the bosom of a woman's dress!

Yes! after the lapse of eight centuries, the Moonstone looks forth once more, over the walls of the sacred city in which its story first began. How it has found its way back to its wild native land—by what accident, or by what crime, the Indians regained possession of their sacred gem, may be in your knowledge, but is not in mine. You have lost sight of it in England, and (if I know anything of this people) you have lost sight of it for ever.

So the years pass, and repeat each other; so the same events revolve in the cycles of time. What will be the next adventures of the Moonstone? Who can tell!

The Amateur Cracksman

by E. W. Hornung

THE IDES OF MARCH

It was about half-past twelve when I returned to the Albany as a last desperate resort. The scene of my disaster was much as I had left it. The baccarat-counters still strewed the table, with the empty glasses and the loaded ash-trays. A window had been opened to let the smoke out, and was letting in the fog instead. Raffles himself had merely discarded his dining-jacket for one of his innumerable blazers. Yet he arched his eyebrows as though I had dragged him from his bed.

'Forgotten something?' said he, when he saw me on the mat.

'No,' said I, pushing past him without ceremony. And I led the way into his room with an impudence amazing to myself.

'Not come back for your revenge, have you. Because I'm afraid I can't give it you single-handed. I was sorry myself that the others—'

We were face to face by his fireside, and I cut him short.

'Raffles,' said I, 'you may well be surprised at my coming back in this way and at this hour. I hardly know you. I was never in your rooms before tonight. But I fagged for you at school, and you said you remembered me. Of course that's no excuse; but will you listen to me—for two minutes?'

In my emotion I had at first to struggle for every word; but his face reassured me as I went on, and I was not mistaken in its expression.

'Certainly my dear fellow,' said he, 'as many minutes as you like. Have a Sullivan and sit down.' And he handed me his silver cigarette-case.

'No,' said I, finding a full voice as I shook my head; 'no, I won't smoke, and I won't sit down, thank you. Nor will you ask me to do either when you've heard what I have to say.'

'Really?' said he, lighting his own cigarette with one clear blue eye upon me. 'How do you know?'

'Because you will probably show me the door,' I cried bitterly; 'and you'll be justified in doing it! But it's no good beating about the bush. You know I dropped over two hundred just now?'

He nodded.

'I hadn't the money in my pocket.'

'I remember.'

'But I had my cheque-book, and I wrote each of you a cheque at that desk.'

'Well?'

'Not one of them was worth the paper it was written on, Raffles. I am overdrawn already at my bank!'

'Surely only for the moment?'

'No. I have spent everything.'

'But somebody told me you were so well off. I heard you had come in for money?'

'So I did. Three years ago. It has been my curse; now it's all gone—every penny! Yes, I've been a fool; there never was nor will be such a fool as I've been. . . . Isn't this enough for you? Why don't you turn me out?' He was walking up and down with a very long face instead.

'Couldn't your people do anything?' he asked at length.

'Thank God,' I cried, 'I have no people! I was an only child. I came in for everything there was. My one comfort is that they're gone, and will never know.'

'I cast myself into a chair and hid my face. Raffles continued to pace the rich carpet that was of a piece with everything else in his rooms. There was no variation in his soft and even footfalls.

'You used to be a literary little cuss,' he said at length; 'didn't you edit the mag before you left? Anyway I recollect fagging you to do my verses; and literature of sorts is the very thing nowadays; any fool can make a living at it.'

I shook my head. 'Any fool couldn't write off my debts,' said I.

'Then you have a flat somewhere?' he went on.

'Yes, in Mount Street.'

'Well, what about the furniture?'

I laughed aloud in my misery. 'There's been a bill of sale on every stick for months!' And at that Raffles stood still, with raised eyebrows and stern eyes that I could meet the better now that he knew the worst; then, with a shrug, he resumed his walk, and for some minutes neither of us spoke. But in his handsome unmoved face I read my fate and death-warrant; and with every breath I cursed my folly and my cowardice in coming to him at all. Because he had been kind to me at school, when he was captain of the eleven, and I his fag, I had dared to look for kindness from him now; because I was ruined, and he rich enough to play cricket all the summer, and do nothing for the rest of the year, I had fatuously counted on his mercy, his sympathy, his help! Yes, I had relied on him in my heart, for all my outward diffidence and humility; and I was rightly served. There was as little of mercy as of sympathy in that curling nostril, that rigid jaw, that cold blue eye which never glanced my way. I caught up my hat. I blundered to my feet. I would have gone without a word, but Raffles stood between me and the door.

'Where are you going?' said he.

'That's my business,' I replied. 'I won't trouble you any more.'

'Then how am I to help you?'

'I didn't ask your help.'

'Then why come to me?'

'Why, indeed!' I echoed. 'Will you let me pass?'

'Not until you tell me where you are going and what you mean to do.'

'Can't you guess?' I cried. And for many seconds we stood staring in each other's eyes.

'Have you got the pluck?' said he, breaking the spell in a tone so cynical that it brought my last drop of blood to the boil.

'You shall see,' said I, as I stepped back and whipped the pistol from my overcoat pocket. 'Now, will you let me pass or shall I do it here?'

The barrel touched my temple, and my thumb the trigger. Mad with excitement as I was, ruined, dishonoured, and now finally determined to make an end of my mis-spent life, my only surprise to this day is that I did not do so then and there. The despicable satisfaction of involving another in one's destruction added its miserable appeal to my baser egoism; and had fear or horror flown to my companion's face, I shudder to think I

340

might have died diabolically happy with that look for my last impious consolation. It was the look that came instead which held my hand. Neither fear nor horror were in it; only wonder, admiration, and such a measure of pleased expectancy as caused me after all to pocket my revolver with an oath.

'You devil!' I said. 'I believe you wanted me to do it!'

'Not quite,' was the reply, made with a little start, and a change of colour that came too late. 'To tell you the truth, though, I half thought you meant it, and I was never more fascinated in my life. I never dreamt you had such stuff in you, Bunny! No, I'm hanged if I let you go now. And you'd better not try that game again, for you won't catch me stand and look on a second time. We must think of some way out, of the mess. I had no idea you were a chap of that sort! There, let me have the gun.'

One of his hands fell kindly on my shoulder, while the other slipped into my overcoat pocket, and I suffered him to deprive me of my weapon without a murmur. Nor was this simply because Raffles had the power of making himself irresistible at will. He was beyond comparison the most masterful man whom I have ever known; yet my acquiescence was due to more than the mere subjection of the weaker nature to the stronger. The forlorn hope which had brought me to the Albany was turned as by magic into an almost staggering sense of safety. Raffles would help me after all! A.J. Raffles would be my friend! It was as though all the world had come round suddenly to my side; so far, therefore, from resisting his action, I caught and clasped his hand with a fervour as uncontrollable as the frenzy which had preceded it.

'God bless you!' I cried. 'Forgive me for everything. I will tell you the truth. I did think you might help me in my extremity, though I well knew that I had no claim upon you. Still—for the old school's sake—the sake of old times—I thought you might give me another chance. If you wouldn't, I meant to blow out my brains—and will still if you change your mind.'

In truth I feared that it was changing, with his expression, even as I spoke, and in spite of his kindly tone and kindlier use of my old school nickname. His next words showed me my mistake.

'What a boy it is for jumping to conclusions! I have my vices, Bunny, but backing and filling is not one of them. Sit down, my good fellow, and have a cigarette to soothe your nerves. I insist. Whisky? The worst thing for you; here's some coffee that I was brewing when you came in. Now listen to me. You speak of ''another chance''. What do you mean? Another chance at baccarat? Not if I know it. You think the luck must turn; suppose it didn't. We should only have made bad worse. No, my dear chap, you've plunged enough. Do you put yourself in my hands or do you not? Very well then, you plunge no more, and I undertake not to present my cheque. Unfortunately, there are the other men; and still more unfortunately, Bunny, I'm as hard up at this moment as you are yourself!'

It was my turn to stare at Raffles. 'You?' I vociferated. 'You hard up? How am I to sit here and believe that?'

'Did I refuse to believe it of you?' he returned, smiling. 'And, with your own experience, do you think that because a fellow has rooms in this place, and belongs to a club or two, and plays a little cricket, he must necessarily have a balance at the bank? I tell you, my dear man, that at this moment I'm as hard up as ever you were. I have nothing but my wits to live on—absolutely nothing else. It was as necessary for me to win some money this evening as it was for you. We're in the same boat, Bunny, we'd better pull together.'

'Together!' I jumped at it. 'I'll do anything in this world for you, Raffles,' I said, 'if you really mean that you won't give me away. Think of anything you like and I'll do it! I was a desperate man when I came here, and I'm just as desperate now. I don't mind what I do if only I can get out of this without a scandal.'

Again I see him, leaning back in one of the luxurious chairs with which his room was furnished. I see his indolent, athletic figure; his pale, sharp, clean-shaven features; his curly black hair; his strong unscrupulous mouth. And again I feel the clear beam of his wonderful eye, cold and luminous as a star, shining into my brain—sifting the very secrets of my heart.

'I wonder if you mean all that!' he said at length. 'You do in your present mood; but who can back his mood to last? Still, there's hope when a chap takes that tone. Now I think of it, too, you were a plucky little devil at school; you once did me rather a good turn, I recollect. Remember it, Bunny? Well, wait a bit, and perhaps I'll be able to do you a better one. Give me time to think.'

He got up, lit a fresh cigarette, and fell to pacing the room once more, but with a slower and more thoughtful step, and for a much longer period than before. Twice he stopped at my chair as though on the point of speaking, but each time he checked himself and resumed his stride in silence. Once he threw up the window, which he had shut some time since, and stood for some moments leaning out into the fog which filled the Albany courtyard. Meanwhile a clock on the chimneypiece struck one, and one again for the half-hour, without a word between us.

Yet I not only kept my chair with patience, but I acquired an incongruous equanimity in that half-hour. Insensibly I had shifted my burden to the broad shoulders of this splendid friend, and my thoughts wandered with my eyes as the minutes passed. The room was the good-sized, square one, with the folding doors, the marble mantelpiece, and the gloomy, old-fashioned distinction peculiar to the Albany. It was charmingly furnished and arranged with the right amount of negligence and the right amount of taste. What struck me most, however, was the absence of the usual insignia of a cricketer's den. Instead of the conventional rack of war-worn bats, a carved oak bookcase, with every shelf in a litter, filled the better part of one wall; and where I looked for cricketing groups, I found reproductions of such works as 'Love and Death' and 'The Blessed Damozel', in dusty frames and different parallels. The man might have been a minor poet instead of an athlete of the first water. But there had always been a fine streak of aestheticism in his complex composition; some of these very pictures I had myself dusted in his study at school; and they set me thinking of yet another of his many sides—and of the little incident to which he had just referred.

Everybody knows how largely the tone of a public school depends on that of the eleven, and on the character of the captain of cricket in particular; and I have never heard it denied that in A.J. Raffles's time our tone was good, or that such influence as he troubled to exert was on the side of the angels. Yet it was whispered in the school that he was in the habit of parading the town at night in loud checks and a false beard. It was whispered, and disbelieved. I alone knew it for a fact; for night after night had I pulled the rope up after him when the rest of the dormitory was asleep, and kept awake by the hour to let it down again on a given signal. Well, one night he was over-bold, and within an ace of ignominious expulsion in the hey-day of his fame. Consummate daring and extraordinary nerve on his part, aided, doubtless, by some little presence of mind on mine, averted that untoward result; and no more need be said of a discreditable incident. But I cannot pretend to have forgotten it in throwing myself on this man's mercy in my desperation. And I was wondering how much of his leniency was owing to the fact that Raffles had not forgotten it either, when he stopped and stood over my chair once more.

'I've been thinking of that night we had the narrow squeak,' he began. 'Why do you start?'

'I was thinking of it too.'

He smiled, as though he had read my thoughts.

'Well, you were the right sort of little beggar then, Bunny; you didn't talk and you didn't flinch. You asked no questions and you told no tales. I wonder if you're like that now?'

'I don't know,' said I, slightly puzzled by his tone. 'I've made such a mess of my own affairs that I trust myself about as little as I'm likely to be trusted by anybody else. Yet I never in my life went back on a friend. I will say that; otherwise perhaps I mightn't be in such a hole tonight.'

'Exactly,' said Raffles, nodding to himself, as though in assent to some hidden train of thought; 'exactly what I remember of you, and I'll bet it's as true now as it was ten years ago. We don't alter, Bunny. We only develop. I suppose neither you nor I are really altered since you used to let down that rope and I used to come up it hand over hand. You would stick at nothing for a pal—what?'

'At nothing in this world,' I was pleased to cry.

'Not even at a crime?' said Raffles, smiling.

I stopped to think, for his tone had changed, and I felt sure he was chaffing me. Yet his eye seemed as much in earnest as ever, and for my part I was in no mood for reservations.

'No, not even at that,' I declared; 'name your crime, and I'm your man.'

He looked at me one moment in wonder, and another moment in doubt; then turned the matter off with a shake of his head, and the little cynical laugh that was all his own.

'You're a nice chap, Bunny! A real desperate character—what? Suicide one moment, and any crime I like the next! What you want is a drag, my boy, and you did well to come to a decent law-abiding citizen with a reputation to lose. None the less we must have that money tonight—by hook or crook.'

'Tonight, Raffles?'

'The sooner the better. Every hour after ten o'clock tomorrow morning is an hour of risk. Let one of those cheques get round to your own bank, and you and it are dishonoured together. No, we must raise the wind tonight and re-open your account first thing tomorrow. And I rather think I know where the wind can be raised.'

'At two o'clock in the morning?'

'Yes.'

'But how—but where—at such an hour?'

'From a friend of mine here in Bond Street.'

'He must be a very intimate friend.'

'Intimate's not the word. I have the run of his place and a latchkey all to myself.'

'You would knock him up at this hour of the night?'

'If he's in bed.'

'And it's essential that I should go in with you?'

'Absolutely.'

'Then I must; but I'm bound to say I don't like the idea, Raffles.'

'Do you prefer the alternative?' asked my companion, with a sneer. 'No, hang it, that's unfair!' he cried apologetically in the same breath. 'I quite understand. It's a beastly ordeal. But it would never do for you to stay outside. I tell you what, you shall have a peg before we start—just one. There's the whisky, here's the syphon, and I'll be putting on an overcoat while you help yourself.'

Well, I daresay I did so with some freedom, for this plan of his was not the less distasteful to me from its apparent inevitability. I must own, however, that it possessed fewer terrors before my glass was empty. Meanwhile Raffles rejoined me, with a covert-coat over his blazer, and a soft felt hat set carelessly on the curly head he shook with a smile as I passed him the decanter.

'When we come back,' said he. 'Work first, play afterwards. Do you see what day it is?' he added, tearing a leaflet from a Shakespearean calendar as I drained my glass. 'March 15th. "The Ides of March, the Ides of March, remember." Eh, Bunny, my boy? You won't forget them, will you?'

And, with a laugh, he threw some coals on the fire before turning down the gas like a careful householder. So we went out together as the clock on the chimneypiece was striking two.

II

Piccadilly was a trench of raw white fog, rimmed with blurred street-lamps, and lined with a thin coating of adhesive mud. We met no other wayfarers on the deserted flag-stones, and were ourselves favoured with a very hard stare from the constable of the beat, who, however, touched his helmet on recognising my companion.

'You see, I'm known to the police,' laughed Raffles as we passed on. 'Poor devils, they've got to keep their weather eye open on a night like this! A fog may be a bore to you and me, Bunny, but it's a perfect godsend to the criminal classes, especially so late in their season. Here we are, though—and I'm hanged if the beggar isn't in bed and asleep after all!'

We had turned into Bond Street, and had halted on the kerb a few yards down on the right. Raffles was gazing up at some windows across the road, windows barely discernible through the mist, and without the glimmer of a light to throw them out. They were over a jeweller's shop, as I could see by the peep-hole in the shop door, and the bright light burning within. But the entire 'upper part', with the private street door next to the shop, was black and blank as the sky itself.

'Better give it up for tonight,' I urged. 'Surely the morning will be time enough!'

'Not a bit of it,' said Raffles. 'I have his key. We'll surprise him. Come along.'

And seizing my right arm, he hurried me across the road, opened the door with his latchkey, and in another moment had shut it swiftly but softly behind us. We stood together in the dark. Outside, a measured step was approaching; we had heard it through the fog as we crossed the street; now, as it drew nearer, my companion's fingers tightened on my arm.

'It may be the chap himself,' he whispered. 'He's the devil of a night-bird. Not a sound, Bunny! We'll startle the life out of him. Ah!'

The measured step had passed without a pause. Raffles drew a deep breath, and his singular grip of me slowly relaxed.

'But still, not a sound,' he continued in the same whisper; 'we'll take a rise out of him, wherever he is! Slip off your shoes and follow me.'

Well, you may wonder at my doing so, but you can never have met A.J. Raffles. Half his power lay in a conciliating trick of sinking the commander in the leader. And it was impossible not to follow one who led with such a zest. You might question, but you followed first. So now, when I heard him kick off his own shoes, I did the same, and was on the stairs at his heels before I realised what an extraordinary way was this of approaching a stranger for money in the dead of night. But obviously Raffles and he were on exceptional terms of intimacy, and I could not infer but that they were in the habit of playing practical jokes on each other.

We groped our way so slowly upstairs that I had time to make more than one note before we reached the top. The stair was uncarpeted. The spread fingers of my right hand encountered nothing on the damp wall: those of my left trailed through a dust that could be felt on the banisters. An eerie sensation had been upon me since we entered the house. It increased with every step we climbed. What hermit were we going to startle in his cell?

We came to a landing. The banisters led us to the left, and to the left again. Four steps more, and we were on another and a longer landing, and suddenly a match blazed from the back. I never heard it struck. Its flash was blinding. When my eyes became accustomed to the light, there was Raffles holding up the match with one hand, and shading it with the other, between bare boards, stripped walls, and the open doors of empty rooms.

'Where have you brought me?' I cried. 'The house is unoccupied!'

'Hush! Wait!' he whispered, and he led the way into one of the empty rooms. His match went out as we crossed the threshold, and he struck another without the slightest noise. Then he stood with his back to me, fumbling with something that I could not see. But, when he threw the second match away, there was some other light in its stead, and a slight smell of oil. I stepped forward to look over his shoulder, but before I could do so he had turned and flashed a tiny lantern in my face.

'What's this?' I gasped. 'What rotten trick are you going to play?'

'It's played,' he answered, with his quiet laugh.

'On me?'

'I'm afraid so, Bunny.'

'Is there no one in the house, then?'

'No one but ourselves.'

'So it was mere chaff about your friend in Bond Street who could let us have that money?'

'Not altogether. It's quite true that Danby is a friend of mine.'

'Danby?'

'The jeweller underneath.'

'What do you mean?' I whispered, trembling like a leaf as his meaning dawned upon me. 'Are you going to get the money from the jeweller?'

'Well, not exactly.'

'What then?'

'The equivalent—from his shop.'

There was no need for another question. I understood everything but my own density. He had given me a dozen hints, and I had taken none. And there I stood staring at him, in that empty room; and there he stood with his dark lantern, laughing at me.

'A burglar!' I gasped. 'You—you!'

'I told you I lived by my wits.'

'Why couldn't you tell me what you were going to do? Why couldn't you trust me? Why must you lie?' I demanded, piqued to the quick for all my horror.

'I wanted to tell you,' said he. 'I was on the point of telling you more than once. You may remember how I sounded you about crime, though you have probably forgotten what you said yourself. I didn't think you meant it at the time, but I thought I'd put you to the test. Now I see you didn't, and I don't blame you. I only am to blame. Get out of it, my dear boy, as quick as you can; leave it to me. You won't give me away, whatever else you do!'

Oh, his cleverness! His fiendish cleverness! Had he fallen back on threats, coercion, sneers, all might have been different even then. But he set me free to leave him in the lurch. He would not blame me. He did not even bind me to secrecy; he trusted me. He knew my weakness and my strength, and was playing on both with his master's touch.

'Not so fast,' said I. 'Did I put this into your head, or were you going to do it in any case?'

'Not in any case,' said Raffles. 'It's true I've had the key for days, but when I won tonight I thought of chucking it; for, as a matter of fact, it's not a one-man job.'

'That settles it. I'm your man.'

'You mean it?'

'Yes—for tonight.'

'Good old Bunny,' he murmured, holding the lantern for one moment to my face; the next he was explaining his plans, and I was nodding, as though we had been fellow cracksmen all our days.

'I know the shop,' he whispered, 'because I've got a few things there. I know this upper part too; it's been to let for a month, and I got an order to view, and took a cast of the key before using it. The one thing I don't know is how to make a connection between the two; at present there's none. We may make it up here, though I rather fancy the basement myself. If you wait a minute I'll tell you.'

He set his lantern on the floor, and crept to a back window, and opened it with scarcely a sound; only to return shaking his head, after shutting the window with the same care.

'That was our one chance,' said he, 'a back window above a back window but it's too dark to see anything, and we daren't show an outside light. Come down after me to the basement; and remember, though there's not a soul on the premises, you can't make too little noise. There—there—listen to that!'

It was the measured tread that we had heard before on the flagstones outside. Raffles darkened his lantern, and again we stood motionless till it had passed.

'Either a policeman,' he muttered, 'or a watchman that all these jewellers run between them. The watchman's the man for us to watch; he's simply paid to spot this kind of thing.'

We crept very gingerly down the stairs, which creaked a bit in spite of us, and we picked up our shoes in the passage; then down some narrow stone steps, at the foot of which Raffles showed his light, and put on his shoes once more, bidding me do the same in rather a louder tone than he had permitted himself to employ overhead. We were now considerably below the level of the street, in a small space with as many doors as it had sides. Three were ajar, and we saw through them into empty cellars; but in the fourth a key was turned and a bolt drawn; this one presently let us out into the bottom of a deep square well of fog. A similar door faced it across this area, and Raffles had the lantern close against it, and was hiding the light with his body, when a short and sudden crash made my heart stand still. Next moment I saw the door wide open, and Raffles standing within and beckoning me with a jemmy.

'Door number one,' he whispered. 'Deuce knows how many more there'll be, but I know of two at least. We won't have to make much noise over them, either; down here there's less risk.'

We were now at the bottom of the exact fellow to the narrow stone stair which we had just descended; the yard, or well, being the one part common to both the private and the business premises. But this flight led to no open passage; instead, a singularly solid mahogany door confronted us at the top.

'I thought so,' muttered Raffles, handing me the lantern, and pocketing a bunch of skeleton keys, after tampering for a few minutes with the lock. 'It'll be an hour's work to get through that!'

'Can't you pick it?'

'No. I know these locks. It's no use trying. We must cut it out, and it'll take us an hour.'

It took us forty-seven minutes by my watch; or rather it took Raffles, and never in my life have I seen anything more deliberately done. My part was simply to stand by with the dark lantern in one hand, and a small bottle of rock-oil in the other. Raffles had produced a pretty embroidered case, intended obviously for his razors, but filled instead with the tools of his secret trade, including the rock-oil. From this case he selected a bit, capable of drilling a hole an inch in diameter, and fitted it to a small but very strong steel brace. Then he took off his covert-coat and his blazer, spread them neatly on the top step—knelt on them—turned up his shirtcuffs—and went to work with brace-and-bit near the keyhole. But first he oiled the bit to minimise the noise, and this he did invariably before beginning a fresh hole, and often in the middle of one. It took thirty-two separate borings to cut round that lock.

I noticed that through the first circular orifice Raffles thrust a forefinger; then, as the circle became an ever-lengthening oval, he got his hand through up to the thumb, and I heard him swear softly to himself.

'I was afraid so!'

'What is it?'

'An iron gate on the other side!'

'How on earth are we to get through that?' I asked in dismay.

'Pick the lock. But there may be two. In that case they'll be top and bottom, and we shall have two fresh holes to make, as the door opens inwards. It won't open two inches as it is.'

I confess I did not feel sanguine about the lock-picking, seeing that one lock had baffled us already; and my disappointment and impatience must have been a revelation to me had I stopped to think. The truth is that I was entering into our nefarious undertaking with an involuntary zeal of which I was myself quite unconscious at the time. The romance and the peril of the whole proceeding held me spellbound and entranced. My moral sense and my sense of fear were stricken by a common paralysis. And there I stood, shining my light and holding my phial with a keener interest than I had ever brought to any honest avocation. And there knelt A.J. Raffles, with his black hair tumbled, and the same watchful, quiet, determined half-smile with which I have seen him send down over after over in a county match!

At last the chain of holes was complete, the lock wrenched out bodily, and a splendid bare arm plunged up to the shoulder through the aperture, and through the bars of the iron gate beyond.

'Now,' whispered Raffles, 'if there's only one lock it'll be in the middle. Joy! Here it is! Only let me pick it, and we're through at last.'

He withdrew his arm, a skeleton key was selected from the bunch, and then back went his arm to the shoulder. It was a breathless moment. I heard the heart throbbing in my body, the very watch ticking in my pocket, and ever and anon the tinkle-tinkle of the skeleton key. Then—at last—there came a single unmistakable click. In another minute the mahogany door and the iron gate yawned behind us, and Raffles was sitting on an office table, wiping his face, with the lantern throwing a steady beam by his side.

We were now in a bare and roomy lobby behind the shop, but separated therefrom by an iron curtain, the very sight of which filled me with despair. Raffles, however, did not appear in the least depressed, but hung up his coat and hat on some pegs in the lobby before examining this curtain with his lantern.

'That's nothing,' said he, after a minute's inspection; 'we'll be through that in no time, but there's a door on the other side which may give us trouble.'

'Another door!' I groaned. 'And how do you mean to tackle this thing?'

'Prise it up with the jointed jemmy. The weak point of these iron curtains is the leverage you can get from below. But it makes a noise, and this is where you're coming in, Bunny; this is where I couldn't do without you. I must have you overhead to knock through when the street's clear. I'll come with you and show a light.'

Well, you may imagine how little I liked the prospect of this lonely vigil; and yet there was something very stimulating in the vital responsibility which it involved. Hitherto I had been a mere spectator. Now I was to take part in the game. And the fresh excitement made me more than ever insensible to those considerations of conscience and of safety which were already as dead nerves in my breast.

So I took my post without a murmur in the front room above the shop. The fixtures had been left for the refusal of the incoming tenant, and fortunately for us they included Venetian blinds, which were already down. It was the simplest matter in the world to stand peeping through the laths into the street, to beat twice with my foot when anybody was approaching, and once when all was clear again. The noises that even I could hear below, with the exception of one metallic crash at the beginning, were indeed incredibly slight; but they ceased altogether at each double rap from my toe, and a policeman passed quite half a dozen times beneath my eyes, and the man whom I took to be the jeweller's watchman oftener still, during the better part of an hour that I spent at the window. Once, indeed, my heart was in my mouth, but only once. It was when the watchman stopped and peered through the peep-hole into the lighted shop. I waited for his whistle. I waited for the gallows or the gaol! But my signals had been studiously obeyed, and the man passed on in undisturbed serenity. In the end I had a signal in my turn, and retraced my steps with lighted matches down the broad stairs, down the narrow ones, across the area, and up into the lobby where Raffles awaited me with an out-stretched hand.

'Well done, my boy!' said he. 'You're the same good man in a pinch, and you shall have your reward. I've got a thousand pounds' worth if I've got a penn'oth. It's all in my pockets. And here's something else I found in this locker; very decent port and some cigars, meant for poor dear Danby's business friends. Take a pull, and you shall light up presently. I've found a lavatory, too, and we must have a wash-and-brush-up before we go, for I'm as black as your boot.'

The iron curtain was down, but he insisted on raising it until I could peep through the glass door on the other side and see his handiwork in the shop beyond. Here two electric lights were left burning all night long, and in their cold white rays I could at first see nothing amiss. I looked along an orderly lane, an empty glass counter on my left, glass cupboards of untouched silver on my right, and facing me the filmy black eye of the peep-hole that shone like a stage moon on the street. The counter had not been emptied by Raffles; its contents were in the Chubb's safe, which he had given up at a glance; nor had he looked at the silver, except to choose a cigarette-case for me. He had confined himself entirely to the shop window. This was in three compartments, each secured for the night by removable panels with separate locks. Raffles had removed them a few hours before their time, and the electric light shone on a corrugated shutter bare as the ribs of an empty carcase. Every article of value was gone from the one place which was invisible from the little window in the door; elsewhere all was as it had been left overnight. And but for a train of mangled doors behind the iron curtain, a bottle of wine and a cigar-box with which liberties had been taken, a rather black towel in the lavatory, a burnt match here and there, and our finger-marks on the dusty banisters, not a trace of our visit did we leave.

'Had it in my head for long?' said Raffles, as we strolled through the streets towards dawn, for all the world as though we were returning from a dance. 'No, Bunny, I never thought of it till I saw that upper part empty about a month ago, and bought a few things in the shop to get the lie of the land. That reminds me that I never paid for them; but, by Jove, I will tomorrow and if that isn't poetic justice, what is? One visit showed me the possibilities of the place, but a second convinced me of its impossibilities without a pal. So I had practically given up the idea, when you came along on the very night and in the very plight for it! But here we are at the Albany, and I hope there's some fire left; for I don't know how you feel, Bunny, but for my part I'm as cold as Keats' owl.'

He could think of Keats on his way from a felony! He could hanker for his fireside like another. Floodgates were loosened within me, and the plain English of our adventure rushed over me as cold as ice. Raffles was a burglar. I had helped to commit one burglary, therefore I was a burglar too. Yet I could stand and warm myself by his fire and watch him empty his pockets, as though we had done nothing wonderful or wicked!

My blood froze. My heart sickened. My brain whirled. How I had liked this villain! How I had admired him! How my liking and admiration must turn to loathing and disgust. I waited for the change. I longed to feel it in my heart. But—I longed and I waited in vain!

I saw he was emptying his pockets; the table sparkled with their hoard. Rings by the dozen, diamonds by the score; bracelets, pendants, aigrettes, necklaces; pearls, rubies, amethysts, sapphires; and diamonds always, diamonds in everything, flashing bayonets of light, dazzling me—blinding me—making me disbelieve because I could no longer forget. Last of all came no gem, indeed, but my own revolver from an inner pocket. And that struck a chord. I suppose I said something—my hand flew out. I can see Raffles now, as he looked at me once more with a high arch over each clear eye. I can see him pick out the cartridges with his quiet, cynical smile, before he would give me my pistol back again.

'You mayn't believe it, Bunny,' said he, 'but I never carried a loaded one before. On the whole I think it gives one confidence. Yet it would be very awkward if anything went wrong; one might use it, and that's not the game at all, though I have often thought that the murderer who has just done the trick must have great sensations before things get too hot for him. Don't look so distressed, my dear chap, I've never had those sensations, and I don't suppose I ever shall.'

'But this much you have done before?' said I, hoarsely.

'Before? My dear Bunny, you offend me! Did it look like a first attempt? Of course I have done it before.'

'Often?'

'Well—no. Not often enough to destroy the charm, at all events; never, as a matter of fact, unless I'm cursedly hard up. Did you hear about the Thimbleby diamonds? Well, that was the last time—and a poor lot of paste they were. Then there was the little business of the Dormer house-boat at Henley last year. That was mine also—such as it was. I've never brought off a really big *coup* yet; when I do I shall chuck it up.'

Yes, I remembered both cases very well. To think that he was their author! It was incredible, outrageous, inconceivable. Then my eyes would fall upon the table, twinkling and glittering in a hundred places, and incredulity was at an end.

'How came you to begin?' I asked, as curiosity overcame mere wonder, and a fascination for his career gradually wove itself into my fascination for the man.

'Ah! that's a long story,' said Raffles. 'It was in the Colonies, when I was out there playing cricket. It's too long a story to tell you now, but I was in much the same fix that you were in tonight, and it was my only way out. I never meant it for anything more; but I'd tasted blood, and it was all over with me. Why should I work when I could steal? Why

THE AMATEUR CRACKSMAN

settle down to some humdrum uncongenial billet, when excitement, romance, danger, and a decent living were all going begging together. Of course, it's very wrong, but we can't all be moralists, and the distribution of wealth is very wrong to begin with. Besides, you're not at it all the time. I'm sick of quoting Gilbert's lines to myself, but they're profoundly true. I only wonder if you'll like the life as much as I do!'

'Like it?' I cried. 'Not I! It's no life for me. Once is enough!'

'You wouldn't give me a hand another time?'

'Don't ask me, Raffles. Don't ask me, for God's sake!'

'Yet you said you would do anything for me! You asked me to name my crime! But I knew at the time you didn't mean it; you didn't go back on me tonight, and that ought to satisfy me, goodness knows! I suppose I'm ungrateful, and unreasonable, and all that. I ought to let it end at this. But you're the very man for me, Bunny, the—very—man! Just think how we got through tonight. Not a scratch—not a hitch! There's nothing very terrible in it, you see; there never would be, while we worked together.'

He was standing in front of me with a hand on either shoulder; he was smiling as he knew so well how to smile. I turned on my heel, planted my elbows on the chimneypiece, and my burning head between my hands. Next instant a still heartier hand had fallen on my back.

'All right, my boy! You are quite right and I'm worse than wrong. I'll never ask it again. Go, if you want to, and come again about midday for the cash. There was no bargain; but, of course, I'll get you out of your scrape—especially after the way you've stood by me tonight.'

I was round again with my blood on fire.

'I'll do it again,' I said through my teeth.

He shook his head. 'Not you,' he said, smiling quite good-humouredly on my insane enthusiasm.

'I will,' I cried with an oath. 'I'll lend you a hand as often as you like! What does it matter now? I've been in it once. I'll be in it again. I've gone to the devil anyhow. I can't go back, and wouldn't if I could. Nothing matters another rap! When you want me I'm your man.'

And that is how Raffles and I joined felonious forces on the Ides of March.

A COSTUME PIECE

London was just then talking of one whose name is already a name and nothing more. Reuben Rosenthall had made his millions on the diamond fields of South Africa, and had come home to enjoy them according to his lights; how he went to work will scarcely be forgotten by any reader of the halfpenny evening papers, which revelled in endless

351

anecdotes of his original indigence and present prodigality, varied with interesting particulars of the extraordinary establishment which the millionaire set up in St John's Wood. Here he kept a retinue of Kaffirs, who were literally his slaves; and hence he would sally with enormous diamonds in his shirt and on his finger, in the convoy of a prize-fighter of heinous repute, who was not, however, by any means the worst element in the Rosenthall *ménage*. So said common gossip; but the fact was sufficiently established by the interference of the police on at least one occasion, followed by certain magisterial proceedings which were reported with justifiable gusto and huge headlines in the news-papers aforesaid. And this was all one knew of Reuben Rosenthall up to the time when the Old Bohemian Club, having fallen on evil days, found it worth its while to organise a great dinner in honour of so wealthy an exponent of the club's principles. I was not at the banquet myself, but a member took Raffles, who told me all about it that very night.

'Most extraordinary show I ever went to in my life,' said he. 'As for the man himself—well, I was prepared for something grotesque, but the fellow fairly took my breath away. To begin with, he's the most astounding brute to look at, well over six feet, with a chest like a barrel and a great hook-nose, and the reddest hair and whiskers you ever saw. Drank like a fire-engine, but only got drunk enough to make us a speech that I wouldn't have missed for ten pounds. I'm only sorry you weren't there too, Bunny, old chap.'

I began to be sorry myself, for Raffles was anything but an excitable person, and never had I seen him so excited before. Had he been following Rosenthall's example? His coming to my rooms at midnight, merely to tell me about his dinner, was in itself enough to excuse a suspicion which was certainly at variance with my knowledge of A. J. Raffles.

'What did he say?' I inquired mechanically, divining some subtler explanation of this visit, and wondering what on earth it could be.

'Say?' cried Raffles. 'What did he not say! He boasted of his rice, he bragged of his riches, and he blackguarded society for taking him up for his money and dropping him out of sheer pique and jealousy because he had so much. He mentioned names, too, with the most charming freedom, and swore he was as good a man as the Old Country had to show—*pace* the Old Bohemians. To prove it he pointed to a great diamond in the middle of his shirt-front with a little finger loaded with another just like it: which of our bloated princes could show a pair like that? As a matter of fact, they seemed quite wonderful stones, with a curious purple gleam to them that must mean a pot of money. But old Rosenthall swore he wouldn't take fifty thousand pounds for the two, and wanted to know where the other man was who went about with twenty-five thousand in his shirt front, and the other twenty-five on his little finger. He didn't exist. If he did, he wouldn't have the pluck to wear them. But he had—he'd tell us why. And before you could say Jack Robinson he had whipped out a whacking great revolver!'

'Not at the table?'

'At the table! In the middle of his speech! But it was nothing to what he wanted to do. He actually wanted us to let him write his name in bullets on the opposite wall to show us why he wasn't afraid to go about in all his diamonds! That brute Purvis, the prize-fighter who is his paid bully, had to bully his master before he could be persuaded out of it.

There was quite a panic for the moment; one fellow was saying his prayers under the table, and the waiters bolted to a man.'

'What a grotesque scene!'

'Grotesque enough, but I rather wish they had let him go the whole hog and blaze away. He was as keen as knives to show us how he could take care of his purple diamonds; and, do you know, Bunny, I was as keen as knives to see.'

And Raffles leant towards me with a sly, slow smile that made the hidden meaning of his visit only too plain to me at last.

'So you think of having a try for his diamonds yourself?'

He shrugged his shoulders.

'It is horribly obvious, I admit. But—yes, I have set my heart upon them! To be quite frank, I have had them on my conscience for some time; one couldn't hear so much of the man, and his prize-fighter, and his diamonds, without feeling it a kind of duty to have a go for them; but when it comes to brandishing a revolver and practically challenging the world, the thing becomes inevitable. It is simply thrust upon one. I was fated to hear that challenge, Bunny, and I, for one, must take it up. I was only sorry I couldn't get on my hind legs and say so then and there.'

'Well,' I said, 'I don't see the necessity as things are with us; but, of course, I'm your man.'

My tone may have been half-hearted. I did my best to make it otherwise. But it was barely a month since our Bond Street exploit, and we certainly could have afforded to behave ourselves for some time to come. We had been getting along so nicely; by his advice I had scribbled a thing or two; inspired by Raffles, I had even done an article on our own jewel robbery; and for the moment I was quite satisfied with this sort of adventure. I thought we ought to know when we were well off, and could see no point in our running fresh risks before we were obliged. On the other hand, I was anxious not to show the least disposition to break the pledge that I had given a month ago. But it was not on my manifest disinclination that Raffles fastened.

'Necessity, my dear Bunny? Does the writer only write when the wolf is at the door? Does the painter paint for bread alone? Must you and I be driven to crime like Tom of Bow and Dick of Whitechapel? You pain me, my dear chap; you needn't laugh, because you do. Art for art's sake is a vile catchword, but I confess it appeals to me. In this case my motives are absolutely pure, for I doubt if we shall ever be able to dispose of such peculiar stones. But if I don't have a try for them—after tonight, I shall never be able to hold up my head again.'

His eye twinkled, but it glittered too.

'We shall have our work cut out,' was all I said.

'And do you suppose I should be keen on it if we hadn't?' cried Raffles. 'My dear fellow, I would rob St Paul's Cathedral if I could, but I could no more scoop a till when the shopwalker wasn't looking than I could bag apples out of an old woman's basket. Even that little business last month was a sordid affair, but it was necessary, and I think its strategy redeemed it to some extent. Now there's some credit, and more sport, in going where they boast they're on their guard against you. The Bank of England, for example, is the ideal crib; but that would need half a dozen of us with years to give to the job; and meanwhile Reuben Rosenthall is high enough game for you and me. We know he's armed. We know how Billy Purvis can fight. It'll be no soft thing, I grant you. But what of that, my good Bunny—what of that? A man's reach must exceed his grasp, dear boy, or what the dickens is a heaven for?'

'I would rather we didn't exceed ours just yet,' I answered laughing, for his spirit was irresistible, and the plan was growing upon me, despite my qualms.

'Trust me for that,' was his reply; 'I'll see you through. After all I expect to find that the difficulties are nearly all on the surface. These fellows both drink like the devil, and that should simplify matters considerably. But we shall see, and we must take our time. There will probably turn out to be a dozen different ways in which the thing might be done, and we shall have to choose between them. It will mean watching the house for at least a week in any case; it may mean lots of other things that will take much longer; but give me a week, and I will tell you more. That's to say if you're really on?'

'Of course I am,' I replied indignantly. 'But why should I give you a week? Why shouldn't we watch the house together?'

'Because two eyes are as good as four, and take up less room. Never hunt in couples unless you're obliged. But don't you look offended, Bunny; there'll be plenty for you to do when the time comes, that I promise you. You shall have your share of the fun, never fear, and a purple diamond all to yourself—if we're lucky.'

On the whole, however, this conversation left me less than lukewarm, and I still remember the depression which came over me when Raffles was gone. I saw the folly of the enterprise to which I had committed myself—the sheer, gratuitous, unnecessary folly of it. And the paradoxes in which Raffles revelled, and the frivolous casuistry which was nevertheless half sincere, and which his mere personality rendered wholly plausible at the moment of utterance, appealed very little to me when recalled in cold blood. I admired the spirit of pure mischief in which he seemed prepared to risk his liberty and his life, but I did not find it an infectious spirit on calm reflection. Yet the thought of withdrawal was not to be entertained for a moment. On the contrary, I was impatient of the delay ordained by Raffles; and, perhaps, no small part of my secret disaffection came of his galling determination to do without me until the last moment.

It made it no better that this was characteristic of the man and of his attitude towards me. For a month we had been, I suppose, the thickest thieves in all London, and yet our intimacy was curiously incomplete. With all his charming frankness, there was in Raffles a vein of capricious reserve which was perceptible enough to be very irritating. He had the instinctive secretiveness of the inveterate criminal. He would make mysteries of matters of common concern; for example, I never knew how or where he disposed of the Bond Street jewels, on the proceeds of which we were both still leading the outward lives of hundreds of other young fellows about town. He was consistently mysterious about that and other details, of which it seemed to me that I had already earned the right to know everything. I could not but remember how he had led me into my first felony, by means of a trick, while yet uncertain whether he could trust me or not. That I could no longer afford to resent, but I did resent his want of confidence in me now. I said nothing about it, but it rankled every day, and never more than in the week that succeeded the Rosenthall dinner. When I met Raffles at the club he would tell me nothing; when I went to his rooms he was out, or pretended to be. One day he told me he was getting on well, but slowly; it was a more ticklish game than he had thought; but when I began to ask questions he would say no more. Then and there, in my annoyance, I took my own decision. Since he would tell me nothing of the result of his vigils, I determined to keep one of my own account, and that very evening found my way to the millionaire's front gates.

The house he was occupying is, I believe, quite the largest in the St John's Wood district. It stands in the angle formed by two broad thoroughfares, neither of which, as it happens, is a 'bus route, and I doubt if many quieter spots exist within the four-mile radius. Quiet also was the great square house, in its garden of grass-plots and shrubs; the lights were low, the millionaire and his friends obviously spending their evening elsewhere. The garden walls were only a few feet high. In one there was a side door opening into a glass passage; in the other two five-barred grained-and-varnished gates, one at either end of the little semi-circular drive, and both wide open. So still was the place that I had a great mind to walk boldly in and learn something of the premises; in fact, I was on the point of doing so, when I heard a quick, shuffling step on the pavement behind me. I turned round and faced the dark scowl and the dirty clenched fists of a dilapidated tramp.

'You fool!' said he. 'You utter idiot!'

'Raffles!'

'That's it,' he whispered savagely; 'tell all the neighbourhood—give me away at the top of your voice!'

With that he turned his back upon me, and shambled down the road, shrugging his shoulders and muttering to himself as though I had refused him alms. A few moments I stood astounded, indignant, at a loss; then I followed him. His feet trailed, his knees gave, his back was bowed, his head kept nodding; it was the gait of a man eighty years of age. Presently he waited for me midway between two lamp-posts. As I came up he was lighting rank tobacco, in a cutty pipe, with an evil-smelling match, and the flame showed me the suspicion of a smile.

'You must forgive my heat, Bunny, but it really was very foolish of you. Here am I trying every dodge—begging at the door one night—hiding in the shrubs the next—doing every mortal thing but stand and stare at the house as you went and did. It's a costume piece, and in you rush in your ordinary clothes. I tell you they're on the look-out for us night and day. It's the toughest nut I ever tackled!'

'Well,' said I, 'if you had told me so before I shouldn't have come. You told me nothing.'

'He looked hard at me from under the broken rim of a battered billycock.

'You're right,' he said at length. 'I've been too close. It's become second nature with me, when I've anything on. But here's an end of it, Bunny, so far as you're concerned. I'm going home now, and I want you to follow me; but for heaven's sake keep your distance, and don't speak to me again till I speak to you. There—give me a start.' And he was off again, a decrepit vagabond, with his hands in his pockets, his elbows squared, and frayed coat-tails swinging raggedly from side to side.

I followed him to the Finchley Road. There he took an omnibus, and I sat some rows behind him on the top, but not far enough to escape the pest of his vile tobacco. That he could carry his character-sketch to such a pitch—he who would only smoke one brand of cigarettes! It was the last, least touch of the insatiable artist, and it charmed away what mortification there still remained in me. Once more I felt the fascination of a comrade who was for ever dazzling one with a fresh and unsuspected facet of his character.

As we neared Piccadilly I wondered what he would do. Surely he was not going into the Albany like that? No, he took another omnibus to Sloane Street, I sitting behind him as before. At Sloane Street we changed again, and were presently in the long lean artery of the King's Road. I was now all agog to know our destination, nor was I kept many more minutes in doubt. Raffles got down. I followed. He crossed the road and disappeared up a dark turning. I pressed after him, and was in time to see his coat-tails as he plunged into a still darker flagged alley to the right. He was holding himself up and stepping out like a young man once more; also, in some subtle way, he already looked less disreputable. But I alone was there to see him, the alley was absolutely deserted, and desperately dark. At the farther end he opened a door with a latchkey, and it was darker yet within.

Instinctively I drew back and heard him chuckle. We could no longer see each other.

'All right, Bunny! There's no hanky-panky this time. These are studios, my friend, and I'm one of the lawful tenants.'

Indeed, in another minute we were in a lofty room with skylight, easels, dressing-cupboard, platform, and every other adjunct save the signs of actual labour. The first thing I saw, as Raffles lit the gas, was its reflection in his silk hat on the pegs beside the rest of his normal garments.

'Looking for the works of art?' continued Raffles, lighting a cigarette and beginning to divest himself of his rags. 'I'm afraid you won't find any, but there's the canvas I'm always going to make a start upon. I tell them I'm looking high and low for my ideal model. I have the stove lit on principle twice a week, and look in and leave a newspaper and a smell of Sullivans—how good they are after shag! Meanwhile I pay my rent and am a good tenant in every way; and it's a very useful little *pied-à-terre*—there's no saying how useful it might be at a pinch. As it is, the billycock comes in and the topper goes out, and nobody takes the slightest notice of either; at this time of night the chances are that there's not a soul in the building except ourselves.'

'You never told me you went in for disguises,' said I, watching him as he cleansed the grime from his face and hands.

'No, Bunny, I've treated you very shabbily all round. There was really no reason why I shouldn't have shown you this place a month ago, and yet there was no point in my doing so, and circumstances are just conceivable in which it would have suited us both for you to be in genuine ignorance of my whereabouts. I have something to sleep on, as you perceive, in case of need, and, of course, my name is not Raffles in the King's Road. So you will see that one might bolt farther and fare worse.'

'Meanwhile you use the place as a dressing-room?'

'It's my private pavilion,' said Raffles. 'Disguises? In some cases they're half the battle, and it's always pleasant to feel that, if the worst comes to the worst, you needn't necessarily be convicted under your own name. Then they're indispensable in dealing with the fences. I drive all my bargains in the tongue and raiment of Shoreditch. If I didn't there'd be the very devil to pay in blackmail. Now, this cupboard's full of all sorts of toggery. I tell the woman who cleans the room that it's for my models when I find 'em. By the way, I only hope I've got something that'll fit you, for you'll want a rig for tomorrow night.'

'Tomorrow night!' I exclaimed. 'Why, what do you mean to do?'

'The trick,' said Raffles. 'I intended writing to you as soon as I got back to my rooms, to ask you to look me up tomorrow afternoon; then I was going to unfold my plan of campaign, and take you straight into action then and there. There's nothing like putting the nervous players in first; it's the sitting with their pads on that upsets their apple cart; that was another of my reasons for being so confoundedly close. You must try to forgive me. I couldn't help remembering how well you played up last trip, without any time to weaken on it beforehand. All I want is for you to be as cool and smart tomorrow night as you were then; though, by Jove, there's no comparison between the two cases!'

'I thought you would find it so.'

'You were right. I have. Mind you, I don't say this will be the tougher job all round; we shall probably get in without any difficulty at all; it's the getting out again that may flummox us. That's the worst of an irregular household!' cried Raffles, with quite a burst of virtuous indignation. 'I assure you, Bunny, I spent the whole of Monday night in the shrubbery of the garden next door looking over the wall, and, if you'll believe me, somebody was about all night long! I don't mean the Kaffirs. I don't believe they ever get to bed at all, poor devils! No, I mean Rosenthall himself, and that pasty-faced beast Purvis. They were up and drinking from midnight when they came in, to broad daylight, when I cleared out. Even then I left them sober enough to slang each other. By the way, they very nearly came to blows in the garden, within a few yards of me, and I heard something that might come in useful and make Rosenthall shoot crooked at a critical moment. You know what an IDB is?'

'Illicit Diamond Buyer?'

'Exactly. Well, it seems that Rosenthall was one. He must have let it out to Purvis in his cups. Anyhow, I heard Purvis taunting him with it, and threatening him with the breakwater at Capetown; and I begin to think our friends are friend and foe. But about tomorrow night: there's nothing subtle in my plan. It's simply to get in while these fellows are out on the loose, and to lie low till they come back, and longer. If possible we must doctor the whisky. That would simplify the whole thing, though it's not a very sporting game to play; still, we must remember Rosenthall's revolver; we don't want him to sign his name on us. With all those Kaffirs about, however, it's ten to one on the whisky, and a hundred to one against us if we go looking for it. A brush with the heathen would spoil everything, if it did no more. Besides, there are the ladies—'

'The deuce there are!'

'Ladies with an "i," and the very voices for raising Cain. I fear, I fear the clamour! It would be fatal to us. *Au contraire*, if we can manage to stow ourselves away unbeknowns, half the battle will be won. If Rosenthall turns in drunk, it's a purple diamond apiece. If he sits up sober, it may be a bullet instead. We will hope not, Bunny; and all the firing wouldn't be on one side; but it's on the knees of the gods.'

And so we left it when we shook hands in Piccadilly—not by any means as much later as I could have wished. Raffles would not ask me to his rooms that night. He said he made it a rule to have a long night before playing cricket and—other games. His final word to me was framed on the same principle.

'Mind, only one drink tonight, Bunny. Two at the outside—as you value your life— and mine!'

I remember my abject obedience, and the endless, sleepless night it gave me; and the roofs of the houses opposite standing out at last against the blue-grey London dawn. I wondered whether I should ever see another, and was very hard on myself for that little expedition which I had made on my own wilful account.

It was between eight and nine o'clock in the evening when we took up our position in the garden adjoining that of Reuben Rosenthall; the house itself was shut up, thanks to the outrageous libertine next door, who, by driving away the neighbours, had gone far towards delivering himself into our hands. Practically secure from surprise on that side, we could watch our house under cover of a wall just high enough to see over, while a fair margin of shrubs in either garden afforded us additional protection. Thus entrenched we had stood an hour, watching a pair of lighted bow-windows with vague shadows flitting continually across the blinds, and listening to the drawing of corks, the clink of glasses, and a gradual crescendo of coarse voices within. Our luck seemed to have deserted us; the owner of the purple diamonds was dining at home and dining at undue length. I thought it was a dinner-party. Raffles differed; in the end he proved right. Wheels grated in the drive, a carriage and pair stood at the steps; there was a stampede from the dining-room, and the loud voices died away, to burst forth presently from the porch.

Let me make our position perfectly clear. We were over the wall, at the side of the house, but a few feet from the dining-room windows. On our right, one angle of the building cut the back lawn in two diagonally; on our left, another angle just permitted us to see the jutting steps and the waiting carriage. We saw Rosenthall come out—saw the glimmer of his diamonds before anything. Then came the pugilist; then a lady with a head of hair like a bath sponge; then another, and the party was complete.

Raffles ducked and pulled me down in great excitement.

'The ladies are going with them,' he whispered. 'This is great!'

'That's better still.'

'The Gardenia!' the millionaire had bawled.

'And that's best of all,' said Raffles, standing upright as hoofs and wheels crunched through the gates and rattled off at a fine speed.

'Now what?' I whispered, trembling with excitement.

'They'll be clearing away. Yes, here come their shadows. The drawing-room windows open on the lawn. Bunny, it's the psychological moment. Where's that mask?'

I produced it with a hand whose trembling I tried in vain to still, and could have died for Raffles when he made no comment on what he could not fail to notice. His own hands were firm and cool as he adjusted my mask for me, and then his own.

'By Jove, old boy,' he whispered cheerily, 'you look about the greatest ruffian I ever saw! These masks alone will down a nigger, if we meet one. But I'm glad I remembered to tell you not to shave. You'll pass for Whitechapel if the worst comes to the worst and you don't forget to talk the lingo. Better sulk like a mule if you're not sure of it and leave the dialogue to me; but, please our stars, there will be no need. Now, are you ready?'

'Quite.'

'Got your gag?'

'Yes.'

'Shooter?'

'Yes.'

'Then follow me.'

In an instant we were over the wall, in another on the lawn behind the house. There was no moon. The very stars in their courses had veiled themselves for our benefit. I crept at my leader's heels to some French windows opening upon a shallow verandah. He pushed. They yielded.

'Luck again,' he whispered; 'nothing but luck! Now for a light.'

And the light came!

A good score of electric burners glowed red for the fraction of a second, then rained merciless white beams into our blinded eyes. When we found our sight, four revolvers covered us, and between two of them the colossal frame of Reuben Rosenthall shook with a wheezy laughter from head to foot.

'Good evening, boys,' he hiccoughed. 'Glad to see ye at last! Shift foot or finger, you on the left, though, and you're a dead boy. I mean you, you greaser!' he roared out at Raffles. 'I know you. I've been waitin' for you. I've been watching you all this week! Plucky smart you thought yerself, didn't you? One day beggin', next time shammin' tight, and next one o' them old pals from Kimberley what never come when I'm in. But you left the same tracks every day, you buggins', an' the same tracks every night, all round the blessed premises.'

'All right, guv' nor,' drawled Raffles; 'don't excite. It's a fair cop. We don't sweat to know 'ow you brung it orf. On'y don't you go for to shoot, 'cos we 'aint awmed, s'help me Gord!'

'Ah, you're a knowin' one,' said Rosenthall, fingering his triggers. 'But you've struck a knowin'er.'

'Ho, yuss, we know all abaht thet! Set a thief to catch a thief—ho, yuss.'

My eyes had torn themselves from the round black muzzles, from the accursed diamonds that had been our snare, the pasty pig-face of the over-fed pugilist, and the flaming cheeks and hook nose of Rosenthall himself. I was looking beyond them at the doorway filled with quivering silk and plush, black faces, white eye-balls, woolly pates. But a sudden silence recalled my attention to the millionaire. And only his nose retained its colour.

'What d'ye mean?' he whispered with a hoarse oath. 'Spit it out, or, by Christmas, I'll drill you!'

'Whort price thet brikewater?' drawled Raffles coolly.

'Eh?'

Rosenthall's revolvers were describing widening orbits.

'What price thet brikewater—old IDB?'

'Where in hell did you get hold o' that?' asked Rosenthall, with a rattle in his thick neck meant for mirth.

'You may well arst,' says Raffles. 'It's all over the plice w'ere I come from.'

'Who can have spread such rot?'

'I dunno,' says Raffles; 'arst the gen'leman on yer left; p'raps 'e knows.'

The gentleman on his left had turned livid with emotion. Guilty conscience never declared itself in plainer terms. For a moment his small eyes bulged like currants in the suet of his face; the next, he had pocketed his pistols on a professional instinct, and was upon us with his fists.

'Out o' the light—out o' the light!' yelled Rosenthall in a frenzy.

He was too late. No sooner had the burly pugilist obstructed his fire than Raffles was through the window at a bound; while I, for standing still and saying nothing, was scientifically felled to the floor.

I cannot have been many moments without my senses. When I recovered them there was great to-do in the garden, but I had the drawing-room to myself. I sat up. Rosenthall and Purvis were rushing about outside, cursing the Kaffirs and nagging at each other.

'Over that wall, I tell yer!'

'I tell you it was this one. Can't you whistle for the police?'

'Police be damned! I've had enough of the blessed police.'

'Then we'd better get back and make sure of the other rotter.'

'Oh, make sure o' yer skin. That's what you'd better do. Jala, you black hog, if I catch you skulkin' . . .'

I never heard the threat. I was creeping from the drawing-room on my hands and knees, my own revolver swinging by its steel ring from my teeth.

For an instant I thought that the hall also was deserted. I was wrong, and I crept upon a Kaffir on all fours. Poor devil, I could not bring myself to deal him a base blow, but I threatened him most hideously with my revolver, and left the white teeth chattering in his black head as I took the stairs three at a time. Why I went upstairs in that decisive fashion, as though it were my only course, I cannot explain. But garden and ground floor seemed alive with men, and I might have done worse.

I turned into the first room I came to. It was a bedroom—empty, though lit up; and never shall I forget how I started as I entered, on encountering the awful villain that was myself at full length in a pier-glass! Masked, armed, and ragged, I was indeed fit carrion for a bullet or the hangman, and to one or the other I made up my mind. Nevertheless, I hid myself in the wardrobe behind the mirror, and there I stood shivering and cursing my fate, my folly, and Raffles most of all—Raffles first and last—for I daresay half an hour. Then the wardrobe door was flung suddenly open; they had stolen into the room without a sound; and I was hauled downstairs, an ignominious captive.

Gross scenes followed in the hall. The ladies were now upon the stage, and at sight of the desperate criminal they screamed with one accord. In truth I must have given them fair cause, though my mask was now torn away and hid nothing but my left ear. Rosenthall answered their shrieks with a roar for silence; the woman with the bath-sponge hair swore at him shrilly in return; the place became a Babel impossible to describe. I remember wondering how long it would be before the police appeared. Purvis and the ladies were for calling them in and giving me in charge without delay. Rosenthall would not hear of it. He swore that he would shoot man or woman who left his sight. He had had enough of the police. He was not going to have them coming there to spoil sport; he was going to deal with me in his own way. With that he dragged me from all other hands, flung me against a door, and sent a bullet crashing through the wood within an inch of my ear.

'You drunken fool! It'll be murder!' shouted Purvis, getting in the way a second time.

'Wha' do I care? He's armed isn't he? I shot him in self-defence. It'll be a warning to others. Will you stand aside, or d'ye want it yourself?'

'You're drunk,' said Purvis, still between us. 'I saw you take a neat tumblerful since you came in, and it's made you drunk as a fool. Pull yourself together, old man. You ain't a-going to do what you'll be sorry for.'

'Then I won't shoot at him, I'll only shoot roun' an' roun' the beggar. You're quite right, ole feller. Wouldn't hurt him. Great mishtake. Roun' an' roun'. There—like that!'

His freckled paw shot up over Purvis's shoulder, mauve lightning came from his ring, a red flash from his revolver, and shrieks from the women as the reverberations died away. Some splinters lodged in my hair.

Next instant the prize-fighter disarmed him; and I was safe from the devil, but finally doomed to the deep sea. A policeman was in our midst. He had entered through the drawing-room window; he was an officer of few words and creditable promptitude. In a twinkling he had the handcuffs on my wrists, while the pugilist explained the situation, and his patron reviled the force and its representative with impotent malignity. A fine watch they kept; a lot of good they did; coming in when all was over and the whole household might have been murdered in their sleep. The officer only deigned to notice him as he marched me off.

'We know all about you, sir,' said he contemptuously, and he refused the sovereign Purvis proffered. 'You will be seeing me again, sir, at Marylebone.'

'Shall I come now?'

'As you please, sir. I rather think the other gentleman requires you more, and I don't fancy this young man means to give much trouble.'

'Oh, I'm coming quietly,' I said.

And I went.

In silence we traversed perhaps a hundred yards. It must have been midnight. We did not meet a soul. At last I whispered:

'How on earth did you manage it?'

'Purely by luck,' said Raffles. 'I had the luck to get clear away through knowing every brick of those back-garden walls, and the double luck to have these togs with the rest over at Chelsea. The helmet is one of a collection I made up at Oxford; here it goes over this wall, and we'd better carry the coat and belt before we meet a real officer. I got them once for a fancy ball—ostensibly—and thereby hangs a yarn. I always thought they might come in useful a second time. My chief crux tonight was getting rid of the cab that brought me back. I sent him off to Scotland Yard with ten bob and a special message to good old Mackenzie. The whole detective department will be at Rosenthall's in about half an hour. Of course I speculated on our gentleman's hatred of the police—another huge slice of luck. If you'd got away, well and good; if not, I felt he was the man to play with his mouse as long as possible. Yes, Bunny, it's been more of a costume piece than I intended, and we've come out of it, with a good deal less credit. But, by Jove, we're jolly lucky to have come out of it at all!'

GENTLEMEN AND PLAYERS

Old Raffles may or may not have been an exceptional criminal, but as a cricketer I dare swear he was unique, Himself, a dangerous bat, a brilliant field, and perhaps the very finest slow bowler of his decade, he took incredibly little interest in the game at large. He never went up to Lord's without his cricket-bag, or showed the slightest interest in the result of a match in which he was not himself engaged. Nor was this mere hateful egotism on his part. He professed to have lost all enthusiasm for the game, and to keep it up only from the very lowest motives.

'Cricket,' said Raffles, 'like everything else, is good enough sport until you discover a better. As a source of excitement it isn't in it with other things you wot of, Bunny, and the involuntary comparison becomes a bore. What's the satisfaction of taking a man's wicket when you want his spoons? Still, if you can bowl a bit your low cunning won't get rusty, and always looking for the weak spot's just the kind of mental exercise one wants. Yes, perhaps there's some affinity between the two things after all. But I'd chuck up cricket tomorrow, Bunny, if it wasn't for the glorious protection it affords a person of my proclivities.'

'How so?, said I. 'It brings you before the public, I should have thought, far more than is either safe or wise.'

'My dear Bunny, that's exactly where you make a mistake. To follow crime with reasonable impunity you simply must have a parallel ostensible career—the more public the better. The principle is obvious. Mr Peace, of pious memory, disarmed suspicion by acquiring a local reputation for playing the fiddle and taming the animals, and it's my profound conviction that Jack the Ripper was a really eminent public man, whose speeches were very likely reported alongside his atrocities. Fill the bill in some prominent part, and you'll never be suspected of doubling it with another of equal prominence. That's why I want you to cultivate journalism, my boy, and sign all you can. And it's the one and only reason why I don't burn my bats for firewood.'

Nevertheless, when he did play there was no keener performer on the field, nor one more anxious to do well for his side. I remember how he went to the nets, before the first match of the season, with his pocket full of sovereigns which he put on the stumps instead of bails. It was a sight to see the professionals bowling like demons for the hard cash, for whenever a stump was hit a pound was tossed to the bowler and another balanced in its stead, while one man took £3 with a ball that spread-eagled the wicket. Raffles's practice cost him either eight or nine sovereigns; but he had absolutely first-class bowling all the time, and he made fifty-seven runs next day.

It became my pleasure to accompany him to all his matches, to watch every ball he bowled, or played, or fielded, and to sit chatting with him in the pavilion when he was doing none of these three things. You might have seen us there, side by side, during the greater part of the Gentlemen's first innings against the Players (who had lost the toss) on the second Monday in July. We were to be seen, but not heard, for Raffles had failed to score, and was uncommonly cross for a player who cared so little for the game. Merely taciturn with me, he was positively rude to more than one member who wanted to know how it had happened, or who ventured to commiserate with him on his luck; there he sat, with a straw hat tilted over his nose and a cigarette stuck between lips that curled disagreeably at every advance. I was, therefore, much surprised when a young fellow of the exquisite type came and squeezed himself in between us, and met with a perfectly civil reception despite the liberty. I did not know the boy by sight, nor did Raffles introduce us; but their conversation proclaimed at once the slightness of acquaintanceship and a licence on the lad's part which combined to puzzle me. Mystification reached its height when Raffles was informed that the other's father was anxious to meet him, and he instantly consented to gratify that whim.

'He's in the Ladies' Enclosure. Will you come round now?'

'With pleasure,' says Raffles. 'Keep a place for me, Bunny.'

And they were gone.

'Young Crowley,' said some voice farther back. 'Last year's Harrow Eleven.'

'I remember him. Worst man in the team.'

'Keen cricketer, however. Stopped till he was twenty to get his colours. Governor made him. Keen breed. Oh, pretty, sir! Very pretty!'

The game was boring me. I only came to see old Raffles perform. Soon I was looking wistfully for his return, and at length I saw him beckoning me from the palings to the right.

'Want to introduce you to old Amersteth,' he whispered, when I joined him. 'They've a cricket week next month, when this boy Crowley comes of age, and we've both got to go down and play.'

'Both!' I echoed. 'But I'm no cricketer!'

'Shut up,' says Raffles. 'Leave that to me. I've been lying for all I'm worth,' he added sepulchrally, as we reached the bottom of the steps. 'I trust to you not to give the show away.'

There was the gleam in his eye that I knew well enough elsewhere, but was unprepared for in those healthy, sane surroundings; and it was with very definite misgivings and surmises that I followed the Zingari blazer through the vast flower-bed of hats that bloomed beneath the ladies' awning.

Lord Amersteth was a fine-looking man with a short moustache and a double chin. He received me with much dry courtesy, through which, however, it was not difficult to read a less flattering tale. I was accepted as the inevitable appendage of the invaluable Raffles, with whom I felt deeply incensed as I made my bow.

'I have been bold enough', said Lord Amersteth, 'to ask one of the Gentlemen of England to come down and play some rustic cricket for us next month. He is kind enough to say that he would have liked nothing better, but for this little fishing expedition of yours, Mr—, Mr—,' and Lord Amersteth succeeded in remembering my name.

It was, of course, the first I had ever heard of that fishing expedition, but I made haste to say that it could easily, and should certainly, be put off. Raffles gleamed approval through his eyelashes. Lord Amersteth bowed and shrugged.

'You're very good, I'm sure,' said he. 'But I understand you're a cricketer yourself?'

'He was one at school,' said Raffles, with infamous readiness.

'Not a real cricketer,' I was stammering meanwhile.

'In the eleven?' said Lord Amersteth.

'I'm afraid not,' said I.

'But only just out of it,' declared Raffles, to my horror.

'Well, well, we can't all play for the Gentlemen,' said Lord Amersteth slyly. 'My son Crowley only just scraped into the eleven at Harrow, and he's going to play. I may even come in myself at a pinch; so you won't be the only duffer, if you are one, and I shall be very glad if you will come down and help us too. You shall flog a stream before breakfast and after dinner, if you like.'

'I should be very proud,' I was beginning, as the mere prelude to resolute excuses; but the eye of Raffles opened wide upon me; and I hesitated weakly, to be duly lost.

'Then that's settled,' said Lord Amersteth, with the slightest suspicion of grimness. 'It's to be a little week, you know, when my son comes of age. We play the Free Foresters, the Dorsetshire Gentlemen, and probably some local lot as well. But Mr Raffles will tell you all about it, and Crowley shall write. Another wicket! By Jove, they're all out! Then I rely on you both.' And, with a little nod, Lord Amersteth rose and sidled to the gangway.

Raffles rose also, but I caught the sleeve of his blazer.

'What are you thinking of?' I whispered savagely. 'I was nowhere near the eleven. I'm no sort of cricketer. I shall have to get out of this!'

'Not you,' he whispered back. 'You needn't play, but come you must. If you wait for me after half-past six, I'll tell you why.'

But I could guess the reason; and I am ashamed to say that it revolted me much less than did the notion of making a public fool of myself on a cricket field. My gorge rose at this as it no longer rose at crime, and it was in no tranquil humour that I strolled about the ground while Raffles disappeared in the pavilion. Nor was my annoyance lessened by a little meeting I witnessed between young Crowley and his father, who shrugged as he stopped and stooped to convey some information which made the young man look a little blank. It may have been pure self-consciousness on my part, but I could have sworn that the trouble was their inability to secure the great Raffles without his insignificant friend.

Then the bell rang, and I climbed to the top of the pavilion to watch Raffles bowl. No subtleties are lost up there; and if ever a bowler was full of them, it was A.J. Raffles on this day, as, indeed, all the cricket world remembers. One had not to be a cricketer one-self to appreciate his perfect command of pitch and break, his beautifully easy action, which never varied with the varying pace, his great ball on the leg-stump—his dropping head-ball—in a word, the infinite ingenuity of that versatile attack. It was no mere exhibition of athletic prowess, it was an intellectual treat, and one with a special significance in my eyes. I saw the 'affinity between the two things', saw it in that after-noon's tireless warfare against the flower of professional cricket. It was not that Raffles took many wickets for few runs; he was too fine a bowler to mind being hit; and time was short, and the wicket good. What I admired, and what I remember, was the combination of resource and cunning, of patience and precision, of head-work and handiwork, which made every over an artistic whole. It was all so characteristic of that other Raffles whom I alone knew!

'I felt like bowling this afternoon,' he told me later—in the cab. 'With a pitch to help me, I'd have done something big; as it is, three for forty-one, out of the four that fell, isn't bad for a slow bowler on a plumb wicket against those fellows. But I felt venomous! Nothing riles me more than being asked about for my cricket as though I were a pro myself.'

'Then why on earth go?'

'To punish them, and—because we shall be jolly hard up, Bunny, before the season's over!'

'Ah!' said I. 'I thought it was that.'

'Of course it was! It seems they're going to have me very devil of a week of it—balls—dinner-parties—swagger house-party—general junketings—and, obviously, a houseful of diamonds as well. Diamonds galore! As a general rule nothing would induce me to abuse my position as a guest. I've never done it, Bunny. But in this case we're engaged like the waiters and the band, and by heaven we'll take our toll! Let's have a quiet dinner somewhere and talk it over.'

'It seems rather a vulgar sort of theft,' I could not help saying; and to this, my single protest, Raffles instantly assented.

'It is a vulgar sort,' said he; 'but I can't help that. We're getting vulgarly hard up again, and there's an end on't. Besides, these people deserve it and can afford it. And don't you run away with the idea that all will be plain sailing; nothing will be easier than getting some stuff, and nothing harder than avoiding all suspicion, as, of course, we must. We may come away with no more than a good working plan of the premises. Who knows? In any case there's weeks of thinking in it for you and me.'

But with those weeks I will not weary you further than by remarking that the 'thinking' was done entirely by Raffles, who did not always trouble to communicate his thoughts to me. His reticence, however, was no longer an irritant. I began to accept it as a necessary convention of these little enterprises. And, after our last adventure of the kind, more especially after its *dénouement*, my trust in Raffles was much too solid to be shaken by a want of trust in me, which I still believe to have been more the instinct of the criminal than the judgment of the man.

It was on Monday, 10 August, that we were due at Milchester Abbey, Dorset; and the beginning of the month found us cruising about that very county, with fly-rods actually in our hands. The idea was that we should acquire at once a local reputation as decent fishermen, and some knowledge of the country-side, with a view to further and more deliberate operations in the event of an unprofitable week. There was another idea which Raffles kept to himself until he had got me down there. Then one day he produced a cricket-ball in a meadow we were crossing, and threw me catches for an hour together. More hours he spent in bowling to me on the nearest green; and, if I was never a cricketer, at least I came nearer to being one, by the end of that week, than ever before or since.

Incident began early on the Monday. We had sallied forth from a desolate little junction within quite a few miles of Milchester, had been caught in a shower, had run for shelter to a wayside inn. A florid over-dressed man was drinking in the parlour, and I could have sworn it was at the sight of him that Raffles recoiled on the threshold, and afterwards insisted on returning to the station through the rain. He assured me, however, that the odour of stale ale had almost knocked him down. And I had to make what I could of his speculative, downcast eyes and knitted brows.

Milchester Abbey is a grey, quadrangular pile, deep-set in rich woody country, and twinkling with triple rows of quaint windows, every one of which seemed alight as we drove up just in time to dress for dinner. The carriage had whirled us under I know not how many triumphal arches in process of construction, and past the tents and flag-poles of a juicy-looking cricket field, on which Raffles undertook to bowl up to his reputation, But the chief signs of festival were within, where we found an enormous house party assembled, including more persons of pomp, majesty, and dominion than I had ever encountered in one room before. I confess I felt overpowered. Our errand and my own pretences combined to rob me of an address upon which I had sometimes plumed myself; and I have a grim recollection of my nervous relief when dinner was at last announced. I little knew what an ordeal it was to prove.

I had taken in a much less formidable young lady than might have fallen to my lot. Indeed, I began by blessing my good fortune in this respect. Miss Melhuish was merely the rector's daughter, and she had only been asked to make an even number. She informed me of both facts before the soup reached us, and her subsequent conversation was characterised by the same engaging candour. It exposed what was little short of a mania for imparting information. I had simply to listen, to nod, and be thankful. When I confessed to knowing very few of those present, even by sight, my entertaining companion proceeded to tell me who everybody was, beginning on my left and working conscientiously round to her right. This lasted quite a long time, and really interested me; but a great deal that followed did not: and, obviously to recapture my unworthy attention, Miss Melhuish suddenly asked me, in a sensational whisper, whether I could keep a secret.

I said I thought I might, whereupon another question followed, in still lower and more thrilling accents:

'Are you afraid of burglars?'

Burglars! I was roused at last. The word stabbed me. I repeated it in horrified query.

'So I've found something to interest you at last!' said Miss Melhuish, in naïve triumph. 'Yes—burglars! But don't speak so loud. It's supposed to be kept a great secret. I really oughtn't to tell you at all!'

'But what is there to tell?' I whispered with satisfactcry impatience.

'You promise not to speak of it?'

'Of course!'

'Well, then, there are burglars in the neighbourhood.'

'Have they committed any robberies?'

'Not yet.'

'Then how do you know?'

'They've been seen. In the district. Two well-known London thieves!'

Two! I looked at Raffles. I had done so often during the evening, envying him his high spirits, his iron nerve, his buoyant wit, his perfect ease and his self-possession. But now I pitied him: through all my own terror and consternation, I pitied him as he sat eating and drinking, and laughing, and talking, without a cloud of fear or of embarrassment on his handsome, taking, dare-devil face. I caught up my champagne and emptied the glass.

'Who has seen them?' I then asked calmly.

'A detective. They were traced down from town a few days ago. They are believed to have designs on the Abbey!'

'But why aren't they run in?'

'Exactly what I asked papa on the way here this evening; he says there is no warrant out against the men at present, and all that can be done is to watch their movements.

'Oh! so they are being watched?'

'Yes, by a detective who is down here on purpose. And I heard Lord Amersteth tell papa that they had been seen this afternoon at Warbeck Junction.'

The very place where Raffles and I had been caught in the rain! Our stampede from the inn was now explained; on the other hand, I was no longer to be taken by surprise by anything that my companion might have to tell me; and I succeeded in looking her in the face with a smile.

'This is really quite exciting, Miss Melhuish,' said I. 'May I ask how you come to know so much about it?'

'It's papa,' was the confidential reply. 'Lord Amersteth consulted him, and he consulted me. But for goodness' sake don't let it get about! I can't think what tempted me to tell you!'

'You may trust me, Miss Melhuish. But—aren't you frightened?'

Miss Melhuish giggled.

'Not a bit! They won't come to the rectory. There's nothing for them there. But look round the table; look at the diamonds. Look at old Lady Melrose's necklace alone!'

The Dowager Marchioness of Melrose was one of the few persons whom it had been unnecessary to point out to me. She sat on Lord Amersteth's right, flourishing her ear-trumpet, and drinking champagne with her usual notorious freedom, as dissipated and kindly a dame as the world has ever seen. It was a necklace of diamonds and sapphires that rose and fell about her ample neck.

'They say it's worth five thousand pounds at least,' continued my companion. 'Lady Margaret told me so this morning (that's Lady Margaret next your Mr Raffles, you know); and the old dear will wear them every night. Think what a haul they would be! No; we don't feel in immediate danger at the rectory.'

When the ladies rose, Miss Melhuish bound me to fresh vows of secrecy; and left me, I should think, with some remorse for her indiscretion, but more satisfaction at the importance which it had undoubtedly given her in my eyes. The opinion may smack of vanity, though, in reality, the very springs of conversation reside in that same human, universal itch to thrill the auditor. The peculiarity of Miss Melhuish was that she must be thrilling at all costs. And thrilling she had surely been.

I spare you my feelings of the next two hours. I tried hard to get a word with Raffles, but again and again I failed. In the dining-room he and Crowley lit their cigarettes with the same match, and had their heads together all the time. In the drawing-room I had the mortification of hearing him talk interminable nonsense into the trumpet-ear of Lady Melrose, whom he knew in town. Lastly, in the billiard-room, they had a great and lengthy pool, while I sat aloof and chafed more than ever in the company of a very serious Scotsman, who had arrived since dinner, and who would talk of nothing but the recent improvements in instantaneous photography. He had not come to play in the matches (he told me), but to obtain for Lord Amersteth such a series of cricket photographs as had never been taken before; whether as an amateur or a professional photographer I was unable to determine. I remember, however, seeking distraction in little bursts of resolute attention to the conversation of this bore. And so at last the long ordeal ended: glasses were emptied, men said goodnight, and I followed Raffles to his room.

'It's all up!' I gasped, as he turned up the gas and I shut the door. 'We're being watched. We've been followed down from town. There's a detective here on the spot!'

'How do you know?' asked Raffles, turning upon me quite sharply, but without the least dismay. And I told him how I knew.

'Of course,' I added, 'it was the fellow we saw in the inn this afternoon.'

'The detective?' said Raffles. 'Do you mean to say you don't know a detective when you see one, Bunny?'

'If that wasn't the fellow, which is?'

Raffles shook his head.

'To think that you've been talking to him for the last hour in the billiard room, and couldn't spot what he was!'

'The Scotch photographer—'

I paused aghast.

'Scotch he is,' said Raffles, 'and photographer he may be. He is also Inspector Mackenzie of Scotland Yard—the very man I sent the message to that night last April. And you couldn't spot who he was in a whole hour! Oh, Bunny, Bunny, you were never built for crime!'

'But,' said I, 'if that was Mackenzie, who was the fellow you bolted from at Warbeck?'

'The man he's watching.'

'But he's watching us!'

Raffles looked at me with a pitying eye, and shook his head again before handing me his open cigarette-case.

'I don't know whether smoking's forbidden in one's bedroom, but you'd better take one of these and stand tight, Bunny, because I'm going to say something offensive.'

I helped myself with a laugh.

'Say what you like, my dear fellow, if it really isn't you and I that Mackenzie's after.'

'Well, then, it isn't, and it couldn't be, and nobody but a born Bunny would suppose for a moment that it was! Do you seriously think he would sit there and knowingly watch his man playing pool under his nose? Well, he might; he's a cool hand, Mackenzie; but I'm not cool enough to win a pool under such conditions. At least, I don't think I am; it would be interesting to see. The situation wasn't free from strain as it was, though I knew he wasn't thinking of us. Crowley told me all about it after dinner, you see, and then I'd seen one of the men for myself this afternoon. You thought it was a detective who made me turn tail at that inn. I really don't know why I didn't tell you at the time, but it was just the opposite. That loud, red-faced brute is one of the cleverest thieves in London, and I once had a drink with him and our mutual fence. I was an East-ender from tongue to toe at the moment, but you will understand that I don't run unnecessary risks of recognition by a brute like that.'

'He's not alone, I hear.'

'By no means; there's at least one other man with him; and it's suggested that there may be an accomplice here in the house.'

'Did Lord Crowley tell you so?'

'Crowley and the champagne between them. In confidence, of course, just as your girl told you; but even in confidence he never let on about Mackenzie. He told me there was a detective in the background, but that was all. Putting him up as a guest is evidently their big secret, to be kept from the other guests because it might offend them, but more particularly from the servants whom he's here to watch. That's my reading of the situation, Bunny, and you will agree with me that it's infinitely more interesting than we could have imagined it would prove.'

'But infinitely more difficult for us,' said I, with a sigh of pusillanimous relief. 'Our hands are tied for this week, at all events.'

'Not necessarily, my dear Bunny, though I admit that the chances are against us. Yet I'm not so sure of that either. There are all sorts of possibilities in these three-cornered combinations. Set A to watch B, and he won't have an eye left for C. That's the obvious theory, but then Mackenzie's a very big A. I should be sorry to have any boodle about me with that man in the house. Yet it would be great to nip in between A and B and score off them both at once! It would be worth a risk, Bunny, to do that; it would be worth risking something merely to take on old hands like B and his men at their old game! Eh, Bunny? That would be something like a match. Gentlemen and Players at single wicket, by Jove!'

His eyes were brighter than I had known them for many a day. They shone with the perverted enthusiasm which was roused in him only by the contemplation of some new audacity. He kicked off his shoes and began pacing his room with noiseless rapidity; not since the night of the Old Bohemian dinner to Reuben Rosenthall had Raffles exhibited such excitement in my presence; and I was not sorry at the moment to be reminded of the fiasco to which that banquet had been the prelude.

'My dear A.J.,' said I in his very own tone, 'you're far too fond of the uphill game; you will eventually fall a victim to the sporting spirit and nothing else. Take a lesson from our last escape, and fly lower as you value our skins. Study the house as much as you like, but do—not—go and shove your head into Mackenzie's mouth!'

My wealth of metaphor brought him to a standstill, with his cigarette between his fingers and a grin beneath his shining eyes.

'You're quite right, Bunny. I won't. I really won't. Yet—you saw old Lady Melrose's necklace? I've been wanting it for years! But I'm not going to play the fool, honour bright, I'm not; yet—by Jove!—to get to windward of the professors and Mackenzie too! It would be a great game, Bunny, it would be a great game!'

'Well, you mustn't play it this week.'

'No, no, I won't. But I wonder how the professors think of going to work? That's what one wants to know. I wonder if they've really got an accomplice in the house? How I wish I knew their game! But it's all right, Bunny; don't you be jealous; it shall be as you wish.'

And with that assurance I went off to my own room and so to bed with an incredibly light heart. I had still enough of the honest man in me to welcome the postponement of our actual felonies, to dread their performance, and to deplore their necessity; which is merely another way of stating the too patent fact that I was an incomparably weaker man than Raffles, while every whit as wicked. I had, however, one rather strong point. I possessed the gift of dismissing unpleasant considerations, not intimately connected with the passing moment, entirely from my mind. Through the exercise of this faculty I had lately been living my frivolous life in town with as much ignoble enjoyment as I had derived from it the year before; and similarly, here at Milchester, in the long-dreaded cricket-week, I had after all a quite excellent time.

It is true that there were other factors in this pleasing disappointment. In the first place, *mirabile dictu*, there were one or two even greater duffers than I on the Abbey cricket field. Indeed, quite early in the week, when it was of most value to me, I gained considerable kudos for a lucky catch; a ball, of which I had merely heard the hum, stuck fast in my hand, which Lord Amersteth himself grasped in public congratulation. This happy accident was not to be undone even by me, and, as nothing succeeds like success, and the constant encouragement of the one great cricketer on the field was in itself an immense stimulus, I actually made a run or two in my very next innings. Miss Melhuish said pretty things to me that night at the great ball in honour of Viscount Crowley's majority; she also told me that was the night on which the robbers would assuredly make their raid, and was full of arch tremors when we sat out in the garden, though the entire premises were illuminated all night long. Meanwhile the quiet Scotsman took countless photographs by day, which he developed by night in a dark room admirably situated in the servants' part of the house; and it is my first belief that only two of his fellow guests knew Mr Clephane of Dundee for Inspector Mackenzie of Scotland Yard.

The week was to end with a trumpery match on the Saturday, which two or three of us intended abandoning early in order to return to town that night. The match, however, was never played. In the small hours of the Saturday morning a tragedy took place at Milchester Abbey.

Let me tell of the thing as I saw and heard it. My room opened upon the central gallery, and was not even on the same floor as that on which Raffles—and I think all the other men—were quartered. I had been put, in fact, into the dressing room of one of the grand suites, and my two near neighbours were old Lady Melrose and my host and hostess. Now, by the Friday evening the actual festivities were at an end, and, for the first time that week I must have been sound asleep since midnight, when all at once I found myself sitting up breathless. A heavy thud had come against my door, and now I heard hard breathing and the dull stamp of muffled feet.

'I've got ye,' muttered a voice. 'It's no use struggling.'

It was the Scotch detective, and a new fear turned me cold. There was no reply, but the hard breathing grew harder still, and the muffled feet beat the floor to a quicker measure. In sudden panic I sprang out of bed and flung open my door. A light burnt low on the landing, and by it I could see Mackenzie swaying and staggering in a silent tussle with some powerful adversary.

'Hold this man!' he cried, as I appeared. 'Hold the rascal!'

But I stood like a fool until the pair of them backed into me, when, with a deep breath, I flung myself on the fellow, whose face I had seen at last. He was one of the footmen who waited at table; and no sooner had I pinned him than the detective loosed his hold.

'Hang on to him,' he cried. There's more of 'em below.'

And he went leaping down the stairs, as other doors opened, and Lord Amersteth and his son appeared simultaneously in their pyjamas. At that my man ceased struggling: but I was still holding him when Crowley turned up the gas.

'What the devil's all this?' asked Lord Amersteth, blinking.

'Who was that ran downstairs?'

'MacClephane!' said I hastily.

'Aha!' said he, turning to the footman. 'So you're the scoundrel, are you? Well done! Well done! Where was he caught?'

I had no idea.

'Here's Lady Melrose's door open,' said Crowley. 'Lady Melrose! Lady Melrose!'

'You forget she is deaf,' said Lord Amersteth. 'Ah! that'll be her maid.'

An inner door had opened; next instant there was a little shriek, and a white figure gesticulated on the threshold.

'Où donc est l'écrin de Madame la Marquise? La fenêtre est ouverte. Il a disparu!'

'Window open and jewel case gone, by Jove!' exclaimed Lord Amersteth. 'Mais comment est Madame la Marquise? Est-elle bien?'

'Oui, milor. Elle dort.'

'Sleeps through it all,' said my lord. 'She's the only one, then!'

'What made Mackenzie—Clephane—bolt?' young Crowley asked me.

'Said there were more of them below.'

'Why the devil couldn't you tell us so before?' he cried, and went leaping downstairs in his turn.

He was followed by nearly all the cricketers, who now burst upon the scene in a body, only to desert it for the chase. Raffles was one of them, and I would gladly have been another, had not the footman chosen this moment to hurl me from him, and to make a dash in the direction from which they had come. Lord Amersteth had hit him in an instant; but the fellow fought desperately, and it took the two of us to drag him downstairs; amid a terrified chorus from half-open doors. Eventually we handed him over to two other footmen who appeared with their night-shirts tucked into their trousers, and my host was good enough to compliment me as he led the way outside.

'I thought I heard a shot,' he added. 'Didn't you?'

'I thought I heard three.'

And out we dashed into the darkness.

I remember how the gravel pricked my feet, how the wet grass numbed them as we made for the sound of voices on an outlying lawn. So dark was the night that we were in the cricketers' midst before we saw the shimmer of their pyjamas, and then Lord Amersteth almost trod on Mackenzie as he lay prostrate in the dew.

'Who's this?' he cried. 'What on earth's happened?'

'It's Clephane,' said a man who knelt over him. 'He's got a bullet in him somewhere.'

'Is he alive?'

'Barely.'

'Good God! Where's Crowley?'

'Here I am,' called a breathless voice. 'It's no good, you fellows. There's nothing to show which way they've gone. Here's Raffles; he's chucked it, too.' And they ran up panting.

'Well, we've got one of them, at all events,' muttered Lord Amersteth. 'The next thing is to get this poor fellow indoors. Take his shoulders somebody. Now his middle. Join hands under him. Altogether now; that's the way. Poor fellow! Poor fellow! His name isn't Clephane at all. He's a Scotland Yard detective, down here for these very villains!'

Raffles was the first to express surprise; but he had also been the first to raise the wounded man. Nor had any of them a stronger or more tender hand in the slow procession to the house. In a little we had the senseless man stretched on a sofa in the library. And there, with ice on his wound and brandy in his throat, his eyes opened and his lips moved.

Lord Amersteth bent down to catch the words.

'Yes, yes,' said he, 'we've got one of them safe and sound. The brute you collared upstairs.' Lord Amersteth bent lower. 'By Jove! Lowered the jewel-case out of the window, did he? And they've got clean away with it! Well, well! I only hope we'll be able to pull this good fellow through. He's off again.'

An hour passed; the sun was rising.

It found a dozen young fellows on the settees in the billard-room, drinking whisky and soda-water in their overcoats and pyjamas, and still talking excitedly in one breath. A time-table was being passed from hand to hand: the doctor was still in the library At last the door opened, and Lord Amersteth put in his head.

'It isn't hopeless,' said he, 'but it's bad enough. There'll be no cricket today.'

Another hour, and most of us were on our way to catch the early train; between us we filled a compartment almost to suffocation. And still we talked all together on the night's event; and still I was a little hero in my way, for having kept my hold on the ruffian who had been taken; and my gratification was subtle and intense. Raffles watched me under lowered lids. Not a word had we had together; not a word did we have until we had left the others at Paddington, and were skimming through the streets in a hansom with noiseless tyres and a tinkling bell.

'Well, Bunny,' said Raffles, 'so the professors have it, eh?'

'Yes,' said I. 'And I'm jolly glad!'

'That poor Mackenzie has a ball in his chest?'

'That you and I have been on the decent side for once.'

He shrugged his shoulders.

'You're hopeless, Bunny, quite hopeless! I take it you wouldn't have refused your share if the boodle had fallen to us? Yet you positively enjoy coming off second best—for the second time running! I confess, however, that the professors' methods were full of interest to me. I, for one, have probably gained as much in experience as I have lost in other things. That lowering the jewel-case out of the window was a very simple and effective expedient; two of them had been wailing below for it for hours.'

'How do you know?' I asked.

'I saw them from my own window, which was just above the dear old lady's. I was fretting for that necklace in particular, when I went up to turn in for our last night— and I happened to look out of the window. In point of fact, I wanted to see whether the one below was open, and whether there was the slightest chance of working the oracle with my sheet for a rope. Of course, I took the precaution of turning my light off first, and it was a lucky thing I did. I saw the pros right down below, and they never saw me. I saw a little tiny luminous disc just for an instant, and then again for an instant a few minutes later. Of course I knew what it was, for I have my own watch-dial daubed with luminous paint; it makes a lantern of sorts when you can get no better. But these fellows were not using theirs as a lantern. They were under the old lady's window. They were watching the time. The whole thing was arranged with their accomplice inside. Set a thief to catch a thief; in a minute I had guessed what the whole thing proved to be.'

'And you did nothing,' I exclaimed.

'On the contrary, I went downstairs and straight into Lady Melrose's room—'

'You did?'

'Without a moment's hesitation. To save her jewels. And I was prepared to yell as much into her ear-trumpet for all the house to hear. But the dear lady is too deaf and too fond of her dinner to wake easily.'

'Well?'

'She didn't stir.'

'And yet you allowed the professors, as you call them, to take her jewels, case and all!'

'All but this,' said Raffles, thrusting his fist into my lap. 'I would have shown it you before, but really, old fellow, your face all day has been worth a fortune to the firm!'

And he opened his fist, to shut it next instant on the bunch of diamonds and of sapphires that I had last seen encircling the neck of Lady Melrose.

LE PREMIER PAS

That night he told me the story of his earliest crime. Not since the fateful morning of the Ides of March, when he had just mentioned it as an unreported incident of a certain cricket tour, had I succeeded in getting a word out of Raffles on the subject. It was not for want of trying; he would shake his head, and watch his cigarette smoke thoughtfully; a subtle look in his eyes, half cynical, half wistful, as though the decent honest days that were no more had had their merits after all. Raffles would plan a fresh enormity, or glory in the last, with the unmitigated enthusiasm of the artist. It was impossible to imagine one throb or twitter of compunction beneath those frankly egoistic and infectious transports. And yet the ghost of a dead remorse seemed still to visit him with the memory of his first felony, so that I had given the story up long before the night of our return from Milchester. Cricket, however, was in the air, and Raffles's cricket-bag back where he sometimes kept it, in the fender, with the remains of an old Orient label still adhering to the leather. My eyes had been on this label for some time, and I suppose his eyes had been on mine, for all at once he asked me if I still burned to hear that yarn.

'It's no use,' I replied. 'You won't spin it. I must imagine it for myself.'

'How can you?'

'Oh, I begin to know your methods.'

'You take it I went with my eyes open, as I do now, eh?'

'I can't imagine your doing otherwise.'

'My dear Bunny, it was the most unpremeditated thing I ever did in my life!'

His chair wheeled back into the books as he sprang up with sudden energy. There was quite an indignant glitter in his eyes.

'I can't believe that,' said I craftily. 'I can't pay you such a poor compliment.'

'Then you must be a fool—'

He broke off, stared hard at me, and in a trice stood smiling in his own despite.

'Or a better knave than I thought you, Bunny, and by Jove, it's the knave! Well—I suppose I'm fairly drawn; I give you best, as they say out here. As a matter of fact, I've been thinking of the thing myself; last night's racket reminds me of it in one or two respects. I tell you what, though, this is an occasion in any case, and I'm going to celebrate it by breaking the one good rule of my life. I'm going to have a second drink!'

The whisky tinkled, the syphon fizzed, and ice plopped home; and seated there in his pyjamas, with the inevitable cigarette, Raffles told me the story that I had given up hoping to hear. The windows were wide open; the sounds of Piccadilly floated in at first. Long before he finished, the last wheels had rattled, the last brawler was removed, we alone broke the quiet of the summer night.

'. . . No, they do you very well indeed. You pay for nothing but drinks, so to speak, but I'm afraid mine were of a comprehensive character. I had started in a hole, I ought really to have refused the invitation; then we all went to the Melbourne Cup, and I had the certain winner that didn't win, and that's not the only way you can play the fool in Melbourne. I wasn't the steady old stager I am now, Bunny: my analysis was a confession in itself. But the others didn't know how hard up I was, and I swore they shouldn't. I tried the Jews, but they're extra fly out there. Then I thought of a kinsman of sorts, a second cousin of my father's whom none of us knew anything about, except that he was supposed to be in one or other of the Colonies. If he were a rich man, well and good, I would work him; if not there would be no harm done. I tried to get on his tracks, and, as luck would have it, I succeeded (or thought I had) at the very moment when I happened to have a few days to myself. I was cut over on the hand, just before the big Christmas match, and couldn't have bowled a ball if they had played me.

'The surgeon who fixed me up happened to ask me if I was any relation of Raffles of the National Bank, and the pure luck of it almost took my breath away. A relation who was a high official in one of the banks, who would finance me on my mere name—could anything be better? I made up my mind that this Raffles was the man I wanted, and was awfully sold to find next moment that he wasn't a high official at all. Nor had the doctor so much as met him, but had merely read of him in connection with a small sensation at the suburban branch which my namesake managed; an armed robber had been rather pluckily beaten off, with a bullet in him, by this Raffles; and the sort of thing was so common out there that this was the first I had heard of it! A suburban branch—my financier had faded into some excellent fellow with a billet to lose if he called his soul his own. Still a manager was a manager, and I said I would soon see whether this was the relative I was looking for, if he would be good enough to give me the name of that branch.

' "I'll do more," says the doctor. "I'll give you the name of the branch he's been promoted to, for I think I heard they've moved him up one already." And the next day he brought me the name of the township of Yea, some fifty miles north of Melbourne; but, with the vagueness which characterized all his information, he was unable to say whether I should find my relative there or not.

' "He's a single man, and his initials are W.F.," said the doctor, who was certain enough of the immaterial points. "He left his old post several days ago, but it appears he's not due at the new one till the New Year. No doubt he'll go before then to take things over and settle in. You might find him up there and you might not. If I were you I should write."

' "That'll lose two days," said I, "and more if he isn't there," for I'd grown quite keen on this up-country manager, and I felt that if I could get at him while the holidays were still on, a little conviviality might help matters considerably.

' "Then," said the doctor, "I should get a quiet horse and ride. You needn't use that hand."

' "Can't I go by train?"

' "You can and you can't. You would still have to ride. I suppose you're a horseman?"

' "Yes."

' "Then I should certainly ride all the way. It's a delightful road, through Whittlesea and over the Plenty Ranges. It'll give you some idea of the bush, Mr Raffles, and you'll see the sources of the water-supply of this city, sir. You'll see where every drop of it comes from, the pure Yan Yean! I wish I had time to ride with you.'

' "But where can I get a horse?"

'The doctor thought a moment.

' "I've a mare of my own that's as fat as butter for want of work," said he. "It would be a charity to me to sit on her back for a hundred miles or so, and then I should know you'd have no temptation to use that hand."

' "You're far too good," I protested.

' "You're A.J. Raffles," he said.

'And if ever there was a prettier compliment, or a finer instance of even Colonial hospitality, I can only say, Bunny, that I never heard of either.'

He sipped his whisky, threw away the stump of his cigarette, and lit another before continuing.

'Well, I managed to write a line to W.F. with my own hand, which, as you will gather, was not very badly wounded; it was simply this third finger that was split and in splints; the next morning the doctor packed me off on a bovine beast that would have done for an ambulance. Half the team came up to see me start; the rest were rather sick with me for not stopping to see the match out, as if I could help them to win by watching them. They little knew the game I'd got on myself, but still less did I know the game I was going to play.

'It was an interesting ride enough, especially after passing the place called Whittlesea, a real wild township on the lower slopes of the ranges, where I recollect having a deadly meal of hot mutton and tea with the thermometer at three figures in the shade. The first thirty miles or so was a good metal road, too good to go half round the world to ride on, but after Whittlesea it was a mere track over the ranges, a track I often couldn't see and left entirely to the mare. Now it dipped into a gully and ran through a creek, and all the time the local colour was inches thick: gum trees galore and parrots all colours of the rainbow. In one place a whole forest of gums had been ring-barked, and were just as though they had been painted white, without a leaf or a living thing for miles. And the first living thing I did meet was the sort to give you the creeps; it was a riderless horse coming full tilt through the bush, with the saddle twisted round and the stirrup-irons ringing. Without thinking, I had a shot at heading him with the doctor's mare, and blocked him just enough to allow a man who came galloping after to do the rest.

' "Thank ye, mister," growled the man, a huge chap in a red checked shirt, with a beard like W. G. Grace, but the very devil of an expression.

' "Been an accident?" said I, reining up.

' "Yes," said he, scowling as though he defied me to ask any more.

' "And a nasty one," I said, "if that's blood on the saddle!"

' "Well, Bunny, I may be a blackguard myself, but I don't think I ever looked at a fellow as that chap looked at me. But I stared him out, and forced him to admit that it was blood on the twisted saddle, and after that he became quite tame. He told me exactly what had happened. A mate of his had been dragged under a branch, and had his nose smashed, but that was all; had sat tight after it till he dropped from loss of blood, another mate was with him in the bush.

'As I've said already, Bunny, I wasn't the old stager that I am now—in any respect—and we parted good enough friends. He asked me which way was I was going, and when I told him, he said I should save seven miles, and get a good hour earlier to Yea, by striking off the track and making for a peak that we could see through the trees, and following a creek that I should see from the peak. Don't smile, Bunny! I began by saying I was a child in those days. Of course, the short cut was the long way round; and it was nearly dark when that unlucky mare and I saw the single street of Yea.

'I was looking for the bank when a fellow in a white suit ran down from the verandah.

' "Mr Raffles?" said he.

' "Mr Raffles!" said I, laughing, as I shook his hand.

' "You're late."

' "I was misdirected."

' "That all? I'm relieved," he said. "Do you know what they are saying? There are some brand-new bushrangers on the road between Whittlesea and this—a second Kelly gang! They'd have caught a Tartar in you, eh?"

' "They would in you," I retorted, and my *tu quoque* shut him up and seemed to puzzle him. Yet there was much more sense in it than in his compliment to me, which was absolutely pointless.

' "I'm afraid you'll find things pretty rough," he resumed, when he had unstrapped my valise, and handed my reins to his man. "It's lucky you're a bachelor like myself."

'I could not quite see the point of this remark either, since, had I been married, I should hardly have sprung my wife upon him in this free-and-easy fashion. I muttered the conventional sort of thing, and then he said I should find it all right when I settled, as though I had come to graze upon him for weeks! "Well," thought I, "these Colonials do take the cake for hospitality!" And, still marvelling, I let him lead me into the private part of the bank.

' "Dinner will be ready in a quarter of an hour," said he, as we entered. "I thought you might like a tub first, and you'll find all ready in the room at the end of the passage. Sing out if there's anything you want. Your luggage hasn't turned up yet, by the way, but here's a letter that came this morning."

' "Not for me?"

' "Yes, didn't you expect one?"

' "I certainly did not!"

' "Well, here it is."

'And, as he lit me to my room, I read my own superscription of the previous day—to W. F. Raffles!

'Bunny, you've had your wind bagged at footer, I daresay; you know what that's like? All I can say is that my moral wind was bagged by that letter as I hope, old chap, I have never yet bagged yours. I couldn't speak. I could only stand with my own letter in my hands until he had the good taste to leave me by myself.

'W. F. Raffles! We had mistaken each other for W. F. Raffles—for the new manager who had not yet arrived! Small wonder we had conversed at cross-purposes; the only wonder was that we had not discovered our mutual mistake. How the other man would have laughed! But I—I could not laugh. By Jove, no, it was no laughing matter for me! I saw the whole thing in a flash, without a tremor, but with the direct depression from my own single point of view. Call it callous if you like, Bunny, but remember that I was in much the same hole as you've since been in yourself, and that I had counted on W. F. Raffles even as you counted on A. J. I thought of the man with the W. G. beard— the riderless horse with the bloody saddle—the deliberate misdirection that had put me off the track and out of the way—and now the missing manager and the report of bush-rangers at this end. But I simply don't pretend to have felt any personal pity for a man whom I had never seen; that kind of pity's usually cant; and besides, all mine was needed for myself.

'I was in as big a hole as ever. What the devil was I to do? I doubt if I have sufficiently impressed upon you the absolute necessity of my returning to Melbourne in funds. As a matter of fact it was less the necessity than my own determination which I can truthfully describe as absolute.

'Money I would have—but how—but how? Would this stranger be open to persuasion—if I told him the truth? No; that would set us all scouring the country for the rest of the night. Why should I tell him? Suppose I left him to find out his mistake . . . would anything be gained? Bunny, I give you my word that I went to dinner without a definite intention in my head, or one premeditated lie upon my lips. I might do the decent, natural thing, and explain matters without loss of time; on the other hand, there was no hurry, I had not opened the letter, and could always pretend I had not noticed the initials; meanwhile something might turn up. I could wait a little and see. Tempted I already was, but as yet the temptation was vague, and its very vagueness made me tremble.

' "Bad news, I'm afraid," said the manager, when at last I sat down at his table.

' "A mere annoyance," I answered—I do assure you—on the spur of the moment and nothing else. But my lie was told; my position was taken; from that moment onward there was no retreat. By implication, without realising what I was doing, I had already declared myself W. F. Raffles. Therefore, W. F. Raffles I would be, in that bank, for that night. And the devil teach me how to use my lie!'

Again he raised his glass to his lips—I had forgotten mine. His cigarette-case caught the gaslight as he handed it to me. I shook my head without taking my eyes from his.

'The devil played up,' continued Raffles, with a laugh. 'Before I tasted my soup I had decided what to do. I had determined to rob that bank instead of going to bed, and be back in Melbourne for breakfast if the doctor's mare could do it. I would tell the old fellow that I had missed my way and been bushed for hours, as I easily might have been, and had never got to Yea at all. At Yea, on the other hand, the personation and robbery would ever after be attributed to a member of the gang that had waylaid and murdered the new manager with that very object. You are acquiring some experience in such matters, Bunny. I ask you, was there ever a better get-out? Last night's was something like it, only never such a certainty. And I saw it from the beginning—saw to the end before I had finished my soup!

'To increase my chances, the cashier, who also lived in the bank, was away over the holidays, had actually gone down to Melbourne to see us play; and the man who had taken my horse also waited at table; for he and his wife were the only servants, and they slept in a separate building. You may depend I ascertained this before we had finished dinner. Indeed, I was by way of asking too many questions (the most oblique and delicate was that which elicited my host's name, Ewbank), nor was I careful enough to conceal their drift.

' "Do you know," said this fellow Ewbank, who was one of the downright sort, "if it wasn't you, I should say you were in a funk of robbers? Have you lost your nerve?"

' "I hope not," said I, turning jolly hot, I can tell you; "but—well, it's not a pleasant thing to have to put a bullet through a fellow!"

' "No?" said he, coolly. "I should enjoy nothing better myself; besides, yours didn't go through."

' "I wish it had!" I was smart enough to cry.

' "Amen!" said he.

'And I emptied my glass; actually I did not know whether my wounded bank-robber was in prison, dead, or at large!

'But, now that I had had more than enough of it, Ewbank would come back to the subject. He admitted that the staff was small; but as for himself, he had a loaded revolver under his pillow all night, under the counter all day, and he was only waiting for his chance.

' "Under the counter, eh?" I was ass enough to say.

' "Yes; so had you!"

'He was looking at me in surprise, and something told me that to say "of course—I had forgotten!" would have been quite fatal, considering what I was supposed to have done. So I looked down my nose and shook my head.

' "But the papers said you had!" he cried.

' "Not under the counter," said I.

' "But it's the regulation!"

'For the moment, Bunny, I felt stumped, though I trust I only looked more superior than before, and I think I justified my look.

' "The regulation!" I said at length, in the most offensive tone at my command. "Yes, the regulation would have us all dead men! My dear sir, do you expect your bank-robber to let you reach for your gun in the place where he knows it's kept? I had mine in my pocket, and I got my chance by retreating from the counter with all visible reluctance.''

'Ewbank stared at me with open eyes and a five-barred forehead, then came down his fist on the table.

' ''By God, that was smart! Still,'' he added, like a man who would not be in the wrong, ''the papers said the other thing, you know!''

' ''Of course,'' I rejoined, ''because they said what I told them. You wouldn't have had me advertise the fact that I improved upon the bank's regulations, would you?''

'So that cloud rolled over, and by Jove it was a cloud with a golden lining! Not silver—real good Australian gold! For old Ewbank hadn't quite appreciated me till then; he was a hard nut, a much older man than myself, and I felt pretty sure he thought me young for the place, and my supposed feat a fluke. But I never saw a man change his mind more openly. He got out his best brandy, he made me throw away the cigar I was smoking and opened a fresh box. He was a convivial-looking party, with a red moustache, and a very humorous face (not unlike Tom Emmett's), and from that moment I laid myself out to attack him on his convivial flank. But he wasn't a Rosenthall, Bunny; he had a treble-seamed, hand-sewn head, and could have drunk me under the table ten times over.

' ''All right,'' I thought, ''you may go to bed sober, but you'll sleep like a timber yard!'' And I threw half he gave me through the open window when he wasn't looking.

'But he was a good chap, Ewbank, and don't you imagine he was at all intemperate. Convivial I called him, and I only wish he had been something more. He did, however, become more and more genial as the evening advanced, and I had not much difficulty in getting him to show me round the bank at what was really an unearthly hour for such a proceeding. It was when he went to fetch the revolver before turning in. I kept him out of his bed another twenty minutes, and I knew every inch of the business premises before I shook hands with Ewbank in my room.

'You won't guess what I did with myself for the next hour. I undressed and went to bed. The incessant strain involved in even the most deliberate impersonation is the most wearing thing I know; then how much more so when the impersonation is impromptu! There's no getting your eye in; the next word may bowl you out; it's batting in a bad light all through. I haven't told you of half the tight places I was in during a conversation that ran into hours and became dangerously intimate towards the end. You can imagine them for yourself, and then picture me spread out on my bed, getting my second wind for the big deed of the night.

'Once more I was in luck, for I had not been lying there long before I heard my dear Ewbank snoring like a harmonium, and the music never ceased for a moment; it was as loud as ever when I crept out and closed my door behind me, as regular as ever when I stopped to listen at his. And I have still to hear the concert that I shall enjoy much more. The good fellow snored me out of the bank, and was still snoring when I again stood and listened under his open window.

'Why did I leave the bank first? To catch and saddle the mare and tether her in a clump of trees close by: to have the means of escape nice and handy before I went to work. I have often wondered at the instinctive wisdom of the precaution; unconsciously I was acting on what has been one of my guiding principles ever since. Pains and patience were required; I had to get my saddle without waking the man, and I was not used to catching horses in a horse-paddock. Then I distrusted the poor mare, and I went back to the stables for a hatful of oats, which I left with her in the clump, hat and all. There was a dog, too, to reckon with (our very worst enemy, Bunny); but I had been cute enough to make immense friends with him during the evening; and he wagged his tail, not only when I came downstairs, but when I reappeared at the back door.

'As the *soi-disant* new manager, I had been able, in the most ordinary course, to pump poor Ewbank about anything and everything connected with the working of the bank, especially in those twenty last invaluable minutes before turning in. And I had made a very natural point of asking him where he kept, and would recommend me to keep, the keys at night. Of course, I thought he would take them with him to his room; but no such thing; he had a dodge worth two of that. What it was doesn't much matter, but no outsider would have found those keys in a month of Sundays.

'I, of course, had them in a few seconds, and in a few more I was in the strong-room itself. I forgot to say that the moon had risen and was letting quite a lot of light into the bank. I had, however, brought a bit of candle with me from my room; and in the strong-room, which was down some narrow stairs behind the counter in the banking chamber, I had no hesitation in lighting it. There was no window down there, and though I could no longer hear old Ewbank snoring, I had not the slightest reason to anticipate disturbance from that quarter. I did think of locking myself in while I was at work, but, thank goodness, the iron door had no keyhole on the inside.

'Well, there was heaps of gold in the safe, but I only took what I needed and could comfortably carry, not much more than a couple of hundred altogether. Not a note would I touch, and my native caution came out also in the way I divided the sovereigns between all my pockets, and packed them up so that I shouldn't be like the old woman of Banbury Cross. Well you think me too cautious still, but I was insanely cautious then. And so it was that, just as I was ready to go, whereas I might have been gone ten minutes, there came a violent knocking at the outer door.

'Bunny, it was the outer door of the banking chamber! My candle must have been seen! And there I stood, with the grease running hot over my fingers, in that brick grave of a strong room!

'There was only one thing to be done. I must trust to the sound sleeping of Ewbank upstairs, open the door myself, knock the visitor down, or shoot him with the revolver I had been new chum enough to buy before leaving Melbourne, and make a dash for that clump of trees and the doctor's mare. My mind was made up in an instant, and I was at the top of the strong-room stairs, the knocking still continuing, when a second sound drove me back. It was the sound of bare feet coming along a corridor.

'My narrow stair was stone, I tumbled down it with little noise, and had only to push open the iron door, for I had left the keys in the safe. As I did so I heard a handle turn overhead, and thanked my gods that I had shut every single door behind me. You see, old chap, one's caution doesn't always let one in!

' "Who's that knocking?" said Ewbank, up above.

'I could not make out the answer, but it sounded to me like the irrelevant supplication of a spent man. What I did hear plainly, was the cocking of the bank revolver before the bolts were shot back. Then, a tottering step, a hard, short, shallow breathing, and Embank's voice in horror:

' "Good Lord! What's happened to you? You're bleeding like a pig!"

' "Not now," came with a grateful sort of sigh.

' "But you have been! What's done it?"

' "Bushrangers."

' "Down the road?"

' "This and Whittlesea—tied to tree—cock-shots—left me—bleed to death. . . ."

'The weak voice failed, and the bare feet bolted. Now was my time—if the poor devil had fainted. But I could not be sure, and there I crouched down below in the dark, at the half-shut iron door, not less spell-bound than imprisoned. It was just as well, for Ewbank wasn't gone a minute.

' "Drink this," I heard him say, and when the other spoke again his voice was stronger.

' "Now I begin to feel alive."

' "Don't talk!"

' "It does me good. You don't know what it was, all those miles alone, one an hour at the outside! I never thought I should come through. You must let me tell you—in case I don't!"

' "Well, have another sip."

' "Thank you. . . . I said bushrangers; of course there are no such things nowadays."

' "What were they, then?"

' "Bank thieves; the one that had the pot-shots was the very brute I drove out of the bank at Coburg, with a bullet in him!" '

'I knew it!'

'Of course you did, Bunny; so did I, down in that strong-room; but old Ewbank didn't, and I thought he was never going to speak again.

' "You're delirious," he says at last. "Who in blazes do you think you are?"

' "The new manager."

' "The new manager's in bed and asleep upstairs!"

' "When did he arrive?"

' "This evening."

' "Call himself Raffles?"

' "Yes."

' "Well, I'm damned!" whispered the real man. "I thought it was just revenge, but now I see what it was. My dear sir, the man upstairs is an imposter—if he's upstairs still! He must be one of the gang. He's going to rob the bank—if he hasn't done so already!"

' "If he hasn't done so already," muttered Ewbank after him; "if he's upstairs still! By God, if he is I'm sorry for him!"

'His tone was quiet enough, but about the nastiest I ever heard. I tell you, Bunny, I was glad I'd brought that revolver. It looked as though it must be mine against his, muzzle to muzzle.

' "Better have a look down here, first," said the new manager.

' "While he gets through his window? No, no, he's not down here."

' "It's easy to have a look."

'Bunny, if you ask me what was the most thrilling moment of my infamous career, I say it was that moment. There I stood at the bottom of those narrow stone stairs inside the strong-room, with the door a good foot open, and I didn't know whether it would creak or not. The light was coming nearer—and I didn't know! I had to chance it. And it didn't creak a bit; it was far too solid and well-hung; and I couldn't have banged it if I'd tried, it was too heavy; and it fitted so close that I felt and heard the air squeeze out in my face. Every shred of light went out, except the streak underneath, and it brightened. How I blessed that door!

' "No, he's not down there," I heard, as though through cotton-wool; then the streak went out too, and in a few seconds I ventured to open once more, and was in time to hear them creeping to my room.

'Well, now, there was not a fifth of a second to be lost; but I'm proud to say I came up those stairs on my toes and fingers, and out of that bank (they'd gone and left the door open) just as gingerly as though my time had been my own. I didn't even forget to put on the hat that the doctor's mare was eating her oats out of, as well as he could with a bit, or it alone would have landed me. I didn't even gallop away, but just jogged off quietly in the thick dust at the side of the road (though I own my heart was galloping), and thanked my stars the bank was at that end of the township, in which I really hadn't set foot. The very last thing I heard was the two managers raising Cain and the coachman. And now, Bunny—'

He stood up and stretched himself, with a smile that ended in a yawn. The black windows had faded through every shade of indigo; they now framed their opposite neighbours, stark and livid in the dawn; and the gas seemed turned to nothing in the globes.

'But that's not all?' I cried.

'I'm sorry to say it is,' said Raffles apologetically. 'The thing should have ended with an exciting chase, I know, but somehow it didn't. I suppose they thought I had got no end of a start; then they had made up their minds that I belonged to the gang, which was not so many miles away; and one of them had got as much as he could carry from that gang as it was. But I wasn't to know all that, and I'm bound to say that there was plenty of excitement left for me. Lord, how I made that poor brute travel when I got among the trees! Though we must have been well over fifty miles from Melbourne, we had done it at a snail's pace; and those stolen oats had brisked the old girl up to such a pitch that she fairly bolted when she felt her nose turned south. By Jove, it was no joke, in and out among those trees, and under branches with your face in the mane! I told you about the forest of dead gums? It looked perfectly ghostly in the moonlight. And I found it as still as I had left it—so still that I pulled up there, my first halt, and lay with my ear to the ground for two or three minutes. But I heard nothing—not a thing but the mare's bellows and my own heart. I'm sorry, Bunny; but if ever you write my memoirs, you won't have any difficulty in working up that chase. Play those dead gum-trees for all they're worth, and let the bullets fly like hail. I'll turn round in my saddle to see Ewbank coming up hell-for-leather in his white suit, and I'll duly paint it red. Do it in the third person, and they won't know how it's going to end.'

'But I don't know myself,' I complained. 'Did the mare carry you all the way back to Melbourne?'

'Every rod, pole, or perch! I had her well seen to at our hotel, and returned her to the doctor in the evening. He was tremendously tickled to hear I had been bushed; next morning he brought me the paper to show me what I had escaped at Yea!'

'Without suspecting anything?'

'Ah!' said Raffles, as he put out the gas; 'that's a point on which I've never made up my mind. The mare and her colour was a coincidence—luckily she was only a bay—and I fancy the condition of the beast must have told a tale. The doctor's manner was certainly different. I'm inclined to think he suspected something, though not the right thing. I wasn't expecting him, and I fear my appearance may have increased his suspicions.'

I asked him why.

'I used to have rather a heavy moustache,' said Raffles, 'but I lost it the day after I lost my innocence.'

WILFUL MURDER

Of the various robberies in which we were both concerned, it is but the few, I find, that will bear telling at any length. Not that the others contained details which even I would hesitate to recount; it is, rather, the very absence of untoward incident which renders them useless for my present purpose. In point of fact our plans were so craftily laid (by Raffles) that the chances of a hitch were invariably reduced to a minimum before we went to work. We might be disappointed in the market value of our haul; but it was quite the exception for us to find ourselves confronted by unforeseen impediments, or involved in a really dramatic dilemma. There was a sameness, even in our spoil; for, of course, only the most precious stones are worth the trouble we took and the risks we ran. In short, our most successful escapades would prove the greatest weariness of all in narrative form; and none more so than the dull affair of the Ardagh emeralds, some eight or nine weeks after the Milchester cricket week. The former, however, had a sequel that I would rather forget than all our burglaries put together.

It was the evening after our return from Ireland, and I was waiting at my rooms for Raffles, who had gone off as usual to dispose of the plunder. Raffles had his own method of conducting this very vital branch of our business, which I was well content to leave entirely in his hands. He drove the bargains, I believe, in a thin but subtle disguise of the flashy-seedy order, and always in the Cockney dialect of which he had made himself a master. Moreover, he invariably employed the same 'fence', who was ostensibly a money-lender in a small (but yet notorious) way, and in reality a rascal as remarkable as Raffles himself. Only lately I also had been to the man, but in my proper person. We had needed capital for the getting of these very emeralds, and I had raised a hundred pounds, on the terms you would expect from a soft-spoken greybeard with an ingratiating smile, an incessant bow, and the shiftiest old eyes that ever flew from rim to rim of a pair of spectacles. So the original sinews and the final spoils of war came in this case from the self-same source—a circumstance which appealed to us both.

But these same final spoils I was still to see, and I waited and waited with an impatience that grew upon me with the growing dusk. At my open window I had played Sister Ann until the faces in the street below were no longer distinguishable. And now I was tearing to and fro in the grip of horrible hypothesis—a grip that tightened when at last the lift-gates opened with a clatter outside—that held me breathless until a well-known tattoo followed on my door.

'In the dark!' said Raffles, as I dragged him in. 'Why, Bunny, what's wrong?'

'Nothing—now you've come,' said I, shutting the door behind him in a fever of relief and anxiety. 'Well? Well? What fetch?'

'Five hundred.'

'Down?'

'Got it in my pocket.'

'Good man!' I cried. 'You don't know what a stew I've been in. I'll switch on the light. I've been thinking of you and nothing else for the last hour. I—I was ass enough to think something had gone wrong!'

Raffles was smiling when the white light filled the room, but for the moment I did not perceive the peculiarity of his smile. I was fatuously full of my own late tremors and present relief, and my first idiotic act was to spill some whisky and squirt the soda-water all over in my anxiety to do justice to the occasion.

'So you thought something had happened?' said Raffles, leaning back in my chair as he lit a cigarette, and looking much amused. 'What should you say if something had? Sit tight, my dear chap! It was nothing of the slightest consequence, and it's all over now. A stern chase and a long one, Bunny, but I think I'm well to wind-ward this time.'

And suddenly I saw that his collar was limp, his hair matted, his boots thick with dust.

'The police?' I whispered aghast.

'Oh dear, no; only old Baird.'

'Baird! But wasn't it Baird who took the emeralds?'

'It was.'

'Then how came he to chase you?'

'My dear fellow, I'll tell you if you give me a chance, it's really nothing to get in the least excited about. Old Baird has at last spotted that I'm not quite the common cracksman I would have him think me. So he's been doing his best to run me to my burrow.'

'And you call that nothing!'

'It would be something if he had succeeded; but he has still to do that. I admit, however, that he made me sit up for the time being. It all comes of going on the job so far from home. There was the old brute with the whole thing in his morning paper. He knew it must have been done by some fellow who could pass himself off for a gentleman, and I saw his eyebrows go up the moment I told him I was the man, with the same old twang that you could cut with a paper knife. I did my best to get out of it—swore I had a pal who was a real swell—but I saw very plainly that I had given myself away. He gave up haggling. He paid my price as though he enjoyed doing it. But I felt him following when I made tracks—though, of course, I didn't turn round to see.'

'Why not?'

'My dear Bunny, it's the very worst thing you can do. As long as you look unsuspecting they'll keep their distance, and so long as they keep their distance you stand a chance. Once show that you know you're being followed, and it's flight or fight for all you're worth. I never even looked round; and mind you never do in the same hole. I just hurried up to Blackfriars and booked for High Street, Kensington, at the top of my voice; and as the train was leaving Sloane Square out I hopped, and up an those stairs like a lamplighter, and round to the studio by the back streets. Well, to be on the safe side, I lay low there all the afternoon, hearing nothing in the least suspicious, and only wishing I had a window to look through instead of that beastly skylight. However, the coast seemed clear enough, and thus far it was my mere idea that he would follow me; there was nothing to show he had. So at last I marched out in my proper rig—almost straight into old Baird's arms!'

'What on earth did you do?'

'Walked past him as though I had never set eyes on him in my life, and didn't then; took a cab in the King's Road, and drove like the deuce to Clapham Junction; rushed on to the nearest platform, without a ticket, jumped into the first train I saw, got out at Twickenham, walked full tilt back to Richmond, took the District to Charing Cross, and here I am! Ready for tub and a change, and the best dinner the club can give us. I came to you first, because I thought you might be getting anxious. Come round with me, and I won't keep you long.'

'You're certain you've given him the slip?' I said, as we put on our hats.

'Certain enough; but we can make assurance doubly sure,' said Raffles, and went to my window, where he stood for a minute or two looking down into the street.

'All right?' I asked him.

'All right,' said he; and we went downstairs forthwith, and so to the Albany arm-in-arm. But we were both rather silent on the way. I, for my part, was wondering what Raffles would do about the studio in Chelsea, whither, at all events, he had been successfully dogged. To me the point seemed one of immediate importance, but when I mentioned it he said there was time enough to think about that. His one other remark was made after we had nodded (in Bond Street) to a young blood of our acquaintance who happened to be getting himself a bad name.

'Poor Jack Rutter!' said Raffles, with a sigh. 'Nothing's sadder than to see a fellow going to the bad like that. He's about mad with drink and debt; did you see his eye? Odd that we should have met him tonight, by the way; it's old Baird who's said to have skinned him. I've a jolly good mind to skin old Baird!'

And his tone took a sudden low fury, made the more noticeable by another long silence, which lasted, indeed, throughout an admirable dinner at the club, and for some time after we had settled down in a quiet corner of the smoking-room with our coffee and cigars. Then at last I saw Raffles looking at me with his lazy smile, and I knew that the morose fit was at an end.

'I daresay you wonder what I've been thinking about all this time?' said he. 'I've been thinking what rot it is to go doing things by halves!'

'Well,' said I, returning his smile, 'that's not a charge that you can bring against yourself, is it?'

'I'm not so sure,' said Raffles, blowing a meditative puff; 'as a matter of fact, I was thinking less of myself than of that poor devil of a Jack Rutter. There's a fellow who does things by halves; he's only half gone to the bad; and look at the difference between him and us! He's under the thumb of a villainous money-lender; we are solvent citizens. He's taken to drink; we're as sober as we are solvent. His pals are beginning to cut him; our difficulty is to keep the pal from the door. *Enfin*, he begs or borrows, which is stealing by halves; and we steal outright and are done with it. Obviously, ours is the more honest course. Yet I'm not sure, Bunny, but we're doing the thing by halves ourselves!'

'Why? What more could we do?' I exclaimed in soft derision, looking round, however, to make sure that we were not overheard.

'What more?' said Raffles. 'Well, murder—for one thing.'

'Rot!'

'A matter of opinion, my dear Bunny; I don't mean it for rot. I've told you before that the biggest man alive is the man who's committed a murder, and not yet been found out; at least he ought to be, but he so very seldom has the soul to appreciate himself. Just think of it! Think of coming here and talking to the men, very likely about the murder itself; and knowing you've done it; and wondering how they'd look if they knew! Oh, it would be great, simply great! But, besides all that, when you were caught, there'd be a merciful and dramatic end of you. You'd fill the bill for a few weeks and then snuff out with a flourish of extra-specials; you wouldn't rust with a vile repose for seven or fourteen years.'

'Good old Raffles!' I chuckled. 'I begin to forgive you for being in bad form at dinner.'

'But I was never more earnest in my life.'

'Go on!'

'I mean it.'

'You know very well that you wouldn't commit a murder, whatever else you might do.'

'I know very well I'm going to commit one tonight!'

He had been leaning back in the saddle-bag chair, watching me with keen eyes sheathed by languid lids; now he started forward, and his eyes leapt to mine like cold steel from the scabbard. They struck home to my slow wits; their meaning was no longer in doubt. I, who knew the man, read murder in his clenched hands, and murder in his locked lips, but a hundred murders in those hard blue eyes.

'Baird?' I faltered, moistening my lips with my tongue.

'Of course.'

'But you said it didn't matter about the room in Chelsea?'

'I told a lie.'

'Anyway you gave him the slip afterwards!'

'That was another. I didn't. I thought I had when I came up to you this evening; but when I looked out of your window—you remember?—to make assurance doubly sure—there he was on the opposite pavement down below.'

'And you never said a word about it!'

'I wasn't going to spoil your dinner, Bunny, and I wasn't going to let you spoil mine.

But there he was as large as life, and, of course, he followed us to the Albany. A fine game for him to play, a game after his mean old heart; blackmail for me, bribes from the police, the one bidding against the other; but he shan't play it with me, he shan't live to, and the world will have an extortioner the less. Waiter! Two Scotch whiskies and sodas. I'm off at eleven, Bunny; it's the only thing to be done.'

'You know where he lives, then?'

'Yes, out Willesden way, and alone; the fellow's a miser among other things. I long ago found out all about him.'

Again I looked around the room; it was a young man's club, and young men were laughing, chatting, smoking, drinking, on every hand. One nodded to me through the smoke. Like a machine I nodded to him, and turned back to Raffles with a groan.

'Surely you will give him a chance!' I urged. 'The very sight of your pistol should bring him to terms.'

'It wouldn't make him keep them.'

'But you might try the effect?'

'I probably shall. Here's a drink for you, Bunny. Wish me luck.'

'I'm coming too.'

'I don't want you.'

'But I must come!'

An ugly gleam shot from the steel-blue eyes.

'To interfere?' said Raffles.

'Not I.'

'You give me your word?'

'I do.'

'Bunny, if you break it—'

'You may shoot me too!'

'I most certainly should,' said Raffles solemnly. 'So you come at your own peril, my dear man; but if you are coming—well, the sooner the better, for I must stop at my rooms on the way.'

Five minutes later I was waiting for him at the Piccadilly entrance to the Albany. I had a reason for remaining outside. It was the feeling—half hope, half fear—that Angus Baird might still be on our trail—that some more immediate and less cold-blooded way of dealing with him might result from a sudden encounter between the money-lender and myself. I would not warn him of his danger; but I would avert tragedy at all costs. And when no such encounter had taken place, and Raffles and I were fairly on our way to Willesden, that, I think, was still my honest resolve. I would not break my word if I could help it, but it was a comfort to feel that I could break it if I liked, on an understood penalty. Alas! I fear my good intentions were tainted with a devouring curiosity, and overlaid by the fascination which goes hand in hand with horror.

I have a poignant recollection of the hour it took us to reach the house. We walked across St James's Park (I can see the lights now, bright on the bridge and blurred on the water), and we had some minutes to wait for the last train to Willesden. It left at 11.21, I remember, and Raffles was put out to find it did not go on to Kensal Rise. We had to get out at Willesden Junction and walk on through the streets into fairly open country that happened to be quite new to me. I could never find the house again. I remember, however, that we were on a dark foot-path between the woods and fields when the clocks began striking twelve.

'Surely,' said I, 'we shall find him in bed and asleep?'

'I hope we do,' said Raffles grimly.

'Then you mean to break in?'

'What else did you think?'

I had not thought about it at all; the ultimate crime had monopolised my mind. Beside it burglary was a bagatelle, but one to deprecate none the less. I saw obvious objections; the man was *au fait* with cracksmen and their ways, he would certainly have fire-arms, and might be the first to use them.

'I could wish nothing better,' said Raffles. 'Then it will be man to man, and devil take the worst shot. You don't suppose I prefer foul play to fair, do you? But die he must, by one or the other, or it's a long stretch for you and me.'

'Better that than this!'

'Then stay where you are my good fellow. I told you I didn't want you; and this is the house. So good-night.'

I could see no house at all, only the angle of a high wall rising solitary in the night, with the starlight glittering on battlements of broken glass; and in the wall a tall green gate, bristling with spikes, and showing a front for battering-rams in the feeble rays of an outlying lamp-post cast across the new-made road. It seemed to me a road of building sites, with but this one house built, all by itself, at one end; but the night was too dark for more than a mere impression.

Raffles, however, had seen the place by daylight, and had come prepared for the special obstacles; already he was reaching up and putting champagne corks on the spikes, and in another moment he had his folded covert coat across the corks. I stepped back as he raised himself, and saw a little pyramid of slates snip the sky above the gate; as he squirmed over I ran forward, and had my own weight on the spikes and corks and covert coat when he gave the latter a tug.

'Coming after all?'

'Rather!'

'Take care then; the place is all bell-wires and springs. It's no soft spring this! There—stand still while I take off the corks.'

The garden was very small and new, with a grass-plot still in separate sods, but a quantity of full-grown laurels stuck into the raw clay beds. 'Bells in themselves,' Raffles whispered; 'there's nothing else rustles so—cunning old beast!' And we gave them a wide berth as we crept across the grass.

'He's gone to bed!'

'I don't think so, Bunny. I believe he's seen us.'

'Why?'

'I saw a light.'

'Where?'

'Downstairs, for an instant, when I—'

His whisper died away; he had seen the light again, and so had I.

It lay like a golden rod under the front door—and vanished. It reappeared like a gold thread under the lintel—and vanished for good. We heard the stairs creak, creak, and cease, also for good. We neither saw nor heard any more, though we stood waiting on the grass till our feet were soaked with the dew.

'I'm going in,' said Raffles at last. 'I don't believe he saw us at all. I wish he had. This way.'

We trod gingerly on the path, but the gravel stuck to our wet soles, and grated horribly in a little tiled verandah with a glass door leading within. It was through this glass that Raffles had first seen the light; and he now proceeded to take out a pane, with the diamond, the pot of treacle, and the sheet of brown paper which were seldom omitted from his impedimenta. Nor did he dispense with my own assistance, though he may have accepted it as instinctively as it was proffered. In any case it was these fingers that helped to spread the treacle on the brown paper, and pressed the latter to the glass until the diamond had completed its circuit and the pane fell gently back into our hands.

Raffles now inserted his long hand, turned the key in the lock, and, by making a long arm, succeeded in drawing the bolt at the bottom of the door; it proved to be the only one, and the door opened, though not very wide.

'What's that?' said Raffles, as something crunched beneath his feet on the very threshold.

'A pair of spectacles,' I whispered, picking them up. I was still fingering the broken lenses and the bent rims when Raffles tripped and almost fell, with a gasping cry that he made no effort to restrain.

'Hush, man, hush!' I entreated under my breath. 'He'll hear you!'

For answer his teeth chattered—even his—and I heard him fumbling with his matches.

'No, Bunny; he won't hear us,' whispered Raffles presently, and he rose from his knees and lit a gas as the match burnt down.

Angus Baird was lying on his own floor, dead, with his grey hairs glued together by his blood; near him a poker with the black end glistening; in a corner his desk, ransacked, littered. A clock ticked noisily on the chimneypiece, for perhaps a hundred seconds there was no other sound.

Raffles stood very still, staring down at the dead, as a man might stare into an abyss after striding blindly to its brink. His breath came audibly through wide nostrils; he made no other sign and his lips seemed sealed.

'That light!' said I hoarsely; 'the light we saw under the door!'

With a start he turned to me.

'It's true. I had forgotten it. It was in here I saw it first!'

'He must be upstairs still!'

'If he is we'll soon rout him out. Come on!'

Instead I laid a hand upon his arm, imploring him to reflect—that his enemy was dead now—that we should certainly be involved—that now or never was our own time to escape. He shook me off a sudden fury of impatience, a reckless contempt in his eyes, and, bidding me save my own skin if I liked, he once more turned back upon me, and this time left me half resolved to take him at his word. Had he forgotten on what errand he himself was here? Was he determined that this night should end in black disaster? As I asked myself these questions his match flared in the hall; in another moment the stairs were creaking under his feet, even as they had creaked under those of the murderer; and the human instinct that inspired him in defiance of his risk was borne in also upon my slower sensibilities. Could we let the murderer go? My answer was to bound up the creaking stairs and to overhaul Raffles on the landing.

But three doors presented themselves; the first opened into a bedroom with the bed turned down but undisturbed; the second room was empty in every sense; the third door was locked.

Raffles lit the landing gas.

'He's in there,' said he, cocking his revolver. 'Do you remember how we used to break into the studies at school? Here goes!'

His flat foot crashed over the keyhole, the lock gave, the door flew open, and in the sudden draught the landing gas heeled over like a cobble in a squall; as the flame righted itself I saw a fixed bath, two bath-towels knotted together—an open window—a cowering figure—and Raffles struck aghast on the threshold.

'Jack—Rutter?'

The words came thick and slow with horror, and in horror I heard myself repeating them, while the cowering figure by the bathroom window rose gradually erect.

'It's you!' he whispered, in amazement no less than our own; 'it's you two! What's it mean, Raffles? I saw you get over the gate; a bell rang, the place is full of them. Then you broke in? What's it all mean?'

'We may tell you that, when you tell us what in God's name you've done, Rutter!'

'Done? What have I done?' The unhappy wretch came out into the light with blood-shot, blinking eyes, and a bloody shirt-front. 'You know—you've seen—but I'll tell you if you like. I've killed a robber; that's all. I've killed a robber, a usurer, a jackal, a black-mailer, the cleverest and the cruellest villain unhung. I'm ready to hang for him. I'd kill him again!'

And he looked us fiercely in the face, a fine defiance in his dissipated eyes; his breast heaving, his jaw like a rock.

'Shall I tell you how it happened?' he went passionately on. 'He's made my life a hell these weeks and months past. You may know that. A perfect hell. Well, tonight I met him in Bond Street. Do you remember when I met you fellows? He wasn't twenty yards behind you; he was on your tracks, Raffles; he saw me nod to you, and stopped me and asked me who you were. He seemed as keen as knives to know, I couldn't think why, and didn't care either, for I saw my chance. I said I'd tell him all about you if he'd give me a private interview. He said he wouldn't. I said he should, and held him by the coat; by the time I let him go you were out of sight, and I waited where I was till he came back in despair. I had the whiphand of him then. I could dictate where the interview should be, and I made him take me home with him, still swearing to tell him all about you when we'd had our talk. Well, when we got here I made him give me something to eat, putting him off and off; and about ten o'clock I heard the gate shut. I waited a bit, and then asked him if he lived alone.

' "Not at all," says he; "did you not see the servant?"

'I said I'd seen her, but I thought I heard her go; if I was mistaken no doubt she would come when she was called; and I yelled three times at the top of my voice. Of course there was no servant to come. I knew that, because I came to see him one night last week, and, he interviewed me himself through the gate, but wouldn't open it. Well, when I had done yelling, and not a soul had come near us, he was as white as that ceiling. Then I told him we could have our chat at last; and I picked the poker out of the fender, and told him how he'd robbed me, but by God he shouldn't rob me any more. I gave him three minutes to write and sign a settlement of all his iniquitous claims against me, or have his brains beaten out over his own carpet. He thought a minute, and then went to his desk for pen and paper. In two seconds he was round like lightning with a revolver, and I went for him bald-headed. He fired two or three times and missed—you can find the holes if you like; but I hit him every time—by God! I was like a savage till the thing was done. And then I didn't care. I went through his desk looking for my own bills, and was coming away when you turned up. I said I didn't care, nor do I; but I was going to give myself up tonight, and shall still; so you see I shan't give you fellows much trouble!'

He was done; and there we stood on the landing of the lonely house, the low, thick, eager voice still racing and ringing through our ears; the dead man below, and in front of us his impenitent slayer. I knew to whom the impenitence would appeal when he had heard the story, and I was not mistaken.

'That's all rot,' said Raffles, speaking after a pause; 'we shan't let you give yourself up.'

'You shan't stop me! What would be the good? The woman saw me; it would only be a question of time; and I can't face waiting to be taken. Think of it; waiting for them to touch you on the shoulder! No, no, no; I'll give myself up and get it over.'

His speech was changed; he faltered, floundered. It was as though a clearer perception of his position had come with the bare idea of escape from it.

'But listen to me,' urged Raffles. 'We're here at our peril ourselves. We broke in like thieves to enforce redress for a grievance like your own. But don't you see? We took out a pane—did the thing like regular burglars. We shall get the credit of all the rest!'

'You mean that I shan't be suspected?'

'I do.'

'But I don't want to get off scot-free,' cried Rutter hysterically. 'I've killed him. I know that. But it was in self-defence; it wasn't murder. I must own up and take the consequences. I shall go mad if I don't.'

His hands twitched; his lips quivered; the tears were in his eyes. Raffles took him roughly by the shoulder.

'Look here, you fool! If the three of us are caught here now, do you know what those consequences would be? We should swing in a row in six weeks' time! You talk as though we were sitting in a club; don't you know it's one o'clock in the morning, and the lights on, and a dead man down below? For God's sake pull yourself together, and do what I tell you, or you're a dead man yourself.'

'I wish I was one!' Rutter sobbed. 'I wish I had his revolver, I'd blow my own brains out. It's somewhere under him! O my God, my God!'

His knees knocked together; the frenzy of reaction was at its height. We had to take him downstairs between us, and so through the front door out into the open air.

All was still outside—all but the smothered weeping of the unstrung wretch upon our hands. Raffles returned for a moment to the house; then all was dark as well. The gate opened from within; we closed it carefully behind us; and so left the starlight shining on broken glass and polished spikes, one and all as we had found them.

We escaped; no need to dwell on our escape. Our murderer seemed set upon the scaffold: drunk with his deed, he was more trouble than six men drunk with wine. Again and again we threatened to leave him to his fate, to wash our hands of him. But incredible and unmerited luck was with the three of us. Not a soul did we meet between that and Willesden; and of those who saw us later, did one think of the two young men with crooked white ties, supporting a third in a seemingly unmistakable condition, when the evening papers apprised the town of a terrible tragedy at Kensal Rise?

We walked to Maida Vale, and thence drove openly to my rooms. But I alone went upstairs; the other two proceeded to the Albany, and I saw no more of Raffles for forty-eight hours. He was not at his rooms when I called in the morning, he had left no word. When he reappeared the papers were full of the murder; and the man who had committed it was on the wide Atlantic, a steerage passenger from Liverpool to New York.

'There was no arguing with him,' so Raffles told me; 'either he must make a clean breast of it or flee the country. So I rigged him up at the studio, and we took the first train to Liverpool. Nothing would induce him to sit tight and enjoy the situation as I should have endeavoured to do in his place; and it's just as well! I went to his diggings to destroy some papers, and what do you think I found? The police in possession; there's a warrant out against him already! The idiots think that window wasn't genuine, and the warrant's out. It won't be my fault if it's ever served!'

Nor, after all these years, can I think it will be mine.

NINE POINTS OF THE LAW

'Well,' said Raffles, 'what do you make of it?'

I read the advertisement once more before replying. It was in the last column of the *Daily Telegraph*, and it ran:

'Two Thousand Pounds Reward.—The above sum may be earned by any one qualified to undertake delicate mission and prepared to run certain risk.—Apply by telegram, Security, London.'

'I think,' said I, 'it's the most extraordinary advertisement that ever got into print!'

Raffles smiled.

'Not quite all that, Bunny; still, extraordinary enough, I grant you.'

'Look at the figure.'

'It is certainly large.'

'And the mission—and the risk!'

'Yes; the combination is frank, to say the least of it. But the really original point is requiring applications by telegram to a telegraphic address! There's something in the fellow who thought of that, and something in his game; with one word he chokes off the million who answer an advertisement every day—when they can raise the stamp. My answer cost me five bob; but then I prepaid another.'

'You don't mean to say that you've applied?'

'Rather,' said Raffles. 'I want two thousand pounds as much as any man.'

'Put your own name?'

'Well—no, Bunny, I didn't. In point of fact, I smell something interesting and illegal, and you know what a cautious chap I am. I signed myself Glasspool, care of Hickey, 38 Conduit Street; that's my tailor, and after sending the wire I went round and told him what to expect. He promised to send the reply along the moment it came. I shouldn't be surprised if that's it!'

And he was gone before a double knock on the outer door had done ringing through the rooms, to return next minute with an open telegram and a face full of news.

'What do you think?' said he. 'Security's that fellow Addenbrooke, the police-court lawyer, and he wants to see me instanter!'

'Do you know him then?'

'Merely by repute. I only hope he doesn't know me. He's the chap who got six weeks for sailing too close to the wind in the Sutton-Wilmer case; everybody wondered why he wasn't struck off the rolls. Instead of that he's got a first-rate practice on the seamy side, and every blackguard with half a case takes it straight to Bennett Addenbrooke. He's probably the one man who would have the cheek to put in an advertisement like that, and the one man who could do it without exciting suspicion. It's simply in his line; but you may be sure there's something shady at the bottom of it. The odd thing is that I have long made up my mind to go to Addenbrooke myself if accidents should happen.'

'And you're going to him now?'

'This minute,' said Raffles, brushing his hat; 'and so are you.'

'But I came in to drag you out to lunch.'

'You shall lunch with me when we've seen this fellow. Come on, Bunny, and we'll choose your name on the way. Mine's Glasspool, and don't you forget it.'

Mr Bennett Addenbrooke occupied substantial offices in Wellington Street, Strand, and was out when we arrived; but he had only just gone 'over the way to the court'; and five minutes sufficed to produce a brisk, fresh-coloured, resolute-looking man, with a very confident, rather festive air, and black eyes that opened wide at the sight of Raffles.

'Mr—Glasspool?' exclaimed the lawyer.

'My name,' said Raffles, with dry effrontery.

'Not up at Lord's, however!' said the other, slyly. 'My dear sir, I have seen you take far too many wickets to make any mistake!'

For a single moment Raffles looked venomous; then he shrugged and smiled, and the smile grew into a little cynical chuckle.

'So you have bowled me out in my turn?' said he. 'Well, I don't think there's anything to explain. I am harder up than I wished to admit under my own name, that's all, and I want that thousand pounds reward.'

'Two thousand,' said the solicitor. 'And the man who is not above an alias happens to be just the sort of man I want; so don't let that worry you, my dear sir. The matter, however, is of a strictly private and confidential character.' And he looked very hard at me.

'Quite so,' said Raffles. 'But there was something about a risk?'

'A certain risk is involved.'

'Then surely three heads will be better than two. I said I wanted that thousand pounds; my friend here wants the other. We are both cursedly hard up, and we go into this thing together or not at all. Must you have his name too? I should give him my real one, Bunny.'

Mr Addenbrooke raised his eyebrows over the card I found for him; then he drummed upon it with his finger-nail, and his embarrassment expressed itself in a puzzled smile.

'The fact is I find myself in a difficulty,' he confessed at last. 'Yours is the first reply I have received; people who can afford to send long telegrams don't rush to the advertisements in the *Daily Telegraph*; but, on the other hand, I was not quite prepared to hear from men like yourselves. Candidly, and on consideration, I am not sure that you are the stamp of men for me—men who belong to good clubs! I rather intended to appeal to the—er—adventurous classes.'

'We are adventurers,' said Raffles gravely.

'But you respect the law?'

The black eyes gleamed shrewdly.

'We are not professional rogues, if that's what you mean,' said Raffles smiling. 'But on our beam-ends we are; we would do a good deal for a thousand pounds apiece, eh, Bunny?'

'Anything,' I murmured.

The solicitor rapped his desk.

'I'll tell you what I want you to do. You can but refuse. It's illegal, but it's illegality in a good cause; that's the risk, and my client is prepared to pay for it. He will pay for the attempt, in case of failure; the money is as good as yours once you consent to run the risk. My client is Sir Bernard Debenham, of Broom Hall, Esher.'

'I know his son,' I remarked.

Raffles knew him too, but said nothing, and his eye drooped disapproval in my direction. Bennett Addenbrooke turned to me.

'Then,' said he, 'you have the privilege of knowing one of the most complete young blackguards about town, and the *fons et origo* of the whole trouble. As you know the son, you may know of the father too, at all events by reputation; and in that case I needn't tell you that he is a very peculiar man. He lives alone in a storehouse of treasures which no eyes but his ever behold. He is said to have the finest collection of pictures in the south of England, though nobody ever sees them to judge; pictures, fiddles, and furniture are his hobby, and he is undoubtedly very eccentric. Nor can one deny that there has been considerable eccentricity in his treatment of his son. For years Sir Bernard paid his debts, and the other day, without the slightest warning, not only refused to do so any more, but absolutely stopped the lad's allowance. Well, I'll tell you what has happened; but first of all you must know, or you may remember, that I appeared for young Debenham in a little scrape he got into a year or two ago. I got him off all right, and Sir Bernard paid me handsomely on the nail. And no more did I hear or see of either of them until one day last week.'

The lawyer drew his chair nearer ours, and leant forward with a hand on either knee.

'On Tuesday of last week I had a telegram from Sir Bernard; I was to go to him at once.

I found him waiting for me in the drive; without a word he led me to the picture-gallery, which was locked and darkened, drew up a blind, and stood simply pointing to an empty picture-frame. It was a long time before I could get a word out of him. Then at last he told me that that frame had contained one of the rarest and most valuable pictures in England—in the world—an original Velasquez. I have checked this,' said the lawyer, 'and it seems literally true; the picture was a portrait of the Infanta Maria Teresa, said to be one of the artist's greatest works, second only to another portrait of one of the Popes of Rome—so they told me at the National Gallery, where they had its history by heart. They say there that the picture is practically priceless. And young Debenham has sold it for five thousand pounds!'

'The deuce he has' said Raffles.

I inquired who had bought it.

'A Queensland legislator of the name of Craggs—the Hon. John Montagu Craggs, MLC, to give him his full title. Not that we knew anything about him on Tuesday last; we didn't even know for certain that young Debenham had stolen the picture. But he had gone down for money on the Monday evening, had been refused, and it was plain enough that he had helped himself in this way; he had threatened revenge, and this was it. Indeed, when I hunted him up in town on the Tuesday night, he confessed as much in the most brazen manner imaginable. But he wouldn't tell me who was the purchaser, and finding out took the rest of the week; but I did find out, and a nice time I've had of it ever since! Backwards and forwards between Esher and the Metropole, where the Queenslander is staying, some-times twice a day; threats, offers, prayers, entreaties, not one of them a bit of good!'

'But,' said Raffles, 'surely it's a clear case? The sale was illegal; you can pay him back his money and force him to give the picture up.'

'Exactly; but not without an action and a public scandal, and that my client declines to face. He would rather lose even his picture than have the whole thing get into the papers; he has disowned his son, but he will not disgrace him; yet his picture he must have by hook or crook, and there's the rub! I am to get it back by fair means or foul. He gives me *carte blanche* in the matter, and, I verily believe, would throw in a blank cheque if asked. He offered one to the Queenslander, but Craggs simply tore it in two; the one old boy is as much a character as the other, and between the two of them I'm at my wits' end.'

'So you put that advertisement in the paper?' said Raffles, in the dry tones he had adopted throughout the interview.

'As a last resort, I did.'

'And you wish us to steal this picture?'

It was magnificently said; the lawyer flushed from his hair to his collar.

'I knew you were not the men!' he groaned. 'I never thought of men of your stamp! But it's not stealing,' he exclaimed heatedly; 'it's recovering stolen property. Besides, Sir Bernard will pay him his five thousand as soon as he has the picture; and, you'll see, old Craggs will be just as loth to let it come out as Sir Bernard himself. No, no—it's an enter-prise, an adventure, if you like—but not stealing.'

'You yourself mentioned the law,' murmured Raffles.

'And the risk,' I added.

'We pay for that,' he said once more.

'But not enough,' said Raffles, shaking his head. 'My good sir, consider what it means to us. You spoke of those clubs; we should not only get kicked out of them, but put in prison like common burglars! It's true we're hard up, but it simply isn't worth it at the price. Double your stakes, and I for one am your man.'

Addenbrooke wavered.

'Do you think you could bring it off?'

'We could try.'

'But you have no—'

'Experience? Well, hardly!'

'And you would really run the risk for four thousand pounds?'

Raffles looked at me. I nodded.

'We would,' said he, 'and blow the odds!'

'It's more than I can ask my client to pay,' said Addenbrooke, growing firm.

'Then it's more than you can expect us to risk.'

'You are in earnest?'

'Yes!'

'Say three thousand if you succeed!'

'Four is our figure, Mr Addenbrooke.'

'Then I think it should be nothing if you fail.'

'Double or quits?' cried Raffles. 'Well, that's sporting. Done!'

Addenbrooke opened his lips, half rose, then sat back in his chair, and looked long and shrewdly at Raffles—never once at me.

'I know your bowling,' said he reflectively. 'I go up to Lord's whenever I want an hour's real rest, and I've seen you bowl again and again—yes, and take the best wickets in England on a plumb pitch. I don't forget the last Gentlemen and Players; I was there. You're up to every trick—every one. . . . I'm inclined to think that if anybody could bowl out this old Australian . . . Damme, I believe you're my very man!'

The bargain was clenched at the Café Royal, where Bennett Addenbrooke insisted on playing host at an extravagant luncheon. I remember that he took his whack of champagne with the nervous freedom of a man at high pressure, and have no doubt I kept him in countenance by an equal indulgence; but Raffles, ever an exemplar in such matters, was more abstemious even than his wont, and very poor company to boot. I can see him now, his eyes in his plate—thinking—thinking. I can see the solicitor glancing from him to me in an apprehension of which I did my best to disabuse him by reassuring looks. At the close Raffles apologised for his preoccupation, called for an ABC time-table, and announced his intention of catching the 3.2 to Esher.

'You must excuse me, Mr Addenbrooke,' said he, 'but I have my own idea, and for the moment I would much prefer to keep it to myself. It may end in fizzle, so I would rather not speak about it to either of you just yet. But speak to Sir Bernard I must, so will you write me one line to him on your card? Of course, if you wish you must come down with me and hear what I say; but I really don't see much point in it.'

And as usual Raffles had his way, though Bennett Addenbrooke showed some temper when he was gone, and I myself shared his annoyance to no small extent. I could only tell him that it was in the nature of Raffles to be self-willed and secretive, but that no man of my acquaintance had half his audacity and determination; that I for my part would trust him through and through and let him gang his own gait every time. More I dared not say, even to remove those chill misgivings with which I knew that the lawyer went his way.

396

That day I saw no more of Raffles, but a telegram reached me when I was dressing for dinner:

'Be in your rooms tomorrow from noon and keep rest of day clear.—Raffles.'

It had been sent off from Waterloo at 6.42.

So Raffles was back in town; at an earlier stage of our relations I should have hunted him up then and there, but now I knew better. His telegram meant that he had no desire for my society that night or the following forenoon; that when he wanted me I should see him soon enough.

And see him I did, towards one o'clock next day. I was watching for him from my window in Mount Street, when he drove up furiously in a cab, and jumped out without a word to the man. I met him next minute at the lift gates, and he fairly pushed me back into my rooms.

'Five minutes, Bunny!' he cried. 'Not a moment more.'

And he tore off his coat before flinging himself into the nearest chair.

'I'm fairly on the rush,' he panted; 'having the very devil of a time! Not a word till I've told you all I've done. I settled my plan of campaign yesterday at lunch. The first thing was to get in with this man Craggs; You can't break into a place like the Metropole, it's got to be done from the inside. Problem one, how to get at the fellow. Only one sort of pretext would do—it must be something to do with this blessed picture, so that I might see where he'd got it and all that. Well, I couldn't go and ask to see it out of curiosity, and I couldn't go as a second representative of the old chap, and it was thinking how I could go that made me such a bear at lunch. But I saw my way before we got up. If I could only lay hold of a copy of the picture I might ask leave to go and compare it with the original. So down I went to Esher to find out if there was a copy in existence, and was at Broom Hall for one hour and a half yesterday afternoon. There was no copy there, but they must exist, for Sir Bernard himself (there's "copy" there!) has allowed a couple to be made since the picture has been in his possession. He hunted up the painters' addresses, and the rest of the evening I spent in hunting up the painters themselves; but their work had been done on commission; one copy had gone out of the country, and I'm still on the track of the other.'

'Then you haven't seen Craggs yet?'

'Seen him and made friends with him, and if possible he's the funnier old cuss of the two; but you should study 'em both. I took the bull by the horns this morning, went in and lied like Ananias, and it was just as well I did—the old ruffian sails for Australia by tomorrow's boat. I told him a man wanted to sell me a copy of the celebrated Infanta Maria Teresa of Velasquez, that I'd been down to the supposed owner of the picture, only to find that he had just sold it to him. You should have seen his face when I told him that! He grinned all round his wicked old head. 'Did old Debenham admit the sale?' says he; and when I said he had he chuckled to himself for about five minutes. He was so pleased that he did just what I hoped he would do; he showed me the great picture—luckily it isn't by any means a large one—also the case he's got it in. It's an iron map-case in which he brought over the plans of his land in Brisbane; he wants to know who would suspect it of containing an Old Master too? But he's had it fitted with a new Chubb's lock, and I managed to take an interest in the key while he was gloating over the canvas. I had the wax in the palm of my hand, and I shall make my duplicate this afternoon.'

Raffles looked at his watch and jumped up saying he had given me a minute too much.

'By the way,' he added, 'you've got to dine with him at the Metropole tonight!'

'I?'

'Yes; don't look so scared. Both of us are invited—I swore you were dining with me. I accepted for us both; but I shan't be there.'

His clear eye was upon me, bright with meaning and with mischief. I implored him to tell me what his meaning was.

'You will dine in his private sitting-room,' said Raffles; 'it adjoins his bedroom. You must keep him sitting as long as possible, Bunny, and talking all the time!'

In a flash I saw his plan.

'You're going for the picture while we're at dinner?'

'I am.'

'If he hears you!'

'He shan't.'

'But if he does!'

And I fairly trembled at the thought.

'If he does,' said Raffles, 'there will be a collision, that's all. Revolvers would be out of place in the Metropole, but I shall certainly take a life-preserver.'

'But it's ghastly!' I cried. 'To sit and talk to an utter stranger and to know that you're at work in the next room!'

'Two thousand apiece,' said Raffles quietly.

'Upon my soul I believe I shall give it away!'

'Not you, Bunny. I know you better than you know yourself.'

He put on his coat and his hat.

'What time have I to be there?' I asked him, with a groan.

'Quarter to eight. There will be a telegram from me saying I can't turn up. He's a terror to talk, you'll have no difficulty to keep the ball rolling; but head him off his picture for all you're worth. If he offers to show it you, say you must go. He locked up the case elaborately this afternoon, and there's no earthly reason why he should unlock it again in this hemisphere.'

'Where shall I find you when I get away?'

'I shall be down at Esher. I hope to catch the 9.55.'

'But surely I can see you again this afternoon?' I cried in a ferment, for his hand was on the door. 'I'm not half coached up yet! I know I shall make a mess of it!'

'Not you,' he said again, 'but I shall if I waste any more time. I've got a deuce of a lot of rushing about to do yet. You won't find me at my rooms. Why not come down to Esher yourself by the last train? That's it—down you come with the latest news! I'll tell old Debenham to expect you: he shall give us both a bed. By Jove! he won't be able to do us too well if he's got his picture.'

'If!' I groaned as he nodded his adieu; and he left me limp with apprehension, sick with fear, in a perfectly pitiable condition of pure stage-fright.

For, after all, I had only to act my part; unless Raffles failed where he never did fail, unless Raffles the neat and noiseless was for once clumsy and inept, all I had to do was indeed to 'smile and smile and be a villain'. I practised that smile half the afternoon. I rehearsed putative parts in hypothetical conversations. I got up stories. I dipped in a book on Queensland at the club. And at last it was 7.45, and I was making my bow to a somewhat elderly man with a small bald head and a retreating brow.

'So you're Mr Raffles's friend?' said he, overhauling me rather rudely with his light small eyes. 'Seen anything of him? Expected him early to show me something, but he's never come.'

No more, evidently, had his telegram, and my troubles were beginning early. I said I had not seen Raffles since one o'clock, telling the truth with unction while I could; even as we spoke there came a knock at the door; it was the telegram at last, and, after reading it himself, the Queenslander handed it to me.

'Called out of town!' he grumbled. 'Sudden illness of near relative! What near relatives has he got?'

I knew of none, and for an instant I quailed before the perils of invention; then I replied that I had never met any of his people, and again felt fortified by my veracity.

'Thought you were bosom pals?' said he, with (as I imagined) a gleam of suspicion in his crafty little eyes.

'Only in town,' said I. 'I've never been to his place.'

'Well,' he growled, 'I suppose it can't be helped. Don't know why he couldn't come and have his dinner first. Like to see the death-bed I'd go to without my dinner; it's a full-skin billet, if you ask me. Well, must just dine without him, and he'll have to buy his pig in a poke after all. Mind touching that bell? Suppose you know what he came to see me about. Sorry I shan't see him again, for his own sake. I liked Raffles—took to him amazingly. He's a cynic. Like cynics. One myself. Rank bad form of his mother, or his aunt, and I hope she will kick the bucket.'

I connect these specimens of his conversation, though they were doubtless detached at the time, and interspersed with remarks of mine here and there. They filled the interval until dinner was served, and they gave me an impression of the man which his every subsequent utterance confirmed. It was an impression which did away with all remorse for my treacherous presence at his table. He was that terrible type, the Silly Cynic, his aim a caustic commentary on all things and all men, his achievement mere vulgar irreverence and unintelligent scorn. Ill-bred and ill-informed, he had (on his own showing) fluked into fortune on a rise in land; yet cunning he possessed, as well as malice, and he chuckled till he choked over the misfortunes of less astute speculators in the same boom. Even now I cannot feel much compunction for my behaviour to the Hon. J. M. Craggs, MLC.

But never shall I forget the private agonies of the situation, the listening to my host with one ear and for Raffles with the other! Once I heard him—though the rooms were not divided by the old-fashioned folding-doors, and though the door that did divide them was not only shut but richly curtained, I could have sworn I heard him once. I spilt my wine and laughed at the top of my voice at some coarse sally of my host's. And I heard nothing more, though my ears were on the strain. But later, to my horror, when the waiter had finally withdrawn, Craggs himself sprang up and rushed to his bedroom without a word. I sat like stone till he returned.

'Thought I heard a door go,' he said. 'Must have been mistaken . . . imagination . . . gave me quite a turn. Raffles tell you of the priceless treasure I've got in there?'

It was the picture at last; up to this point I had kept him to Queensland and the making of his pile. I tried to get him back there now, but in vain. He was reminded of his great ill-gotten possession. I said that Raffles had just mentioned it, and that set him off. With the confidential garrulity of a man who has dined too well, he plunged into his darling topic, and I looked past him at the clock. It was only a quarter to ten.

In common decency I could not go yet. So there I sat (we were still at port) and learnt what had originally fired my host's ambition to possess what he was pleased to call a 'real, genuine, twin-screw, double-funnelled, copper-bottomed Old Master'; it was to 'go one better' than some rival legislator of pictorial proclivities. But even an epitome of his monologue would be so much weariness; suffice it that it ended inevitably in the invitation I had dreaded all the evening.

'But you must see it. Next room. This way.'

'Isn't it packed up?' I inquired hastily.

'Lock and key. That's all.'

'Pray don't trouble,' I urged.

'Trouble be hanged!' said he. 'Come along.'

And all at once I saw that to resist him further would be to heap suspicion upon myself against the moment of impending discovery. I therefore followed him into his bedroom without further protest, and suffered him first to show me the iron map-case which stood in one corner; he took a crafty pride in this receptacle, and I thought he would never cease descanting on its innocent appearance and its Chubb's lock. It seemed an interminable age before the key was in the latter. Then the ward clicked, and my pulse stood still.

'By Jove!' I cried the next instant.

The canvas was in its place among the maps!

'Thought it would knock you,' said Craggs, drawing it out and unfolding it for my benefit. 'Grand thing, ain't it? Wouldn't think it had been painted two hundred and thirty years? It has, though, my word! Old Johnson's face will be a treat when he sees it; won't go bragging about his pictures much more. Why, this one's worth all the pictures in Colony o' Queensland put together. Worth fifty thousand pounds, my boy—and I got it for five!'

He dug me in the ribs, and seemed in the mood for further confidences. My appearance checked him, and he rubbed his hands.

'If you take it like that,' he chuckled, 'how will old Johnson take it? Go out and hang himself to his own picture-rods, I hope!'

Heaven knows what I contrived to say at last. Struck speechless first by my relief, I continued silent from a very different cause. A new tangle of emotions tied my tongue. Raffles had failed—could I not succeed? Was it too late? Was there no way?

'So long,' he said, taking a last look at the canvas before he rolled it up—'so long till we get to Brisbane.'

The flutter I was in as he closed the case!

'For the last time,' he went on, as his keys jingled back into his pocket. 'It goes straight into the strong-room on board.'

For the last time! If I could but send him out to Australia with only its legitimate contents in his precious map-case! If I could but succeed where Raffles had failed!

We returned to the other room. I have no notion how long he talked, or what about. Whisky and soda-water became the order of the hour. I scarcely touched it, but he drank copiously, and before eleven I left him incoherent. And the last train for Esher was the 11.50 out of Waterloo.

I took a cab to my rooms. I was back at the hotel in thirteen minutes. I walked upstairs. The corridor was empty; I stood an instant on the sitting-room threshold, heard a snore within, and admitted myself softly with my gentleman's own key, which it had been a very simple matter to take away with me.

Craggs never moved; he was stretched on the sofa fast asleep. But not fast enough for me. I saturated my handkerchief with the chloroform I had brought, and I laid it gently over his mouth. Two or three stertorous breaths, and the man was a log.

I removed the handkerchief; I extracted the keys from his pocket. In less than five minutes I put them back, after winding the picture about my body beneath my Inverness cape. I took some whisky and soda-water before I went.

The train was easily caught—so easily that I trembled for ten minutes in my first-class smoking carriage, in terror of every footstep on the platform—in unreasonable terror till the end. Then at last I sat back and lit a cigarette, and the lights of Waterloo reeled out behind.

Some men were returning from the theatre. I can recall their conversation even now. They were disappointed with the piece they had seen. It was one of the later Savoy operas, and they spoke wistfully of the days of *Pinafore* and *Patience*. One of them hummed a stave, and there was an argument as to whether the air was out of *Patience* or the *Mikado*. They all got out at Surbiton, and I was alone with my triumph for a few intoxicating minutes. To think that I had succeeded where Raffles had failed! Of all our adventures this was the first in which I had played a commanding part; and, of them all, this was infinitely the least discreditable. It left me without a conscientious qualm; I had but robbed a robber, when all was said. And I had done it myself, single-handed—*ipse egomet*!

I pictured Raffles, his surprise, his delight. He would think a little more of me in future. And that future, it should be different. We had two thousand pounds apiece—surely enough to start afresh as honest men—and all through me.

In a glow I sprang out at Esher, and took the one belated cab that was waiting under the bridge. In a perfect fever I beheld Broom Hall, with the lower storey still lit up, and saw the front door open as I climbed the steps.

'Thought it was you,' said Raffles cheerily. 'It's all right. There's a bed for you. Sir Bernard's sitting up to shake your hand.'

His good spirits disappointed me. But I knew the man; he was one of those who wear their brightest smile in the blackest hour. I knew him too well by this time to be deceived.

'I've got it!' I cried in his ear. 'I've got it!'

'Got what?' he asked, stepping back.

'The picture?'

'What?'

'The picture. He showed it to me. You had to go without it; I saw that. So I determined to have it. And here it is.'

'Let's see,' said Raffles grimly.

I threw off my cape and unwound the canvas from about my body. While I was doing so an untidy old gentleman made his appearance in the hall, and stood looking on with raised eyebrows.

'Looks pretty fresh for an Old Master, doesn't she?' said Raffles.

His tone was strange. I could only suppose that he was jealous of my success.

'So Craggs said. I hardly looked at it myself.'

'Well, look now—look closely. By Jove, I must have faked her better than I thought!'

'It's a copy!' I cried.

'It's the copy,' he answered. 'It's the copy I've been tearing all over the country to procure. It's the copy I faked back and front, so that, on your own showing, it imposed upon Craggs, and might have made him happy for life. And you go and rob him of that!'

I could not speak.

'How did you manage it?' inquired Sir Bernard Debenham.

'Have you killed him?' asked Raffles sardonically.

I did not look at him; I turned to Sir Bernard Debenham, and to him I told my story, hoarsely, excitedly, for it was all that I could do to keep from breaking down. But as I spoke I became calmer, and I finished in mere bitterness, with the remark that another time Raffles might tell me what he meant to do.

'Another time!' he cried instantly. 'My dear Bunny, you speak as though we were going to turn burglars for a living!'

'I trust you won't,' said Sir Bernard smiling, 'for you are certainly two very daring young men. Let us hope our friend from Queensland will do as he said, and not open his map-case till he gets back there. He will find my cheque awaiting him, and I shall be very much surprised if he troubles any of us again.'

Raffles and I did not speak till I was in the room which had been prepared for me. Nor was I anxious to do so then. But he followed me and took my hand.

'Bunny,' said he, 'don't you be hard on a fellow! I was in the deuce of a hurry, and didn't know that I should get what I wanted in time, and that's a fact. But it serves me right that you should have gone and undone one of the best things I ever did. As for your handiwork, old chap, You won't mind my saying that I didn't think you had it in you. In future—'

'Don't talk to me about the future!' I cried. 'I hate the whole thing! I'm going to chuck it up!'

'So am I,' said Raffles, 'when I've made my pile.'

THE RETURN MATCH

I had turned into Piccadilly, one thick evening in the following November, when my guilty heart stood still at the sudden grip of a hand upon my arm. I thought—I was always thinking—that my inevitable hour was come at last. It was only Raffles, however, who stood smiling at me through the fog.

'Well met!' said he; 'I've been looking for you at the club.'

'I was just on my way there,' I returned, with an attempt to hide my tremors. It was an ineffectual attempt, as I saw from his broader smile, and by the indulgent shake of his head.

'Come up to my place instead,' said he. 'I've something amusing to tell you.'

I made excuses, for his tone foretold the kind of amusement, and it was a kind against which I had successfully set my face for months. I have stated before, however, and I can but reiterate, that to me, at all events, there was never anybody in the world so irresistible as Raffles when his mind was made up. That we had both been independent of crime since our little service to Sir Bernard Debenham—that there had been no occasion for that masterful mind to be made up in any such direction for many a day—was the undeniable basis of a longer spell of honesty than I had hitherto enjoyed during the term of our mutual intimacy. Be sure I would deny it if I could; the very thing I am to tell you would discredit such a boast. I made my excuses, as I have said. But his arm slid through mine, with his little laugh of light-hearted mastery. And even while I argued we were on his staircase in the Albany.

His fire had fallen low. He poked and replenished it after turning on the lights. As for me, I stood by sullenly in my overcoat until he dragged it off my back.

'What a chap you are!' said Raffles playfully. 'One would really think I had proposed to crack another crib, this blessed night! Well, it isn't that, Bunny; so get into that chair, and take one of these Sullivans and sit tight.'

He held the match to my cigarette; he brought me a whisky and soda. Then he went out in the lobby, and, just as I was beginning to feel happy, I heard a bolt shot home. It cost me an effort to remain in that chair; next moment he was straddling another and gloating over my discomfiture across his folded arms.

'You remember Milchester, Bunny, old boy?'

His tone was as bland as mine was grim when I answered that I did.

'We had a little match there that wasn't down on the card. Gentlemen and Players, if you recollect?'

'I don't forget it.'

'Seeing that you never got an innings, so to speak, I thought you might. Well, the Gentlemen scored pretty freely, but the Players were all caught—'

'Poor devils!'

'Don't be too sure. You remember the fellow we saw in the inn? The florid, overdressed chap who I told you was one of the cleverest thieves in town?'

'I remember him. Crawshay his name turned out to be.'

'Well, it was certainly the name he was convicted under, so Crawshay let it be. You needn't waste any pity on him, old chap; he escaped from Dartmoor yesterday afternoon.'

'Well done!'

Raffles smiled, but his eyebrows had gone up and his shoulders followed suit.

'You are perfectly right; it was very well done indeed. I wonder you didn't see it in the paper. In a dense fog on the moor yesterday good old Crawshay made a bolt for it, and got away without a scratch under heavy fire. All honour to him, I agree; a fellow with that much grit deserves his liberty. But Crawshay has a good deal more. They hunted him all night long; couldn't find him for nuts; and that was all you missed in the morning papers.'

He unfolded a *Pall Mall*, which he had brought in with him.

'But listen to this; here's an account of the escape; with just the addition which puts the thing on a higher level. "The fugitive has been traced to Totnes, where he appears to have committed a peculiarly daring outrage in the early hours of this morning. He is reported to have entered the lodgings of the Rev A. H. Ellingworth, curate of the parish, who missed his clothes on rising at the usual hour; later in the morning those of the convict were discovered neatly folded at the bottom of a drawer. Meanwhile Crawshay had made good his second escape, though it is believed that so distinctive a guise will lead to his recapture during the day." What do you think of that, Bunny?'

'He is certainly a sportsman,' said I, reaching for the paper.

'He's more,' said Raffles; 'he's an artist, and I envy him. The curate, of all men! Beautiful—beautiful! But that's not all. I saw just now on the board at the club that there's been an outrage on the line near Dawlish. Parson found insensible in the six-foot way. Our friend again. The telegram doesn't say so, but it's obvious; he's simply knocked some other fellow out, changed clothes again, and come on gaily to town. Isn't it great? I do believe it's the best thing of the kind that's ever been done!'

'But why should he come to town?'

In an instant the enthusiasm faded from Raffles's face: clearly I had reminded him of some prime anxiety, forgotten in his impersonal joy over the exploit of a fellow criminal. He looked over his shoulder towards the lobby before replying.

'I believe,' said he, 'that the beggar's on my tracks!'

And as he spoke he was himself again—quietly amused—cynically unperturbed— characteristically enjoying the situation and my surprise.

'But look here, what do you mean?' said I. 'What does Crawshay know about you?'

'Not much; but he suspects.'

'Why should he?'

'Because, in his way, he's very nearly as good a man as I am; because, my dear Bunny, with eyes in his head and brains behind them, he couldn't help suspecting. He saw me once in town with old Baird. He must have seen me that day in the pub, on the way to Milchester, as well as afterwards on the cricket field. As a matter of fact, I know he did, for he wrote and told me so before his trial.'

'He wrote to you! And you never told me!'

The old shrug answered the old grievance.

'What was the good, my dear fellow? It would only have worried you.'

'Well, what did he say?'

'That he was sorry he had been run in before getting back to town, as he had proposed doing himself the honour of paying me a call; however, he trusted it was only a pleasure deferred, and he begged me not to go and get lagged myself before he came out. Of course he knew the Melrose necklace was gone, though he hadn't got it; and he said that the man who could take that and leave the rest was a man after his own heart. And so on, with certain little proposals for the far future, which I fear may be the very near future indeed! I'm only surprised he hasn't turned up yet.'

He looked again towards the lobby, which he had left in darkness, with the inner door shut as carefully as the outer one. I asked him what he meant to do.

'Let him knock—if he gets so far. The porter is to say I'm out of town; it will be true, too, in another hour or so.'

'You're going off tonight?'

'By the 7.15 from Liverpool Street. I don't say much about my people, Bunny, but I have the best of sisters married to a country parson in the eastern counties. They always make me welcome, and let me read the lessons for the sake of getting me to church. I'm sorry you won't be there to hear me on Sunday, Bunny. I've figured out some of my best schemes in that Parish, and I know of no better port in a storm. But I must pack. I thought I'd just let you know where I was going, and why, in case you cared to follow my example.'

He flung the stump of his cigarette into the fire, stretched himself as he rose, and remained so long in the inelegant attitude that my eyes mounted from his body to his face; a second later they had followed his eyes across the room, and I also was on my legs. On the threshold of the folding doors that divided bedroom and sitting-room, a well-built man stood in ill-fitting broadcloth, and bowed to us until his bullet head presented an unbroken disc of short red hair.

Brief as was my survey of this astounding apparition, the interval was long enough for Raffles to recover his composure; his hands were in his pockets, and a smile upon his face, when my eyes flew back to him.

'Let me introduce you, Bunny,' said he, 'to our distinguished colleague, Mr Reginald Crawshay.'

The bullet head bobbed up, and there was a wrinkled brow above the coarse, shaven face, crimson, also I remember, from the grip of a collar several sizes too small. But I noted nothing consciously at the time. I had jumped to my own conclusion, and I turned on Raffles with an oath.

'It's a trick!' I cried. 'It's another of your cursed tricks. You got him here, and then you got me. You want me to join you, I suppose? I'll see you damned!'

So cold was the stare which met this outburst that I became ashamed of my words while they were yet upon my lips.

'Really, Bunny!' said Raffles, and turned his shoulder with a shrug.

'Lord love yer,' cried Crawshay, ' 'e knew nothin'. 'E didn't expect me; 'e's all right. And you're the cool canary, you are,' he went on to Raffles. 'I knoo you were, but, do me proud, you're one after my own kidney.' And he thrust out a shaggy hand.

'After that,' said Raffles, taking it, 'what am I to say? But you must have heard my opinion of you. I am proud to make your acquaintance. How the deuce did you get in?'

'Never you mind,' said Crawshay, loosening his collar; 'let's talk about how I'm to get out. Lord love yer, but that's better!' There was a livid ring round his bull-neck, that he fingered tenderly. 'Didn't know how much longer I might have to play the gent,' he explained, 'didn't know who you'd bring in.'

'Drink whisky and soda?' inquired Raffles, when the convict was in the chair from which I had leapt.

'No, I drink it neat,' replied Crawshay, 'but I talk business first. You don't get over me like that, Lor' love yer!'

'Well, then, what can I do for you?'

'You know without me tellin' you.'

'Give it a name.'

'Clean heels, then; that's what I want to show, and I leaves the way to you. We're brothers in arms, though I ain't armed this time. It ain't necessary. You've too much sense. But brothers we are, and you'll see a brother through. Let's put it at that. You'll see me through in your own way. I leaves it all to you.'

His tone was rich with conciliation and concession; he bent over and tore a pair of button boots from his bare feet, which he stretched towards the fire, painfully uncurling his toes.

'I hope you take a larger size than them,' said he. 'I'd have had a see if you'd given me time. I wasn't in long afore you.'

'And you won't tell me how you got in?'

'Wot's the use? I can't teach you nothin'. Besides I want out. I want out of London, an' England, an' bloomin' Europe too. That's all I want of you, mister. I don't arst how you go on the job. You know w'ere I come from, 'cos I heard you say; you know w'ere I want to 'ead for, 'cos I've just told yer; the details I leaves entirely to you.'

'Well,' said Raffles, 'we must see what can be done.'

'We must,' said Mr Crawshay, and leaned back comfortably, and began twirling his stubby thumbs.

Raffles turned to me with a twinkle in his eye; but his forehead was scored with thought, and resolve mingled with resignation in the lines of his mouth. And he spoke exactly as though he and I were alone in the room.

'You seize the situation, Bunny? If our friend here is "copped", to speak his language, he means to "blow the gaff" on you and me. He is considerate enough not to say so in so many words, but it's plain enough, and natural enough for that matter. I would do the same in his place. We had the bulge before; he has it now; it's perfectly fair. We must take on this job; we aren't in a position to refuse it: even if we were, I should take it on. Our friend is a great sportsman; he has got clear away from Dartmoor; it would be a thousand pities to let him go back. Nor shall he; not if I can think of a way of getting him abroad.'

'Any way you like,' murmured Crawshay, with his eyes shut. 'I leaves the 'ole thing to you.'

'But you'll have to wake up and tell us things.'

'All right, mister; but I'm fair on the rocks for a sleep!'

And he stood up blinking.

'Think you were traced to town?'

'Must have been.'

'And here?'

'Not in this fog—not with any luck.'

Raffles went into the bedroom, lit the gas there, and returned next minute.

'So you got in by the window?'

'That's about it.'

'It was devilish smart of you to know which one; it beats me how you brought it off in daylight, fog or no fog! But let that pass. Don't you think you were seen?'

'I don't think it, sir.'

'Well, let's hope you are right. I shall reconnoitre and soon find out. And you'd better come too, Bunny, and have something to eat and talk it over.'

As Raffles looked at me, I looked at Crawshay, anticipating trouble; and trouble brewed in his blank, fierce face, in the glitter of his startled eyes, in the sudden closing of his fists.

'And what's to become of me?' he cried out with an oath.

'You wait here.'

'No, you don't,' he roared, and at a bound had his back to the door. 'You don't get round me like that, you cuckoos!'

Raffles turned to me with a twitch of the shoulders.

'That's the worst of these professors,' said he; 'they never will use their heads. They see the pegs, and they mean to hit 'em; but that's all they do see and mean, and they think we're the same. No wonder we licked them last time!'

'Don't talk through yer neck,' snarled the convict. 'Talk out straight, curse you!'

'Right,' said Raffles. 'I'll talk as straight as you like. You say you put yourself in my hands—you leave it all to me—yet you don't trust me an inch! I know what's to happen if I fail. I accept the risk. I take this thing on. Yet you think I'm going straight out to give you away and make you give me away in turn. You're a fool, Mr Crawshay, though you have broken Dartmoor; you've got to listen to a better man, and obey him. I see you through in my own way, or not at all. I come and go as I like, and with whom I like, without your interference; you stay here and lie just as low as you know how, be as wise as your word, and leave the whole thing to me. If you won't—if you're fool enough not to trust me—there's the door. Go out and say what you like, and be damned to you!'

Crawshay slapped his thigh.

'That's talking!' said he. 'Lord love yer, I know where I am when you talk like that. I'll trust yer. I know a man when he get's his tongue between his teeth; you're all right. I don't say so much about this other gent, though I saw him along with you on the job that time in the provinces; but if he's a pal of yours, Mr Raffles, he'll be all right too. I only hope you gents ain't too stony—'

And he touched his pockets with a rueful face.

'I only went for their togs,' said he. 'You never struck two such stony-broke cusses in yer life.'

'That's all right,' said Raffles. 'We'll see you through properly. Leave it to us, and you sit tight.'

'Rightum!' said Crawshay. 'And I'll have a sleep time you're gone. But no sperrits—no, thank'ee—not yet! Once let me loose on lush, and, Lord love yer, I'm a gone coon!'

Raffles got his overcoat, a long, light driving coat, I remember, and even as he put it on our fugitive was dozing in the chair; we left him murmuring incoherently, with the lights out, and his bare feet toasting.

'Not such a bad chap, that professor,' said Raffles on the stairs; 'a real genius in his way, too, though his methods are a little elementary for my taste. But technique isn't everything; to get out of Dartmoor and into the Albany in the same twenty-four hours is a whole that justifies its parts. Good Lord!'

We had passed a man in the foggy courtyard, and Raffles had nipped my arm.

'Who was it?'

'The last man we want to see! I hope to heaven he didn't hear me!'

'But who is it, Raffles?'

'Our old friend Mackenzie, from the Yard!'

I stood still with horror.

'Do you think he's on Crawshay's track?'

'I don't know. I'll find out.'

And before I could remonstrate he had wheeled me round; when I found my voice he merely laughed, and whispered that the bold course was the safe one every time.

'But it's madness—'

'Not it. Shut up! Is that you, Mr Mackenzie?'

The detective turned about and scrutinized us keenly; and through the gaslit mist I noticed that his hair was grizzled at the temples, and his face still cadaverous, from the wound that had nearly been his death.

'Ye have the advantage o' me, sirs,' said he.

'I hope you're fit again,' said my companion. 'My name is Raffles, and we met at Milchester last year.'

'Is that a fact?' cried the Scotsman, with quite a start. 'Yes, now I remember your face, and yours too, sir. Ay, yon was a bad business, but it ended vera well, an' that's the main thing.'

His native caution had returned to him. Raffles pinched my arm.

'Yes, it ended splendidly, but for you,' said he. 'But what about this escape of the leader of the gang, that fellow Crawshay? What do you think of that, eh?'

'I havena the parteeculars,' replied the Scot.

'Good!' cried Raffles. 'I was only afraid you might be on his tracks once more!'

Mackenzie shook his head with a dry smile, and wished us good evening, as an invisible window was thrown up and a whistle blown softly through the fog.

'We must see this out,' whispered Raffles. 'Nothing more natural than a little curiosity on our part. After him, quick!'

And he followed the detective into another entrance on the same side as that from which we had emerged, the left-hand side on one's way to Piccadilly; quite openly we followed him, and at the foot of the stairs met one of the porters of the place. Raffles asked him what was wrong.

'Nothing, sir,' said the fellow glibly.

'Rot!' said Raffles. 'That was Mackenzie, the detective. I've just been speaking to him. What's he here for? Come on, my good fellow; we won't give you away, if you've instructions not to tell.'

The man looked quaintly wistful, the temptation of an audience hot upon him; a door shut upstairs, and he fell.

'It's like this,' he whispered. 'This afternoon a gen'leman comes arfter rooms, and I sent him to the orfice; one of the clurks, 'e goes round with 'im an' shows 'im the empties, an' the gen'leman's partic'ly struck on the set the coppers is up in now. So he sends the clurk to fetch the manager, as there was one or two things he wished to speak about; an' when they come back, blowed if the gent isn't gone! Beg your pardon, sir, but he's clean disappeared off the face of the premises!' And the porter looked at us with shining eyes.

'Well?' said Raffles.

'Well, sir, they looked about, an' at larst they give him up for a bad job; thought he'd changed his mind an' didn't want to tip the clurk; so they shut up the place and come away. An' that's all till about 'alf an hour ago, when I takes the manager his extry-speshul *Star*; in about ten minutes he comes running out with a note an' sends me with it to Scotland Yard in a hansom. An' that's all I know, sir—straight. The coppers is up there now, and the tec. and the manager, and they think their gent is about the place somewhere still. Least, I reckon that's their idea; but who he is, or what they want him for, I dunno,'

'Jolly interesting!' said Raffles. 'I'm going up to inquire. Come on, Bunny; there should be some fun.'

'Beg your pardon, Mr Raffles, but you won't say nothing about me?'

'Not I; you're a good fellow. I won't forget it if this leads to sport. Sport!' he whispered, as we reached the landing. 'It looks like precious poor sport for you and me, Bunny!'

'What are you going to do?'

'I don't know. There's no time to think. This, to start with.'

And he thundered on the shut door; a policeman opened it. Raffles strode past him with the air of a chief commissioner, and I followed before the man had recovered from his astonishment. The bare boards rang under us; in the bedroom we found a knot of officers stooping over the window-ledge with a constable's lantern. Mackenzie was the first to stand upright, and he greeted us with a glare.

'May I ask what you gentlemen want?' said he.

'We want to lend a hand,' said Raffles briskly. 'We lent one once before, and it was my friend here who took over from you and the fellow who split on all the rest and held him tight. Surely that entitles him, at all events, to see any fun that's going? As for myself, well it's true I only helped to carry you to the house; but for old acquaintance I do hope, my dear Mr Mackenzie, that you will permit us to share such sport as there may be. I myself can only stop a few minutes, in any case.'

'Then ye'll not see much,' growled the detective, 'for he's not up here. Constable, go and stand at the foot o' the stairs, and let no other body come up on any conseederation; these gentlemen may be able to help us after all.'

'That's kind of you, Mackenzie!' cried Raffles warmly. 'But what is it all? I questioned a porter I met coming down, but could get nothing out of him, except that somebody had been to see these rooms and not since been seen himself.'

'He's a man we want,' said Mackenzie. 'He's concealed himself somewhere about these premises, or I'm vera much mistaken. D'ye reside in the Albany, Mr Raffles?'

'I do.'

'Will your rooms be near these?'

'On the next staircase but one.'

'Ye'll just have left them?'

'Just.'

'Been in all the afternoon, likely?'

'Not all.'

'Then I may have to search your rooms, sir. I am prepared to search every room in the

Albany! Our man seems to have gone for the leads; but unless he's left more marks outside than in, or we find him up there, I shall have the entire building to ransack.'

'I will leave you my key,' said Raffles at once. 'I am dining out, but I'll leave it with the officer down below.'

I caught my breath in mute amazement. What was the meaning of this insane promise? It was wilful, gratuitous, suicidal; it made me catch at his sleeve in open horror and disgust; but, with a word of thanks, Mackenzie had returned to his window-sill, and we sauntered unwatched through the folding doors in the adjoining room. Here the window looked down into the courtyard; it was still open; and as we gazed out in apparent idleness, Raffles reassured me.

'It's all right, Bunny; you do what I tell you and leave the rest to, me. It's a tight corner, but I don't despair. What you've got to do is to stick to these chaps, especially if they search my rooms; they mustn't poke about more than necessary, and they won't if you're there.'

'But where will you be? You're never going to leave me to be landed alone?'

'If I do, it will be to turn up trumps at the right moment. Besides, there are such things as windows, and Crawshay's the man to take his risks. You must trust me, Bunny; you've known me long enough.'

'And you're going now?'

'There's no time to lose. Stick to them, old chap, don't let them suspect you, whatever else you do.' His hand lay an instant on my shoulder; then he left me at the window, and recrossed the room.

'I've got to go now,' I heard him say; 'but my friend will stay and see this through, and I'll leave the light on in my rooms—and my key with the constable downstairs. Good luck, Mackenzie; only wish I could stay.'

'Good-bye, sir,' came in a preoccupied voice, 'and many thanks.'

Mackenzie was still busy at his window, and I remained at mine, a prey to mingled fear and wrath, for all my knowledge of Raffles and of his infinite resource. By this time I felt that I knew more or less what he would do in any given emergency; at least I could conjecture a characteristic course of equal cunning and audacity. He would return to his rooms, put Crawshay on his guard, and—stow him away? No—there were such things as windows. Then why was Raffles going to desert us all? I thought of many things—lastly of a cab. These bedroom windows looked into a narrow side-street; they were not very high; from them a man might drop on to the roof of a cab—even as it passed—and be driven away—even under the noses of the police! I pictured Raffles driving that cab, unrecognizable in the foggy night; the vision came to me as he passed under the window, tucking up the collar of his great driving-coat on the way to his rooms; it was still with me when he passed again on his way back, and stopped to hand the constable his key.

'We're on his track,' said a voice behind me. 'He's got up on the leads, sure enough, though how he managed it from yon window is a myst'ry to me. We're going to lock up here and try what like it is from the attics. So you'd better come with us if you've a mind.'

The top floor at the Albany, as elsewhere, is devoted to the servants—a congeries of little kitchens and cubicles, used by many as lumber-rooms—by Raffles among the many. The annexe in this case was, of course, empty as the rooms below; and that was lucky, for we filled it, what with the manager, who now joined us, and another tenant whom he brought with him to Mackenzie's undisguised annoyance.

'Better let in all Piccadilly at a crown a head,' said he. 'Here, my man, out you go on the roof to make one less, and have your truncheon handy.'

We crowded to the little window, which Mackenzie took care to fill; and a minute yielded no sound but the crunch and slither of constabulary boots upon sooty slates. Then came a shout.

'What now?' cried Mackenzie.

'A rope,' we heard, 'hanging from the spout by a hook!'

'Sirs,' purred Mackenzie, 'yon's how he got up from below! He would do it with one o' they telescope sticks, an' I never thocht o't! How long a rope, my lad?'

'Quite short. I've got it.'

'Did it hang over a window? Ask him that!' cried the manager. 'He can see by leaning over the parapet.'

The question was repeated by Mackenzie; a pause, then, 'Yes, it did.'

'Ask him how many windows along!' shouted the manager in high excitement.

'Six, he says,' said Mackenzie the next minute; and he drew in his head and shoulders. 'I should just like to see those rooms, six windows along.'

'Mr Raffles's,' announced the manager after a mental calculation.

'Is that a fact?' cried Mackenzie. 'Then we shall have no difficulty at all. He's left me his key down below.'

The words had a dry, speculative intonation, which even then I found time to dislike; it was as though the coincidence had already struck the Scotsman as something more.

'Where is Mr Raffles?' asked the manager, as we all filed downstairs.

'He's gone out to his dinner,' said Mackenzie.

'Are you sure.'

'I saw him go,' said I. My heart was beating horribly. I would not trust myself to speak again. But I wormed my way to a front place in the little procession, and was, in fact, the second man to cross the threshold that had been the Rubicon of my life. As I did so I uttered a cry of pain, for Mackenzie had trod back heavily on my toes; in another second I saw the reason, and saw it with another and a louder cry.

A man was lying at full length before the fire, on his back, with a little wound in the white forehead, and the blood draining into his eyes. And the man was Raffles himself!

'Suicide,' said Mackenzie calmly. 'No—here's the poker—looks more like murder.' He went on his knees and shook his head quite cheerfully. 'An' it's not even murder,' said he, with a shade of disgust in his matter-of-fact voice; 'yon's no more than a fleshwound, and I have my doubts whether it felled him; but, sirs, he just stinks o' chloryform!'

He got up and fixed his keen grey eyes upon me; my own were full of tears, but they faced him unashamed.

'I understood ye to say ye saw him go out?' said he sternly.

'I saw that long driving-coat; of course I thought he was inside it.'

'And I could ha' sworn it was the same gent when he gave me the key!'

It was the disconsolate voice of the constable in the background; on him turned Mackenzie, white to the lips.

'You'd think anything, some of you damned policemen,' said he. 'What's your number, you rotter? P 34? You'll be hearing more of this, Mr P 34! If that gentleman were dead—instead of coming to himself while I'm talking—do you know what you'd be? Guilty of his manslaughter, you stuck pig in buttons! Do you know who you've let slip, butter-fingers? Crawshay—no less—him that broke Dartmoor yesterday. By the God that made ye, P 34, if I lose him I'll hound ye from the forrce!'

Working face—shaking fist—a calm man on fire. It was a new side of Mackenzie, and one to mark and to digest. Next moment he had flounced from our midst.

'Difficult thing to break your own head,' said Raffles later; 'infinitely easier to cut your own throat. Chloroform's another matter; when you've used it on others, you know the dose to a nicety. So you thought I was really gone? Poor old Bunny! But I hope Mackenzie saw your face?'

'He did,' said I. I would not tell him all Mackenzie must have seen, however.

'That's all right. I wouldn't have had him miss it for worlds; and you mustn't think me a brute, old boy, for I fear that man; and, you know, we sink or swim together.'

'And now we sink or swim with Crawshay too,' said I dolefully.

'Not we!' cried Raffles with conviction. 'Old Crawshay's a true sportsman, and he'll do by us as we've done by him; besides, this makes us quits; and I don't think, Bunny, that we'll take on the professors again!'

THE GIFT OF THE EMPEROR

I

When the King of the Cannibal Islands made faces at Queen Victoria, and a European monarch set the cables tingling with his compliments on the exploit, the indignation in England was not less than the surprise, for the thing was not so common as it has since become. But when it transpired that a gift of peculiar significance was to follow the congratulations, to give them weight, the inference prevailed that the white potentate and the black had taken simultaneous leave of their fourteen senses. For the gift was a pearl of price unparalleled, picked aforetime by British cutlasses from a Polynesian setting, and presented by British royalty to the sovereign who seized this opportunity of restoring it to its original possessor.

The incident would have been a godsend to the Press a few weeks later. Even in June there were leaders, letters, large headlines, leaded type; the *Daily Chronicle* devoted half its literary page to a charming drawing of the island capital which the new *Pall Mall*, in a leading article headed by a pun, advised the Government to blow to flinders. I was myself driving a poor but not dishonest quill at the time, and the topic of the hour goaded me into satiric verse which obtained a better place than anything I had yet turned out. I had let my flat in town, and taken inexpensive quarters at Thames Ditton, on a plea of a disinterested passion for the river.

'First-rate, old boy,' said Raffles (who must needs come and see me there), lying back in the boat while I sculled and steered. 'I suppose they pay you pretty well for these, eh?'

'Not a penny.'

'Nonsense, Bunny! I thought they paid so well? Give them time, and you'll get your cheque.'

'Oh, no, I shan't,' said I gloomily. 'I've got to be content with the honour of getting in; the editor wrote to say so, in so many words,' I added. But I gave the gentleman his distinguished name.

'You don't mean to say you've written for payment already?'

No; it was the last thing I had intended to admit. But I had done it. The murder was out; there was no sense in further concealment. I had written for my money because I really needed it; if he must know, I was cursedly hard up. Raffles nodded as though he knew already. I warmed to my woes. It was no easy matter to keep your end up as a raw free lance of letters; for my part, I was afraid I wrote neither well enough nor ill enough for success. I suffered from a persistent ineffectual feeling after style. Verse I could manage; but it did not pay. To personal paragraphs or to baser journalism I could not and I would not stoop.

Raffles nodded again, this time with a smile that stayed in his eyes as he leant back watching me. I knew that he was thinking of other things I had stooped to, and I thought I knew what he was going to say. He had said it before so often; he was sure to say it again. I had my answer ready, but evidently he was tired of asking the same question. His lids fell, he took up the paper he had dropped, and I sculled the length of the old red wall of Hampton Court before he spoke again.

'And they gave you nothing for these! My dear Bunny, they're capital, not only *qua* verses, but for crystallising your subject and putting it in a nutshell. Certainly you've taught me more about it than I knew before. But is it really worth fifty thousand pounds—a single pearl?'

'A hundred, I believe; but that wouldn't scan.'

'A hundred thousand pounds!' said Raffles, with his eyes shut. And again I made certain what was coming, but again I was mistaken. 'If it's worth all that,' he cried at last, 'there would be no getting rid of it at all; it's not like a diamond that you can subdivide. But I beg your pardon, Bunny. I was forgetting!'

And we said no more about the emperor's gift; for pride thrives on an empty pocket, and no privation would have drawn from me the proposal which I had expected Raffles to make. My expectation had been half a hope, though I only knew it now. But neither did we touch again on what Raffles professed to have forgotten—my 'apostasy', 'my lapse into virtue', as he had been pleased to call it. We were both a little silent, a little constrained, each preoccupied with his own thoughts. It was months since we had met, and, as I saw him off towards eleven o'clock that Sunday night, I fancied it was for more months that we were saying good-bye.

But as we waited for the train I saw those clear eyes peering at me under the station lamps, and when I met their glance Raffles shook his head.

'You don't look well on it, Bunny,' said he. 'I never did believe in this Thames Valley. You want a change of air.'

I wished I might get it.

'What you really want is a sea voyage.'

'And a winter at St Moritz, or do you recommend Cannes or Cairo? It's all very well, A.J., but you forget what I told you about my funds.'

'I forget nothing. I merely don't want to hurt your feelings. But, look here, a sea voyage you shall have. I want a change myself, and you shall come with me as my guest. We'll spend July in the Mediterranean.'

'But you're playing cricket—'

'Hang the cricket!'

'Well, if I thought you meant it—'

'Of course I mean it. Will you come?'

'Like a shot—if you go.'

And I shook his hand, and waved mine in farewell, with the perfectly good-humoured conviction that I should hear no more of the matter. It was a passing thought, no more, no less. I soon wished it were more; that week found me wishing myself out of England for good and all. I was making nothing. I could but subsist on the difference between the rent I paid for my flat and the rent at which I had sublet it, furnished, for the season. And the season was near its end, and creditors awaited me in town. Was it possible to be entirely honest? I had run no bills when I had money in my pocket, and the more downright dishonesty seemed to me less the ignoble.

But from Raffles, of course, I heard nothing more; a week went by, and half another week; then, late on the second Wednesday night, I found a telegram from him at my lodgings, after seeking him vainly in town, and dining with desperation at the solitary club to which I still belonged.

'Arranged to leave Waterloo by North German Lloyd special,' he wired, '9.25 a.m. Monday next will meet you Southampton aboard *Uhlan* with tickets, am writing.'

And write he did, a light-hearted letter enough, but full of serious solicitude for me and for my health and prospects; a letter almost touching in the light of our past relations, in the twilight of their complete rupture. He said that he had booked two berths to Naples, that we were bound for Capri, which was clearly the Island of the Lotos-eaters, that we would bask there together, 'and for a while forget'. It was a charming letter. I had never seen Italy; the privilege of initiation should be his. No mistake was greater than to deem it an impossible country for the summer. The Bay of Naples was never so divine, and he wrote of 'faery lands forlorn', as though the poetry sprang unbidden to his pen. To come back to earth and prose, I might think it unpatriotic of him to choose a German boat, but on no other line did you receive such attention and accommodation for your money. There was a hint of better reasons. Raffles wrote, as he had telegraphed, from Bremen; and I gathered that the personal use of some little influence with the authorities there had resulted in a material reduction in our fares.

Imagine my excitement and delight! I managed to pay what I owed at Thames Ditton, to squeeze a small editor for a very small cheque, and my tailors for one more flannel suit. I remember that I broke my last sovereign to get a box of Sullivan's cigarettes for

Raffles to smoke on the voyage. But my heart was as light as my purse on the Monday morning, the fairest morning of an unfair summer, when the special whirled me through the sunshine to the sea.

A tender awaited us at Southampton. Raffles was not on board, nor did I really look for him till we reached the liner's side. And then I looked in vain. His face was not among the many that fringed the rail; his hand was not of the few that waved to friends. I climbed aboard in a sudden heaviness. I had no ticket, nor the money to pay for one. I did not even know the number of my room. My heart was in my mouth as I waylaid a steward and asked if a Mr Raffles was on board. Thank heaven—he was! But where? The man did not know; was plainly on some other errand, and a-hunting I must go. But there was no sign of him on the promenade deck, and none below in the saloon; the smoking-room was empty but for a little German with a red moustache twisted into his eyes; nor was Raffles in his own cabin, whither I inquired my way in desperation, but where the sight of his own name on the baggage was certainly a further reassurance. Why he himself kept in the background, however, I could not conceive, and only sinister reasons would suggest themselves in explanation.

'So there you are! I've been tooking for you all over the ship!'

Despite the graven prohibition, I had tried the bridge as a last resort; and there, indeed, was A. J. Raffles, seated on a skylight, and leaning over one of the officers' long chairs, in which reclined a girl in a white drill coat and skirt—a slip of a girl with a pale skin, dark hair, and rather remarkable eyes. So much I noted as he rose and quickly turned; thereupon I could think of nothing but the swift grimace which preceded a start of well-feigned astonishment.

'Why—Bunny?' cried Raffles. 'Where have you sprung from?'

I stammered something as he pinched my hand.

'And you are coming in this ship? And to Naples too? Well, upon my word! Miss Werner, may I introduce my friend?'

And he did so without a blush, describing me as an old school-fellow whom he had not seen for months, with wilful circumstance and gratuitous detail that filled me at once with confusion, suspicion, and revolt. I felt myself blushing for us both, and I did not care. My address utterly deserted me, and I made no effort to recover it, to carry the thing off. All I would do was to mumble such words as Raffles actually put into my mouth, and that I doubt not with a thoroughly evil grace.

'So you saw my name in the list of passengers, and came in search of me? Good old Bunny! I say, though, I wish you'd share my cabin? I've got a beauty on the promenade deck, but they wouldn't promise to keep me by myself. We ought to see about it before they shove in some alien. In any case we shall have to get out of this.'

For a quartermaster had entered the wheel-house, and even while we had been speaking the pilot had taken possession of the bridge; as we descended, the tender left us with flying handkerchiefs and shrill good-byes; and as we bowed to Miss Werner on the promenade deck there came a deep, slow throbbing underfoot, and our voyage had begun.

It did not begin pleasantly between Raffles and me. On deck he had overborne my stubborn perplexity by dint of a forced though forceful joviality; in his cabin the gloves were off.

'You idiot,' he snarled. 'You've given me away again!'

'How have I given you away?'

I ignored the separate insult in his last word.

'How? I should have thought any clod could see that I meant us to meet by chance!'

'After taking both tickets yourself?'

'They know nothing about that on board; besides, I hadn't decided when I took the tickets.'

'Then you should have let me know when you did decide. You lay your plans, and never say a word, and expect me to tumble to them by light of nature. How was I to know you had anything on?'

I had turned the tables with some effect. Raffles almost hung his head.

'The fact is, Bunny, I didn't mean you to know. You—you've grown such a pious rabbit in your old age!'

My nickname and his tone went far to mollify me, other things went further, but I had much to forgive him still.

'If you were afraid of writing,' I pursued, 'it was your business to give me the tip the moment I set foot on board. I would have taken it all right. I am not so virtuous as all that.'

Was it my imagination, or did Raffles look slightly ashamed? If so, it was for the first and last time in all the years I knew him; nor can I swear to it even now.

'That', said he, 'was the very thing I meant to do—to lie in wait in my room and get you as you passed. But—'

'You were better engaged?'

'Say otherwise.'

'The charming Miss Werner?'

'She is quite charming.'

'Most Australian girls are,' said I.

'How did you know she was one?' he cried.

'I heard her speak.'

'Brute!' said Raffles, laughing; 'she has no more twang than you have. Her people are German, she has been to school in Dresden, and is on her way out alone.'

'Money?' I inquired.

'Confound you!' he said, and, though he was laughing, I thought it was a point at which the subject might be changed.

'Well,' I said, 'it wasn't for Miss Werner you wanted us to play strangers, was it? You have some deeper game than that, eh?'

'I suppose I have.'

'Then hadn't you better tell me what it is?'

Raffles treated me to the old cautious scrutiny that I knew so well; the very familiarity of it, after all these months, set me smiling in a way that might have reassured him; for dimly already I divined his enterprise.

'It won't send you off in the pilot's boat, Bunny?'

'Not quite.'

'Then—you remember the pearl you wrote the—'

I did not wait for him to finish his sentence.

'You've got it!' I cried, my face on fire, for I caught sight of it that moment in the state-room mirror.

Raffles seemed taken aback.

416

'Not yet,' said he; 'but I mean to have it before we get to Naples.'

'Is it on board?'

'Yes.'

'But how—where—who's got it?'

'A little German officer, a whipper-snapper with perpendicular moustaches.'

'I saw him in the smoke-room.'

'That's the chap; he's always there. Herr Captain Wilhelm von Heumann, if you look in the list. Well, he's the special envoy of the emperor, and he's taking the pearl out with him!'

'You found this out in Bremen?'

'No, in Berlin, from a newspaper man I know there. I'm ashamed to tell you, Bunny, that I went there on purpose!'

I burst out laughing.

'You needn't be ashamed. You are doing the very thing I was rather hoping you were going to propose the other day on the river.'

'You were hoping it?' said Raffles, with his eyes wide open. Indeed, it was his turn to show surprise, and mine to be much more ashamed than I felt.

'Yes,' I answered, 'I was quite keen on the idea; but I wasn't going to propose it.'

'Yet you would have listened to me the other day?'

Certainly I would, and I told him so without reserve; not brazenly, you understand; not even now with the gusto of a man who savours such an adventure for its own sake, but doggedly, defiantly, through my teeth, as one who had tried to live honestly and had failed. And, while I was about it, I told him much more. Eloquently enough I daresay, I gave him chapter and verse of my hopeless struggle, my inevitable defeat; for hopeless and inevitable they were to a man with my record, even though that record was written only in one's own soul. It was the old story of the thief trying to turn honest man; the thing was against nature, and there was an end of it.

Raffles entirely disagreed with me. He shook his head over my conventional view. Human nature was a board of chequers; why not reconcile one's self to alternate black and white? Why desire to be all one thing or all the other, like our forefathers on the stage or in the old-fashioned fiction? For his part, he enjoyed himself on all squares of the board, and liked the light the better for the shade. My conclusion he considered absurd.

'But you err in good company, Bunny, for all the cheap moralists who preach the same twaddle; old Virgil was the first and worst offender of you all. I back myself to climb out of Avernus any day I like, and sooner or later I shall climb out for good. I suppose I can't very well turn myself into a Limited Liability Company. But I could retire and settle down and live blamelessly ever after. I'm not sure that it couldn't be done on this pearl alone!'

'Then you don't still think it too remarkable to sell?'

'We might take a fishery and haul it up with smaller fry. It would come after months of ill-luck, just as we were going to sell the schooner; by Jove, it would be the talk of the Pacific!'

'Well, we've got to get it first. Is this von What's-his-name a formidable cuss?'

'More so than he looks; and he has the cheek of the devil!'

As he spoke, a white drill skirt fluttered past the open state-room door, and I caught a glimpse of an upturned moustache beyond. 'But is he the chap we have to deal with? Won't the pearl be in the purser's keeping?'

Raffles stood at the door, frowning out upon the Solent, but for an instant he turned to me with a sniff.

'My good fellow, do you suppose the whole ship's company knows there's a gem like that aboard? You said that it was worth a hundred thousand pounds; in Berlin they say it's price-less. I doubt if the skipper himself knows that von Heumann has it on him.'

'And he has?'

'Must have.'

'Then we have only him to deal with?'

He answered me without a word. Something white was fluttering past once more, and Raffles, stepping forth, made the promenaders three.

II

I do not ask to set foot aboard a finer steamship than the *Uhlan* of the Norddeutscher Lloyd, to meet a kindlier man than her then commander or better fellows than his officers. This much at least let me have the grace to admit. I hated the voyage. It was no fault of anybody connected with the ship; it was no fault of the weather, which was monotonously ideal. Not even in my own heart did the reason reside; conscience and I were divorced at last, and the decree made absolute. With my scruples had fled all fear, and I was ready to revel between bright skies and sparkling sea with the light-hearted detachment of Raffles himself. It was Raffles himself who prevented me, but not Raffles alone. It was Raffles and that Colonial minx on her way home from school.

What he could see in her—but that begs the question. Of course he saw no more than I did, but to annoy me, or perhaps to punish me for my long defection, he must turn his back on me and devote himself to this chit from Southampton to the Mediterranean. They were always together. It was too absurd. After breakfast they would begin, and go on until eleven or twelve at night; there was no intervening hour at which you might not hear her nasal laugh, or his quiet voice talking soft nonsense into her ear. Of course it was nonsense! Is it conceivable that a man like Raffles, with his knowledge of the world, and his experience of women (a side of his character upon which I have purposely never touched, for it deserves another volume); is it credible, I ask, that such a man could find anything but nonsense to talk by the day together to a giddy young schoolgirl? I would not be unfair for the world. I think I have admitted that the young person had points. Her eyes, I suppose, were really fine, and certainly the shape of the little brown face was charming, so far as mere contour can charm. I admit also more audacity than I cared about, with enviable health, mettle, and vitality. I may not have occasion to report any of this young lady's speeches (they would scarcely bear it), and am therefore the more anxious to describe her without injustice. I confess to some little prejudice against her. I resented her success with Raffles, of whom, in consequence, I saw less and less each day. It is a mean thing to have to confess, but there must have been something not unlike jealousy rankling within me.

Jealousy there was in another quarter—crude, rampant, undignified jealousy. Captain von Heumann would twirl his moustaches into twin spires, shoot his white cuffs over his rings, and stare at me insolently through his rimless eye-glasses; we ought to have consoled each other, but we never exchanged a syllable. The captain had a murderous scar across one of his cheeks, a present from Heidelberg, and I used to think how he must long to have Raffles there to serve the same. It was not as though von Heumann never had his innings. Raffles let him go in several times a day, for the malicious pleasure of bowling him out as he was 'getting set'; those were his words when I taxed him disingenuously with obnoxious conduct towards a German on a German boat.

'You'll make yourself disliked on board!'

'By von Heumann merely.'

'But is that wise when he's the man we've got to diddle?'

'The wisest thing I ever did. To have chummed up with him would have been fatal—the common dodge.'

I was consoled, encouraged, almost content. I had feared Raffles was neglecting things, and I told him so in a burst. Here we were near Gibraltar, and not a word since the Solent. He shook his head with a smile.

'Plenty of time, Bunny, plenty of time. We can do nothing before we get to Genoa, and that won't be till Sunday night. The voyage is still young, and so are we; let's make the most of things while we can.'

It was after dinner on the promenade deck, and as Raffles spoke he glanced sharply fore and aft, leaving me next moment with a step full of purpose. I retired to the smoking-room, to smoke and read in a corner, and to watch von Heumann, who very soon came to drink beer and to sulk in another.

Few travellers tempt the Red Sea at midsummer; the *Uhlan* was very empty indeed. She had, however, but a limited supply of cabins on the promenade deck, and there was just that excuse for my sharing Raffles's room. I could have had one to myself downstairs, but I must be up above. Raffles had insisted that I should insist on the point. So we were together, I think, without suspicion, though also without any object that I could see.

On the Sunday afternoon I was asleep in my berth, the lower one, when the curtains were shaken by Raffles, who was in his shirt-sleeves on the settee.

'Achilles sulking in his bunk!'

'What else is there to do?' I asked him as I stretched and yawned. I noted, however, the good-humour of his tone, and did my best to catch it.

'I have found something else, Bunny.'

'I daresay!'

'You misunderstand me. The whipper-snapper's making his century this afternoon. I've had other fish to fry.'

I swung my legs over the side of my berth and sat forward, as he was sitting, all attention. The inner door, a grating, was shut and bolted, and curtained like the open port-hole.

'We shall be at Genoa before sunset,' continued Raffles. 'It's the place where the deed's got to be done.'

'So you still mean to do it!'

'Did I ever say I didn't?'

'You have said so little either way.'

'Advisedly so, my dear Bunny; why spoil a pleasure trip by talking unnecessary shop? But now the time has come. It must be done at Genoa or not at all.'

'On land?'

'No, on board, tomorrow night. Tonight would do, but tomorrow is better, in case of mishap. If we were forced to use violence we could get away by the earliest train, and nothing be known till the ship was sailing and von Heumann found dead or drugged—'

'Not dead!' I exclaimed.

'Of course not,' assented Raffles, 'or there would be no need for us to bolt; but if we should have to bolt, Tuesday morning is our time when the ship has got to sail, whatever happens. But I don't anticipate any violence. Violence is a confession of terrible incompetence. In all these years how many blows have you known me strike? Not one, I believe; but I have been quite ready to kill my man every time, if the worst came to the worst.'

I asked him how he proposed to enter von Heumann's stateroom unobserved, and even through the curtained gloom of ours his face lighted up.

'Climb into my bunk, Bunny, and you shall see.'

I did so, but could see nothing. Raffles reached across me and tapped the ventilator, a sort of trapdoor in the wall above his bed, some eighteen inches long and half that height. It opened outwards into the ventilating shaft.

'That', said he, 'is our door to fortune. Open it if you like; you won't see much, because it doesn't open far; but loosening a couple of screws will set that all right. The shaft, as you may see, is more or less bottomless; you pass under it whenever you go to your bath, and the top is a skylight on the bridge. That's why this thing has to be done while we're at Genoa, because they keep no watch on the bridge in port. The ventilator opposite ours is von Heumann's. It again will only mean a couple of screws and there's a beam to stand on while you work.'

'But if anybody should look from below?'

'It's extremely unlikely that anybody will be astir below, so unlikely that we can afford to chance it. No, I can't have you there to make sure. The great point is that neither of us should be seen from the time we turn in. A couple of ship's boys do sentry-go on these decks, and they shall be our witnesses; by Jove, it'll be the biggest mystery that ever was made!'

'If von Heumann doesn't resist.'

'Resist! He won't get the chance. He drinks too much beer to sleep light, and nothing is so easy as to chloroform a heavy sleeper; you've even done it yourself on an occasion of which it's perhaps unfair to remind you. Von Heumann will be past sensation almost as soon as I get my hand through his ventilator. I shall crawl in over his body, Bunny, my boy!'

'And I?'

'You will hand me what I want, and hold the fort in case of accidents, and generally lend me the moral support you've made me require. It's a luxury, Bunny, but I found it devilish difficult to do without it after you turned pi!'

He said that von Heumann was certain to sleep with a bolted door, which he, of course, would leave unbolted, and spoke of other ways of laying a false scent while rifling the cabin. Not that Raffles anticipated a tiresome search. The pearl would be about von

Heumann's person; in fact, Raffles knew exactly where and in what he kept it. Naturally, I asked how he could have come by such knowledge, and his answer led up to a momentary unpleasantness.

'It's a very old story, Bunny. I really forget in what book it comes: I'm only sure of the Testament. But Samson was the unlucky hero, and one Delilah the heroine.'

And he looked so knowing that I could not be in a moment's doubt as to his meaning.

'So the fair Australian has been playing Delilah?' said I.

'In a very harmless, innocent sort of way.'

'She got his mission out of him?'

'Yes, I've forced him to score all the points he could, and that was his great stroke, as I hoped it would be. He has even shown Amy the pearl.'

'Amy, eh! and she promptly told you?'

'Nothing of the kind. What makes you think so? I had the greatest trouble in getting it out of her.'

His tone should have been a sufficient warning to me. I had not the tact to take it as such. At last I knew the meaning of his furious flirtation, and stood wagging my head and shaking my finger, blinded to his frowns by my own enlightenment.

'Wily worm!' said I. 'Now I see through it all; how dense I've been!'

'Sure you're not still?'

'No; now I understand what has beaten me all the week. I simply couldn't fathom what you saw in that little girl. I never dreamt it was part of the game.'

'So you think it was that and nothing more?'

'You deep old dog—of course I do!'

'You didn't know she was the daughter of a wealthy squatter?'

'There are wealthy women by the dozen who would marry you tomorrow.'

'It doesn't occur to you that I might like to draw stumps, start clean, and live happily ever after—in the bush?'

'With that voice? It certainly does not!'

'Bunny!' he cried so fiercely that I braced myself for a blow.

But no more followed.

'Do you think you would live happily?' I made bold to ask him.

'God knows!' he answered. And with that he left me, to marvel at his look and tone, and, more than ever, at the insufficiently exciting cause.

III

Of all the mere feats of cracksmanship which I have seen Raffles perform, at once the most delicate and most difficult was that which he accomplished between one and two o'clock on the Tuesday morning, aboard the North German steamer *Uhlan*, lying at anchor in Genoa harbour.

Not a hitch occurred. Everything had been foreseen; everything happened as I had been assured everything must. Nobody was about below, only the ship's boys on deck, and nobody on the bridge. It was twenty-five minutes past one when Raffles, without a stitch of clothing on his body, but with a glass phial, corked with cotton-wool, between his teeth, and a tiny screw-driver behind his ear, squirmed feet first through the ventilator over his berth; and it was nineteen minutes to two when he returned, head first, with the phial still between his teeth, and the cotton-wool rammed home to still the rattling of that which lay like a great grey bean within. He had taken screws out and put them in again; he had unfastened von Heumann's ventilator and had left it fast as he had found it—fast as he instantly proceeded to make his own. As for von Heumann, it had been enough to place the drenched wad first on his moustache, and then to hold it between his gaping lips; thereafter the intruder had climbed both ways across his shins without eliciting a groan.

And here was the prize—this pearl as large as a filbert—with a pale pink tinge like a lady's finger-nail—this spoil of the filibustering age—this gift from a European emperor to a South Sea chief. We gloated over it when all was snug. We toasted it in whisky and soda-water laid in overnight in view of the great moment. But the moment was greater, more triumphant, than our most sanguine dreams. All we had now to do was to secrete the gem (which Raffles had prised from its setting, replacing the latter), so that we could stand the strictest search and yet take it ashore with us at Naples; and this Raffles was doing when I turned in. I myself would have landed incontinently, that night, at Genoa, and bolted, with the spoil; he would not hear of it, for a dozen good reasons which will be obvious.

On the whole I do not think that anything was discovered or suspected before we weighed anchor; but I cannot be sure. It is difficult to believe that a man could be chloroformed in his sleep and feel no tell-tale effects, sniff no suspicious odour, in the morning. Nevertheless, von Heumann reappeared as though nothing had happened to him, his German cap over his eyes and his moustaches brushing the peak. And by ten o'clock we were quit of Genoa; the last lean, blue-chinned official had left our decks; the last fruitseller had been beaten off with bucketsful of water and left cursing us from his boat; the last passenger had come aboard at the last moment—a fussy greybeard who kept the big ship waiting while he haggled with his boatman over half a lira. But at length we were off, the tug was shed, the lighthouse passed, and Raffles and I leaned together over the rail, watching our shadows on the pale green, liquid, veined marble that again washed the vessel's side.

Von Heumann was having his innings once more; it was part of the design that he should remain in all day, and so postponed the inevitable hour; and, though the lady looked bored, and was for ever glancing in our direction, he seemed only too willing to avail himself of his opportunities. But Raffles was moody and ill at ease. He had not the air of a successful man. I could but opine that the impending parting at Naples sat heavily on his spirit. He would neither talk to me, nor would he let me go.

'Stop where you are, Bunny. I've things to tell you. Can you swim?'

'A bit.'

'Ten miles?'

'Ten?' I burst out laughing. 'Not one! Why do you ask?'

'We shall be within a ten miles' swim of the shore most of the day.'

'What on earth are you driving at, Raffles?'

'Nothing; only I shall swim for it if the worst comes to the worst. I suppose you can't swim under water at all?'

I did not answer his question. I scarcely heard it; cold beads were bursting through my skin.

'Why should the worst come to the worst?' I whispered. 'We aren't found out, are we?'

'No.'

'Then why speak as though we were?'

'We may be; an old enemy of ours is on board.'

'An old enemy?'

'Mackenzie.'

'Never.'

'The man with the beard who came aboard last.'

'Are you sure?'

Sure! I was only sorry to see you didn't recognize him too.'

I took my handkerchief to my face; now that I thought of it, there had been something familiar in the old man's gait, as well as something rather youthful for his apparent years; his very beard seemed unconvincing, now that I recalled it in the light of this horrible revelation. I looked up and down the deck, but the old man was nowhere to be seen.

'That's the worst of it,' said Raffles. 'I saw him go into the captain's cabin twenty minutes ago.'

'But what can have brought him?' I cried miserably. 'Can it be a coincidence—is it somebody else he's after?'

Raffles shook his head.

'Hardly, this time.'

'Then you think he's after you?'

'I've been afraid of it for some weeks.'

'Yet there you stand!'

'What am I to do? I don't want to swim for it before I must. I begin to wish I'd taken your advice, Bunny, and left the ship at Genoa. But I've not the smallest doubt that Mac was watching both ship and station till the last moment. That's why he ran it so fine.'

He took a cigarette and handed me the case, but I shook my head impatiently.

'I still don't understand,' said I. 'Why should he be after you? He couldn't come all this way about a jewel which was perfectly safe for all he knew. What's your own theory?'

'Simply that he's been on my track for some time, probably ever since friend Crawshay slipped clean through his fingers last November. There have been other indications. I am really not unprepared for this. But it can only be pure suspicion. I'll defy him to bring anything home, and I'll defy him to find the pearl! Theory, my dear Bunny! I know how he's got here as well as though I'd been inside that Scotsman's skin, and I know what he'll do next. He found out I'd gone abroad, and looked for a motive; he found out about von Heumann and his mission, and here was his motive cut and dried. Great chance—to nab me on a new job altogether. But he won't do it, Bunny; mark my words, he'll search the ship and search us all, when the loss is known; but he'll search in vain. And there's skipper beckoning the whipper-snapper to his cabin; the fat will be in the fire in five minutes!'

Yet there was no conflagration, no fuss, no searching of the passengers, no whisper of what had happened in the air; instead of a stir there was portentous peace; and it was clear to me that Raffles was not a little disturbed at the falsification of all his predictions. There was something sinister in silence under such a loss, and the silence was sustained for hours, during which Mackenzie never reappeared. But he was abroad during the luncheon-hour—he was in our cabin! I had left my book in Raffles's berth, and in taking it after lunch I touched the quilt. It was warm from the recent pressure of flesh and blood, and on an instinct I sprang to the ventilator; as I opened it the ventilator opposite was closed with a snap.

I waylaid Raffles. 'All right. Let him find the pearl.'

'Have you dumped it overboard?'

'That's a question I shan't condescend to answer.'

He turned on his heel, and at subsequent intervals I saw him making the most of his last afternoon with the inevitable Miss Werner. I remember that she looked both cool and smart in quite a simple affair of brown holland, which toned well with her complexion, and was cleverly relieved with touches of scarlet. I quite admired her that afternoon, for her eyes were really very good, and so were her teeth, yet I had never admired her more directly in my own despite. For I passed them again and again in order to get a word with Raffles, to tell him I knew there was danger in the wind; but he would not so much as catch my eye. So at last I gave it up. And I saw him next in the captain's cabin.

They had summoned him first; he had gone in smiling; and smiling I found him when they summoned me. The stateroom was spacious, as befitted that of a commander. Mackenzie sat on the settee, his beard in front of him on the polished table; but a revolver lay in front of the captain; and, when I had entered, the chief officer, who had summoned me, shut the door and put his back to it. Von Heumann completed the party, his fingers busy with his moustache.

Raffles greeted me.

'This is a great joke!' he cried. 'You remember the pearl you were so keen about, Bunny, the emperor's pearl, the pearl money wouldn't buy? It seems it was entrusted to our little friend here, to take out to Canoodle Dum, and the poor little chap's gone and lost it; *ergo*, as we're Britishers, they think we've got it!'

'But I know ye have,' put in Mackenzie, nodding to his beard.

'You will recognize that loyal and patriotic voice,' said Raffles. Mon, 'tis our auld acquaintance Mackenzie, o' Scoteland Yarrd an' Scoteland itsel'!'

'Dat is enought,' cried the captain. 'Have you submid to be searge, or do I vorce you?'

'What you will,' said Raffles, 'but it will do you no harm to give us fair play first. You accuse us of breaking into Captain von Heumann's stateroom during the small hours of this morning, and abstracting from it this confounded pearl. Well, I can prove that I was in my own room all night long, and I have no doubt my friend can prove the same.'

'Most certainly I can,' said I indignantly. 'The ship's boys can bear witness to that.'

Mackenzie laughed, and shook his head at his reflection in the polished mahogany.

'That was vera clever,' said he, 'and like enough it would ha' served ye had I not stepped aboard. But I've just had a look at they ventilators, and I think I know how ye worrked it. Anyway, captain, it makes no matter. I'll just be clappin' the darbies on these young sparks, an' then—'

'By what right?' roared Raffles in a ringing voice, and I never saw his face in such a blaze. 'Search us if you like; search every scrap and stitch we possess; but you dare to lay a finger on us without a warrant!'

'I wouldna' dare,' said Mackenzie gravely, as he fumbled in his breast-pocket, and Raffles dived his hand into his own. 'Haud his wrist!' shouted the Scotsman; and the huge Colt that had been with us many a night, but had never been fired in my hearing, clattered on the table and was raped in by the captain.

'All right,' said Raffles savagely to the mate. 'You can let go now. I won't try it again. Now Mackenzie, let's see your warrant!'

'Ye'll no mishandle it?'

'What good would that do me? Let me see it,' said Raffles, peremptorily, and the detective obeyed. Raffles raised his eyebrows as he perused the document; his mouth hardened, but suddenly relaxed; and it was with a smile and a shrug that he returned the paper.

'Wull that do for ye?' inquired Mackenzie.

'It may. I congratulate you, Mackenzie; it's a strong hand, at any rate. Two burglaries and the Melrose necklace, Bunny!' And he turned to me with a rueful smile.

'An' all easy to prove,' said the Scotsman, pocketing the warrant. 'I've one o' these for you,' he added, nodding to me, 'only not such a long one.'

'To thingk,' said the captain reproachfully, 'that my shib should be made a den of thiefs! It shall be a very disagreeable madder. I have been obliged to pud you both in irons until we ged to Nables.'

'Surely not!' exclaimed Raffles. 'Mackenzie, intercede with him; don't give your countrymen away before all hands! Captain, we can't escape; surely you could hush it up for the night? Look here, here's everything I have in my pockets; you empty yours too, Bunny, and they shall strip us stark if they suspect we've weapons up our sleeves. All I ask is that we are allowed to get out of this without gyves upon our wrists!'

'Webbons, you may not have,' said the captain; 'bud wad about de bearl dat you were sdealing?'

'You shall have it!' cried Raffles. 'You shall have it this minute if you guarantee no public indignity on board!'

'That I'll see to,' said Mackenzie, 'as long as you behave yourselves. There now, where is't?'

'On the table under your nose.'

My eyes fell with the rest, but no pearl was there; only the contents of our pocket—our watches, pocket-books, pencils, penknives, cigarette-cases—lay on the shiny table along with the revolvers already mentioned.

'Ye're humbuggin' us,' said Mackenzie. 'What's the use?'

'I'm doing nothing of the sort,' laughed Raffles. 'I'm testing you. Where's the harm?'

'It's here, joke apart?'

'On that table, by all my gods.'

Mackenzie opened the cigarette-cases and shook each particular cigarette. Thereupon Raffles prayed to be allowed to smoke one, and, when his prayer was heard, observed that the pearl had been on the table much longer than the cigarettes. Mackenzie promptly caught up the Colt and opened the chamber in the butt.

'Not there, not there,' said Raffles; 'but you're getting hot. Try the cartridges.'

Mackenzie emptied them into his palm, and shook each one at his ear without result.

'Oh, give them to me!'

And, in an instant, Raffles had found the right one, had bitten out the bullet, and placed the emperor's pearl with a flourish in the centre of the table.

'After that you will perhaps show me such little consideration as is in your power. Captain, I have been a bit of a villain, as you see, and as such I am ready and willing to lie in irons all night if you deem it requisite for the safety of the ship. All I ask is that you do me one favour first.'

'That shall debend on wad der vafour has been.'

'Captain, I've done a worse thing aboard your ship than any of you know. I have become engaged to be married, and I want to say good-bye!'

I suppose we were all equally amazed; but the only one to express his amazement was von Heumann, whose deep-chested German oath was almost his first contribution to the proceedings. He was not slow to follow it, however, with a vigorous protest against the proposed farewell; but he was overruled, and the masterful prisoner had his way. He was to have five minutes with the girl, while the captain and Mackenzie stood within range (but not earshot), with their revolvers behind their backs. As we were moving from the cabin in a body, he stopped and gripped my hand.

'So I've let you in at last, Bunny—at last and after all! If you knew how sorry I am . . . But you won't get much—I don't see why you should get anything at all. Can you forgive me? This may be for years, and it may be for ever, you know! You were a good pal always when it came to the scratch; some day or other you mayn't be so sorry to remember you were a good pal at the last!'

There was a meaning in his eye that I understood; and my teeth were set, and my nerves strung ready, as I wrung that strong and cunning hand for the last time in my life.

How that last scene stays with me, and will stay to my death! How I see every detail, every shadow on the sunlit deck! We were among the islands that dot the course from Genoa to Naples; that was Elba falling back on our starboard quarter, that purple patch with the hot sun setting over it. The captain's cabin opened to starboard, and the starboard promenade deck, sheeted with sunshine and scored with shadow, was deserted but for the group of which I was one, and for the pale, slim, brown figure farther aft with Raffles. Engaged? I could not believe it, cannot to this day. Yet there they stood together, and we did not hear a word; there they stood out against the sunset, and the long, dazzling highway of sunlit sea that sparkled from Elba to the *Uhlan*'s plates; and their shadows reached almost to our feet.

Suddenly—an instant—and the thing was done—a thing I have never known whether to admire or to detest. He caught her—he kissed her before us all—then flung her from him so that she almost fell. It was that action which foretold the next. The mate sprang after him, and I sprang after the mate.

Raffles was on the rail, but only just.

'Hold him, Bunny!' he cried. 'Hold him tight!'

And, as I obeyed that last behest with all my might, without a thought of what I was doing, save that he bade me do it, I saw his hands shoot up and his head bob down, and his lithe, spare body cut the sunset as cleanly and precisely as though he had plunged at his leisure from a diver's board!

*

Of what followed on deck I can tell you nothing, for I was not there. Nor can my final punishment, my long imprisonment, my everlasting disgrace, concern or profit you, beyond the interest and advantage to be gleaned from the knowledge that I at least had my deserts. But one thing I must set down, believe it who will—one more thing only and I am done.

It was into a second-class cabin, on the starboard side, that I was promptly thrust in irons, and the door locked upon me as though I were another Raffles. Meanwhile a boat was lowered, and the seas scoured to no purpose, as is doubtless on record elsewhere. But either the setting sun, flashing over the waves, must have blinded all eyes, or else mine were victims of a strange illusion.

For the boat was back, the screw throbbing, and the prisoner peering through his port-hole across the sunlit waters that he believed had closed for ever over his comrade's head. Suddenly the sun sank behind the Island of Elba, the lane of dancing sunlight was instantaneously quenched and swallowed in the trackless waste, and in the middle distance, already miles astern, either my sight deceived me or a black speck bobbed amid the grey. The bugle had blown for dinner; it may well be that all save myself had ceased to strain an eye. And now I lost what I had found, now it rose, now sank, and now I gave it up utterly. Yet anon it would rise again, a mere mote dancing in the dim grey distance, drifting towards a purple island, beneath a fading western sky, streaked with dead gold and cerise. And night fell before I knew whether it was a human head or not.

Room 13

by Edgar Wallace

1

Over the grim stone archway were carved the words:

PARCERE SUBJECTIS

In cold weather, and employing the argot of his companions Johnny Gray translated this as 'Parky Subjects'—it certainly had no significance as 'Spare the Vanquished', for he had been neither vanquished nor spared.

Day by day, he and Lal Morgon had pulled a heavy handcart up the steep slope, and day by day had watched absently the gate-warder put his key in the big polished lock and snap open the gates. And then the little party had passed through, an armed warder leading, an armed warder behind, and the gate had closed.

And at four o'clock he had walked back under the archway and halted whilst the gate was unlocked and the handcart admitted.

Every building was hideously familiar. The gaunt 'halls', pitch painted against the Dartmoor storms, the low-roofed office, the big, barn-like laundry, the ancient bakery, the exercise yard with its broken asphalt, the ugly church, garishly decorated, the long, scrubbed benches with the raised seats for the warders . . . and the graveyard where the happily released lifers rested from their labours.

One morning in spring, he went out of the gate with a working-party. They were building a shed, and he had taken the style and responsibility of bricklayer's labourer. He liked the work because you can talk more freely on a job like that, and he wanted to hear all that Lal Morgon had to say about the Big Printer.

'Not so much talking today,' said the warder in charge, seating himself on a sack-covered brick heap.

'No, sir,' said Lal.

He was a wizened man of 50 and a lifer, and he had one ambition, which was to live long enough to get another 'lagging'.

'But not burglary, Gray,' he said, as he leisurely set a brick in its place; 'and not shootin', like old Legge got his packet. And not faking Spider King, like you got yours.'

'I didn't get mine for faking Spider King,' said Johnny calmly. 'I didn't know that Spider King had been rung in when I took him on the course. They framed up Spider King to catch me. I'm not complaining.'

'I know you're innocent—everybody is,' said Lal soothingly. 'I'm the only guilty man in boob. That's what the governor says. "Morgon," he says, "it does my heart good to meet a guilty man that ain't the victim of circumstantiality. Like everybody else is in boob," he says.'

Johnny did not pursue the subject. There was no reason why he should. This fact was beyond dispute. He had known all about the big racecourse swindles that were being worked, and had been an associate of men who backed the rung in horses. He accepted his three years' sentence without appeal or complaint. Not because he was guilty of the act for which he was charged—there was another excellent reason.

'If they lumbered you with the crime, it was because you was a mug,' said old Lal complacently. 'That's what mugs are for—to be lumbered. What did old Kane say?'

'I didn't see Mr Kane,' said Johnny shortly.

'He'd think you was a mug, too.' said Lal with satisfaction —'hand me a brick, Gray, and shut up! That nosey screw's coming over.'

The 'nosey screw' was no more inquisitive than any other warder. He strolled across, the handle of his truncheon showing from his pocket, the well-worn strap dangling.

'Not so much talking,' he said mechanically.

'I was asking for a brick, sir,' said Lal humbly. 'These bricks ain't so good as the last lot.'

'I've noticed that,' said the warder, examining a half-brick with a professional and disapproving eye.

'Trust you to notice that, sir,' said the sycophant with the right blend of admiration and awe. And, when the warder had passed:

'That boss-eyed perisher don't know a brick from a gas-stove,' said Lal without heat. 'He's the bloke that old Legge got straightened when he was in here—used to have private letters brought in every other day. But then, old Legge's got money. Him and Peter Kane smashed the strong-room of the *Orsonic* and got away with a million dollars. They never caught Peter, but Legge was easy. He shot a copper and got life.'

Johnny had heard Legge's biography a hundred times, but Lal Morgon had reached the stage of life when every story he told was new.

'That's why he hates Peter,' said the garrulous bricklayer. 'That's why young Legge and him are going to get Peter. And young Legge's hot! Thirty years of age by all accounts, and the biggest printer of slush in the world! And it's not ord'nary slush. Experts get all mixed up when they see young Legge's notes—can't tell 'em from real Bank of England stuff. And the police *and* the secret service after him for years—and then never got him!'

The day was warm, and Lal stripped off his working jacket.

'You've never met young Jeff?' stated rather than asked Lal, smoothing a dab of mortar with a leisurely touch.

'I've seen him—I haven't met him,' said Johnny grimly, and something in his tone made the old convict look up.

'He shopped me,' said Johnny, and Lal indicated his surprise with an inclination of his head that was ridiculously like a bow.

'I don't know why, but I do know that he shopped me,' said Johnny. 'He was the man who fixed up the fake, persuaded me to bring the horse on to the course, and then squeaked. until then I didn't know that the horse they called Spider King was really Boy Saunders cleverly camouflaged.'

'Squeaking's hidjus,' said the shocked Lal, and he seemed troubled. 'And Emanuel Legge's boy, too! Why did he do it—did you catch him over money?'

Johnny shook his head.

'I don't know. If it's true that he hates Peter Kane he may have done it out of revenge, knowing that I'm fond of Peter, and . . . well, I'm fond of Peter. He warned me about mixing with the crowd I ran with—'

'*Stop that talking, will you?*'

They worked for some time in silence. Then:

'That screw will get somebody hung one of these days,' said Lal in a tone of quiet despair. 'He's the feller that little Lew Morse got a bashing for—over clouting him with a spanner in the blacksmith's shop. He was nearly killed. What a pity! Lew wasn't much account, an' he's often said he'd as soon be dead as sober.'

At four o'clock the working-party fell in and marched or shuffled down the narrow road to the prison gates.

Parcere Subjectis.

Johnny looked up and winked at the grim jest, and he had the illusion that the archway winked back at him. At half-past four he turned into the deep-recessed doorway of his cell, and the yellow door closed on him with a metallic snap of a lock.

It was a big, vaulted cell, and the colour of the folded blanket ends gave it a rakish touch of gaiety. On a shelf in one corner was a photograph of a fox terrier, an intelligent head turned inquiringly towards him.

He poured out a mugful of water and drank it, looking up at the barred window. Presently his tea would come, and then the lock would be put on for over twelve hours. And for all those hours he must amuse himself as best he could. He could read whilst the light held—a travel book was on the ledge that served as a table. Or he could write, or draw horses and dogs, or work out interminable problems in mathematics, or write poetry . . . or think.

That was the worst exercise of all. He crossed the cell and took down the photograph. The mount had worn limp with much handling, and he looked with a half-smile into the big eyes of the terrier.

'It's a pity you can't write, old Spot,' he said.

Other people could write, and did, he thought as he replaced the photograph. But Peter Kane never once mentioned Marney, and Marney had not written since . . . a long time. It was ominous, informative, in some ways decisive. A brief reference, 'Marney is well,' or 'Marney thanks you for your inquiry,' and that was all.

The whole story was clearly written in those curt phrases, the story of Peter's love for the girl, and his determination that she should not marry a man with the prison taint. Peter's adoration of his daughter was almost a mania—her happiness and her future came first, and must always be first. Peter loved him—Johnny had sensed that. He had given him the affection that a man might give his grown son. If this tragic folly of his had not led to the entanglement which brought him to a convict prison, Peter would have given Marney to him, as she was willing to give herself.

'That's that,' said Johnny, in his role of philosopher.

And then came tea and the final lock-up, and silence . . . and thoughts again.

Why did young Legge trap him? He had only seen the man once; they had never even met. It was only by chance that he had ever seen this young printer of forged notes. He could not guess that he was known to the man he shopped, for Jeff Legge was an elusive person. One never met him in the usual rendezvous where the half-underworld forgather to boast and plot or drink and love.

A key rattled in the lock, and Johnny got up. He forgot that it was the evening when the chaplain visited him.

'Sit down, Gray.' The door closed on the clergyman, and he seated himself on Johnny's bed.

It was curious that he should take up the thread of Johnny's interrupted thoughts.

'I want to get your mind straight about this man Legge . . . the son, I mean. It's pretty bad to brood on grievances, real or fancied, and you're nearing the end of your term of imprisonment, when your resentment will have a chance of expressing itself. And, Gray, I don't want to see you here again.'

Johnny Gray smiled.

'You won't see me *here*!' he emphasized the word. 'As to Jeff Legge, I know little about him, though I've done some fairly fluent guessing and I've heard a lot.'

The chaplain shook his head thoughtfully.

'I've heard a little; he's the man they call the Big Printer, isn't he? Of course, I know that Europe is being flooded with spurious notes, and that the police haven't caught the man who's circulating them. Is that Jeff Legge?'

Johnny did not answer, and the chaplain smiled somewhat sadly.

' "Thou shalt not squeak"—the eleventh commandment, isn't it?' he asked good-humouredly. 'I'm afraid I've been indiscreet. When does your sentence end?'

'In six months,' replied Johnny, 'and I'll not be sorry.'

'What are you going to do? Have you any money?'

The convict's lips twitched.

'Yes. I've three thousand a year,' he said quietly. 'That is a fact which didn't come out at the trial, for certain reasons. No, padre, money isn't my difficulty. I suppose I shall travel. I certainly shall not attempt to live down my grisly past.'

'That means you're not going to change your name,' said the chaplain with a twinkle in his eye. 'Well, with three thousand a year, I can't see you coming here again.' Suddenly he remembered. Putting his hand in his pocket, he took out a letter. 'The Deputy gave me this, and I'd nearly forgotten. It arrived this morning.'

The letter was opened, as were all letters that came to convicts, and Johnny glanced carelessly at the envelope. It was not, as he had expected, a letter from his lawyer. The bold handwriting was Peter Kane's—the first letter he had written for six months. He waited until the door had closed on the visitor, and then he took the letter from the envelope. There were only a few lines of writing.

Dear Johnny, I hope you are not going to be very much upset by the news I am telling you. Marney is marrying Major Floyd of Toronto, and I know that you're big enough and fine enough to wish her luck. This man really is a good fellow and I know that he will make her happy.

Johnny put the letter on the ledge, and for ten minutes paced the narrow length of his cell, his hands clasped behind him. Marney to be married! His face was white, tense, his eyes dark with gloom. He stopped and poured out a mugful of water with a hand that shook, then raised the mug to the barred window that looked eastward.

'Good luck to you, Marney!' he said huskily, and drank the mug empty.

2

Two days later, Johnny Gray was summoned to the Governor's office and heard the momentous news.

'Gray, I've good news for you. You're to be released immediately. I've just had the authority.'

Johnny inclined his head.

'Thank you, sir,' he said.

A warder took him to a bathroom, where he stripped and, with a blanket about him, came out to a cubicle where his civilian clothes were waiting. He dressed with a strange air of unfamiliarity, and went back to his cell: there the warder brought him a looking-glass and a razor, and he shaved.

The rest of the day was his own. He was a privileged man, and could wander about the prison in his strangely-feeling attire, the envy of men whom he had come to know and to loathe; the half madmen who for a year had been whispering their futilities into his ear.

As he stood there in the hall, the door was flung open violently and a group of men staggered in. In the midst of them was a howling, shrieking thing that was neither man nor beast, his face bloody, his wild arms gripped by struggling warders.

He watched the tragic group as it made its way to the punishment cells.

'Fenner,' said somebody under his breath. 'He coshed a screw, but they can't give him another bashing.'

'Isn't Fenner that twelve-year man, that's doing his full time?' asked Johnny, remembering the convict. 'And he's going out tomorrow, too!'

'That's him,' said his informant, one of the hall sweepers. 'He'd have got out with nine, but old Legge reported him. Game to the last, eh? They can't bash him after tomorrow, and the visiting justices won't be here for a week.'

Johnny remembered the case. Legge had witnessed a brutal assault on the man by one of the warders, who had since been discharged from the service. In desperation the unfortunate Fenner had hit back, and had been tried. Legge's evidence might have saved him from the flogging which followed, but Legge was too good a friend of the warders— or they were too good friends of his—to betray a screw. So Fenner had gone to the triangle, as he would not go again.

Johnny could not sleep that last night in the cell. His mind was on Marney. He did not reproach her for a second. Nor did he feel bitter towards her father. It was only right and proper that Peter Kane should do what was best for his daughter. The old man's ever-present fear for her future was almost an obsession. Johnny guessed that when this presentable Canadian had come along, Peter had done all in his power to further the match.

Johnny Gray walked up the steep slope for the last time. A key turned in the big lock, and he stood outside the gates, a free man. The red-bearded head warder put out his hand.

'Good luck to you,' he said gruffly. 'Don't you come over the Alps again.'

'I've given up mountain climbing,' said Johnny.

He had taken his farewell of the Governor, and now the only thing to remind him of his association with the grim prison he had left was the warder who walked by his side to the station. He had some time to wait, and Johnny tried to get some information from another angle.

'No, I don't know Jeff Legge,' said the warder, shaking his head. 'I knew the old man: he was here until twelve months ago—you were here, too, weren't you, Gray?'

Johnny nodded.

'Mr Jeff Legge has never been over the Alps, then?' he asked sardonically.

'No, not in this prison, and he wasn't in Parkhurst or Portland so far as I can remember. I've been at both places. I've heard the men talking about him. They say he's clever, which means that he'll be putting out his tins one morning. Goodbye, Gray, and be good!'

Johnny gripped the outstretched hand of the man, and, when he was in the carriage, took out his handkerchief and wiped his hand of the last prison contact.

His valet was waiting for him at Paddington when he arrived that afternoon, and with him, straining at a leash, a small, lop-eared fox terrier, who howled his greeting long before Johnny had seen the group. In another second the dog was struggling in his arms, licking his face, his ears, his hair, and whining his joy at the reunion. There were tears in Johnny's eyes when he put the dog down on the platform.

'There are a number of letters for you, sir. Will you dine at home?'

The excellent Parker might have been welcoming his master from a short sojourn at Monte Carlo, so very unemotional was he.

'Yes, I'll dine at home,' said Johnny. He stepped into the taxi that Parker had hired and Spot leapt after him.

'There is no luggage, sir?' asked Parker gravely through the open window.

'There is no luggage,' said Johnny as gravely. 'You had better ride back with me, Parker.'

The man hesitated.

'It would be a very great liberty, sir,' he said.

'Not so great a liberty as I've had taken with me during the past year and nine months,' said Johnny.

As the cab came out into dismal Chapel Street, the greatly daring Parker asked:

'I hope you have not had too bad a time, sir?'

Johnny laughed.

'It hasn't been pleasant, Parker. Prisons seldom are.'

'I suppose not, sir,' agreed Parker, and added unnecessarily, 'I have never been in prison, sir.'

Johnny's flat was in Queen's Gate, and at the sight of the peaceful luxury of his study he caught his breath.

'You're a fool,' he said aloud to himself.

'Yes, sir,' said the obliging Parker.

That night many men came furtively to the flat in Queen's Gate, and Johnny, after admitting the first of these, called Parker into his small dining-room.

'Parker, I am told that during my absence in the country even staid men have acquired the habit of going out in the evening?'

'Well, sir, I sometimes like to go to the cinema myself,' admitted Parker.

'Then go and find one that lasts until eleven o'clock,' said Johnny.

'You mean, sir—?'

'I mean I don't want you here tonight.'

Parker's face fell, but he was a good servant.

'Very good, sir,' he said, and went out, wondering sorrowfully what desperate plans his master was hatching.

At half past ten the last of the visitors took his leave.

'I'll see Peter tomorrow,' said Johnny, tossing the end of his cigarette into the hall fire-place. 'You know nothing of this wedding, when it is to take place?'

'No, Captain. I only know Peter slightly.'

'Who is the bridegroom?'

'A swell, by all accounts—Peter is a plausible chap, and he'd pull in the right kind. A major in the Canadian Army, I've heard, and a very nice man. Peter can catch mugs easier than some people can catch flies—'

'Peter was never a mug-catcher,' said John Gray sharply.

'I don't know,' said the other. 'There's one born every minute.'

'But they take a long time to grow up, and the women get first pluck,' said Johnny good-humouredly.

Parker, returning at 11.15, found his master sitting in front of a fireplace which was choked with burnt paper.

Johnny reached Horsham the next afternoon soon after lunch, and none who saw the athletic figure striding up the Horsham Road would guess that less than two days before he had been the inmate of a prison cell.

He had come to make his last desperate fight for happiness. How it would end, what argument to employ, he did not know. There was one, and one only, but that he could not use.

As he turned into Down Road he saw two big cars standing one behind the other, and wondered what social event was in progress.

Manor Hill stood aloof from its suburban neighbours, a sedate, red-brick house, its walls gay with clematis. Johnny avoided the front gates and passed down a sidepath which, as he knew, led to the big lawn behind, where Peter loved to sun himself at this hour.

He paused as he emerged into the open. A pretty maid was talking to an elderly man, who wore without distinction the livery of a butler. His lined face was puckered uncomfortably, and his head was bent in a listening attitude, though it was next to impossible for a man totally deaf to miss hearing all that was said.

'I don't know what sort of houses you've been in, and what sort of people you've been working for, but I can tell you that if I find you in my room again, looking in my suitcases, I shall tell Mr Kane. I won't have it, Mr Ford!'

'No, miss,' said the butler, huskily.

It was not, as Johnny knew, emotion which produced the huskiness. Barney Ford had been husky from his youth—probably squawed huskily in his cradle.

'If you're a burglar and trying to keep your hand in, I'd understand it,' the girl continued hotly, 'but you're supposed to be a respectable man! I won't have this underhand prying and sneaking. Understand that! I won't have it!'

'No, miss,' said the hoarse Barney.

John Gray surveyed the scene with amusement. Barney he knew very well. He had quitted the shadier walks of life when Peter Kane had found it expedient to retire from his hazardous calling. Ex-convict, ex-burglar and ex-prizefighter, his seamy past was in some degree redeemed by his affection for the man whose bread he ate and in whose service he pretended to be, though a worse butler than Barney had never put on uniform.

The girl was pretty, with hair of dull gold and a figure that was both straight and supple. Now her face was flushed with annoyance, and the dark eyes were ablaze. Barney certainly had prying habits, the heritage of his unregenerate days. Other staff had left the house for the same reason, and Peter had cursed and threatened without wholly reforming the servitor.

The girl did not see him as she turned and flounced into the house, leaving the old man to stare after her.

'You've made her cross,' said John, coming up behind him.

Barney Ford spun round and stared. Then his jaw dropped.

'Good Lord, Johnny, when did *you* come down from college?'

The visitor laughed softly.

'Term ended yesterday,' he said. 'How's Peter?'

Before he replied Barney blew his nose violently, all the time keeping his eye on the newcomer.

'How long have you bin here?' he asked at length.

'I arrived at the tail-end of your conversation,' said Johnny, amused. 'Barney, you haven't reformed!'

Barney Ford screwed up his face into an expression of scorn.

'They think you're a hook even if you ain't one,' he said. 'What does she know about life? You ain't seen Peter? He's in the house; I'll tell him in a minute. *He's* all right. All beans and bacon about the girl. That fellow adores the ground she walks on. It's not natural, being fond of your kids like that. I never was.' He shook his head despairingly. 'There's too much lovey-dovey and not enough strap nowadays. Spare the rod and spoil the child, as the good old poet says.'

John Gray turned his head at the sound of a foot upon a stone step. It was Peter, Peter radiant yet troubled. Straight as a ramrod, for all his sixty years and white hair. He was wearing a morning coat and pearl-grey waistcoat—an innovation. For a second he hesitated, the smile struck from his face, frowning, and then he came quickly his hand outstretched.

'Well, Johnny boy, had a rotten time?'

His hand fell on the young man's shoulder, his voice had the old pleasure of pride and affection.

'Fairly rotten,' said Johnny; 'but any sympathy with me is wasted. Personally, I prefer Dartmoor to Parkhurst—it's more robust, and there are fewer imbeciles.'

Peter took his arm and led him to a chair beneath the big umbrella planted on the lawn. There was something in his manner, a certain awkwardness which the newcomer could not understand.

'Did you meet anybody . . . there . . . that I know, Johnny boy?'

'Legge,' said the other laconically, his eyes on Peter's face.

'That's the man I'm thinking of. How is he?'

The tone was careless, but Johnny was not deceived. Peter was intensely interested.

'He's been out six months—didn't you know?'

The other's face clouded.

'Out six months? Are you sure?'

Johnny nodded.

'I didn't know.'

'I should have thought you'd have heard from him,' said John quietly. 'He doesn't love you!'

Peter's slow smile broadened.

'I know he doesn't; did you get a chance of talking with him?'

'Plenty of chances. He was in the laundry, and he straightened a couple of screws so that he could do what he liked. He hates you, Peter. He says you shopped him.'

'He's a liar,' said Peter calmly. 'I wouldn't shop my worst enemy. He shopped himself, Johnny; the police get a reputation for smartness but the truth is every other criminal arrests himself. Criminals aren't clever. They wear gloves to hide their finger-prints, and then write their names in the visitors' book. Legge and I smashed the strong-room of the *Orsonic* and got away with a hundred and twenty thousand pounds in American currency—it was the last job I did. It was dead easy getting away, but Emanuel started boasting what a clever fellow he was—and he drank a bit. An honest man can drink and wake up in his own bed. But a crook who drinks says good morning to the gaoler.'

He dropped the subject abruptly, and again his hand fell on the younger man's shoulder.

'Johnny, you're not feeling sore, are you?'

Johnny did not answer.

'Are you?'

And now the fight was to begin. John Gray steeled himself for the forlorn hope.

'About Marney? No, only—'

'Old boy, I had to do it.' Peter's voice was urgent, pleading. 'You know what she is to me. I liked you well enough to take a chance, but after they dragged you I did some hard thinking. It would have smashed me, Johnny, if she'd been your wife then. I couldn't bear to see her cry even when she was quite a little baby. Think what it would have meant to her. It was bad enough as it was. And then this fellow came along—a good, straight boy. And well, I'll tell you the truth—I helped him. You'll like him. He's the sort of man anybody would like. And she loves him, Johnny.'

There was a silence.

'I don't bear him any ill-will. It would be absurd if I did. Only, Peter, before she marries I want to say—'

'Before she marries?' Peter Kane's voice shook. 'John, didn't Barney tell you? She was married this morning.'

3

'Married?'

Johnny repeated the word dully.

Marney married . . .! It was incredible, impossible to comprehend. For a moment the stays and supports of existence dissolved into dust, and the fabric of life fell into chaos.

'Married this morning, Johnny. You'll like him. He isn't one of us, old boy. He's as straight as . . . well, you understand, Johnny boy? I've worked for her and planned for her all these years; I'd have been rotten if I took a chance with her future.'

Peter Kane was pleading, his big hand on the other's shoulder, his fine face clouded with anxiety and the fear that he had hurt this man beyond remedy.

'I should have telephoned . . .'

'It would have made no difference,' said Peter Kane almost doggedly. 'Nothing could have been changed, Johnny, nothing. It had to be. If you'd been convicted innocently—I don't say you weren't—I couldn't have the memory of your imprisonment hanging over her; I couldn't have endured the uncertainty myself. Johnny, I've been crook all my life—up to fifteen years ago. I take a broader view than most men because I am what I am. But she doesn't know that. Craig's here today—'

'Craig—the Scotland Yard man?'

Peter nodded, a look of faint amusement in his eyes.

'We're good friends; we have been for years. And do you know what he said this morning? He said, "Peter, you've done well to marry that girl into the straight way," and I know he's right.'

Johnny stretched back in the deep cane chair, his hand shading his eyes, as though he found the light too strong for him.

'I'm not going to be sorry for myself,' he said with a smile, and stretching out his hand, gripped Kane's arm. 'You'll not have another vendetta on your hands, Peter. I have an idea that Emanuel Legge will keep you busy—'

He stopped suddenly. The ill-fitted butler had made a stealthy appearance.

'Peter,' he began in his husky whisper, 'he's come. Do you want to see him?'

'Who?'

'Emanuel Legge—uglier than ever.'

Peter Kane's face set, mask-like.

'Where is Miss Marney—Mrs Floyd?'

'She's gettin' into her weddin' things and falderals for the photogrypher,' said Barney. 'She had 'em off once, but the photogrypher's just come, and he's puttin' up his things in the front garden. I sez to Marney—'

'You're a talkative old gentleman,' said Peter grimly. 'Send Emanuel through. Do you want to see him, Johnny?'

John Gray rose.

'No,' he said. 'I'll wander through your alleged rosary. I want nothing to remind me of the Awful Place, thank you.'

Johnny had disappeared through an opening of the box hedge at the lower end of the lawn when Barney returned with the visitor.

Mr Emanuel Legge was a man below middle height, thin of body and face, grey and a little bald. On his nose perched a pair of horn-rimmed glasses. He stood for a second or two surveying the scene, his chin lifted, his thin lips drawn in between his teeth. His attire was shabby and, as if to emphasize the rustiness of his wrinkled suit, he wore shoes that were patently new and vividly yellow. Hat in hand, he waited, his eyes slowly sweeping the domain of his enemy, until at last they came to rest on his host.

It was Peter Kane who broke the deadly silence.

'Well, Emanuel? Come over and sit down.'

Legge moved slowly towards his host.

'Quite a swell place, Peter. Everything of the best, eh? Trust you! Still got old Barney, I see. Has he reformed too? That's the word, ain't it—"reformed"?'

His voice was thin and complaining. His pale blue eyes blinked coldly at the other.

'He doesn't go thieving any more, if that's what you mean.' said Peter shortly, and a look of pain distorted the visitor's face.

'Don't use that word; it's low—'

'Let me take your hat.' Peter held out his hand, but the man drew his away.

'No, thanks. I promised a young friend of mine that I wouldn't lose anything while I was here. How long have you been at this place, Peter?'

'About fourteen years.'

Peter sat down, and the unwelcome guest followed his example, pulling his chair round so that he faced the other squarely.

'Ah!' he said thoughtfully. 'Living very comfortable, plenty to eat, go out and come in when you like. Good way of spending fourteen years. Better than having the key on you six o'clock in the evening. Princetown's the same old place—oh, I forgot you'd never been there.'

'I've driven through,' said Peter coolly, deliberately, and knew that he had touched a raw place before the lips of the man curled back in a snarl.

'Oh, you've driven through!' he sneered. 'I wish I'd known; I'd have hung my flags out! They ought to have decorated Princetown that day, Peter. You drove through!' he almost spat the words.

'Have a cigar?'

Emanuel Legge waved aside the invitation.

'No, thanks. I've got out of the habit—you do in fifteen years. You can get into some, too. Fifteen years is a long time out of a life.'

So Emanuel had come to make trouble, and had chosen his day well. Peter took up the challenge.

'The man you shot would have been glad of a few—he died two years after,' he said curtly, and all the pent fury of his sometime comrade flamed in his eyes.

'I hope he's in hell,' he hissed, 'the dirty flattie!' With an effort he mastered himself. 'You've had a real good time, Peter? Nice house, that wasn't bought for nothing. Servants and what not *and* motoring through the moor! You're clever!'

'I admit it.'

The little man's hands were trembling, his thin lips twitched convulsively.

'Leave your pal in the lurch and get away yourself, eh? Every man for himself—well, that's the law of nature, ain't it? And if you think he's going to squeak, send a line to the busies in charge of the case and drop a few hundred to 'em and there you are!' He paused, but no reply came. 'That's how it's done, ain't it, Peter?'

Kane shrugged his shoulders indifferently.

'I don't know—I'm never too old to learn.'

'But that's the way it's done?' insisted the man, showing his teeth again. 'That's the way you keep out of boob, ain't it?'

Peter looked at his tormentor, outwardly untroubled.

'I won't argue with you,' he said.

'You can't,' said the other. 'I'm logical.' He gazed around. 'This house cost a bit of money. What's half of two hundred thousand? I'm a bad counter!' Peter did not accept the opening. 'It's a hundred thousand, ain't it? I got sixty thousand—you owe me forty.'

'We got less than a hundred and twenty thousand pounds, if you're talking about the ship job. You got sixty thousand, which was more than your share. I paid it into your bank the day you went down.'

Legge smiled sceptically.

'The newspapers said a million dollars,' he murmured.

'You don't believe what you read in the newspapers, do you? Emanuel, you're getting childish.' Then suddenly: 'Are you trying to put the black on me?'

'Blackmail?' Emanuel was shocked. 'There's honour amongst—friends surely, Peter. I only want what's right and fair.'

Peter laughed softly, amusedly.

'Comic, is it? You can afford to laugh at a poor old fellow who's been in stir for fifteen years.'

The master of Manor Hill snapped round on him.

'If you'd been in hell for fifty I should still laugh.'

Emanuel was sorry for himself. That was ever a weakness of his; he said as much.

'You wouldn't, would you? You've got a daughter, haven't you? Young? Married today, wasn't she?'

'Yes.'

'Married money—a swell?'

'Yes. She married a good man.'

'He doesn't know what you are, Peter?' Emanuel asked the question carelessly, and his host fixed him with a steely glance.

'No. What's the idea? Do you think you'll get 40,000 that way?'

'I've got a boy. You've never sat in a damp cell with the mists of the moor hanging on the walls and thought and thought till your heart ached? You can get people through their children.' He paused. 'I could get you that way.'

In a second Peter Kane was towering above him, an ominous figure.

'The day my heart ached,' he said slowly, 'yours would not beat! You're an old man, and you're afraid of death! I can see it in your eyes. I am afraid of nothing. I'd kill you!'

Legge shrank farther into his chair.

'What's all this talk about killing? I only want what's fair. Fond of her, ain't you, Peter? I'll bet you are. They say that you're crazy about her. Is she pretty? I don't suppose she takes after you. Young Johnny Gray was sweet on her too. Peter, I'll get you through her—'

So far he got, and then a hand like a steel clamp fell on his neck, and he was jerked from his chair.

Peter spoke no word but, dragging the squirming figure behind him, as if it had neither weight nor resistance, he strode up the narrow pathway by the side of the house, across the strip of garden, through the gate and into the road. A jerk of his arm, and Emanuel Legge was floundering in the dusty road.

'Don't come back, Emanuel,' he said, and he did not stop to listen to the reply.

*   *   *   *   *

John Gray passed out of sight and hearing of the two men, being neither curious to know Legge's business nor anxious to renew a prison acquaintance.

Below the box hedge were three broad terraces, blazing with colour, blanketed with the subtle fragrance of flowers. Beyond that, a sloping meadow leading to a little river. Peter had bought his property wisely. A great cedar of Lebanon stood at the garden's edge; to the right, massed bushes were patched with purple and heliotrope blooms.

He sat down on a marble seat, glad of the solitude which he shared only with a noisy thrush and a lark invisible in the blue above him.

Marney was married. That was the beginning and the end of him. But happy. He recognized his very human vanity in the instant doubt that she could be happy with anybody but him.

How dear she was! And then a voice came to him, a shrill, hateful voice. It was Legge's—he was threatening the girl, and Johnny's blood went cold. Here was the vulnerable point in Peter Kane's armour; the crevice through which he could be hurt.

He started to his feet and went up the broad steps of the terrace three at a time. Tile garden was empty, save for Barney setting a table. Kane and his guest had disappeared. He was crossing the lawn when he saw something white shining in the gloom beyond the open French windows of a room. Something that took glorious shape. A girl in bridal white, and her hands were outstretched to him. So ethereal, so unearthly was her beauty, that at first he did not recognize her.

'Johnny!'

A soldierly figure was at her side, Peter Kane was behind her, but he had no eyes for any but Marney.

She came flying toward him, both his hands were clasped in hers.

'Oh, Johnny . . . Johnny!'

Then he looked up into the smiling face of the bridegroom, that fine, straight man to whom Peter had entrusted his beloved girl. For a second their eyes met, the debonair Major Floyd and his. Not by a flicker of eyelash did Johnny Gray betray himself.

The husband of the woman he loved was Jeff Legge, forger and traitor, the man sworn with his father to break the heart of Peter Kane.

4

Had he betrayed himself? he wondered. All his will power was exercised to prevent such a betrayal. Though a tornado of fury swept through and through him, though he saw the face of the man distorted and blurred, and brute instinct urged his limbs to savage action, he remained outwardly unmoved. It was impossible for the beholder to be sure whether he had paled, for the sun and wind of Dartmoor had tanned his lean face the colour of mahogany. For a while so terrific was the shock that he was incapable of speech or movement.

'Major Floyd' was Jeff Legge! This was Emanuel's revenge—to marry his crook son to the daughter of Peter Kane.

Jeff was watching him narrowly, but by no sign did Johnny betray his recognition, it was all over in a fraction of a second. He brought his eyes back to the girl, smiling mechanically. She seemed oblivious to her surroundings. That her new husband stood by, watching her with a gleam of amusement in his eyes, that Peter was frowning anxiously, and that even old Barney was staring open-mouthed, meant nothing.

'Johnny, poor Johnny! You aren't hating me, are you?'

John smiled and patted the hand that lay in his.

'Are you happy?' he asked in a low voice.

'Yes, oh yes, I'm happily married—that's what you mean, isn't it? I'm very happy . . . Johnny, was it terrible? I haven't stopped thinking about you, I haven't. Though I didn't write . . . after . . . Don't you think I was horrible? I know I was. Johnny, did it hurt you?'

He shook his head.

'There's one thing you mustn't be in Dartmoor—sorry for yourself. Are you happy?'

She did not meet his eyes.

'That is twice you've asked in a minute! Isn't it disloyal to say that I am? Don't you want to meet Jeffrey?'

'Why, of course, I want to meet Jeffrey.'

He crossed to the man, and Jeff Legge watched him.

'I want you to meet Captain Gray, a very old friend of mine,' she said with a catch in her voice.

Jeffrey Legge's cold hand gripped his.

'I'm glad to meet you, Captain Gray.'

Had he been recognized? Apparently not, for the face turned to him was puckered in an embarrassed smile.

'You've just come back from East Africa, haven't you? Get any shooting?'

'No, I didn't do any shooting,' said Johnny.

'Lots of lions, aren't there?' said Jeff.

The lips of the ex-convict twitched.

'In that part of the country where I was living, the lions are singularly tame,' he said dryly.

'Marney, darling, you're glad to see Gray on your wedding day, aren't you?—it was good of you to come, Gray. Mrs Floyd has often spoken about you.'

He put his arm round the girl, his eyes never leaving Johnny's face. He designed to hurt—to hurt them both. She stood rigidly, neither yielding nor resisting, tense, breathless, pale. She knew! The realization came to John Gray like a blow. She knew that this man was a liar and a villain. She knew the trick that had been played upon her father!

'Happy, darling?'

'Very—oh, very.'

There was a flutter in her voice. and now Johnny was hurt, and the fight to hold himself in became terrific. It was Peter who for the moment saved the situation.

'Johnny, I want you to know this boy. The best in the world. And I want you to think with me that he's the best husband in the world for Marney.'

Jeff Legge laughed softly.

'Mr Kane, you embarrass me terribly. I'm not nearly good enough for her—I'm just an awkward brute that doesn't deserve my good luck.'

He bent and kissed the white-faced girl. Johnny did not take his eyes from the man.

'Happy, eh? I'll bet you're happy, you rascal,' chuckled Kane.

Marney pulled herself away from the encircling arm.

'Daddy, I don't think this is altogether amusing Johnny.' Her voice shook. The man from Dartmoor knew that she was on the verge of tears.

'It takes a lot to bore me.' John Gray found his voice. 'Indeed, the happiness of young people—I feel very old just now—is a joy. You're a Canadian, Major Floyd?'

'Yes—a French Canadian, though you wouldn't guess that from my name. My people were *habitant* and went west in the last century—to Alberta and Saskatchewan, long before the railway came. You ought to go to Canada; you'd like it better than the place you've been to.'

'I'm sure I should.'

Peter had strolled away, the girl's arm in his.

'No lions in Canada, tame or wild,' said Jeff, regarding him from under his drooped eyelids.

Gray had lit a cigarette. He was steady now, steady of nerve and hand.

'I should feel lonely without lions,' he said coolly, and then: 'If you will forgive my impertinence, Major Floyd, you have married a very nice girl.'

'The very, very best.'

'I would go a long way to serve her—a long way. Even back to the lions.'

Their eyes met. In the bridegroom's was a challenge; in Johnny Gray's cold murder. Jeff Legge's eyes fell and he shivered.

'I suppose you like—hunting?' he said. 'Oh, no, you said you didn't. I wonder why a man of your—er—character went abroad?'

'I was sent,' said Johnny, and he emphasized every word. 'Somebody had a reason for sending me abroad—they wanted me out of the way. I should have gone, anyhow, but this man hurried the process.'

'Do you know who it was?'

The East African pretence had been tacitly dropped. Jeff might do so safely, for he would know that the cause of John Gray's retirement from the world was no secret.

'I don't know the man. He was a stranger to me. Very few people know him personally.

In his set—our set—not half a dozen people could identify him. Only one man in the police knows him—'

'Who's that?' interrupted the other quickly.

'A man named Reeder. I heard that in prison—of course you knew I'd come from Dartmoor?'

Jeff nodded with a smile.

'That's the fellow who is called The Great Unknown,' he said, striving to thin the contempt from his voice. 'I've heard about him in the club. He's a very stupid person of middle-age, who lives in Peckham. So he isn't as much unknown as *your* mystery man!'

'It's very likely,' said the other. 'Convicts invest their heroes and enemies with extraordinary gifts and qualities. I only know what I've been told. At Dartmoor they say Reeder knows everything. The Government gave him carte blanche to find the Big Printer—'

'And has he found him?' asked Jeff Legge innocently.

'He'll find him,' said Johnny. 'Sooner or later there will be a squeak.'

'May I be there to hear it,' said Jeff Legge, and showed his white teeth in a mirthless smile.

5

Johnny was alone in the lower garden sitting on a corner of the marble bench, out of sight but not out of hearing of the guests who were assembling on the lawn. He had to think, and think quickly. Marney knew! But Marney had not told, and Johnny guessed why.

When had Jeff Legge told her? On the way back from the church, perhaps. She would not let Peter know—Peter, who believed her future assured, her happiness beyond question. What had Jeff said? Not much, Johnny guessed. He had given her just a hint that the charming Major Floyd she had known was not the Major Floyd with whom she was to live.

Johnny was cool now—icy cold was a better description. He must be sure, absolutely sure, beyond any question of doubt. There might be some resemblance between Jeff Legge and this Major Floyd. He had only seen the crook once, and that at a distance.

He heard footsteps and looked round quickly. It was the maid he had seen quarreling with Barney.

'Mr Kane says, would you care to be in the group that is being photographed, Captain Gray?' she asked.

He did not immediately reply. His eyes were scanning her with a new interest.

'Tell him I'd rather not, and come back.'

'Come back, sir?' she repeated in astonishment.

'Yes, I want to talk to you,' said Johnny with a smile. 'Have mercy on a disgruntled guest, who can find nobody to entertain him.'

She stood, hesitating. He could see the indecision in her face.

'I don't know if Mr Kane would like that,' she said, and a smile trembled at the corner of her mouth. 'Very well, I'll come back.'

It was not till ten minutes later, when he judged the photograph had been taken and the guests had gone again to the house, that she appeared, demure but curious.

'Sit down,' said Johnny. He threw away his cigarette and moved to the end of the stone bench.

'How long have you been here?' he asked.

'With Mr Kane? About six months,' she said.

'Pretty good job?' he asked carelessly.

'Oh, yes, sir, very.'

'What's your name?'

'My name's Lila. Why do you ask?'

'I think you and I ought to get better acquainted, Lila,' he said, and took her unresisting hand.

Secretly she was amused; on the surface she showed some sign of being shocked.

'I didn't know you were that type of flirting man, Mr Gray—you're a Captain, though, aren't you?'

' "Captain" is a purely honorary title, Lila,' said Johnny. 'I suppose you'll miss your lady?'

'Yes, I shall miss her,' said Lila.

'A nice girl, eh?' bantered Johnny.

'And a very nice husband,' she said tartly.

'Do you think so?'

'Yes, I suppose he is a nice fellow. I don't know much about him.'

'Good-looking?' suggested Johnny.

The woman shrugged her shoulders.

'I suppose he is.'

'And very much in love with Miss Kane. That fellow adores her,' said Johnny. 'In fact, I don't know that I've ever seen a man so much in love with a woman.'

She suppressed a sigh.

'Oh, yes, I suppose he is,' she said impatiently. 'Do you want me any more, Captain Gray, because I've a lot of work to do?'

'Don't run away,' said Johnny in his most gentle voice. 'Weddings always make me romantic.' He took up the thread where it was interrupted. 'I don't expect the Major will have eyes for any other girl for years,' he said. 'He's head over heels in love, and why shouldn't he be? I suppose,' he said reminiscently, avoiding her eyes, 'he's the sort of man who would have had many love affairs in the past.' He shrugged his shoulders. 'With the kind of girls that one picks up and puts down at pleasure.'

Now a flush, deep and even, had come to her face, and her eyes held a peculiar brightness.

'I don't know anything about Major Floyd,' she said shortly, and was rising, but his hand fell on her arm.

'Don't run away, Lila.'

'I'm not going to stay,' she said with sudden vehemence. 'I don't want to discuss Major Floyd or anybody else. If you want me to talk to you—'

'I want to talk to you about the honeymoon. Can't you picture them, say, on Lake Como in a bower of roses? Can't you imagine him forgetting all that's past, all the old follies, all the old girls—?'

She wrenched her arm from his grip and stood up, and her face was deadly white.

'What are you getting at, Gray?' she asked, all the deference, all the demureness gone from her voice.

'I'm getting at you, Miss Lila Sain,' he said, 'and if you attempt to get away from me, I'll throttle you!'

She stared at him, her breath coming quickly.

'You're supposed to be a gentleman, too,' she said.

'I'm supposed to be Johnny Gray from Dartmoor. Sit down. What's the graft, Lila?'

'I don't understand what you're talking about.'

'What's the graft?' asked Johnny with deadly calm. 'Jeff Legge put you here to nose the house for him, and keep him wise about what was going on.'

'I don't know Jeff Legge,' she faltered.

'You're a liar,' said Johnny ungently. 'I know you, Lila. You run with Legge and you're a cheap squeak. I've seen you a dozen times. Who is Major Floyd?'

'Go and ask him,' she said defiantly.

'Who's Major Floyd?'

The grip on her arm tightened.

'You know,' she said sullenly. 'It's Jeff Legge.'

'Now listen, Lila. Come here.' He had released her, and now he crooked his finger. 'Go and blow to Jeff, and I'll squeak on you both—you understand that? I'll put Jeff just where I want him to be—there's a vacant cell at Dartmoor, anyway. That worries you, doesn't it? You're in love with Jeff?'

She did not reply.

'I'll put him where I want him to be,' he repeated slowly and deliberately, 'unless you do as I tell you.'

'You're going to put the black on him?' she said, her lips curling.

'Black doesn't mean anything in my young life,' said Johnny. 'But I tell you this, that I'll find Reeder and squeak a whole pageful unless I have my way.'

'What do you want?' she asked.

'I want to know where they're going, and where they're staying. I want to know their plans for the future. Are you married to him, by any chance?'

A glance at her face gave him the answer.

'You're not? Well, you may be yet, Lila. Aren't you tired of doing his dirty work?'

'Perhaps I am and perhaps I'm not,' she replied defiantly. 'You can't do anything to him now, anyway, Johnny Gray. He's got your girl, and if you squeaked like a garden of birds you couldn't undo what that old God-man did this morning! Jeff's too clever for you. He'll get you, Gray—'

'If he knows,' said Johnny quietly. 'But if he knows, Reeder knows too. Do you get that?'

'What are you going to do?' she asked after a silence.

'I'm having one of my little jokes,' said Johnny between his teeth. 'A real good joke! It's starting now. I can't tell Peter, because he'd kill your young man, and I have a particular objection to Peter going to the drop. And *you* can't tell Jeff, because there'd be a case for a jury, and when Jeff came out you'd be an old woman. That's not a good prospect, is it? Now tell me all you've got to tell, and speak slowly, because I don't write shorthand.'

He whipped a small notebook from his pocket, and as she spoke, reluctantly, sulkily, yet fearfully, he wrote rapidly. When he had finished:

'You can go now, my gentle child,' he said, and she stood up, her eyes blazing with rage.

'If you squeak, Johnny Gray, I'll kill you. I never was keen on this marriage business— naturally. I knew old Legge wanted him to marry Peter's daughter, because Legge wanted to get one back on him. But Jeff's been good to me; and the day the busies come for Legge I'll come for you, and I'll shoot you stone dead, Johnny, as God's my judge!'

'Beat it!' said Johnny tersely.

He waited till she was gone through one of the openings in the box hedge, then passed along to the other and stopped. Peter Kane was standing in the open, shielded from view by the thin box bush, and Peter's face was inscrutable.

6

'Hallo Johnny! Running for the compensation stakes?'

Johnny laughed.

'You mean the maid? She is rather pretty, isn't she?'

'Very,' said the other.

Had he heard? That was a question and a fear in Johnny's mind. The marble bench was less than six feet from the bush where Peter Kane stood. If he had been there any time—

'Been waiting long for me, Peter?' he asked.

'No; I just saw you take a farewell of Lila—very nice girl, that, Johnny—an extraordinary nice girl. I don't know when I've met a nicer. What did you find to talk about?'

'The weather, dicky-birds and the course of true love,' said Johnny, as Kane took his arm and led him across the lawn.

'Everything variable and flighty, eh?' said Peter with a smile. 'Come and eat, Johnny. These people are going away soon. Marney is changing now. What do you think of my new son-in-law?'

His old jovial manner held. When they came into the big reception-room and Peter Kane's arm went round his son-in-law's shoulder, Johnny breathed a sigh of relief. Thank God he did not know! He had sweated in his fear of what might follow a discovery.

Thirty-six people sat down in the dining-room and, contrary to convention, Marney, who sat at the head of the table, was wearing her going-away dress. John shot a quick glance at her as he came in, but she averted her eyes. Her father sat on her left; next to him was the clergyman who had performed the ceremony. Next came a girl friend, and then a man, by whose side Johnny sat.

He recognized the leathery features instantly.

'Been away, Johnny?' Detective-Superintendent Craig asked the question in a voice so carefully pitched that it did not reach any farther than the man to whom he spoke.

The chatter and buzz of conversation, the little ripples of laughter that ran up and down the table, did something to make the privacy of their talk assured.

As Old Barney bent over to serve a dish, Craig gave a side-long glance at his companion.

'Peter's got old Barney still—keeping honest, Barney?'

'I'm naturally that way,' said Barney *sotto voce*. 'It's not meeting policemen that keeps me straight.'

The hard features of the detective relaxed.

'There are lots of other people who could say that, Barney,' he said, and when the man had passed to the next guest: 'He's all right. Barney never was a bad man. I think he only did one stretch—he wouldn't have done that if he'd had Peter's imagination, Johnny.'

'Peter's imagination?'

'I'm not referring to his present imagination, but the gift he had fourteen–fifteen years ago. Peter was the cleverest of them all. The brilliant way his attack was planned, the masterly line of retreat, the wonderful alibis, so beautifully dove-tailed into one another that, if we had pinched him, he'd not only have been discharged, but he would have got something from the poor box! It used to be the life ambition of every young officer to catch him, to find some error of judgment, some flaw in his plan. But it was police-proof and fool-proof.'

'He'd blush to hear you,' said the other dryly.

'But it's true, Johnny! The clever letters he used to write, all to fool us. He did a lot of work with letters—getting people together, luring 'em to the place he wanted 'em and where their presence served him best. I remember how he got my chief to be at Charing Cross under the clock at ten past nine, and showed up himself and made him prove his alibi!' He laughed gently.

'I suppose,' said Gray, 'people would think it remarkable that you and he are such good friends?'

'They wouldn't say it was remarkable; they'd say it was damned suspicious!' growled the other. 'Having a drink?' he said suddenly, and pulled a wine bottle across the table.

'No, thanks—I seldom drink. We have to keep a very clear head in our business. We can't afford to dream.'

'We can't afford anything else,' said Craig. 'Why our business, Johnny? You're out of that?'

Johnny saw the girl look toward him. It was only a glance—but in that brief flash he saw all that he feared to see—the terror, the bewilderment, the helplessness. He set his teeth and turned abruptly to the detective.

'How is *your* business?' he asked.

'Quiet.'

'I'm sorry to hear that,' said John Gray with mock concern. 'But trade's bad everywhere, isn't it?'

'What sort of time did you have—in the country?' asked Craig, and his companion grinned.

'Wonderful! My bedroom wanted papering, but the service was quite good.'

Craig sighed.

'Ah well, we live and learn,' he said heavily. 'I was sorry about it, Johnny, very sorry. It's a misfortune, but there's no use grieving about it. You were one of the unlucky ones. If all the people who deserved prison were *in* prison—why, there wouldn't be any housing problems. I hear there were quite a lot of stars there,' Craig went on. 'Harry Becker, and young Lew Storing—why, old Legge must have been there in your time. And another fellow—now, what's his name? The slush man—ah, Carper, that's it. Ever see him?'

'Yes; he and I once pulled the same cart.'

'Ah!' said Craig encouragingly. 'I'll bet you heard a few things. He'd talk to you.'

'He did.'

Craig bent towards him, lowering his voice.

'Suppose I told you a certain party coppered you, and suppose I said I've reason to believe that your copper is the man I want. Now couldn't we exchange confidences?' he asked.

'Yes, we might squeak together, and it would sound like modern music. But we won't. Honestly, Craig, I can't tell you about the Big Printer. Reeder ought to know all about him!'

'Reeder!' said the other scornfully. 'An amateur! All this nonsense about secret service men gets my goat! If they'd left the matter to the police, we'd have had the Big Printer—ever seen him, Johnny?'

'No,' said Johnny untruthfully.

'Reeder, eh?' said the thoughtful detective. 'They used to have an office man named Golden once, an old fellow that thought he could catch slushers by sitting in an office and thinking hard. Reeder isn't much better by all accounts. I saw him once, a soft fellow on the edge of senile decay!'

Craig sighed deeply, looked up and down the happy board with a bleak and grudging glance, and then:

'Just for a little heart-to-heart talk, I know where you could get an easy monkey, Johnny,' he said softly.

Johnny did not smile.

'It would have to be a monkey on a stick, Craig—'

'We're both men of the world,' interrupted the detective imploringly.

'Yes,' said Johnny Gray, 'but not the same world, Craig.'

One last despairing effort the detective made, though he knew that, in angling for a squeak, he might as well have tried Peter himself.

'The Bank of England will pay a thousand pounds for the information I want.'

'And who can afford it better?' said Johnny heartily. 'Now, shut up, Craig; somebody's going to make a speech.'

It was a mild and beatific oration delivered by the officiating clergymen. When it came to its machine-made peroration Craig, who was intensely interested in the sonorous platitudes, looked round and saw that his companion had gone from his side—later he saw him leaning over Peter's chair, and Peter was nodding vigorously. Then Johnny passed through the door.

Somebody else was watching him. The bridegroom, twiddling the stem of his wine-glass between his fingers, saw him go, and was more than ordinarily interested. He was sufficiently curious, at any rate, to catch the eye of the pretty maid and look significantly at the door. At that signal Lila followed Johnny Gray. He was not in the hall, and she went out into the road, but here saw no sign of the man she sought. There was, however, somebody else and she obeyed his call to her.

'Tell Jeff I want him before he starts on that honeymoon of his,' snarled Emanuel Legge, glaring at her through his glasses. 'He's been talking to that girl—I saw her face. What did he say?'

'How do I know?' she snapped back. 'You and your Jeff! I wish to God I'd never come into this job. What's the graft anyway? That flash crook knows all about it, Legge.'

'Wh—Johnny Gray? Is he here? He did come, then?'

She nodded.

'What do you mean—"he knows"?'

'He knows Jeff—recognized him first pop,' said the girl inelegantly, and Emanuel Legge whistled.

'Does Jeff know that he's been recognized?'

The harsh features of Emanuel Legge were drawn and tense.

'What's the use of asking me? I haven't had a word with him. He's so taken up with this girl—'

'Forget it,' said Legge with a gesture. 'Tell me what this Johnny Gray says.'

'I'll tell you one thing that amused me,' said the girl grimly. 'He said he'd throttle me if I squeaked! And he's got a fascinating pair of hands. I shouldn't like to play rough with that fellow—there's no use in tut-tutting me, Emanuel. I've told you all he said. He knows Jeff; he must have seen him before he went over the Alps.'

The old man was thinking, his brow furrowed, his lips pursed.

'It's pretty bad if he guesses, because he's sweet on the girl, and there's going to be trouble. Get Jeff out quick!'

'If you stay here, Peter will see you,' she warned him. 'Go down the lane and turn into the private path. I'll send Jeff to you in the lower garden.'

Nodding, he hurried away. It took her some time to find an opportunity but presently she signalled the man with her eyes, and he followed her to the lawn.

'The old man's waiting down in the lower garden,' she said in a low voice. 'Hurry.'

'What's wrong?' he asked quickly, sensing trouble.

'He'll tell you.'

With a glance round Jeff hurried on to the terrace just as his father reached the rendezvous.

'Jeff, Gray knows.'

The man drew a quick breath.

'Me?' he said incredulously. 'He didn't so much as bat a lid when I met him.'

Emanuel nodded.

'That fellow's hell cool—the most dangerous crook in the world. I was in the Awful

Place with him, and I know his reputation. There's nothing he's afraid of. If he tells Peter . . . shoot first! Peter won't be carrying a gun, but he's sure to have one within travelling distance—and Peter's a quick mover. I'll cover you; I've got two boys handy that mind me, and Johnny . . . Well, he'll get what's coming.'

'What am I to do?'

Jeff Legge was biting his nails thoughtfully.

'Get the girl away—you're due to leave by car, ain't you? Get her to the Charlton Hotel. You're supposed to stay there a week—make it a day. Clear to Switzerland tomorrow and stop her writing. I'll fix Peter. He'll pay.'

'For what?'

'To get his girl back; forty thousand—maybe more.'

Jeff Legge whistled.

'I didn't see that side of the graft before. It's a new variety of black.'

'It's what I choose to call it!' hissed his father. 'You're in fifty-fifty. You can have the lot so far as I care. *You make that girl eat dirt*, d'ye hear? Put her right down to earth, Jeff . . . Peter will pay.'

'I promised Lila . . .' began the other, hesitant.

'Promise your Aunt Rebecca Jane!' Emanuel almost screamed. 'Lila! That trash, and you the big man, too—what are ye running? A girls' refuge society? Get!'

'What about Gray?'

'I'll fix Gray!'

7

The old man made his way back to the road and passed quickly along until he came to the main highway. Two men were seated in the shade of a bush, eating bread and cheese. They came quickly enough when he whistled them, tall, broad-shouldered men whose heavy jowls had not felt a razor for days.

'Either of you boys know Johnny Gray?' he asked.

'I was on the moor with him,' said one gruffly, 'if he's the fellow that went down for ringing in horses?'

Emanuel nodded.

'He's in the house, and it's likely he'll walk to the station, and likely enough take the short cut across the fields. That'll be easy for you. He's got to be coshed—you understand? Get him good, even if you have to do it in the open. If there's anybody with him, get him in London. But get him.'

Emanuel came back to his observation post as the first of the cars went into the drive. Jeff was moving quickly—and there was need.

Presently the car came out. Emanuel caught a glimpse of Jeff and the frightened face of the girl, and rubbed his hands in an ecstasy of satisfaction. Peter was standing in the middle of the road, watching the car. If he knew! The smile vanished from the old man's face. Peter did not know; he had not been told. Why? Johnny would not let her go, knowing. Perhaps Lila was lying. You can never trust women of that kind; they love sensation. Johnny . . . dangerous. The two words left one impression. And there was Johnny, one hand resting on a walking stick, the other waving at the car as it came into brief view on the Shoreham road, as unconcerned as though he were the least interested.

A second car went in and came out. Some guests were leaving. Now, if Johnny had sense, he would be driven to London with a party. But Johnny hadn't sense. He was just a poor sucker, like all cheap crooks are. He came out alone, crossed the road and went down the narrow passage that led to the field path.

Emanuel looked backward. His bulldogs had seen and were moving parallel to the unconscious Gray.

From the road two paths led to the field, forming a Y where they met. Johnny had passed the fork when he heard the footsteps behind him. Glancing back, he saw a familiar face and did some shrewd guessing. He could run and easily out-distance these clumsy men. He preferred to face them, and turned, holding his walking stick in both hands.

' 'Lo, Gray,' said the bigger of the men. 'Wher'n thunder are you going in such a hurry? I want to talk with you, you dirty squeaker! You're the fellow that told the deputy I was getting tobacco in through a screw!'

It was a crude invention, but good enough to justify the rough house that was booked to follow. They carried sticks in their hands, pliable canes, shotted at the end.

The blow missed Johnny as he stepped back, and then something long and bright glittered in the afternoon sun. The scabbard of the sword cane he held defensively before him, the sword, thin and deadly, was pointed to the nearer of his enemies. They stopped, Saxon-like, appalled by the sight of steel.

'Bad boy!' said Johnny reproachfully.

The razor-pointed rapier flickered from face to face, and the men stumbled back, getting into one another's way. One of the men felt something wet on his cheek, and put up his hand. When it came down it was wet and red.

'Beast, you have my brand!' said Johnny with deadly pleasantry. 'Come when I call you.'

He clicked the sword back in its wooden sheath and strode away. His indifference, his immense superiority, was almost as tremendously impressive as his cold toleration.

'He's ice, that fellow,' said the man with the cut cheek. A sob of rage softened the rasp of his voice. 'By God I'll kill him for that!'

But he made no attempt to follow, and his companion was glad.

John Gray increased his pace, and after a while emerged into the outskirts of the town. Here he found a taxi and reached the station in time to see the train pull out. He had made a mistake; the time-table had been changed that day, but in half an hour there was a fast train from Brighton that stopped only at Horsham.

He crossed the station yard to an hotel and was in the telephone booth for a quarter of an hour before he emerged, his collar limp, perspiration streaming down his face.

There was no sign of a familiar face when he came back to the platform. He expected to see Emanuel eventually, and here he was not disappointed, for Emanuel arrived a few minutes before the Brighton train came in.

Officially, it was their first meeting since they had been members of the same farm gang at Dartmoor, and Legge's expression of surprise was therefore appropriate.

'Why, if it isn't Gray! Well, fancy meeting you, old man! Well, this is a surprise! When did you come out?'

'Cease your friendly badinage,' said Johnny shortly. 'If we can get an empty compartment, I've got a few words to say to you, Emanuel.'

'Been down to the wedding?' asked the old man slyly. 'Nice girl, eh? Done well for herself? They tell me he's a Canadian millionaire. Ain't that Peter's luck! That fellow would fall off rock and drop in feathers, he's that lucky.'

Johnny made no answer. When the train stopped and he found himself opposite a first-class carriage, he opened the door and Emanuel hopped in.

'If you're short of money—' began Legge.

'I'm not,' said the other curtly. 'I'm short of nothing except bad company. Now listen, Emanuel'—the train was puffing slowly from the station when he spoke again—'I'm going to give you a chance.'

The wide-eyed astonishment of Emanuel Legge was very convincing, but Johnny was not open to conviction at the moment.

'I don't get you, Johnny,' he said. 'What's all this talk about giving me a chance? Have you been drinking?'

Johnny had seated himself opposite the man, and now he leant forward and placed his hand on the other's knee.

'Emanuel,' he said gently, 'call off that boy, and there'll be no squeak. Take that wounded fawn look from your face, because I haven't any time for fooling. You call off Jeff and send the girl back home tonight, or I squeak. Do you understand that?'

'I understand your words, Johnny Gray, but what they mean is a mystery to me.' Emanuel Legge shook his head. 'What boy are you talking about? I've only got one boy, and he's at college—'

'You're a paltry old liar. I'm talking about Jeff Legge, who married Peter's daughter today. I've tumbled to your scheme, Emanuel. You're getting even with Peter. Well, get even with him, but try some other way.'

'She's married him of her own free will,' began the man. 'There's no law against that, is there, Johnny? Fell in love with him right on the spot! That's what I like to see, Johnny—young people in love.'

If he hoped to rattle his companion he was disappointed.

'Now he can unmarry of his own free will,' said Johnny calmly. 'Listen to me, Emanuel Legge. When you arrive in London, you'll go straight away to the Charlton Hotel and talk very plainly to your son. He, being a sensible man, will carry out your instructions—'

'*Your* instructions,' corrected Emanuel, his mouth twisted in a permanent smile. 'And what happens if I don't, Johnny?'

'I squeak,' said Johnny, and the smile broadened.

'They're married, old man. You can't divorce 'em. You can turn a brown horse into a black 'un, but you can't turn Mrs Jeffrey Legge into Miss Marney Kane, clever as you are.'

Johnny leant forward.

'I can turn Mr Jeffrey Legge into Dartmoor Jail,' he said unpleasantly, 'and that's what I propose to do.'

'On what charge?' Emanuel raised his eyebrows. 'Give us a little rehearsal of this squeal of yours, Gray.'

'He's the Big Printer,' said Johnny, and the smile slowly dissolved. 'The Government has spent thousands to catch him; they've employed the best secret service men in the world to pull him down, and I can give them just the information they want. I know where his stuff is planted. I know where it's printed; I know at least four of his agents. You think Jeff's secret is his own and yours, but you're mistaken, Emanuel. Craig knows he's the Big Printer; he told me so at lunch. All he wants is evidence, and that evidence I can give him. Old Reeder knows—you think he's a fool, but he knows. I could give him a squeak that would make him the cleverest lad in the world.'

Emanuel Legge licked his dry lips.

'Going in for the con. business, Johnny?' he asked banteringly. There was no amusement in his voice. 'What a confidence man you'd make! You look like a gentleman, and talk like one. Why, they'd fall for you and never think twice! But that confidence stuff doesn't mean anything to me, Johnny, I'm too old and too wide to be bluffed—'

'There's no bluff here,' interrupted Johnny. 'I've got your boy like that!' He held out his hand and slowly clenched it.

For fully five minutes Emanuel Legge sat huddled in a corner of the compartment, staring out upon the flying scenery.

'You've got him like that, have you, Johnny boy?' he said gently. 'Well, there's no use deceiving you, I can see. Slush is funny stuff—they call it phoney in America. Did you know that? I guess you would, because you're well educated. But it's good slush, Johnny. Look at this. Here's a note. Is it good or bad?'

His fingers had gone into his waistcoat pocket and he withdrew a folded five-pound note. He opened it out and caressed the paper with finger and thumb. The eyes behind the powerful glasses gleamed; the thin-lined face softened with pride.

'Is it good or bad, Johnny?'

Though the day was bright and hot, and not a cloud was in the sky, the lights in the carriage lit up suddenly. In the powerful light of day they seemed pale ghosts of flame, queerly dim. As the sunshine fell upon them their shadows were cast on the white cornice of the carriage.

'There's a tunnel coming,' said Emanuel. 'It'll give you a chance of seeing them at their best—feel 'em, Johnny! The real paper; bankers have fallen for 'em . . .'

With a roar the train plunged into the blackness of the tunnel. Emanuel stood with his back to the carriage door, the note held taut between his hands.

'There's only one flaw—the watermark. I'm giving away secrets, eh? Look!'

He stretched his arms up until he held the note against one of the bracket lamps. To see, John Gray had to come behind him and peer over his shoulder. The thunder of the train in the narrow tunnel was almost deafening.

'Look at the "F",' shouted Emanuel. 'See . . . that "F" in "Five"—it's printed too shallow . . .'

As Johnny bent forward the old man thrust at him with his shoulder, and behind that lurch of his was all the weight and strength of his body. Taken by surprise, John Gray was thrown from his balance. He staggered back against the carriage door, felt it give and tried to recover his equilibrium. But the thrust was too well timed. The door flew open, and he dropped into the black void, clutching as he did so the window ledge. For a second he swayed with the in and out swinging of the door. Then Legge's clenched fist hammered down on his fingers, and he dropped. . . .

8

He struck a layer of thick sand and turned a complete somersault. The wall of the tunnel caught and almost dislocated his arm, and he rebounded toward the whirling wheels. One wheel flicked him back against the wall, and he slid, his arms covering his face, the flint ballast ripping his sleeves to ribbons . . .

He was alive. The train had passed. He saw the red tail-lights closing to one another. Gingerly he moved first one leg and then the other; then he rolled over towards the wall and lay on his back without further movement. His heart was pounding furiously; he felt a soreness working through the numb overlay of shock. Shock . . . shock sometimes killed men. His heart was going faster yet; he experienced a horrible nausea, and he found himself trembling violently.

The proper thing to do was to inject hydrocortisone into his veins—his thoughts were curiously well ordered—Doctors did that; he remembered the doctor telling him at Dartmoor.

But there was no hydrocortisone to be had . . . Ten minutes later he lifted his body on his elbow and struggled to a sitting position. His head swam, but it did not ache; his arms . . . he felt them carefully. They were very sore; but no bones were broken.

A roadman at the exit of the tunnel nearly dropped with amazement as a grimy young man whose clothes were in rags emerged, limping.

'I fell out,' said Johnny. 'Can you tell me if there is anywhere I can hire a car?'

The roadman was going off duty and was willing to act as guide. Johnny hobbled up the steep slopes of the railway cutting, and with the assistance of the interested workman, traversed a wide field to the road. And then came a blessed sportsman on his way back from Gatwick Races, and he was alone in his car.

At first he looked suspiciously at the bruised and ragged figure that had waved him down. In the end he flung open the door by his side.

'Step in,' he said.

To the railway worker Johnny had a few words to say.

'Here's five,' he said. 'Two for your help and three to stop your talking. I don't want this business to be reported, you understand? The truth is, I'd been looking on the wine when it was red and gaveth its colour aright.'

Johnny had evidently touched a sympathetic chord.

'You mean you was boozed?' said the man. 'You can trust me.'

The angel who drove him to London was not a talkative angel. Beyond expressing the wish that something drastic had happened to *him* before he went racing, and the advancement of his view that all racing was crooked and all jockeys thieves, he contributed little to the entertainment of his passenger, and the passenger was glad.

At the first cab-rank they struck—it was in Sutton—Johnny insisted on getting out.

'I'll take you home if you like,' said his gloomy benefactor.

Gently the other declined.

'My name is Lawford,' said the driver in a sudden outburst of confidence. 'I've got an idea I know your face. Haven't I seen you on the track?'

'Not for some time,' said Johnny.

'Rather like a fellow I once met . . . well, introduced to . . . fellow named Gay or Gray . . . regular villain. He got time.'

'Thanks,' said Johnny, 'that was me,' and the hitherto reticent Mr Lawford became almost conversational in his apologies.

The young man finished the journey in a taxi and reached Queen's Gate late in the afternoon.

Parker, who opened the door to him, asked no questions.

'I have laid out another suit for you, sir,' he returned to the study to say—the only oblique reference he made to his employer's disorder.

As he lay in a hot bath, soaking the stiffness out of his limbs, Johnny examined his injuries. They were more or less superficial, but he had had a terribly narrow escape from death, and he was not wholly recovered from the violence of it. Emanuel had intended his destruction. The attempt did not surprise him. Men of Legge's type worked that way. He met them in Dartmoor. They would go to a killing without fire of rage or frenzy of despair. Once he had seen a convict select with deliberation and care a large jagged stone and drop it on the head of a man working in the quarry below. Fortunately, a warder had seen the act, and his shout saved the intended victim from mutilation. The assailant had only one excuse. The man he had attacked had slighted him in some way.

In the hearts of these men lived a cold beast. Johnny often pictured it, an obscene shape with pale, lidless eyes and a straight slit of a mouth. He had seen the beast staring at him from a hundred distorted faces, had heard its voice, had seen its hatefulness expressed in actions that he shivered to recall. Something of the beast had saturated into his own soul.

When he came from his bath, the masseur whom Parker had summoned was waiting, and for half an hour he groaned under the kneading hands.

The evening newspaper that Parker procured contained no news of the 'accident'— Emanuel was hardly likely to report the matter, even for his own protection. There were explanations he could offer—Johnny thought of several.

Free from the hands of the masseur, he rested in his dressing-gown.

'Has anybody called?' he asked.

'A Mr Reeder, sir.'

Johnny frowned.

'Mr Reeder?' he repeated. 'What did he want?'

'I don't know, sir. He merely asked for you. A middle-aged man, with rather a sad face,' said Parker. 'I told him you were not at home, and that I would take any message for you, but he gave none.'

His employer made no reply. For some reason, the call of the mysterious Mr Reeder worried him more than the memory of the tragic happening of that afternoon, more, for the moment, than the marriage of Marney Kane.

9

Marney made her journey to London that afternoon in almost complete silence. She sat in a corner of the car and felt herself separated from the man she had married by a distance which was becoming immeasurable. Once or twice she stole a timid glance at him, but he was so preoccupied with his thoughts that he did not even notice. They were not pleasant thoughts, to judge by his unchanging scowl. All the way up he nibbled at his nails; a wrinkle between his eyes.

It was not until the big car was bowling across one of the river bridges that the strain was relieved, and he turned his head, regarding her coldly.

'We're going abroad tomorrow,' he said, and her heart sank.

'I thought you were staying in London for a week, Jeff,' she asked, trouble in her eyes. 'I told father—'

'Does it matter?' he said roughly, and then she found courage to ask him a question that had been in her mind during that dreary ride.

'Jeff, what did you mean this morning, on the way back from the church . . .? You frightened me.'

Jeff Legge chuckled softly.

'I frightened you, did I?' he sneered. 'Well, if that's all that's going to happen to you, you're a lucky girl!'

'But you're so changed . . .' she was bewildered. 'I—I didn't want to marry you . . . I thought you wanted . . . and father was so very anxious. . . .'

'Your father was very anxious that you should marry a man in good society with plenty of money,' he said, emphasizing every word. 'Well, you've married him, haven't you? When I told you this morning that I'd got your father like that'—he put out his thumb suggestively—'I meant it. I suppose you know your father's a crook?'

The beautiful face flushed and went pale again.

'How dare you say that?' she asked, her voice trembling with anger. 'You know it isn't true. You know!'

Jeffrey Legge closed his eyes wearily.

'There's a whole lot of revelations coming to you, my dear,' he said, 'but I guess we'd better wait till we reach the hotel.'

Silence followed, until the car drew up before the awning of the Charlton, and then Jeff became his smiling, courteous self, and so remained until the door of their sitting-room closed upon them.

'Now, you've got to know something, and you can't know it too soon,' he said. 'My name isn't Floyd at all. I'm Jeffrey Legge. My father was a convict until six months ago. He was put in prison by Peter Kane.'

She listened, open-mouthed, stricken dumb with amazement and fear.

'Peter Kane is a bank robber—or he was till fifteen years ago, when he did a job with my father, got away with a million dollars, and squeaked on his pal.'

'Squeaked?' she said, bewildered.

'Your father betrayed him,' said Jeffrey patiently. 'I'm surprised that Peter hasn't made you acquainted with the technical terms of the business. He squeaked on his pal, and my father went down for twenty years.'

'It's not true,' she said indignantly. 'You're inventing this story. My father was a broker. He never did a dishonest thing in his life. And if he had, he would never have betrayed his friend!'

The answer seemed to amuse Legge.

'Broker, was he? I suppose that means he's a man who's broken into strong-rooms? That's the best joke I've heard for a long time! Your father's crook! Johnny knows he's crook. Craig knows he's crook. Why in hell do you think a broker should be a pal of a busy. And take that look off your face—a busy is a detective. Peter has certainly neglected your education!'

'Johnny knows?' she faltered. 'Johnny knows father is—I don't believe it! All you've told me is lies. If it were so, why should you want to marry me?'

Suddenly she realized the truth and stood, frozen with horror, staring back at the smiling man.

'You've guessed, eh? We've been waiting to get under Peter's skin for years. And I guess we've got there. And now, if you like, you can tell him. There's a telephone; call him up. Tell him I'm Jeff Legge, and that all the wonderful dreams he has had of seeing you happy and comfortable are gone! Phone him! Tell him you never wanted to marry me, and it was only to make him happy that you did—you've got to break his heart, anyway. You might as well start now.'

'He'd kill you,' she breathed.

'Maybe he would. And that'd be a fine idea too. We'd have Peter on the trap. It would be worth dying for. But I guess he wouldn't kill me. At the sight of a gun in his hands, I'd shoot him like a dog. But don't let that stop you telling him, Marney darling.'

'You planned it all . . . this was your revenge?'

He nodded.

'But Johnny . . . Johnny doesn't know.'

She saw the change in the man's face, that suave assurance of his vanish.

'He does know.' She pointed an accusing finger at him. 'He knows!'

'He knows, but he let you go, honey,' said Jeff. 'He's one of us, and we never squeak. One of us!' he repeated the words mechanically.

She sat down and covered her face with her hands, and Jeffrey, watching her, thought at first that she was crying. When she raised her face, her eyes were dry. And, more extraordinary to him, the fear that he had seen was no longer there.

'Johnny will kill you,' she said simply. 'He wouldn't let me go . . . like that . . . if he knew. It isn't reasonable to suppose that he would, is it?'

It was Jeff Legge's turn to be uncomfortable. Not at the menace of Johnny's revenge, but at her utter calmness. She might have been discussing the matter impartially with a third person. For a moment he lost his grip of the situation. All that she said was so obviously, so patently logical, and instinctively he looked round as though he expected to find Johnny Gray at his elbow. The absurdity of the situation struck him, and he chuckled nervously.

'Johnny!' he sneered. 'What do you expect Johnny to do, eh? He's just out of bird— that's jail; it's sometimes called boob—I see there's a whole lot of stuff you've got to learn before you get right into the family ways.'

He lounged toward her and dropped his hands on her shoulders.

'Now, old girl,' he said, 'there are two things you can do. You can call up Peter and put him wise, or you can make the best of a bad job.'

'I'll call father,' she said, springing up. Before she could reach the telephone, his arm was round her, and he had swung her back.

'You'll call nothing,' he said. 'There's no alternative, my little girl. You're Mrs Legge, and I lowered myself to marry the daughter of such a squealing old dog! Marney, give me a kiss. You've not been very free with your tokens of affection, and I haven't pressed you, for fear of scaring you off. Always the considerate gentleman—that's Jeff Legge.' Suddenly she was in his arms, struggling desperately. He tried to reach her lips, but she buried her face in his coat until, with a savage jerk that almost dislocated her shoulder, he had flung her at arm's distance. She looked up at the inflamed face and shuddered.

'I've got you, Marney.' His voice was hoarse with triumph. 'I've got you properly . . . legally. You're my wife! You realize that? No man can come between you and me.'

He pulled her towards him, caught her pale face between his hands, and turned it up to his. With all the strength of utter horror and loathing, she tore herself free, fled to the door. flung it open, and stood back, wide-eyed with amazement.

In the doorway stood a tall, broad woman, with vividly red hair and a broad, good-humoured face. From her uniform she was evidently one of the chambermaids of the hotel. From her voice she was most obviously Welsh.

'What are you doing here?' demanded Jeff. 'Get out, damn you!'

'Why do you talk so at me now, look you? I will not have this bad language. The maid of this suite I am!'

Marney saw her chance of escaping and, running into the bedroom, she slammed the door and locked it.

10

For a moment Jeff Legge stood, helpless with rage. Then he flung all his weight against the door, but it did not yield. He took up the telephone, but changed his mind. He did not want a scandal. Least of all did he wish to be advertised as Jeffrey Legge. Compromise was a blessed word—he knocked at the door.

'Marney, come out and be sensible,' he said, 'I was only joking. The whole thing was just to try you—'

She offered no reply. There was probably a telephone in the bedroom, he thought. Would she dare call her father? He heard another door unlocked. The bedroom gave on to the corridor, and he went out, to see the big chambermaid emerging. She was alone, and no sooner was she outside the door than it was locked upon her.

'I'll report you to the management,' he said furiously. He could have murdered her without compunction. But his rage made no impression upon the phlegmatic Welsh woman.

'A good character I have, look you, from all my employers. To be in the bedroom, it was my business. You shall not use bad language to me, look you, or I will have the law on you!'

Jeffrey thought quickly. He waited in the corridor until the woman had disappeared, then he beckoned from the far end a man who was evidently the floor waiter.

'Go down to the office and ask the manager, with my compliments, if I can have a second set of keys to my rooms,' he said suavely. 'My wife wishes to have her own.'

He slipped a bill into the man's hand, of such magnitude that the waiter was overwhelmed.

'Certainly, sir. I think I can arrange,' he said.

'And perhaps you would lend me your pass key,' said Jeff carelessly.

'I haven't a pass key, sir. Only the management have that,' replied the man; 'but I believe I can get you what you want.'

He came back in a few minutes to the sitting-room with many apologies. There were no duplicate sets of keys.

Jeff closed the sitting-room door on the man and locked it. Then he went over to the bedroom door.

'Marney!' he called, and this time she answered him. 'Are you going to be sensible?'

'I think I'm being very sensible,' was her reply.

'Come out and talk to me.'

'Thank you, I'd rather remain here.'

There was a pause.

'If you go to your father, I shall follow and kill him. I've got to shoot first, you know, Marney, after what you've told me.'

There was a silence, and he knew that his words had impressed her.

'Think it over,' he suggested. 'Take your time about it.'

'Will you promise to leave me alone?' she asked.

'Why, sure, I'll promise anything,' he said, and meant it. 'Come out, Marney,' he wheedled. 'You can't stay there all day. You've got to eat.'

'The woman will bring me my dinner,' was the instant reply, and Jeffrey cursed her softly.

'All right, have it your own way,' he said. 'But I tell you this, that if you don't come out tonight, there will be trouble in your happy family.'

He was satisfied, even though she did not answer him, that Marney would make no attempt to communicate with her father—that night, at least. After that night, nothing mattered.

He got on to the telephone, but the man he sought had not arrived. A quarter of an hour later, as he was opening his second bottle of champagne, the telephone bell tinkled and Emanuel Legge's voice answered him.

'She's giving me trouble,' he said in a low voice, relating what had happened.

He heard his father's click of annoyance and hastened to excuse his own precipitancy. 'She had to know sooner or later.'

'You're a fool,' snarled the old man. 'Why couldn't you leave it?'

'You've got to cover me here,' said Jeff urgently. 'If she phones Peter, there's going to be trouble. And Johnny—'

'Don't worry about Johnny,' said Emanuel Legge unpleasantly. 'There won't be any kick coming from him.'

He did not offer any explanation, and Jeff was too relieved by the assurance in his father's voice to question him on the subject.

'Take a look at the keyhole,' said Emanuel, 'and tell me if the key's in the lock. Anyway, I'll send you a couple of tools, and you'll open that door in two jiffs—but you've got to wait until the middle of the night, when she's asleep.'

Half an hour later a small package arrived by district messenger and Jeffrey, cutting the sealed cord, opened the little box and picked out two curiously wrought instruments. For an hour he practised on the door of the second bedroom leading from the saloon, and succeeded in turning the key from the reverse side. Towards dinner-time he heard voices in Marney's bedroom. He crept to the door and listened. It was the Welsh woman, and there came to his ears the clatter of plates and cutlery, and he smiled.

He had hardly got back to his chair and his newspaper when the telephone bell rang. It was the reception clerk.

'There's a lady to see you. She asked if you'd come down. She says it is very important.'

'Who is it?' asked Jeffrey, frowning.

'Miss Lila.'

'Lila!' He hesitated. 'Send her up, please,' he said, and drew a heavy velvet curtain across the door of Marney's room.

At the first sight of Peter Kane's maid he knew that she had left Horsham in a hurry. Under the light coat she wore, he saw the white collar of her uniform.

'What's the trouble with you, Lila?' he asked.

'Where's Marney?' she asked.

He nodded to the curtained room.

'Have you locked her in?'

'To be exact, she locked herself in,' said Jeff with a twisted smile.

The eyes of the woman narrowed.

'Oh, it's like that, is it?' she asked harshly. 'You haven't lost much time, Jeff.'

'Don't get silly ideas in your nut,' he said coolly. 'I told her who I was, and there was a row—that's all there is to it. Now, what's the trouble?'

'Peter Kane's left Horsham with a gun in his pocket—that's all,' she said, and Jeffrey paled.

'Sit down and tell me just what you mean.'

'After you'd gone I went up to my room, because I was feeling mighty bad,' she said. 'I've got my feelings, and there isn't a woman breathing that can see a man go away with another girl—'

'Cut out all the sentiment and let's get right down to the facts,' commanded Jeff.

'I'll tell it in my own way if you don't mind, Jeffrey Legge,' said Lila.

'Well, get on with it,' he said impatiently.

'I wasn't there long before I heard Peter in his room—it's underneath mine—and he was talking to himself. I guess curiosity got the better of my worry, and I went down and listened. I couldn't hear what he was saying, and so I opened the door of his room a little bit. He'd just changed. The moment I went in he was slipping the magazine in the butt of a Browning—I saw him put it in his coat pocket, and then I went downstairs. After a while he came down too and, Jeff, I didn't like the look of his face. It was all grey and pinched, and if ever I saw a devil in a man's eyes I saw it in Peter Kane's. I heard him order the car, and then I went down into the kitchen, thinking he was going at once. But he didn't leave for about half an hour.'

'What was he doing?'

'He was in his own room, writing. I don't know what he was writing, because he always uses a black blotting-pad. He must have written a lot, because I know there was half a dozen sheets of stationery in the rack, and when I went in after he'd left they'd all gone. There was nothing torn up in the waste-paper basket, and he'd burnt nothing, so he must have taken all the stuff with him. I tried to get you on the phone, but you hadn't arrived, and I decided to come up.'

'How did you come up—by train or car?'

'By taxi. There wasn't a train for nearly two hours.'

'You didn't overtake Peter by any chance?'

She shook her head.

'I wouldn't. He was driving himself; his car is a Bentley, and it moves!'

Jeff bit his nails.

'That gun of Peter's worries me a little,' he said after a while, 'because he isn't a gunman. Wait.'

He took up the telephone and again called his father, and in a few words conveyed the story which Lila had brought.

'You'll have to cover me now,' he said anxiously. 'Peter knows.'

A long pause.

'Johnny must have told him. I didn't dream he would,' said Emanuel. 'Keep to the hotel, and don't go out. I'll have a couple of boys watching both entrances, and if Peter shows his nose in Pall Mall he's going to be hurt.'

Jeff hung up the receiver slowly and turned to the girl.

'Thank you, Lila. That's all you can do for me.'

'It is not all you can do for me,' said Lila. 'Jeff, what's going to happen now? I've tried

464

to pin you down, but you're a little too shifty for me. You told me that this was going to be one of those high-class platonic marriages which figure in the divorce courts, and, Jeff, I'm beginning to doubt.'

'Then you're a wise woman,' said Jeffrey calmly.

For a moment she did not understand the significance of the words.

'I'm a wise woman?' she repeated. 'Jeff, you don't mean—

'I'm entitled to my adventures,' said Jeffrey, settling himself comfortably in the big armchair and crossing his legs. 'I have a dear little wife, and for the moment, Lila, our little romance is finished.'

'You don't mean that?' she asked unsteadily. 'Jeff, you're kidding. You told me that all you wanted was to get a share of Peter's money, and Emanuel told me the same. He said he was going to put the black on Peter and get away with 40,000.'

'In the meantime I've got away with the girl,' said Jeffrey comfortably, 'and there's no sense in kicking up a fuss, Lila. We've had a good time, and change is everything in life.'

She was on her feet now, glaring down at him.

'And have I been six months working as a maid, nosing for you, Jeffrey Legge, to be told that our little romance is finished?' she asked shrilly. 'You've double-crossed me, you dirty thief! And if I don't fix you, my name's not Lila.'

'It isn't,' said Jeffrey. He reached for a cigar and lit it. 'And never was. Your name's Jane—that is, if you haven't been telling me lies. Now, Lila, be an intelligent human being. I've put aside 500 for you—'

'Real money, I hope,' she sneered. 'No, you're not going to get away with it so easy, Mr Jeffrey Legge. You've fooled me from beginning to end, and you either carry out your promise or I'll—'

'Don't say you'll squeak,' said Jeffrey, closing his eyes in mock resignation. 'You're all squeakers. I'm tired of you! You don't think I'd give you anything to squeak about, do you? That I'd trust you farther than I could fling you? No, my girl, I'm four kinds of a fool, but not that kind. You know just as much about me as the police know, or as Johnny Gray knows. You can't tell my new wife, because she knows too. And Peter knows—in fact, I shouldn't be surprised if somebody didn't write a story about it in the newspapers tomorrow!'

He took out his pocket-case, opened it, and from a thick wad of notes he counted fifty, which he flung on to the table.

'There's your monkey, and au revoir, beauteous maiden,' he said.

She took up the notes slowly, and put them in her bag. Her eyes were burning fires, her face colourless.

If she had flown at him in a fury he would have understood and he was, in fact, prepared. But she said nothing until she stood, the knob of the door in her hand.

'There are three men after you, Jeffrey Legge,' she said, 'and one will get you. Reeder, or Johnny, or Peter—and if they fail, you look out for me!'

And on this threat she took her departure, slamming the door behind her; and Jeffrey settled down again to his newspaper, with the feeling of satisfaction which comes to a man who has got through a very unpleasant task.

11

In a long sedate road in suburban Brockley lived a man who had apparently no fixed occupation. He was tall, thin, somewhat cadaverous, and he was known locally as a furtive night-bird. Few had seen him in the daytime, and the inquisitive who, by skilful cross-examination, endeavoured to discover his business from a reticent housekeeper learnt comparatively little, and that little inaccurate. Policemen on night duty, morning way-farers had seen him walking up Brockley Road in the early hours, coming apparently from the direction of London. He was known as Mr J. G. Reeder. Letters in that name came addressed to him—large blue letters, officially stamped and sealed; and in consequence it was understood in postal circles that he held a Government position.

The local police force never troubled him. He was one of the subjects which it was not permissible to discuss. Until the advent of Emanuel Legge that afternoon, nobody ever remembered Mr Reeder having a caller.

Emanuel had come from prison to the affairs of the everyday world with a clearer perception of values than his son. He was too old a criminal to be under any illusions. Sooner or later, the net of the law would close on Jeffrey, and the immunity which he at present enjoyed would be at an end. To every graft came its inevitable lagging. Emanuel, wise in his generation, had decided upon taking the boldest step of his career. And that he did so was not flattering to the administration of justice; nor could it be regarded as a tribute to the integrity of the police.

Emanuel had straightened many a young detective, and not a few who were advanced in years. He knew the art of dropping to perfection. In all his life he had only met three or four men who were superior to the well-camouflaged bribe. A hundred here and there makes things easier for the big crook; a thousand will keep him out of the limelight; but, once the light is on him, not a million can disturb the inevitable march of justice. Emanuel was working in the pre-limelight stage, and hoped for success.

If his many inquiries were truthfully answered, the police had not greatly changed since his young days. Secret service men were new to him. He had thought, in spite of the enormous sums allocated to that purpose in every year's budget, that the secret service was an invention of the sensational novelist; and even now, he imagined Mr Reeder to be one who was subsidized from the comparatively private resources of the banks rather than from the Treasury.

It was Emanuel's action to grasp the nettle firmly. 'In-fighting is not much worse than hugging,' was a favourite saying of his, and once he had located Mr J. G. Reeder, the night-hawk—and that had been the labour of months—the rest was easy. Always providing that Mr Reeder was amenable to argument.

The middle-aged woman who opened the door to him gave him an unpromising reception.

'Mr Reeder is engaged,' she said, 'and he doesn't want to see any visitors.'

'Will you kindly tell him,' said Emanuel with his most winning smile and a beam of benevolence behind his thick glasses, 'that Mr Legge from Devonshire would like to see him on a very particular matter of business?'

She closed the door in his face, and kept him waiting so long that he decided that even the magic of his name and its familiar association (he guessed) had not procured him an entry. But here he was mistaken. The door was opened for him, closed and bolted behind him, and he was led up a flight of stairs to the first floor.

The house was, to all appearances, well and comfortably furnished. The room into which he was ushered, if somewhat bare and official-looking, had an austerity of its own. Sitting behind a large writing-table, his back to the fireplace, was a man whom he judged to be between fifty and sixty. His face was thin, his expression sad. A pair of horn-rimmed glasses slid down his nose. His hair was of that peculiar tint, red turning to grey, and his ears were large and prominent, seeming to go away from his head at right angles. All this Emanuel noted in a glance.

'Good morning, or good afternoon, Mr Legge,' said the man at the desk. He half rose and offered a cold and lifeless hand. 'Sit down, will you?' he said wearily. 'I don't as a rule receive visitors, but I seem to remember your name. Now where have I heard it?'

He dropped his chin to his chest and looked over his spectacles dolefully. Emanuel's expansive smile struck against the polished surface of his indifference and rebounded. He felt for the first time the waste of expansiveness.

'I had a little piece of information I thought I'd bring to you, Mr Reeder,' he said. I suppose you know that I'm one of those unfortunate people who, through the treachery of others, have suffered imprisonment?'

'Yes, yes, of course,' said Mr Reeder in his weak voice, his chin still bent, his pale blue eyes fixed unwaveringly on the other. 'Of course, I remember. You were the man who robbed the strong-room. Of course you were. Legge, Legge? I seem to remember the name too. Haven't you a son?'

'I have a son, the best boy in the world,' said Emanuel fervently.

There was a telephone by Mr Reeder's right hand and throughout the interview he was polishing the black base with the cuff of his coat, a nervous little trick which first amused and then irritated the caller.

'He has never been in trouble, Mr Legge? Oh, that's a blessing,' he sighed. 'So many young people get into trouble nowadays.'

If there was one person whom Legge did not want to discuss it was his son. He got off the subject as well as he could.

'I understand, Mr Reeder, that you're doing special work for the Government—in the police department?'

'Not in the police department,' murmured the other. 'No, no, certainly not—not in the police department. I scarcely know a policeman. I see them often in the streets, and very picturesque figures they are. Mostly young men in the vigour and prime of youth. What a wonderful thing is youth, Mr Legge! I suppose you're very proud of your son!'

'He's a good boy,' said Emanuel shortly, and Mr Reeder sighed again.

'Children are a great expense,' he said. 'I often wonder whether I ought to be glad that I never married. What is your son by occupation, Mr Legge?'

'An export agent,' said Emanuel promptly.

'Dear, dear!' said the other, and shook his head.

Emanuel did not know whether he was impressed or only sympathizing.

'Being in Dartmoor, naturally I met a number of bad characters,' said the virtuous Emanuel; 'men who did not appeal to me, since I was perfectly innocent and only got my stretch—lagging—imprisonment through a conspiracy on the part of a man I've done many a good turn to—'

'Ingratitude,' interrupted Mr Reeder, drawing in his breath. 'What a terrible thing is ingratitude! How grateful your son must be that he has a father who looks after him, who has properly educated him and brought him up in the straight way, in spite of his own deplorable lapses!'

'Now, look here, Mr Reeder.' Emanuel thought it was time to get more definitely to business. 'I'm a very plain man, and I'm going to speak plainly to you. It has come to my knowledge that the gentlemen you are acting for are under the impression that my boy's got something to do with the printing of slush—counterfeit notes. I was never more hurt in my life than when I heard this rumour. I said to myself: "I'll go straight away to Mr Reeder and discuss the matter with him. I know he's a man of the world, and he will understand my feelings as a father." Some people, Mr Reeder'—his elbows were on the table and he leant over and adopted a more confidential tone—'some people get wrong impressions. Only the other day somebody was saying to me: "That Mr Reeder is broke. He's got three county court summonses for money owed—" '

'A temporary embarrassment,' murmured Mr Reeder. 'One has those periods of financial—er—depression.'

He was polishing the base of the telephone more vigorously.

'I don't suppose you're very well paid? I'm taking a liberty in making that personal statement, but as a man of the world you'll understand. I know what it is to be poor. I've had some of the best society people in my office'—Emanuel invented the office on the spur of the moment—'the highest people in the land, and if they've said: "Mr Legge, can you oblige me with a thousand or a couple of thousand?" why, I've pulled it out, as it were, like this.'

He put his hand in his pocket and withdrew it, holding a large roll of money fastened with a rubber band.

For a second Mr J. G. Reeder allowed his attention to be distracted, and surveyed the pile of wealth with the same detached interest which he had given to Emanuel. Then, reaching out his hand cautiously, he took the note from the top, felt it, fingered it, rustled it, and looked quickly at the water-mark.

'Genuine money,' he said in a hushed voice, and handed the note back with apparent reluctance.

'If a man is broke,' said Legge emphatically, 'I don't care who he is or what he is, I say: "Is a thousand or two thousand any good to you?"—'

'And is it?' asked Mr Reeder.

'Is what?' said Emanuel, taken off his guard.

'Is it any good to him?'

'Well, of course it is,' said Legge. 'My point is this: a gentleman may be very hard pressed, and yet be the most solvent person in the world. If he can only get a couple of thousand just when he wants it—why, there's no scandal, no appearance in court which might injure him in his job—'

'How very true. How very, very true!' Mr Reeder seemed profoundly touched. 'I hope you pass on these wise and original statements to your dear son, Mr Legge?' he said. 'What a splendid thing it is that he has such a father!'

Emanuel cursed him under his breath.

468

'Two thousand pounds,' mused Mr Reeder. Now, if you had said five thousand pounds—'

'I do say five thousand,' said Emanuel eagerly. 'I'm not going to spoil the ship for a ha'porth of tar.'

'If you had said five thousand pounds,' Mr Reeder went on, 'I should have known that three thousand was slush, or shall we say phoney—because you only drew two thousand from the City and Birmingham Bank this morning, all in ten-pound notes, series A.19 900021 to A.19 900220. Correct me if I'm wrong. Of course, you might have some other genuine money stowed away in your little hotel, Mr Legge; or your dear boy may have given you another three thousand as a sort of wedding present—I forgot, though, a bridegroom doesn't give wedding presents, does he? He receives them. How foolish of me! Put away your money, Mr Legge. This room is very draughty, and it might catch cold. Do you ever go to the Hilly Fields? It is a delightful spot. You must come to tea with me one Sunday, and we will go up there. It is a very inexpensive but satisfactory method of spending two hours. As to those judgment summonses'—he coughed, and rubbed his nose with his long forefinger—'those summonses were arranged in order to bring you here. I *did so* want to meet you, and I knew the bait of my impecuniosity would be almost irresistible.'

Emanuel Legge sat, dumbfounded.

'Do you know a man named "Golden"? Ah, he would be before your time. Have you ever heard of him? He was my predecessor. I don't think you met him. He had a great saying—set a brief to catch a thief. We called a note a brief in those days. Good afternoon, Mr Legge. You will find your way down.'

Legge rose, and with that the sad-faced man dropped his eyes and resumed the work he had been at when the visitor had interrupted him.

'I only want to say this, Mr Reeder—' began Legge.

'Tell my housekeeper,' pleaded Reeder weakly, and he did not look up. 'She's frightfully interested in fairy stories—I think she must be getting towards her second childhood. Good afternoon, Mr Legge.'

12

Emanuel Legge was half-way home before he could sort out his impressions. He went back to the Bloomsbury hotel where he was staying. There was no message for him, and there had been no callers. It was now seven o'clock. He wondered whether Jeff had restrained his impatience. Jeff must be told and warned. Johnny Gray, dead or maimed in a hospital, had ceased to be a factor. Peter Kane, for all his cunning and his vengefulness, might be dismissed as a source of danger. It was Mr J.G. Reeder who filled his thoughts; the bored Civil Servant with a weak voice, who had such a surprising knowledge of things, and whose continuous pointed references to Jeffrey filled him with unquiet. Jeffrey must clear out of the country and he must go while the going was good. If he hadn't been such a fool, he would have moved that night. Now, that was impossible.

Peter had not arrived at the Charlton, or the men whom Legge had set to watch would have reported. If it had not been for the disturbing interview he had had with Reeder, he would have been more worried about Peter Kane; for when Peter delayed action, he was dangerous.

At eight o'clock that night, a small boy brought him a note to the hotel. It was addressed 'E. Legge', and the envelope was grimy with much handling. Emanuel took the letter to his room and locked the door before he opened it. It was from a man who was very much on the inside of things, one of Jeff's shrewd but illiterate assistants, first lieutenant of the Big Printer and a man to be implicitly trusted.

There were six closely written pages, ill-spelt and blotted. Emanuel read the letter a dozen times, and when he finished, there was panic in his heart.

'Johnny Gray got out of the tunnel all right and he's going to squeak to Reeder,' was the dramatic beginning, and there was a great deal more . . .

Emanuel knew a club in the West End of London, and his name was numbered amongst the members, even in the days when he had little opportunity of exercising his membership. It was a club rather unlike any other and it occupied the third and fourth floor of a building, the lower floors being in the possession of an Italian *restaurateur*. Normally, the proprietor of a fairly popular restaurant would not hire out his upper floors to so formidable a rival; but the proprietors of the club were also proprietors of the building, the restaurant keeper being merely a tenant.

It suited the membership of the Highlow Club to have their premises a little remote. It suited them better that no stairway led from the lower to the upper floors. Members of the club went down a narrow passage by the side of the restaurant entrance. From the end of the passage ran a small elevator, which carried them to the third floor. The County Council, in granting this concession, insisted on a very complete fire escape system outside the building—a command which very well suited the members. Some there were who found it convenient to enter the premises by this latter method, and a window leading into the club was left unfastened day and night against such a contingency.

On the flat roof of the building was a small superstructure, which was never used by the club members; whilst another part of the building, which also belonged exclusively to the Highlow, was the basement, to which the restaurant proprietor had no access—much to his annoyance, since it necessitated the building of a wine storage room in the limited space in the courtyard behind.

Stepping out of the elevator into a broad passage, well carpeted, its austere walls hung with etchings, Emanuel Legge was greeted respectfully by the liveried porter who sat behind a desk within sight of the lift. There was every reason why Emanuel should be respected at the Highlow for he was, in truth, the proprietor of the club, and his son had exercised control of the place during many of the years his father had been in prison.

The porter, who was a big ex-prize-fighter, expressly engaged for the purpose for which he was frequently required, hurried from his tiny perch to stand deferentially before his master.

'Anybody here?' asked Legge.

The man mentioned a few names.

'Let me see the engagement book,' said the other, and the man produced from beneath the ledge of his desk a small, red book; Emanuel turned the pages. The old man's hand ran down the list, and suddenly stopped.

'Oh, yes,' he said softly, closing the book and handing it back.

'Are you expecting anybody, Mr Legge?' asked the porter.

'No, I'm not expecting anybody . . . only I wondered . . .'

'Mr Jeffrey got married today, I hear, sir? I'm sure all the staff wish him joy.'

All the staff did not wish Mr Jeffrey Legge joy, for neither he nor his father were greatly popular, even in the tolerant society of the Highlow and moreover, strange as it may appear, very few people knew him by sight.

'That's very good of you, very good indeed,' murmured Emanuel absently.

'Are you dining here, sir?'

'No, no. I'm not dining here. I just looked in, that is all.'

He stepped back into the elevator, and the porter watched it drop with pleasure. It was half-past eight; the glow was dying in the sky, and the lights were beginning to twinkle in the streets, as Emanuel walked steadily towards Shaftesbury Avenue.

Providentially, he was at the corner of a side street when he saw Peter Kane. He was near enough to note that under his thin overcoat Peter was in evening dress. Slipping into the doorway, he watched the man pass. Peter was absorbed in thought; his eyes were on the ground and he had no interest for anything but the tremendous problem which occupied his mind.

Legge came back to the corner of the street and watched him furtively. Opposite the club, Peter stopped, looked up for a while, and passed on. The watcher laughed to himself. That club could have no pleasant memories for Peter Kane that night; it was in the Highlow that he had met the 'young Canadian officer' and had 'rescued' him, as he had thought, from his dangerous surroundings. There had Peter been trapped, for the introduction of Jeff Legge was most skilfully arranged. Going into the club one night, Peter saw, as he thought, a young, good-looking boy in the hands of a gang of cardsharpers, and the 'rescued officer' had been most grateful, and had called on Peter at the earliest opportunity. So simple, so very simple, to catch Peter. It would be a more difficult matter, thought Emanuel, for Peter to catch *him*.

He waited until the figure had disappeared in the gloom of the evening, and then walked back to the Avenue. This comedy over, there remained the knowledge of stark tragedy, of danger to his boy, the upsetting of all his plans and, the most dreadful of all possibilities, the snaring of the Big Printer. This night would the battle be fought, this night of nights would victory or defeat be in his hands. Reeder— Johnny—Peter Kane— all opposed him, innocent of their cooperation, and in his hands a hostage beyond price—the body and soul of Marney Legge.

He had scarcely disappeared when another person known to him came quickly along the quiet street, turned into the club entrance and, despite the expostulations of the elevator man, insisted on being taken up. The porter had heard the warning bell and stood waiting to receive her when the door of the elevator opened.

'Where's Emanuel?' she asked.

'Just gone,' said the porter.

'That's a lie. I should have seen him if he'd just gone.'

She was obviously labouring under some emotion, and the porter, an expert on all stages of feminine emotionalism, shrewdly diagnosed the reason for her wildness of manner and speech.

'Been a wedding today, hasn't there?' he asked with heavy jocularity. 'Now, Lila, what's the good of kicking up a fuss? You know you oughtn't to come here. Mr Legge gave orders you weren't to be admitted while you were at Kane's.'

'Where's Emanuel?' she asked.

'I tell you he's just gone out,' said the porter in a tone of ponderous despair. 'What a woman you are! You don't believe anything!'

'Has he gone back to his hotel?'

'That's just where he has gone. Now be wise, girl, and beat it. Anybody might be coming here—Johnny Gray was in last night, and he's a pal of Peter's.'

'Johnny knows all about me,' she said impatiently. 'Besides, I've left Peter's house.'

She stood undecidedly at the entrance of the open elevator and then, when the porter was preparing some of his finest arguments for her rapid disappearance, she stepped into the lift and was taken down.

The Highlow was a curious club, for it had no common room. Fourteen private dining-rooms and a large and elegantly furnished card-room constituted the premises. Meals were served from the restaurant below, being brought up by service lift to a small pantry. The members of the club had not the club feeling in the best sense of the word. They included men and women, but the chief reason for the club's existence was that it afforded a safe and not unpleasant meeting-place for members of a certain class, and gave necessary seclusion for the slaughter of such innocents as came within the influence of its more dexterous members. How well its inner secrets were kept is best illustrated by the fact that Peter Kane had been a member for twenty years without knowing that his sometime companion in crime had any official connection with its control. Nor was it ever hinted to him that the man who was directing the club's activities during Emanuel's enforced absence, was his son.

Peter was a very infrequent visitor to the Highlow; and indeed, on the occasion of his first meeting with the spurious Major Floyd, he had been tricked into coming, though this he did not know.

The porter was busy until half past nine. Small parties came, were checked off in the book, and then—he looked at his watch.

'Twenty-five to ten,' he said, and pushed a bell button.

A waiter appeared from the side passage.

'Put a bottle of wine in No. 13,' he said.

The waiter looked at him surprised.

'No. 13?' he said, as if he could not believe his ears.

'I said it,' confirmed the porter.

*   *   *   *   *

Jeffrey ate a solitary dinner. The humour of the situation did not appeal to him. On his honeymoon, he and his wife were dining, a locked door between them. But he could wait.

Again he tried the odd-shaped pliers on the key of the second bedroom. The key turned readily. He put the tool into his pocket with a sense of power. The clatter of a table being cleared came to him from the other room, and presently he heard the outer door close and a click of the key turning. He lit his fourth cigar and stepped out on to the balcony, surveying the crowded street with a dispassionate interest. It was theatre time. Cars were rolling up to the Haymarket; the long queue that he had seen waiting for the cheaper seats had disappeared; a restaurant immediately opposite was blazing with lights; and on a corner of the street three aged ex-soldiers were playing the overture of 'Lohengrin'.

Glancing down into the street, he distinguished one of the 'minders' his father had put there for his protection, and grinned. Peter could not know; he would have been here before. As to Johnny . . .? Emanuel had been very confident that Johnny presented no danger, and it rather looked as though Emanuel's view was right. But if Peter knew, why hadn't he come?

He strolled back to the room, looked at the girl's door and walked towards it.

'Marney!' he called softly.

There was no answer. He knocked on the panel.

'Marney, come along. I want to talk to you. You needn't open the door. I just wanted to ask you something.'

Still there was no answer. He tried the door; it was locked.

'Are you there?' he called sharply, but she did not reply.

He pulled the pliers from his pocket and, pushing the narrow nose into the keyhole, gripped the end of the key and turned it. Then, flinging open the door, he rushed in.

The room was empty, and the big bathroom that led out of the suite was empty also. He ran to the passage door: it was locked—locked from the outside. In a sweat of fear he flew through the sitting-room into the corridor, and the first person he saw was the floor waiter.

'Madam, sir? Yes, she went out a little time ago.'

'Went out, you fool? Where?' stormed Jeff.

'I don't know, sir. She just went out. I saw her going along the corridor.'

Jeff went down the stairs three at a time. The reception clerk had not seen the girl, nor had any of the pages, or the porter on the door. Oblivious to any immediate danger, he dashed out into the street and, looking up and down, saw the minder and called him.

'She hasn't come out this entrance. There's another in Pall Mall,' he explained. 'Jimmy Low's there.'

But the second man on the Pall Mall entrance had not seen her either. Jeff went back to interview the manager.

'There is no other way out, sir, unless she went down the service stairs.'

'It was that cursed maid, the Welsh woman,' snarled Jeffrey. 'Who is she? Can I see her?'

'She went off duty this afternoon, sir,' said the manager. 'Is there anything I can do? Perhaps the lady has gone out for a walk? Does she know London?'

Jeff did not stop to reply: he fled up the stairs, back to the room, and made a quick search. The girl's dressing-case, which he knew had been taken into the bedroom, was gone. Something on the floor attracted his attention. He picked it up, and read the few scribbled lines, torn from a notebook; and as he read a light came into his eyes. Very carefully he folded the crumpled sheet and put it into his pocket. Then he went back to his sitting-room, and sat for a long time in the big arm-chair, his legs thrust out before him, his hands deep in his trousers pockets, and his thoughts were not wholly unpleasant.

The light was now nearly gone, and he got up.

'Room 13,' he said. 'Room 13 is going to hold a few surprises tonight!'

13

To Parker, the valet, as he laid out Johnny's dress clothes, there was a misfortune and a tragedy deeper than any to which Johnny had been a spectator. Johnny, loafing into his bedroom, a long, black cigarette-holder between his teeth, found his man profoundly agitated.

'The buckle of your white dress waistcoat has in some unaccountable way disappeared,' he said in a hushed voice. 'I'm extremely sorry, sir, because this is the only white dress waistcoat you have.'

'Be cheerful,' said Johnny. 'Take a happier view of life. You can tie the tapes behind. You could even sew me together, Parker. Are you an expert needle worker, or do you crochet?'

'My needlework has been admired, sir,' said Parker complacently. 'I think yours is an excellent suggestion. Otherwise, the waistcoat will not sit as it should. Especially in the case of a gentleman with your figure.'

'Parker,' said Johnny, as he began to dress, 'have you ever killed a man?'

'No, sir, I have never killed a man,' said Parker gravely. 'When I was a young man, I once ran over a cat—I was a great cyclist in my youth.'

'But you never killed a man? And, what is more, you've never even wanted to kill a man?'

'No, sir, I can't say that I ever have,' said Parker after a few moments' consideration, as though it were possible that some experience had been his which had been overlooked in the hurry of his answering.

'It is quite a nice feeling, Parker. Is there a hip pocket to these—yes, there is,' he said, patting his trousers.

'I'm sorry there is,' said Parker, 'very sorry indeed. Gentlemen get into the habit of carrying their cigarette cases in the hip pocket, with the result that the coat tail is thrown out of shape. That is where the dinner jacket has its advantages—the Tuxedo, as the American gentlemen call it, though I've never understood why a dinner jacket should be named after a Scottish town.'

'Tuxedo is in Dixie,' said Johnny humorously, 'and Dixie is America's lost Atlantis. Don't worry about the set of my coat tail. I am not carrying my cigarette case there.'

'Anything more bulky would of course be worse, sir,' said Parker, and Johnny did not carry the discussion any farther.

'Get me a cab,' he ordered.

When Parker returned, he found his master was fully dressed.

Johnny dismissed his taxi in Shaftesbury Avenue and walked down towards the club. It was dark now; half past nine had chimed as he came along Piccadilly.

It was a point of honour with all members of the Highlow that nobody drove up to the club, and its very existence was unknown to the taxidrivers. That was a rule that had been made, and most faithfully adhered to; and the members of the Highlow observed their rules for, if a breach did not involve a demand for their resignation, it occasionally brought about a broken head.

Just before he reached the club, he saw somebody cross the road. It was not difficult to recognize Jeff Legge. Just at that moment it would have been rather embarrassing for Johnny to have met the man. He turned and walked back the way he had come, to avoid the chance of their both going up in the elevator together.

Jeff Legge was in a hurry: the elevator did not move fast enough for him, and he stepped out on to the third floor and asked a question.

'No, sir, nobody has come. If they do, I'll send them along to you. Where will you be? You haven't a room engaged—your own room is taken. We don't often let it, but we're full tonight, and Mr Legge raised no objection.'

'No, I don't object,' said Jeff; 'but don't you worry about that. Let me see the book.'

Again the red-covered engagement book was opened. Jeff read and nodded.

'Fine,' he said. 'Now tell me again who is here.'

'There is Mr George Kurlu, with a party of friends in No. 3; there's Mr Bob Albutt and those two young ladies he goes about with—they're in No. 4.' And so he recited until he came to No. 13.

'I know all about No. 13,' said Jeff Legge between his teeth. 'You needn't bother about me, however. That will do.'

He strode along the carpeted hallway, turned abruptly into the right-angled passage, and presently stopped before a door with a neat golden '13' painted on its polished panel. He opened the door and went in. On the red-covered table was a bottle of wine and two glasses.

It was a moderately large room, furnished with a sofa, four dining chairs and a deep easy chair, whilst against one wall was a small buffet. The room was brilliantly lighted. Six bracket lamps were blazing; the centre light above the table, with its frosted bulbs, was full on. He did not shut the door, leaving it slightly ajar. There was too much light for his purpose. He first switched out the bracket lamps, and then all but one of the frosted bulbs in the big shaded lamp over the table. Then he sat down, his back to the door, his eyes on the empty firegrate.

Presently he heard a sound, the whining of the elevator, and smiled. Johnny stepped out to the porter's desk with a friendly nod.

'Good evening, Captain,' said the porter with a broad grin. 'Glad to see you back, sir. I wasn't here last night when you came in. Hope you haven't had too bad a time in the country?'

'Abroad, my dear fellow, abroad,' murmured the other reproachfully, and the porter chuckled. 'Same old crowd, I suppose?'

'Yes, sir.'

'Same old bolt down the fire-escape when the busies call—or have you got all the busies straightened?'

'I don't think there's much trouble, sir,' said the porter. 'We often have a couple of those gentlemen in here to dinner. The club's very convenient sometimes. I shouldn't think they'll ever shut us up.'

'I shouldn't think so, either,' said Johnny. 'Which of the busies do you get?'

'Well, sir, we get Mr Craig, and—once we had that Reeder. He came here alone, booked a table and came alone! Can you beat it? Came and had his dinner, saw nobody and went away again. I don't think he's right up there'—he tapped his forehead significantly. 'Anything less like a busy I've never seen.'

'I don't know whether he is a detective,' said Johnny carelessly. 'From all I've heard, he has nothing whatever to do with the police.'

'Private, is he?' said the other in a tone of disappointment.

'Not exactly private. Anyway,' with a smile, 'he's not going to bother you or our honourable members. Anybody here?'

The porter looked to left and right, and lowered his voice.

'A certain person you know is here,' he said meaningly.

Johnny laughed.

'It would be a funny club if there wasn't somebody I knew,' he said. 'Don't worry about me; I'll find a little corner for myself. . . .'

Jeff looked at his watch; it was a quarter to ten, and he glanced up at the light; catching a glimpse of himself in the mirror of the buffet, was satisfied.

Room 13! And Marney was his wife! The blood surged up into his face, gorging the thick veins in his temples at the thought. She should pay! He had helped the old man, as he would help him in any graft, but he had never identified himself so completely with the plan as he did at that moment.

'Put her down to the earth,' had said Emanuel, and by God he would do it. As for Johnny Gray. . . .

The door opened stealthily, and a hand came in, holding a Browning. He heard the creak of the door but did not look round, and then:

'*Bang!*'

Once the gun fired. Jeff felt a sharp twitch of pain, exquisite, unbearable, and fell forward on his knees.

Twice he endeavoured to rise, then with a groan fell in a huddled heap, his head in the empty fireplace.

14

The doors and the walls of the private dining-rooms were almost sound-proof. No stir followed the shot. In the hall outside, the porter lifted his head and listened.

'What was that?' he asked the waiting elevator man.

'Didn't hear anything,' said the other laconically. 'Somebody slammed a door.'

'Maybe,' said the porter, and went back to his book. He was filling in the names of that night's visitors, an indispensable record in such a club, and he was filling them in with pencil, an equally necessary act of caution, for sometimes the club members desired a quick expungement of this evidence.

In Room 13 silence reigned. A thin blue cloud floated to the ceiling; the door opened a little farther and Johnny Gray came in, his right hand in his overcoat pocket.

Slowly he crossed the room to where the huddled figure lay and, stooping, turned it on its back. Then, after a brief scrutiny, his quick hands went through the man's pockets. He found something, carried it to the light, read with a frown and pushed the paper into his own pocket. Going out, he closed the door carefully behind him and strolled back to the hall.

'Not staying, Captain?' asked the porter in surprise.

'No, nobody I know here. Strange how the membership changes.'

The man on duty was too well trained to ask inconvenient questions.

'Excuse me, Captain.' He went over to Johnny and bent down. 'You've got some blood on your cuff.'

He took out his handkerchief and wiped the stain clean. Then his frowning eyes met the young man's.

'Anything wrong, Captain?'

'Nothing that I can tell you about,' said Johnny. 'Good night.'

'Good night, sir,' said the porter.

He stood by his desk, looking hard at the glass doors of the elevator, heard the rattle of the gate as it opened, and the whine of the lift as it rose again.

'Just stay here, and don't answer any rings till I come back,' he said.

He hurried along the corridor into the side passage and, coming to No. 13, knocked. There was no answer. He turned the handle. One glance told him all he wanted to know. Gently he closed the door and hurried back to the telephone on his desk.

Before he raised the receiver he called the gaping lift-boy.

'Go to all the rooms, and say a murder has been committed. Get everybody out.'

He was still clasping the telephone with damp hands when the last frightened guest crowded into the elevator, then:

'Highlow Club speaking. *Is* that the Charing Cross Hospital? . . . I want an ambulance here . . . Yes, 38, Boburn Street . . . There's been an accident.'

He rung off and called another number.

'Highlow Club. Is that the police station? . . . It's the porter at the Highlow Club speaking, sir. One of our members has shot himself.'

He put down the instrument and turned his face to the scared elevator man who had returned to the high level. At the end of the passage stood a crowd of worried waiters.

'Benny,' he said, 'Captain Gray hasn't been here tonight. You understand? Captain—Gray—has—not—been—here—tonight.'

The guest-book was open on the desk. He took his pencil and wrote, on the line where Johnny Gray's name should have been, 'Mr William Brown of Toronto.'

15

The last of the guests had escaped, when the police came, and, simultaneously with the ambulance, Divisional-Inspector Craig, who had happened to be making a call in the neighbourhood. The doctor who came with the ambulance made a brief examination.

'He isn't dead, though he may be before he reaches hospital,' he said.

'Is it a case of suicide?'

The doctor shook his head.

'Suicides do not, as a rule, shoot themselves under the right shoulder-blade. It would be a difficult operation: try it yourself. I should say he'd been shot from the open doorway.'

He applied a rough first dressing, and Jeffrey was carried into the elevator. In the bottom passage a stretcher was prepared, and upon this he was laid and, covered with a blanket, carried through the crowd which had assembled at the entrance.

'Murder, or attempted murder, as the case may be,' said Craig. 'Someone has tipped off the guests. You, I suppose, Stevens? Let me see your book.'

The inspector ran his finger down the list, and stopped at Room 13.

'Mr William Brown of Toronto. Who is Mr Brown of Toronto?'

'I don't know, sir. He engaged a room by telephone. I didn't see him go.'

'That old fire-escape of yours still working?' asked Craig sardonically. 'Anybody else been here? Who's the wounded man? His face seemed familiar to me.'

'Major Floyd, sir.'

'Who?' asked Craig sharply. 'Impossible! Major Floyd is—'

It *was* Floyd! He remembered now. Floyd, with whom he had sat that day—that happily-married man!

'What was he doing here?' he asked. 'Now, spill it, Stevens, unless you want to get yourself into pretty bad trouble.'

'I've spilled all I know, sir,' said Stevens doggedly. 'It was Major Floyd.'

And then an inspiration came to him.

'If you want to know who it was, it was Jeff Legge. Floyd's his fancy name.'

'Who?'

Craig had had many shocks in his life, but this was the greatest he had had for years.

'Jeff Legge? Old Legge's son?'

Stevens nodded.

'Nobody knows that but a couple of us,' he said. 'Jeff doesn't work in the light.'
The officer nodded slowly.
'I've never seen him,' he admitted. 'I knew Legge had a son, but I didn't know he was running crook. I thought he was a bit of a boy.'
'He's some boy, let me tell you!' said Stevens.
Craig sat down, his chin in his hands.
'Mrs Floyd will have to be told. Good God! Peter Kane's daughter! Peter didn't know that he'd married her to Legge's son?'
'I don't know whether he knew or not,' said Stevens, 'but if I know old Peter, he'd as soon known that she'd gone to the devil as marry her to a son of Emanuel Legge's. I'm squeaking in a way,' he said apologetically, 'but you've got to know—Emanuel will tell you as soon as he gets the news.'
'Come here,' said Craig. He took the man's arm and leading him from the passage where the detectives could hear, opened the door of a private room, the table giving evidence of the hasty flight of the diners. 'Now,' he said, closing the door, 'What's the strength of this story?'
'I don't know it all, Mr Craig, but I know they were putting a point on Peter Kane a long time ago. Then one night they brought Peter along and kidded him into thinking that Jeff was a sucker in the hands of the boys. Peter had never seen Jeff before—as a matter of fact, I didn't know he was Jeff at the time; I'd heard a lot about him, but like a lot of other people, I hadn't seen him. Well, they fooled Peter all right. He took the lad away with him. Jeff was wearing a Canadian officer's uniform and, of course, Jeff told the tale. He wouldn't be the son of his father if he didn't. That's how he got to know the Kanes, and was taken to their home. When I heard about the marriage, I thought Peter must have known. I never dreamt they were playing a trick on him.'
'Peter didn't know,' said Craig slowly. 'Where's the girl?'
'I can't tell you. She's in London somewhere.'
'At the Charlton,' nodded the other. 'Now, you've got to tell me, Stevens, who is Mr Brown of Toronto? It's written differently from your usual hand—written by a man who has had a bad scare. In other words, it was written after you'd found the body.'
Stevens said nothing.
'You saw him come out; who was he?'
'If I die this minute—' began Stevens.
'You might in a few months, as "accessary after",' said the other ominously; 'and that's what you'll do if you conceal a murderer. Who is Mr Brown?'
Stevens was struggling with himself, and after a while it came out.
'Johnny was here tonight,' he said huskily. 'Johnny Gray.'
Craig whistled.
There was a knock at the door. A police officer, wanting instructions.
'There's a woman down below, pretty nigh mad. I think you know her, sir.'
'Not Lila?' blurted Stevens.
'That's the girl. Shall I let her come up?'
'Yes,' said Craig. 'Bring her in here.'
She came in a minute, distracted, incoherent, her hair dishevelled, her hands trembling.

'Is he dead?' she gasped. 'For God's sake tell me. I see it in your face—he's dead. Oh, Jeff, Jeff!'

'Now you sit down,' said the kindly Craig. 'He's no more dead than you or I are. Ask Stevens. Jeff's doing very well indeed. Just a slight wound, my dear—nothing to worry about. What was the trouble? Do you know anything about it?'

She could not answer him.

'He's dead,' she moaned. 'My God, I killed him! I saw him and followed him here!'

'Give her a glass of wine, Stevens.'

The porter poured out a glass of white wine from one of the many deserted bottles on the table, and put it to her chattering teeth.

'Now, Lila, let's get some sense out of you. I tell you, Jeff's not dead. What is he to you, anyway?'

'Everything,' she muttered. She was shivering from head to foot. 'I married him three years ago. No, I didn't,' she said in a sudden frenzy.

'Go on; tell us the truth,' said Craig. 'We're not going to pull him for bigamy, anyway.'

'I married him three years ago,' she said. 'He wasn't bad to me. It was the old man's idea, his marrying this girl, and there was a thousand in it for me. He put me down in Horsham to look after her, and see that there wasn't any letters going to Johnny. There wasn't any need of that, because she never wrote. I didn't like the marriage idea, but he swore to me that it was only to get Peter's money, and I believed him. Then tonight he told me the truth, knowing I wouldn't squeak. I wish to God I had now, I wish I had! He is dead, isn't he? I know he's dead!'

'He's not dead, you poor fish,' said Craig impatiently. 'I might be congratulating you if he was. No, he's got a bit of a wound.'

'Who shot him?'

'That's just what I want to know,' said Craig. 'Was it you?'

'Me!' Her look of horror supplied a satisfactory answer to his question. 'No, I didn't. I didn't know he was here, or coming here. I thought he was at the hotel, till I saw him. Yet I had a feeling that he was coming here tonight, and I've been waiting about all evening. I saw Peter and dodged him.'

'Peter? Has he been near the club?'

She shook her head.

'I don't know. He was on his way. I thought he was going to the Highlow. There's nowhere else he'd go in this street—I saw him twice.'

Craig turned his bright, suspicious eyes upon the porter.

'Peter been here? I didn't see anything about Mr Brown of Montreal?' he asked sarcastically.

'No, he hasn't. I haven't seen Peter since the Lord knows when,' said the porter emphatically. 'That's the truth. You can give the elevator boy permission to tell you all he knows, and if Peter was here tonight you can hang me.'

Craig considered for a long time.

'Does Peter know his way in by the easy route?' he asked.

'You mean the fire-escape? Yes, Peter knows that way but members never come in by the back nowadays. They've got nothing to hide.'

Craig went out of the room and walked down the passage, stopping at No. 13. Immediately opposite the door was a window, and it was wide open. Beyond was the grille of the fire-escape landing. He stepped out through the window and peered down into the dark yard where the escape ended. By the light of a street lamp he saw a stout gate, in turn pierced by a door, and this led to the street. The door was open, a fact which might be accounted for by the presence in the yard of two uniformed policemen, the flash of whose torches he saw. He came back into the corridor and to Stevens.

'Somebody may have used the fire-escape tonight, and they may not,' he said. 'What time did Gray come in? Who came in first?'

'Jeff came first, about five minutes before Gray.'

'Then what happened?'

'I had a chat with Captain Gray,' said the porter, after a second's hesitation. 'He went round into the side passage—'

'The same way that Jeff had gone?'

The porter nodded.

'About a minute later—in fact, it was shorter than a minute—I heard what I thought was a door slammed. I remarked on the fact to the elevator man.'

'And then?'

'I suppose four or five minutes passed after that, and Captain Gray came out. Said he might look in later.'

'There was no sign of a struggle in Captain Gray's clothes?'

'No, sir. I'm sure there was no struggle.'

'I should think not,' agreed Craig. 'Jeff Legge never had a chance of showing fight.'

The girl was lying on the sofa, her head buried in her arms, her shoulders shaking, and the sound of her weeping drew the detective's attention to her.

'Has she been here before tonight?'

'Yes, she came, and I had to throw her out—Emanuel told me she was not to be admitted.'

Craig made a few notes in his book, closed it with a snap and put it in his pocket.

'You understand, Stevens, that, if you're not under arrest, you're under open arrest. You'll close the club for tonight and admit no more people. I shall leave a couple of men on the premises.'

'I'll lock up the beer,' said Stevens facetiously.

'And you needn't be funny,' was the sharp retort. 'If we close this club you'll lose your job—and if they don't close it now they never will.'

He took aside his assistant.

'I'm afraid Johnny's got to go through the hoop tonight,' he said. 'Send a couple of men to pull him in. He lives at Albert Mansions. I'll go along and break the news to the girl, and somebody'll have to tell Peter—I hope there's need for Peter to be told,' he added grimly.

16

A surprise awaited him when he came to the Charlton. Mrs Floyd had gone—nobody knew where. Her husband had followed her some time afterwards, and neither had returned. Somebody had called her on the telephone, but had left no name.

'I know all about her husband not returning,' said Craig. 'But haven't you the slightest idea where the lady is?'

The negative reply was uncompromising.

'Her father hasn't been here?'

His informant hesitated.

'Yes, sir; he was on Mrs Floyd's floor when she was missing—in fact, when Major Floyd was down here making inquiries. The floor waiter recognized him, but he didn't see him come or go.'

Calling up the house at Horsham he learnt, what he already knew, that Peter was away from home. Barney, who answered him, had heard nothing of the girl; indeed, this was the first intimation he had had that all was not well. And a further disappointment lay in store for Craig. The detective he had sent to find Johnny returned with the news that the quarry had gone. According to the valet, his master had returned and changed in a hurry and, taking a small suitcase, had gone off to an unknown destination.

An inquiry late that night elicited the fact that Jeff was still living, but unconscious. The bullet had been extracted, and a hopeful view was taken of the future. His father had arrived early in the evening, and was half mad with anxiety and rage.

'And if he isn't quite mad by the morning, I shall be surprised,' said the surgeon. 'I'm going to keep him here and give him a little bromide to ease him down.'

'Poison him,' suggested Craig.

When the old detective was on the point of going home, there arrived a telephone message from the Horsham police, whom he had enlisted to watch Peter's house.

'Mr Kane and his daughter arrived in separate cars at a quarter past twelve,' was the report. 'They came within a few minutes of one another.'

Craig was on the point of getting through to the house, but thought better of it. A fast police car got him to Horsham under the hour, the road being clear and the night a bright one. Lights were burning in Peter's drawing-room, and it was he himself who, at the sound of the car wheels, came to the door.

'Who's that?' he asked, as Craig came up the dark drive, and at the sound of the detective's voice he came half-way down to meet him. 'What's wrong, Craig? Anything special?'

'Jeff's shot. I suppose you know who Jeff is?'

'I know, to my sorrow,' said Peter Kane promptly. 'Shot? How? Where?'

'He was shot this evening between a quarter to ten and ten o'clock, at the Highlow Club.'

'Come in. You'd better not tell my girl—she's had as much as she can bear tonight. Not that I'm worrying a damn about Jeff Legge. He'd better die, and die quick, for if I get him—'

He did not finish his sentence, and the detective drew the man's arm through his.

'Now, listen, Peter, you've got to go very slow on this case, and not talk such a darned lot. You're under suspicion too, old man. You were seen in the vicinity of the club.'

'Yes, I was seen in the vicinity of the club,' repeated Peter, nodding. 'I was waiting there—well, I was waiting there for a purpose. I sent to the Charlton, but my girl had gone—I suppose they told you—and then I went on to the Highlow, and saw that infernal Lila—by the way, she's one of Jeff's women, isn't she?'

'To be exact,' said the other quietly, 'she's his wife.'

Peter Kane stopped dead.

'His wife?' he whispered. 'Thank God for that! Thank God for that! I forgive her everything. Though how a woman could allow—but I can't judge her. That graft has always been dirty to me. It is hateful and loathsome. But, thank God she's his wife, Craig!' Then: 'Who shot this fellow?'

'I don't know. I'm going to pull Johnny for it.'

They were in the hall, and Peter Kane spun round.

'You're going to pull Johnny?' he said. 'Do you know what you're saying, Craig? You're mad! Johnny didn't do it. Johnny was nowhere near—'

'Johnny was there. And, what is more, Johnny was in the room, either at the moment of the shooting or immediately after. The elevator boy has spoken what's in his mind, which isn't much, but enough to convict Johnny if this fellow dies.'

'Johnny there!' Peter's voice did not rise above a whisper.

'I tell you frankly, Peter, I thought it was you.'

Craig was facing him squarely, his keen eyes searching the man's pallid face. 'When I heard you were around, and that you'd got to know that this fellow was a fake. Why were you waiting?'

'I can't tell you that—not now. I should have seen Johnny if he was there. I saw this girl Lila and I was afraid she'd recognize me. I think she did, too. I went straight on into Shaftesbury Avenue, to a bar I know. I was feeling quite ill over this—this discovery of mine. I can prove I was there from a quarter to ten till ten, if you want any proof. Oh, Johnny, Johnny!'

All this went on in the hall. Then came a quick patter of footsteps, and Marney appeared in the doorway.

'Who is it—Johnny? Oh, it's you, Mr Craig? Has anything happened?' She looked in alarm from face to face. 'Nothing has happened to Johnny?'

'No, nothing has happened to Johnny,' said Craig soothingly. He glanced at Peter. 'You ought to know this, Marney,' he said. 'I can call you Marney—I've known you since you were five. Jeff Legge has been shot.'

He thought she was going to faint, and moved to catch her, but with an effort of will she recovered.

'Jeff shot?' she asked shakily. 'Who shot him?'

'I don't know. That's just what we are trying to discover. Perhaps you can help us. Why did you leave the hotel? Was Johnny with you?'

She shook her head.

'I haven't seen Johnny,' she said, 'but I owe him—everything. There was a woman in the hotel.' She glanced timidly at her father. 'I think she was an hotel thief or something of the sort. She was there to—to steal. A big Welsh woman.'

'A Welsh woman?' said Craig quickly. 'What's her name?'

'Mrs Gwenda Jones. Johnny knew about her, and telephoned her to tell her to take care of me until he could get to me. She got me out of the hotel, and then we walked down the Duke of York steps into the Mall. And then a curious thing happened—I was just telling daddy when you came. Mrs Jones—she's such a big woman—'

'I know the lady,' said Craig.

'Well, she disappeared. She wasn't exactly swallowed up by the earth,' she said with a faint smile, 'and she didn't go without warning. Suddenly she said to me: "I must leave you now, my dear. I don't want that man to see me." I looked round to find who it was that she was so afraid of, and there seemed to be the most harmless lot of people about. When I turned, Mrs Jones was running up the steps. I didn't want to call her back, I felt so ridiculous. And then a man came up to me, a middle-aged man with the saddest face you could imagine. I told you that, Daddy?'

He nodded.

'He took his hat off—his hair was almost white—and asked me if my name was Kane. I didn't tell him the other name,' she said with a shiver. ' "May I take you to a place of safety, Miss Kane?" he said. "I don't think you ought to be seen with that raw-boned female." I didn't know what to do, I was so frightened, and when he called a taxi I got in without the slightest hesitation. He was such a gentle soul, Mr Craig. He talked of nothing but the weather and chickens! I think we talked about chickens all the way to Lewisham.'

'Are you sure it was Lewisham?'

'It was somewhere in that neighbourhood. What other places are there there?'

'New Cross, Brockley—' began Craig.

'That's the place—Brockley. It was the Brockley Road. I saw it printed on the corner of the street. He took me into his house. There was a nice, motherly old woman whom he introduced to me as his housekeeper.'

'And what did he talk about?' asked the fascinated Craig.

'Chickens,' she said solemnly. 'Do you know what chickens lay the best eggs? I'm sure you don't. Do you know the best breed for England and the best for America? Do you know the most economical chickens to keep? I do! I wondered what he was going to do with me. I tried to ask him, but he invariably turned me back to the question of incubators and feeds, and the cubic space that a sitting hen requires as compared with an ordinary hen. It was the quaintest, most fantastic experience. It seems now almost like one of Alice's dreams! Then, at ten o'clock, I found a car had come for me. "I'm sending you home, young lady," he said.'

'Were you with him all the time, by the way?' asked Craig.

She shook her head.

'No, some part of the time I was with his housekeeper, who didn't even talk about chickens, but knitted large and shapeless jumpers, and sniffed. That was when he was telephoning; I knew he was telephoning because I could hear the drone of his voice.'

'He didn't bring you back?'

'No, he just put me into the car and told me that I should be perfectly safe. I arrived just a few minutes ahead of daddy.'

The detective scratched his chin, irritated and baffled.

'That's certainly got me,' he said. 'The raw-boned lady I know, but the chicken gentleman is mysterious. You didn't hear his name, by any chance?'

She shook her head.

'Do you know the number of the house?'

'Yes,' she said frankly, 'but he particularly asked me to forget it, and I've forgotten it.' Then, in a more serious tone: 'Is my—my—'

'Your nothing,' interrupted Peter. 'The blackguard was married—married to Lila. I think I must have gone daft, not realizing that this woman was planted in my house for a purpose. That type of girl wouldn't come at the wages if she'd been genuine. Barney was always suspicious of her, by the way.'

'Have you seen Johnny?' the girl asked Craig.

'No, I haven't seen him,' said Craig carefully. 'I thought of calling on him pretty soon.'

Then it came to her in a flash, and she gasped.

'You don't think Johnny shot this man? You can't think that?'

'Of course he didn't shoot him,' said Peter loudly. 'It's a ridiculous idea. But you'll understand that Mr Craig has to make inquiries in all sorts of unlikely quarters. You haven't been able to get hold of Johnny tonight?'

A glance passed between them, and Peter groaned.

'What a fool! What a fool!' he said. 'Oh, my God, what a fool!'

'Father, Johnny hasn't done this? It isn't true, Mr Craig. Johnny wouldn't shoot a man. Did anybody see him? How was he shot?'

'He was shot in the back.'

'Then it wasn't Johnny,' she said. 'He couldn't shoot anyone in the back!'

'I think, young lady,' said Craig with a smile, 'that you'd better go to bed and dream about butterflies. You've had a perfect hell of a day, if you'll excuse my language. Say the firm word to her, Peter. Who's that?' He turned his head, listening.

'Barney,' said Peter. 'He has a distressing habit of wearing slippers. You can hear him miles away. He's opening the door to somebody—one of your people, perhaps. Or he's taking your chauffeur a drink. Barney has an enormous admiration for chauffeurs. They represent mechanical genius to him.'

The girl was calmer now.

'I've too much to thank God for today, for this terrible thing to be true,' she said in a low voice. 'Mr Craig, there's a mistake, I'm sure. Johnny couldn't have committed such a crime. It was somebody else—one of Jeffrey Legge's associates, somebody who hated him. He told me once that lots of people hated him, and I thought he was joking; he seemed so nice, so considerate. Daddy, I was mad to go through that, even to make you happy.'

Peter Kane nodded.

'If you were mad, I was criminal, Marney,' he said. 'There was only one man in the world for you—'

The door opened slowly, and Barney sidled in.

'Johnny to see you folks,' he said, and pulled the door wider.

John Gray was standing in the passage, and his eyes fell on Craig with a look of quiet amusement.

17

In another second the girl was in his arms, clinging to him, weeping convulsively on his shoulder, her face against his, her clasped hands about his neck.

Craig could only look, wondering and fearing. Johnny would not have walked into the net unwarned. Barney would have told him that he was there. What amazed Craig, as the fact slowly dawned on him, was that Johnny was still in evening dress. He took a step towards him, and gently Johnny disengaged the girl from his arms.

'I'd like to see the right cuff of your shirt, Johnny,' said Craig.

Without a word, Gray held up his arm, and the inspector scrutinized the spotless linen, for spotless it was. No sign of a stain was visible.

'Either somebody's doing some tall lying, or you're being extraordinarily clever, Johnny. I'll see that other cuff if I may.'

The second scrutiny produced no tangible result.

'Didn't you go home and change tonight?'

'No, I haven't been near my flat,' he said.

Craig was staggered.

'But your man said that you came in, changed, took a suitcase and went away.'

'Then Parker has been drinking,' was the calm reply. 'I have been enjoying the unusual experience of dining with the detective officer who was responsible for my holiday in Devonshire.'

Craig took a step back.

'With Inspector Flaherty?' he asked.

Johnny nodded.

'With the good Inspector Flaherty. We've been exchanging confidences about our mutual acquaintances.'

'But who was it who went to your flat?' asked the bewildered Craig.

'My double. I've always contended that I have a double,' said Johnny serenely.

He stood in the centre of the astounded group. Into Marney's heart had crept a wild hope.

'Johnny,' she said, 'was it this man who committed the crime for which you were punished?'

To her disappointment he shook his head.

'No, I am the gentleman who was arrested and sent to Dartmoor—my double stops short of these unpleasant experiences, and I can't say that I blame him.'

'But do you mean to say that he deceived your man?'

'Apparently,' said Johnny, turning again to the detective who had asked the question.

'I take your word, of course, Johnny, as an individual.'

Johnny chuckled.

'I like the pretty distinction. As an official, you want corroboration. Very well, that is not hard to get. If you take me back to Flaherty, he will support all I have told you.'

Peter and the detective allowed him to take leave of the girl without the embarrassment of their presence.

'It beats me—utterly beats me. Have you ever heard of this before, Peter?'

'That Johnny had a double? No, I can't say that I have.'

'He may have invented the story for the sake of the girl. But there is the fact: he's in evening dress, whilst his valet distinctly described him as wearing a grey tweed suit. There's no mark of blood on his cuff, and I'm perfectly certain that Stevens wouldn't have tried to get Johnny in bad. He's very fond of the boy. Of course, he may be spinning this yarn for the sake of Marney, but it'll be easy enough to corroborate. I'll use your phone, Peter,' he said suddenly. 'I've got Flaherty's number in my book.'

The biggest surprise of the evening came when a sleepy voice, undeniably Flaherty's, answered him.

'Craig speaking. Who have you been dining with tonight, Flaherty?'

'You don't mean to tell me that you've called me up in the middle of the night,' began the annoyed Irishman, 'to ask me who I've been dining with?'

'This is serious, Flaherty. I want to know.'

'Why, with Johnny, of course—Johnny Gray. I asked him to come to dinner.'

'What time did he leave you?'

'Nearer eleven than ten,' was the reply. 'No, it was after eleven.'

'And he was with you all that time? He didn't leave for a quarter of an hour?'

'Not for a quarter of a minute. We just talked and talked . . .'

Craig replaced the receiver and turned away from the instrument, shaking his head.

'Any other alibi would have hanged you, Johnny. But Flaherty's the straightest man in the CID.'

In view of what followed when Johnny reached his flat in the early hours of the morning, this testimony to the integrity of inspector Flaherty seemed a little misguided.

'Nobody else been here?'

'No, sir,' said Parker.

'What did you do with the shirt I took off?'

'I cut off the cuffs and burnt them, sir. I did it with a greater pleasure, because the rounded corner cuff is just a little—how shall I call it?—theatrical.'

'The rest of the shirt—?'

'The rest of the shirt, sir,' said Parker deferentially, 'I am wearing. It is rather warm to wear two shirts, but I could think of no other way of disposing of it, sir. Shall I put your bath ready?'

Johnny nodded.

'If you will forgive the impertinence, did you succeed in persuading the gentleman you were going to see, to support your statement?'

'Flaherty? Oh, yes. Flaherty owes me a lot. Good night, Parker.'

'Good night, sir. I hope you sleep well. Er—may I take that gun out of your pocket, sir? It is spoiling the set of your trousers. Thank you very much.'

He took the Browning gingerly between his finger and thumb and laid it on Johnny's writing-table.

'You don't mind my being up a little late, sir?' he said. 'I think I would like to clean this weapon before I retire.'

18

Jeff Legge reclined in a long cane chair on a lawn which stretched to the edge of a cliff. Before him were the blue waters of the Channel, and the more gorgeous blue of an unflecked sky. He reached out his hand and took a glass that stood on the table by his side, sipped it with a wry face and called a name pettishly.

It was Lila who came running to his side.

'Take this stuff away, and bring me a whisky-and-soda,' he said.

'The doctor said you weren't to have anything but lime juice. Oh, Jeff, you must do as he tells you,' she pleaded.

'I'll break your head for you when I get up,' he snarled. 'Do as you're told. Where's the old man?'

'He's gone into the village to post some letters.'

He ruminated on this, and then:

'If that busy comes, you can tell him I'm too ill to be seen.'

'Who—Craig?'

'Yes,' he growled, 'the dirty, twisting thief! Johnny would've been in boob for this if he hadn't straightened Craig. If he didn't drop a thousand to keep off the moor, I'm a dead man!'

She pulled up a low chair to his side.

'I don't think Johnny did it,' she said. 'The old man thinks it was Peter. The window was found open after. He could have come in by the fire-escape—he knows the way.'

He grumbled something under his breath, and very discreetly she did not press home her view.

'Where's Marney—back with her father?'

She nodded.

'Who told him I was married to you?'

'I don't know, Jeff,' she said.

'You liar! You told him; nobody else could have known. If I get bird for this marriage, I'll kill you, Lila. That's twice you've squeaked on me.'

'I didn't know what I was saying. I was half mad with worry.'

'I wish you'd gone the whole journey,' he said bitterly. 'It isn't the woman—I don't care a darn about that. It's the old man's quarrel, and he's got to get through with it. It's the other business being disorganized that's worrying me. Unless it's running like clockwork, you'll get a jam; and when you've got a jam, you collect a bigger crowd than I want to see looking at my operations. You didn't squeak about that, I suppose?'

'No, Jeff, I didn't know.'

'And that's the reason you didn't squeak, eh?'

He regarded her unfavourably. And now she turned on him.

'Listen, Jeff Legge. I'm a patient woman, up to a point, and I'll stand for all your bad temper while you're ill. But you're living in a new age, Jeff, and you'd better wake up to the fact. All that Bill Sikes and Nancy stuff never did impress me. I'm no clinger. If you got really rough with me, I'd bat you, and that's a fact. It may not be womanly, but it's wise. I never did believe in the equality of the sexes, but no girl is the weaker vessel if she gets first grip of the kitchen poker.'

Very wisely he changed the subject.

'I supposed they searched the club from top to bottom?' he said.

'They did.'

'Did they look in the loft?'

'I believe they did. Stevens told me that they turned everything inside out.'

He grunted.

'They're clever,' he said. 'It must be wonderful to be clever. Who's this?' He scowled across the lawn at a strange figure that had appeared, apparently by way of the cliff gate.

She rose and walked to meet the stooping stranger, who stood, hat in hand, waiting for her and smiling awkwardly.

'I'm so sorry to intrude,' he said. 'This is a beautiful place, is it not? If I remember rightly, this is the Dellsea Vicarage? I used to know the vicar—a very charming man. I suppose you have taken the house from him?'

She was half amused, half annoyed.

'This is Dellsea Vicarage,' she said curtly. 'Do you want to see anybody?'

'I wanted to see Mr Jeffrey'—he screwed up his eyes and stared at the sky, as though trying to withdraw from some obscure cell of memory a name that would not come without special effort—'Mr Jeffrey Legge—that is the name—Mr Jeffrey Legge.'

'He's very ill and can't see anyone.'

'I'm sorry to hear that,' said the stranger, his mild face expressing the intensest sympathy. 'Very sorry indeed.'

His big, round glasses were for effect apparently, because he looked over them at her.

'I wonder if he would see me for just a few minutes. I've called to inquire about his health.'

'What is your name?' she asked.

'Reeder—J. G. Reeder.'

The girl felt her colour go, and turned quickly.

'I'll ask him,' she said.

Jeff heard the name and pursed his lips.

'That's the man the bank are running—or maybe it's the Government—to trail me,' he said in a low tone. 'Slip him along, Lila.'

Mr Reeder was beckoned across the lawn, and came with quick, mincing steps.

'I'm so sorry to see that you're in such a deplorable condition, Mr Legge,' he said. 'I hope your father is well?'

'Oh, you've met the old man, have you?' said Jeffrey in surprise.

Mr Reeder nodded.

'Yes; I have met your father,' he said. 'A very entertaining and a very ingenious man. Very!' The last word was spoken with emphasis.

Jeff was silent at this tribute to his parent's amiability.

'There has been a lot of talk in town lately about a certain nefarious business that is being carried on—surreptitiously, of course,' said Mr Reeder, choosing his words with care. 'I who live out of the world, and in the backwater of life, hear strange rumours about the distribution of illicit money—I think the cant term is slush or slosh—probably it is slush.'

'It is slush,' agreed Jeff, not knowing whether to be amused or alarmed, and watching the man all the time.

'Now I feel sure that the persons who are engaged in this practice cannot be aware of the enormously serious nature of their offence,' said Mr Reeder confidentially.

He broke off his lecture to look around the lawn and well-stocked garden that flanked it on either side.

'How beautiful is the world, Mr Jeff—I beg your pardon, Mr Legge,' he said. 'How lovely those flowers are! I confess that the sight of bluebells always brings a lump to my throat. I don't suppose they are bluebells,' he added, 'for it is rather late in the year. But that peculiar shade of blue. And those wonderful roses—I can smell them from here.'

He closed his eyes, raised his nose and sniffed loudly—a ludicrous figure; but Jeff Legge did not laugh.

'I know very little, but I understand that in Dartmoor Prison there are only a few potted flowers, and that those are never seen by the prisoners, except by one privileged man whose task it is to tend them. A lifer, generally. Life without flowers must be very drab, Mr Legge.'

'I'm not especially fond of flowers,' said Jeffrey.

'What a pity!' said the other regretfully. 'What a thousand pities! But there is no sea view from that establishment, no painted ships upon a painted ocean—which is a quotation from a well-known poem; no delightful sense of freedom; nothing really that makes life durable for a man under sentence, let us say, of fifteen or twenty years.'

Jeff did not reply.

'Do you love rabbits?' was the surprising question that was put to him.

'No, I can't say that I do.'

Lila sat erect, motionless, all her senses strained to hear and understand.

Mr Reeder sighed.

'I am very fond of rabbits. Whenever I see a rabbit in a cage or in a hutch, I buy it, take it to the nearest wood and release it. It may be a foolish kindness, because, born and reared in captivity, it may not have the necessary qualities to support itself amongst its wilder fellows. But I like letting rabbits loose; other people like putting rabbits in cages.' He shook his finger in Jeffrey's face. 'Never be a rabbit in a cage, Mr Jeffrey—or is it Mr Legge? Yes, Mr Legge.'

'I'm neither a rabbit, nor a chicken, nor a fox, nor a skylark,' said Jeffrey. 'The cage hasn't been built that could hold me.'

Again Mr Reeder sighed.

'I remember another gentleman saying that some years ago. I forget in what prison he was hanged. Possibly it was Wandsworth—yes, I am sure it was Wandsworth. I saw his grave the other day. Just his initials. What a pity! What a sad end to a promising career! He is better off, I think, for twenty long years in a prison cell, that is a dreadful fate, Mr Legge! And it is a fate that would never overtake a man who decided to reform. Suppose, let us say, he was forging Bank of England notes, and decided that he would burn his paper and his water-markers, dismiss all his agents . . . I don't think we should worry very much about that type of person. We should meet him generously and liberally, especially if his notes were of such excellent quality that they were difficult for the uninitiated to detect.'

'What has happened to Golden?' asked Jeffrey boldly.

The eyes of the elderly man twinkled.

'Golden was my predecessor,' he said. 'A very charming fellow, by some accounts—'
Again Jeffrey cut him short.

'He used to be the man who was looking after the slush for the police. Is he dead?'

'He has gone abroad,' said Mr Reeder gravely. 'Yes, Mr Golden could not stand this climate. He suffered terribly from asthma, or it may have been sciatica. I know there was an "a" at the end of it. Did you ever meet him? Ah! You missed a very great opportunity,' said Mr Reeder. 'Golden was a nice fellow—not as smart, perhaps, as he might have been, or as he should have been, but a very nice fellow. He did not work, perhaps, so much in the open as I do; and there I think he was mistaken. It is always an error to shut yourself up in an office and envelop yourself in an atmosphere of mystery. I myself am prone to the same fault. Now, my dear Mr Legge, I am sure you will take my parable kindly, and will give it every thought and consideration.'

'I would, if I were a printer of slush, but, unfortunately, I'm not,' said Jeffrey Legge with a smile.

'You're not, of course,' the other hastened to say. 'I wouldn't dream of suggesting you were. But with your vast circle of acquaintances—and, I'm sure, admirers—you may perhaps be able to convey my simple little illustration. I don't like to see rabbits in cages, or birds in cages, or anything else behind bars. And I think that Dartmoor is so—what shall I say?—unaesthetic. And it seems *such* a pity to spend all the years in Devonshire. In the spring, of course, it is delightful; in the summer it is hot; in the winter, unless you're at Torquay, it is deplorable. Good morning, Mr Legge.'

He bowed low to the girl and as he bowed his glasses fell off. Stooping, he picked them up with an apology, and backed away; and they watched him in silence till he had disappeared from view.

19

'What do you think of him for a busy?' asked Jeffrey contemptuously.

She did not answer. Contact with the man had frightened her. It was not like Lila to shiver in the presence of detectives.

'I don't know what he is,' she said a little breathlessly. 'He's something like a . . . good-natured snake. Didn't you feel that, Jeffrey?'

'Good-natured nothing,' said the other with a curl of his lip. 'He's worse than Golden. These big corporations fall for that kind of man. They never give a chance to a real clever busy.'

'Who was Golden?' she asked.

'He was an old fellow too. They fired him.' He chuckled to himself. 'And I was responsible for firing him. Then they brought in Mr J. G. Reeder with a flourish of trumpets. He's been on the game three years, and he's just about as near to making a pull as he ever was.'

'Jeff, isn't there danger?' Her voice was very serious.

'Isn't there always danger? No more danger than usual,' he said. 'They can't touch me. Don't worry! I've covered myself so that they can't see me for overcoats! Once the stuff's printed, they can never put it back on me.'

'Once it's printed.' She nodded slowly. 'Then you *are* the Big Printer, Jeff?'

'Talk about something else,' he said.

When Emanuel returned, as he did soon after, Lila met him at the gate and told him of Reeder's visit. To her surprise, he took almost the same view as Jeff had taken.

'He's a fool, but straight—up to five thousand, anyway. No man is straight when you reach his figure.'

'But why did he come to Jeff?' she asked.

'Doesn't everybody in the business know that Jeff's the Big Printer? Haven't they been trying to put it on him for years? Of course he came. It was his last, despairing stroke. How's the boy?' he asked.

'He's all right, but a little touchy.'

'Of course he's a little touchy,' said Emanuel indignantly. 'You don't suppose he's going to get better in a day, do you? The club's running again.'

'Has it been closed?'

'It hasn't exactly been closed, but it has been unpopular,' he said, showing his teeth in that smile of his. 'Listen.' He caught her arm on the edge of the lawn. 'Get your mind off that shooting, will you? I'll fix the man responsible for that.'

'Do you know?' she asked.

It was the first time he had ever discussed the matter calmly, for the very mention of the attack upon Jeff had hitherto been sufficient to drive him to an incoherent frenzy.

'Yes, I know,' he said gratingly. 'It was Peter Kane, but you needn't say anything about that—I'll fix him, I tell you.'

'Jeff thinks it was—'

'Never mind what Jeff thinks,' he said impatiently. 'Do as I tell you.'

He sent her into the house to brew him a cup of tea—Emanuel was a great drinker of tea—and in her absence he had something to say to his son.

'Jeff, there's a big call for your stuff,' he said, 'I've had a letter from Harvey. He says there's another man started in the north of England, and he's turning out pretty good material. But they want yours—they can place half a million on the Continent right away. Jeff, what Harvey says is right. If there's a slackening of supply while you're ill, the busy fellows are going to tumble to you.'

'I've thought of that,' said Jeffrey. 'You can tell anybody who's interested that there'll be a printing next week.'

'Are you well enough to go up?' asked his father anxiously.

Jeffrey nodded, and shifted himself more erect, but winced in the process.

'Reeder's been here; did she tell you?'

Emanuel nodded.

'I'm not worried much about Reeder. Down in Dartmoor he's a bogey; but then they bogey any man they don't know. And they've got all sorts of stories about him. It's very encouraging to get near to the real thing.'

They laughed together, and for the rest of the day discussed ways and means.

Jeffrey had said no more than was true when he had told the girl he was well covered. In various parts of the country he had twelve banking accounts, each in a different name, and at one of the safe deposits, an enormous sum in currency, ready for an emergency.

'You've got to stop some time, I suppose,' said his father, 'but it's mighty tempting to carry on with those profits. It's a bigger graft than I ever attempted, Jeff.' And his son accepted this respectful tribute with a smirk.

The old man sat, his clasped hands between his knees, staring out over the sea.

'It's got to end some day, and that would be a fine end, but I can't quite see how it could be done.'

'What are you talking about?' asked the other curiously.

'I'm thinking about Peter—the respectable Mr Peter Kane. Not quite so respectable in that girl's eyes as he used to be, but respectable enough to have busies to dinner, and that crook, Johnny Gray—Johnny will marry the girl, Jeff.'

Jeffrey Legge winced.

'She can marry the devil so far as I'm concerned,' he said.

'But she can't marry without divorcing you. Do you realize that, my son? That's the law. And she can't divorce you without shopping you for bigamy. That's the law too. And the question is, will she delay her action until Johnny's made a bit, or will she start right in? If she gives me just the time I want, Jeff, you'll have your girl and I'll have Peter Kane. She's your wife in the eyes of the law.'

There was a significance in his words that made the other man look at him quickly.

'What's the great idea?' he asked.

'Suppose Peter was the Big Printer?' said Emanuel, speaking in a tone that was little above a whisper. 'Suppose he was caught with the goods? It could be done. I don't mean by planting the stuff in his house—nobody would accept that; but getting him right on the spot, so that his best friend at Scotland Yard couldn't save him? How's that for an idea?'

'It couldn't be done,' said the other immediately.

'Oh, couldn't it?' sneered Emanuel. 'You can do any old thing you want, if you make up your mind to do it. Or if you're game to do it.'

'That wouldn't get me the girl.'

Emanuel turned his head slowly towards his heir.

'If they found the Big Printer, they'll have to find the big printing,' he said deliberately. 'That means we should all have to skip, and skip lively. We might have a few hours' start, and in these days three hours is twelve hundred miles. Jeff, if we're caught, and they guess I've been in this printing all the time, I shall never see outside again. And you'll go down for life. They can't give you any worse than that—not if you took the girl away with you.'

'By force?' asked the other in surprise. The idea had not occurred to him.

The father nodded.

'If we have to skip, that's the only thing for you to do, son. It's no offence—remember that. She's your wife.' He looked to left and right, to see if there was the faintest shadow of a chance that he would be overheard, and then: 'Suppose we ask Peter and his girl *and* Johnny Gray to dinner? A nice little dinner party, eh?'

'Where?' asked the other suspiciously.

'In Room 13,' said Emanuel Legge. 'In Room 13, Jeff, boy! A nice little dinner. What do you think? And then two whiffs of sleep stuff—'

'You're mad,' said the other angrily. 'What's the good of talking that way? Do you think he's going to come to dinner and bring his girl? Oh, you're nutty to think it!'

'Trust me,' said Emanuel Legge.

20

Walking down Regent Street one morning, Johnny Gray saw a familiar face—a man standing on the kerb selling trinkets. The face was oddly familiar, but he had gone on a dozen paces before he recalled where he had seen him before, and then he turned back. The man knew him; at any rate, his uncouth features twisted in a smile.

'Good morning, my lord,' he said. 'What about a toy balloon for the baby?'

'Your name is Fenner, isn't it?' said Johnny with a good-humoured gesture of refusal.

'That's me, Captain. I didn't think you'd recognized me. How's business?'

'Quiet,' said Johnny conventionally. 'What are you doing?'

The man shrugged his enormous shoulders.

'Selling these, and filling in the time with a little sluicing.'

Johnny shook his head reprovingly. Sluicing in the argot indicates a curious method of livelihood. In public wash-places, where men strip off their coats to wash their hands there are fine pickings to be had by a man with quick fingers and a knowledge of human nature.

'Did you ever get your towelling?'[1]

'No,' said the other contemptuously and with a deep growl. 'I knew they couldn't, that's why I coshed the screw. I was too near my time. If I ever see old man Legge, by God I'll—'

Johnny raised his fingers. A policeman was strolling past, and was eyeing the two suspiciously. Apparently, if he regarded Fenner with disfavour, Johnny's respectability redeemed the association.

'Poor old flattie!' said Fenner as the officer passed. 'What a life!'

The man looked him up and down amusedly.

'You seem to have struck it, Gray,' he said, with no touch of envy. 'What's your graft?'

'It is one you'll find difficult to understand, Fenner. I'm being honest!'

1. Flogging.

'That's certainly a new one on me,' said the other frankly. 'Have you seen old Emanuel?' His voice was now quite calm. 'Great fellow, Emanuel! And young Emanuel—Jeffrey— what a lad!'

There was a glint in his eyes which told Johnny that he knew much more of recent happenings than he was prepared to state. And his next words supported that view.

'You keep away from the Legge lot, Captain,' he said earnestly. 'They're no good to anybody, and least of all to a man who's had an education like yours. I owe Legge one, and I'll get him, but I'm not thinking about that so much as young Jeff. You're the fellow he'd go after, because you dress like a swell and you look like a swell—the very man to put slush about without anybody tumbling.'

'The Big Printer?' asked Johnny, with a smile.

'The Big Printer,' repeated the other gravely, 'And he *is* a big printer. You hear all sorts of lies down on the moor, but that's true. Jeff's got the biggest graft that's ever been worked in this country. They'll get him sooner or later, because there never was a crook game yet that hadn't got a squeak about it somewhere. And the squeak has started, judging by what I can read in the papers. Who shot him?' he asked bluntly.

Johnny shook his head.

'That is what is known as a mystery,' he said and, seeing the man's eyes keenly searching his face, he laughed aloud. 'It wasn't me, Fenner. I'll assure you on that point. And as to me being a friend of Jeff'—he paused—'that isn't like me either. How are you off for money?'

'Rotten,' said the other laconically, and Johnny slipped two five-pound notes on to the tray.

He was turning away when the man called him back.

'Keep out of boob,' he said significantly. 'And don't think I'm handing round good advice. I'm not thinking of Dartmoor. There are other boobs that are worse—I can tell you that, because I've seen most of them.'

He gathered up the money on the tray without so much as a word of thanks, and put it in his waistcoat pocket.

'Keytown Jail is the worst prison in England,' he said, not looking at his benefactor but staring straight ahead. 'The very worst—don't forget that, Gray. Keytown Prison is the worst boob in England; and if you ever find yourself there, do something to get out. So long!'

The mentality of the criminal had been a subject for vicarious study during Johnny's stay in Dartmoor, and he mused on the man's words as he continued his walk along Regent Street. Here was a man offering advice which he himself had never taken. The moral detachment of old lags was no new phenomenon to Johnny. He had listened for hours to the wise admonitions and warnings of convicts, who would hardly be free from the fusty cell of the prison before they would be planning new villainies, new qualifications for their return.

He had never heard of Keytown Jail before, but it was not remarkable that Fenner should have some special grudge against a particular jail. The criminal classes have their likes and their dislikes; they loathed Wandsworth and preferred Pentonville, or vice versa, for no particular reason. There were those who swore by Parkhurst; others regarded Dartmoor as home, and bitterly resented any suggestion that they should be transferred to the island prison.

So musing, he bumped into Craig. The collision was not accidental, for Craig had put himself in the way of the abstracted young man.

'What are you planning, Johnny—a jewel robbery, or just ringing the changes on the Derby favourite?'

Johnny chuckled.

'Neither. I was at that moment wondering what there was particularly bad about Keytown Jail. Where is Keytown Jail, by the way?'

'Keytown? I don't remember—oh, yes, I do. Just outside Oxford. Why?'

'Somebody was telling me it was the worst prison in England.'

'They are all the worst, Johnny,' said Craig. 'And if you're thinking out a summer holiday, I can't recommend either. Keytown was pretty bad,' he admitted. 'It's a little country jail, but it's no longer in the Prison Commissioners' hands. They sold it after the war, when they closed down so many of these little prisons. The policy now is to enlarge the bigger places and cut out these expensive little boobs that cost money to staff. They closed Hereford Jail in the same way, and half a dozen others, I should think. So you needn't bother about Keytown,' he smiled bleakly. 'One of your criminal acquaintances has been warning you, I guess?'

'You've guessed right,' said Johnny, and advanced no information, knowing that, if Craig continued his walk, he would sooner or later see the kerb seller.

'Mr Jeffrey Legge is making a good recovery,' said the detective, changing the subject: 'and there are great rejoicings at Scotland Yard. If there is one man we want to keep alive until he is hanged in a scientific and lawful manner, it is Mr Jeffrey Legge. I know what you're going to say—we've got nothing on him. That's true. Jeffrey has been too clever for us. He's got his father skinned to death in that respect. He makes no mistakes—a rare quality in a forger; he carries no slush, keeps none at his home. I can tell you that, because we've pulled him in twice on suspicion, and searched him from occiput to *tendo achilles*. Forgive the anatomical terms, but anatomy is my hobby. Hallo!'

He was looking across the street at a figure which was not unfamiliar to Johnny. Mr Reeder wore a shabby black coat and badly creased striped trousers. Beneath his arm he carried a partially furled umbrella. His hands, covered in grey cotton gloves (at a distance Johnny thought they were suède), were clasped behind him. His spectacles were, as usual, so far down his nose that they seemed in danger of slipping over.

'Do you know that gentleman?'

'Man named Reeder, isn't it? He's a busy.'

Craig's lips twitched.

'He's certainly a busy of sorts,' he said dryly, 'but not of our sort.'

'He's a bank man, isn't he?' asked Johnny, watching Mr Reeder's slow and awkward progress.

'He is in the employ of the bank,' said the detective, 'and he's not such a fool as he looks. I happen to know. He was down seeing young Legge yesterday. I was curious enough to put a man on to trail him. And he knows more about young Legge than I gave him credit for.'

When Johnny parted from the detective, Mr Reeder had passed out of sight. Crossing Piccadilly Circus, however, he saw the elderly man waiting in a bus queue, and interestedly stood and watched him until the bus arrived and Mr Reeder boarded the vehicle and disappeared into its interior. As the bus drew away, Johnny raised his eyes to the destination board and saw that it was Victoria.

'I wonder,' said Johnny, speaking his thought aloud.

For Victoria is the station for Horsham.

21

Mr Reeder descended from the bus at Victoria Station, bought a third-class return ticket to Horsham. He then went to the bookstall, purchased a copy of the *Economist* and the *Poultry World* and, thus fortified for the journey, passed through the barrier, and finding an empty carriage, ensconced himself in one corner. And until the train drew into Horsham Station, he was apparently alternately absorbed in the eccentricities of Rhode Island Reds and the fluctuations of the mark.

There were many taxis at the station, willing and anxious to convey him to his destination; but Mr Reeder was deaf to all the urgent offers which were made to him and, using his umbrella as a walking-stick, he set out to walk the distance between the station and Peter Kane's residence.

Peter was in his library, smoking a meditative cigar, when Barney came in with the news.

'There's an old guy wants to see you, Peter. I don't know who he is, but he says his name's Reeder.'

Peter's brows met.

'Reeder?' he said sharply. 'What sort of man is he?'

'An old fellow,' said Barney. 'Too shaky for a busy. He looks as if he's trying to raise subscriptions for the organ fund.'

'It was not an unfair description, as Peter knew.

'Bring him here, Barney, and keep your mouth shut. And bear in mind that this is the busiest busy you are ever likely to meet.'

'A copper?' said Barney incredulously.

Peter nodded.

'Where's Marney?' he asked quickly.

'Up in her boojar,' said Barney with relish. 'She's writing letters. She wrote one to Johnny. It started "Dearest".'

'How do you know?' asked Peter sharply.

'Because I read it,' said Barney without shame. 'I'm a pretty good reader: I can read things upside down, owing to me having been in the printing business when I was a kid.'

'Bring in Mr Reeder,' interrupted Peter ominously. 'And remember, Barney, that if I ever catch you reading anything of mine upside down, you *will* be upside down! And don't argue.'

Barney left the room, uttering a mechanical defiance which such threats invariably provoked.

Mr Reeder came in, his shabby hat in one hand, his umbrella in the other, and a look of profound unhappiness on his face.

'*Good* morning, Mr Kane,' he said, laying down his impediments. 'What a beautiful morning it is for a walk! It is a sin and a shame to be indoors on a day like this. Give me a garden, with roses, if I may express a preference, and just a faint whiff of heliotrope . . .'

'You'd like to see me in the garden, eh?' said Peter. 'Perhaps you're wise.'

Barney, his inquisitive ears glued to the keyhole, cursed softly.

'I was in a garden yesterday,' murmured Mr Reeder, as they walked across the lawn towards the sunken terraces. 'Such a lovely garden! One bed was filled with blue flowers. There is something about a blue flower that brings a lump into my throat. Rhododendrons infuriate me: I have never understood why. There is that about a clump of rhododendrons which rouses all that is evil in my nature. Daffodils, on the other hand, and especially daffodils intermingled with hyacinths, have a most soothing effect upon me. The garden to which I refer had the added attraction of being on the edge of the sea—a veritable Garden of Eden, Mr Kane, although'—he wagged his head from side to side disparagingly—'there were more snakes than is customary. There was a snake in a chair, and a snake who was posting letters in the village, and another official snake who was hiding behind a clump of bushes and had followed me all the way from London— sent, I think, by that misguided gentleman, Mr Craig.'

'Where were you, Mr Reeder?'

'At a seaside villa, a beautiful spot. A truly earthly paradise,' sighed Mr Reeder. 'The very place an intelligent man would go to if he were convalescent, and the gentleman on the chair was certainly convalescent.'

'You saw Jeff Legge, eh? Sit down.'

He pointed to the marble bench where Johnny had sat and brooded unhappily on a certain wedding day.

'I think not,' said Mr Reeder, shaking his head as he stared at the marble seat. 'I suffer from rheumatism, with occasional twinges of sciatica. I think I would rather walk with you, Mr Kane.' He glanced at the hedge. 'I do not like people who listen. Sometimes one listens and hears too much. I heard the other day of a very charming man who happened to be standing behind a bush, and heard the direful character of his son-in-law revealed. It was not good for him to hear so much.'

Peter knew that the man was speaking about him, but gave no sign.

'I owe you something, Mr Reeder, for the splendid way you treated my daughter—'

Mr Reeder stopped him with a gesture.

'A very charming girl. A very lovely girl,' he said with mild enthusiasm. 'And so interested in chickens! One so seldom meets with women who take a purely sincere interest in chickens.'

They had reached a place where it was impossible they could be overheard. Peter, who realized that the visitor would not have called unless he had something important to say, waited for the next move. Mr Reeder returned to the subject of eavesdropping.

'My friend—if I may call him my friend—who learnt by accident that his son-in-law was an infernal rascal—if you will excuse that violent expression—might have got himself into serious trouble, very serious trouble.' He shook his heard solemnly. 'For you see,' he went on, 'my friend—I do hope he will allow me to call him my friend?—has something of a criminal past, and all his success has been achieved by clever strategy. Now, was it clever strategy'—he did not look at Peter, and his faded eyes surveyed the landscape gloomily—'was it clever of my friend to convey to Mr Emanuel Legge the astounding information that at a certain hour, in a certain room—I think its number was thirteen, but I am not sure—Mr John Gray was meeting Mr J. G. Reeder to convey information which would result in Emanuel Legge's son going to prison for a long period? Was it wise to forge the handwriting of one of Emanuel Legge's disreputable associates, and induce the aforesaid Emanuel to mount the fire-escape at the Highlow Club and shoot, as he thought, Mr John Gray, who wasn't Mr Gray at all, but his own son? I ask you, was it wise?'

Peter did not answer.

'Was it discreet, when my friend went to the hotel where his daughter was staying, and found her gone, to leave a scribbled note on the floor, which conveyed to Mr Jeffrey Legge the erroneous information that the young lady was meeting Johnny Gray in Room 13 at nine-thirty? I admit,' said Mr Reeder handsomely, 'that by these clever manoeuvres, my friend succeeded in getting Jeffrey Legge just where he wanted him at the proper time; for Jeffrey naturally went to the Highlow Club in order to confront and intimidate his wife. You're a man of the world, Mr Kane, and I'm sure you will see how terribly indiscreet my friend was. For Jeffrey might have been killed.' He sighed heavily. 'His precious life might have been lost; and if the letters were produced at the trial, my friend himself might have been tried for murder.'

He dusted the arms of his coat tenderly.

'The event had the elements of tragedy,' he said, 'and it was only by accident that Jeff's face was turned away from the door; and it was only by accident that Emanuel was not seen going out. And it was only by the sheerest and cleverest perjury that Johnny Gray was not arrested.'

'Johnny was not there,' said Peter sharply.

'On the contrary, Johnny was there—please admit that he was there?' pleaded Mr Reeder. 'Otherwise, all my theories are valueless. And a gentleman in my profession hates to see his theories suffer extinction.'

'I'll not admit anything of the sort,' said Peter sharply. 'Johnny spent that evening with a police officer. It must have been his double.'

'His treble perhaps,' murmured the other. 'Who knows? Humanity resembles, to a very great extent, the domestic fowl, *gallus domesticus*. One man resembles another—it is largely a matter of plumage.'

He looked up to the sky as though he were seeking inspiration from heaven itself.

'Mr Jeffrey Legge has not served you very well, Mr Kane,' he said. 'In fact, I think he has served you very badly. He is obviously a person without principle or honour, and deserves anything that may come to him.'

Peter waited, and suddenly the man brought his eyes to the level of his.

'You must have heard, in the course of your travels, a great deal about Mr Legge?' he suggested. 'Possibly more has come to you since this unfortunate—indeed, dastardly—happening, of which I cannot remind you without inflicting unnecessary pain. Now,

Mr Kane, don't you think that you would be rendering a service to human society if—'

'If I squeaked,' said Peter Kane quietly. 'I'll put your mind at rest on that subject immediately. I know nothing of Jeffrey Legge except that he's a blackguard. But if I did, if I had the key to his printing works, if I had evidence in my pocket of his guilt—' he paused.

'And if you had all these?' asked Mr Reeder gently.

'I should not squeak,' said Peter with emphasis, 'because that is not the way. A squeak is a squeak, whether you do it in cold blood or in the heat of temper.'

Again Mr Reeder sighed heavily, took off his glasses, breathed on them and polished them with gentle vigour, and did not speak until he had replaced them.

'It is all very honourable,' he said sadly. 'This—er—faith and—er—integrity . . . Again the poultry parallel comes to my mind. Certain breeds of chickens hold together and have nothing whatever to do with other breeds; and, though they may quarrel amongst themselves, will fight to the death for one another. Your daughter is well, I trust?'

'She is very well,' said Peter emphatically, 'surprisingly so, I thought she would have a bad time—here she is.' He turned at that moment and waved his hand to the girl, who was coming down the steps of the terrace. 'You know Mr Reeder?' said Peter as the girl came smiling towards the chicken expert with outstretched hand.

'Why, of course I know him,' she said warmly. 'Almost you have persuaded me to run a poultry farm!'

'You might do worse,' said Mr Reeder gravely. There are very few women who take an intelligent interest in such matters. Men are much more interested in chickens.'

Peter looked at him sharply. There was something in his tone, a glint of unsuspected humour in his eyes, that lit and died in a second, and Peter Kane was nearer to understanding the man at that moment that he had ever been before.

And here Peter took a bold step.

'Mr Reeder is a detective,' he said, 'employed by the banks to try and track down the people who have been putting so many forged notes on the market.'

'A detective!'

Her eyes opened wide in surprise, and Mr Reeder hastened to disclaim the appellation.

'Not a detective. I beg of you not to misunderstand, Miss Kane. I am merely an investigator, an inquiry agent, not a detective. "Detective" is a term which is wholly repugnant to me. I have never arrested a man in my life, nor have I authority to do so.'

'At any rate, you don't look like a detective, Mr Reeder,' smiled the girl.

'Thank you,' said Mr Reeder gratefully. 'I should not wish to be mistaken for a detective. It is a profession which I admire, but do not envy.'

He took from his pocket a large note-case and opened it. Inside, fastened by a rubber band in the centre, was a thick wad of bank notes. Seeing them, Peter's eyebrows rose.

'You're a bold man to carry all that money about with you, Mr Reeder,' he said.

'Not bold,' disclaimed the investigator. 'I am indeed a very timid man.'

He slipped a note from under the elastic band and handed it to his wondering host. Peter took it.

'A fiver,' he said.

Mr Reeder took another, Peter saw it was a ten-pound note before he held it in his hand.
'Would you cash that for me?'

Peter Kane frowned.

'What do you mean?'

'Would you cash it for me?' asked Mr Reeder. 'Or perhaps you have no change?'

'I'll change it for you with pleasure,' said Peter, and was taking out his own note-case when Mr Reeder stopped him with a gesture.

'Forged,' he said briefly.

Peter looked at the note in his hand.

'Forged? Impossible! That's a good note.'

He rustled it scientifically and held it up to the light. The watermark was perfect. The secret marks on the face of the note which he knew very well were there. He moistened the corner of the note with his thumb.

'You needn't trouble,' said Reeder. 'It answers all the tests.'

'Do you mean to tell me this is slush—I mean a forgery?'

The other nodded, and Peter examined the note again with a new interest. He who had seen so much bad money had to admit that it was the most perfect forgery he had ever handled.

'I shouldn't have hesitated to change that for you. Is all the other money the same?'

Again the man nodded.

'But is that really bad money?' asked Marney, taking the note from her father. 'How is it made?'

Before the evasive answer came she guessed. In a flash she pieced together the hints, the vague scraps of gossip she had heard about the Big Printer.

'Jeffrey Legge!' she gasped, going white. 'Oh!'

'Mr Jeffrey Legge,' nodded Reeder. 'Of course we can prove nothing. Now perhaps we can sit down.'

It was he who suggested that they should go back to the garden seat. Not until, in his furtive way, he had circumnavigated the clump of bushes that hid the lawn from view did he open his heart.

'I am going to tell you a lot, Mr Kane,' he said, 'because I feel you may be able to help me, in spite of your principles. There are two men who could have engraved this note, one man who could manufacture the paper. Anybody could print it—anybody, that is to say, with a knowledge of printing. The two men are Lacey and Burns. They have both been in prison for forgery; they were both released ten years ago, and since then they have not been seen. The third man is a paper maker, who was engaged in the bank-note works at Wellington. He went to prison for seven years for stealing bank-note paper. He also has been released a very considerable time, and he also has vanished.'

'Lacey and Burns? I've heard of them. What's the other man's name?' asked Peter.

Mr Reeder told him.

'Jennings? I never heard of him.'

'You wouldn't because he is the most difficult type of criminal to track. In other words, he's not a criminal in the ordinary sense of the word. I am satisfied that he is on the Continent because, to be making paper, it is necessary that one should have the most up-to-date machinery. The printing is done here.'

'Where?' asked the girl innocently, and for the first time she saw Mr Reeder smile.

'I want this man very badly, and it is a matter of interest for you, young lady, because I could get him tomorrow—for bigamy. He saw the girl flush. 'Which I shall not do. I want Jeff the Big Printer, not Jeff the bigamist. And oh, I want him badly!'

A sound of loud coughing came from the lawn, and Barney appeared at the head of the steps.

'Anybody want to see Emanuel Legge?'

They looked at one another.

'I don't want to see him,' said Mr Reeder decidedly. He nodded at the girl. 'And you don't want to see him. I fear that leaves only you, Mr Kane.'

22

Peter was as cool as ice when he came into the drawing-room and found Emanuel examining the pictures on the wall with the air of a connoisseur. He turned, and beamed a benevolent smile on the man he hated.

'I didn't think you'd come here again, Legge,' said Peter with dangerous calm.

'Didn't you now?' Emanuel seemed surprised. 'Well, why not? And me wanting to fix things up, too! I'm surprised at you, Peter.'

'You'll put nothing right,' said the other. 'The sooner you recognize that fact and clear, the better it will be for everybody.'

'If I'd known,' Emanuel went on, unabashed, 'if only I'd dreamt that the young woman Jeffrey had taken up with was your daughter, I'd have stopped it at once, Peter. The boy had been brought up straight and never had met you. It's funny the number of straight people that never met Peter Kane. Of course, if he'd been on the crook, he'd have known at once. Do you think my boy would have married the daughter of a man who twisted his father? Is it likely, Peter? However, it's done now, and what's done can't be undone. The girl's fond of him, and he's fond of the girl—'

'When you've finished being comic, you can go,' said Peter. 'I never laugh before lunch.'

'Don't you, Peter? And not after? I've come at a very bad time, it seems to me. Now listen, Peter. Let's talk business.'

'I've no business with you.' Peter opened the door.

'Haste was always your weakness, Peter,' said Emanuel, not budging from where he stood. 'Never lose your temper. I lost my temper once and shot a copper, and did fifteen years for it. Fifteen years, whilst you were sitting here in luxury, entertaining the lords and ladies of the neighbourhood, and kidding 'em you were straight. I'm going to ask you a favour, Peter.'

'It is granted before you ask,' said the other sardonically.

'I'm going to ask you and Johnny boy to come and have a bit of dinner with me and Jeffrey, and let's fix this thing up. You're not going to have this girl brought into the divorce court, are you? And you've got to get a divorce, whether he's married or whether he isn't. As a matter of fact, he isn't married at all. I never dreant you'd be such a mug as to fall for the story that Lila was properly married to Jeff. All these girls tell you the same thing. It's vanity, Peter, a human weakness, if I may so describe it.'

'Perhaps it was the vanity of the registrar who signed their marriage certificate, and the vanity of the people who witnessed the marriage,' said Peter. 'Your son was married to this girl at Greenwich Registry Office; I've got a copy of the certificate—you can see it if you like.'

Still the smile on Emanuel's face did not fade.

'Ain't you smart?' he said admiringly. 'Ain't you the quickest grafter that ever grafted? Married or not, Peter, the girl's got to go into the court for the marriage to be—what do you call it?—annulled, that's the word. And she can't marry till she does. And they'll never annul the marriage until you get my boy caught for bigamy, and that you won't do, Peter, because you don't want to advertise what a damned fool you are. Take my advice, come and talk it over. Bring Johnny with you—'

'Why should I bring Johnny? I can look after myself.'

'Johnny's an interested party,' said the other. 'He's interested in anything to do with Marney, eh?' He chuckled and for a second Peter Kane had all his work to maintain his calm.

'I'm not going to discuss Marney with you. I'll meet you and the Printer, and I don't suppose Johnny will mind either. Though what you can do that the law can't do, I don't know.'

'I can give you evidence that you can't get any other way,' said the other. 'The fact is, Peter, my poor boy has realized he's made a mistake. He married a girl who was the daughter of a respectable gentleman, and when I broke it to him, Peter, that he'd married into a crook family, he was upset! He said I ought to have told him.'

'I don't know what funny business you're going to try,' said Peter Kane, 'but I'm not going to run away from it. You want me to meet you and your son—where?'

'What about the old Highlow?' suggested Emanuel. 'What about Room 13, where a sad accident nearly occurred?'

'Where you shot your son?' asked Peter coolly, and only for a second did the man's self-possession leave him. His face turned a dusky red and then a pale yellow.

'I shot my son there, did I? Peter, you're getting old and dopey. You've been dreaming again, Peter. Shot my son!'

'I'll come to this fool dinner of yours.'

'And Marney?' suggested the other.

'Marney doesn't put her foot inside the doors of the Highlow,' said Peter calmly. 'You're mad to imagine I would allow that. I can't answer for Johnny, but I'll be there.'

'What about Thursday?' suggested the old man.

'Any day will suit me,' said Peter impatiently. 'What time do you want us?'

'Half past eight. Just a snack and a talk. We may as well have a bit of food to make it cheerful, eh, Peter? Remember that dinner we had a few days before we smashed the Southern Bank? That must be twenty years ago. You split fair on that, didn't you? I'll bet you did—I had the money! No taking a million dollars and calling it a hundred and twenty thousand pounds, eh, Peter?'

This time Peter stood by the door, and the jerk of his head told Emanuel Legge that the moment for persiflage had passed.

'I want to settle this matter.' The earnestness of his manner did not deceive Peter. 'You see, Peter, I'm getting old, and I want to go abroad and take the boy with me. And I want to give him a chance too—a good-looking lad like that ought to have a chance. For I'll tell you the truth—he's a single man.'

Peter smiled.

'You can laugh! He married Lila—you've got a record of that, but have you taken a screw at the divorce list? That takes the grin off your face. They were divorced a year after they were married. Lila got tired of the other man and came back to Jeff. You're a looker-up; go and look up that! Ask old Reeder—'

'Ask him yourself,' said Peter. 'He's in the garden.'

He had no sooner said the words than he regretted them. Emanuel was silent for a while.

'So Reeder's here, in the garden, is he! He's come for a squeak. But you can't, because you've nothing to squeak about. What does he want?'

'Why don't you ask him?'

'That fellow spends his life wandering about other people's gardens,' grumbled Emanuel.

A disinterested observer might have imagined that Mr Reeder's passion for horticulture was the only grievance against him.

'He was round my garden yesterday. I dare say he told you? Came worrying poor Jeff to death. But you always were fond of busies, weren't you, Peter? How's your old friend Craig? I can't stand them myself, but then I'm a crook. Thursday will suit you, Peter? That gives you six days.'

'Thursday will suit me,' said Peter. 'I hope it will suit you.'

As he came back on to the lawn Reeder and the girl were coming into view up the steps, and without preliminary he told them what had passed.

'I fear,' said Mr Reeder, shaking his head sadly, 'that Emanuel is not as truthful a man as he might be. There was no divorce. I was sufficiently interested in the case to look up the divorce court records.' He rubbed his chin thoughtfully. 'I think your dinner party at the Highlow—is that the name?—will be an interesting one,' he said. 'Are you sure he did not invite me?' And again Peter saw that glint of humour in his eyes.

23

Mr Emanuel Legge had a great deal of business to do in London. The closing of the club had sadly interfered with the amenities of the Highlow, for many of its patrons and members were, not unnaturally, reluctant to be found on premises subject, at any moment, to the visitation of inquisitive police officers. Stevens, the porter, had been reinstated, though his conduct, in Emanuel's opinion, had been open to the gravest suspicion. In other ways he was a reliable man, and one whose services were not lightly to be dispensed with. To his surprise, when he had come to admonish the porter, that individual had taken the wind out of his sails by announcing his intention of retiring unless the staff was changed. And he had his way, the staff in question being the elevator boy, Benny.

'Benny squeaked on me,' said Stevens briefly, 'and I'm not going to have a squeaker round.'

'He squeaked to me, my friend,' said Emanuel, showing his teeth unpleasantly. 'He told me you tried to shield Johnny Gray.'

'He's a member, ain't he?' asked the porter truculently. 'How do I know what members you want put away, and what members you want hidden? Of course, I helped the Captain—or thought I was trying to help him. That's my job.'

There was a great deal of logic in this. Benny the elevator boy, was replaced.

Stepping out of the lift, Emanuel saw the prints of muddy shoes in the hall, and they were wet.

'Who's here?' he asked.

'Nobody in particular.'

Legge pointed to the footprints.

'Somebody has been here recently,' he said.

'They're mine,' said Stevens without hesitation. 'I went out to get a cab for Monty Ford.'

'Are there any mats?' snapped Emanuel.

Stevens did not answer.

There was a great deal of work for Emanuel to do. For example, there was the matter of a certain house in Berkeley Square to be cleared off. Though he was no longer in active work, he did a lot of crooked financing, and the house had been taken with his money. It was hired furnished for a year, and it was the intention of his associates to run an exclusive gambling club. Unfortunately, the owner, who had a very valuable collection of paintings and old jewellery, discovered the character of the new tenant—a dummy of Legge's—and had promptly cancelled the agreement. Roughly, the venture had cost Emanuel a thousand, and he hated losing good money.

It was late that night when he left the club. He was sleeping in London, intending to travel down to his convalescent son by an early train in the morning. It had been raining heavily, and the street was empty when he went out of the club, pulling the collar of his raincoat about his neck.

He had taken two strides when a man stepped out of the shadow of a doorway and planted himself squarely in his path. Emanuel's hand dropped to his pocket, for he was that rarest variety of criminal, an English gunman.

'Keep your artillery opt of action, Legge,' said a voice that was strangely familiar.

He peered forward, but in the shadow he could not distinguish the stranger's face.
'Who are you?'

'An old friend of yours,' was the reply. 'Don't tell me you've forgotten all your pals!
Why, you'll be passing a screw in the street one of these days without touching your hat
to him.'

And then it dawned on Emanuel.

'Oh . . . you're Fenner, aren't you?'

'I'm Fenner,' admitted the man. 'Who else could I be? I've been waiting to see you,
Mr Emanuel Legge. I wondered if you would remember a fellow you sent to the triangle
. . . fifteen lashes I had. You've never had a bashing have you, Legge? It's not so nice as
you'd think. When they'd took me back to my cell and put that big bit of lint on my
shoulder, I laid on my face for a week. Naturally, that interfered with my sleeping,
though it helped me a whole lot to think. And what I thought was this, Emanuel, that a
thousand a stroke wouldn't be too much to ask from a man who got it for me.'

Legge's lip twisted in a sneer.

'Oh, it's the black you're after, is it? Fifteen thousand pounds, is that your price?'

'I could do a lot with fifteen thousand, Legge. I can go abroad and have a good time—
maybe, take a house in the country.'

'What's the matter with Dartmoor?' snarled Emanuel. 'You'll get no fifteen thousand
from me—not fifteen thousand cents, not fifteen thousand grains of sand. Get out of
my way!'

He lurched forward, and the man slipped aside. He had seen what was in the old
man's hand.

Legge turned as he passed, facing him and walking sideways, alert to meet any attempt
which was launched.

'That's a pretty gun of yours, Legge,' drawled the convict. 'Maybe I shall meet you one
of these days when you won't be in a position to pull it.'

A thought struck Emanuel Legge, and he walked slowly back to the man, and his tone
was mild, even conciliatory.

'What's the good of making a fuss, Fenner? I didn't give you away. Half a dozen
people saw you cosh that screw.'

'But half a dozen didn't come forward, did they?' asked Fenner wrathfully. 'You were
the only prisoner; there wasn't a screw in sight.'

'That's a long time ago,' said Emanuel after a pause. 'You're not going to make any
trouble now, are you? Fifteen thousand pounds is out of the question. It's ridiculous to
ask me for that. But if a couple of hundred will do you any good, why, I'll send it to you.'

'I'll have it now,' said Fenner.

'You won't have it now, because I haven't got it,' replied Emanuel. 'Tell me where
you're to be found, and I'll send a boy along with it in the morning.'

Fenner hesitated. He was surprised even to touch for a couple of hundred.

'I'm staying at Rowton House, Wimborne Street, Pimlico.'

'In your own name?'

'In the name of Fenner,' the other evaded, 'and that's good enough for you.'

Emanuel memorized the address.

'It'll be there at ten o'clock,' he said. 'You're a mug to quarrel with me. I could put you on to a job where you could have made not fifteen, but twenty thousand.'

All the anger had died out of the burglar's tone when he asked:

'Where?'

'There's a house in Berkeley Square,' said Emanuel quickly, and gave the number. It was providential that he had remembered that white elephant of his. And he knew, too, that at the moment the house was empty but for a caretaker.

'Just wait here,' he said, and went back into the club and to his little office on the third floor.

Opening a drawer of his desk, he took out a small bunch of keys, the duplicates that had been made during the brief period that the original keys had been in his possession. He found Fenner waiting where he had left him.

'Here are the keys. The house is empty. One of our people borrowed the keys and got cold feet at the last minute. There's about eight thousand pounds' worth of jewellery in a safe—you can't miss it. It's in the principal drawing-room—in show cases—go and take a look at it. And there's plate worth a fortune.'

The man jingled the keys in his hand.

'Why haven't you gone after it, Emanuel?'

'Because it's not my graft,' said Emanuel. 'I'm running straight now. But I want my cut, Fenner. Don't run away with any idea that you're getting this for nothing. You've got a couple of nights to do the job; after that, you haven't the ghost of a chance, because the family will be coming back.'

'But why do you give it to me?' asked Fenner, still suspicious.

'Because there's nobody else,' was the almost convincing reply. 'It may be that the jewellery is not there at all,' went on Emanuel frankly. 'It may have been taken away. But there's plenty of plate. I wouldn't have given it to you if I'd got the right man—I doubt whether I'm going to get my cut from you.'

'You'll get your cut,' said the other roughly. 'I'm a fool to go after this, knowing what a squeaker you are, but I'll take the risk. If you put a point on me over this, Emanuel, I'll kill you. And I mean it.'

'I'm sick of getting news about my murder,' said Emanuel calmly. 'If you don't want to do it, leave it. I'll send you up a couple of hundred in the morning, and that's all I'll do for you. Give me back those keys.'

'I'll think about it,' said the man, and turned away without another word.

It was one o'clock and Emanuel went back to the club, working the automatic lift himself to the second floor.

'Everybody gone, Stevens?' he asked.

The porter stifled a yawn and shook his head.

'There's a lady and a gentleman'—he emphasized the word —'in No. 8. They've been quarrelling since nine o'clock. They ought to be finished by now.'

'Put my office through to the exchange,' said Emanuel.

Behind the porter's desk was a small switchboard, and Stevens thrust in the two plugs. Presently the disc showed him that Emanuel was through.

Mr Legge had many friends among the minor members of the Criminal Investigation Department. They were not inexpensive acquaintances, but they could on occasion be extremely useful. That night, in some respects, Emanuel's luck was in, when he found

Sergeant Shilto in his office. There had been a jewel theft at one of the theatres, which had kept the sergeant busy.

'Is that you, Shilto?' asked Legge in a low voice. 'It's Manileg.' He gave his telegraphic address, which also served as a *nom de plume* when such delicate negotiations as these were going through.

'Yes, Mr Manileg?' said the officer, alert, for Emanuel did not call up police head-quarters unless there was something unusual afoot.

'Do you want a cop—a real one?' asked Legge in a voice little above a whisper. 'There's a man named Fenner—'

'The old lag?' asked Shilto. 'Yes, I saw him today. What's he doing?'

'He's knocking off a little silver, from 973, Berkeley Square. Be at the front door: you'll probably see him go in. You want to be careful, because he's got a gun. If you hurry, you'll get there in front of him. Good night.'

He hung up the receiver and smiled. The simplicity of the average criminal always amused Emanuel Legge.

24

Peter wrote to tell of the invitation which Legge had extended to him. Johnny Gray had the letter by the first post. He sat in his big armchair, his silk dressing-gown wrapped around him, his chin on his fists; and seeing him thus, the discreet Parker did not intrude upon his thoughts until Johnny, reading the letter again, tore it in pieces and threw it into the wastepaper-basket.

He had a whimsical practice of submitting most of his problems, either in parable form or more directly, to his imperturbable manservant.

'Parker, if you were asked to take dinner in a lion's den, what dress would you wear?'

Parker looked down at him thoughtfully, biting his lip.

'It would largely depend, sir, on whether there were ladies to be present,' he said. 'Under those extraordinary circumstances, one should wear full dress and a white tie.'

Johnny groaned.

'There have been such dinners, sir,' Parker hastened to assure him in all seriousness. 'I recall that, when I was a boy, a visiting menagerie came to our town, and one of the novelties was a dinner which was served in a den of ferocious lions; and I distinctly remember that the lion-tamer wore a white dress bow and a long tail coat. He also wore top boots,' he said, after a moment's consideration, 'which, of course, no gentleman could possibly wear in evening dress. But then, he was an actor.'

'But supposing the lion-tamer had a working arrangement with the lions? Wouldn't you suggest a suit of armour?' asked Johnny without smiling.

Parker considered the problem for a moment.

'That would rather turn it into a fancy-dress affair, sir,' he said, 'where, of course, any costume is permissible. Personally,' he added. 'I should never dream of dining in a den of lions under any circumstances.'

'That's the answer I've been waiting for; it's the most intelligent thing you've said this morning,' said Johnny. 'Nevertheless, I shall not follow your excellent advice. I'll be dining at the Highlow Club on Thursday. Get me the morning newspaper: I haven't seen it.'

He turned the pages apathetically, for the events which were at the moment agitating political London meant nothing in his life. On an inner page he found a brief paragraph which, however, did interest him. It was in the latest news column, and related to the arrest of a burglar, who had been caught red handed breaking into a house in Berkeley Square. The man had given his name as Fenner. Johnny shook his head sadly. He had no doubt as to the identity of the thief, for burglary was Fenner's graft. Since the news had come in the early hours of the morning, there were no details, and he put the paper aside and fell into a train of thought.

Poor Fenner! He must go back to that hell, which was only better than Keytown Jail. He would be spared the ordeal of Keytown, at any rate, if what Craig had said was true. Glancing at the clock, he saw that it was nearly eleven o'clock and jumped up. He was taking Marney to lunch and a matinée that day. Peter was bringing her up, and he was to meet them at Victoria.

Since his release from Dartmoor, Johnny had had no opportunity of a quiet talk with the girl, and this promised to be a red-letter day in his life. He had to wait some time, for the train was late; and as he stood in the broad hall, watching with abstracted interest the never-ceasing rush and movement and life about him, he observed, out of the corner of his eye, a man sidling towards him.

Johnny had that sixth sense which is alike the property of the scientist, the detective and the thief. He was immediately sensitive to what he called the approaching spirit, and long before the shabby stranger had spoken to him, he knew that he was the objective. Nearer at hand, he recognized the stranger as a man he had seen in Dartmoor, and remembered that he had come to prison at the same time as Fenner and for the same offence, though he had been released soon after Johnny had passed through that grim gateway.

'I followed you down here, Mr Gray, but I didn't like to talk to you in the street,' said the stranger, apparently immersed in an evening newspaper and talking, as such men talk, without moving his lips.

Johnny waited, wondering what the communication was, and not doubting that it had to do with Fenner.

'Old Fenner's been shopped by Legge,' said the man. 'He went to knock off some silver from a house in Berkeley Square, and Shilto was waiting in the hall for him.'

'How do you know Legge shopped him?' asked Johnny, interested.

'It was a shop all right,' said the other without troubling to explain. 'If you can put in a good word for Fenner, he'd be much obliged.'

'But, my dear fellow,' said Johnny with a smile, 'to whom can I put in a good word? In the present circumstances I couldn't put a word in for my own maiden aunt. I'll see what I can do.'

There was no need to tell the furtive man to go. With all a thief's keen perceptions he had seen the eyes of Johnny Gray light up, and with a sidelong glance assured himself of the cause. Johnny went towards the girl with long strides, and, oblivious to curious spectators and Peter Kane alike, took both her hands in his. Her loveliness always came to him in the nature of a glorious surprise. The grace and poise of her were indefinite quantities that he could not keep exactly in his mind, and inevitably she surpassed his impressions of her.

After he had handed the girl into a taxi, the older man beckoned him aside.

'I'm not any too sure about this Highlow dinner,' he said. 'Love feasts are not Emanuel's specialities, and there's a kick coming somewhere, Johnny. I hope you're prepared for it?'

Johnny nodded.

'Emanuel isn't usually so obvious,' he said. 'In fact, the whole thing is so patent and so crude that I can't suspect anything more than an attempt to straighten matters as far as Marney is concerned.'

Peter's face clouded.

'There will be no straightening there,' he said shortly. 'If he has committed bigamy, he goes down for it. Understand that, Johnny. It will be very unpleasant because of Marney's name being dragged into the light, but I'm going through with it.'

He turned away with a wave of his hand, and Johnny returned to the girl.

'What is the matter with father?' she asked as the taxi drew out of the station. 'He is so quiet and thoughtful these days. I suppose the poor dear's worrying about me, though he needn't, for I never felt happier.'

'Why?' asked Johnny, indiscreetly.

'Because—oh, well, because,' she said, her face flushing the faintest shade of pink. 'Because I'm unmarried, for one thing. I hated the idea, Johnny. You don't know how I hated it. I understand now poor daddy's anxiety to get me married into respectable society.' Her sense of humour, always irrepressible, overcame her anxiety. 'I wonder if you understand my immoral sense of importance at the discovery that poor father has done so many illegal things! I suppose it's some kick that he has transmitted to me.'

'Was it a great shock to you, Marney?' interrupted the young man quietly.

She nodded.

'Yes, but shocks are like blows—they hurt and they fade. It isn't pleasant to be twisted violently to another angle of view. It pains horribly, Johnny. But I think when I found—' She hesitated.

'When you found that I was a thief.'

'When I found that you were—oh, Johnny, why did you? You had so many advantages; you'd been to the University; you weren't poor—Johnny, it wasn't big of you. There's an excuse for daddy; he told me about his youth and his struggles and the fearful hardness of living. But you had opportunities that he never had. Easy money isn't good money, is it, Johnny?'

He was silent, and then, with a quick breath-catching sigh, she smiled again.

'I haven't come out to lecture you, and I shan't even ask you if, for my sake, you'll go straight in the future. Because, Johnny'—she dropped a cool palm on the back of his hand—'I'm not going to do anything like the good fairy and try to save you from yourself.'

'I'm saved,' said Johnny, with a quizzical smile. 'You're perfectly right: there was no reason why I should be a thief. I was the victim of circumstances. It was possibly the fascination of the game—no, no, it wasn't that. One of these days I'll tell you why I left the straight path of virtue. It's a long and curious story.'

She made no further reference to the matter, and throughout the lunch was her own gay self. Looking down at her hand, Johnny saw, with satisfaction, that the platinum wedding-ring she had worn had been replaced by a small, plain gold ring, ornamented with a single turquoise, and his breath came faster. He had first met her at a gymkhana, a country fair which had been organized for charity, and the ring had been the prize he had won at a shooting match, one of the gymkhana features—though it was stretching terminology to absurd lengths so to describe the hotch-potch of contests which went to the making of the programme—he had offered it to her as whimsically as it had been accepted. Its value was small; to Johnny, all the millions in the world would not have given him the joy that its appearance on her finger gave him now.

After lunch she returned to the unpleasant side of things.

'Johnny, you're going to be very careful, aren't you? Daddy says that Jeff Legge hates you, and he's quite serious about it. He says that there are no lengths to which Jeffrey and his father will not go to hurt you—and me,' she added.

Johnny bent over the table, lowering his voice.

'Marney, when this matter is settled—I mean, the release from your marriage—will you take me—whatever I am?'

She met his eyes steadily and nodded. It was the strangest of all proposals, and Jeffrey Legge who had watched the meeting at the station, and was now overlooking them from one of the balconies of the restaurant, flushed a deeper red, guessing all that that scene meant.

25

On Thursday afternoon, Emanuel Legge came out of the elevator at the Highlow Club and, with a curt nod to Stevens, walked up the heavily-carpeted corridor, unlocked the door of his tiny office and went in. For half an hour he sat before his desk, his hands clasped on the blotting-pad before him, motionless, his mind completely occupied by his thoughts. At last he opened his desk and pressed a bell by his side. He had hardly taken his fingers from the push when the head waiter of the establishment came in, a tall, unpleasant-looking Italian.

'Fernando, you have made all the arrangements about the dinner tonight?'

'Yes,' said the man.

'All the finest wines, eh? The best in the house?'

He peered at the waiter, his teeth showing in a smile.

'The very best,' said Fernando briskly.

'There will be four: myself and Major Floyd, Mr Johnny Gray and Peter Kane.'

'The lady is not coming?' asked Fernando.

'No, I don't think she'll be dining with us tonight,' said Emanuel carefully.

When the waiter had gone, he rose and bolted the door and returned to an idle examination of the desk. He found extraordinary pleasure in opening the drawers and looking through the little works of reference which filled a niche beneath the pigeon-holes. This was Jeffrey's desk, and Jeff was the apple of his eye.

Presently he rose and walked to a nest of pigeon-holes which stood against the wall. He put his hand into one, turned a knob and pulled. The nest opened like a door, exposing a narrow, spiral staircase which led upward and downward. He left the secret door open and pulled down a switch, which gave him light above and below. For a second he hesitated whether he should go up or down, and decided on the latter course.

At the foot of the stairs was another door, which he opened, passing into the cellar basement of the house. As the door moved, there came to him a wave of air so super-heated that for a moment he found difficulty in breathing. The cellar in which he found himself was innocent of furnishing, except for a table placed under a strong light, and a great, enclosed furnace which was responsible for the atmosphere of the room. It was like a Turkish bath, and he had not gone two or three paces before the perspiration was rolling down his cheeks.

A broad-shouldered, undersized man was sitting at the table, a big book open before him. He had turned at the sound of the key in the door, and now he came towards the intruder. He was a half-caste and, beyond the pair of blue dungaree trousers, he wore no clothing. His yellow skin and his curiously animal face gave him a particularly repulsive appearance.

'Got the furnace going, eh, Pietro?' said Emanuel mildly, taking off his glasses to wipe the moisture which had condensed on the lenses.

Pietro grunted something and, picking up an iron bar, lifted open the big door of the furnace. Emanuel put up his hands to guard his face from the blast of heat that came forth.

'Shut it, shut it!' he said testily, and when this was done, he went nearer to the furnace.

Two feet away there ran a box-like projection, extending from two feet above the floor to the ceiling. A stranger might have imagined that this was an air shaft, introduced to regulate the ventilation. Emanuel was not a stranger. He knew that the shaft ran up to the roof, and that it had a very simple explanation.

'That's a good fire you've got, eh, Pietro? You could burn up a man there?'

'Burn anything,' growled the other, 'but not man.'

Emanuel chuckled.

'Scared I'm going to put a murder point on you, are you? Well, you needn't be,' he said. 'But it's hot enough to melt copper, eh, Pietro?'

'Melt it down to nothing.'

'Burnt any lately?'

The man nodded, rubbing his enormous arms caressingly.

'They came last Monday week, after the boss had been shot,' said the other. He had a curious impediment in his speech which made his tone harsh and guttural. 'The fellows upstairs knew they were coming, so there was nothing to see. The furnace was nearly out.'

Emanuel nodded.

'The boss said the furnace was to be kept going for a week,' said Pietro complainingly.

'That's pretty tough on me, Mr Legge. I feel sometimes I'd nearly die, the heat's so terrible.'

'You get the nights off,' said Emanuel, 'and there are weeks when you do no work. Tonight I shall want you. . . . Mr Jeff has told you?'

The dwarf nodded. Emanuel passed through the door, closing it behind him; and, contrasted with the heat of the room, it seemed that he had walked into an ice wall. His collar was limp, his clothes were sticking to him, as he made his way up the stairs and, passing the open door of his office, continued until he reached the tiny landing which scarcely gave him foothold. He knocked twice on the door, for of this he had no key. After a pause came an answering knock, a small spyhole opened and an inquiring and suspicious eye examined him.

When at last the door was opened, he found he was in a small room with a large skylight, heavily barred. At one end of the skylight was a rolled blind, which could be drawn across at night and effectively veil the glare of light which on occasions rose from this room.

The man who grinned a welcome was little and bald. His age was in the region of sixty, and the grotesqueness of his appearance was due less to his shabby attire and diminutive stature than to the gold-rimmed monocle fixed in his right eye.

In the centre of the room was a big table, littered with paraphernalia, ranging from a small microscope to a case filled with little black bottles. Under the brilliant overhead light which hung above the table, and clamped to the wood by glass-headed pins, was an oblong copper plate, on which the engraver had been working—the engraving tool was in his hand as he opened the door.

'Good morning, Lacey. What are you working at now?' asked Emanuel with a benevolent air of patronage appropriate to the proprietor in addressing a favourite workman.

'The new fives,' said the other. 'Jeff wants a big printing. Jeff's got brains. Anybody else would have said, "Work from a photographic plate"—you know what that means. After a run of a hundred, the impression goes wrong, and before you know where you are, there's a squeak, But engraving is engraving,' he said with pride. 'You can get all the new changes without photography. I never did hold with this new method—boobs are full of fellows who think they can make slush with a camera and a zinc plate!'

It was good to hear praise of Jeffrey, and Emanuel Legge purred. He examined the half-finished plate through his powerful glasses, and though the art of the engraver was one with which he was not well acquainted, he could admire the fine work which this expert forger was doing.

To the left of the table was an aperture like the opening of a service lift. It was a continuation of the shaft which led from the basement, and it had this value that however clever the police might be, long before they could break into the engraver's room all evidence of his guilt would have been flung into the opening and consumed in the furnace fire.

'Jeffrey's idea. What a mind!' said the admiring Lacey. 'It reduces risk to what I might term a minimum. It's a pleasure working for Jeff, Mr Legge. He takes no chances.'

'I suppose Pietro is always on the spot?'

Mr Lacey smiled. He took up a plate from the table and examined it back and front.

'This is one I spoilt this morning,' he said. 'Spilt some acid on it. Look!'

He went to the opening, put in his hand, and evidently pressed a bell, for a faint tinkle came from the mouth of the shaft. When he withdrew his hand, the plate that it held had disappeared. There came the buzz of a bell from beneath the table.

'That plate's running like water by now,' he said. 'There's no chance of a squeak if Pietro's all right. Wide! That's Jeffrey! As wide as Broad Street! Why, Mr Legge, would you believe that I don't know to this day where the stuff's printed? And I'll bet the printer hasn't got the slightest idea where the plates are made. There isn't a man in this building who's got so much as a smell of it.'

Emanuel passed down to his office, a gratified father and, securely closing the pigeon-hole door, he went out into the club premises to look at Room 13. The table was already laid; a big rose-bowl, overflowing with the choicest blooms, filled the centre; an array of rare glass, the like of which the habitués of the club had never seen on their tables, stood before each plate.

His brief inspection of the room satisfied him, and he returned, not to his office but to Stevens, the porter.

'What's the idea of telling the members that all the rooms are engaged tonight?' asked Stevens. 'I've had to put off Lew Brady, and he pays.'

'We're having a party, Stevens,' said Emanuel, 'and we don't want any interruption. Johnny Gray is coming. And you can take that look off your face; if I thought he was a pal of yours, you wouldn't be in this club two minutes. Peter Kane's coming too.'

'Looks to me like a rough house,' said Stevens. 'What am I to do?' he asked sarcastically. 'Bring in the police at the first squeal?'

'Bring in your friend from Toronto,' snapped Emanuel, and went home to change.

26

Johnny was the first of the guests to arrive, and Stevens helped him to take off his raincoat. As he did so, he asked in a low voice:

'Got a gun, Captain?'

'Never carry one, Stevens. It's a bad habit to get into.'

'I never thought you were a mug,' said Stevens in the same voice.

'Any man who has been in prison is, *ex officio*, one of the Ancient Order of Muggery,' said Johnny, adjusting his tie in the mirror by the porter's desk. 'What's going?'

'I don't know,' said the other, bending down to wipe the mud from Johnny's shoes. 'But curious things have happened in No. 13; and don't sit with your back to the buffet. Do you get that?'

Johnny nodded.

He had reached the end of the corridor when he heard the whine of the ascending lift, and stopped. It was Peter Kane, and to him in a low voice, Johnny passed on the porter's advice.

'I don't think they'll start anything,' said Peter under his breath. 'But if they do, there's a nurse at Charing Cross Hospital who's going to say: "What, you here again!" '

As Johnny had expected, his two hosts were waiting in Room 13. The silence which followed their arrival was, for one member of the party, an awkward one.

'Glad to see you, Peter,' said Emanuel at last, though he made no pretence of shaking hands. 'Old friends ought to keep up acquaintances. There's my boy, Jeffrey. I think you've met him,' he said with a grin.

'I've met him,' said Peter, his face a mask.

Jeffrey Legge had apparently recovered fully from his unpleasant experience.

'Now sit down, everybody,' said Emanuel, bustling around, pulling out the chairs. 'You sit here, Johnny.'

'I'd rather face the buffet; I like to see myself eat,' said Johnny, and, without invitation, sat down in the position he had selected.

Not waiting, Peter seated himself on Johnny's left, and it was Emanuel himself, a little ruffled by this preliminary upset to his plans, who sat with his back to the buffet. Johnny noticed the quick exchange of glances between father and son; he noticed, too, that the buffet carried none of the side dishes for which it was designed, and wondered what particular danger threatened from that end of the room.

By the side of the sideboard, in one corner, hung a long, blue curtain, which, he guessed, hid a door leading to No. 12. Peter, who was better acquainted with the club, knew that No. 12 was the sitting-room, and that the two made one of those suites which were very much in request when a lamb was brought to the killing.

'Now, boys,' said Emanuel with spurious joviality, 'there is to be no bickering and quarrelling. We're all met round the festive board, and we've nothing to do but find a way out that leaves my boy's good name unsullied, if I may use that word.'

'You can use any word you like,' said Peter. 'It'll take more than a dinner party to restore his tarnished reputation.'

'What long words you use, Peter!' said Emanuel admiringly. 'It's my own fault that I don't know them, because I had plenty of time to study when I was away over the Alps. Never been over the Alps, have you, Peter? Well, when they call it time, they use the right word. The one thing you've got there is time!'

Peter did not answer, and it was Jeffrey who took up the conversation.

'See here, Peter,' he said, 'I'm not going to make a song about this business of mine. I'm going to put all my cards on the table. I want my wife.'

'You know where Lila is better than I,' said Peter. 'She's not in my employment now.'

'Lila nothing!' retorted Jeffrey. 'If you fall for that stuff, you're getting soft. I certainly married Lila, but she was married already, and I can give you proof of it.'

The conversation flagged here, for the waiter came in to serve the soup.

'What wine will you have, sir?'

'The same as Mr Emanuel,' said Peter.

Emanuel Legge chuckled softly.

'Think I'm going to knock you out, eh, Peter! What a suspicious old man you are!'

'Water,' said Johnny softly when the waiter came to him.

'On the water-wagon, Johnny? That's good. A young man in your business has got to keep his wits about him. I'll have champagne, Fernando, and so will Major Floyd. Nothing like champagne to keep your heart up,' he said.

Peter watched, all his senses alert, as the wine came, bubbling and frothing, into the long glasses.

'That will do, Fernando,' said Emanuel, watching the proceedings closely.

As the door closed, Johnny could have sworn he heard an extra click.

'Locking us in?' he asked pleasantly, and Emanuel's eyebrows rose.

'Locking you in, Johnny? Why, do you think I'm afraid of losing you, like you're afraid of losing Marney?'

Johnny sipped the glass of water, his eyes fixed on the old man's face. What was behind that buffet? That was the thought which puzzled him. It was a very ordinary piece of furniture, of heavy mahogany, a little shallow, but this was accounted for by the fact that the room was not large, and, in furnishing, the proprietors of the club had of necessity to economize space.

There were two cupboard doors beneath the ledge on which the side dishes should have been standing. Was it his imagination that he thought he saw one move the fraction of an inch?

'Ever been in bird before, Johnny?'

It was Emanuel who did most of the talking.

'I know they gave you three years, but was that your first conviction?'

'That was my first conviction,' said Johnny.

The old man looked up at the ceiling, pulling at his chin.

'Ever been in Keytown?' he demanded. 'No good asking you, Peter, I know. You've never been in Keytown or any bad boob, have you? Clever old Peter!'

'Let's talk about something else,' said Peter. 'I don't believe for one moment the story you told me about Lila having been married before. You've told me a fresh lie every time the matter has been discussed. I'm going to give you a show, Emanuel, for old times' sake. You've been a swine, and you've been nearer to death than you know because, if your plan had come off as you expected it would, I'd have killed you.'

Emanuel chuckled derisively.

'Old Peter's going to be a gunman,' he said. 'And after all the lectures you've given me! I'm surprised at you, Peter. Now I'll tell you what I'm going to do.' He rested his elbows on the table and cupped his chin in his hands, his keen eyes, all the keener for the magnification of his spectacles, fixed hardly upon his sometime friend. 'By my reckoning, you owe me 40,000 pounds, and I know I'm not going to get it without a struggle. Weigh in with that money, and I'll make things easy for my son's wife.' He emphasized the last word.

'You can cut that out!'

It was Jeffrey whose rough interruption checked his father's words.

'There's no money in the world that's going to get Marney from me. Understand that.' He brought his hand down with a crash upon the table. 'She belongs to me, and I want her, Peter. Do you get it? And what is more, I'm going to take her.'

Johnny edged a little farther from the table; he folded his arms across his chest and his lips parted in a smile. His right hand reached for the gun that he carried under his armpit:

a little Browning, but a favourite one of Johnny's in such crises as these. For the cupboard door had moved again, and the door of the room was locked: of that he was certain. All this talk of Marney was sheer blind to keep them occupied.

It had long passed the time when the plates should have been cleared and the second course make its appearance. But there was to be no second course, at that dinner. Emanuel was speaking chidingly, reproachfully.

'Jeffrey, my boy, you mustn't spoil a good deal,' he said. 'The truth is—'

And then all the lights of the room went out. Instantly Johnny was on his feet, his back to the wall, his gun fanning the dark.

'What's the game?' asked Peter's voice sharply. 'There'll be a real dead man here if you start fooling.'

'I don't know,' said Emanuel, speaking from the place where he had been. 'Ring the bell, Jeff. I expect the switch has gone.'

There was somebody else in the room: Johnny felt the presence instinctively—a stealthy somebody who was moving toward him. Holding out one hand, ready to pounce the moment it touched, he waited. A second passed—five seconds—ten seconds—and then the lights went on again.

Peter was also standing with his back to the wall, and in his hand a murderous looking Webley. Jeffrey and his father were side by side in the places they had been when the lights went out. There was no fifth man in the room.

'What's the game?' asked Peter suspiciously.

'The game, my dear Peter? What a question to ask! You don't make me responsible for the fuses, do you? I'm not an electrician. I'm a poor old crook who has done time that other people should have done—that's all,' said Emanuel pleasantly. 'And look at the hardware! Bad idea, carrying guns. Let an old crook give you a word of advice, Peter,' he bantered. 'I'm not surprised at Johnny, because he might be anything. Sit down, you damned fools,' he said jocularly. 'Let's talk.'

'I'll talk when you open that door,' said Johnny quietly. 'And I'll put away my gun on the same condition.'

In three strides, Emanuel was at the door. There was a jerk of his wrist, and it flew open.

'Have the door open if you're frightened,' he said contemptuously. 'I guess it's being in boob that makes you scared of the dark. I got that way myself.'

As he had turned the handle, Johnny had heard a second click. He was confident that somebody stood outside the door, and that the words Legge had uttered were intended for the unknown sentry. What was the idea?

Peter Kane was sipping his champagne, with an eye on his host. Had he heard the noise, too? Johnny judged that he had. The extinguishing of the lights had not been an accident. Some secret signal had been given, and the lights cut off from the controlling switchboard. The doors of the buffet cupboard were still. Turning his head, Johnny saw that Jeffrey's eyes were fixed on his with a hard concentration which was significant. What was he expecting?

The climax, whatever it might be, was at hand.

'It's a wonder to me, Gray, that you've never gone in for slush,' Jeffrey was speaking slowly and deliberately. 'It's a good profession, and you can make money that you couldn't dream of getting by faking racehorses.'

'Perhaps you will tell me how to start in that interesting profession,' said Johnny coolly.

'I'll put it on paper for you, if you like. It'll be easier to make a squeak about. Or, better still, I'll show you how it's done. You'd like that?'

'I don't know that I'm particularly interested, but I'm sure my friend Mr Reeder—'

'Your friend Mr Reeder!' sneered the other. 'He's a pal of yours too, is he?'

'All law-abiding citizens are pals of mine,' said Johnny gravely.

He had put his gun back in his jacket pocket, and his hand was on it.

'Well, how's this for a start?'

Jeffrey rose from the table and went to the buffet. He bent down and must have touched some piece of mechanism; for without any visible assistance, the lid of the buffet turned over on some invisible axis, revealing a small but highly complicated piece of machinery, which Johnny recognized instantly as one of those little presses employed by bank-note printers when a limited series of notes, generally of a high denomination, were being made.

The audacity of this revelation momentarily took his breath away.

'You could pull that buffet to pieces,' continued Jeffrey, 'and then not find it.'

He pressed a switch, and the largest of the wheels began to spin, and with it a dozen tiny platens and cylinders. Only for a few minutes, and then he cut off the current, pressed the hidden mechanism again, the machine turned over out of sight, and the two astonished men stared at the very ordinary looking surface of a very ordinary buffet.

'Easy money, eh, Gray?' said Emanuel, with an admiring smirk at his son. 'Now listen, boys.' His tone grew suddenly practical and businesslike as he came back to his chair. 'I want to tell you something that's going to be a lot of good to both of you, and we'll leave Marney out of it for the time being.'

Johnny raised his glass of water, still watchful and suspicious.

'The point is—' said Emanuel, and at that moment Johnny took a long sip from the glass.

The liquid had hardly reached his throat when he strove vainly to reject it. The harsh tang of it he recognized, and, flinging the glass to the floor, jerked out his gun.

And then some tremendous force within him jerked at his brain, and the Browning dropped from his paralyzed hand.

Peter was on his feet, staring from one to the other.

'What have you done?'

He leapt forward, but before he could make a move, Emanuel sprang at him like a cat. He tried to fight clear, but he was curiously lethargic and weak. A vicious fist struck him on the jaw, and he went down like a log.

'Got you!' hissed Emanuel, glaring down at his enemy. 'Got you, Peter, my boy! Never been in boob, have you? I'll give you a taste of it!'

Jeffrey Legge stooped and jerked open the door of the cupboard, and a man came stooping into the light. It was a cat-like Pietro, grinning from ear to ear in sheer enjoyment of the part he had played. Emanuel dropped his hand on his shoulder.

'Good boy,' he said. 'The right stuff for the right man, eh? To every man his dope, Jeff. I knew that this Johnny Gray was going to be the hardest, and if I'd taken your advice and given them both a knock-out, we'd have only knocked out one. Now they know why the lights went out. Pick 'em up.'

The little half-caste must have been enormously strong, for he lifted Peter without an effort and propped him into an armchair. This done, he picked up the younger man and laid him on the sofa, took a little tin box from his pocket and, filling a hypodermic syringe from a tiny phial, looked round for instructions.

Jeffrey nodded, and the needle was driven into the unfeeling flesh. This done, he lifted the eyelid of the drugged man and grinned again.

'He'll be ready to move in half an hour,' he said. 'My knock-out doesn't last longer.'

'Could you get him down the fire-escape into the yard?' asked Emanuel anxiously. 'He's a pretty heavy fellow, that Peter. You'll have to help him, Jeff boy. The car's in the yard. And, Jeff, don't forget you've an engagement at two o'clock.'

His son nodded.

Again the half-caste swung up Peter Kane, and Jeffrey, holding the door wide, helped him to carry the unconscious man through the open window and down the steel stairway, though he needed very little help, for the strength of the man was enormous.

He came back, apparently unmoved by his effort, and hoisted Johnny on to his back. Again unassisted, he carried the young man to the waiting car below, and flung him in.

He was followed this time by Jeffrey, wrapped in a dark raincoat, a chauffeur's cap pulled down over his eyes. Jeffrey got behind the wheel of the car and Pietro opened the gate and glanced out. There were few people about, and the car swung out and sped at full speed towards Oxford Street.

Closing and locking the gate, the half-caste went up the stairs of the fire-escape two at a time and reported to his gratified master.

Emanuel was gathering the coats and hats of his two guests into a bundle. This done, he opened a cupboard and flung them in, and they immediately disappeared.

'Go down and burn them,' he said laconically. 'You've done well, Pietro. There's fifty for you tonight.'

'Good?' asked the other laconically.

Emanuel favoured him with his benevolent smile. He took the two glasses from which the men had drunk, and these followed the clothes. A careful search of the room brought to light no further evidence of their presence. Satisfied, Emanuel sat down and lit a long, thin cigar. His night's work was not finished. Jeff had left to him what might prove the hardest of all the tasks.

From a small cupboard he took a telephone, and pushed in the plug at the end of a long flex. He had some time to wait for the number, but presently he heard a voice which he knew was Marney's.

'Is that you, Marney?' he asked softly, disguising his voice so cleverly that the girl was deceived.

'Yes, Daddy. Are you all right? I've been so worried about you.'

'Quite all right, darling. Johnny and I have made a very interesting discovery. Will you tell Barney to go to bed, and will you wait up for me—open the door yourself?'

'Is Johnny coming back with you?'

'No, no, darling; I'm coming alone.'

'Are you sure everything is all right?' asked the anxious voice.

'Now, don't worry, my pet. I shall be with you at two o'clock. When you hear the car stop at the gate, come out. I don't want to come into the house. I'll explain everything to you.'

'But—'

'Do as I ask you, darling,' he said, and before she could reply had rung off.

But could Jeff make it? He would like to go himself, but that would mean the employment of a chauffeur, and he did not know one he could trust. He himself was not strong enough to deal with the girl and, crowning impossibility, driving was a mystery—that was one of the accomplishments which a long stay in Dartmoor had denied to him.

But could Jeff make it? He took a pencil from his pocket and worked out the times on the white tablecloth. Satisfied, he put away his pencil, and was pouring out a glass of champagne when there was a gentle tap-tap-tap at the door. He looked up in surprise. The man had orders not under any circumstances to come near Room 13, and it was his duty to keep the whole passage clear until he received orders to the contrary.

Tap-tap-tap.

'Come in,' he said.

The door opened. A man stood in the doorway. He was dressed in shabby evening clothes; his bow was clumsily tied; one stud was missing from his white shirt-front.

'Am I intruding upon your little party?' he asked timidly.

Emanuel said nothing. For a long time he sat staring at this strange apparition. As if unconscious of the amazement and terror he had caused, the visitor sought to readjust his frayed shirt-cuffs, which hung almost to the knuckles of his hands. And then:

'Come in, Mr Reeder,' said Emanuel Legge a little breathlessly.

27

Mr Reeder sidled into the room apologetically, closing the door behind him.

'All alone, Mr Legge?' he asked. I thought you had company?'

'I had some friends, but they've gone.'

'Your son gone, too?' Reeder stared helplessly from one corner of the room to the other. 'Dear me, this is a disappointment, a great disappointment.'

Emanuel was thinking quickly. In all probability the shabby detective had been watching the front of the house, and would know that they had not left that way. He took a bold step.

'They left a quarter of an hour ago. They went down the fire-escape—my boy's car was in the yard. We never like to have a car in front of the club premises; people talk so much. And after the publicity we've had—'

Mr Reeder checked him with a mild murmur of agreement.

'That was the car, was it? I saw it go and wondered what it was all about—Number 9712 XC, blue saloon—Daimler—I may be wrong, but it seemed like a Daimler to me; I know so little about cars that I could be very easily mistaken, and my eyesight is not as good as it used to be.'

Emanuel cursed him under his breath.

'Yes, it was a Daimler,' he said, 'one we bought cheap at a sale.'

The absent-minded visitor's eyes were fixed on the table.

'Took their wine-glasses with them?' he asked gently. 'I think it is a pretty custom, taking souvenirs of a great occasion. I'm sure they were very happy.'

How had he got in? wondered Emanuel. Stevens had strict orders to stop him, and Fernando was at the end of the L-shaped passage. As if he divined the thought that was passing through Legge's mind, Mr Reeder answered the unspoken question.

'I took the liberty of coming up the fire-escape, too,' he said. 'It was an interesting experience. One is a little old to begin experiments, and I am not the sort of man that cares very much for climbing, particularly at night.'

Following the direction of his eyes, Emanuel saw that a small square of the rusty trousers had been torn, and through the opening a bony white knee.

'Yes, I came up the fire-escape, and fortunately the window was open. I thought I would give you a pleasant surprise. By the way, the escape doesn't go any higher than this floor! That is curious, because you know, my dear Mr Legge, it might well happen, in the event of fire, that people would be driven to the roof. If I remember rightly, there is nothing on the roof but a square superstructure—store-room, isn't it? Let me think. Yes, it's a store-room, I'm sure.'

'The truth is,' interrupted Emanuel, 'I had two old acquaintances here, Johnny Gray and Peter Kane. I think you know Peter?'

The other inclined his head gently.

'And they got just a little too merry. I suppose Johnny's not used to wine, and Peter's been a teetotaller for years.' He paused. 'In fact, they were rather the worse for drink.'

'That's very sad.' Mr Reeder shook his head. 'Personally, I am a great believer in prohibition. I would prohibit wine and beer, and crooks and forgers, tale-tellers, poisoners'—he paused at the word—'druggers would be a better word,' he said. 'They took their glasses with them, did they? I hope they will return them. I should not like to think that people I—er—like would be guilty of so despicable a practice as—er—the petty theft of—er—wine-glasses.'

Again his melancholy eyes fell on the table.

'And they only had soup! It is very unusual to get bottled before you've finished the soup, isn't it? I mean, in respectable circles,' he added apologetically.

He looked back at the open door over his glasses.

'I wonder,' he mused, 'how they got down that fire-escape in the dark in such a sad condition?'

Again his expressionless eyes returned to Emanuel.

'If you see them again, will you tell them that I expect both Mr Kane and Mr Johnny—what is his name?—Gray, that's it! to keep an appointment they made with me for tomorrow morning? And that if they do not turn up at my house at half past ten . . .'

He stopped, pursing up his lips as though he were going to whistle. Emanuel wondered what was coming next, and was not left long in doubt.

'Did you feel the cold very much in Dartmoor? They tell me that the winters are very trying, particularly for people of an advanced age. Of course,' Mr Reeder went on, 'one can have friends there; one can even have relations there. I suppose it makes things much easier if you know your son or some other close relative is living on the same landing—there are three landings, are there not? But it is much nicer to live in comfort in London, Mr Legge—to have a cosy little suite in Bloomsbury, such as you have got; to go where you like without a screw following you—I think screw is a very vulgar word, but it means warder, does it not?'

'He walked to the door and turned slowly.

'You won't forget that I expect to meet Mr Peter Kane and Mr Johnny Gray tomorrow at my house at half past ten—you won't forget, will you?'

He closed the door carefully behind him and, with his great umbrella hooked on to his arm, passed along the corridor into the purview of the surprised Fernando and astounded the jailers on guard at the end.

'Good evening,' murmured Mr Reeder as he passed.

Fernando was too overcome to make a courteous reply.

Stevens saw him as he came into the main corridor, and gasped.

'When did you come in, Mr Reeder?'

'Nobody has ever seen you come in, but lots of people see you go out,' said Reeder good-humouredly. 'On the other hand, there are people who are seen coming into this club whom nobody sees go out. Mr Gray didn't pass this way, or Mr Kane?'

'No, sir,' said Stevens in surprise. 'Have they gone?'

Reeder sighed heavily.

'Yes, they've gone,' he said. 'I hope not for long, but they've certainly gone. Good night, Stevens. By the way, your name isn't Stevens, is it? I seem to remember you'—he screwed up his eyes as though he had difficulty in recalling the memory—'I seem to remember your name wasn't Stevens, let us say, eight years ago.'

Stevens flushed.

'It is the name I'm known as now, sir.'

'A very good name, too, an excellent name,' murmured Mr Reeder as he stepped into the elevator. 'And after all, we must try to live down the past. And I'd be the last to remind you of your—er—misfortune.'

When he reached the street, two men who had been standing on the opposite sidewalk crossed to him.

'They've gone,' said Mr Reeder. 'They were in that car, as I feared. All stations must be warned, and particularly the town stations just outside of London, to hold up the car. You have its number. You'd better watch this place till the morning,' he said to one of them.

'Very good, sir.'

'I want you especially to follow Emanuel, and keep him under observation until tomorrow morning.'

The detective left on duty waited with that philosophical patience which is the greater part of the average detective's equipment, until three o'clock in the morning; and at that hour, when daylight was coming into the sky, Emanuel had not put in an appearance. Stevens went off duty half an hour after Mr Reeder's departure. At two o'clock the head waiter and three others left, Fernando locking the door. Then, a few minutes before three o'clock, the squat figure of Pietro, muffled up in a heavy overcoat, and he too locked the door behind him, disappearing in the direction of Shaftesbury Avenue. At half past three the detective left a policeman to watch the house, and got on the phone to Mr Reeder, who was staying in London.

'Dear me!' said Mr Reeder, an even more incongruous sight in pyjamas which were a little too small for him, though happily there were no spectators of his agitation. 'Not gone, you say? I will come round.'

It was daylight when he arrived. The gate in the yard was opened with a skeleton key (the climb so graphically described by Mr Reeder was entirely fictitious, and the cut in his trousers was due to catching a jagged nail in one of the packing-cases with which the yard was littered), and he mounted the iron stairway to the third floor.

The window through which he had made his ingress on the previous evening was closed and fastened but, with the skill of a professional burglar, Mr Reeder forced back the catch and, opening the window, stepped in.

There was enough daylight to see his whereabouts. Unerringly he made for Emanuel's office. The door had been forced, and there was no need to use the skeleton key.

There was no sign of Emanuel, and Reeder came out to hear the report of the detective, who had made a rapid search of the club.

'All the doors are open except No. 13, sir,' he said. 'That's bolted on the inside. I've got the lock open.'

'Try No. 12,' said Reeder. 'There are two ways in — one by way of a door, which you'll find behind a curtain in the corner of the room, and the other way through the buffet, which communicates with the buffet in No. 13. Break nothing if you can help it, because I don't want my visit here advertised.'

He followed the detective into No. 12, and found that there was no necessity to use the buffet entrance, for the communicating door was unlocked. He stepped into No. 13; it was in complete darkness.

'Humph!' said Mr Reeder, and sniffed. 'One of you go along this wall and find the switch. Be careful you don't step on something.'

'What is there?'

'I think you'll find . . . however, turn on the light.'

The detective felt his way along the wall, and presently his finger touched a switch and he turned it down. And then they saw all that Mr Reeder suspected. Sprawled across the table was a still figure—a horrible sight, for the man who had killed Emanuel Legge had used the poker which, twisted and blood-stained, lay amidst the wreckage of rare glass and once snowy napery.

28

It was unnecessary to call a doctor to satisfy the police. Emanuel Legge had passed beyond the sphere of his evil activities.

'The poker came from—where?' mused Mr Reeder, examining the weapon thoughtfully. He glanced down at the little fireplace. The poker and tongs and shovel were intact, and this was of a heavier type than was used in the sitting-rooms.

Deftly he searched the dead man's pockets, and in the waistcoat he found a little card inscribed with a telephone number, 'Horsham 98753'. Peter's. That had no special significance at the moment, and Reeder put it with the other documents that he had extracted from the dead man's pockets. Later came an inspector to take charge of the case.

'There was some sort of struggle, I imagine,' said Mr Reeder. 'The right wrist, I think you'll find, is broken. Legge's revolver was underneath the table. He probably pulled it, and it was struck from his hand. I don't think you'll want me any more, inspector.'

He was examining the main corridor when the telephone switchboard at the back of Stevens' little desk gave him an idea. He put through a call to Horsham and, in spite of the earliness of the hour, was almost immediately answered.

'Who is that?' he asked.

'I'm Mr Kane's butler,' said a husky voice.

'Oh, is it Barney? Is your master at home yet?'

'No, sir. Who is it speaking?'

'It is Mr Reeder. . . . Will you tell Miss Kane to come to the telephone?'

'She's not here either. I've been trying to get on to Johnny Gray all night, but his man says he's out.'

'Where is Miss Kane?' asked Reeder quickly.

'I don't know, sir. Somebody came for her in the night in a car and she went away, leaving the door open. It was the wind slamming it that woke me up.'

It was so long before Mr Reeder answered that Barney thought he had gone away.

'Did nobody call for her during the evening? Did she have any telephone messages?'

'One sir, about ten o'clock. I think it was her father from the way she was speaking.'

Again a long interval of silence, and then:

'I will come straight down to Horsham,' said Mr Reeder, and from the pleasant and conversational quality of his voice, Barney took comfort; though, if he had known the man better, he would have realized that Mr Reeder was most ordinary when he was most perturbed.

Mr Reeder pushed the telephone away from him and stood up.

So they had got Marney. There was no other explanation. The dinner party had been arranged to dispose of the men who could protect her. Where had they been taken?

He went back to the old man's office, which was undergoing a search at the hands of a police officer.

'I particularly want to see immediately any document referring to Mr Peter Kane,' he said, 'any road maps which you may find here, and especially letters addressed to Emanuel Legge by his son. You know, of course, that this office was broken into? There should be something in the shape of clues.'

The officer shook his head.

'I'm afraid, Mr Reeder, we won't find much here,' he said. 'So far, I've only come across old bills and business letters which you might find in any office.'

The detective looked round.

'There is no safe?' he asked.

All the timidity and deference in his manner had gone.

'Yes, sir, the safe's behind that panelling. I'll get it open this morning. But I shouldn't imagine that Legge would leave anything compromising on the premises. Besides, his son has had charge of the Highlow for years. Previous to that, they had a manager who's now doing time. Before him, if I remember right, that fellow Fenner, who's been in boob for burglary.'

'Fenner?' said the other sharply. 'I didn't know he ever managed this club.'

'He used to, but he had a quarrel with the old man. I've got an idea they were in jug together.'

Fenner's was not the type of mentality one would expect to find among the officers of a club, even a club of the standing of the Highlow: but there was this about the Highlow, that it required less intelligence than sympathy with a certain type of client.

Reeder was assisting the officer by taking out the contents of the pigeon-holes, when his hand touched a knob.

'Hallo, what's this?' he said, and turned it.

The whole desk shifted slightly and, as he pulled, it revealed the door to the spiral staircase.

'This is very interesting,' he said. He ascended as far as the top landing. There was evidently a door here, but every effort he made to force it ended in failure. He came down again, continuing to the basement, and this time he was joined by the inspector in charge of the case.

'Rather hot,' said Mr Reeder, as he opened the door. 'I should say there is a fire burning here.'

It took him some time to discover the light connections, and when he did, he whistled. For, lying by the side of the red-hot stove, he saw a piece of shining metal and recognized it. It was an engraver's plate, and one glance told him that it was the finished plate from which £5 notes could be printed.

The basement was empty, and for a second the mystery of the copper plate baffled him.

'We may not have found the Big Printer, but we've certainly found the Big Engraver,' he said. 'This plate was engraved somewhere upstairs.' He pointed to the shaft. 'What is it doing down here? Of course!' He slapped his thigh exultantly. 'I never dreamt he was right—but he always is right!'

'Who?' asked the officer.

'An old friend of mine, whose theory was that the plates from which the slush was printed were engraved within easy reach of a furnace, into which, in case of a police visitation, they could be pushed and destroyed. And, of course, the engraving plant is somewhere upstairs. But why they should throw down a perfectly new piece of work, and at a time when the attendant was absent, is beyond me. Unless . . . Get me an axe; I want to see the room on the roof.'

The space was too limited for the full swing of an axe, and it was nearly an hour before at last the door leading to the engraver's room was smashed in. The room was flooded with sunshine, for the skylight had not been covered. Reeder's sharp eyes took in the table with a glance, and then he looked beyond, and took a step backward. Lying by the wall, dishevelled, mud-stained, his white shirt crumpled to a pulp, was Peter Kane, and he was asleep!

They dragged him to a chair, bathed his face with cold water, but even then he took a long time to recover.

'He has been drugged: that's obvious,' said Mr Reeder, and scrutinised the hands of the unconscious man for a sign of blood. But though they were covered with rust and grime, Reeder found not so much as one spot of blood; and the first words that Peter uttered, on recovering consciousness, confirmed the view that he was ignorant of the murder.

'Where is Emanuel?' he asked drowsily. 'Have you got him?'

'No; but somebody has got him,' said Reeder gently, and the shock of the news brought Peter Kane wide awake.

'Murdered!' he said unbelievingly. 'Are you sure? Of course, I'm mad to ask you that.' He passed his hand wearily across his forehead. 'No, I know nothing about it. I suppose you suspect me, and I don't mind telling you that I was willing to murder him if I could have found him.'

Briefly he related what had happened at the dinner.

'I knew that I was doped, but dope works slowly on me, and the only chance I had was to sham dead. Emanuel gave me a thump in the jaw, and that was my excuse for going out. They got me downstairs into the yard and put me into the car first. I slipped out the other side as soon as the dwarf went up to get Johnny. There were a lot of old cement sacks lying about, and I threw a couple on to the floor, hoping that in the darkness they'd mistake the bundle for me. Then I lay down amongst the packing-cases and waited. I guessed they'd brought down Johnny, but I was powerless to help him. When the car had gone, and Pietro had gone up again, I followed. I suppose the dope was getting busy, and if I'd had any sense, I should have got over the gate. My first thought was that they might have taken my gun away and left it in the room. I tried to open the door, but it was locked.'

'Are you sure of that, Peter?'

'Absolutely sure.'

'How long after was this?'

'About half an hour. It took me all that time to get up the stairs, because I had to fight the dope all the way. I heard somebody moving about and I slipped into one of the other rooms, and then I heard the window pulled down and locked. I didn't want to go to sleep, for fear they discovered me; but I must have dozed, for when I woke up, it was dark and cold, and I heard no sound at all. I tried the door of 13 again, but I could make no impression on it. So I went to Emanuel's office. I know the place very well: I used to go in there in the old days, before Emanuel went to jail, and I knew all about the spiral staircase to the roof. All along I suspected that the hut they'd put on the roof was the place where the slush was printed. But I was wrong about that because as soon as I got into the room I saw that it was where the engraver worked. There was a plate on the edge of a shaft. I suppose I was still dizzy, because I fumbled at it. It slipped through my hand and I heard a clang come up from somewhere below.'

'How did you get into this room?'

'The door was open,' was the surprising reply. 'I have an idea that it's one of those doors that can only be opened and closed from the inside. The real door of the room is in the room in Emanuel's office. It's the only way in, and the only way out, both from the basement and the room on the roof. I don't know what happened after that. I must have lain down, and by now the dope was working powerfully. I ought to let Marney know I'm all right. She'll be worried.'

He saw something in the detective's face, something that made his heart sink.

'Marney! Is anything wrong with Marney?' he asked quickly.

'I don't know. She went out last night—or rather, early this morning—and she hasn't been seen since.'

Peter listened, stricken dumb by the news. It seemed to Mr Reeder that he aged ten years in as few minutes.

'Now, Kane, you've got to tell me all you know about Legge,' said Reeder kindly. 'I haven't any doubt that Jeffrey's taken her to the big printing place. Where is it?'

Peter shook his head.

'I haven't the least idea,' he said. 'The earlier slush was printed in this building; in fact, it was printed in Room 13. I've known that for a long time. But as the business grew, young Legge had to find another works. Where he has found it is a mystery to me, and to most other people.'

'But you must have heard rumours?' persisted Reeder.

Again Peter shook his head.

'Remember that I mix very little with people of my own profession, or my late profession,' he said. 'Johnny and old Barney are about the only crooks I know, outside of the Legge family. And Stevens, of course—he was in jail ten years ago. I've lost touch with all the others, and my news has come through Barney, though most of Barney's gossip is unreliable.'

They reached Barney by telephone, but he was unable to give any information that was of the slightest use. All that he knew was that the printing works were supposed to be somewhere in the West.

'Johnny knows more about it than I do, or than anybody. All the boys agree about that,' said Barney. 'They told him a lot in boob.'

Leaving Peter to return home, Mr Reeder made a call at Johnny's flat. Parker was up. He had been notified earlier in the morning of his master's disappearance, but he had no explanation to offer.

He was preparing to give a list of the clothes that Johnny had been wearing, but Reeder cut him short impatiently.

'Try to think of Mr Gray as a human being, and not as a tailor's dummy,' he said wrathfully. 'You realise that he is in very grave danger?'

'I am not at all worried, sir,' said the precise Parker. 'Mr Gray was wearing his new sock suspenders—'

For once Mr Reeder forgot himself.

'You're a damned fool, Parker,' he said.

'I hope not, sir,' said Parker as he bowed him out.

29

It was five minutes past two in the morning when Marney, sitting in the drawing-room at the front of the house, heard the sound of a car stopping outside. She went into the hall, opened the door and stood on the step, peering into the darkness.

'Is that you, father?' she asked.

There was no reply, and she walked quickly up the garden path to the gate. The car was unfamiliar but as she looked over the gate, she saw a hand come out and beckon her, and heard a voice whisper:

'Don't make a noise. Come in here; I want to talk to you. I don't want Barney to see me.'

Bewildered, she obeyed. Jerking open the door, she stepped into the dark interior, by the side of the man at the wheel.

'What is it?' she asked.

Then, to her amazement, the car began to move towards the main road. It had evidently circled before it had stopped.

'What's the matter, father?' she asked.

And then she heard a low chuckle that made her blood run cold.

'Go into the back and stay there. If you make a row, I'll spoil that complexion of yours, Marney Legge!'

'Jeffrey!' she gasped.

She gripped the inside handle of the door and had half turned it when he caught her with his disengaged hand and flung her into the back of the car.

'I'll kill you if you make me do that again.' There was a queer sob of pain in his voice, and she remembered his wound.

'Where are you taking me?' she asked.

'I'm taking you to your father,' was the unexpected reply. 'Will you sit quiet? If you try to get away, or attempt to call assistance, I'll drive you at full speed into the first tree I see and we'll finish the thing together.'

From the ferocity of his tone she did not doubt that he would carry his threat into execution. Mile after mile the car sped on, flashing through villages, slowing through the sparsely peopled streets of small towns. It was nearing three o'clock when they came into the street of a town and, looking through the window, she saw a grey façade and knew she was in Oxford.

In ten minutes they were through the city and traversing the main western road. And now, for the first time, Jeffrey Legge became communicative.

'You've never been in boob have you, angel?' he asked.

She did not answer.

'Never been inside the little bird-house with the other canaries, eh? Well, that's an experience ahead of you. I am going to put you in jail, kid. Peter's never been in jail either, but he nearly had the experience tonight.'

'I don't believe you,' she said. 'My father hasn't broken the law.'

'Not for a long time, at any rate,' agreed Jeffrey, dexterously lighting a cigarette with one hand. 'But there's a little boob waiting for him all right now.'

'A prison,' she said, incredulously. 'I don't believe you.'

'You've said that twice, and you're the only person living that's called me a liar that number of times.'

He turned off into a side road, and for a quarter of an hour gave her opportunity for thought.

'It might interest you to know that Johnny is there,' he said. 'Dear little Johnny! The easiest crook that ever fell—and this time he's got a lifer.'

The car began to move down a sharp declivity and, looking through the rain-spattered windscreen, she saw a squat, dark building ahead.

'Here we are,' he said, as the car stopped.

Looking through the window she saw, with a gasp of astonishment, that he had spoken the truth. They were outside a prison. The great, black, iron-studded gates were opening as she looked, and the car passed through under the deep archway and stopped.

'Get out,' said Jeff, and she obeyed.

A narrow black door led from the archway and, following her, he caught her by the arm and pushed her through. She was in a narrow room, the walls of which were covered with stained and discoloured whitewash. A large fireplace, overflowing with ashes, a rickety chair and a faded board screwed to the wall were the only furniture. In the dim light of a carbon lamp she saw the almost indistinguishable words: 'HM Prison, Keytown', and beneath, row after row of closely set regulations. A rough-looking, powerfully-built man had followed her into the room, which was obviously the gate-keeper's lodge.

'Have you got the cell ready?'

'Yes, I have,' said the man. 'Does she want anything to eat?'

'If she does, she'll want,' said Jeff curtly.

He took off his greatcoat and hung it on a nail, and then, with his hand gripping her arm, he led her again into the archway and across a small courtyard, through an iron grille gate and a further door.

A solitary light that burnt in a bracket near the door, showed her that she was in a small hall. Around this, at the height of about nine feet from the ground, ran a gallery, which was reached by a flight of iron stairs. There was no need to ask the meaning of those two rows of black doors that punctured the wall. They were cells. She was in a prison!

While she was wondering what it all meant, a door near at hand was unlocked, and she was pushed in. The cell was a small one, the floor of worn stone, but a new bedstead had been fitted up in one corner. There was a washstand; and, as she was to discover, the cell communicated with another containing a stone bath and washplace.

'The condemned cell,' explained Jeffrey Legge with relish. 'You'll have plenty of ghosts to keep you company tonight, Marney.'

In her heart she was panic-stricken, but she showed none of her fear as she faced him.

'A ghost would be much less repulsive to me than you, Jeffrey Legge,' she said, and he seemed taken aback by the spirit she displayed.

'You will have both,' he said, as he slammed the door on her and locked it.

The cell was illuminated by a feeble light that came through an opaque pane of glass by the side of the door. Presently, when her eyes grew accustomed to the semi-darkness, she was able to take stock of her surroundings. The prison must have been a very old one, for the walls were at one place worn smooth, probably by the back of some condemned unfortunate who had waited day after day for the hour of doom. She shuddered, as her imagination recalled to her the agony of soul which these four walls had held.

By standing on the bed she could reach a window. That also was of toughened glass, set in small, rusty frames. Some of the panes were missing, but she guessed that the outlook from the window would not be particularly promising, even supposing she could force the window.

The night had been unusually cold and raw for the time of year and, pulling a blanket from the bed, she wrapped it about her and sat down on the stool, waiting for the light to grow.

And so, sitting, her weary eyes closing involuntarily, she heard a stealthy tapping. It came from above, and her heart fluttered at the thought that possibly, in the cell above her, her father was held . . . or Johnny.

Climbing on to the bed, she rapped with her knuckles on the stone ceiling. Somebody answered. They were tapping a message in Morse, which she could not understand. Presently the tapping ceased. She heard footsteps above. And then, looking by chance at the broken pane of the window, she saw something come slowly downward and out of view. She leapt up, gripping the window pane, and saw a piece of black silk. With difficulty two fingers touched it at last and drew it gently in through the window pane. She pulled it up and, as she suspected, found a piece of paper tied to the end.

It was a bank-note. Bewildered, she gazed at it until it occurred to her that there might be a message written on the other side. The pencil marks were faint, and she carried the note as near to the light as she could get.

Who is there? Is it you Peter? I am up above. Johnny.

She suppressed the cry that rose to her lips. Both Johnny and her father were here. Then Jeffrey had not lied.

How could she answer? She had no pencil. Then she saw that the end of the cotton was weighted by a small yellow pencil, the kind that accompanies a diary or address book. With this unsatisfactory medium she wrote a reply and pushed it through the window, and after a while she saw it drawn up. Johnny was there—and Johnny knew. She felt strangely comforted by his presence, impotent though he was.

For half an hour she waited at the window, but now the daylight had come, and evidently Johnny thought it was too dangerous to make any further communications.

Exhausted, she lay down on the bed, intending to remain awake, but within five minutes she was sleeping heavily. The sound of a key in the lock made her spring to her feet. It was the man she had seen in the early morning; he was carrying a big tray, set with a clumsy cup and saucer, six slices of bread and butter, and an enormous teapot. He put it down on the bed, for want of a table, and without a word went out. She looked at the little platinum watch on her wrist: it was ten o'clock. Half an hour later the man came and took away the tray.

'Where am I?' she asked.

'You're in boob,' he said, with quiet amusement. 'But it's better than any other boob you've ever been in, young lady. And don't try to ask me questions, because you'll not get a civil answer if you do.'

At two o'clock came another meal, a little more tastily served this time. It seemed, from the appearance of the plate, that Jeffrey had sent into Oxford for a new service specially for her benefit. Again she attempted to discover what had happened to her father, but with no more satisfactory result.

The weary day dragged through; every minute seemed an hour, every hour interminable. Darkness had fallen again when the last of the visits was made, and this time it was Jeffrey Legge. At the sight of his face, all her terror turned to wonder. He was ghastly pale, his eyes burnt strangely, and the hand that came up to his lips was trembling as though he were suffering from a fever.

'What do you want?' she asked.

'I want you,' he said brokenly. 'I want you for the life of my father!'

'What do you mean?' she gasped.

'Peter Kane killed my father last night,' he said.

You're mad,' she gasped. 'My father is here—you told me.'

'I told you a lie. What does it matter what I told you, anyway? Peter Kane escaped on the way to Keytown, and he went back to the club and killed my father!'

30

The girl looked at him, speechless.

'It isn't true!' she cried.

'It's not true, isn't it?' Jeffrey almost howled the words. He was mad with hate, with grief, with desire for vengeance. 'I'll show you whether it's not true, my lady. You're my wife—do you understand that? If you don't, you're going to.'

He flung out of the cell, turning to voice his foul mind, and then the door clanged on her, and he strode out of the hall into the little house that was once the Governor's residence, and which was now the general headquarters of the Big Printer.

He poured himself out a stiff dose of whisky and drank it undiluted, and the man who had accompanied him watched him curiously.

'Jeff, it looks to me as if it's time to make a get-away. We can't keep these people here very long. The men are scared, too.'

'Scared, are they?' sneered Jeffrey Legge. 'I guess they'd be more scared if they were in front of a judge and jury.'

'That's the kind of scare they're anxious to avoid,' said his lieutenant calmly. 'Anyway, Jeff, we're getting near the end, and it seems to me that it's the time for all sensible men to find a little home on the other side of the water.'

Legge thought for a long time, and when he spoke his voice was more calm.

'Perhaps you're right,' he said. 'Tell them they can clear tonight.'

The other man was taken aback by the answer.

'Tonight?' he said. 'Well, I don't know that there's that hurry.'

'Tell 'em to clear tonight. They've got all the money they want. I'm shutting this down.'

'Who killed your father?'

'Peter Kane,' snarled Legge. 'I've got the full strength of it. The police are hiding him up, but he did the killing all right. They found him on the premises in the morning.'

He sat awhile, staring moodily at the glass in his hand.

'Let them go tonight,' he said. 'Every one of them. I'll tell them myself.'

'Do you want me to go?' asked the other.

Legge nodded.

'Yes; I want to be alone. I'm going to fix two people tonight,' he said, between his teeth, 'and I'm fixing them good.'

'Some of the men like Johnny Gray; they were in boob with him,' suggested his assistant, but Jeffrey stopped him with an oath.

'That's another reason they can get out,' he said, 'and they can't know too soon.'

He jumped to his feet and strode out of the room, the man following at a distance.

There were two halls to the prison, and it was into the second that he turned. This was brilliantly illuminated. The doors had been removed from most of the cells, and several of them were obviously sleeping-rooms for the half a dozen men who sat about a table playing cards. At only four places were the cell doors intact, for behind these were the delicate printing presses which from morning till night were turning out and numbering French, American and English paper currency. Every one of the men at the table, and each of those who came to the doors of their cubicles, attracted by the unusual appearance of Legge, had served long terms of imprisonment on forgery charges. Jeffrey had recruited them as carefully as the producer of a musical recruits his chorus. They were men without homes, without people, mainly without hope; men inured to the prison system and who found, in this novel method of living, a delightful variation of the life to which they were most accustomed.

It was believed by the authorities that Keytown Jail was in the hands of a syndicate engaged in experimental work of a highly complicated character, and no obstacle had been placed in the way of laying additional power cables to the 'laboratories'. Jeff had found the safest asylum in the land, and one which was more strongly guarded than any he could have built.

His speech was short and to the point.

'Boys, I guess that the time has come when we've got to make the best of our way home. You've all enough money to live comfortably on for the rest of your lives, and I advise you to get out of the country as soon as you can. You have your passports; you know the way; and there's no time like the present.'

'Do you mean that we've got to go tonight, Jeff?' asked a voice.

'I mean tonight. I'll have a car run you into London; you'll have to leave your kit behind, but you can afford that.'

'What are you going to do with the factory?'

'That's my business,' said Jeff.

The proposal did not find universal favour, but they stood in such awe of the Big Printer that, though they demurred, they obeyed. By ten o'clock that night the prison was empty, except for Jeffrey and his assistant.

'I didn't see Bill Holliss go,' said the latter; but Jeffrey Legge was too intent on his plans to give the matter a moment's thought.

'Maybe you'll see yourself go now, Jenkins,' said he. 'You can take your sports car and run anywhere you like.'

'Let me stay till the morning,' asked the man.

'You'll go tonight. Otherwise, what's the use of sending the other fellows away?'

He closed the big gate upon the car. He was alone with his wife and with the man he hated. He could think calmly now. The madness of rage had passed. He made a search of a little storeroom and found what he was looking for. It was a stout rope. With this over his arm, and a torch in his hand, he went out into the yard and came to a little shed built against the wall. Unlocking the rusty padlock, he pulled the doors apart. The shed was empty; the floor was inches thick with litter. He went back, found a broom and swept it clean. With the aid of a ladder he mounted to a beam that ran transversely across the roof, and fastened one end of the rope securely. Coming down, he spent half an hour in making a noose.

He was in the death-house. Under his feet was the fatal trap that a pull of the rusty lever would spring. He wanted to make the experiment, but the trap would take a lot of time to pull up. His face was pouring with perspiration when he had finished for the night was close, and a flicker of lightning illuminated for a second the gloomy recesses of the prison yard.

As he entered the hall a low growl of thunder came to him, but the storm in his heart was more violent than any nature could provide.

He walked softly up the iron stairs to the landing, and came at last to No. 4 and hesitated. His enemy could wait. Creeping down the stairs again, his heart beating thunderously, he stood outside the door of the condemned cell. The key trembled as he inserted it in the lock. No sound broke the stillness as the door opened stealthily, and he slipped into the room.

He waited, holding his breath, not knowing whether she were awake or asleep, and then crept forward to the bed. He saw the outline of a figure.

'Marney,' he said huskily, groping for her face.

And then two hands like steel clamps caught him by the throat and flung him backward.

'I want you, Jeffrey Legge,' said a voice—the voice of Johnny Gray.

31

Johnny Gray came to consciousness with a violent headache and a sense of suffocating restriction, which he discovered was due to his tie knot holding tightly in spite of the rough usage that had been his. This fact would have been pleasing to Parker, but was intensely discomforting to the wearer, and in a minute he had stripped it from his neck, loosened his shirt and had risen unsteadily to his feet.

The room in which he was had a familiar appearance. It was a cell, and—

Keytown Jail! He remembered Fenner's warning. So Fenner knew! Keytown Jail, sold by the Government to—Jeffrey Legge! The idea was preposterous; but why not? Some time ago a timber merchant had bought a jail at Hereford; a firm of caterers had purchased an old prison in the North of England, and were serving afternoon teas in the cells.

Now he understood. Keytown Prison was the headquarters of the Big Printer. The one place in the world that the police would never dream of searching, particularly if, as he guessed, Jeffrey Legge had offered some specious excuse for his presence and the presence of his company in this isolated part of the world.

The sound of voices came faintly up to him, and he heard a door bang and the clicking of locks; and with that sound he recalled the happenings of the evening. It must be Peter: they had got him too. In spite of his discomfiture, in spite of the awful danger in which he knew he was, he laughed softly to himself.

Above his bed was a window with scarcely a whole pane. But there was no escape that way. A thought struck him and, leaning down, he tapped a Morse message on the floor. If it was Peter, he would understand. He heard the answering tap which came feebly, and when he signalled again he knew that whoever was in the cell below had no knowledge of the Morse code. He searched his pockets and found a tiny scrap of pencil but could find no paper, except a bundle of five-pound notes; which his captors had not troubled to remove. Here was both stationery and the means of writing, but how could he communicate with the occupant of the cell below? Presently a plan suggested itself, and he tore off the lapel of his dinner-jacket and unravelled the silk. Tying the pencil to the end to give it weight he slowly lowered his message, hoping, though it seemed unlikely, that his fellow-prisoner would be able to see the paper.

To his joy he felt a tug, and when, a few minutes later, he carefully drew up the message, it was to find, written underneath his own, one which left him white and shaking.

Marney here! He groaned aloud at the thought. It was too light now to risk any further communication. There was a ewer of water and a basin in the cell, and with this he relieved the aching in his head; and when breakfast came, he was ready.

The man who brought in the tray was a stranger to him, as also was the man who stood on guard at the door, revolver in hand.

'What's the great idea?' asked Johnny coolly, sitting on the bed and swinging his legs. 'Has Jeff bought a jail to practise in? Wouldn't it have been cheaper to have gone over the Alps?'

'You shut up, Johnny Gray,' growled the man. 'You'll be sorry for yourself before you're out of here.'

'Who isn't?' asked Johnny. 'How's Peter?'

'You know damned well Peter has escaped,' said the other before he could check himself.

'Escaped!' said the delighted Johnny. 'You don't mean that?'

'Never mind what I mean,' growled the man, realizing he had said too much. 'You keep a civil tongue in your head, Gray, and you'll be treated square. If you don't, there are plenty of men on the spot to make Dartmoor a paradise compared with Keytown.'

The door slammed in Johnny Gray's face, but he was so absorbed in the news which the man had unwillingly given to him that he had to force himself to eat.

Soon the man came to take away the tray.

'What's your name, bo', anyway?' said Johnny carelessly. 'I hate calling you "face"—it's low.'

'Bill's my name,' said the man, 'and you needn't call me Bill either. You say "sir" to me.'

'Woof!' said Johnny admiringly. 'You're talking like a real screw!'

The door slammed in his face. He had further time to consider his plans. They had taken away his watch, his gold cigarette-case and the small penknife he carried, but these losses did not worry him in the slightest. His chief anxiety was to know the exact character of Keytown Prison. And that he determined to learn at the earliest opportunity.

It was late in the afternoon; he guessed it was somewhere in the neighbourhood of four when his lunch came, and he was quite ready to eat it, though a little suspicious of its possible accessories.

'No poison in this, Bill?' he asked pleasantly as he took the bread and cheese from the man's hand.

'There's no need to poison you; we could starve you, couldn't we?' said the other. 'If Jeff was here, maybe I'd get a rapping for giving you anything.'

'Gone away, has he? Well, prisons are more pleasant when the governor's away. Am I right, Bill? Now, what do you say to a couple of hundred of real money?'

'For what?' asked the man, stopping at the door. 'If you mean it's for letting you make a get-away, why, you're crazy! You're going to stay here till Jeff fixes you.'

All the day Johnny had heard, or rather felt, a peculiar whirr of sound coming from some remote quarter of the prison.

'Got everything electric here, Bill?' he said conversationally.

'Yes, we have,' said the other. 'This is a model boob, this is.'

'I'll bet it is,' said Johnny grimly. 'Are you running any electric radiators in my cell tonight, or do you want all the power for the press?'

He saw the man's face twitch.

'Of course, you're running the slush factory here—everybody knows that. Take my advice, Bill—go while the going's good. Or the bulls will have you inside the realest boob you've seen.'

He had made the guard more than a little uncomfortable, as he saw, and he sought to press home the impression he had created.

'Jeffrey's going to shop you sooner or later, because he's a natural born shopper. And he's got the money, Bill, to get away with, and the cars and aeroplanes. You haven't got that. You'll have to walk on your own pads. And the bulls will get you half-way over the field.'

'Oh, shut up!' said the man uncomfortably, and the conversation ended, as in the morning, with the slamming of the door.

Presently a little spy-hole in the cell door opened.

'What made you think this is a print-shop?' asked Bill's voice.

'I don't think anything about it; I know,' said Johnny decisively. 'If you like to come to me this evening I'll tell you the name of every worker here, the position of every press, and the length of the lagging you'll get.'

The cover of the spy-hole dropped.

Jeffrey was away; that was all to the good. If he remained away for the whole of the night. . . . He was worried about Marney, and it required all his strength of will not to fret himself into a state of nerves.

In an hour Bill returned, and this time he brought no guard but himself, but for safety's sake he carried on his conversation through a little grille in the door.

'You're bluffing, Johnny Gray. We've got a fellow here who was in boob with you, and he says you're the biggest bluffer that ever lived. You don't know anything.'

'I know almost everything,' said Johnny immodestly. 'For instance, I know you've got a young lady in the cell below. How's she doing?'

The man was taken aback for a moment.

'Who told you?' he asked suspiciously. 'Nobody else has been here, have they?'

'Nobody at all. It's part of my general knowledge. Now listen, Bill. How are you treating that lady? And your life hangs on your answer—don't forget it.'

'She's all right,' said Bill casually. 'They've given her the condemned cell, with a bath-room and all, and a proper bed—not like yours. And you can't scare me, Gray.'

'I'll bet I can't,' said Johnny. 'Bring me some water.'

But the water was not forthcoming, and it was dark before the man made his reappearance. Johnny listened at the door; he was coming alone. Johnny pulled up the leg of his trousers and showed those suspenders which were Parker's pride. They were not ordinary suspenders. Strapped to the inside of the calf was a small holster. The automatic it carried was less than four inches in length, but its little blunt-nosed bullets were man-stoppers of a peculiarly deadly kind.

The door swung open, and Bill stepped in.

'Jeff's back—' he began, and then:

'Step in, and step lively,' said Johnny.

His arm had shot out, and the gun hand of the jailer was pinned to his side.

'This gun may look pretty paltry, but it would blow a square inch out of your heart, and that's enough to seriously inconvenience you for the remainder of your short life.'

With a turn of his wrist he wrenched the revolver from the man's grasp.

'Sit over there,' he said. 'Is anybody in the hall?'

'For God's sake, don't let Jeff see you. He'll kill me,' pleaded the agitated prisoner.

'I'd hate for him to do that,' said Johnny.

He looked out into the hall: it was empty, and he went back to his prisoner.

'Stand against the wall. I'm going to give you the twice-over.'

His hands searched quickly but effectively. The key he was putting in his pocket when he noticed the design of the ward.

'Pass-key, I fancy. Now, don't make a fuss, Bill, because you'll be let out first thing in the morning, and maybe I'll have a good word to say for you at the Oxford Assizes. There's something about you that I like. Give me the simple criminal, and the Lord knows you're simple enough!'

He stepped out of the cell, snapped the lock of the door and, keeping in the shadow, walked swiftly along the gallery until he came to the open stairway on to the floor below.

The hall was untenanted. Apparently Bill was the only jailer. He had reached the floor when the door at the end of the hall opened and somebody came in. He flattened himself in one of the recessed cell doorways. Two men entered, and one, he guessed was Jeff. One, two, three, four—the fourth door from the end. That was Marney's door, immediately under his own. He saw Jeffrey stop, heard the too-familiar grind of the lock, and his enemy disappeared, leaving the second man on guard outside.

If Jeffrey had made an attempt to close the door behind him, Johnny would have shot down the guard and taken the consequences. But the man was absent for only a few minutes. When he came out, he was shouting incoherently threats that made the hair rise on Johnny Gray's neck. But they were only threats.

The hall door closed on Jeffrey Legge and Johnny moved swiftly to No. 4. As the door opened, the girl shrank back against the wall.

'Don't touch me!' she cried.

'Marney!'

At the sound of his voice she stood rooted to the spot. The next second she was laughing and crying in his arms.

'But, Johnny, how did you get here? . . . where were you? . . . you won't leave me?'

He soothed her and quietened her as only Johnny Gray could.

'I'll stay . . . I think this fellow will come back. If he does, he'll wish he hadn't!'

And Jeffrey came. As the grip of strong hands closed on his throat, and the hateful voice of his enemy came to his ears, Johnny's prophecy was justified.

32

For a second Legge was paralysed with rage and fear. Then, in the wildness of his despair, he kicked at the man, who had slipped from the bed and was holding him. He heard an exclamation, felt for a second the fingers relax and, slipping like an eel from the grasp, flew to the door and closed it. He stood, breathless and panting by the doorway, until he heard the sound of steel against the inner keyhole, and in a flash realised that Johnny had secured the pass-key. Quick as lightning, he slipped his own key back into the lock and turned it slightly, so that it could not be pushed out from the other side.

Johnny Gray! How had he got there? He fled up the stairs and hammered on the door of the cell where he thought his prisoner was held safe. A surly voice replied to him.

'You swine!' he howled. 'You let him go! You twister! You can stay there and starve, damn you!'

'I didn't let him go. He held me up. Look out, Jeff, he's got a gun.'

The news staggered the man. The search of Johnny's clothing had been of a perfunctory nature, but he had thought that it was impossible that any kind of weapon could have been concealed.

'Let me out, guv'nor,' pleaded the prisoner. 'You've got a key.'

There was a third key in his house, Jeffrey remembered. Perhaps this man might be of use to him. He was still weak from his wound, and would need assistance.

'All right, I'll get the key. But if you shopped me—'

'I didn't shop you, I tell you. He held me up—'

Legge went back to his room, found the key and, taking another stiff dose of whisky, returned and released his man.

'He's got my gun, too,' explained Bill. 'Where are all the fellows? We'll soon settle with him.'

'They've gone,' said Jeffrey.

What a fool he had been! If he had had the sense to keep the gang together only for a few hours—. But he was safe, unless Johnny found a means of getting through the window.

'In my room you'll find a gun, it's in the top right-hand corner of my desk,' he said quickly. 'Take it and get outside Johnny's cell—on the yard side. If he tries to escape that way, shoot. Because, if he escapes, you're going a long journey, my friend.'

Inside the cell, a chagrined Johnny Gray sat down on the girl's bed to consider the possibilities of the position.

'My dear, there's going to be serious trouble here, and I don't want you to think otherwise,' he said. 'I should imagine there were quite a number of men in this prison, in which case, though I shall probably get two or three of them, they'll certainly get me in the end.'

She sat by his side, holding his hand, and the pressure of her fingers was eloquent of the faith she had in him.

'Johnny, dear, does it matter very much what happens now? They can't come in, and we can't get out. How long will it take to starve us to death?'

Johnny had already considered that problem.

'About three days,' he said, in such a matter-of-fact tone that she laughed. 'My only hope, Marney, is that your father may know more about this place than he has admitted.'

'Did you know anything about it?' she asked.

He hesitated.

'Yes, I think I did. I wasn't sure, though I was a fool not to locate it just as soon as Fenner warned me against Keytown Jail. These chaps like to speak in parables, and mystery is as the breath of their nostrils. Besides, I should have been certain that Fenner knew the jail had been taken over from the Government.'

He made a careful examination of the bars about the window, but without instruments or tools to force them, he knew that escape that way was impossible. When, in the early hours of the morning, he saw the patient figure of Bill, he realized the extent of the impossibility.

'Good morning, William. I see you're out,' he greeted the scowling sentry, who immediately jumped to cover, flourishing his long-barrelled weapon.

'Don't you show your nose, or I'll blow it off,' he threatened. 'We've got you, Mr Gray.'

'They've got you, alas, my poor William,' said Johnny sadly. 'The busies will be here at nine o'clock—you don't suppose that I should have let myself come into a trap like this? Of course, I didn't. I squeaked! It was my only chance, William. And *your* only chance is to sneak away at the earliest opportunity, and turn State's evidence. I'm addressing you as a friend.'

'You'll never get away from here alive,' said the man. 'Jeff's going to fix you.'

'Indeed?' the prisoner began politely, when a scream made him turn.

'Johnny!'

The shutter which hid the grille in the door was swung back, and the muzzle of Jeffrey's Browning had been pushed through one of the openings. As Johnny dropped flat on the bed, he was stunned by the deafening sound of an explosion. Something hit the wall, ricocheted to the roof, and fell almost at the girl's feet. Before the gun could be withdrawn, Johnny Gray had fired. A jagged end of iron showed where his bullet struck.

'The time for persiflage,' said Johnny cheerfully, 'is past. Now you will sit in that corner, young lady, and you will not budge without permission.' He pointed to the wall nearest the door, which afforded perfect cover and, dragging up a stool, he seated himself by her side. 'Jeffrey's got quite a tough proposition,' he said in his conversational tone. 'He can't burn the prison, because there's nothing to burn. He can't come in, and he mustn't go out. If he would only for one moment take away that infernal key—'

'There's another door going out from the bathroom,' she said suddenly. 'I think it leads to an exercise ground. You can just see a little railed-off space through the window.'

Johnny went into the bathroom and examined the door. Screwing his head, he could see, through a broken pane, ten square yards of space, where in olden times a condemned prisoner took his exercise, removed from the gaze of his fellows. He tried the key, and to his delight, it turned. Another minute and he was in the little paved yard.

Looking round, he saw a high and narrow gateway, which seemed to be the only exit from the courtyard. And on the other side of that gateway was William, the sentry, well armed and sufficiently terrified to be dangerous. Slipping off his shoes, Johnny crept to the gate and listened. The sound of the man's footsteps pacing the flagged walk came to him. He stooped, squinted through the keyhole and saw Bill standing, his back towards him, some six yards away. There was no time to be lost. He inserted the key, and the gate was opened before the man could turn to face the levelled revolver.

'Don't shout,' whispered Johnny. 'You're either discreet or dead. Hand over that gun, you unfortunate man.' He moved swiftly towards the terrified criminal, and relieved him of his weapon.

With a gesture, Johnny directed him to the exercise yard.

'Get in and stay,' he said, and locked the door, and for the second time, Bill (Johnny never discovered that his other name was Hollis) was a prisoner.

Skirting the building, he came to the entrance of the hall. The door was open and with his hand on the uplifted hammer of the gun and his finger pressing the trigger, Johnny leapt into the building.

'Hands up!' he shouted.

At the words, Jeffrey Legge spun round. There was a boom of sound, something whistled past Gray's face, and he fired twice. But now the man was running, zigzagging to left and right, and Johnny hesitated to fire. He disappeared through the door at the farther end of the hall, shutting it behind him, and Johnny raced after him.

He was in the courtyard now, facing the grille-covered archway. As he came into view, Jeffrey disappeared through the lodge-keeper's door. Johnny tried the grille, but in vain, for a pass-key operated on all locks save the lock of the entrance gate of a prison. That alone is distinct, and may not be opened save by the key that was cut for it.

Covering the lodge-keeper's door with his gun, Johnny waited and, waiting, heard a rumbling sound. Something was coming down the centre of the archway. The straight line of it came lower and lower. A hanging gate! He had forgotten that most old country prisons were so equipped. Under the cover of this ancient portcullis, Legge could escape, for it masked the entrance of the lodge.

He turned back to the girl.

'Keep out of sight. He's got away,' he warned her. 'This fellow isn't finished yet.'

The gate was down. . . . Jeffrey put on the overcoat he had left in the lodge, put his gun into his pocket and opened the great gates. He had at least a dozen hours' start, he thought, as he stepped into the open. . . .

'Please do not put your hand in your pocket, Mr Jeffrey,' said a plaintive voice. 'I should *so* hate to shoot a fellow-creature. It would be a deed utterly repugnant to my finest feelings.'

Jeffrey raised his hands to their fullest extent, for Mr Reeder was not alone. Behind him were four armed policemen, a cordon of police cars, cutting off all avenues of escape. And, most ominous of all, Peter Kane, who stood at Reeder's right hand.

33

For the first time Jeffrey Legge felt the cold contact of handcuffs. He was led back to the porter's lodge, while two of the policemen worked at the windlass that raised the hanging gate.

'It's a cop, Craig,' he said, for the inspector in charge was that redoubtable thief-catcher. 'But I'm going to squeak all I know. Johnny Gray is in this. He's been working my slush for years. You'll find the presses in the second hall, but the other birds have done some quick flying.'

'They've all flown into the police station at Oxford,' said Craig, 'and they're singing their pretty little songs merrily. The Oxford police took a whole carload of them about eleven o'clock last night. Unfortunately, they weren't so ready to squeak as you.'

'Johnny Gray's in it, I tell you.'

'Oh, how can you say such a thing?' said the shocked Mr Reeder. 'I'm perfectly sure Mr Gray is quite innocent.'

Jeffrey regarded him with a sneer of contempt.

'You're a pretty funny busy. I suppose Craig brought you here?'

'No,' murmured Mr Reeder, 'I brought myself here.'

'The only thing I can say about you,' said Jeffrey Legge, 'is that you're smarter than old Golden—and that's not saying much.'

'Not very much,' murmured Mr Reeder.

'But you're not smart enough to know that Johnny Gray has been in this business for years.'

'Even while he was in prison?' suggested Mr Reeder innocently. 'The opportunities are rather restricted, don't you think? But don't let us quarrel, Mr Jeffrey.'

The portcullis was raised now, and in a few minutes the girl was in her father's arms.

'Johnny, you've had a narrow escape,' said Craig, as he shook the man's hand, 'and there's some talk about you being in this slush business, but I'll not believe it till I get proof.'

'Who killed old Legge?' asked Johnny.

The detective shook his head.

'We don't know. But Stevens has disappeared, and Stevens was Fenner's brother. I got it from Mr Reeder, who seems to have remarkable sources of information.'

'Not at all,' disclaimed the apologetic Reeder. 'I certainly have a remarkable source of information, and to that all credit must go. But I think you will confirm my statement, John, that Stevens is Fenner's brother?'

To Peter's surprise, Johnny nodded.

'Yes, I knew they were brothers; and it is unnecessary to say that their name was neither Stevens nor Fenner. It's pretty well established that the old man gave Fenner away— shopped him for the Berkeley Square job—and possibly Stevens got to know of this and waited his opportunity to settle accounts with Emanuel. Have you caught Stevens?'

'Not yet,' said Craig.

'I hope you won't,' said Johnny. 'What are you going to do about me, Peter?'

He put his arm round the girl's shoulder, and Peter smiled.

'I suppose I'll have to let her marry you, Johnny, whether you're a crook or honest. I want you to go straight, and I'll make it worth while—'

'That I can promise you.' It was Mr Reeder who spoke. 'And may I offer an apology. I'm rather a wolf in sheep's clothing, or a sheep in wolf's clothing. The truth is, my name is Golden.'

'Golden!' gasped Craig. 'But I thought Golden was out of this business?'

'He is out of it, and yet he is in it,' explained Mr Reeder carefully. 'I am an excellent office man,' he confessed, in that mincing manner of his, staring owlishly over his glasses, 'but a very indifferent seeker of information, and although, when Mr John Gray Reeder was appointed over me as chief inspector of my department—'

'Here, stop!' said the dazed Craig. 'John Gray Reeder? Who's Inspector John Gray Reeder?'

Mr Golden's hand went out in the direction of the smiling Johnny.

'Johnny! You a busy!' said the bewildered Peter. 'But you went to jail sure enough?'

'I certainly went to jail,' said Johnny. 'It was the only place I could get any news about the Big Printer, and I found out all I wanted to know. It was a trying two years, but well worth it, though I nearly lost the only thing in the world that made life worth living,' he said. 'You've got to forgive me, Peter, because I spied on you—a good spy doesn't play favourites. I've been watching you and every one of your pals, and I watched Marney most of all. And now I'm going to watch her for years and years!'

'You see,' said Mr Golden, who seemed most anxious to exculpate himself from any accusation of cleverness. 'I was merely the listener-in, if I may use the expression, to the information which John broadcast. I knew all about this marriage, and I was the person who appointed a woman detective to look after her at the Charlton Hotel—but on Johnny's instructions. That is why he was able to prove his alibi, because naturally, that section of the police which knows him, is always ready to prove alibis for other officers of the police who are mistakenly charged with being criminals.'

'How did you guess about the prison?'

'Fenner squeaked,' said Mr Golden with a gesture of deprecation. ' "Squeak" is not a word I like, but it's rather expressive. Yes, Fenner squeaked.'

Two happy people drove home together in the car which had brought Marney to Keytown. The country between Oxford and Horsham is the most beautiful in the land. The road passes through great aisles of tall trees, into which a car may be turned and be hidden from the view of those who pass along the road. Johnny slowed down at an appropriate spot, and put the car towards the thickest part of the wood. And Marney, who sat by his side, did not seek any explanation for his eccentricity.